Twist Me

The Complete Trilogy

Anna Zaires

♠ Mozaika Publications ♠

Published by Mozaika Publications, an imprint of Mozaika LLC.
www.mozaikallc.com

Edited by Mella Baxter
Cover by Najla Qamber Designs
www.najlaqamberdesigns.com

E-ISBN: 978-1-63142-118-1
ISBN: 978-1-63142-119-8

Printed in Great Britain
by Amazon

Twist Me

Twist Me: Book 1

PROLOGUE

*B*lood.

It's everywhere. The pool of dark red liquid on the floor is spreading, multiplying. It's on my feet, my skin, my hair . . . I can taste it, smell it, feel it covering me. I'm drowning in blood, suffocating in it.

No! Stop!

I want to scream, but I can't draw in enough air. I want to move, but I'm restrained, tied in place, the ropes cutting into my skin as I struggle against them.

I can hear her screams, though. Inhuman shrieks of pain and agony that slice me open, leaving my mind as raw and mangled as her flesh.

He lifts the knife one last time, and the pool of blood turns into an ocean, the rip current sucking me in—

I wake up screaming his name, my sheets soaked through with cold sweat.

For a moment, I'm disoriented . . . and then I remember.

He will never come for me again.

CHAPTER ONE

Eighteen Months Earlier

I'm seventeen years old when I first meet him.

Seventeen and crazy about Jake.

"Nora, come on, this is boring," Leah says as we sit on the bleachers watching the game. Football. Something I know nothing about, but pretend I love because that's where I see him. Out there on that field, practicing every day.

I'm not the only girl watching Jake, of course. He's the quarterback and the hottest guy on the planet—or at least in the Chicago suburb of Oak Lawn, Illinois.

"It's not boring," I tell her. "Football is a lot of fun."

Leah rolls her eyes. "Yeah, yeah. Just go talk to him already. You're not shy. Why don't you just make him notice you?"

I shrug. Jake and I don't run in the same circles. He's got cheerleaders climbing all over him, and I've been watching him long enough to know that he goes for tall blond girls, not short brunettes.

Besides, for now it's kind of fun to just enjoy the attraction. And I know that's what this feeling is. Lust. Hormones, pure and simple. I have no idea if I'll like Jake as a person, but I certainly love how he looks without his shirt. Whenever he walks by, I feel my heart beating faster from excitement. I feel warm inside, and I want to squirm in my seat.

I also dream about him. Sexy dreams, sensual dreams, where he holds my hand, touches my face, kisses me. Our bodies touch, rub against each other. Our clothes come off.

I try to imagine what sex with Jake would be like.

Last year, when I was dating Rob, we nearly went all the way, but then I found out he slept with another girl at a party while drunk. He groveled profusely when I confronted him about it, but I couldn't trust him again and we broke up. Now I'm much more careful about the guys I date, although I know not all of them are like Rob.

Jake might be, though. He's just too popular not to be a player. Still, if there's anybody I'd want to have my first time with, it's definitely Jake.

"Let's go out tonight," Leah says. "Just us girls. We can go to Chicago, celebrate your birthday."

"My birthday is not for another week," I remind her, even though I know she's got the date marked on her calendar.

"So what? We can get a head start."

I grin. She's always so eager to party. "I don't know. What if they throw us out again? Those IDs are just not that good—"

"We'll go to another place. It doesn't have to be Aristotle."

Aristotle is by far the coolest club in the city. But Leah was right—there were others.

"Okay," I say. "Let's do it. Let's get a head start."

* * *

Leah picks me up at 9 p.m.

She's dressed for clubbing—dark skinny jeans, a sparkly black tube-top, and over-the-knee high-heeled boots. Her blond hair is perfectly smooth and straight, falling down her back like a highlighted waterfall.

In contrast, I'm still wearing my sneakers. My clubbing shoes I hide in the backpack that I intend to leave in Leah's car. A thick sweater hides the sexy top I'm wearing. No makeup and my long brown hair in a ponytail.

I leave the house like that to avoid any suspicion. I tell my parents I'm going to hang out with Leah at a friend's house. My mom smiles and tells me to have fun.

4

Now that I'm almost eighteen, I don't have a curfew anymore. Well, I probably do, but it's not a formal one. As long as I come home before my parents start freaking out—or at least if I let them know where I am—it's all good.

Once I get into Leah's car, I begin my transformation.

Off goes the thick sweater, revealing the slinky tank-top I have on underneath. I wore a push-up bra to maximize my somewhat-undersized assets. The bra straps are cleverly designed to look cute, so I'm not embarrassed to have them show. I don't have cool boots like Leah's, but I did manage to sneak out my nicest pair of black heels. They add about four inches to my height. I need every single one of those inches, so I put on the shoes.

Next, I pull out my makeup bag and pull down the windshield visor, so I can get access to the mirror.

Familiar features stare back at me. Large brown eyes and clearly defined black eyebrows dominate my small face. Rob once told me that I look exotic, and I can kind of see that. Even though I'm only a quarter Latino, my skin always looks lightly tanned and my eyelashes are unusually long. Fake lashes, Leah calls them, but they're entirely real.

I don't have a problem with my looks, although I often wish I were taller. It's those Mexican genes of mine. My abuela was petite and so am I, even though both of my parents are of average height. I wouldn't care, except Jake likes tall girls. I don't think he even sees me in the hallway; I'm literally below his eye level.

Sighing, I put on lip gloss and some eye shadow. I don't go crazy with makeup because simple works best on me.

Leah cranks up the radio, and the latest pop songs fill the car. I grin and start singing along with Rihanna. Leah joins me, and now we're both belting out S&M lyrics.

Before I know it, we arrive at the club.

We walk in like we own the place. Leah gives the bouncer a big smile, and we flash our IDs. They let us through, no problem.

We've never been to this club before. It's in an older, slightly rundown part of downtown Chicago.

"How did you find this place?" I yell at Leah, shouting to be heard above the music.

"Ralph told me about it," she yells back, and I roll my eyes.

Ralph is Leah's ex-boyfriend. They broke up when he started acting weird, but they still talk for some reason. I think he's into drugs or something these days. I'm not sure, and Leah won't tell me out of some misplaced loyalty to him. He's the king of shady, and the fact that we're here on his recommendation is not super-comforting.

But whatever. Sure, the area outside is not the best, but the music is good and the crowd is a nice mix of people.

We're here to party, and that's exactly what we do for the next hour. Leah gets a couple of guys to buy us shots. We don't have more than one drink each. Leah—because she has to drive us home. And me—because I don't metabolize alcohol well. We may be young, but we're not stupid.

After the shots, we dance. The two guys who bought us drinks dance with us, but we gradually migrate away from them. They're not that cute. Leah finds a group of college-age hotties, and we sidle up to them. She strikes up a conversation with one of them, and I smile, watching her in action. She's good at this flirting business.

In the meantime, my bladder tells me I need to visit the ladies' room. So I leave them and go.

On my way back, I ask the bartender for a glass of water. I am thirsty after all the dancing.

He gives it to me, and I greedily gulp it down. When I'm done, I put down the glass and look up.

Straight into a pair of piercing blue eyes.

He's sitting on the other side of the bar, about ten feet away. And he's staring at me.

I stare back. I can't help it. He's probably the most handsome man I've ever seen.

His hair is dark and curls slightly. His face is hard and masculine, each feature perfectly symmetrical. Straight dark eyebrows over those strikingly pale eyes. A mouth that could belong to a fallen angel.

I suddenly feel warm as I imagine that mouth touching my skin, my lips. If I were prone to blushing, I would've been beet-red.

He gets up and walks toward me, still holding me with his gaze. He walks leisurely. Calmly. He's completely sure of himself. And why not? He's gorgeous, and he knows it.

As he approaches, I realize that he's a large man. Tall and well built. I don't know how old he is, but I'm guessing he's closer to thirty than twenty. A man, not a boy.

He stands next to me, and I have to remember to breathe.

"What's your name?" he asks softly. His voice somehow carries above the music, its deeper notes audible even in this noisy environment.

"Nora," I say quietly, looking up at him. I am absolutely mesmerized, and I'm pretty sure he knows it.

He smiles. His sensuous lips part, revealing even white teeth. "Nora. I like that."

He doesn't introduce himself, so I gather my courage and ask, "What's your name?"

"You can call me Julian," he says, and I watch his lips moving. I've never been so fascinated by a man's mouth before.

"How old are you, Nora?" he asks next.

I blink. "Twenty-one."

His expression darkens. "Don't lie to me."

"Almost eighteen," I admit reluctantly. I hope he doesn't tell the bartender and get me kicked out of here.

He nods, like I confirmed his suspicions. And then he raises his hand and touches my face. Lightly, gently. His thumb rubs against my lower lip, as though he's curious about its texture.

I'm so shocked that I just stand there. Nobody has ever done that before, touched me so casually, so possessively. I feel hot and cold at the same time, and a tendril of fear snakes down my spine. There is no hesitation in his actions. No asking for permission, no pausing to see if I would let him touch me.

He just touches me. Like he has the right to do so. Like I belong to him.

I draw in a shaky breath and back away. "I have to go," I whisper, and he nods again, watching me with an inscrutable expression on his beautiful face.

I know he's letting me go, and I feel pathetically grateful—because something deep inside me senses that he could've easily gone further, that he doesn't play by the normal rules.

That he's probably the most dangerous creature I've ever met.

I turn and make my way through the crowd. My hands are trembling, and my heart is pounding in my throat.

I need to leave, so I grab Leah and make her drive me home.

As we're walking out of the club, I look back and I see him again. He's still staring at me.

There is a dark promise in his gaze—something that makes me shiver.

CHAPTER TWO

The next three weeks pass by in a blur. I celebrate my eighteenth birthday, study for finals, hang out with Leah and my other friend Jennie, go to football games to watch Jake play, and get ready for graduation.

I try not to think about the club incident again. Because when I do, I feel like a coward. Why did I run? Julian had barely touched me.

I can't fathom my strange reaction. I had been turned on, but ridiculously frightened at the same time.

And now my nights are restless. Instead of dreaming of Jake, I often wake up feeling hot and uncomfortable, throbbing between my legs. Dark sexual images invade my dreams, stuff I've never thought about before. A lot of it involves Julian doing something to me, usually while I'm helplessly frozen in place.

Sometimes I think I'm going crazy.

Pushing that disturbing thought out of my mind, I focus on getting dressed.

My high school graduation is today, and I'm excited. Leah, Jennie, and I have big plans for after the ceremony. Jake is throwing a post-graduation party at his house. It will be the perfect opportunity to finally talk to him.

I'm wearing a black dress under my blue graduation gown. It's simple, but it fits me well, showing off my small curves. I'm also wearing my four-inch heels. A little much for the graduation ceremony, but I need the added height.

My parents drive me to the school. This summer I'm hoping to save enough money to buy my own car for college. I'm going to a local community college because it's cheaper that way, so I'll still be living at home.

I don't mind. My parents are nice, and we get along well. They give me a lot of freedom—probably because they think I'm a good kid, never getting in trouble. They're mostly right. Other than the fake IDs and the occasional clubbing excursions, I lead a pretty sedate life. No heavy drinking, no smoking, no drugs of any kind—although I did try pot once at a party.

We arrive and I find Leah. Lining up for the ceremony, we wait patiently for our names to be called. It's a perfect day in early June—not too hot, not too cold.

Leah's name is called first. Luckily for her, her last name starts with 'A.' My last name is Leston, so I have to stand for another thirty minutes. Fortunately, our graduating class is only a hundred people. One of the perks of living in a small town.

My name is called and I go to receive my diploma. Looking out onto the crowd, I smile and wave to my parents. I'm pleased that they look so proud.

I shake the principal's hand and turn to go back to my seat.

And in that moment, I see him again.

My blood freezes in my veins.

He's sitting in the back, watching me. I can feel his eyes on me, even from a distance.

Somehow I make my way down from the stage without falling. My legs are trembling, and my breathing is much faster than normal. I take a seat next to my parents and pray that they don't notice my state.

Why is Julian here? What does he want from me? Taking a deep breath, I tell myself to calm down. Surely he's here because of someone else. Maybe he has a brother or a sister in my graduating class. Or some other relative.

But I know I'm lying to myself.

I remember that possessive touch, and I know he's not done with me.

He wants me.

A shudder runs down my spine at the thought.

* * *

I don't see him again after the ceremony, and I'm relieved. Leah drives us to Jake's house. She and Jennie are chattering the entire way, excited to be done with high school, to start the next phase of our lives.

I would normally join in the conversation, but I'm too disturbed by seeing Julian, so I just sit there quietly. For some reason, I hadn't told Leah about meeting him in the club. I only said that I had a headache and wanted to go home.

I don't know why I can't talk to Leah about Julian. I have no problem spilling my guts about Jake. Maybe it's because it's too difficult for me to describe how Julian makes me feel. She wouldn't understand why he frightens me.

I don't really understand it myself.

At Jake's house, the party is in full swing when we arrive. I am still resolved to talk to Jake, but I'm too freaked out from seeing Julian earlier. I decide that I need some liquid courage.

Leaving the girls, I walk over to the keg and pour myself a cup of punch. Sniffing it, I determine that it definitely has alcohol, and I drink the full cup.

Almost immediately, I start to feel buzzed. As I had discovered in the past few years, my alcohol tolerance is virtually nonexistent. One drink is just about my limit.

I see Jake walking to the kitchen, and I follow him there.

He's cleaning up, throwing away some extra cups and dirty paper plates.

"Do you want some help with that?" I ask.

He smiles, his brown eyes crinkling at the corners. "Oh, sure, thanks. That would be awesome." His sun-streaked hair is a little long and flops over his forehead, making him look particularly cute.

I melt a little inside. He's so handsome. Not in the disturbing Julian way, but in a pleasantly comfortable sense. Jake is tall and muscular, but he's not all that big for a quarterback. Not big enough to play ball in college, or at least that's what Jennie once told me.

I help him clean up, brushing some chip crumbs off the counter and wiping up the punch that had spilled on the floor. The entire time, my heart is beating faster from excitement.

"Nora, right?" Jake says, looking at me.

He knows my name!

I give him a huge grin. "That's right."

"That's really awesome of you to help, Nora," he says sincerely. "I like throwing parties, but the cleaning is always a bitch the next day. So now I try to clean a little during, before it gets really nasty."

My grin widens further, and I nod. "Of course."

That makes total sense to me. I love the fact that he seems so nice and thoughtful, so much more than just a jock.

We start chatting. He tells me about his plans for next year. Unlike me, he's going away to college. I tell him I'm planning to stay local for the next two years to save money. Afterwards, I want to transfer to a real university.

He nods approvingly and says that it's smart. He'd thought about doing something like that, but he was lucky enough to get a full-ride scholarship to the University of Michigan.

I smile and congratulate him. On the inside, I'm jumping up and down in joy.

We're clicking. We're really clicking! He likes me, I can tell. Oh, why hadn't I approached him before?

We talk for about twenty minutes before someone comes into the kitchen looking for Jake.

"Hey, Nora," Jake says before he goes back to the party, "are you doing anything tomorrow?"

I shake my head, holding my breath.

"How about we go see a movie?" Jake suggests. "Maybe grab dinner at that little seafood place?"

I grin and nod like an idiot. I'm too afraid to say something stupid, so I keep my mouth shut.

"Great," Jake says, grinning back at me. "Then I'll pick you up at six."

He goes back to being the party host, and I rejoin the girls. We stay for another couple of hours, but I don't talk to Jake again. He's surrounded by his jock friends, and I don't want to interrupt.

But every now and then, I catch him looking my way and smiling.

* * *

I'm floating on air for the next twenty-four hours. I tell Leah and Jennie all about what happened. They're excited for me.

In preparation for our date, I put on a cute blue dress and a pair of high-heeled brown boots. They're a cross between cowboy boots and something a bit dressier, and I know I look good in them.

Jake picks me up at six o'clock sharp.

We go to Fish-of-the-Sea, a popular local joint not too far from the movie theater. It's a nice sit-down place, not too formal.

Perfect for a first date.

We have a great time. I learn more about Jake and his family. He asks me questions too, and we discover that we like the same types of movies. I can't stand chick flicks for some reason, and I really enjoy cheesy end-of-the-world stories with lots of special effects. So does Jake, apparently.

After dinner, we go see a movie. Unfortunately, it's not about an apocalypse, but it's still a pretty good action film. During the movie, Jake puts his arm around my shoulders, and I can barely suppress my excitement. I hope he kisses me tonight.

When the movie is done, we go for a walk in the park. It's late, but I feel completely safe. The crime rate in our town is negligible, and there are plenty of streetlights.

We're walking and Jake is holding my hand. We're discussing the movie. Then he stops and just looks at me.

I know what he wants. It's what I want, too.

I look up at him and smile. He smiles back, puts his hands on my shoulders, and leans down to kiss me.

His lips feel soft, and his breath smells like the minty gum he was chewing earlier. His kiss is gentle and pleasant, everything I hoped it would be.

Then, in a blink of an eye, everything changes.

I don't even know what happened or how it happened. One minute, I'm kissing Jake, and the next, he's lying on the ground, unconscious. A large figure is looming over him.

I open my mouth to scream, but I can't get more than a peep out before a big hand covers my mouth and nose.

I feel a sharp prick on the side of my neck, and my world goes completely dark.

CHAPTER THREE

I wake up with a pounding headache and queasy stomach. It's dark, and I can't see a thing.

For a second, I can't remember what happened. Did I have too much to drink at a party? Then my mind clears, and the events of last night come rushing in. I remember the kiss and then . . . *Jake!* Oh dear God, what happened to Jake?

What happened to me?

I'm so terrified that I just lie there, shaking.

I am lying on something comfortable. A bed with a good mattress, most likely. I'm covered by a blanket, but I can't feel any clothes on my body, just the softness of cotton sheets against my skin. I touch myself and confirm that I'm right: I'm completely naked.

My shaking intensifies.

I use one hand to check between my legs. To my huge relief, everything feels the same. No wetness, no soreness, no indication that I've been violated in any way.

For now, at least.

Tears burn my eyes, but I don't let them fall. Crying wouldn't help my situation now. I need to figure out what's going on. Are they planning to kill me? Rape me? Rape me and then kill me? If it's ransom they're after, then I'm as good as dead. After my dad got laid off during the recession, my parents can barely pay their mortgage as is.

I hold back hysteria with effort. I don't want to start screaming. That would attract their attention.

Instead I just lie there in the dark, every horrifying story I've seen on the news running through my mind. I think of Jake and his warm smile. I think of my parents and how devastated they'll be when the police tell them I'm missing. I think of all my plans, and how I will probably never get a chance to attend a real university.

And then I start to get angry. Why did they do this? Who are they, anyway? I assume it's 'they' instead of 'he' because I remember seeing a dark figure looming over Jake's body. Someone else must've grabbed me from the back.

The anger helps hold back the panic. I'm able to think a little. I still can't see anything in the dark, but I can feel.

Moving quietly, I carefully start exploring my surroundings.

First, I determine that I'm indeed lying on a bed. A big bed, probably king-sized. There are pillows and a blanket, and the sheets are soft and pleasant to the touch. Likely expensive.

For some reason, that scares me even more. These are criminals with money.

Crawling to the edge of the bed, I sit up, holding the blanket tightly around me. My bare feet touch the floor. It's smooth and cold to the touch, like hardwood.

I wrap the blanket around me and stand up, ready to do further exploration.

At that moment, I hear the door opening.

A soft light comes on. Even though it's not bright, I'm blinded for a minute. I blink a few times, and my eyes adjust.

And I see *him*.

Julian.

He stands in the doorway like a dark angel. His hair curls a little around his face, softening the hard perfection of his features. His eyes are trained on my face, and his lips are curved in a slight smile.

He's stunning.

And utterly terrifying.

My instincts had been right—this man is capable of anything.

"Hello, Nora," he says softly, entering the room.

I cast a desperate glance around me. I see nothing that could serve as a weapon.

My mouth is dry like the desert. I can't even gather enough saliva to talk. So I just watch him stalk toward me like a hungry tiger approaches its prey.

I am going to fight if he touches me.

He comes closer, and I take a step back. Then another and another, until I'm pressed against the wall. I'm still huddling in the blanket.

He lifts his hand, and I tense, preparing to defend myself.

But he's merely holding a bottle of water and offering it to me.

"Here," he says. "I figured you must be thirsty."

I stare at him. I'm dying of thirst, but I don't want him to drug me again.

He seems to understand my hesitation. "Don't worry, my pet. It's just water. I want you awake and conscious."

I don't know how to react to that. My heart is hammering in my throat, and I feel sick with fear.

He stands there, patiently watching. Holding the blanket tightly with one hand, I give in to my thirst and take the water from him. My hand shakes, and my fingers brush against his in the process. A wave of heat rolls through me, a strange reaction that I ignore.

Now I have to unscrew the cap—which means I have to let go of the blanket. He's observing my dilemma with interest and no small measure of amusement. Thankfully, he's not touching me. He's standing less than two feet away and simply watching me.

I press my arms tightly against my body, holding the blanket that way, and unscrew the cap. Then I hold the blanket with one hand and lift the bottle to my lips to drink.

The cool liquid feels amazing on my parched lips and tongue. I drink until the entire bottle is gone. I can't remember the last time water tasted so good. Dry mouth must be the side effect of whatever drug he used to get me here.

Now I can talk again, so I ask him, "Why?"

To my huge surprise, my voice sounds almost normal.

He lifts his hand and touches my face again. Just like he did at the club. And again, I stand there helplessly and let him. His fingers are gentle on my skin, his touch almost tender. It's such a stark contrast to the whole situation that I'm disoriented for a moment.

"Because I didn't like seeing you with him," Julian says, and I can hear the barely suppressed rage in his voice. "Because he touched you, laid his hands on you."

I can barely think. "Who?" I whisper, trying to figure out what he's talking about. And then it hits me. "Jake?"

"Yes, Nora," he says darkly. "Jake."

"Is he—" I don't know if I can even say it out loud. "Is he . . . alive?"

"For now," Julian says, his eyes burning into mine. "He's in the hospital with a mild concussion."

I'm so relieved I slump against the wall. And then the full meaning of his words hits me. "What do you mean, for now?"

Julian shrugs. "His health and wellbeing are entirely dependent on you."

I swallow to moisten my still-dry throat. "On me?"

His fingers caress my face again, push the hair back behind my ear. I'm so cold I feel like his touch is burning my skin. "Yes, my pet, on you. If you behave, he'll be fine. If not . . ."

I can barely draw in a breath. "If not?"

Julian smiles. "He'll be dead within a week."

His smile is the most beautiful and frightening thing I've ever seen.

"Who are you?" I whisper. "What do you want from me?"

He doesn't answer. Instead, he touches my hair, lifts a thick brown strand to his face. Inhales, as though smelling it.

I watch him, frozen in place. I don't know what to do. Do I fight him now? And if so, what would that accomplish? He hasn't hurt me yet, and I don't want to provoke him. He's much larger than me, much stronger. I can see the thickness of his muscles under the black T-shirt he's wearing. Without my heels on, I barely come up to his shoulder.

While I contemplate the merits of fighting someone who probably outweighs me by a hundred pounds, he makes the decision for me. His hand leaves my hair and tugs at the blanket I'm holding so tightly.

I don't let go. If anything, I clutch it harder. And I do something embarrassing.

I beg.

"Please," I say desperately, "please, don't do this."

He smiles again. "Why not?" His hand is continuing to pull at the blanket, slowly and inexorably. I know he's doing it this way to prolong the torture. He could easily rip the blanket away from me with one strong tug.

"I don't want this," I tell him. I can barely draw in air through the constriction in my chest, and my voice comes out sounding unexpectedly breathy.

He looks amused, but there's a dark gleam in his eyes. "No? You think I couldn't feel your reaction to me in the club?"

I shake my head. "There was no reaction. You're wrong . . ." My voice is thick with unshed tears. "I only want Jake—"

In an instant, his hand is wrapped around my throat. He doesn't do anything else, doesn't squeeze, but the threat is there. I can feel the violence within him, and I'm terrified.

He leans down toward me. "You don't want that boy," he says harshly. "He can never give you what I can. Do you understand me?"

I nod, too scared to do anything else.

He releases my throat. "Good," he says in a softer tone. "Now let go of the blanket. I want to see you naked again."

Again? He must've been the one to undress me.

I try to plaster myself even closer to the wall. And still don't let go of the blanket.

He sighs.

Two seconds later, the blanket is on the floor. As I had suspected, I don't stand a chance when he uses his full strength.

I resist the only way I can. Instead of standing there and letting him look at my naked body, I slide down the wall until I'm sitting on the floor, my knees drawn up to my chest. My arms wrap around my legs, and I sit there like that, trembling all over. My long, thick hair streams down my back and arms, partially covering me.

I hide my face against my knees. I'm terrified of what he'll do to me now, and the tears burning my eyes finally escape, running down my cheeks.

"Nora," he says, and there is a steely note in his voice. "Get up. Get up right now."

I shake my head mutely, still not looking at him.

"Nora, this can be pleasurable for you or it can be painful. It's really up to you."

Pleasurable? Is he insane? My entire body is shaking with sobs at this point.

"Nora," he says again, and I hear the impatience in his voice. "You have exactly five seconds to do what I'm telling you."

He waits, and I can almost hear him counting in his head. I'm counting too, and when I get to four, I get up, tears still streaming down my face.

I'm ashamed of my own cowardice, but I'm so afraid of pain. I don't want him to hurt me.

I don't want him to touch me at all, but that is clearly not an option.

"Good girl," he says softly, touching my face again, brushing my hair back over my shoulders.

I tremble at his touch. I can't look at him, so I keep my eyes down.

He apparently objects to that, because he tilts my chin up until I have no choice but to meet his gaze with my own.

His eyes are dark blue in this light. He's so close to me that I can feel the heat coming off his body. It feels good because I'm cold. Naked and cold.

Suddenly, he reaches for me, bending down. Before I can get really scared, he slides one arm around my back and another under my knees.

Then he lifts me effortlessly in his arms and carries me to the bed.

* * *

He puts me down, almost gently, and I curl into a ball, shaking. He starts to undress, and I can't help watching him.

He's wearing jeans and a T-shirt, and the T-shirt comes off first.

His upper body is a work of art, all broad shoulders, hard muscles, and smooth tan skin. His chest is lightly dusted with dark hair. Under some other circumstances, I would've been thrilled to have such a good-looking lover.

Under these circumstances, I just want to scream.

His jeans are next. I can hear the sound of his zipper being lowered, and it galvanizes me into action.

In a second, I go from lying on the bed to scrambling for the door—which he'd left open.

I may be small, but I'm fast on my feet. I did track for ten years and was quite good at it. Unfortunately, I hurt my knee during one of the races, and now I'm limited to more leisurely runs and other forms of exercise.

I make it out the door, down the stairs, and I'm almost to the front door when he catches me.

His arms close around me from behind, and he squeezes me so hard that I can't breathe for a moment. My arms are completely restrained, so I can't even fight him. He lifts me, and I kick back at him with my heels. I manage to land a few kicks before he turns me around to face him.

I'm sure he's going to hurt me now, and I brace myself for a blow.

Instead, he just pulls me into his embrace and holds me tightly. My face is buried in his chest, and my naked body is pressed against his. I can smell the clean, musky scent of his skin and feel something hard and warm against my stomach.

His erection.

He's fully naked and turned on.

With the way he's holding me, I'm almost completely helpless. I can neither kick nor scratch him.

But I can bite.

So I sink my teeth into his pectoral muscle and hear him curse before he yanks on my hair, forcing me to release his flesh.

Then he holds me like that, one arm wrapped around my waist, my lower body tightly pressed against him. His other hand is fisted in my hair, holding my head arched back. My hands are pushing at his chest in a futile attempt to put some distance between us.

I meet his gaze defiantly, ignoring the tears running down my face. I have no choice but to be brave now. If I die, I want to at least retain some dignity.

His expression is dark and angry, his blue eyes narrowed at me.

I am breathing hard, and my heart is beating so fast I feel like it might jump out of my chest. We look at each other—predator and prey, the conqueror and the conquered—and in that moment, I feel an odd sort of connection to him. Like a part of myself is forever altered by what's happening between us.

Suddenly, his face softens. A smile appears on his sensuous lips.

Then he leans toward me, lowers his head, and presses his mouth to mine.

I am stunned. His lips are gentle, tender as they explore mine, even as he holds me with an iron grip.

He's a skilled kisser. I've kissed quite a few guys, and I've never felt anything like this. His breath is warm, flavored with something sweet, and his tongue teases my lips until they part involuntarily, granting him access to my mouth.

I don't know if it's the aftereffects of the drug he gave me or the simple relief that he's not hurting me, but I melt at that kiss. A strange languor spreads through my body, sapping my will to fight.

He kisses me slowly, leisurely, as though he has all the time in the world. His tongue strokes against mine, and he lightly sucks on my lower lip, sending a surge of liquid heat straight to my core. His hand eases its grip on my hair and cradles the back of my head instead. It's almost like he's making love to me.

I find my hands holding on to his shoulders. I have no idea how they got there, but I'm now clinging to him instead of pushing him away. I don't understand my own reaction. Why am I not cringing away from his kiss in disgust?

It just feels so good, that incredible mouth of his. It's like kissing an angel. It makes me forget the situation for a second, enables me to push the terror away.

He pulls away and looks down on me. His lips are wet and shiny, a little swollen from our kiss. Mine probably are too.

He no longer seems angry. Instead, he looks hungry and pleased at the same time. I can see both lust and tenderness on his perfect face, and I can't tear my eyes away.

I lick my lips, and his eyes drop down to my mouth for a second. He kisses me again, just a brief brush of his lips against mine.

Then he picks me up again and carries me upstairs to his bed.

CHAPTER FOUR

When I look back on this day, my behavior doesn't make sense to me. I don't understand why I didn't fight him harder, why I didn't try to get away again. It wasn't a rational decision on my part—it wasn't a conscious choice to cooperate in order to avoid pain.

No, I am acting purely on instinct.

And my instinct is to submit to him.

He puts me down on the bed, and I just lie there. I'm too worn out from our earlier struggle, and I still feel woozy from the drug.

There is something so surreal about what's happening that my mind can't process it fully. I feel like I'm watching a play or a movie. It can't possibly be me in this situation. I can't be this girl who was drugged and kidnapped, and who is letting her kidnapper touch her, stroke her all over her body.

We're lying on our sides, facing each other. I can feel his hands on my skin. They're slightly rough, callused. Warm on my frozen flesh. Strong, though he's not using that strength right now. He could subdue me with ease, like he did before, but there is no need. I'm not fighting him. I'm floating in a hazy, sensual fog.

He's kissing me again, and caressing my arm, my back, my neck, my outer thigh. His touch is gentle, yet firm. It's almost like he's giving me a massage, except I can feel the sexual intent in his actions.

He kisses my neck, lightly nibbling on the sensitive spot where my neck and shoulder join, and I shiver from the pleasurable sensation.

I close my eyes. It's disarming, that surprising gentleness of his. I know I should feel violated—and I do—but I also feel oddly cherished.

With my eyes closed, I pretend that this is just a dream. A dark fantasy, like the kind I sometimes have late at night. It makes it more palatable, the fact that I'm letting this stranger do this to me.

One of his hands is now on my buttocks, kneading the soft flesh. His other hand is traveling up my belly, my rib cage. He reaches my breasts and cups the left one in his palm, squeezes it lightly. My nipples are already hard, and his touch feels good, almost soothing. Rob has done this to me before, but it's never been like this. It's never felt like this.

I continue to keep my eyes shut as he rolls me onto my back. He's partially on top of me, but most of his weight is resting on the bed. He doesn't want to crush me, I realize, and I feel grateful.

He kisses my collarbone, my shoulder, my stomach. His mouth is hot, and it leaves a moist trail on my skin.

Then he closes his lips around my right nipple and sucks on it. My body arches, and I feel tension low in my belly. He repeats the action with my other nipple, and the tension inside me grows, intensifies.

He senses it. I know he does because his hand ventures between my thighs and feels the moisture there. "Good girl," he murmurs, stroking my folds. "So sweet, so responsive."

I whimper as his lips travel down my body, his hair tickling my skin. I know what he intends, and my mind blanks out when he reaches his destination.

For a second, I try to resist, but he effortlessly pulls my legs apart. His fingers pat me gently, then pull apart my nether lips.

And then he kisses me there, sending a surge of heat through my body. His skilled mouth licks and nibbles around my clitoris until I'm moaning, and then he closes his lips around it and lightly sucks.

The pleasure is so strong, so startling that my eyes fly open.

I don't understand what's happening to me, and it's frightening. I'm burning inside, throbbing between my legs. My heart is beating so fast I can't catch my breath, and I find myself panting.

I start struggling, and he laughs softly. I can feel the puffs of air from his breath on my sensitive flesh. He easily holds me down and continues what he's doing.

The tension inside me is becoming unbearable. I'm squirming against his tongue, and my motions seem to be bringing me closer to some elusive edge.

Then I go over with a soft scream. My entire body tightens, and I'm swamped by a wave of pleasure so intense that my toes curl. I can feel my inner muscles pulsing, and I realize that I just had an orgasm.

The first orgasm of my life.

And it was at the hands—or rather the mouth—of my captor.

I'm so devastated that I just want to curl up and cry. I squeeze my eyes shut again.

But he's not done with me yet. He crawls up my body and kisses my mouth again. He tastes differently now, salty, with a slightly musky undertone. It's from me, I realize. I'm tasting myself on his lips. A hot wave of embarrassment rolls through my body even as the hunger inside me intensifies.

His kiss is more carnal than before, rougher. His tongue penetrates my mouth in an obvious imitation of the sexual act, and his hips settle heavily between my legs. One of his hands is holding the back of my head, while another one is between my thighs, lightly rubbing and stimulating me again.

I still don't really resist, although my body tenses as the fear returns. I can feel the heat and hardness of his erection pushing against my inner thigh, and I know he's going to hurt me.

"Please," I whisper, opening my eyes to look at him. My vision is blurred by tears. "Please . . . I've never done this before—"

His nostrils flare, and his eyes gleam brighter. "I'm glad," he says softly. Then he shifts his hips a little and uses his hand to guide his shaft toward my opening.

I gasp as he begins to push inside. I'm wet, but my body resists the unfamiliar intrusion. I don't know how big he is, but he feels enormous as the head of his cock slowly enters my body.

It begins to hurt, to burn, and I cry out, pushing at his shoulders.

His pupils expand, making his eyes look darker. There are beads of sweat on his forehead, and I realize he's actually restraining himself. "Relax, Nora," he whispers harshly. "It will hurt less if you relax."

I'm trembling. I can't follow his advice because I'm too nervous—and because it hurts so much, having even a little bit of him inside me.

He continues to press, and my flesh slowly gives way, reluctantly stretching for him. I'm writhing now, sobbing, my nails scratching at his back, but he's relentless, working his cock in inch by slow inch.

Then he pauses for a second, and I can see a vein pulsing near his temple. He looks like he's in pain. But I know that it's pleasurable for him, this act that's hurting me so much.

He lowers his head, kissing my forehead. And then he pushes past my virginal barrier, tearing through the thin membrane with one firm thrust. He doesn't stop until his full length is buried inside me, his pubic hair pressing against my own.

I almost black out from the pain. My stomach twists with nausea, and I feel faint. I can't even scream; all I can do is try to take small, shallow breaths to avoid passing out. I can feel his hardness lodged deep inside me, and it's the most agonizingly invasive thing I've ever experienced.

"Relax," he murmurs in my ear, "just relax, my pet. The pain will pass, it will get better . . ."

I don't believe him. It feels like a heated pole has been shoved inside my body, tearing me open. And I can't do anything to escape, to make it hurt less. He's so much larger than me, so much stronger. All I can do is lie there helplessly, pinned underneath him.

He doesn't move his hips, doesn't thrust, even though I can feel the tension in his muscles. Instead, he gently kisses my forehead again. I close my eyes, bitter tears streaming down my temples, and feel the light brush of his lips against my eyelids.

I don't know how long we stay there like this. He's raining soft kisses on my face, my neck. His hands embrace me, caress my skin in a parody of a lover's touch. And all the while, his cock is buried deep inside me, its uncompromising hardness hurting me, burning me from within.

I don't know at what point the pain starts to change. My treacherous body slowly softens, begins to respond to his kisses, to the tenderness in his touch.

The evil bastard senses it. And he slowly begins to move, partially withdrawing from my body and then working himself back in.

Initially, his movements make it worse, only adding to my agony. And then he reaches between our bodies with one hand, and uses one finger to press against my clit, keeping the pressure light and steady. His thrusts move my hips, causing me to rub against his finger in a rhythmic way.

To my horror, I feel the tension gathering inside me again. The pain is still there, but so is the pleasure. I'm writhing in his arms, but now I'm fighting myself as well. His thrusts get harder, deeper, and I'm screaming from the unbearable intensity. The pain and the pleasure mix, until they're indistinguishable from one another—until I exist in a world of pure, overwhelming sensation. And then I explode, the orgasm ripping through my body with such force that my vision darkens for a moment.

Suddenly, I can hear him groaning against my ear and feel him getting even thicker and longer inside me. His cock is pulsing and jerking deep within me, and I know that he found his release as well.

In the aftermath, he rolls off me and gathers me to him, holding me close.

And I cry in his arms, seeking solace from the very person who is the cause of my tears.

* * *

Afterwards, my mind is foggy, my thoughts strangely jumbled. He carries me somewhere, and I lie limply in his arms, like a rag doll.

Now he's washing me. I'm standing in the shower with him. I'm vaguely surprised that my legs can hold me upright.

I feel numb, detached somehow.

There is blood on my thighs. I can see it mixing with the water, running down the drain. Also, there's something sticky between my legs. His semen, most likely. He hadn't used protection.

I might now have an STD. I should be horrified by the thought, but I just feel numb. At least pregnancy isn't something I have to be concerned about. As soon as I got serious with Rob, my mom insisted on taking me to the doctor to get a birth control implant in my arm. As a nursing assistant at a nonprofit women's clinic, she saw far too many teenage pregnancies and wanted to make sure the same thing didn't happen to me.

I'm so grateful to her right now.

While I'm pondering all this, Julian washes me thoroughly, shampooing and conditioning my hair. He even shaves my legs and armpits.

Once I'm squeaky clean and smooth, he shuts off the water and guides me out of the shower.

He dries me with a towel first and then himself. Afterwards, he wraps me in a fluffy robe and carries me to the kitchen to feed me.

I eat what he puts in front of me. I don't even taste it. It's a sandwich of some kind, but I don't know what's in it. He also gives me a glass of water, which I gulp down eagerly.

I vaguely hope that he's not drugging me, but I don't really care if he is. I'm so tired I just want to pass out.

After I'm done eating and drinking, he leads me back to the bathroom.

"Go ahead, brush your teeth," he says, and I stare at him. He cares about my oral hygiene?

I do want to brush my teeth, though, so I do as he says. I also use the restroom to pee. He considerately leaves me alone for that.

Then he takes me back to the room. Somehow the bed now has fresh sheets on it, with no traces of blood anywhere. I'm thankful for that.

He kisses me lightly on the lips, leaves the room, and locks the door.

I'm so exhausted that I walk over to the bed, lie down, and instantly fall asleep.

CHAPTER FIVE

When I wake up, my mind is completely clear. I remember everything, and I want to scream.

I jump out of bed, noticing that I'm still wearing the robe from last night. The sudden movement makes me aware of a deep inner soreness, and my lower body tightens at the memory of how I got to be that sore. I can still feel his fullness inside me, and I shudder at the recollection.

I am sickened and disgusted with myself. What is wrong with me? How could I have just lain there and let Julian have sex with me? How could I have found pleasure in his embrace?

Yes, he's good-looking, but that's no excuse. He's evil. I know it. I sensed it from the very beginning. His outer beauty hides a darkness inside.

I have a feeling he's only begun to reveal his true nature to me.

Yesterday I had been too frightened, too traumatized to pay attention to my surroundings. I'm feeling much better today, so I carefully study this room.

There is a window. It's covered by thick ivory shades, but I can still see a little sunlight peeking through.

I rush to it, pulling open the shades, and blink at the sudden bright light. It takes a few seconds for my eyes to adjust, and then I look outside.

The bottom drops out of my stomach.

The window is not hermetically sealed or anything like that. In fact, it looks like I could easily open it and climb out. This room is on the second floor, so I could maybe even make it to the ground without breaking anything.

No, the window is not the problem.

It's the view outside.

I can see palm trees and a white sandy beach. Beyond it, there is a large body of water, blue and shimmering in the bright sun.

It's beautiful and tropical.

And about as different as possible from my little town in the Midwest.

* * *

I'm cold again. So cold that I'm shivering. I know it's from stress because the temperature must be somewhere in the eighties.

I'm pacing up and down the room, occasionally pausing to look out the window.

Every time I look, it's like a punch to the stomach.

I don't know what I'd been hoping. I honestly hadn't had a chance to think about my location. I'd just sort of assumed that he would keep me somewhere in the area, maybe near Chicago where we'd first met. I'd thought that all I had to do in order to escape is find a way out of this house.

Now I realize it's far more complicated than that.

I try the door again. It's locked.

A few minutes ago, I had discovered a small bathroom attached to this room. I used it to take care of my basic needs and to brush my teeth. It had been a nice distraction.

Now I'm pacing like a caged animal, growing more terrified and angry with every minute that passes.

Finally, the door opens, and a woman comes inside.

I'm so shocked that I simply stare. She's fairly young—maybe in her early thirties—and pretty.

She's holding a tray of food and smiling at me. Her hair is red and curly, and her eyes are a soft brown color. She's bigger than me, probably at least five inches taller, with an athletic build. She's dressed very casually, in a pair of jean shorts and a white tank top, with flip-flops on her feet.

I think about attacking her. She's a woman, and I have a small chance of winning against her in a fight. I have no chance against Julian.

Her smile widens, as though she's reading my mind. "Please don't jump me," she says, and I can hear the amusement in her voice. "It's quite pointless, I promise. I know you want to escape, but there is really nowhere to go. We're on a private island in the middle of the Pacific Ocean."

The sinking feeling in my stomach worsens. "Whose private island?" I ask, though I already know the answer.

"Why, Julian's, of course."

"Who is he? Who are you people?" My voice is relatively steady as I speak to her. She doesn't make me nervous the way Julian does.

She puts down the tray. "You'll learn everything in due time. I'm here to take care of you and the property. My name is Beth, by the way."

I take a deep breath. "Why am I here, Beth?"

"You're here because Julian wants you."

"And you don't see anything wrong with that?" I can hear the hysterical edge in my tone. I don't understand how this woman is going along with that madman, how she's acting like this is normal.

She shrugs. "Julian does whatever he wants. It's not for me to judge."

"Why not?"

"Because I owe him my life," she says seriously and walks out of the room.

* * *

I eat the food Beth brought me. It's pretty good actually, even though it's not traditional breakfast food. There is grilled fish in some kind of mushroom sauce and roasted potatoes with a side of green salad. For dessert, there's some cut-up mango. Local fruit, I'm guessing.

Despite my inner turmoil, I manage to eat everything. If I were less of a coward, I would resist by refusing to eat his food—but I fear hunger as much as I fear pain.

So far he hasn't really hurt me. Well, it did hurt when he put his cock inside me, but he hadn't been purposefully rough. I suspect it would've hurt the first time regardless of the circumstances.

The first time. It suddenly dawns on me that it had been my first time. Now I'm no longer a virgin.

Strangely, I don't feel like I lost anything. The thin membrane inside me had never held any particular meaning for me. I never intended to wait until marriage or anything else like that. I regret that my first time was with a monster, but I don't mourn the loss of the 'virgin' designation. I would've gladly gone all the way with Jake, if I'd only had a chance.

Jake! My stomach lurches. I can't believe I haven't thought about him since Julian told me he was safe. The guy I've been crazy about for months had been the furthest thing from my mind when I was in the arms of my captor.

Hot shame burns inside me. Shouldn't I have been thinking of Jake last night? Shouldn't I have been picturing his face when Julian touched me so intimately? If I truly wanted Jake, shouldn't he have been the one on my mind during my forced sexual encounter?

I'm suddenly filled with bitter hatred for the man who did this to me—the man who shattered my illusions about the world, about myself. I'd never thought much about what I would do if I got kidnapped, how I would react. Who thinks about stuff like that? But I guess I'd always assumed I would be brave, fighting to my last breath. Isn't that what they do in all the books and movies? Fight, even when it's useless, even when doing so means getting hurt? Shouldn't I have done that too? Yes, he's stronger than me, but I didn't have to give in so easily. He didn't tie me up; he didn't threaten me with a knife or a gun. All he'd done was chase me down when I tried to run.

That run had been the grand total of my resistance thus far.

I don't recognize this person who had given in so easily. And yet I know she's me. A part of me that had never come to light before. A part of me that I would've never known if Julian hadn't taken me.

Thinking about this is so upsetting that I focus on my captor instead. Who is he? How can someone afford to have an entire private island? How does Beth owe him her life? And, most importantly, what does he intend to do with me?

A million different scenarios run through my mind, each one more horrifying than the next. I know there's such a thing as human trafficking. It happens all the time, especially to women from poorer countries. Is that the fate that awaits me? Am I going to end up in a brothel somewhere, drugged out of my mind and used daily by dozens of men? Is Julian simply sampling the merchandise before he delivers it to its final destination?

Before panic can take over my mind, I inhale deeply and try to think logically. While the human trafficking is a possibility, it doesn't seem likely to me. For one thing, Julian appears to be very possessive of me—far too possessive for someone just testing out the merchandise. And besides, why bring me here, to his private island, if he's just planning to sell me?

My pet, he had called me. Is that just a meaningless endearment, or is that how he sees me? Does he have some fetish that involves keeping women captive? I think about it for a while, and decide that he probably does. Why else would a wealthy, good-looking man do this? Surely he has no problem getting dates the usual way. In fact, I might've gone out with him myself if I hadn't gotten that strange vibe from him in the club.

If he hadn't touched me like he owned me.

Is that his thing? Ownership? Does he want a sex slave? If so, why did he choose me? Was it because of my reaction to him at the club? Did he guess that I would be a coward, that I would let him do whatever he wanted to me? Did I somehow bring this upon myself?

The thought is so sickening that I push it away and get up, determined to explore my prison further.

The door is still locked, which doesn't surprise me. I'm able to open the window, and warm, ocean-scented air fills the room.

I can't open the screen on the window, though. I would need to do that in order to climb out. I don't try too hard. If Beth is to be believed, escaping from this room wouldn't help me at all.

I look for something that could be used as a weapon. There's no knife, but there's a fork left over from my meal. Beth would probably notice if I hide it. Still, I take a chance and do it, concealing the utensil behind a stack of books on a tall bookshelf that lines one of the walls.

Next I explore the bathroom, hoping to find a bottle of hairspray or something else along those lines. But there's only soap, toothbrush, and toothpaste. In the shower stall, I find body wash, shampoo, and conditioner—all nice, expensive brands. My captor is clearly not stingy.

Then again, anyone who owns a private island can probably afford a fifty-dollar shampoo. He might even be able to afford a thousand-dollar shampoo, if such a thing exists.

The fact that I'm thinking about shampoo amazes me. Shouldn't I be screaming and crying? *Oh, wait, I did that yesterday.* I guess there's only so much crying a person can do. I seem to be all out of tears, at least for now.

After exploring every nook and cranny of the room, I get bored, so I take one of the books from the bookshelf. A Sidney Sheldon novel, something about a woman betrayed who seeks revenge on her enemies.

It's engrossing enough that I'm able to mentally escape my prison for the next couple of hours.

* * *

Beth comes and brings me lunch. She also brings me some clothes, folded in a stack.

I'm glad. I've been wearing the bathrobe all morning, and I would like to dress normally.

When she puts the clothes on the dresser, I again think about tackling her and trying to escape. Maybe using the fork I've got stashed away.

"Nora, give me the fork," she says.

I jump a little and give her a startled look. Could she actually be a mind-reader?

And then I realize that she's simply looking at the empty tray and noticing that the utensil is missing.

I decide to play dumb. "What fork?"

She lets out a sigh. "You know what fork. The one you hid behind the books. Give it to me."

Another one of my assumptions proven wrong. I don't know why I'd thought I had any privacy.

I look up at the ceiling, studying it carefully, but I can't see where the cameras are.

"Nora . . ." Beth prompts.

I retrieve the fork and throw it at her. I think I'm secretly hoping it spears her in the eye.

But Beth catches it and shakes her head at me, as though disappointed in my behavior. "I was hoping you wouldn't act this way," she says.

"Act what way? Like a victim of kidnapping?" I really, really want to hit her right now.

"Like a spoiled brat," she clarifies, putting the fork in her pocket. "You think it's so awful, being here on this beautiful island? You think you're suffering by being in Julian's bed?"

I stare at her like she's a lunatic. Does she honestly expect me to be okay with this situation? To meekly go along with this and never utter a word of protest?

She stares back at me, and for the first time, I notice some lines on her face. "You don't know the real meaning of suffering, little girl," she says softly, "and I hope you never find out. Be nice to Julian, and you just might be able to continue living a charmed life."

She leaves the room, and I swallow to get rid of the sudden dryness in my throat.

For some reason, her words make my hands shake.

CHAPTER SIX

It's evening now. With every minute that passes, I'm starting to get more and more anxious at the thought of seeing my captor again.

The novel that I've been reading can no longer hold my interest. I put it down and walk in circles around the room.

I am dressed in the clothes Beth had given me earlier. It's not what I would've chosen to wear, but it's better than a bathrobe. A sexy pair of white lacy panties and a matching bra for underwear. A pretty blue sundress that buttons in the front. Everything fits me suspiciously well. Has he been stalking me for a while? Learning everything about me, including my clothing size?

The thought makes me sick.

I am trying not to think about what's to come, but it's impossible. I don't know why I'm so sure he'll come to me tonight. It's possible he has an entire harem of women stashed away on this island, and he visits each one only once a week, like sultans used to do.

Yet somehow I know he'll be here soon. Last night had simply whetted his appetite. I know he's not done with me, not by a long shot.

Finally, the door opens.

He walks in like he owns the place. Which, of course, he does.

I am again struck by his masculine beauty. He could've been a model or a movie star, with a face like his. If there was any fairness in the world, he would've been short or had some other imperfection to offset that face.

But he doesn't. His body is tall and muscular, perfectly proportioned. I remember what it feels like to have him inside me, and I feel an unwelcome jolt of arousal.

He's again wearing jeans and a T-shirt. A grey one this time. He seems to favor simple clothing, and he's smart to do so. His looks don't need any enhancement.

He smiles at me. It's his fallen angel smile—dark and seductive at the same time. "Hello, Nora."

I don't know what to say to him, so I blurt out the first thing that pops into my head. "How long are you going to keep me here?"

He cocks his head slightly to the side. "Here in the room? Or on the island?"

"Both."

"Beth will show you around tomorrow, take you swimming if you'd like," he says, approaching me. "You won't be locked in, unless you do something foolish."

"Such as?" I ask, my heart pounding in my chest as he stops next to me and lifts his hand to stroke my hair.

"Trying to harm Beth or yourself." His voice is soft, his gaze hypnotic as he looks down at me. The way he's touching my hair is oddly relaxing.

I blink, trying to break his spell. "And what about on the island? How long will you keep me here?"

His hand caresses my face, curves around my cheek. I catch myself leaning into his touch, like a cat getting petted, and I immediately stiffen.

His lips curl into a knowing smile. The bastard knows the effect he has on me. "A long time, I hope," he says.

For some reason, I'm not surprised. He wouldn't have bothered bringing me all the way here if he just wanted to fuck me a few times. I'm terrified, but I'm not surprised.

I gather my courage and ask the next logical question. "Why did you kidnap me?"

The smile leaves his face. He doesn't answer, just looks at me with an inscrutable blue gaze.

I begin to shake. "Are you going to kill me?"

"No, Nora, I won't kill you."

His denial reassures me, although he could obviously be lying.

"Are you going to sell me?" I can barely get the words out. "Like to be a prostitute or something?"

"No," he says softly. "Never. You're mine and mine alone."

I feel a tiny bit calmer, but there is one more thing I have to know. "Are you going to hurt me?"

For a moment, he doesn't answer again. Something dark briefly flashes in his eyes. "Probably," he says quietly.

And then he leans down and kisses me, his warm lips soft and gentle on mine.

For a second, I stand there frozen, unresponsive. I believe him. I know he's telling the truth when he says he'll hurt me. There's something in him that scares me—that has scared me from the very beginning.

He's nothing like the boys I've gone on dates with. He's capable of anything.

And I'm completely at his mercy.

I think about trying to fight him again. That would be the normal thing to do in my situation. The brave thing to do.

And yet I don't do it.

I can feel the darkness inside him. There's something wrong with him. His outer beauty hides something monstrous underneath.

I don't want to unleash that darkness. I don't know what will happen if I do.

So I stand still in his embrace and let him kiss me. And when he picks me up again and takes me to bed, I don't try to resist in any way.

Instead, I close my eyes and give in to the sensations.

* * *

He's again gentle with me. I should be terrified of him—and I am—but my body seems to enjoy the dual sensation of fear and arousal. I don't know what that says about me.

I lie there with my eyes closed as he takes off my clothes, layer by layer. First he unbuttons the front of the dress, like he's unwrapping a present. His hands are strong and sure; there's no hint of awkwardness or hesitation in his movements. He's clearly had a lot of practice with women's clothing.

After the dress is unbuttoned, he pauses for a second. I sense his gaze on me, and I wonder what he's seeing. I know I have a good body; it's slim and toned, even though it's not as curvy as I would like.

He trails his fingers down my stomach, making me tremble. "So pretty," he says softly. "Such lovely skin. You should always wear white. It suits you."

I don't respond, just squeeze my eyes tighter. I don't want him looking at me, don't want him enjoying the sight of my body in the undergarments he picked out for me. I wish he would just fuck me and get it over with, instead of engaging in this twisted parody of lovemaking.

But he has no intention of making it easy for me.

His mouth follows the same path as his fingers. It feels hot and moist on my belly, and then he moves lower, to where my legs are instinctively squeezed tightly together. He doesn't seem to like that, and his hands are rough as they pull my thighs apart, his fingers digging into my tender flesh.

I whimper at the hint of violence, and try to relax my legs to avoid angering him further.

His grip eases, his hands becoming gentler. "My sweet, beautiful girl," he whispers, and I can feel his hot breath on my sensitive folds. "You know I'll make it good for you."

And then his lips are on me, and his tongue is swirling around my clit, his mouth sucking and nibbling. His hair brushes against my inner thighs, tickling me, and his hands hold my legs spread wide open. I twist and cry out, the pleasure so intense that I forget everything but the incredible heat and tension inside me.

He brings me close to the edge, but doesn't let me go over. Every time I feel my orgasm approaching, he stops or changes the rhythm, driving me crazy with frustration. I find myself pleading, begging, my body arching mindlessly toward him. When he finally lets me reach the peak, it's such a relief that my entire body spasms, shuddering and twisting from the intensity of the release.

For some reason, I start crying when it's over. Tears leak from the outer corners of my eyes and run down my temples, soaking into my hair and then the pillow. He appears to like it because he crawls up my body and kisses the wet trails on my face, then licks them.

His large hands stroke my body, rubbing my skin, caressing me all over. It would be soothing if it weren't for the hardness of his cock prodding at my entrance.

I'm not fully healed inside, so it hurts again when he starts to push in. Even though I'm wet from the orgasm, he can't slip into me easily, not without tearing me open. Instead, he has to go slowly, working himself in gradually until I have a chance to adjust to the intrusion.

I bite my lower lip, trying to cope with the burning, too-full feeling. Would I ever be able to accept him easily? Would I ever experience pleasure without pain in his arms?

"Open your eyes," he orders in a harsh whisper.

I obey him, even though I can barely see through the veil of tears.

He's staring at me as he slowly begins to move inside me, and there's something triumphant in his gaze. The heat of his body surrounds me, his weight presses me down on the bed. He's inside me, on top of me, all around me. I can't even escape into the privacy of my mind.

And in that moment, I feel possessed by him, like he's taking more than just my body. Like he's laying claim to something deep within me, bringing out a side of me that I never knew existed.

Because in his arms, I experience something I have never felt before.

A primitive and completely irrational sense of belonging.

* * *

He takes me twice more during the night. By morning I'm so sore I feel raw inside—and yet I've had so many orgasms I lost count.

He leaves me at some point in the morning. I'm so exhausted I'm not even aware of his departure. I sleep deeply and dreamlessly, and when I wake up, it's already past noon.

I get up, brush my teeth, and take a shower. On my thighs, I can see dried bits of semen. He didn't use a condom this night either.

I wonder again about STDs. Does Julian care about this at all? He probably isn't worried about catching anything from me, given my lack of experience, but I'm certainly worried about getting it from him. Lifting my left arm, I peer at the tiny mark where my birth control implant was inserted. Thank God for my mom's pregnancy paranoia. If I didn't have it . . . I shudder at the thought.

Right after I exit the bathroom, Beth comes into my room carrying another food tray and more clothes. This time, it's more traditional breakfast food: an omelet with vegetables and cheese, a piece of toast, and fresh tropical fruit.

She's again smiling at me, apparently determined to ignore the fork incident. "Good morning," she says cheerfully.

My eyebrows rise. "And good morning to you too," I say, my voice thick with sarcasm.

At my obvious attempt to needle her, Beth's smile widens further. "Oh, don't be such a grump. Julian said you get to leave the room today. Isn't that nice?"

It actually *is* nice. It would give me a chance to explore my prison a bit, to see if this place is really an island. Maybe there are other people here besides Beth—people who would be more sympathetic to my plight.

Alternatively, maybe I'll find a phone or a computer. If I could just send a text or an email to my parents, they could pass it along to the police and then I might be rescued.

At the thought of my family, my chest feels tight and my eyes burn. They must be so worried about me, wondering what happened, whether I am still alive. I'm an only child, and my mom always said she'd die if anything happened to me. I hope she didn't mean it.

I hate him.

And I hate this woman, who's smiling at me right now.

"Sure, Beth," I say, wanting to claw at her face until that smile turns into a grimace. "It's always nice to leave a small cage for a bigger one."

She rolls her eyes and sits down on a chair. "So dramatic. Just eat your food and then I'll show you around."

I think about not eating just to spite her, but I am hungry. So I eat, polishing off all the food on the tray.

"Where is Julian?" I ask between bites. I'm curious how he spends his days. So far, I've only seen him in the evenings.

"He's working," Beth explains. "He has a lot of business interests that require his attention."

"What kind of business interests?"

She shrugs. "All kinds."

"Is he a criminal?" I ask bluntly.

She laughs. "Why would you assume that?"

"Um, maybe because he kidnapped me?"

She laughs again, shaking her head as though I said something funny.

I want to hit her, but I restrain myself. I need to learn more about my surroundings before I try anything like that. I don't want to end up locked up in the room if I can avoid it. My chances of escape are much better if I have more freedom.

So I just get up and give her a cold look. "I'm ready to go."

"Then put on a swimming suit," she says, gesturing toward the clothes she had brought, "and we can go."

* * *

Before we walk out, Beth shows me the rest of the house. It's spacious and tastefully furnished. The decor is modern, with just a hint of tropical influence and subtle Asian motifs. Light hues predominate, although here and there, I see an unexpected pop of color in the form of a red vase or a bright blue dragon sculpture. There are four bedrooms—three upstairs and one downstairs. The kitchen on the first floor is particularly striking, with top-of-the-line appliances and gleaming granite countertops.

There is also one room that Beth says is Julian's office. It's on the first floor, and it's apparently off-limits to anyone but him. That's where he supposedly takes care of his business affairs. The door is closed when we walk past it.

After we're done with the house tour, Beth spends the next two hours showing me the island. And it's definitely an island—she didn't lie to me about that.

It's only about two miles across and a mile wide. According to Beth, we're somewhere in the Pacific Ocean, with the nearest populated piece of land over five hundred miles away. She emphasizes that fact a couple of times, as though she's afraid I might take it into my head to try to swim away.

I wouldn't do that. I'm not a strong enough swimmer, nor am I suicidal.

I would try to steal a boat instead.

We go up to the highest point of the island. It's a small mountain—or a large hill, depending on one's definition of these things. The view from there is amazing—all bright blue water wherever the eye can see.

On one side of the island, the water is a different shade of blue, more turquoise, and Beth tells me it's a shallow cove that's great for snorkeling.

Julian's house is the only one on the island. It's sitting on one side of the mountain, a little ways back from the beach and somewhat elevated. That's the most sheltered location, Beth explains; the house is protected from both strong winds and the ocean there. It has apparently survived a number of typhoons with minimal damage.

I nod, as though I care. I have no intention of being here for the next typhoon. The desire to escape burns brightly within me. I didn't see any phones or computers when Beth was showing me the house, but that doesn't mean they're not there. If Julian is able to work from the island, then there's definitely internet connectivity. And if they're foolish enough to let me roam this island freely, I will find a way to reach the outside world.

We end the tour at the beach near the house.

"Want to go for a swim?" Beth asks me, stripping off her shorts and T-shirt. Underneath, she's wearing a blue bikini. Her body is lean and toned. She's in such great shape that I wonder about her age. Her figure could belong to a teenager, but her face seems older.

"How old are you?" I ask straight out. I would never be so tactless under normal circumstances, but I don't care if I offend this woman. What do social conventions matter when you're being held captive by a pair of crazy people?

She smiles, not the least bit upset at my impolite question. "I'm thirty-seven," she says.

"And Julian?"

"He's twenty-nine."

"Are you two lovers?" I don't know what makes me ask this. If she's in any way jealous of my position as Julian's sexual plaything, she's certainly not showing it.

Beth laughs. "No, we're not."

"Why not?" I can't believe I'm being so forward. I've been raised to always be polite and well-mannered, but there's something liberating about not caring what people think. I have always been a people-pleaser, but I don't want to please this woman in any way.

She stops laughing and gives me a serious look. "Because I'm not what Julian needs or wants."

"And what is that?"

"You'll learn someday," she says mysteriously, then walks into the water.

I stare after her, curiosity eating at me, but she appears to be done talking. Instead, she dives in and starts swimming with a sure athletic stroke.

It's hot outside, and the sun is beaming down on me. The sand is white and looks soft, and the water is sparkling, tempting me with its coolness. I want to hate this place, to despise everything about my captivity, but I have to admit that the island is beautiful.

I don't have to go swimming if I don't want to. It doesn't seem like Beth is going to force me. And it seems wrong to enjoy myself at the beach while my family is undoubtedly worried sick about me, grieving about my disappearance.

But the lure of the water is strong. I've always loved the ocean, even though I've been to the tropics only a couple of times in my life. This island is my idea of paradise, despite the fact that it belongs to a snake.

I deliberate for a minute, then I take off my dress and kick off my sandals. I could deny myself this small pleasure, but I'm too pragmatic. I have no illusions about my status here. At any moment, Julian and Beth could lock me up, starve me, beat me. Just because I've been treated relatively well so far doesn't mean it will continue to be that way. In my precarious situation, every moment of joy is precious—because I don't know what the future holds for me, whether I will ever again experience anything resembling happiness.

So I join my enemy in the ocean, letting the water wash away my fear and cool the helpless anger burning in the pit of my stomach.

We swim, then lounge on the hot sand, and then swim again. I don't ask any more questions, and Beth seems content with the silence.

We stay on the beach for the next two hours and then finally head back to the house.

CHAPTER SEVEN

This time, Julian is supposed to join me for dinner. Beth sets a table for us downstairs and prepares a meal of local fish, rice, beans, and plantains. It's her Caribbean recipe, she tells me proudly.

"Are you having dinner with us?" I ask, watching as she carries the plates over to the table.

I'm showered and dressed in the clothes Beth provided for me. It's another white lacy bra-and-panties set and a yellow dress with white flowers on it. On my feet, I'm wearing white high-heeled sandals. The outfit is sweet and feminine, very different from the jeans and dark tops I normally wear. It makes me look like a pretty doll.

I still can't believe they're letting me walk around the house freely. There are knives in the kitchen. I could steal one and use it on Beth at any point. I'm tempted, even though my stomach churns at the thought of blood and violence.

Perhaps I'll do it soon, once I've had a chance to learn a bit more about this place.

I'm learning something interesting about myself. I apparently don't believe in grand, but pointless gestures. A cool, rational voice inside me tells me that I need a plan, a way to get off the island before I try anything. Attacking Beth right now would be stupid. It could result in my being locked up or worse.

No, this is much better. Let them think I'm harmless. I stand a much greater chance of escape that way.

For the past hour, I've been sitting in the kitchen, watching Beth prepare food. She's very good, very efficient. Spending time with her is distracting me from thoughts of Julian and the night to come.

"No," she says, answering my question. "I'll be in my room. Julian wants some alone time with you."

"Why? Does he think we're dating or something?"

She grins. "Julian doesn't date."

"No kidding." My tone is beyond sarcastic. "Why date when you can kidnap and rape instead?"

"Don't be ridiculous," Beth says sharply. "Do you really think he has to force women? Even you can't be that naive."

I stare at her. "You mean to tell me he doesn't make a habit of stealing women and bringing them here?"

Beth shakes her head. "You're the only person besides me who has ever been here. This island is Julian's private sanctuary. Nobody knows it even exists."

A chill runs down my spine at those words. "So why am I so lucky?" I ask slowly, my pulse picking up. "What makes me worthy of this great honor?"

She smiles. "You'll find out someday. Julian will tell you when he wants you to know."

I'm sick of all this 'someday' bullshit, but I know she's too loyal to my captor to tell me anything. So I try to learn something else instead. "What did you mean when you said you owe him your life?"

Her smile fades and her expression hardens, her face settling into harsh, bitter lines. "That's none of your business, little girl."

And for the next ten minutes while she's finishing setting the table, she doesn't speak to me at all.

* * *

After everything is ready, she leaves me alone in the dining room to wait for Julian. I'm both nervous and excited. For the first time, I'm going to have a chance to interact with my captor outside the bedroom.

I have to admit to a kind of sick fascination with him. He frightens me, yet I'm unbearably curious about him. Who is he? What does he want from me? Why did he choose me to be his victim?

A minute later, he walks into the room. I'm sitting at the table, looking out the window. Before I even see him, I feel his presence. The atmosphere turns electric, heavy with expectation.

I turn my head, watching him approach. This time, he's wearing a soft-looking grey polo shirt and a pair of white khaki pants. We could be having dinner at a country club.

My heart is beating rapidly in my chest, and I can feel blood rushing through my veins. I'm suddenly much more aware of my body. My breasts feel more sensitive, my nipples tightening underneath the lacy confines of my bra. The soft fabric of the dress brushes against my bare legs, reminding me of the way he touched me there. Of the way he touched me everywhere.

Warm moisture gathers between my thighs at the memory.

He comes up to me and bends down, giving me a brief kiss on the mouth. "Hello, Nora," he says when he straightens, his beautiful lips curved in a darkly sensual smile. He's so breathtaking that I'm unable to think for a moment, my mind clouded by his nearness.

His smile widens, and he walks over to sit down across the table from me. "How was your day, my pet?" he asks, reaching for a piece of fish and putting it on his plate. His movements are confident and oddly graceful.

It's hard to believe that evil wears such a beautiful mask.

I gather my wits. "Why do you call me that?"

"Call you what? My pet?"

I nod.

"Because you remind me of a kitten," he says, his blue eyes glittering with some strange emotion. "Small, soft, and very touchable. You make me want to stroke you just to see if you will purr in my arms."

My cheeks get hot. I feel flushed all over, and I hope my skin tone hides my reaction. "I'm not an animal—"

"Of course you're not. I'm not into bestiality."

"Then what are you into?" I blurt out, then cringe internally. I don't want to make him mad. He's not Beth. He scares me.

Fortunately, he just looks amused at my daring. "At the moment," he says softly, "I'm into you."

I look away and reach for the rice, my hand shaking slightly.

"Here, let me help you with that." He takes the plate from me, his fingers briefly brushing against mine. Before I can say anything, my plate is filled with a healthy portion of everything that's on the table.

He puts the plate back in front of me, and I stare at it in dismay. I'm too nervous to eat in front of him. My stomach is all tied into knots.

When I look up, I see that he has no such problem. He's eating with gusto, clearly enjoying Beth's cooking.

"What's the matter?" he asks between bites. "You're not hungry?"

I shake my head, even though I was ravenous before he came.

He frowns, putting down his fork. "Why not? Beth said you spent the day at the beach and swam quite a bit. Shouldn't you be hungry after all that exercise?"

I shrug. "I'm okay." I'm not about to tell him that he's the cause of my lack of appetite.

His eyes narrow at me. "Are you playing games with me? Eat, Nora. You're already slim. I don't want you to lose weight."

I gulp nervously and start to pick at the food. There's something about him that makes me think it would be unwise to oppose him on this issue.

On any issue, really.

My instincts are screaming that this man is as dangerous as they come. He hasn't really been cruel to me, but there is cruelty within him. I can sense it.

"Good girl," he says approvingly after I eat a few bites.

I continue eating, even though I don't really taste the food and I have to force each bite past the restriction in my throat. I keep my eyes trained on my plate. I have an easier time eating if I don't see his piercing blue gaze.

"So Beth tells me you had a nice day swimming," he comments after I've had a chance to eat about half of my portion.

I nod in response and look up to find him staring at me.

"What do you think of the island?" he asks, as though genuinely interested in my opinion. He's studying me with a thoughtful look on his face.

"It's pretty," I tell him honestly. Then, pausing for a second, I add, "But I don't want to be here."

"Of course." He looks almost understanding. "But you'll get used to it. This is your new home, Nora. The sooner you come to terms with that, the better."

My stomach lurches, and I feel like the food that I just ate is in danger of coming up. I swallow convulsively, trying to control the sick feeling inside me. "And my family?" The words come out low and bitter. "How are they supposed to come to terms with it?"

Some emotion flickers briefly across his face. "What if they didn't think you were dead?" he asks quietly, holding my gaze. "Would that make you feel better, my pet?"

"Of course it would!" I can hardly believe what I'm hearing. "Can you do that? Can you let them know I'm alive? Maybe I can just call them and—"

He reaches out to cover my hand with his own, stopping my hopeful rambling. "No." His tone leaves no room for arguments. "I will contact them myself."

I swallow my disappointment. "What are you going to tell them?"

"That you are alive and well." His large thumb is gently massaging the inside of my palm, his touch distracting me, turning my bones to jelly.

"But"—I almost moan when he presses on one particularly sensitive spot—"but they wouldn't believe you—"

"They would." He withdraws his hand, leaving me feeling strangely bereft. "You can trust me on that."

Trust him? *Yeah, right.* "Why are you doing this to me?" I ask in frustration. "Is it because I talked to you in the club?"

He shakes his head. "No, Nora. It's because you're you. You're everything I've been looking for. Everything I've always wanted."

"You know that's crazy, right?" I'm so upset I forget to be afraid for a moment. "You don't even know me!"

"That's true," he says softly. "But I don't need to know you. I just need to know what I feel."

"Are you saying you're in love with me?" For some reason, that idea frightens me more than when I thought he just had weird sexual preferences.

He laughs, throwing his head back. I stare at him, irrationally offended. I don't want him to be in love with me, but does he have to find the idea so funny?

"Of course not," he says after he's finally done laughing. He's still grinning, though.

"Then what are you talking about?" I ask in frustration.

His smile slowly fades. "It doesn't matter, Nora," he says quietly. "All you need to know is that you're special to me."

"So why didn't you just ask me out on a date?" I'm struggling to comprehend the incomprehensible. "Why did you have to kidnap me?"

"Because you went on a date with that boy." There is sudden rage in Julian's voice, and icy terror spreads through my veins. "You kissed him when you were already mine."

I swallow. "But I didn't even know you wanted me." My voice shakes a little. "I only saw you at the club—"

"And at your graduation."

"And at my graduation," I agree, my heart hammering in my chest. "But I thought you might've been there for someone else. Like a younger brother or sister . . ."

He takes a deep breath, and I can see that he's much more calm now. "It doesn't matter now, Nora. I wanted you here, with me, not out there. It's much safer for you—and for that boy."

"Safer for Jake?"

Julian nods. "If you had gone out with him again, I would've killed him. It's best for everyone that you're here, away from him and others who might want you."

He's completely serious about killing Jake. It's not an idle threat. I can see it on his face.

My lips feel dry, so I lick them. His eyes follow my tongue, and I can see his breathing changing. My simple action clearly turned him on.

Suddenly, a crazy and desperate idea occurs to me. He obviously wants me. He's even willing to do things to make me happy—like letting my family know I'm alive. What if I use that fact to my advantage? I'm inexperienced, but I'm not completely naive. I know how to flirt with guys. Could I do this? Could I somehow seduce Julian into letting me go?

I'm going to have to be careful about it. I can't have a sudden about-face. I can't act like I despise him one minute and love him the next. He needs to believe that he can take me off the island and that I would willingly remain with him for as long as he wants me. That I would never look at Jake or another man again.

I'm going to have to take my time and convince Julian of my devotion.

CHAPTER EIGHT

For the rest of the dinner, I continue acting scared and intimidated. It's not really an act because I do feel that way. I'm in the presence of a man who casually talks about killing innocent people. How else am I supposed to feel?

However, I also try to be seductive. It's small things, like the way I brush my hair back while looking at him. The way I bite into a piece of papaya that Beth cut up for our dessert and lick the juice off my lips.

I know my eyes are pretty, so I look at him shyly, through half-closed eyelids. I've practiced that look in front of the mirror, and I know my eyelashes look impossibly long when I tilt my head at exactly the right angle.

I don't go overboard because he wouldn't find that believable. I just do little things that he might find arousing and appealing.

I also try to avoid any other confrontational topics. Instead, I ask him about the island and how he came to own it.

"I came across this island five years ago," Julian explains, his lips curving into a charming smile. "My Cessna was having a mechanical problem, and I needed a place to land. Luckily, there's a flat, grassy area right on the other side, near the beach. I was able to bring down the plane without crashing it completely and make the necessary repairs. It took me a couple of days, so I got a chance to explore the island. By the time I was able to fly away, I knew this place was exactly what I wanted. So I purchased it."

I widen my eyes and look impressed. "Just like that? Isn't that expensive?"

He shrugs. "I can afford it."

"Do you come from a wealthy family?" I'm genuinely curious. My captor is a huge mystery to me. I stand a much better chance of manipulating him if I understand him at least a little bit.

His expression cools a little. "Something like that. My father had a successful business, which I took over after his death. I changed its direction and expanded it."

"What kind of business?"

Julian's mouth twists slightly. "Import-export."

"Of what?"

"Electronics and other things," he says, and I realize that he's not going to reveal more than that for now. I strongly suspect that 'other things' is a euphemism for something illegal. I don't know much about business, but I somehow doubt that selling TVs and MP3 players results in this kind of wealth.

I steer the conversation toward a more innocuous topic. "Does the rest of your family also use the island?"

His gaze goes flat and hard. "No. They're all dead."

"Oh, I'm sorry . . ." I don't really know what to say. What can you say that will make something like that better? Yes, he kidnapped me, but he's still a human being. I can't even imagine suffering that kind of loss.

"It's all right." His tone is unemotional, but I can sense the pain underneath. "It happened a long time ago."

I nod sympathetically. I genuinely feel bad for him, and I don't try to hide the glimmer of tears in my eyes. I'm too soft—Leah says that every time I cry at a depressing movie—and I can't help the sadness I feel at Julian's suffering.

It ends up working in my favor, because his expression warms slightly. "Don't pity me, my pet," he says softly. "I've gotten over it. Why don't you tell me about yourself instead?"

I blink at him slowly, knowing that the gesture draws attention to my eyes. "What would you like to know?" Didn't he find out everything about me in the process of stalking me?

He smiles. It makes him look so beautiful that I feel a tiny squeezing sensation in my chest. *Stop it, Nora. You're the one seducing him, not the other way around.*

"What do you like to read?" he asks. "What kind of movies do you like to watch?"

And for the next thirty minutes, he learns all about my enjoyment of romance novels and detective thrillers, my hatred of romantic comedies, and my love of epic movies with lots of special effects. Then he asks me about my favorite food and music, and listens attentively as I talk about my preference for eighties' bands and deep-dish pizza.

In a weird way, it's almost flattering, the way he's so utterly focused on me, hanging on to my every word. The way his blue eyes are glued to my face. It's as though he wants to really understand me, as though he truly cares. Even with Jake, I didn't get the sense that I was anything more than a pretty girl whose company he enjoyed.

With Julian, I feel like I'm the most important thing in the world to him. I feel like I truly matter.

* * *

After dinner, he leads me upstairs to his bedroom. My heart begins to pound in fear and anticipation.

Like the other two nights, I know I won't fight him. In fact, tonight I will go even further as part of my escape-by-seduction plan.

I will pretend to make love to him of my own free will.

As we walk into the room, I decide to brave a topic that has been nagging at the back of my mind. "Julian..." I ask, purposefully keeping my voice soft and uncertain. "What about protection? What if I get pregnant or something?"

He stops and turns toward me. There's a small smile on his lips. "You won't, my pet. You have that implant, don't you?"

My eyes widen in shock. "How do you know about that?" The implant is a tiny plastic rod underneath my skin, completely invisible except for a small mark where it was inserted.

"I accessed your medical history before bringing you here. I wanted to make sure you don't have any life-threatening medical conditions, like diabetes."

I stare at him. I should feel furious at this invasion of my privacy, but I feel relieved instead. It seems that my kidnapper is quite considerate—and more importantly, not trying to impregnate me.

"And you don't have to worry about any diseases," he adds, understanding my unspoken concern. "I've been recently tested, and I have always used condoms in the past."

I don't know if I believe that. "Why aren't you using them with me, then? Is it because I was a virgin?"

He nods, and there is a possessive gleam in his eyes. He lifts his hand and strokes the side of my face, making my heart beat even faster. "Yes, exactly. You're completely mine. I'm the only one who's ever been inside your pretty little pussy."

My breath catches in my throat, and I feel a gush of liquid warmth between my thighs.

I can't believe the strength of my physical response to him. Is this normal, that I get so aroused by someone I fear and despise? Is this why Julian was drawn to me at the club? Because he sensed this about me? Because he somehow knew about my weakness?

Of course, given my plan, it's not necessarily a bad thing that he turns me on so much. It would be far worse if he disgusted me, if I couldn't bear to have him touch me.

No, this is for the best. I can be the perfect little captive, obedient and responsive, slowly falling in love with my captor.

So instead of standing stiff and scared, I give in to my desire and lean a little into his hand, as though involuntarily responding to his touch.

Something like triumph briefly flashes in his eyes, and then he lowers his head, touching his lips to mine. His strong arms wrap around me, molding me against his powerful body. He's fully aroused; I can feel the hard ridge of his erection against the softness of my belly. He's stroking my mouth with his lips, his tongue. He tastes sweet, from the papaya we just had.

Fire surges through my veins, and I close my eyes, losing myself in the overwhelming pleasure of his kiss. My hands creep up to his chest, touch it shyly. I can feel the heat of his body, smell the scent of his skin—male and musky, strangely appealing. His chest muscles flex under my fingers, and I can feel his heart beating faster.

He backs me toward the bed, and we fall on it. Somehow my hands are buried in his thick, silky hair, and I'm kissing him back, passionately, desperately. I'm not thinking about my grand seduction plan—I'm not thinking at all.

He bites my lower lip, sucks it into his mouth. His hand closes around my right breast, kneads it, squeezes the nipple through the dual barrier of the bra and the dress. His roughness is perversely arousing, even though I should be frightened by it.

I moan, and he flips me over, onto my stomach. One of his hands presses me down, pushing me into the mattress, while the other one lifts my skirt, exposing my underwear.

And then he pauses for a second, looking at my butt, lightly stroking it with his large palm. "Such curvy little cheeks," he murmurs. "So pretty in white."

His fingers reach between my legs, feel the wetness there. I can't help squirming at the light touch. I'm so turned on I just need a little bit more before I come.

He pulls down my underwear, leaving it hanging around my knees. His hand caresses my buttocks again, soothing me, arousing me. I'm trembling with anticipation.

Suddenly, I hear a loud smack and feel a sharp, stinging slap on my butt. I cry out, startled, more from the unexpected nature of the attack than from any real pain.

He pauses, rubs the area soothingly, and then does it again, slapping my right cheek with his open palm. Twenty slaps in quick succession, each one harder than the rest. It hurts; this is not a light, playful spanking.

He means to cause me pain.

Forgetting all about my resolution to play along, I begin to struggle, frightened. He holds me down easily, then transfers his attention to my other butt cheek, slapping it twenty times with equal force.

By the time he pauses, I'm sobbing into the mattress, begging him to stop. My backside feels like it's burning, throbbing in agony.

Even worse than the pain is the irrational sense of betrayal. To my horror, I realize that I had begun to trust my captor, to feel like I knew him a bit.

He'd caused me pain before, but I didn't think it was on purpose. I thought it was just because I was so new to sex. I hoped my body would adjust and there would be only pleasure in the future.

I was obviously a fool.

My entire body is shaking, and I can't stop crying. He's still holding me down, and I'm terrified of what he'll do next.

What he does next is as shocking as what he did before.

He turns me over and lifts me into his arms. Then he sits down, holding me on his lap, and rocks me back and forth. Gently, sweetly, like I'm a child that he's trying to console.

And despite everything, I bury my face against his shoulder and sob, desperately needing that illusion of tenderness, craving comfort from the one who made me hurt.

* * *

After I'm a bit more calm, he stands up and places me on my feet. My legs feel weak and shaky, and I sway a little as he carefully undresses me.

I wait for him to say something. Maybe to apologize or to explain why he hurt me. Was he punishing me? If so, I want to know what I did, so I can avoid doing it in the future.

But he doesn't speak—he simply takes off my clothes. When I'm naked, he begins to undress himself.

I watch him with a strange mixture of distress and curiosity. His body is still a mystery to me because I've kept my eyes closed for the last two nights. I haven't even seen his sex yet, even though I've felt it inside me.

So now I look at him.

His figure is magnificent. Completely male. Wide shoulders, a narrow waist, lean hips. He's powerfully muscled all over, but not in a steroid-enhanced bodybuilder way. Instead, he looks like a warrior. For some reason, I can easily picture him swinging a sword, cutting down his enemies. I notice a long scar on his thigh and another one on his shoulder. They only add to the warrior impression.

His skin is tan all over, with just the right amount of hair on his chest. There's more dark hair around his navel and trailing down to his groin area. His skin color makes me think he either goes around naked, or he's naturally darker, like me. Perhaps he has some Latino ancestry, too.

He's also fully aroused. I can see his cock jutting out at me. It's long and thick, similar to the ones I've seen in porn. No wonder I'm sore. I can't believe he's even able to fit inside me.

After we're both naked, he guides me to the bed. "I want you on all fours," he says quietly, giving me a light push.

My heart jumps in panic, and I resist for a second, turning to look at him instead. "Are you—" I swallow hard. "Are you going to hurt me again?"

"I haven't decided," he murmurs, lifting his hand to cup my breast. His thumb rubs my nipple, makes it harden. "I think it's probably enough for now."

Enough for now? I want to scream.

"Are you a sadist?" The question escapes me before I can think, and I freeze in place waiting for his answer.

He smiles at me. It's his beautiful Lucifer smile. "Yes, my pet," he says softly. "Sometimes I am. Now be a good girl and do as I asked. You might not like what happens otherwise . . ."

Before he even finishes speaking, I scramble to obey, getting on my hands and knees on the bed. Despite the warmth in the room, I'm shivering, trembling from head to toe.

Violent, gruesome images fill my mind, making me feel ill. I don't know much about S&M. *Fifty Shades* and a few other books of its ilk are the extent of my experience with the subject, but none of those romances depicted anything like my situation now. Even in my darkest, most secret fantasies, I've never imagined being held captive by a self-admitted sadist.

What is he going to do? Whip me? Torture me? Chain me in a dungeon? Is there even a dungeon on this island? I picture a stone chamber filled with torture instruments, like in a movie about the Spanish Inquisition, and I want to puke. I'm sure normal BDSM is nothing like that, but there's nothing normal about my situation with Julian. He can literally do anything he wants to me.

He gets on the bed behind me and strokes my back. His touch is slow, gentle. It would be soothing, except I'm cringing, expecting a blow at any moment.

He probably realizes it because he leans over me and whispers in my ear, "Relax, Nora. I won't do anything else tonight."

I almost collapse on the bed in relief. Tears run down my face again. This time, they're tears of relief and gratitude. I'm pathetically grateful that he won't hurt me again. At least, not tonight.

And then I'm horrified. Horrified and disgusted—because when he starts kissing my neck, my body begins to respond to him as though nothing had happened. As though it's never known a moment of pain at his hands.

My stupid body doesn't care that he's a depraved bastard. That he's going to hurt me again and again. No, my body wants pleasure, and it doesn't care about anything else.

His warm mouth moves from my neck to my shoulders, then over my back. My breathing is shallow, erratic. Despite his reassurance, I'm still afraid of him, and the fear somehow makes me wetter.

His lips move to my buttocks, kiss the area that he hurt just a few minutes earlier. His hand pushes on my lower back, and I arch slightly under his touch, understanding his unspoken command. His fingers slip between my legs, and one long finger finds its way into my slippery channel, entering deeply.

He curves that finger inside me, and I gasp as he presses on some sensitive spot deep inside. It makes me tense and tremble—but this time, not from fear.

As he pushes that curved finger in and out, I feel a pressure gathering inside me. My heartbeat skyrockets, and I suddenly feel hot, as though I'm burning from within. And then a powerful orgasm tears through my body, originating at my core and spreading outward. It's so strong that my vision blurs for a moment and I almost collapse on the bed.

Before my pulsations even stop, he gets on his knees behind me and begins to push in.

I'm wet and his entry is relatively easy, though he still feels huge inside me. My inner tissues feel tender and sore from last night's hard use, and I can't help a slight gasp of pain at the invasion. When he's in fully, his groin presses against my burning bottom, adding to the discomfort.

Grasping my hips, he begins to move in and out, slowly and rhythmically. Despite the initial pain, my body appears to like the feeling of fullness, of being stretched, and responds by producing even more lubrication. As his pace picks up, my breathing accelerates and helpless moans escape my throat each time he pushes deeply into me.

Suddenly, with no warning, my muscles tighten as my senses reach fever-pitch. The release ripples through me, the pleasure stunning in its intensity. Behind me, I can hear his groan as my climax provokes his own—and feel the warm spurt of his seed inside me.

And then we both collapse on the bed, his body heavy and slick with perspiration on top of mine.

CHAPTER NINE

I wake up slowly, in stages. First, I feel the tickling sensation of my hair on my face. Then the warmth of the sun on my uncovered arm. For a moment, my mind is floating in that soft, comfortable limbo between sleep and wakefulness, between dreams and reality.

I keep my eyes closed, not wanting to wake fully, because this is so nice.

Then I realize I can smell pancakes cooking in the kitchen.

My lips curl in a smile. It's the weekend, and my mom decided to spoil us again. She makes pancakes on special occasions and sometimes just because.

The hair tickles me again, and I reluctantly move my arm to push it off my face.

I'm more awake now, and the warm feeling inside me dissipates, replaced by harsh, gnawing fear.

No, please let it all be a dream. Please let it all be a bad dream.

I open my eyes.

It's not a dream. I can still smell the pancakes, but there's no way it could be my mom cooking them.

I'm on an island in the middle of the Pacific Ocean, held captive by a man who derives pleasure from hurting me.

I stretch carefully, taking stock of my body. Other than a slight tenderness in my bottom, I seem to be mostly fine. He had only taken me once last night, for which I am grateful.

Getting up, I walk naked to the mirror and look at my back. There are faint bruises on my buttocks, but nothing major. That's one of the benefits of my golden-tinted skin—I don't bruise easily. By tomorrow, it should look completely normal.

All in all, I seem to have survived another night in my captor's bed.

As I brush my teeth, I think back to last evening. The dinner, my silly plan to seduce him, my feeling of betrayal at his actions . . .

I can't believe I had begun to trust him even a tiny bit. Normal men don't kidnap girls from the park. They don't drug them and bring them to a private island. Men who like normal, consensual sex don't keep women captive.

No, Julian is not normal. He's a sadistic control freak, and I can never forget it. The fact that he hasn't hurt me badly yet doesn't mean anything. It's just a matter of time before he does something truly awful to me.

I need to escape before that happens, and I can't take my sweet time seducing Julian. He's far too dangerous and unpredictable.

I need to find a way off this island.

* * *

After I take a quick shower and brush my teeth, I go downstairs for breakfast. Beth must've already been in my room because there is another fresh set of clothes laid out. A swimsuit, flip-flops, and another sundress.

Beth herself is in the kitchen, and so are the pancakes I'd smelled earlier.

At my entrance, she smiles at me, yesterday's tension apparently forgotten. "Good morning," she says cheerfully. "How are you feeling?"

I give her an incredulous look. Does she know what Julian did to me? "Oh, just great," I say sarcastically.

"That's good." She seems oblivious to my tone. "Julian was afraid you might be a bit sore this morning, so he left me a special cream to give you just in case."

She does know.

"How do you live with yourself?" I ask, genuinely curious. How can a woman stand by and watch another woman being abused like this? How can she work for this cruel man?

Instead of answering, Beth places a large, fluffy pancake on a plate and brings it to me. There is also sliced mango on the table, right next to a bottle of maple syrup.

"Eat, Nora," she says, not unkindly.

I give her a bitter look and dig into the pancake. It's delicious. I think she added bananas to the batter because I can taste their sweetness. I don't even need the maple syrup, although I do add a few slices of mango for additional flavor.

Beth smiles again, and goes back to doing various kitchen chores.

After breakfast, I leave the house and explore the island on my own. Beth doesn't stop me. I still find it shocking that they're letting me wander around like this. They must be completely confident there is no way off the island.

Well, I intend to find a way.

I walk tirelessly for hours in the hot sun, until the flip-flops I'm wearing give me a blister. I stick close to the beach, hoping to find a boat tied somewhere, maybe in a cave or a lagoon.

But I find nothing.

How did I get here? Was it by plane or helicopter? Julian did mention yesterday that he had originally discovered this place while flying a plane. Maybe that's how he brought me here, via a private plane?

That would not be good. Even if I found the plane sitting somewhere, how would I fly it? I imagine it must be at least somewhat complicated.

Then again, with sufficient incentive, I might be able to figure it out. I'm not stupid, and flying a plane is not rocket science.

But I don't find the plane either. There is a flat grassy area on the other side of the island with a structure at the end of it, but there's nothing inside the structure. It's completely empty.

Tired, thirsty, and with the blister beginning to bother me more with each step, I head back to the house.

* * *

"Julian left a couple of hours ago," Beth tells me as soon as I walk in.

Stunned, I stare at her. "What do you mean, he left?"

"He had some urgent business to take care of. If all goes well, he should be back within a week."

I nod, trying to keep a neutral expression, and go upstairs to my room.

He's gone! My tormentor is gone!

It's just Beth and me on this island. No one else.

My mind is whirling with possibilities. I can steal one of the kitchen knives and threaten Beth until she shows me a way off the island. There's probably internet here, and I might be able to reach out to the outside world.

I'm so excited I could scream.

Do they truly think I'm that harmless? Did my meek behavior thus far lull them into thinking I would continue to be a nice, obedient captive?

Well, they couldn't be more mistaken.

Julian is the one I'm afraid of, not Beth. With the two of them on this island, attacking Beth would've been pointless and dangerous.

Now, however, she's fair game.

* * *

An hour later, I quietly sneak into the kitchen. As I had expected, Beth is not there. It's too early to prepare dinner and too late for lunch.

My feet are bare, to minimize any sound. Cautiously looking around, I slide open one of the drawers and take out a large butcher knife. Testing it with my finger, I determine that it's sharp.

A weapon. Perfect.

The sundress that I'm wearing has a slim belt at the waist, and I use it to tie the knife to myself at the back. It's a very crude holster, but it holds the knife in place. I hope I don't cut my butt with the naked blade, but even if I do, it's a risk worth taking.

A large ceramic vase is my next acquisition. It's heavy enough that I can barely lift it over my head with two arms. I can't imagine a human skull would be a match for something like this.

Once I have those two things, I go look for Beth.

I find her on the porch, curled up with a book on a long, comfy-looking outdoor couch, enjoying the fresh air and the beautiful ocean view. She doesn't look when I poke my head outside through the open door, and I quickly go back in, trying to figure out what to do next.

My plan is simple. I need to catch Beth off-guard and bash her over the head with the vase. Maybe tie her up with something. Then I could use the knife to threaten her into letting me contact the outside world. This way, by the time Julian returns, I could already be rescued and pressing charges.

All I need now is a good spot for my ambush.

Looking around, I notice a little nook near the kitchen entrance. If you're coming in off the porch—like I think Beth will be—then you don't really see anything in that nook. It's not the best place to conceal oneself, but it's better than attacking her openly. I go there and press myself flat against the wall, the vase standing on the floor next to me where I can easily grab it.

Taking a deep breath, I try to still the fine trembling in my hands. I'm not a violent person, yet here I am, about to smash this vase into Beth's head. I don't want to think about it, but I can't help picturing her skull split open, blood and gore everywhere, like in some horror movie. The image makes me ill. I tell myself that it won't be like that, that she'll most likely end up with a nasty bruise or a mild concussion.

The wait seems interminable. It goes on and on, each second stretching like an hour. My heart is pounding and I'm sweating, even though the temperature in the house is much cooler than the heat outside.

Finally, after what feels like several hours, I hear Beth's footsteps. Grabbing the vase, I carefully lift it over my head and hold my breath as Beth steps through the open door leading from the porch.

As she walks by me, I grip the vase tightly and bring it down on her head.

And somehow I miss. At the last moment, Beth must've heard me move because the vase hits her on the shoulder instead.

She cries out in pain, clutching her shoulder. "You fucking bitch!"

I gasp and try to lift the vase again, but it's too late. She grabs for the vase, and it falls down, breaking into a dozen pieces between us.

I jump back, my right hand frantically scrambling for the knife. *Shit, shit, shit.* I manage to grab the handle and pull it out, but before I can do anything, she grabs my arm, moving as quickly as a snake. Her grip is like a steel band around my right wrist.

Her face is flushed and her eyes are glittering as she twists my arm painfully backward. "Drop the knife, Nora," she orders harshly, her voice filled with fury.

Panicking, I try to hit her in the face with my other hand, but she catches that arm too. She clearly knows how to fight—and she's also obviously stronger than me.

My right arm is screaming in pain, but I try to kick at her. I can't lose this fight. This is my best chance at escape.

My feet make contact with her legs, but I'm not wearing shoes and I do more damage to my toes than to her shins.

"Drop the knife, Nora, or I will break your arm," she hisses, and I know that she's telling the truth. My shoulder feels like it's about to pop out of its socket, and my vision darkens as waves of pain radiate down my arm.

I hold out for one more second, and then my fingers release the knife. It falls to the floor with a loud thunk.

Beth immediately lets me go and bends down to pick it up.

I back away, breathing harshly, tears of pain and frustration burning in my eyes. I don't know what she's going to do to me now, and I don't want to find out.

So I run.

* * *

I am fast on my feet and in good shape. I can hear Beth chasing after me, calling my name, but I doubt she's ever done track before.

I run out of the house and down to the beach. Rocks, twigs, and gravel dig into my feet, but I barely feel them.

I don't know where I'm running, but I can't let Beth catch me. I can't be locked up in the room or worse.

"Nora!"

Fuck, she's a good runner too. I put on a burst of speed, ignoring the pain in my feet.

"Nora, don't be an idiot! There's nowhere to go!"

I know that's true, but I can't be a passive victim any longer. I can't sit meekly in that house, eat Beth's food, and wait for Julian to return.

I can't allow him to hurt me again and then make my body crave him.

My leg muscles are screaming, and my lungs are straining for air. I divorce myself from the discomfort, pretend I'm in a race with the finish line only a hundred yards away.

It feels like I'm running forever. When I glance back, I see that Beth is falling further and further behind.

My pace eases a little bit. I can't sustain that speed much longer. Without thinking too much, I head for the rocky side of the island, where I can clamber up the rocks and disappear in the heavily wooded area above them.

It takes me another ten minutes to get there. By then, I can no longer see Beth behind me.

I slow down and climb up the rocks. Now that I'm out of immediate danger, I can feel the cuts and bruises on my bare feet.

It's a slow and torturous climb. My legs are quivering from unaccustomed exertion, and I can feel a post-adrenaline slump coming on. Nevertheless, I manage to get myself up the rocky hill and into the woods.

Tropical vegetation, lush and thick, is all around me, hiding me from view. I go deeper into the brush, seeking a good spot to collapse in exhaustion. It wouldn't be easy to find me here. From what I remember during my earlier exploration, this forest covers a large portion of this side of the island.

I should be safe here for now.

As the darkness begins to fall, I take shelter under a large tree, where the underbrush is particularly impenetrable. I clear a little patch of ground for myself, making sure I'm not near any ant hills or anything else that could bite me. Then I lie down, ignoring the throbbing pain in my lacerated feet.

Not for the first time in my life, I'm grateful to my dad for taking me camping when I was a child. Thanks to his tutelage, I'm comfortable with nature in all its glory. Bugs, snakes, lizards—none of these bother me. I know I should be careful around certain species, but I don't fear them as a whole.

I'm far more scared of the snakes who brought me to this island.

Now that I'm away from Beth, I can think a little more clearly.

That lean, toned body of hers is clearly not from doing light cardio and yoga in the gym. She's strong—probably as strong as some men— and definitely much stronger than me.

She also seems to have had some kind of special training. Martial arts, maybe? I clearly made a mistake trying to take her prisoner. I should've slipped that knife into her back when she wasn't looking.

It's not too late, though. I can still sneak back into the house and surprise her there. I need access to that internet, and I need it now, before Julian returns.

I don't know what he'll do to me for attacking Beth—and I certainly don't want to find out.

CHAPTER TEN

A strange sensation wakes me up the next morning. It feels almost like—

"Oh shit!"

I jump up, trying to shake off the long-legged spider that's leisurely strolling up my arm.

The spider flies off, and I frantically brush at my face, hair, and body, trying to get rid of any other potential creepy-crawlies.

Okay, so I'm not exactly afraid of spiders, but I really, really don't like them on me.

This is definitely not the most pleasant way to wake up.

My heart rate gradually returns to normal, and I take stock of my situation. I'm thirsty, and my entire body aches from sleeping on the hard ground. I also feel grimy, and my feet hurt. Lifting up one leg, I peer at the sole of the foot. I'm pretty sure there's dried blood on there.

My stomach is rumbling with hunger. I didn't have dinner last night, and I'm absolutely starving.

On the plus side, Beth hasn't found me yet.

I'm not really sure what I'm going to do next. Perhaps make my way back to the house and try to ambush Beth there again?

I think about it and decide it's probably the best course of action at this point. Sooner or later, Beth or Julian will find me. The island is not that big, and I would not be able to hide from them for long. And I can't risk procrastinating, in case Julian returns sooner than expected. Two against one are terrible odds.

I'm also getting hungrier by the minute, and I tend to get light-headed if I don't eat regularly. I could probably find fresh water to drink, but food is more iffy. I don't know where Beth gets those mangos from. If I try to hide for another couple of days, I might be too weak to attack anyone, much less a woman who could be a freaking warrior princess.

Besides, she might not be expecting me quite yet, and I could really use an element of surprise.

So I take a deep breath and start walking—or rather, limping—back toward the house. I know this might not end well for me, but I have no choice. I either fight now, or I will forever be a victim.

It takes me about two hours to get back. I end up having to stop and take breaks when I can no longer tolerate the agony in my feet.

It's kind of ironic that I escaped because I'm afraid of pain, and I ended up hurting myself so badly in the process. Julian would probably love to see me like this. *That perverted bastard.*

Finally, I reach the house and crouch behind some large bushes near the front door. I don't know if it's locked or not, but I don't think I can just stroll in through the main entrance. For all I know, Beth is right there in the living room.

No, I need to be more strategic about it.

After a few minutes, I carefully make my way to the back of the house, toward the large screened porch where I had attacked Beth yesterday.

To my relief, no one is there.

Taking care not to make a sound, I open the screen door and slip inside. In my hand I'm holding a large rock. I would much rather have a knife or a gun, but a rock will have to do for now.

Crab-walking to one of the windows, I glance inside and am gratified to find the living room empty.

Straightening, I walk up to the glass door that leads to the living room, quietly slide it open, and step inside.

The house is completely silent. There's no one cooking in the kitchen or setting the table.

The digital clock in the living room reads 7:12. I'm hoping that Beth is still asleep.

Still clutching the rock, I sneak into the kitchen and find another knife. Holding both, I carefully head upstairs.

Beth's bedroom is the first one on the left. I know because she showed it to me during the house tour.

Holding my breath, I quietly push open the door . . . and freeze.

Sitting there on the bed is the person I fear most.

Julian.

He's back early.

* * *

"Hello, Nora."

His voice is deceptively soft, his perfect face expressionless. Yet I can feel the rage burning quietly underneath.

For a second, I just stare at him, paralyzed by terror. I can't hear anything but the roaring of my own heartbeat in my ears. And then I start to back away, still keeping my eyes trained on his face. My hands are raised defensively in front of me, rock and knife clutched tightly in each.

At that moment, steely hands grip my arms from behind, painfully squeezing my wrists. I scream, struggling, but Beth is too strong. The knife twists backward in my hand, nearly reaching my shoulder.

In a flash, Julian is on me, and both the knife and the rock are wrenched out of my hands. Beth releases me and Julian grabs me, holding me tightly as I scream and writhe hysterically in his arms.

The harder I fight, the tighter his arms become around me, until I go limp, almost fainting from lack of air.

Then he picks me up and carries me out of Beth's room.

To my surprise, he brings me downstairs and stops in front of the door that leads to his office. A tiny panel opens on the side, and I can see a red light moving over Julian's face, like a laser at a supermarket checkout.

Then the door slides open.

I stifle a gasp of surprise. His office door opens via a retina scan— something I've only seen before in spy movies.

As he carries me inside, I try to struggle again, but it's futile. His arms are completely immovable, holding me securely in his grip.

I'm once again helpless in his embrace.

Tears of bitter frustration slide down my face. I hate being so weak, so easily handled. He's not even winded from our struggle.

I'm not sure what I'm expecting him to do. Perhaps beat me, or brutally take me.

But he simply places me on my feet when we're inside his office.

As soon as he releases me, I take a few steps back, needing to put at least some distance between us.

He smiles at me, and there's something disturbing in the beauty of that smile. "Relax, my pet. I won't hurt you. Not now, at least."

And as I watch, he walks over to a large desk and slides open the drawer, taking out a remote control. Then he points it at a wall behind me.

I turn around warily and stare at two large flat-panel TV screens. They look very high-tech, not at all like the ones I'm used to seeing at home.

The left screen lights up. The image is strange because it's so unexpected.

It looks like a regular bedroom in someone's house. The bed is unmade, sheets bunched up carelessly on the mattress. Posters of various football players line the walls, and there is a laptop sitting on the desk.

"Do you recognize it?" Julian asks.

I shake my head.

"Good," he says. "I'm glad about that."

"Whose bedroom is it?" I ask, a sick feeling appearing in my stomach.

"Can't you guess?"

I stare at him, feeling colder by the minute. "Jake's?"

"Yes, Nora. Jake's."

I begin to shake inside. "Why is it on your TV?"

"Do you remember when I told you that Jake is safe as long as you behave?"

I stop breathing for a second. "Yes . . ." My whisper is barely audible.

Truthfully, I had forgotten about his initial threat to Jake, too consumed with the experience of my own captivity. I don't think I took the threat seriously to begin with, certainly not after I learned we were on an island thousands of miles away from my hometown. Somewhere in the back of my mind, I had been convinced Julian can't really harm Jake. Not from a distance, at least.

"Good," Julian says. "Then you'll understand why I'm doing this. I don't want to keep you locked up, unable to go anywhere or do anything. This island is your new home, and I want you to be happy here—"

Happy here? I'm more than ever convinced that he's crazy.

"—but I can't have you trying to hurt Beth in pointless escape attempts. You need to learn that there are consequences to your actions—"

The sick feeling inside me spreads throughout my body. "I'm sorry! I won't do it anymore! I won't, I promise!" My words are hurried and jumbled. I don't know if I can prevent what's about to happen, but I have to try. "I won't hurt Beth, and I won't try to escape. Please, Julian, I learned my lesson . . ."

Julian looks at me almost sadly. "No, Nora. You haven't. I had to come back today, cutting short my business trip because of what you did. Beth is not here to be your jailer. That's not her role. She's here to take care of you, to make sure you're comfortable and content. I can't have you repaying her kindness by trying to kill her—"

"I wasn't trying to kill her! I just wanted . . ." I stop, not wanting to reveal my plan to him.

"You thought you could take her hostage?" Julian looks amused now. "To do what? Get her to take you off the island? Help you reach the outside world?"

I look at him, neither denying nor admitting it.

"Well, Nora, let me explain something to you. Even if your attack had succeeded—which it wouldn't have, because Beth is more than capable of handling one small girl—she wouldn't have been able to help you. When I leave, the plane leaves with me. There's no boat or any other way off the island."

His words confirm what I had already suspected from my explorations. But I'm still hoping that—

"And I'm the only one who has access to my office. There's no computer or communication equipment anywhere else in the house. All Beth can do is send me a direct message on a special line that we have set up. So you see, my pet, she would've been quite useless as a hostage."

So much for that hope. Each sentence feels like a nail getting pounded deeper into my coffin. If he's not lying to me, then my situation is far, far worse than I feared.

Unless Julian chooses to let me go, I'll be stuck on his island forever.

I want to scream, cry, and throw things, but I can't let myself fall apart right now. Instead, I nod and pretend to be calm and rational. "I understand. I'm sorry, Julian. I didn't know any of this before. I won't try to escape again, and I won't hurt Beth. Please believe me . . ."

"I'd like to, Nora." He looks almost regretful. "But I can't. You don't know me yet, so you're not sure if you can believe me. I need to show you that I'm a man of my word. The sooner you accept the inevitable, the happier you'll be."

And with that, he reaches into his pocket and pulls out something that looks like a phone. Pressing a button, he waits a couple of seconds, then says curtly, "You can proceed."

Then he turns his attention to the screen.

I do the same, a hollow sense of dread in my stomach.

The TV still shows an empty room, but a few seconds later, the door opens and Jake walks in.

He looks terrified. One of his eyes is swollen shut, and his nose is off-center, like it's broken. He's followed by a large masked figure toting a gun.

A horrified gasp escapes my lips. "Please, no . . ." I'm not even cognizant of moving, but my hands are somehow on Julian's arm, tugging at him in desperation.

"Watch, Nora." There's no emotion on Julian's face as he pulls me into his arms, holding me so that I'm facing the TV. "I want you to learn once and for all that actions have consequences."

On the screen, the masked henchman suddenly reaches for Jake—

"No!"

—and hits him hard across the face with the handle of the gun. Jake stumbles backward, blood trickling out of the corner of his mouth.

"Please, no!" I'm sobbing and struggling in Julian's iron grip, my eyes glued to the violent scene taking place thousands of miles away.

Jake's attacker is relentless, hitting him over and over. I scream, feeling each blow inside my heart. Every brutal strike against Jake's body is killing something inside me, some belief in a brighter future that has held me together thus far.

When Jake falls to his knees, the man kicks him in the ribs, and I can hear Jake's pained groan.

"Please, Julian," I whisper in defeat, slumping in his arms. "Please, stop . . ." I know I'm begging for mercy from a man who has none. He's murdering Jake in front of my eyes, and there's absolutely nothing I can do about it.

My captor lets the beating proceed for another minute before he releases me and pulls out his phone. I stare at him, trembling from head to toe. I don't even dare hope.

Julian quickly types in a text. On the screen, I see Jake's assailant pausing and reaching into his pocket.

Then he stops completely and leaves Jake's room.

Jake is left lying on the floor, covered in blood. I remain glued to the screen, needing to know that he is alive. After a minute, I hear his groan and see him getting up. He hobbles toward the house phone, moving like an old man instead of an athletic young guy.

And then I hear him calling 911.

I sink to the floor and bury my face in my hands.

Julian has won.

I know that my life will never be my own again.

CHAPTER ELEVEN

When I wake up the next morning, Julian is gone again.

I don't really remember what happened after I collapsed in Julian's office yesterday. The rest of the day is fuzzy in my memory. It's like my brain had switched off, unable to process the violence I had witnessed. I think I vaguely recall Julian picking me up off the floor and bringing me to the shower. He must've washed me and bandaged my feet because they're wrapped in gauze this morning and hurting a lot less when I walk.

I'm not sure if he had sex with me last night. If he did, then he must've been unusually gentle because I don't have any soreness this morning. I do remember sleeping with him in my bed, with his large body curved around mine.

In some ways, what happened simplifies things. When there's no hope, when there's no choice, everything becomes remarkably clear. The fact of the matter is that Julian holds all the cards. I'm his for as long as he wishes to keep me. There's no escape for me, no way out.

And once I accept that fact, my life becomes easier. Before I know it, I have been on the island for nine days.

Beth tells me so over breakfast this morning.

I've grown to tolerate her presence. I have no choice—without Julian there, she's my only source of human interaction. She feeds me, clothes me, and cleans after me. She's almost like my nanny, except she's young and sometimes bitchy. I don't think she's forgiven me fully for trying to bash her head in. It hurt her pride or something.

I try not to bug her too much. I leave the house during the day, spending most of my time on the beach or exploring the woods. I come back to the house for meals and to pick up a new book to read. Beth told me Julian will bring me more books when I'm done with the hundred or so that are currently in my room.

I should be depressed. I know that. I should be bitter and raging all the time, hating Julian and the island. And sometimes I do. But it takes so much energy, constantly being a victim. When I'm lying in the hot sun, absorbed in a book, I don't hate anything. I just let myself get carried away by some author's imagination.

I try not to think about Jake. The guilt is almost unbearable. Rationally, I know Julian is the one who did this, but I can't help feeling responsible. If I had never gone out with Jake, this would've never happened to him. If I hadn't approached him during that party, he wouldn't have been savagely beaten.

I still don't know what Julian is or how he's able to have such a long reach. He's as much of a mystery to me today as he's ever been.

Maybe he's in the Mafia. That would explain the thugs he has in his employ. Of course, he could simply be a wealthy eccentric with sociopathic tendencies. I truly don't know.

Sometimes I cry myself to sleep at night. I miss my family, my friends. I miss going out and dancing at a club. I miss human contact. I'm not a loner by nature. Back home, I was always in touch with people—Facebook, Twitter, just hanging out with friends at the mall. I like to read, but it's not enough for me. I need more.

It gets so bad that I try talking to Beth about it.

"I'm bored," I tell her over dinner. It's fish again. I learned that Beth catches it herself near the cove on the other side of the island. This time, it's with mango salsa. It's a good thing I'm a seafood fan because I get a lot of it here.

"You are?" She seems amused. "Why? Don't you have enough books to read?"

I roll my eyes. "Yes, I still have seventy or so left. But there's nothing else to do . . ."

"Want to help me fish tomorrow?" she asks, giving me a mocking look. She knows she's not my favorite person, and she fully expects me to turn her down immediately. However, she doesn't realize the extent to which I need human interaction.

"Okay," I say, obviously surprising her. I've never been fishing, and I can't imagine it's a particularly fun activity, especially if Beth is going to be snarky the entire time. Still, I'd do just about anything to break the routine at this point.

"Okay, then," she says. "The best time to catch these fuckers is right around dawn. Think you're up for it?"

"Sure," I say. I normally hate waking up early, but I get so much sleep here that I'm sure it won't be too bad. I probably sleep close to ten hours at night and also catch an occasional nap in the afternoon sun. It's kind of ridiculous, really. My body seems to think I'm on vacation at some relaxing retreat. There are apparently perks to not having internet or other distractions; I don't think I've felt so well-rested in my entire life.

"Then you better go to sleep soon because I'll come by your room early," she warns.

I nod, finishing up my dinner. Then I head upstairs to my room and cry myself to sleep again.

* * *

"When is Julian coming back?" I ask, watching Beth as she carefully arranges the bait at the end of the hook. What she's doing looks disgusting, and I'm glad she's not making me help her.

"I don't know," Beth says. "He'll come back when he's done taking care of business."

"What kind of business?" I've asked this before, but I'm hoping one of these days Beth will answer me.

She sighs. "Nora, stop prying."

"What's the big deal if I know?" I give her a frustrated look. "It's not like I'm going anywhere anytime soon. I just want to know what he is, that's all. Don't you think it's normal to be curious in my situation?"

She sighs again and casts the lure into the ocean with a smooth, practiced motion. "Of course it is. But Julian will tell you everything himself if he wants you to know."

I take a deep breath. I'm obviously not going to get anywhere with that line of questioning. "You're really loyal to him, huh?"

"Yes," Beth says simply, sitting down beside me. "I am."

Because he saved her life. I'm curious about that too, but I know she's touchy on that subject. So instead I ask, "How long have you known him?"

"About ten years," she says.

"Since he was nineteen?"

"Yes, exactly."

"How did you two meet?"

Her jaw hardens. "That's none of your business."

Uh-huh. I sense I'm again approaching the difficult subject. I decide to proceed anyway. "Was that when he saved your life? Is that how you met him?"

She gives me a narrow-eyed look. "Nora, what did I tell you about prying?"

"Okay, fine . . ." Her non-answer is answer enough for me. I move on to another topic of interest. "So why did Julian bring me here? To this island, I mean? He's not even here himself."

"He'll come back soon enough." She gives me an ironic look. "Why, do you miss him?"

"No, of course not!" I give her an offended glare.

She raises her eyebrows. "Really? Not even a little bit?"

"Why would I miss that monster?" I hiss at her, uncontrollable anger suddenly boiling up from the pit of my stomach. "After what he did to me? To Jake?"

She laughs softly. "Methinks the lady doth protest too much . . ."

I jump to my feet, unable to bear the mockery in her voice any longer. In this moment, I hate her so much I would've gladly stabbed her with a knife if I had it handy. I've never had much of a temper, but something about Beth brings out the worst in me.

Thankfully, I regain control over myself before I storm off and make a complete fool of myself. Taking a deep breath, I pretend that I intended to get up all along. Walking to the water, I test the temperature with my toe and then walk back toward Beth, sitting down again.

"Really warm water on this side of the island," I say calmly, as though I'm not still burning with anger inside.

"Yeah, the fish seem to like it here," she replies in the same even tone. "I always catch some nice ones in this area."

I nod and look out over the water. The sound of the waves is soothing, helping me control whatever it was that came over me. I don't fully understand why I reacted so strongly to her teasing. Surely I should've just given her a contemptuous look and coldly dismissed her ridiculous suggestion. Instead I'd risen to her bait.

Could there be some truth to her words? Is that why they irritated me so much? Am I actually missing Julian?

The idea is so sickening that I want to throw up.

I try to think about it rationally for a bit, to sort through the confusing jumble of feelings in my chest.

Okay, yes, a small part of me does resent the fact that he left me here on this island, with only Beth for company. For someone who supposedly wanted me enough to steal me, Julian is certainly not being very attentive.

Not that I want his attentions. I want him to stay as far away from me as possible. But at the same time, I am oddly insulted that he's staying away. It's like I'm not desirable enough for him to want to be here.

As soon as I analyze it all logically, I see the absurdity of my contradictory emotions. The whole thing is so silly, I have to mentally kick myself.

I'm not going to be one of those girls who falls in love with their kidnapper. I refuse to be. I know being here on this island is screwing with my head, and I'm determined not to let it.

Perhaps I can't escape from Julian, but I can keep him from getting under my skin.

* * *

Two days later, Julian returns.

I learn about it when he wakes me up from my nap on the beach.

At first, I think I'm having a dream. In my dream, I'm warm and safe in my bed. Gentle hands start stroking my body, soothing me, caressing me. I arch toward them, loving their touch on my skin, reveling in the pleasure they're giving me.

And then I feel hot lips on my face, my neck, my collarbone. I moan softly, and the hands become more demanding, pulling at the straps of my bikini top, tugging the bikini bottoms off my legs . . .

The realization of what's happening filters through to my half-conscious brain, and I wake up with a sudden gasp, adrenaline rushing through my veins.

Julian is crouched over me, looking down at me with that darkly angelic smile of his. I'm already naked, lying on top of the large beach towel that Beth gave me this morning. He's naked too—and fully aroused.

I stare up at him, my heart racing with a mixture of excitement and dread. "You're back," I say, stating the obvious.

"I am," he murmurs, leaning down and kissing my neck again. Before I can gather my scattered thoughts, he's already lying on top of me, his knee parting my thighs and his erection prodding at my tender opening.

I squeeze my eyes shut as he begins to push inside me. I'm wet, but I still feel uncomfortably stretched as he slides in all the way. He pauses for a second, letting me adjust, and then he begins to move, slowly at first and then with increasing pace.

His thrusts press me into the towel, and I can feel the sand shifting under my back. I clutch at his hard shoulders, needing something to hold on to as the familiar tension starts to gather low in my belly. The head of his cock brushes against that sensitive spot somewhere inside me, and I gasp, arching to take him deeper, needing more of that intense sensation, wanting him to bring me over the edge.

"Did you miss me?" he breathes into my ear, slowing down just enough to prevent me from reaching my peak.

I'm coherent enough to shake my head.

"Liar," he whispers, and his thrusts become harder, more punishing. He's ruthlessly driving me higher and higher until I'm screaming, my nails raking down his back in frustration as the elusive release hovers just beyond my reach.

And then I'm finally there, my body flying apart as a powerful orgasm sweeps through me, leaving me weak and panting in its wake.

With a suddenness that startles me, he pulls out and flips me over, onto my stomach.

I cry out, frightened, but he merely pushes inside me again and resumes fucking me from behind, his body large and heavy on top of mine. I am surrounded by him; my face is pressed into the towel and I can hardly breathe. All I can feel is him: the back-and-forth movement of his thick cock inside my body, the heat emanating from his skin. In this position, he goes deep, even deeper than usual, and I can't help the pained gasps that escape my throat as the head of his cock bumps against my cervix with each thrust of his hips. Yet the discomfort doesn't seem to prevent the pressure growing inside me again, and I climax again, my inner muscles clenching helplessly around his shaft.

He groans harshly, and then I can feel him coming too, his cock pulsing and jerking within me, his pelvis grinding into my buttocks. It enhances my own orgasm, draws out my pleasure. It's like we're linked together, because my contractions don't stop until his are fully over.

Afterwards, he rolls over onto his back, releasing me, and I draw in a shaky breath. With limbs that feel weak and heavy, I get up on all fours and find my bikini, then pull it on while he watches me, a lazy smile on his beautiful lips. He doesn't seem to be in a rush to get dressed himself, but I can't stand to be naked around him. It makes me feel too vulnerable.

The irony of that doesn't escape me. Of course I'm vulnerable. I'm as vulnerable as a woman can be: completely at the mercy of a ruthless madman. A couple of tiny patches of material aren't going to protect me from him.

Nothing will, if he decides to really hurt me.

I decide not to think about that. Instead I ask, "Where were you?"

Julian's smile widens. "You did miss me after all."

I give him a sardonic look, trying to ignore the fact that he's naked and sprawled out only a couple of feet away from me. "Yeah, I missed you."

He laughs, not the least bit put off by my snarky attitude. "I knew you would," he says. Then he gets up and pulls on a pair of swimming trunks that were lying on the sand next to us. Turning toward me, he offers me his hand. "A swim?"

I stare at him. Is he serious? He expects me to go for a swim with him like we're friends or something?

"No, thanks," I say, taking a step back.

He frowns a little. "Why not, Nora? You can't swim?"

"Of course I can swim," I say indignantly. "I just don't want to swim with you."

He raises his eyebrows. "Why not?"

"Um . . . maybe because I hate you?" I don't know why I'm being so brave today, but it seems like the time apart made me less afraid of him. Or maybe it's because he appears to be in a light, playful mood, and is thus just a bit less scary.

He smiles again. "You don't know what hatred is, my pet. You might not like my actions, but you don't hate me. You can't. It's not in your nature."

"What do you know about my nature?" For some reason, I find his words offensive. How dare he say that I can't hate my kidnapper? Who does he think he is, telling me what I can and cannot feel?

He looks at me, his lips still curved in that smile. "I know you've had what they call a normal upbringing, Nora," he says softly. "I know that you were raised in a loving family, that you had good friends, decent boyfriends. How could you possibly know what real hatred is?"

I stare at him. "And you know? You know what real hatred is?"

His expression hardens. "Unfortunately, yes," he says, and I can hear the truth in his voice.

A sick feeling floods my stomach. "Am I the one you hate?" I whisper. "Is that why you're doing this to me?"

To my huge relief, he looks surprised. "Hate you? No, of course I don't hate you, my pet."

"Then why?" I ask again, determined to get some answers. "Why did you kidnap me and bring me here?"

He looks at me, his eyes impossibly blue against his tan skin. "Because I wanted you, Nora. I already told you that. And because I'm not a very nice man. But you already figured that out, didn't you?"

I swallow and look down at the sand. He's not even the least bit ashamed of his actions. Julian knows what he's doing is wrong, and he simply doesn't care.

"Are you a psychopath?" I don't know what prompts me to ask this. I don't want to make him angry, but I can't help wanting to understand. Holding my breath, I look up at him again.

Thankfully, he doesn't seem offended by the question. Instead, he looks thoughtful as he sits down on the towel next to me. "Perhaps," he says after a couple of seconds. "One doctor thought I might be a borderline sociopath. I don't check all the boxes, so there's no definitive diagnosis."

"You saw a doctor?" I don't know why I'm so shocked. Maybe because he doesn't seem like the type to go to a shrink.

He grins at me. "Yeah, for a bit."

"Why?"

He shrugs. "Because I thought it might help."

"Help you be less of a psychopath?"

"No, Nora." He gives me an ironic look. "If I were a true psychopath, nothing could help that."

"So then what?" I know I'm prying into some very personal matters, but I feel like he owes me some answers. Besides, if you can't get personal with a man who just fucked you on the beach, then when can you?

"You're a curious little kitten, aren't you?" he says softly, putting his hand on my thigh. "Are you sure you really want to know, my pet?"

I nod, trying to ignore the fact that his fingers are only inches away from my bikini line. His touch is both arousing and disturbing, playing havoc with my equilibrium.

"I went to a therapist after I killed the men who murdered my family," he says quietly, looking at me. "I thought it might help me come to terms with it."

I stare at him blankly. "Come to terms with the fact that you killed them?"

"No," he says. "With the fact that I wanted to kill more."

My stomach turns over, and my skin feels like it's crawling where Julian is touching me. He has just admitted to something so horrible that I don't even know how to react.

As if from a distance, I hear my own voice asking, "So did it help you come to terms with it?" I sound calm, like we're discussing nothing more tragic than the weather.

He laughs. "No, my pet, it didn't. Doctors are useless."

"You've killed more?" The numbness encasing me is fading, and I can feel myself beginning to shake.

"I have," he says, a dark smile playing on his lips. "Now aren't you glad you asked?"

My blood turns to ice. I know I should stop talking now, but I can't. "Are you going to kill me?"

"No, Nora." He sounds exasperated for a moment. "I've already told you that."

I lick my dry lips. "Right. You're just going to hurt me whenever you feel like it."

He doesn't deny it. Instead he gets up again and looks at me. "I'm going for a swim. You can join me if you like."

"No, thanks," I say dully. "I don't feel like swimming right now."

"Suit yourself," he says, and then walks away, striding into the water.

Still in a state of shock, I watch his tall, broad-shouldered frame as he goes deeper into the ocean, his dark hair shining in the sun.

The devil does indeed wear a beautiful mask.

CHAPTER TWELVE

After Julian's revelations on the beach, I don't feel like asking any more questions for a while. I already knew I was being held by a monster, and what I learned today just solidifies that fact. I don't know why he was so open with me, and that scares me.

At dinner, I mostly keep quiet, only answering questions posed directly to me. Beth is eating with us today, and the two of them are carrying on a lively conversation, mostly about the island and how she and I have been spending our time.

"So you're bored?" Julian asks me after Beth tells him about my lack of interest in reading all the time.

I lift my shoulders in a shrug, not wanting to make a big deal of it. After what I learned earlier, I'd take boredom over Julian's company any time.

He smiles. "Okay, I'll have to remedy that. I'll bring you a TV and a bunch of movies the next time I make a trip."

"Thanks," I say automatically, staring down into my plate. I feel so miserable that I want to cry, but I have too much pride to do it in front of them.

"What's the matter?" Beth asks, finally noticing my uncharacteristic behavior. "Are you feeling okay?"

"Not really," I say, gladly latching on to the excuse she gave me. "I think I got too much sun."

Beth sighs. "I told you not to sleep on the beach mid-day. It's ninety-five degrees out."

It's true; she had warned me about that. But my misery today has nothing to do with the heat and everything with the man sitting across the table from me. I know that when the dinner is over, he's going to take me upstairs and fuck me again. Maybe hurt me.

And I will respond to him, like I always do.

That last part is the worst. He beat up Jake in front of my eyes. He admitted to being a murdering sociopath. I should be disgusted. I should look at him with nothing but fear and contempt. The fact that I can feel even a smidgen of desire for him is beyond sick.

It's downright twisted.

So I sit there, picking at my food, my stomach filled with lead. I would get up and go to my room, but I'm afraid it will just speed up the inevitable.

Finally, the meal is over. Julian takes my hand and leads me upstairs. I feel like I'm going to my execution, though that's probably too dramatic. He said he wouldn't kill me.

When we're in the room, he sits down on the bed and pulls me between his legs. I want to resist, to put up at least some kind of fight, but my brain and my body don't seem to be on speaking terms these days. Instead, I stand there mutely, trembling from head to toe, while he looks at me. His eyes trace over my facial features, lingering on my mouth, then drop down to my neckline, where my nipples are visible through the thin fabric of my sundress. They're peaked, as though from arousal, but I think it's because I'm chilled. Beth must've turned on air-conditioning for the night.

"Very pretty," he says finally, lifting his hand and stroking the edge of my jaw with his fingers. "Such soft golden skin."

I close my eyes, not wanting to look at the monster in front of me. *I wanted to kill more . . . I wanted to kill more . . .* His words repeat over and over in my mind, like a song that's stuck on replay. I don't know how to turn it off, how to go back in time and scrub the memories of this afternoon from my mind. Why did I insist on knowing this about him? Why did I probe and pry until I got these kind of answers? Now I can't think about anything but the fact that the man touching me is a ruthless killer.

He leans closer to me, and I can feel his hot breath on my neck. "Are you sorry you asked me all those questions today?" he whispers in my ear. "Are you, Nora?"

I flinch, my eyes flying open. Does he also read minds?

At my reaction, he pulls back and smiles. There's something in that smile that makes my chill ten times worse. I don't know what's going on with him tonight, but whatever it is, it frightens me more than anything he's done before.

"You're scared of me, aren't you, my pet?" he says softly, still holding me prisoner between his legs. "I can feel you shaking like a leaf."

I want to deny it, to be brave, but I can't. I *am* scared, and I *am* shaking. "Please," I whisper, not even knowing why I'm begging. He hasn't done anything to me yet.

He gives me a light push then, releasing me from his hold. I take a few steps back, glad to put some distance between us.

He gets up off the bed and walks out of the room.

I stare after him, unable to believe he just left me alone. Could it be that he doesn't want sex right now? He did already have me once on the beach earlier today.

And just as I'm about to let myself feel relief, Julian returns, a black gym bag in his hands.

All blood drains from my face. Horrifying thoughts run through my mind. What does he have in there—knives, guns, some kind of torture devices?

When he takes out a blindfold and a small dildo, I'm almost grateful. *Sex toys.* He just has some sex toys in that bag. I would take sex over torture any day of the week.

Of course, with Julian the two are not necessarily separate, as I learn this night.

"Strip, Nora," he tells me, walking over to sit down on the bed again. He lays the blindfold and the dildo on the mattress. "Take off your clothes, slowly."

I freeze. He wants me to disrobe while he watches? For a moment, I think about refusing, but then I start to undress with clumsy fingers. He has already seen me naked today. What would I achieve by being modest now? Besides, I'm still sensing that strange vibe from him. His eyes are glittering with excitement that goes beyond simple lust.

It's an excitement that makes my blood run cold.

He watches as the dress falls off my body and I kick off my flip-flops. My movements are wooden, stiff with fear. I doubt a normal man would find this striptease arousing, but I can see that it turns Julian on. Under the dress, I'm wearing only a pair of cream-colored lacy panties. The cold air washes over my skin, making my nipples harden even more.

"Now the underwear," he says.

I swallow and push the panties down my legs. Then I step out of them.

"Good girl," he says approvingly. "Now come here."

This time I'm unable to obey him. My self-preservation instinct is screaming that I need to run, but there's nowhere to run to. Julian would catch me if I tried to make it out the door right now—and it's not like I can get off this island anyway.

So I just stand there, naked and shivering, frozen in place.

Julian gets up himself. Contrary to my expectations, he doesn't look angry. Instead he seems almost . . . pleased. "I see that I was right to begin training you tonight," he says as he comes up to me. "I've been too soft with you because of your inexperience. I didn't want to break you, to damage you beyond repair—"

My shaking intensifies as he circles around me like a shark.

"—but I need to start molding you into what I want you to be, Nora. You're already so close to perfection, but there are these occasional lapses . . ." He traces his fingers down my body, ignoring the way I'm cringing from his touch.

"Please," I whisper, "please, Julian, I'm sorry." I don't know what I'm sorry for, but I will say anything right now to avoid this training, whatever it may be.

He smiles at me. "It's not a punishment, my pet. I just have certain needs, that's all—and I want you to be able to satisfy them."

"What needs?" My words are barely audible. I don't want to know, I truly don't, yet I can't seem to stop myself from asking.

"You'll see," he says, wrapping his fingers around my upper arm and leading me toward the bed. When we get there, he reaches for the blindfold and ties it around my eyes. My hands automatically try to go to my face, but he pulls them down, so that they're hanging by my sides.

I hear rustling sounds, as though he's searching for something in that bag. Terror rips through me again, and I make a convulsive movement to free my eyes, but he catches my wrists. Then I feel him binding them behind my back.

At this point I start to cry. I don't make a sound, but I can feel the blindfold getting wet from the moisture escaping my eyes. I know I was helpless before, even without being blindfolded and tied up, but the sense of vulnerability is a thousand times worse now. I know there are women who are into this, who play these types of games with their partners, but Julian is not my partner. I've read enough books that I know the rules—and I know that he's not following them. There's nothing safe, sane, or consensual about what's going on here.

And yet, when Julian reaches between my legs and strokes me there, I'm horrified to realize that I'm wet.

That pleases him. He doesn't say anything, but I can feel the satisfaction emanating from him as he begins to play with my clit, occasionally dipping the tip of one finger inside me to monitor my physical response to his stimulation. His movements are sure, not the least bit hesitant. He knows exactly what to do to enhance my arousal, how to touch me to make me come.

I hate that, his expertise in bringing me pleasure. How many women has he done this to? Surely it takes practice to get so good at making a woman orgasm despite her fear and reluctance.

None of this matters to my body, of course. With each stroke of his skilled fingers, the tension inside me builds and intensifies, the insidious pressure starting to gather low in my belly. I moan, my hips involuntarily pushing toward him as he continues to play with my sex. He's not touching me anywhere else, just there, but it seems to be enough to drive me insane.

"Oh yes," he murmurs, bending down to kiss my neck. "Come for me, my pet."

As though obeying his command, my inner muscles contract . . . and then the climax rushes through me with the force of a freight train. I forget to be afraid; I forget everything in that moment except the pleasure exploding through my nerve endings.

Before I can recover, he pushes me onto the bed, face down. I hear him moving, doing something, and then he lifts me and arranges me on top of a mound of pillows, elevating my hips. Now I'm lying on my stomach with my ass sticking out and my hands tied behind my back, even more exposed and vulnerable than before. I turn my head sideways, so I don't suffocate in the mattress.

My tears, which had almost stopped before, begin again. I have a terrible suspicion I know what he's going to do to me now.

When I feel something cool and wet between my butt cheeks, my suspicion is confirmed. He's spreading lube on me, preparing me for what's to come.

"Please, don't." The words are wrenched out of me. I know that begging is useless. I know that he has no mercy, that it turns him on to see me like this—but I can't help it. I can't accept that additional violation. I just can't. "Please."

"Hush, baby," he murmurs, stroking the curve of my buttocks with his large palm. "I'll teach you to enjoy this too."

I hear more sounds, and then I feel something pushing into me, into that other opening. I tense, clenching my muscles with all my might, but the pressure is too much to resist and the thing begins to penetrate me.

"Stop," I moan as a burning pain begins, and Julian actually listens this time, pausing for a second.

"Relax, my pet," he says softly, caressing my leg with one of his hands. "It'll go much better if you relax."

"Take it out," I beg. "Please take it out."

"Nora," he says, his tone suddenly harsh. "I told you to relax. It's nothing but a small toy. It won't hurt you if you relax."

"Isn't hurting me the whole point?" I ask bitterly. "Isn't that what gets your rocks off?"

"Do you want me to hurt you?" His voice is soft, almost hypnotic. "It would get my rocks off, you're right . . . Is that what you want, my pet? For me to hurt you?"

No, I don't. I don't want that at all. I give an almost imperceptible shake of my head and do my best to relax. I don't think I'm successful at it. It's just too wrong, the feeling of something pushing in there from the outside.

Nonetheless, Julian seems pleased with my efforts. "Good," he croons. "Good girl, there we go . . ." He applies steady pressure, and the thing goes deeper into me, past the resistance of my sphincter, inch by slow inch. When it's all the way in, he pauses, letting me get used to the sensation.

The burning pain is still there, as is the almost nauseating feeling of fullness. I focus on taking small, even breaths and not moving. After about a minute, the pain begins to subside, leaving only the disorienting sensation of a foreign object lodged inside my body.

Julian leaves the toy in place and starts stroking me all over, his touch oddly gentle. He starts with my feet, rubbing them, finding all the kinks and massaging them away. Then he moves up my calves and thighs, which are almost vibrating with tension. His hands are skilled and sure on my body; what he's doing is better than any massage I've ever had. Despite everything, I feel myself melting into his touch, my muscles turning to mush under his fingers. By the time he gets to my neck and shoulders, I'm as relaxed as I've been since waking up on this island. If I hadn't been blindfolded, bound, and sodomized, I would've thought I was in a spa.

When he removes the toy some twenty minutes later, it slides right out, without even a hint of discomfort. He pushes it back in again, and this time, the pain is minimal. If anything, it feels . . . interesting . . . particularly when his fingers find my clit and begin stimulating it again.

I don't resist the pleasure those fingers bring me. Why bother? I would take pleasure over pain any day of the week. Julian is going to do whatever he wants, and I might as well enjoy some parts of it.

So I divorce my mind from the wrongness of it all and let myself simply feel. I can't see anything with the blindfold, and I can't put up much of a fight with my hands tied behind my back. I'm completely helpless—and there's something peculiarly liberating in that. There's no point in worrying, no point in thinking. I'm simply drifting in the darkness, high on post-massage endorphins.

He fucks me with the toy, pushing it in and out of me at the same time as his fingers press on my clit. His movements are rhythmic, coordinated, and I moan as my sex starts to throb, the pressure inside me growing with each thrust. Abruptly, the tension gets to be too much, and there's a sudden, intense burst of pleasure, starting at my core and radiating outward. My muscles clamp down on the toy, and the unusual sensation only intensifies my orgasm. Unable to control myself, I cry out, grinding against Julian's fingers. I want the ecstasy to last forever.

All too soon, though, it's over, and I'm left limp and shaking in the aftermath. Julian is not done with me, of course, not by a long shot. Just as I'm starting to recover, he withdraws the toy and presses a different, larger object to my back opening. It's his cock, I realize, tensing again as he begins to push in.

"Nora . . ." There is a warning note in his voice, and I know what he wants from me, but I don't know if I can do it. I don't know if I can relax enough to let him in. It's too much; he's too thick, too long. I don't understand how something that big can enter me there without ripping me apart.

But he's relentless, and I feel my muscles slowly giving in, unable to resist the pressure he's applying. The head of his cock pushes past the tight ring of my sphincter, and I cry out at the burning, stretching sensation. "Shh," he says soothingly, stroking my back as he slowly goes deeper. "Shh . . . it's all good . . ."

By the time he's in all the way, I'm a trembling, sweating mess. There's pain, yes, but there's also the novelty of having something so large invading my body in this weird, unnatural way. I know people do this—and supposedly even derive pleasure from this act—but I can't imagine ever doing this willingly.

He pauses, letting me adjust to the sensations, and I sob softly into the mattress, wanting nothing more than for this to be over. He's patient, though, his strong hands caressing me, relaxing me, until my tears subside and I no longer feel like passing out.

He senses it when my discomfort begins to ease, and starts to move inside me, slowly, carefully. I can hear his harsh breathing, and I know that he's exerting a lot of control over himself, that he probably wants to fuck me harder but is trying not to 'damage me beyond repair.' Nevertheless, his movements cause my insides to twist and churn, causing me to cry out with every stroke.

And just when I think I can't bear it anymore, he slides one hand under my hips and finds my swollen clit again. His fingers are gentle, his touch butterfly-soft, and I begin to feel a familiar warmth in my belly, my body responding to him despite the violation. What he's doing isn't taking away the pain, but it's distracting me from it, allowing me to focus on the pleasure. I never knew pleasure and pain could co-exist like that, but there's something strangely addictive in that combination, something dark and forbidden that resonates with a part of myself I never knew existed.

His pace picks up, and somehow that makes it better. Maybe some nerve endings are desensitized by now—or maybe I'm simply getting used to having him inside me—but the pain lessens, almost disappears. All that's left is a host of other sensations—strange, unfamiliar sensations that are intriguing in their own way. That, and the pleasure from his clever fingers playing with my sex, arousing me until I'm crying out for a different reason, until I'm begging Julian to do it, to send me over the edge again.

And he does. My entire body tightens and explodes, shuddering with the force of my release. He groans as my muscles clamp down on his shaft, and I feel the liquid warmth from his seed bathing my insides, the saltiness of it stinging my raw flesh.

"Good girl," he whispers in my ear, his cock softening within me. He kisses my earlobe, and the tender gesture is such a contrast to what he'd just done that I feel disoriented. Is this normal kidnapper behavior? When he withdraws from me, I feel empty and cold, almost as if I'm missing the heat from his body pressing me down.

He doesn't leave me alone for long, though. He unties my hands first and rubs them lightly, then he takes off my blindfold. I blink, letting my eyes adjust to the soft light in the room, and move my arms, bracing myself on my elbows.

"Come," he says softly, wrapping his fingers around my upper arm. "Let's get you into the shower."

I let him tug me to my feet and lead me into the bathroom. My legs feel shaky, and I'm glad he's holding me. I don't know if I could've walked there by myself.

He turns on the shower, waits for the water to heat up for a few seconds, and leads us into the large stall. Then he thoroughly washes every part of my body, rinsing away all traces of lube and semen. He even shampoos and conditions my hair, his fingers massaging my skull and relaxing me again. By the time he's done, I feel clean and cared for.

"Now it's your turn," he says, turning up my palm and pouring some body wash into it.

"You want me to wash you?" I say incredulously, and he nods, a small smile curving his lips. With the water running down his muscular body, he's even more gorgeous than usual, like some kind of a sea god.

A sea monster, I correct myself. A beautiful sea monster.

He continues looking at me expectantly, waiting to see if I will do as he asked, and I mentally shrug. Why not wash him, really? It won't hurt me in the least. And besides, as much as I hate him, I can't deny that I am curious about his body—that touching him is something I find exciting.

So I rub my hands together and run them over his chest, spreading the soap all over his bronzed skin. He raises his arms, and I wash his sides and underarms, then his back.

His skin is mostly smooth, roughened in just a few places by dark, masculine hair. I can feel the powerful muscles bunching under my fingers, and I find myself enjoying this experience. In this moment, I can almost pretend that I want to be here, that this stunning creature is my lover instead of my captor.

I wash him as thoroughly as he washed me, my soapy hands gliding over his legs, his feet. By the time I get to his sex, his cock begins to harden again, and I freeze, realizing that my ministrations unintentionally aroused him.

He correctly interprets my reaction as fear. "Relax, my pet," he murmurs, his voice filled with amusement. "I'm only human, you know. As delicious as you are, I need more than a few minutes to recover fully."

I swallow and turn away, rinsing my hands under the water spray. What the hell am I doing? He hadn't forced me to touch him. I had done it of my own accord. He'd asked, but I am pretty sure I could've refused and he would've let it slide. The dark undercurrent I'd sensed in him earlier this evening is not there now. In fact, Julian seems to be in a good mood, his manner almost playful.

I want to get out of the shower now, so I make a move to slide past him. He stops me, his arm blocking my way.

"Wait," he says softly, tilting my chin up with his fingers. Then he bends his head and kisses me, his lips sweet and gentle on mine. A now-familiar response warms my body, making me want to rub myself against him like a cat in heat. He doesn't let it go far, though. After about a minute, he lifts his head and smiles down at me, his blue eyes gleaming with satisfaction. "Now you can go."

Utterly confused, I step out of the shower, dry myself off, and escape into my room as quickly as I can.

CHAPTER THIRTEEN

That night I learn about Julian's nightmares.

After the shower, he joins me in my bed, his muscular body curving around me from the back, one heavy arm draping over my torso. I stiffen at first, unsure of what to expect, but all he does is go to sleep while holding me close to him. I can hear the even rhythm of his breathing as I stare into the darkness, and then I gradually fall asleep too.

I wake up to a strange noise. It startles me out of deep sleep, and my eyes fly open, my heart pounding from an adrenaline surge.

What was that? For a moment, I don't dare breathe, but then I realize that the sounds are coming from the other side of the bed—from the man sleeping beside me.

I sit up in bed and peer at him. It looks like he rolled away from me in the night, gathering all the blankets to himself. I'm completely naked and uncovered, and I actually feel a little chilly with the air-conditioning running at full blast.

The sounds escaping his throat are muffled, but there is a raw quality to them that gives me goosebumps. They remind me of an animal in pain. He's breathing hard, almost gasping for air.

"Julian?" I say uncertainly. I don't really know what to do in this situation. Should I wake him up? He's clearly having a bad dream. I recall him telling me about his family, that they were all murdered, and I can't help feeling pity for this beautiful, twisted man.

He cries out, his voice low and hoarse, and flops over onto his back, one arm hitting the pillow only a few inches away from me.

"Um, Julian?" I reach out cautiously and touch his hand.

He mumbles and turns his head, still deeply asleep. If we were anywhere but on this island, this would be the perfect moment for me to try to escape. As it stands, however, there's really no point in going anywhere, so I just watch Julian warily, wondering if he's going to wake up on his own or if I should try harder to wake him.

For a few moments, it seems like he's settling down, his breathing calming a bit. Then he suddenly cries out again.

It's a name this time.

"Maria," he rasps out. "Maria . . ."

For one shocking second, I feel a hot tide of jealousy sweeping over me. *Maria . . .* He's dreaming of another woman.

Then my rational side reasserts itself. Maria could easily be his mother or his sister—and even if she's not, why should I care that he's dreaming of her? It's not like he's my boyfriend or anything.

So I swallow and reach for him again, suppressing the residual pangs of jealousy. "Julian?"

As soon as my fingers touch his arm, he grabs me, his motions so fast and startling that only a small gasp escapes me as he pulls me toward him. His arms around me are inescapable, his embrace almost suffocating, and I can feel him shaking as he holds me tightly against him, my face pressed into his shoulder. His skin is cold and clammy with sweat, and I can hear his heart galloping in his chest.

"Maria," he mumbles into my hair, his fingers digging into my back with such force that I'm sure there will be bruises there tomorrow. Yet somehow I don't mind because I know he's not doing this on purpose. He's in the grip of his nightmare and he's seeking comfort—and I'm the only one who can provide it right now.

After a while, I can hear his breathing easing. His arms relax a little, no longer squeezing me with such desperation, and his frantic heartbeat begins to slow. "Maria," he whispers again, but there's less pain in his voice now, as though he's reliving happier times with her, whatever those may be.

I let him hold me, not moving lest I wake him from his now-peaceful rest. He's not the only one receiving comfort here. Despite everything he's done to me, I can't deny that a part of me wants this from him, this feeling of closeness, of safety. He's the only thing I have to fear; logically, I know that. It doesn't matter, though, because right now I feel like he's holding the darkness at bay, keeping me safe from whatever other monsters may be lurking out there.

Just as I'm keeping him safe from his nightmares.

* * *

When I wake up the next morning, Julian is gone again.

"Where is he?" I ask Beth at breakfast, watching as she cuts up a mango for me. I still feel an occasional twinge of discomfort when I move, a reminder of my captor's more exotic proclivities.

"A work emergency," she says, her hands moving with a graceful efficiency that I can't help but admire. "He should be back in a couple of days."

"What kind of work emergency?"

Beth shrugs. "I don't know. You can ask Julian that when he returns."

I look at her, trying to understand what motivates her ... and Julian. "You said I'm the first girl he brought here, to this island," I say, keeping my tone casual. "So what did he do with the others?"

"There were no others." She's done with the mango, and she's placing the plate in front of me before sitting down to eat her own breakfast.

"So why is he doing this to me? I know he's got peculiar tastes, but surely there are women who are into that—"

Beth grins at me, showing even white teeth. "Of course. But he wants you."

"Why? What's so special about me?"

"You'll have to ask Julian that."

Again that non-answer. Her evasiveness makes me want to scream. I spear a piece of mango with my fork and chew it slowly, thinking this over.

"Is it because of Maria?" I'm not sure what makes me ask this, except that I can't get that name out of my head.

It's apparently the right question, though, because it stops Beth in her tracks. "Julian told you about Maria?" She sounds shocked.

"He mentioned her." It's not really a lie. Her name did come up, even though Julian doesn't know it. "Why does that surprise you?"

She shrugs again, no longer looking so shocked. "I guess it doesn't, now that I think about it. If he's going to tell anyone, it would probably be you."

Me? Why? I'm burning with curiosity, but I try to keep my expression impassive, like none of this is news to me. "Of course," I say calmly, eating my mango.

"Then you understand, Nora," she says, looking at me. "You have to understand at least a little bit. Your resemblance to her is uncanny. I saw the photo, and she could've been your younger sister."

"That similar?" I struggle to keep the shock out of my voice. My heart is pounding in my chest. This is so much more than I could've hoped for, and Beth just handed me this information on a silver platter.

She frowns. "He didn't tell you that?"

"No," I say. "He didn't tell me much. Just a little bit." Just her name, uttered in the throes of a nightmare.

Beth's eyes widen as she realizes that she probably revealed more than she should have. She looks unhappy for a moment, but then her expression smooths out. "Oh well," she says. "I guess now you know. I'll have to tell Julian about this, of course."

I swallow, and the piece of mango slides down my throat like a rock. I don't want her to tell Julian anything. I don't know what he'll do to me when he finds out that I know about Maria—that I saw him when he was at his most vulnerable.

My stupid curiosity.

"Why?" I say, trying not to sound anxious. "You're the one he's going to be upset with, not me."

"I wouldn't be too sure of that, Nora," Beth says, giving me a slightly malicious smile. "And besides, I don't ever keep secrets from Julian. He's very good at prying them out of people."

And getting up, she starts washing the dishes.

* * *

I spend the next two days alternating between speculating about Maria and worrying about Julian's return.

Who is she? Someone who looks a lot like me, apparently. So similar that she could be my younger sister, Beth said. How old is this girl? Who is she to Julian? The questions gnaw at me, interfering with my sleep. He took me because of my resemblance to her—that much is obvious to me. But why? What happened to her? Why is she in his nightmares?

I want to know, I want to understand, yet I'm afraid of Julian's reaction when he returns and finds out that I snooped. I could try to explain that I learned all of this accidentally, that I didn't mean to invade his privacy, but I strongly suspect my captor is not the understanding type.

Beth doesn't tell me anything else about Maria. In fact, she doesn't talk to me much at all. She's one of those rare individuals who seems happy being by herself. If I were her, I would go crazy being stuck here on this island, doing nothing but cooking, cleaning, and looking after Julian's sex toy, but she seems perfectly fine with it.

I, on the other hand, am far from fine. I am constantly thinking about my old life, missing my family and friends. They probably think I'm dead at this point. I'm guessing there was a big search for me, but I doubt it yielded any results.

I also think about Jake, wondering if he recovered from his beating. It had looked so brutal, what Julian's thug had done to him. Does Jake know that it was my fault? That he got attacked in his house because of me?

Taking a deep breath, I tell myself that it doesn't matter if he knows or not. Whatever Jake and I could've had together is over. I belong to Julian now, and there's no point in thinking about any other man.

In a way, I am lucky. I know that. I'm sure many girls end up in far worse circumstances than me. I once saw a documentary about sexual slavery, and the images of those hollow-eyed women had haunted me for days. They'd seemed broken, completely and utterly crushed by whatever had been done to them, and even the fact that they'd been rescued didn't seem to dispel the suffering etched into their faces.

My captivity is different. It's much nicer, much more comfortable. Julian is not trying to break me, and I'm grateful for that. I may be his sex slave, but at least he's my only master. Things could definitely be much worse.

Or so I tell myself as I wait for his return, desperately hoping that Julian's reaction to my prying won't be as bad as I fear.

CHAPTER FOURTEEN

Julian comes back in the middle of the night. I must've been sleeping lightly because I wake up as soon as I hear the quiet murmur of conversation downstairs. My captor's deeper tones are interspersed with Beth's more feminine ones, and I have a strong suspicion I know what they're talking about.

I sit up in bed, my heart galloping in my chest. Getting up, I quickly pull on yesterday's clothes and run to the bathroom to freshen up. I don't know why I care about brushing teeth right now, but I do. I want to be as awake and prepared as possible for whatever Julian decides to do to me.

Then I just sit on the bed and wait.

Finally, the door to my room opens and Julian walks in. He looks unusually tired, with dark shadows under his eyes and a hint of stubble on his normally clean-shaven face. These flaws should've diminished his beauty, but they only humanize him a bit, somehow enhancing his attractiveness.

"You're awake." He sounds surprised.

"I heard voices," I explain, watching him warily.

"And you decided to greet me. How nice of you, my pet."

I know he's mocking me, so I don't say anything, just continue looking at him. My palms are sweating, but I'm doing my best to project a calm demeanor.

He sits down on the bed next to me and lifts his hand to touch my hair. "Such a sweet pet," he murmurs, lifting a thick strand and playfully tickling my cheek with it. "Such a curious little kitten . . ."

I swallow, my breathing fast and shallow. What is he going to do to me?

He gets up and starts to undress while I watch him, frozen in place by a mixture of fear and strange anticipation. His clothes come off, revealing the powerfully masculine body underneath, and I feel a wave of desire rolling through me, heating up my core.

I want him. Despite everything, I want him, and that's the most screwed-up thing of all. He's probably going to do something awful to me, but I still want him more than I could've ever imagined wanting anyone.

In for a penny, in for a pound. "Did you do this to Maria?" I ask quietly. "Did you also keep her as your pet?"

He looks at me, his eyes as blue and mysterious as the ocean. "Are you sure you want to go there, Nora?" His voice is soft, deceptively calm.

I stare at him, feeling uncharacteristically reckless. "Why, yes, Julian, I do." My tone is bitterly sarcastic, and I realize that part of my boldness stems from jealousy, that I hate the idea of this Maria being special to Julian. But even that realization is not enough to stop me. "Who is she? Some other girl you abused?"

His expression darkens, and I hold my breath, waiting to see what he would do now. In a way, I want to provoke him. I want him to punish me, to hurt me. I want it because I need him to be nothing more than a monster—because I need to hate him for the sake of my sanity.

He walks over and sits down on the bed next to me. I fight the urge to flinch when he reaches for me and wraps his strong fingers around my neck. Gripping my throat, he leans over and brushes his cheek against mine, back and forth, as though enjoying the soft texture of my skin against the roughness of his stubble-covered jaw. His fingers don't squeeze, but the threat is there, and I can feel myself shaking, my breathing speeding up in terrified anticipation.

He chuckles softly, and I feel the gust of air against my ear. Despite his weary appearance, his breath is fresh and sweet, as though he had just been chewing gum. I close my eyes, trying to convince myself that Julian wouldn't really kill me, that he's just toying with me right now.

He kisses my ear, nibbling lightly on my earlobe. His touch in that sensitive area sends pleasurable chills down my spine, and my breathing changes again, becomes slower and deeper as I get more aroused. I can smell the warm, musky scent of his skin, and my nipples tighten, reacting to his nearness. The ache between my thighs is growing, and I squirm a little, trying to relieve the pressure building inside me.

"You want me, don't you?" he whispers in my ear, slipping his hand under the skirt of my dress and lightly stroking my sex. I know he can feel the moisture there, and I suppress a moan as one long finger pushes inside me, rubbing against my slick inner wall. "Don't you, Nora?"

"Yes." I gasp as he touches a particularly sensitive spot.

"Yes, what?" His voice is harsh, demanding. He wants my complete surrender.

"Yes, I want you," I admit in a broken whisper. I can't deny it any longer. I want Julian. I want the man who kidnapped me, who hurt me. I want him, and I hate myself for it.

He withdraws his finger then and lets go of my throat. Startled, I open my eyes and meet his gaze. He lifts his hand to my face, pressing his finger against my lips. It's the same finger that was just inside me. "Suck it," he orders, and I obediently open my mouth, sucking the finger in. I can taste myself, my own desire, and it makes me even more turned on.

When he's satisfied that the finger is clean, he removes it from my mouth, grasping my chin with his hand instead, forcing me to meet his gaze. I stare up at him, mesmerized by the dark blue striations in his irises. My body is throbbing with need, desperately craving his possession. I want him to take me, to fill the aching emptiness within.

But all he does is look at me, a mocking half-smile playing on his beautiful lips. "You think I'm going to punish you tonight, Nora?" he asks softly. "Is that what you're expecting me to do?"

I blink, startled by the question. Of course I expect him to do that. I did something that upset him, and he's not shy about hurting me when I'm on my best behavior.

Apparently reading the answer on my face, he smiles wider. "Well, sorry to disappoint you, my pet, but I'm far too exhausted to do your punishment justice tonight. All I want right now is your mouth." And with that, he fists his hand in my hair and pushes me down, so that I'm kneeling between his legs, his erection at my eye level.

"Suck it," he murmurs, looking down at me. "Just like you did my finger."

I'm no stranger to blow-jobs, having given quite a few to my ex-boyfriend, so I know what to do. I close my lips around the thick column of his shaft and swirl my tongue around the tip. He tastes a little salty, a little musky, and I look up, watching his face as I cup his balls in my hand and squeeze them lightly. He groans, his eyes closing and his hand tightening in my hair, and I continue, moving my mouth up and down on his cock, swallowing him deeper every time.

For some reason, I don't mind pleasuring him this way. In fact, I find it strangely enjoyable. Even though it's an illusion, I feel like he's at *my* mercy at the moment, that I am the one who has the power right now. I love the helpless groans that escape his throat as I use my hands, my lips, and my tongue to bring him to the very brink of orgasm before slowing down. I love the agonized expression on his face when I take his balls into my mouth and suck on them, feeling them tightening in my mouth. I love the way he shudders when I lightly scrape my fingernails on the underside of his balls, and when he finally explodes, I love the way he grabs my head, holding me in place as he comes, his cock pulsing and throbbing in my mouth.

When he releases me, I lick my lips, cleaning off the traces of semen while looking up at him the whole time.

He stares down at me, still breathing heavily. "That was good, Nora." His voice is low and raspy. "Very good. Who taught you to do that?"

I shrug. "It's not like I was a nun before I met you," I say without thinking.

His eyes narrow, and I realize that I just made a mistake. This is a man who seems to revel in the fact that he was my first, who likes the idea that I belong to him and only to him. Any references to ex-boyfriends are best kept to myself.

To my relief, he doesn't seem inclined to punish me for this transgression either. Instead, he pulls me up, back onto the bed. Then he undresses me, turns off the light, and puts his arm around me, holding me close as he drifts off to sleep.

* * *

My punishment doesn't take place until the following night. Julian again spends the day in his office, and I don't see him until dinnertime.

For some reason, I'm not as frightened as I was before. The little interlude last night—and sleeping in Julian's arms afterwards—soothed my anxiety, making me think the punishment won't be as bad as I'd initially feared. He didn't seem particularly angry that I'd found out about Maria, which is a big relief. I hope he'll forgo punishing me altogether, particularly if I do my best to behave today.

The three of us have dinner again, and I listen to Julian and Beth discussing the latest developments in the Middle East. It surprises me how well informed both of them seem to be about the topic. Before my kidnapping, I was pretty good about following current events, but I've never heard most of the politicians' names they're mentioning. Then again, if Julian really does run an international import-export company, then it makes sense for him to have his finger on the pulse of world politics.

My curiosity gets the best of me again, and I ask if Julian's company does a lot of business in the Middle East.

He smiles at me as he spears a piece of shrimp with his fork. "Yes, my pet, it does."

"Is that where you went on this trip?"

"No," he says, biting into the juicy shrimp. "I was in Hong Kong this time."

I make a mental note of that. Hong Kong had to be close enough to the island for him to fly there, conduct his business, and fly back—all within two days. I picture a map of the Pacific Ocean in my head. It's a bit fuzzy, as geography is not my strong point, but I think this island must not be that far from the Philippines.

Beth offers me some curried potatoes to go with my shrimp, and I take them, thanking her with a smile. I've noticed that we get more food variety shortly after Julian comes back from the mainland. I'm guessing he brings us food supplies from wherever he goes to.

Beth smiles back at me, and I see that she's in a good mood. In general, she seems happier when Julian is here, more lighthearted. I'm sure it's not fun for her, dealing with my attitude all the time. One could almost feel bad for her—'almost' being the key word.

"I've never been to Asia," I tell Julian. "Is Hong Kong really how they show it in movies?"

Julian grins at me. "Pretty much. It's amazing. Probably one of my favorite cities. The architecture is fascinating, and the food . . ." He makes a show of licking his lips. "The food is just to die for." He rubs his belly, and I laugh, charmed despite myself.

The rest of the dinner passes in the same pleasant manner. Julian tells me amusing stories about the different places he's been to in Asia, and I listen in fascination, occasionally gasping and laughing at some of the more outrageous tales. Beth sometimes chimes in, but for the most part, it's as though it's just Julian and me, having fun on a date.

Like that time when we had dinner alone, I find myself falling under Julian's spell. He's more than charming; he's simply mesmerizing. His allure goes beyond his looks, although I can't deny the physical attraction between us. When he laughs or gives me one of his genuine smiles, I feel a warm glow, like he's the sun and I'm basking in his rays. Everything about him appeals to me—the way he talks, how he gestures to emphasize a point, the way his eyes crinkle at the corners when he grins at me. He's also an excellent storyteller, and three hours simply fly by as he entertains me with tales of his adventures in Japan, where he once lived for a year as a teenager.

I don't want this dinner to end, so I try to stretch it out as much as I can, helping myself to second, third, and fourth helpings of the fruit Beth prepared as dessert. I'm sure Julian is aware of my delaying tactics, but he doesn't seem to mind.

Finally, everything has been eaten, and Beth gets up to wash the dishes. Julian smiles at me, and for the first time this evening, I feel a flicker of fear. I can again sense that dark undercurrent in his smile, and I realize that it's been present all along—that it's always there with Julian. The charming man that I've just spent three hours with is about as real as a figment of my imagination.

Still smiling, he offers me his hand. It's a courtly gesture, but I can't help the chill that runs down my spine as I see a familiar gleam in his blue eyes. He again looks like a dark angel, his sublime beauty tinted with a faint shadow of evil.

Swallowing to get rid of the sudden knot in my throat, I place my hand in his and let him lead me upstairs. It's better this way, more civilized. It allows me to pretend for a few moments longer—to hold on to the illusion of having a choice.

When we enter my room, he has me undress and lie down on the bed, on my stomach. Then he ties me up again, binding my wrists tightly behind my back. A blindfold goes over my eyes, and pillows under my hips. It's the exact same position in which he took me last time, and I can't help tensing as I remember the agony—and the ecstasy—of his possession.

Is that what he's going to do? Have anal sex with me again? If so, it's not that bad. I survived the last time, and I'm sure I'll be fine again.

So when I feel the coolness of lube between my cheeks, I try to relax, to let him do whatever he wants. A toy slides in, the invasion startling but not particularly painful. I can definitely tolerate it. As before, he leaves the toy inside me as he gives me a massage, relaxing me, arousing me with his touch. He kisses the back of my neck, nibbles on the sensitive spot near my shoulder, and then his mouth travels down my spine, kissing each vertebrae. At the same time, his finger slips into my vaginal opening, adding to the tension coiling low in my belly.

My release, when it comes, is so powerful that I buck against the mattress, my entire body shuddering and convulsing. While I'm recovering from the aftershocks, Julian withdraws his finger, and I feel cool air on my back as he leans away from me for a second.

The lick of fire along my buttocks is as sharp as it is sudden. Startled, I cry out, trying to twist away, but I don't get far, and the second hit is even more painful than the first, landing on my thighs. He's whipping me with something, I realize. I don't know what it is, but I can hear the swish in the air as he brings it down on my defenseless ass, again and again while I sob and try to roll away.

Apparently tired of chasing me all over the bed, he unties my hands and then ties them above my head, securing my wrists to the wooden headboard.

"Julian, please, I'm sorry!" I plead, desperate to make him stop. "Please, I'm sorry I was prying. Please, I won't do it again, I won't—"

"Of course you will, my pet," he whispers in my ear, his breath warm on my neck. "You're as curious as a little cat. But sometimes you should let things slide. For your own good, you understand?"

"Yes! Yes, I do. Please, Julian—"

"Shh," he soothes, kissing my neck again. "You need to accept your punishment like a good girl." And with that, he pulls back again, leaving my back and buttocks exposed to him.

I try to scramble away, but he catches my legs, holding my ankles together with one hand. He's strong, far stronger than I could've imagined, because he's able to hold my flailing legs with just one arm while whipping me with the other.

I can hear the swishing sound his prop makes, and I can't help the screams that escape my throat each time it lands on my ass. My butt and thighs feel like they're on fire, and the blindfold is soaked with my tears. I want it to stop, I'm begging him to stop, but Julian is immune to my pleas.

It seems to go on forever, until I'm too hoarse to scream and too exhausted to struggle. I can't even gather enough energy to keep my muscles tense, and somehow that seems to help the pain. I relax further, make my body go limp, and the pain becomes more manageable, each lash feeling less like a bite and more like a stroke.

As the whipping proceeds, my world seems to narrow until nothing exists outside of the present moment. I'm not thinking anymore; I'm simply feeling, simply being. There's something surreal, yet incredibly addictive in the experience. Each swish brings with it a sharp sensation that pulls me deeper into this strange state, making me feel like I'm floating. The pain is no longer unbearable; instead it's comforting in some perverse way. It's grounding me, providing me with what I need at that moment. A warm glow spreads throughout my body, and all my worries, all my fears disappear. It's a high unlike anything I've ever experienced before.

When Julian finally stops and unties me, I cling to him, trembling all over. Without the blindfold and the restraints, I feel lost, overwhelmed. As though knowing what I need, he pulls me onto his lap and cradles me gently in his arms, letting me cry against his shoulder until I no longer feel like I'm going to fall apart.

After a while, I become cognizant of the hard length of his erection pressing into my buttocks, which are sore and throbbing from the whipping. The little toy he put in my ass before is still there, lodged securely inside me, and I realize that the warm glow within me is different now, more sexual in nature.

Apparently sensing the shift in my mood, Julian carefully lifts me and positions me so that I'm facing him while straddling his lap. My hands are on his shoulders, and I can feel the powerful muscles playing under his skin. With my thighs spread wide, the tip of his cock presses against my sex. The smooth head slides between my folds and rubs against my clit, intensifying my arousal. I moan, my head arching back, and he slowly enters me, penetrating me inch by slow inch. With the toy in my ass, he feels even bigger than usual, and I gasp as he goes deeper, filling me with his thickness.

It feels good, so unbelievably good, and I moan again, tightening my inner muscles around his shaft. He groans, closing his eyes, and I do it again, wanting more of the sensation.

He opens his eyes and stares at me, his face taut with lust and his eyes glittering. I hold his gaze, fascinated by the fierce need I see there. He's as much in my thrall right now as I am in his, and the realization adds to my desire, further heating up my core.

Raising his hand, he curves his palm around my cheek, wiping away the remnants of tears with his thumb. Then he bends his head and kisses me, as tenderly as I've ever been kissed. I revel in that kiss; his affection is like a drug to me right now—I need it with a desperation I don't fully understand.

I close my eyes, and my hands slide up his shoulders, finding their way into his hair. It's thick and soft to the touch, like dark satin. Pressing closer to him, I rub my naked breasts against his powerfully muscled chest, delighting in the feel of his hair-roughened skin against my sensitive nipples. His lips are firm and warm on mine, and the cock inside me is unbelievably hard, stretching me, filling me to the brim.

Still kissing me, he begins to rock back and forth, causing his shaft to move within me ever so slightly, sending waves of heat throughout my body. However, each movement also serves as a reminder of the earlier beating, and a pained moan escapes my throat as my sore buttocks rub against his hard thighs. He swallows the sound, his mouth now consuming mine with unrestrained hunger.

His hand slides into my hair, holding it tightly as he devours me with his kiss, his hips rocking harder, adding to the pressure building within my core. His other hand moves down my body, and then he presses on the toy, pushing it deeper inside my rear passage.

I fly apart. My orgasm is so strong, I can't even make a sound. For a few blissful seconds, I'm completely swamped by pleasure, by ecstasy so intense that it's almost agonizing. My body shudders and undulates on top of Julian's, and my movements trigger his own release.

In the aftermath, he holds me, stroking my sweat-dampened hair. I can feel his shaft softening within me, and then he reaches between my butt cheeks and tugs on the toy, carefully pulling it out.

Then he makes me get up and leads me into the shower.

CHAPTER FIFTEEN

He takes care of me in the shower again, washing me, soothing me with his touch. He's especially careful around the tender area of my thighs and buttocks, making sure not to add to my discomfort. To my relief, it doesn't look like the skin is broken anywhere. My ass is pink with some reddish welts, and I'm sure there will be bruising, but there is no trace of blood anywhere.

When I'm clean and dry, he guides me back to bed. He's silent and so am I. I'm still not fully out of that strange state I was in earlier. It's as though my mind is partially disconnected from my body. The only thing holding me together is Julian and his oddly gentle touch.

We lie down together, and Julian turns off the lights, wrapping us in darkness. I lie on my stomach, because any other position is too painful. He pulls me closer to him, so that my head is pillowed on his chest and my arm is draped over his ribcage, and I close my eyes, wanting nothing more than the oblivion of sleep.

"My father was one of the most powerful drug lords in Colombia." Julian's voice is barely audible, his breath ruffling the fine hair near my forehead. I had already begun to fall asleep, but I'm suddenly wide awake, my heart hammering in my chest.

"He started grooming me to be his successor when I was four years old. I held my first gun when I was six." Julian pauses, his hand lightly stroking my hair. "I killed my first man when I was eight."

I'm so horrified that I just lie there, frozen in place by shock.

"Maria was the daughter of one of the men in my father's organization," Julian continues, his voice low and emotionless. "I met her when I was thirteen, and she was twelve. She was everything that I was not. Beautiful, sweet . . . innocent. You see, unlike my father, her parents sheltered her from the reality of their lives. They wanted her to be a child, to know nothing about the ugliness of our world.

"But she was bright, like you. And curious. So very, very curious . . ." His voice trails off for a second, as though he's lost in some memory. Then he shakes it off and resumes his story. "She followed her father one day to see what he was doing. Hid in the back of his car. I found her there because it was my job to be a lookout, to guard the meeting spot."

I can barely breathe, unable to believe that Julian is telling me all this. Why now? Why tonight?

"I could've told her father, gotten her in trouble, but she begged so prettily, looked at me so sweetly with her big brown eyes that I couldn't do it. I made one of my father's guards take her home instead.

"After that, she came to see me on purpose. She wanted to get to know me better, she said. To be friends with me." There is a note of remembered disbelief in Julian's voice, as though nobody in their right mind could've wanted something like that.

I swallow, my heart stupidly aching for the young boy he had been once. Had he even had friends, or had his father stolen that from him too, just as he had destroyed Julian's childhood?

"I tried to tell her that it wasn't a good idea, that I wasn't somebody she should be around, but she wouldn't listen to me. She'd find me somewhere almost every week, until I had no choice but to give in and start spending time with her. We went fishing together, and she showed me how to draw." He pauses for a second, his hand still stroking my hair. "She was very good at drawing."

"What happened to her?" I ask when he doesn't say anything else for a minute. My voice is strangely hoarse. I clear my throat and try again. "What happened to Maria?"

"One of my father's rivals learned that she was seeing me. We had just raided his warehouse, and he was pissed. So he decided to teach my father a lesson . . . through me."

Every little hair on my body is standing on end, and I feel a chill roughening my skin with goosebumps. I can already see where this story is heading, and I want to tell Julian to stop, to go no further, but I can't get a single word past the constriction in my throat.

"They found her body in an alley near one of my father's buildings." His voice is steady, but I can sense the agony buried deeply within. "She had been raped, then mutilated. It was meant to be a message to me and my father. *Back the fuck off*, it said."

I squeeze my eyelids together, trying to keep the tears burning my eyes from leaking out, but it's a futile effort. I know Julian can probably feel the wetness on his chest. "A message? To a thirteen-year-old boy?"

"By that time, I was already fourteen." I can't see Julian's bitter smile, but I can sense it. "And age didn't matter. Not to my father . . . and certainly not to his rival."

"I'm sorry." I don't know what else to say. I want to cry—for him, for Maria, for that young boy who'd lost his friend in such a brutal manner. And I want to cry for myself, because I now understand my captor better—and I realize that the darkness in his soul is worse than anything I could've imagined.

Julian shifts underneath me, and I become aware of the fact that my hand is now on his shoulder and my nails are digging into his skin. I force myself to unclench my fingers and take a deep breath. I need to get a hold on myself, or I'm going to burst out sobbing.

"I killed those men." His tone is casual now, almost conversational, though I can feel the tension in his body. "The ones who raped her. I tracked them down and killed them, one by one. There were seven of them. After that, my father sent me away, first to America, then to Asia and Europe. He was afraid all that killing would be bad for business. I didn't come back until years later, when he and my mother were killed by yet another rival."

I focus on controlling my breathing and keeping the bile in my throat down. "Is that why you don't have a Spanish accent?" My question comes totally out of the left field. I don't even know what makes me ask something so trivial at a moment like this.

But it's apparently the right thing to do because Julian relaxes slightly, some of the tension leaving his muscles. "Yes. That's partially why, my pet. Also, my mother was an American, and she taught me English from a young age."

"An American?"

"Yes. She was a model in her youth, a tall, beautiful blond. They met in New York, when my father was there on a business trip. He swept her off her feet, and they were married before he told her anything about his business."

"What did she do when she found out?" I know I'm probably focusing on the wrong things here, but I need to distract myself from the gruesome images filling my mind—images of a dead girl who's a younger version of me . . .

"There was nothing she could do," Julian says. "She was already married to him, and living in Colombia."

He doesn't explain further, but he doesn't need to. It's clear to me that his mother was as much of a prisoner as I am—except that she'd chosen her captivity, at least initially.

For a few minutes, we just lie there quietly, without talking. I'm no longer drowsy. I don't know if I'll be able to sleep tonight at all. The ache in my body is nothing compared to the despair in my heart.

"So is that what you do now? Drugs?" I ask, finally breaking the silence. It's not far from my original supposition that he's part of the Mafia or some other criminal organization.

"No," he says, to my surprise. "That part of my life ended when my parents were killed. I took the family business in a different direction."

"Which direction?" I remember him telling me something about an import-export organization, but I can't imagine Julian doing something as innocuous as selling electronics. Not after what I've just learned about his upbringing.

He chuckles, as though amused at my persistence. "Weapons," he says. "I'm an arms dealer, Nora."

I blink, surprised. I know a little—or at least, I think I know—about drug dealers, thanks to some popular TV shows. Arms dealers, however, are a complete mystery to me. I strongly suspect Julian isn't talking about a few guns here or there.

I have a million questions about his profession, but there's something I need to know first, while Julian seems to be in a sharing mood. "Why did you steal me? Is it because I remind you of Maria?"

"Yes," he says softly, his voice wrapping around me like a cashmere scarf. "When I first saw you in that club, you looked so much like her, it was uncanny. Except you were older—and even more beautiful. And I wanted you. I *needed* you. For the first time in years, I was truly feeling. Of course, the emotions you evoked in me were nothing like what I'd once felt for her. She was my friend, but you . . ." He inhales deeply, his chest moving under my head. "I just needed you to be mine, Nora. When I touched you that day, when I felt the silkiness of your skin, I so badly wanted to take you, to strip off those tight clothes you were wearing and fuck you senseless right then and there, on the floor of that club. And I wanted to hurt you . . . the way I sometimes like to hurt women, the way they ask me to hurt them . . . I wanted to hear you scream—in pain and in pleasure."

His hand continues playing with my hair, and the caressing touch keeps me calm enough to listen. In the darkness, none of this is real. There's only Julian and his voice, telling me things that a normal person would find frightening—things that somehow make me wet instead.

"I brought you here, to my island, because it's the safest place for you. My business associates are always looking for signs of weakness, and you, my pet, are a weakness of mine. I've never felt this way about another woman. I've never been so"—he pauses for a moment, as though searching for the right word—"so fucking *obsessed*. Just the thought of another man touching you, kissing you, drove me crazy. I tried to stay away, to put you out of my mind, but I couldn't resist seeing you one more time at your graduation. And when I saw you there, I knew you felt it too, this connection between us—and I knew then that it was inevitable . . . that I would take you, and you would always be mine."

His words wash over me like a warm ocean wave, bringing with it trepidation and a kind of unhealthy excitement. Some twisted part of me revels in the fact that I'm special to Julian, that he's as helplessly drawn to me as I am to him.

For some strange reason, I feel compelled to reciprocate his openness. "I was afraid of you," I tell him quietly. "In the club, and then when I saw you at my graduation, I was afraid."

"Only afraid?" He sounds amused and mildly disbelieving.

"Afraid and attracted," I admit. This seems to be the night for revelations. Besides, he already knows the truth. Despite my fear, I desire him. I've wanted him from the very beginning, and nothing he's done since changes that fact.

"Good." He runs his hand lightly down my back. "That's very good, my pet. It'll make things easier for both of us."

Easier? I consider that statement. Easier for him, certainly. But for me? I'm not so sure.

"Did you ever contact my family?" I ask, thinking of his promise all those days ago. "Do they know that I'm alive?"

"Yes." His hand pauses at the curve of my spine. "They know."

I wonder what he told them and how they reacted. I wonder if it made it better for them or worse.

"Will you ever let me go?" I already know the answer, but I need to hear him say it anyway.

"No, Nora," he replies, and I can feel his smile in the darkness. "Never."

And bringing me closer, he holds me until we both eventually fall asleep.

CHAPTER SIXTEEN

Over the next few months, my life on the island falls into a routine of sorts. When Julian is there, my world revolves around him. His moods, his needs and desires, rule my days and nights.

He's an unpredictable lover—gentle one day, cruel the next. And sometimes he's a mix of both, a combination that I find particularly devastating. I understand what he's doing to me, but understanding doesn't make it any less effective. He's training me to associate pain with pleasure, to enjoy whatever he does to me, no matter how shocking and perverted it is. And always afterwards, there's that unsettling tenderness. He turns me inside out, takes me apart, and puts me back together—all in the span of one night.

And his training is working. I go into his arms willingly now, craving that high I often get from a particularly brutal session. Julian tells me that I'm a natural submissive with latent masochistic tendencies. I don't know if I believe him—I know that I certainly don't *want* to believe him—but I can't deny that his peculiar brand of lovemaking resonates with me on some level. Toys, whips, canes— he's used them all, and I have invariably found pleasure in some part of what he was doing.

Of course, he's not always sadistic. Sometimes he's almost sweet, massaging me all over, kissing me until I melt, and then making love to me when I'm nearly out of my mind with need. On days like that, I don't want to leave the island. All I want is for Julian to keep holding me, caressing me . . . loving me, in whichever way he can.

Perhaps that is the most disturbing part of it all—the fact that I now crave my captor's love. I don't even know if he's capable of that emotion, but I can't help needing it from him. He wants me, I know that, but it's not enough. Somewhere along the way, I've lost my hatred for him, and I don't even know how or when it happened. I still resent my captivity, but those feelings are now separate from the way I feel about Julian.

Instead of dreading his visits to the island, I now eagerly await them. His business keeps him away more than I like, and I begin to understand how pets feel, waiting for their owner to come home from work.

"Why can't you conduct more of your business from here?" I ask him one day, after we wake up together in the morning. He always sleeps with me now. He likes holding me during the night; it helps him with his nightmares.

"I do as much remotely as I can. Why, do you want me here, my pet?" His gaze is coolly mocking as he turns his head to look at me. He doesn't like it when I question him about his business. It's a part of his life that he seems to want to keep separate. In general, I get the sense that he's sheltering me and Beth from some of the uglier parts of his world. Beth is fully aware of what Julian does, of course, but I don't know if she knows much more about arms dealing than I do.

"Yes," I tell him honestly. "I want you here." It's pointless to pretend otherwise; Julian knows exactly how I feel. He's very good at reading me—and manipulating me. I have no doubt that he's enjoying my growing attachment to him and likely doing his best to facilitate it.

Sure enough, at my admission, his lips curve in a sensual smile. "All right, baby," he says softly, "I'll try to be here more." And reaching for me, he brings me toward him for a kiss that makes me dissolve in his embrace.

* * *

With each day that passes, my old life seems further and further away, fading into that nebulous time known as the past. When Julian is gone, I occupy myself by reading, swimming, hiking all around the island, and the occasional fishing expeditions with Beth. Julian brought us a large-screen TV with a DVD player and hundreds of movies, so Beth and I have something to do during rainy weather, too.

We're still not exactly friends, Beth and I, but we've definitely grown closer. Partially, I think she likes the fact that I no longer try to escape. After my one failed attempt to bash her over the head—and the horrible incident with Jake that followed—I've been a model prisoner.

Of course, it would be foolish to be anything else. Even during Julian's visits, when his plane is here, it's locked inside the hangar I found on the other side of the island. I'm pretty sure Julian keeps the keys to the hangar in his office, where only he can access them. And even if I somehow got my hands on the keys, I sincerely doubt there would be an operating manual conveniently stored inside the plane, teaching me how to fly it.

No, my captor knew exactly what he was doing when he brought me to this island. It's as secure a prison as any I could imagine.

As days turn into weeks and then into months, I try to find more activities to fill up my free time—and to prevent myself from pining after Julian when he's not there.

The first thing I do is start running again.

I begin with short distances at first, to make sure I don't strain my knee, and then I slowly increase both speed and distance. I run either in the mornings or at night, when it's cooler, and it's not long before I am in as good of a shape as I'd been during my days on the track team. I can do a three-mile run in under seventeen minutes—an accomplishment that makes me ridiculously happy.

I also take up painting. Not because I remember Julian saying that Maria was good at drawing, but because I find it both entertaining and relaxing. I had enjoyed art classes in school, but I was always too busy with friends and other activities to give painting a serious attempt. Now, however, I have plenty of time on my hands, so I start learning how to properly draw and paint. Julian brings me a ton of art supplies and several instructional videos, and I soon find myself absorbed in trying to capture the beauty of the island on canvas.

"You know, you're very good at this," Beth says thoughtfully one day, coming up to me on the porch as I'm finishing a painting of the sunset over the ocean. "You've got the colors down exactly—that glowing orange shaded with the deep pink."

I turn and give her a big smile. "You really think so?"

"I do," Beth says seriously. "You're doing well, Nora."

I get the sense that she's talking about more than just the painting. "Thanks," I say dryly. Should I add that to my list of achievements— the fact that I'm able to thrive in captivity?

She grins in response, and for the first time, I feel like we truly understand each other. "You're welcome."

Walking over to the outdoor couch, she curls up on it, pulling out her book. I watch her for a few seconds, then go back to painting, trying to replicate the multidimensional shimmer of the water—and thinking about the puzzle that is Beth.

She still hasn't told me much about her past, but I get the sense that for her, this island is a retreat of sorts, a sanctuary. She sees Julian as her rescuer, and the outside world as an unpleasant and hostile place. "Don't you miss going to the mall?" I asked her once. "Having dinner with your friends? Going dancing? You're not a prisoner here; you could leave at any time. Why don't you have Julian take you with him on one of his trips? Do something fun before you come back here again?"

Her response was to laugh at me. "Dancing? Fun? Letting men put their hands all over my body—that's supposed to be fun?" Her voice turned mocking. "Should I also shop for sexy clothes and make-up, so I look all pretty for them? And what about pollution, drive-by shootings, and muggings—should I miss those, too?" Laughing again, she shook her head. "No, thanks. I'm perfectly happy right here."

And that's as much as she would say on that topic.

I don't know what happened to make her so bitter, but I strongly suspect Beth hasn't had an easy life. When we were watching *Pretty Woman*, she kept making snide comments about how real prostitution is nothing like the fairy tale they were showing. I didn't ask her about it then, but I've been curious ever since. Could she have been a prostitute in the past?

Putting down my brush, I turn and look at Beth. "Can I paint you?"

She looks up from her book, startled. "You want to paint me?"

"Yes, I do." It would be a nice change of pace from all those landscapes I've been focusing on lately—and it might also give me a chance to get to know her better.

She stares at me for a few seconds, then shrugs. "All right. I guess."

She seems uncertain about this, so I give her an encouraging smile. "You don't have to do anything—just sit there like that, with your book. It makes for a nice visual."

And it's true. The rays of the setting sun turn her red curls into a blazing flame, and with her legs tucked under, she looks young and vulnerable. Much more approachable than usual.

I set aside the painting I was working on and put up a blank canvas. Then I begin to sketch, trying to capture the symmetric angles of her face, the lean lines and curves of her body. It's an absorbing task, and I don't stop until it gets too dark for me to see anything.

"Are you done for today?" Beth asks, and I realize that she's been sitting in the same position for the past hour.

"Oh, yeah, sure," I say. "Thanks for being such a good model."

"No problem." She gives me a genuine smile as she gets up. "Ready for dinner?"

* * *

For the next three days, I work on Beth's portrait. She patiently models for me, and I find myself so busy that I hardly think about Julian at all. It's only at night that I have a chance to miss him—to feel the cold emptiness of my king-sized bed as I lie there aching for his embrace. He's gotten me so addicted that a week without him feels like a cruel punishment—one that I find infinitely worse than any sexual torture my captor has doled out thus far.

"Did Julian say when he's going to be back?" I ask Beth as I'm putting the final touches on the painting. "He's already been gone for seven days."

She shakes her head. "No, but he'll be here as soon as he can manage. He can't stay away from you, Nora, you know that."

"Really? Has he said something to you?" I can hear the eagerness in my voice, and I mentally kick myself. How pathetic can one get? I might as well put a stamp on my forehead: *another stupid girl who fell for her kidnapper*. Of course, I doubt many kidnappers have Julian's lethal charm, so maybe I should cut myself some slack.

Thankfully, Beth doesn't tease me about my obvious infatuation. "He doesn't need to say it," she says instead. "It's perfectly obvious."

I put down my brush for a second. "Obvious how?" This conversation is fulfilling a need I didn't even know I had—that for a real girl-to-girl gossip session about men and their inexplicable emotions.

"Oh, please." Beth is starting to sound exasperated. "You know Julian is fucking crazy about you. Whenever I talk to him, it's Nora this, Nora that . . . Does Nora need anything? Has Nora been eating well?" She lowers her voice comically, mimicking Julian's deeper tones.

I grin at her. "Really? I didn't know this." And I didn't. I mean, I knew that Julian is crazy about fucking me—and he definitely admitted to a certain obsession with me because of my resemblance to Maria—but I didn't know I was this much on his mind outside of the bedroom.

Beth rolls her eyes. "Yeah, right. You're not nearly as naive as you pretend to be. I've seen you batting those long lashes at him over dinner, trying to wrap him around your little finger."

I give her my best wide-eyed-innocent look. "What? No!"

"Uh-huh." Beth doesn't seem fooled in the least.

She's right, of course; I do flirt with Julian. Now that I'm no longer quite so afraid of my captor, I am again doing my best to get into his good graces. Somewhere in the back of my mind, there is a persistent hope that if he trusts me enough—if he cares for me enough—he might take me off the island.

When this plan had first occurred to me—in those terrifying first few days of my captivity—I had been playacting. As soon as I found myself off the island, I would've done my best to escape, regardless of any promises I might've made. Now, however, I don't even know what I would do if Julian took me with him. Would I try to leave him? Do I even *want* to leave him? I honestly have no idea.

"Have you ever been in love?" I ask Beth, picking up my brush again.

To my surprise, a dark shadow passes over her face. "No," she says curtly. "Never."

"But you have loved . . . someone, right?" I don't know what makes me ask that, but I've apparently touched a nerve, because Beth's entire body tightens, like I just struck her a blow.

To my surprise, however, instead of snapping at me, she just nods. "Yes," she says quietly. "Yes, Nora, I have loved." Her eyes are unnaturally bright, as though glittering with unspilled moisture.

And I realize then that she's suffering—that whatever happened to her had left deep, indelible scars on her psyche. Her thorny exterior is just a mask, a way to protect herself from further hurt. And right now, for whatever reason, that mask has slipped, exposing the real woman underneath.

"What happened to this person?" I ask, my voice soft and gentle. "What happened to the one you loved?"

"She died." Beth's tone is expressionless, but I can sense the bottomless well of agony in that simple statement. "My daughter died when she was two."

I inhale sharply. "I'm sorry, Beth. Oh God, I'm so sorry . . ." Setting down my brush again, I walk over to Beth's couch and sit down, putting my arms around her.

At first, she's stiff and rigid, as though not used to human contact, but she doesn't push me away. She needs this right now; I know better than anyone how soothing a warm embrace can be when your emotions are all over the place. Julian delights in making me fall apart, so he can then be the one to mend me and put me back together.

"I am sorry," I repeat softly, rubbing her back in a slow circular motion. "I am so sorry."

Gradually, some of the tension drains out of Beth's body. She lets herself be soothed by my touch. After a while, she seems to regain her equilibrium, and I let her go, not wanting her to feel awkward about the hug.

Scooting back a bit, she gives me a small, embarrassed smile. "I'm sorry, Nora. I didn't mean to—"

"No, it's all right," I interrupt. "I'm sorry I was prying. I didn't know—"

And then we both look at each other, realizing that we could apologize until the end of time and it wouldn't change anything.

Beth closes her eyes for a second, and when she opens them, her mask is firmly back in place. She's my jailer again, as independent and self-contained as ever.

"Dinner?" she asks, getting up.

"Some of this morning's catch would be great," I say casually, walking over to put away my art supplies.

And we continue on, as though nothing had happened.

CHAPTER SEVENTEEN

After that day, my relationship with Beth undergoes a subtle, but noticeable change. She's no longer quite so determined to keep me out, and I slowly get to know the person behind the prickly walls.

"I know you think you got a rough deal," she says one day as we're fishing together, "but believe me, Nora, Julian really does care about you. You're very lucky to have someone like him."

"Lucky? Why?"

"Because no matter what he's done, Julian is not really a monster," Beth says seriously. "He doesn't always act in a way that society deems acceptable, but he's not evil."

"No? Then what is evil?" I'm genuinely curious how Beth defines the word. To me, Julian's actions are the very epitome of something an evil man might do—my stupid feelings for him notwithstanding.

"Evil is someone who would murder a child," Beth says, staring at the bright blue water. "Evil is someone who would sell his thirteen-year-old daughter to a Mexican brothel . . ." She pauses for a second, then adds, "Julian is *not* evil. You can trust me on that."

I don't know what to say, so I just watch the waves pounding against the shore. My chest feels as though it's being squeezed in a vise. "Did Julian save you from evil?" I ask after a while, when I'm certain that I can keep my voice reasonably steady.

She turns her head to look at me. "Yes," she says quietly. "He did. And he destroyed the evil for me. He handed me a gun and let me use it on those men—on the ones who killed my baby daughter. You see,

Nora, he took a used-up, broken street whore and gave her her life back."

I hold Beth's gaze, feeling like I'm crumbling inside. My stomach is churning with nausea. She's right: I didn't know the real meaning of suffering. What she's been through is not something I can comprehend.

She smiles at me, apparently enjoying my shocked silence. "Life is nothing more than a fucked-up roulette," she says softly, "where the wheel keeps spinning and the wrong numbers keep coming up. You can cry about it all you want, but the truth of the matter is that this is as close to a winning ticket as it gets."

I swallow to get rid of the knot in my throat. "That's not true," I say, and my voice sounds a bit hoarse. "It's not always like this. There is a whole other world out there—the world where normal people live, where nobody tries to hurt you—"

"No," Beth says harshly. "You're dreaming. That world is about as real as a Disney fairy tale. You might have lived like a princess, but most people don't. Normal people suffer. They hurt, they die, and they lose their loved ones. And they hurt each other. They tear at each other like the savage predators they are. There is no light without darkness, Nora; the night ultimately catches up with us all."

"No." I don't believe it. I don't want to believe it. This island, Beth, Julian—it's all an anomaly, not the way things always are. "No, that's not—"

"It's true," Beth says. "You might not realize it yet, but it's true. You need Julian just as much as he needs you. He can protect you, Nora. He can keep you safe."

She seems utterly convinced of that fact.

* * *

"Good morning, my pet," a familiar voice whispers in my ear, waking me up, and I open my eyes to see Julian sitting there, leaning over me. He must've come here straight from some formal business meeting, because he's wearing a dress shirt instead of his usual more casual attire. A surge of happiness blazes through me. Smiling, I lift my arms and twine them around his neck, pulling him closer toward me.

He nuzzles my neck, his warm heavy weight pressing me into the mattress, and I arch against him, feeling the customary stirrings of desire. My nipples harden, and my core turns into a pool of liquid need, my entire body melting at his proximity.

"I missed you," he breathes in my ear, and I shiver with pleasure, barely suppressing a moan as his talented mouth moves down my neck and nibbles at a tender spot near my collarbone. "I love it when you're like this," he murmurs, raining gentle kisses on my upper chest and shoulders, "all warm, soft and sleepy . . . and mine . . ."

I do moan now, as his mouth closes around my right nipple and sucks on it strongly, applying just the right amount of pressure. His hand slips under the blanket and between my thighs, and my moans intensify as he begins to stroke my folds, his finger drawing teasing circles around my clit.

"Come for me, Nora," he orders softly, pressing down on my clit, and I shatter into a thousand pieces, my body tensing and peaking, as though on his command. "Good girl," he whispers, continuing to play with my sex, drawing out my orgasm. "Such a good, sweet girl . . ."

When my aftershocks are over, he steps back and begins undressing. I watch him hungrily, unable to tear my eyes away from the sight. He's beyond gorgeous, and I want him so badly. His shirt comes off first, exposing his broad shoulders and washboard stomach, and I can no longer contain myself. Sitting up, I reach for the zipper of his dress pants, my hands shaking with impatience.

He draws in a sharp breath as my palm brushes against his engorged cock. As soon as I succeed in freeing it, I wrap my fingers around the shaft and bend my head, taking him into my mouth.

"Fuck, Nora!" he groans, grasping my head and thrusting his hips at me. "Oh, fuck, baby, that's good . . ." His fingers slide through my hair, tangling in the unbrushed strands, and I slowly suck him in deeper, opening my throat to take in as much of his length as I can.

"Oh fuck . . ." His raspy moan fills me with delight, and I squeeze his balls lightly, reveling in the heavy feel of them in my palm. His cock gets even harder, and I know he's on the verge of coming, but, to my surprise, he pulls away, taking a step back.

He's breathing heavily, his eyes glittering like blue diamonds, but he manages to control himself long enough to get rid of his remaining clothing before he climbs on top of me. His strong hands wrap around my wrists, stretching them above my head, and his hips settle heavily between my open thighs, his thick shaft nudging against my vulnerable entrance. I stare up at him with a mixture of apprehension and excitement; he looks magnificent and savage, with his dark hair disheveled and his beautiful face drawn tight with lust. He's not going to be particularly gentle today—I can already see that.

And I'm right. He enters me with one powerful thrust, sliding so deep inside me that I gasp, feeling like he's splitting me in half. And yet my body responds to him, producing more lubrication, easing his way. He fucks me brutally, without mercy, but my screams are those of pleasure, the tension inside me spiraling out of control one more time before he finally comes.

* * *

At breakfast, I'm a little sore, but happy regardless. Julian is here, and all is right with my world. He seems to be in a good mood as well, teasing me about watching an entire season of *Friends* in one week and asking about my latest running times. He likes it that I'm so much into fitness lately—or rather, he likes the results of it.

Physically, I'm in the best shape I have ever been, and it shows. My body is lean and toned, and I'm a walking testament to the benefits of a healthy diet, lots of fresh air, and regular exercise. My thick brown hair is growing without any sign of split ends, and my skin is perfectly smooth and tan. I can't remember the last time I had so much as a pimple.

"My last three-mile run was 16:20," I tell Julian without false modesty. "I bet not many guys can beat that."

"That's true," he agrees, his blue eyes dancing with laughter. "I probably couldn't."

"Really?" I'm intrigued by the idea of beating Julian at something. "Want to try? I'd be glad to race you."

"Don't do it, Julian," Beth says, laughing. "She's fast. She was quick before, but now she's like a fucking rocket."

"Oh yeah?" He lifts one eyebrow at me. "A fucking rocket, huh?"

"That's right." I give him a challenging look. "Want to race, or are you too chicken?"

Beth begins to make clucking noises, and Julian grins, throwing a piece of bread at her. "Shut up, you traitor."

Laughing at their antics, I throw a piece of bread at Julian, and Beth scolds both of us. "I'm the one who has to clean up this whole mess," she grumbles, and Julian promises to help her with the bread crumbs, soothing her temper with one of his megawatt smiles.

When he's like this, his charm is like a living thing, drawing me in, making me forget the truth about my situation. On the back of my mind, I know that none of this is real—that this sense of connection, this camaraderie is nothing more than a mirage—but with each day that passes, it starts to matter less and less. In a strange way, I feel like I'm two people: the woman who's falling in love with the gorgeous, ruthless killer sitting at the breakfast table and the one who's observing the whole thing with a sense of horror and disbelief.

After breakfast, I change into my running clothes—a pair of shorts and a sports bra—and go read a book on the porch, so I can digest my food before the run. Julian goes into his office as usual. His business doesn't wait just because he's on the island; an illegal arms empire requires constant attention.

While Julian rarely talks about his work, I've managed to glean a few things over the past several months. From what I understand, my captor is the head of an international operation specializing in the manufacture and distribution of cutting-edge weapons and certain types of electronics. His clients are those organizations and individuals who cannot obtain weapons by legitimate means.

"He deals with some really dangerous motherfuckers," Beth told me once. "Psychopaths, many of them. I wouldn't trust them as far as I can throw them."

"So why does he do this?" I asked. "He's so rich. I'm sure he doesn't need the money . . ."

"It's not about the money," Beth explained. "It's about the thrill of it, the challenge. Men like Julian thrive on that."

I wonder sometimes if that's what Julian likes about me—the challenge of making me bend to his will, of shaping me to become whatever it is he thinks he needs. Does he find it thrilling, the knowledge that I'm his captive and that he can do whatever he wants with me? Does the illegal aspect of the whole thing excite him?

"Ready to go?" Julian's voice interrupts my thoughts, and I look up from my book to see him standing there, dressed in only a pair of black running shorts and sneakers. His naked torso ripples with thick, perfectly defined muscles, and his smooth golden skin gleams in the sunlight, making me want to touch him all over.

"Um, yeah." I get up, putting down my book and begin to stretch, watching Julian doing the same out of the corner of my eye. His body is incredible, and I wonder what he does to keep in shape. I've never seen him working out here on the island.

"Do you do some kind of exercise when you go on your trips?" I ask, shamelessly staring as he bends over and touches his toes with surprising flexibility. "How do you stay so fit?"

He straightens and grins at me. "I train with my men when I can. I guess you could call it exercise."

"Your men?" I immediately think of the thug who had beaten up Jake. The memory makes me sick, and I push it away, not wanting to think about such dark matters now. I have to do this sometimes, to separate this new life of mine into neat little sections, keeping the good times apart from the bad. It's my own patented coping mechanism.

"My bodyguards and certain other employees," Julian explains as we head out toward the beach, walking fast to warm up. "Some of them are former Navy SEALs, and training with them is no picnic, believe me."

"You train with Navy SEALs?" I stop and give Julian a hard look. "You were just kidding earlier, weren't you? About not being able to beat me in a race?"

His lips curve in a slightly mischievous—and utterly seductive—smile. "I don't know, my pet," he says softly. "Was I? Why don't you race me and see?"

"All right," I say, determined to give it my best shot. "Let's do this."

* * *

We start our race near a tree that I marked specifically for this purpose. On the other side of the island, there is another tree that serves as the finish line. If we run on the sand, along the ocean, it's exactly three miles from here to that point.

Julian counts to five, I set my stopwatch, and we're off, each starting at a reasonably fast pace that's not our top speed. As I run, I feel my muscles easing into the rhythm of the movement, and I gradually pick up the pace, pushing myself harder than I usually do at this point in the run. Julian runs beside me, his longer stride enabling him to keep up with me with ease.

We run silently, not talking, and I keep sneaking glances at Julian out of the corner of my eye. We're halfway through the course, and I'm sweating and breathing hard, but my gorgeous captor seems to be barely exerting himself. He's in phenomenal shape, his smooth muscles glistening with light drops of perspiration, bunching and releasing with every movement. He runs lightly, landing on the balls of his feet, and I envy his easy stride, wishing that I had even a quarter of his obvious strength and endurance.

As we get into the last half-mile, I put on a burst of speed, determined to try to beat him despite the obvious futility of the effort. He's not even winded yet, and I'm already gasping for breath. He picks up his speed too, and no matter how hard I run, I can't put any distance between us. He's practically glued to my side.

By the time we get within a hundred yards of the tree, I am dripping with sweat and every muscle in my body is screaming for oxygen. I'm on the verge of collapse and I know it, but I make one last heroic attempt and sprint for the finish line.

And just as my hand is about to touch the tree, marking me the race winner, Julian's palm slaps the bark, literally a second before mine.

Frustrated, I whirl around and find myself with my back pressed against the tree and Julian leaning over me. "Gotcha," he says, his eyes gleaming, and I see that he's breathing almost normally.

Gasping for air, I push at him, but he doesn't back away. Instead, he steps closer, and his knee wedges between my thighs. At the same time, his hands grab the backs of my knees, lifting me up against him, my thighs spread wide as he grinds his erection against my pelvis.

Our little race apparently turned him on.

Panting, I stare up at him, my hands grabbing at his shoulders. I can barely remain upright, and he wants to fuck?

The answer is obviously yes, because he sets me down on my feet for a second, pulls down my shorts and underwear, and then does the same thing to his own clothes. I sway on my feet, my legs shaking from the exertion. I can't believe this is happening. Who fucks right after a race? All I want to do is lie down and drink a gallon of water.

But Julian has other ideas. "Get on your knees," he orders hoarsely, pushing me down before I have a chance to comply.

I land on my knees heavily and brace myself with my hands. The position actually helps me regain my breath somewhat, and I gratefully suck in air. My head is spinning from the heat outside—and from the aftermath of a hard run—and I hope I don't end up passing out.

A hard, muscular arm slides under my hips, holding me in place, and then I feel his cock pressing against my buttocks. Dizzy and trembling, I wait for the thrust that will join us together, my treacherous sex wet and throbbing with anticipation. My body's response to Julian is insane, ridiculous, given my overall physical state.

He brushes my sweat-soaked hair off my back and leans forward to kiss my neck, covering me with his heavy body. "You know," he whispers, "you're beautiful when you run. I've been wanting to do this since the first mile." And with that, he pushes deep inside me, his thickness stretching me, filling me all the way.

I cry out, my hands clutching at the dirt as he begins thrusting, both of his hands now holding my hips as he rams into me. My senses narrow, focusing only on this—the rhythmic movements of his hips, the pleasure-pain of his rough possession . . . I feel like I'm burning inside, dying from the violent brew of heat and lust. The pressure building inside me is too much, unbearable, and I throw my head back with a scream as my entire body explodes, the release rocketing through me with so much force that I literally pass out.

By the time I become conscious again, I am cradled on Julian's lap. He's got his back pressed against the finish-line tree, and he's feeding me small sips of water, making sure that I don't choke. "You okay, baby?" he asks, looking down at me with what appears to be genuine concern on his beautiful face.

"Um, yeah." My throat still feels dry, but I'm definitely feeling better—and more than a little embarrassed about my fainting spell.

"I didn't realize you'd gotten this dehydrated," he says, a small frown bisecting his brow. "Why did you push yourself so hard?"

"Because I wanted to win," I admit, closing my eyes and breathing in the scent of his skin. He smells like sex and sweat, an oddly appealing combination.

"Here, drink some more water," he says, and I open my eyes again, obediently drinking when he presses a bottle to my lips. The bottle is from the cooler I keep stashed on this side of the island to keep hydrated after my runs.

After a few minutes—and an entire bottle of water—I feel well enough to start walking back. Except Julian doesn't let me walk. Instead, as soon as I get to my feet, he bends down and lifts me into his arms as effortlessly as if I were a doll. "Hold on to my neck," he orders, and I wrap my arms around him, letting him carry me back home.

CHAPTER EIGHTEEN

The next morning I wake up to the luxurious sensation of having my feet massaged. It feels so incredible that, for a few seconds, I think I'm dreaming and try to avoid waking up. The feel of strong fingers kneading my foot is all too real, however, and I moan in bliss as each individual toe is rubbed and stroked with just the right amount of pressure.

Opening my eyes, I see Julian sitting on the bed, gloriously naked and holding a bottle of massage oil. Pouring some into his palm, he bends over me and starts massaging my ankles and calves next.

"Good morning," he purrs, looking at me. I stare back at him, mute with surprise. Julian has given me massages in the past, but usually only as a way to relax me before doing something that would make me scream. He's never woken me up in this pleasurable way before.

There is a half-smile on his sensuous lips, and I can't help feeling nervous. "Um, Julian," I say uncertainly, "what . . . what are you doing?"

"Giving you a massage," he says, his eyes gleaming with amusement. "Why don't you relax and enjoy it?"

I blink, watching as his hands slowly move up my calves. He has large hands—strong and masculine. My legs look impossibly slender and feminine in his grasp, though I have well-defined muscles from all the running. I can feel the calluses on his palms scratching lightly against my skin, and I swallow, the unbidden thought that those hands belong to a killer entering my mind.

"Turn over," he says, tugging on my legs, and I plop over on my belly, still feeling nervous. What is he up to? I don't like surprises when it comes to Julian.

He starts kneading the back of my legs, unerringly finding the areas most sore from yesterday's race, and I groan as tight muscles begin to loosen up under his skilled fingers. Still, I can't relax completely; Julian is far too unpredictable for my peace of mind.

Apparently sensing my unease, he bends over me and whispers in my ear, "It's just a massage, my pet. No need to be so worried about it."

Somewhat reassured, I let myself relax, sinking into the comfort of my mattress. Julian's hands are magic; I've had professional massages that were nowhere near as good. He's completely attuned to me, paying attention to the slightest change in my breathing, to the most minute twitch in my muscles... After several minutes of this, I no longer care about his strange behavior; I'm simply wallowing in the bliss of this experience.

When my entire body has been thoroughly massaged and I'm lying there in limp contentment, Julian stops and shepherds me into the shower. Then he goes down on me, pleasuring me with his mouth until I explode in mind-blowing release.

At breakfast, I'm practically humming with contentment. This is the best morning I've had in months, maybe even years. By some strange coincidence, Beth made my favorite food—Eggs Benedict with crab cakes. I haven't had anything this decadent since my arrival on the island. The food Beth cooks for us is good, but it's usually on the healthy side. Fruits, vegetables, and fish seem to make up the majority of our diet. I can't remember the last time I had something as rich and satisfying as the Hollandaise sauce Beth made today.

"Mmm, this is so good," I moan around a mouthful. "Beth, this is amazing. These are probably the best eggs I've ever had."

She grins at me. "They did come out well, didn't they? I wasn't sure if I got the recipe right, but it seems like I might have."

"Oh, you did," I reassure her before I serve myself another portion. "This is great."

Julian smiles, his eyes gleaming with warm amusement. "Hungry, my pet?" He himself has already eaten a sizable serving, but I'm on the verge of catching up to him.

"Starving," I tell him, bringing another forkful to my mouth. "I guess I burned a lot of calories yesterday."

"I'm sure you did," he says, his smile widening, and then he tells Beth about how I almost won the race, leaving out the part about our fucking and my passing out afterwards.

When the breakfast is over, I'm so stuffed I can't eat another bite. Thanking Beth for the meal, I stand up, about to go get a book for a relaxing reading session on the porch, when Julian surprises me by wrapping his hand around my wrist. "Wait, Nora," he says softly, pulling me back down into my seat. "There's one more thing Beth prepared today." And he shoots Beth an indecipherable look—at which point she immediately gets up and goes into the kitchen.

"Um, okay." I'm beyond confused. She had prepared something, but didn't serve it during the actual meal?

At that moment, Beth comes back to the table, carrying a tray with a large chocolate cake—a cake with a bunch of burning candles.

"Happy birthday, Nora," Julian says with a smile as Beth places the cake in front of me. "Now make a wish and blow out those candles."

* * *

I blow out the candles on autopilot, barely registering the fact that it takes me three attempts to do this. Beth cheers, clapping her hands, and I hear the sounds as though they're coming from a distance. My mind is whirling, yet I feel oddly numb, as if nothing can touch me right now. All I can think about, all I can concentrate on is the fact that it's my birthday.

My birthday. It's my birthday. Today I turned nineteen.

The realization makes me want to scream.

I met Julian shortly before my last birthday—and he brought me to this island shortly thereafter. If it's my birthday today, then nearly a year has passed since my abduction—since I've been here, at Julian's mercy and entirely isolated from the rest of the world.

A year of my life has passed in captivity.

I feel like I'm suffocating, like all air had left the room, but I know it's just an illusion. There's plenty of oxygen here; I simply can't seem to breathe in any.

"Nora?" Beth's voice somehow penetrates the din in my ears. "Nora, are you all right?"

I finally manage to draw in some much-needed air, and I look up from the cake. Beth is staring at me with a puzzled frown on her face, and Julian is no longer smiling. Instead he looks like a dangerous stranger again, his gaze filled with something dark and disturbing.

Holding myself together with superhuman effort, I squeeze out a shaky smile. "Of course. Thank you for the cake, Beth."

"We wanted to surprise you," she says, her features smoothing out as she takes my words at face value. "I hope you have some room left for dessert. Chocolate cake is your favorite, right?"

The ringing in my ears intensifies. "Um, yes." Despite my best attempts, my voice sounds choked. "And you definitely surprised me."

"Leave us, Beth," Julian says sharply, glancing at her. "Nora and I need to be alone right now."

Beth blinks, obviously taken aback by Julian's tone. I've never heard him speak like that to her before. Nevertheless, she obeys immediately, practically running up the stairs to her room.

I haven't seen Julian this angry in a while and I know I should be frightened, but at this moment, I can't seem to bring myself to care about what's to come. Every muscle in my body is trembling with the effort to contain the terrible storm I can feel brewing inside me, and it's a relief to have Beth away from here. *A year. It's been a fucking year.* The rage that's building inside me is unlike anything I've ever experienced before; it's like a dam has broken and would not be contained. A red mist descends on me, veiling my vision, and the ringing in my ears grows louder as my emotions spin out of control.

As soon as Beth is out of sight, I explode. I'm no longer rational or sane; instead I'm fury personified. I grab at the nearest thing I can reach—the chocolate cake—and throw it across the room, the dark-colored icing splattering everywhere. My plate and cup follow, hitting the wall and shattering into a million pieces, and all the while, I hear screaming, coming at me from far away. Some still-functioning part of my brain realizes that it's me—that it's my own screams and curses I'm hearing—but I can't stop it any more than I can contain a typhoon. All the anger, terror, and frustration of the past year has boiled to the surface, erupting in a lava of fierce rage.

I don't know how long I exist in that mindless state before steely arms wrap around me from the back, imprisoning me in a familiar embrace. I kick and scream until my voice grows hoarse, but my struggles are futile. Julian is far, far stronger than me, and he uses that strength now to subdue me, to hold me tight until I completely exhaust myself and slump against him in defeat, tears running down my face.

"Are you done?" he whispers in my ear, and I can hear the familiar dark note in his tone. As usual, I find it both sinister and arousing, my body now conditioned to crave the pain that's to come—and the mind-shattering bliss that inevitably accompanies it.

I shake my head in response to his question, but I know that I *am* done, that whatever it was that came over me has passed, leaving me drained and empty.

Julian turns me around in his arms, so that I'm facing him. I stare up at him, my tear-glazed gaze helplessly drawn to the perfect symmetry of his features. His high cheekbones are tinged with a hint of color, and there is something disquieting in the way he looks at me—as though he wants to devour me, to tear out my soul and swallow it whole. Our eyes meet, and I know that I'm standing on the edge of a precipice right now, that a sinkhole is opening up underneath my feet.

And in that moment, I see things clearly.

I am not angry because I've been imprisoned on the island for an entire year. No, my rage goes far, far deeper. What burns me up inside is not the fact that I've been a captive this whole time—it's that I've grown to like my captivity.

Over the past few months, I have somehow come to terms with my new life. I've grown to enjoy the calm, relaxing rhythms of the island. The ocean, the sand, the sun—it's about as close to paradise as anything I can imagine. Freedom and all that it implies is now just a vague, impossible dream. I can barely picture the faces of those I left behind; they are just blurry, shadowy figures in my mind. The only thing that matters to me now is the man holding me in his hard embrace.

Julian—my captor, my lover.

"Why, Nora?" he asks, almost soundlessly. His arms tighten around me, his fingers digging into the soft skin of my back. When I don't reply, his expression darkens further. "Why?"

I remain silent, unwilling to take that last, irrevocable step. I can't bare myself to Julian like that. I just can't. He's already taken far too much from me; I can't let him have this too.

"Tell me," he orders, one hand sliding up to twist in my hair, forcing my neck to bend backwards. "Tell me now."

"I hate you," I croak, gathering the last shreds of my defiance. My voice is like sandpaper, hoarse from all the screaming. "I hate you—"

His eyes flash with blue fire. "Is that right?" he whispers, leaning over me, still holding me arched helplessly against him. "You hate me, my pet?"

I hold his gaze, refusing to blink. In for a penny, in for a pound. "Yes," I hiss, "I hate you!" I need to convince him of my hatred because the alternative is unthinkable. He can't know the truth. He just can't.

Julian's face hardens, turning to ice. In one swift motion, he sweeps the remaining dishes off the kitchen table onto the floor and pushes me onto the table, forcing me to bend over, my face sliding on the smooth wooden surface. I try to kick back with my legs, but it's useless. He's gripping the back of my neck with one strong hand, and then I hear the menacing sound of a belt being unbuckled.

I kick back harder, and actually manage to make contact with his leg. Of course, it gains me nothing. I can't escape from Julian. I will never be able to escape from Julian.

He leans over me, pressing me into the table, his hard fingers tightening around the back of my neck. "You're mine, Nora," he says harshly, his large body dominating me, arousing me. "You belong to me, do you understand? Each and every single part of you is mine." His erection presses against my buttocks, its uncompromising hardness both a threat and a promise.

He rears back, still holding me down with one hand on my neck, and I hear the sibilant whisper of a belt being pulled from its loops. A moment later, my dress is flipped up, exposing my lower body. I squeeze my eyes shut, bracing for what's to come.

Thwack. Thwack. The belt descends on my ass, over and over again, each strike like fire licking at my thighs and buttocks. I can hear my own cries, feel my body tensing with each blow, and then the pain propels me into that strange state where everything is turned upside down—where pain and pleasure collide, become indistinguishable from one another, and my tormentor is my only solace. My body softens, melts, each stroke of the belt starting to feel more like a caress, and I know that I somehow need this right now—that Julian has tapped into that dark, secret part of myself that is a mirror image of his own twisted desires. It's a part of me that longs to give up control, to lose myself completely and just be *his*.

By the time Julian stops and turns me over, there isn't an ounce of defiance left in my body. My head is swimming from an endorphin rush more powerful than anything I have ever experienced, and I'm clinging to him, desperate for comfort, for sex, for anything resembling love and affection. My arms twine around Julian's neck, pulling him down on the table with me, and I revel in the taste of him, in the deep, hungry kisses with which he consumes my mouth. My backside feels like it's on fire, but it doesn't diminish my lust one bit; if anything, it intensifies it. Julian has trained me well. My body is conditioned to crave the pleasure that I know comes next.

He fumbles with his jeans, opening the zipper, and then he's inside me, entering me with one powerful thrust. I shudder with relief, with ecstasy that borders on agony, and wrap my legs around his waist, taking him deeper, needing him to fuck me, to claim me in the most primitive way possible.

"Tell me, baby," he whispers in my ear, his lips brushing against my temple. His right hand slides into my hair, holding me immobile. "Tell me how much you hate me." His other hand finds the place where we're joined, rubs there, then moves down a couple of inches to my other opening. "Tell me . . ."

I gasp as his finger pushes into my anus, my senses overwhelmed by all the conflicting sensations. Dazed, I open my eyes and stare at Julian, seeing my own dark need reflected on his face. He wants to possess me, to break me so he could put me back together, and I can no longer fight him on this.

"I don't hate you." My words come out low and raspy, and I swallow to moisten my dry throat. "I don't hate you, Julian."

Something like triumph flashes on his face. His hips thrust forward, his shaft burrowing deeper inside me, and I suppress a moan, still holding his gaze.

"Tell me," he orders again, his voice deepening. His eyes are burning into mine, and I can no longer resist the demand I see there. He wants all of me, and I have no choice but to give it to him.

"I love you." My voice is barely audible, each word feeling like it's being wrenched out of my very soul. "I don't hate you, Julian . . . I can't . . . I can't because I love you."

I can see his pupils dilating, turning his eyes darker. His cock swells within me, even thicker and harder than before, and then he pulls out and slams back inside, making me gasp from the savagery of his possession.

"Tell me again," he groans, and I repeat what I said, the words coming easier the second time around. There's no point in hiding from the truth anymore, no reason to lie. I have fallen head over heels for my sadistic captor, and nothing in the world can change that fact.

"I love you," I whisper, my hand moving up to cradle his cheek. "I love you, Julian."

His eyes darken further, and then he bends his head, taking my mouth in a deep, all-consuming kiss.

Now I am truly his, and he knows it.

CHAPTER NINETEEN

The next three months fly by.

After that day—after what I think of as the Birthday Incident—my relationship with Julian undergoes a noticeable change, becoming more . . . *romantic*, for lack of a better word.

It's a fucked-up romance, I know that. I may be addicted to Julian, but I'm not so far gone that I don't realize how unhealthy this is. I am in love with the man who kidnapped me, the man who is still holding me prisoner.

The man who seems to need my love as much as he needs my body.

I don't know if he loves me back. I don't even know if he's capable of that emotion. How can you love someone whose freedom you stole without a second thought? And yet I can't help feeling that he must care for me, that his obsession with me is not only sexual in nature. It's there in the way I catch him looking at me sometimes, in the way he tries to anticipate my every need.

He constantly brings me my favorite foods, my favorite books and music. If I so much as mention needing a hand lotion, he buys it for me on his next trip. I am about as pampered as a girl can be. He even takes pride in my accomplishments, praising my artwork and going so far as to take several paintings with him off the island to hang in his office in Hong Kong.

He also misses me when we're not together. I know because he tells me so—and because every time he returns, he falls on me like a starving man just getting out of prison. That, more than anything, gives me hope that his feelings for me go beyond that of owner for his possession.

"Do you see other women? Out there, in the real world?" I ask him at breakfast after one night when he takes me three times in a row. The question had been eating at me for months, and I simply can't contain myself any longer. My captor is more than gorgeous; he's got that dangerous, magnetic appeal that probably draws women to him by the dozen. I can easily imagine him sleeping with a different beauty every night—a thought that makes me want to stab something. Even with his sadistic proclivities, I know he would have no trouble finding bed partners; there are probably plenty of women who, like me, derive pleasure from erotic pain.

He smiles at me with dark amusement, not the least bit put off by my obvious display of jealousy. "No, my pet," he says softly. Reaching over, he takes my hand, stroking the inside of my wrist with his thumb. "Why would I want to fuck someone else when I have you? I haven't been with another woman since the day we met."

"You haven't?" I can't conceal my shock. Julian had been faithful to me this whole time?

He looks at me, his lips curved in a sinfully delicious smile. "No, baby, I have not," he says—and in that moment, I feel like the happiest woman in the world.

I love it when he calls me 'baby.' It's a common endearment, I know, but somehow when Julian says it, it sounds different—like he's caressing me with that word. I much prefer 'baby' to being called 'my pet.'

Ultimately, though, I know that's what I am to him—his pet, his possession. He likes the idea that I belong to him, that he's the only man who gets to touch me, to see me. He likes dressing me in the clothes that he provides for me, feeding me the food that he brings. I am completely dependent on him, utterly at his mercy, and I think something about that appeals to him, appeasing the demons I frequently sense lurking beneath the surface.

Truthfully, I don't mind being possessed. It's a disturbing realization, but some part of me seems to like this kind of dynamic. I feel safe and cared for, even though logic tells me I'm far from safe with a man who deals in weapons for a living—a man who admitted to killing without any regret. The hands that touch me at night are those that brought death to others, but there is a certain piquancy in that. It makes everything more intense somehow, helps me feel more alive.

Besides, despite his need to hurt me, Julian has never truly harmed me—not physically, at least. When he's in one of his sadistic moods, I end up with marks and bruises on my skin, but those fade quickly. He's careful never to scar my body, even though I know that blood and tears—my tears—excite him, turn him on.

When I share some of my feelings with Beth, she doesn't seem surprised in the least.

"I knew the two of you were made for each other from the first moment I saw you together," she says, giving me a wry look. "When you and Julian are in the same room, the air practically sizzles. I've never seen such chemistry between two people before. What you have together is rare and special. Don't fight it, Nora. He's your destiny—and you are his."

She seems completely convinced of that.

* * *

On the night my life irrevocably changes, everything starts out as normal.

Julian is on the island, and we share a delicious meal together before he brings me upstairs for a lengthy lovemaking session. It's one of those times when he's gentle, worshipping me with his body like I'm a goddess, and I fall asleep relaxed and satisfied, held tightly in his embrace.

When I wake up in the middle of the night to use the restroom, I become aware of a dull pain near my navel. Relieving myself, I wash my hands and crawl back into bed, stretching out next to Julian's sleeping form. I feel slightly nauseous too, and I wonder if I'm having indigestion. Could I have gotten food poisoning somehow?

I try to fall asleep, but the pain seems to get worse with every minute that passes. It migrates down into my lower right abdomen, becoming sharp and agonizing. I don't want to wake up Julian, but I can't bear it anymore. I need a painkiller of some kind, any kind.

"Julian," I whisper, reaching for him. "Julian, I think I'm sick."

He wakes up immediately and sits up in bed, turning on the bedside lamp. There's no trace of confusion on his face; he's as alert as if it's the middle of the day instead of three o'clock in the morning. "What's wrong?"

I curl into a little ball as the pain intensifies. "I don't know," I manage to say. "My stomach hurts."

His eyebrows snap together. "Where does it hurt, baby?" he says softly, pushing me onto my back.

"My . . . my side," I gasp, tears of pain starting to roll down my face.

"Here?" he asks, pressing on one side, and I shake my head no.

"Here?"

"Yes!" Somehow he has unerringly found the exact area that's in agony.

He immediately gets up and starts getting dressed. "Beth!" he yells. "Beth, I need you here right now!"

She runs into the room thirty seconds later, pulling on a bathrobe over her pajamas. "What happened?"

She sounds scared, and I am terrified too. I've never seen Julian like this before. He seems almost . . . frightened.

"Get ready," he says tersely. "I'm taking her to the clinic, and you're coming with us. It might be her appendix."

Appendicitis! Now that he said it, I realize it's the most probable explanation, but it's beyond scary. I'm no doctor, but I know that if my appendix bursts before they cut it out, I'm pretty much toast. It would be frightening even if I were an hour away from medical attention, but I'm on a private island in the middle of the Pacific. What if I don't make it to the hospital in time?

Julian must be thinking the same thing because the expression on his face is grim as he wraps me in a robe and picks me up, carrying me out of the room.

"I can walk," I protest weakly, my stomach roiling as Julian swiftly walks down the stairs.

"Like hell you can." His tone is unnecessarily harsh, but I don't take offense. I know he's worried about me right now, and even with my insides in agony, I feel warmed by the thought.

By the time we reach the hangar, Beth has opened the gates for us and is already waiting in the back of the airplane. Julian straps me into the passenger seat, and I realize that my greatest wish is about to be granted.

I'm getting off the island.

My stomach lurches, and I grab for the brown paper bag that's lying conveniently in front of me. Sudden hot nausea boils up in my throat, and I vomit into the bag, my entire body sweating and shaking.

I can hear Julian swearing as the plane begins to take off, and I'm so embarrassed I just want to die. "I'm sorry," I whisper, my eyes burning. I have never been so miserable in my entire life.

"It's all right," Julian says curtly. "Don't worry about it."

"Here." Beth hands me a wet wipe from the back. "This should make you feel a little better."

But it doesn't. Instead, as the plane climbs higher, I get nauseous again. Moaning, I clutch at my stomach, the pain in my right side intensifying.

"Fuck," Julian mutters. "Fuck, fuck, fuck." His knuckles are white where he's clutching the controls.

I vomit again.

"How long until we get there?" Beth's voice is unusually high-pitched.

"Two hours," Julian says grimly. "If the wind cooperates."

Those two hours turn out to be the longest ones of my life. By the time the plane begins its descent, I have thrown up five times and am long past the point of embarrassment. The pain in my stomach has long since morphed into agony, and I'm not cognizant of anything but my own bone-deep misery.

Strong hands reach for me, pulling me out of the airplane, and I am vaguely aware that Julian is carrying me somewhere, holding me cradled against his broad chest. There is a babble of voices speaking in a mixture of English and some foreign language, and then I'm placed on a gurney and wheeled through a long hallway into a white, sterile-looking room.

Several people in white coats bustle around me, one man barking out orders in that same strangely mixed language, and I feel a sharp prick in my arm as an IV needle is attached to my wrist. Dazed, I look up to see Julian standing in the corner, his face oddly pale and his eyes glittering . . . and then the darkness swallows me whole again.

CHAPTER TWENTY

When I regain consciousness, I am feeling only a little bit better. My head appears to be stuffed with wool, and the nagging pain in my side remains, though it feels different now, less sharp and more like an ache. For a second, I think that I fell asleep feeling sick and dreamed the whole thing, but the smell convinces me otherwise. It's that unmistakable antiseptic odor that you only encounter in doctor's offices and hospitals.

That odor means I'm alive . . . and off the island.

My heart starts racing at the thought.

"She's awake," an unfamiliar female voice says in accented English, apparently addressing someone else in the room.

I hear footsteps and feel someone sitting down on the side of my bed. Warm fingers reach out and stroke my cheek. "How are you feeling, baby?"

Opening my eyes with some effort, I gaze at Julian's beautiful features. "Like I've been cut open and sewn back together," I manage to croak out. My throat is so dry and sore that it actually hurts to talk, and I can feel a dull, throbbing ache in my right side.

"Here." Julian is holding out a cup with a bent straw in it. "You must be thirsty."

He brings it toward my face, and I obediently close my lips around the straw, sucking down a little water. My mind is still hazy, and for a moment, the wall between the good and the bad memories crumbles. I remember that first day on the island, when Julian had offered me a bottle of water, and an involuntary shiver runs down my spine. In that moment, Julian is not the man I love; he is again my enemy, the one who stole me, the one who made me his against my will.

"Cold?" he asks, taking the cup away before leaning over to pull the blanket higher up, covering my shoulders.

"Um, yeah, a little." *I'm off the island. Oh my God, I'm off the island.* My mind is spinning. I feel torn, like I'm two different people—the terrified girl who insists this is her chance to escape and the woman who desperately craves Julian's touch.

"They took out your appendix," Julian says, brushing back a strand of hair that had been tickling my forehead. "The operation went smoothly, and there shouldn't be any complications. Isn't that right, Angela?" He looks up to the left.

"Yes, Mr. Esguerra."

Esguerra? Is that Julian's last name? Recognizing the voice from before, I turn my head to see a petite young woman in white scrubs. Her smooth skin is a beautiful light brown color, and her hair and eyes are dark, nearly black. To me, she looks Filipino or maybe Thai—not that I can pretend to be an expert on either nationality.

What I do know is that she's the first person I've seen in fifteen months who is neither Beth nor Julian.

I'm off the island. Oh my God, I'm off the island. For the first time since my abduction, there is a real possibility of escape.

"Where am I?" I ask, staring at the young nurse. I can't believe Julian is letting someone else see me—me, the girl he kidnapped.

"You're in a private clinic in the Philippines," Julian replies when the woman merely smiles at me. "Angela is the nursing assistant who will be looking after you."

At that moment, the door opens and Beth walks in. "Oh, look who's awake," she exclaims, coming up to my bedside. "How are you feeling?"

"Okay, I think," I tell her cautiously. *Holy shit, I'm off the fucking island.*

"They said Julian got you here just in time," Beth tells me, pulling up a chair and sitting down next to my bed. "Your appendix was getting ready to go. They cut it out and sewed you right back up, so you should be right as rain."

I let out a nervous chuckle... and immediately groan, the movement tugging at the stitches in my side.

"Are you hurting?" Julian gives me a concerned look. Turning to Angela, he orders, "Give her more painkillers."

"I'm okay, just a little sore," I try to reassure him. "Seriously, I don't need any drugs." The last thing I want is something clouding my mind right now. I'm off the island, and I need to figure out what to do. I'm doing my best to remain calm, but it's taking all of my willpower not to scream or do something stupid. Freedom is so close, I can practically taste it.

"Of course, Mr. Esguerra." Angela completely ignores my protests and comes up to the bed, fiddling with the clear bag that's feeding into my IV tube.

Julian leans over the bed and lightly kisses me on the lips. "You need to rest," he says softly. "I want you healthy. Do you understand me?"

I nod, my eyelids growing heavy as I feel the medicine beginning to work. For a moment, I feel like I'm floating, all pain gone, and then I'm not aware of anything else.

* * *

When I wake up again, I'm alone in the room. Bright sunlight is streaming through the clear large windows and several plants are blooming merrily on the windowsill. It's actually quite cozy. If it weren't for that hospital smell and the various machines and monitors, I would've thought I was in someone's bedroom. Whatever this private clinic is, it's quite luxurious—a fact that I didn't have a chance to really appreciate before.

The door opens and Angela walks into the room. Giving me a wide smile, she says in a cheerful voice, "How are you feeling, Nora?"

"Okay," I reply, a little warily. "Where is Julian?" Something about this woman rubs me the wrong way, and I can't quite figure out what. I know she's probably my best chance to escape, but I don't know if I can trust her. For one thing, she could easily be in Julian's employ, like Beth.

"Mr. Esguerra had to leave for a couple of hours," she says, still smiling at me. "Beth is here, however. She just went to the restroom."

"Oh, good." I stare at her, trying to gather my courage. I have to tell her that I've been kidnapped. I simply have to. This is my one opportunity to escape. She might be loyal to Julian, but I still have to try because I may never get a better shot at freedom.

Angela comes up to the bed and hands me the cup with the bent straw. "Here you go," she says in that same cheerful voice. "I'll bring you some food in a bit."

I lift my arm and take the cup from her, wincing a little as the movement pulls at the stitches. "Thanks," I say, greedily gulping down the water. I really, really need to tell her to call the police, or whatever the local law enforcement officials are called, but for some reason, I don't. Instead, I drink the water and watch as she walks out of the room, leaving me alone once again.

I groan mentally. What is wrong with me? Freedom is a real possibility for the first time in over a year, and here I am, waffling and procrastinating. I tell myself it's because I'm being cautious, because I don't want to risk anyone getting hurt—not Angela and certainly not anyone back home—but deep inside, I know the truth.

As alluring as freedom seems, it's also frightening. I've been a captive for so long that I actually long for the comfort of my cage; being here in this unfamiliar room makes me stressed, anxious, and there is a part of me that just wants to go back to the island, to my regular routine. Most importantly, however, freedom means leaving Julian, and I can't bring myself to do that.

I don't want to leave the man who kidnapped me.

I should be rejoicing at the thought of the police coming to arrest him, but I feel horrified instead. I don't want Julian behind bars. I don't want to be separated from him, not even for a minute.

Closing my eyes, I tell myself that I'm a fool, a brainwashed idiot, but it doesn't matter.

As I lie there in that hospital bed, I come to terms with the fact that I'm no longer an unwilling captive. Instead, I am simply a woman who belongs to Julian—just as he now belongs to me.

* * *

I recuperate in the clinic for the next week. Julian visits me every day, spending several hours by my side, and so does Beth. Angela takes care of me most of the time, although a couple of doctors have dropped by to view my charts and adjust my painkiller dosage.

I still have not told anyone about being a victim of kidnapping, nor am I planning to do so anymore. For one thing, I get the sense that the clinic staff is paid to be discreet. Nobody seems the least bit curious about what an American girl is doing in the Philippines, nor are they inclined to question me in any way. The only thing Angela wants to know is whether I'm in pain, thirsty, hungry, or need to use the bathroom. I'm pretty sure that if I ask her to call the police for me, she would just smile and give me more painkillers.

I have also seen a number of guards stationed in the hallway outside the room. I catch glimpses of them when the door opens. They're armed to the teeth and look like scary sons of bitches, reminding me of the thug who beat up Jake.

When I ask Julian about them, he freely admits that they're his employees. "They're there for your protection," he explains, sitting down on the side of my bed. "I told you I have enemies, right?"

He did tell me, but I hadn't grasped the full extent of the danger before. According to Beth, there is a small army of bodyguards stationed at and around the clinic, all protecting us from whatever threat Julian is concerned about.

"What enemies?" I ask curiously, looking at him. "Who is after you?"

He smiles at me. "That's none of your concern, my pet," he says gently, but there is something cold and deadly lurking beneath the warmth of his smile. "I will deal with them soon."

I shudder a little, and hope that Julian doesn't notice. Sometimes my lover can be very, very scary.

"We're going home tomorrow," he says, changing the topic. "The doctors said you'll need to take it easy for the next few weeks, but there is no need for you to stay here. You can recover at home just as well."

I nod, my stomach tightening with a mixture of dread and anticipation. Home . . . Home on the island. This strange interlude at the clinic—so close to freedom—is almost over.

Tomorrow my real life begins again.

CHAPTER TWENTY-ONE

Pop! Pop! The explosive sound of a car backfiring jerks me out of sound sleep. My heart hammering, I jackknife up to a sitting position, then clutch at the stitches in my side with a hiss of pain.

Pop! Pop! Pop! The sound continues, and I freeze. No car backfires like that.

I'm hearing gunshots. Gunshots and occasional screams.

It's dark, the only light coming from the monitors hooked up to me. I'm on the bed in the middle of the room—the first thing someone would see upon opening the door. It occurs to me that I might as well be sitting there with a bull's eye painted in the middle of my forehead.

Trying to control my ragged breathing, I pull the IV from my arm and get to my feet. It still hurts to walk, but I ignore the pain. I'm certain bullets would hurt a lot worse.

Padding barefoot toward the door, I open it just a tiny bit and peek out into the hallway. My stomach sinks. There isn't a single bodyguard in sight; the hallway in front of me is completely empty.

Shit. Shit, shit, shit.

Casting a frantic glance around, I look for a hiding spot, but the only cupboard in the room is too small for me to fit into. There is no other place to conceal myself. Staying here would be suicidal. I need to get out, and I need to do so now.

Pulling the hospital gown tighter around myself, I cautiously step out into the hallway. The floor is cold under my bare feet, adding to the icy chill inside me. Out here, I feel even more exposed and vulnerable, and the urge to hide grows stronger. Spotting a bunch of doors on the other end of the hallway, I choose one at random, opening it carefully. To my relief, there is no one inside, and I go in, closing the door quietly behind me.

The sound of gunfire continues at random intervals, coming closer each time. I step into the corner behind the door and plaster myself against the wall, trying to control my rising panic. I have no idea who the gunmen are, but the possibilities that occur to me are not reassuring.

Julian has enemies. What if it's them out there? What if he's fighting them right now alongside his bodyguards? I imagine him injured, dead, and the coldness inside me spreads, penetrating deep into my bones. *Please, God, no. Please, anything but that.* I would sooner die than lose him.

My entire body is trembling, and I feel cold sweat sliding down my back. The gunfire has stopped, and the silence is more ominous than the deafening noise from before. I can taste the fear; it's sharp and metallic on my tongue, and I realize that I'd bitten the inside of my cheek hard enough to draw blood.

Time moves at a painful crawl. Every minute seems to stretch into an hour, every second into eternity. Finally, I hear voices and heavy footsteps out in the hallway. It sounds like there are several men, and they're speaking in a language I don't understand—a language that sounds harsh and guttural to my ears.

I can hear doors opening, and I know they're looking for something ... or someone. Hardly daring to breathe, I try to meld into the wall, to make myself so small I would be invisible to the gunmen prowling out in the hallway.

"Where is she?" a harsh male voice demands in strongly accented English. "She's supposed to be here, on this floor."

"No, she's not." The voice answering him is Beth's, and I stifle a terrified gasp, realizing that the men have somehow captured her. She sounds defiant, but I catch an undertone of fear in her voice. "I told you, Julian already took her away—"

"Don't fucking lie to me," the man roars, his accent getting thicker. The sound of a slap is followed by Beth's pained cry. "Where the fuck is she?"

"I don't know," Beth sobs hysterically. "She's gone, I told you, gone—"

The man barks out something in his own language, and I hear more doors opening. They're coming closer to the room where I'm hiding, and I know it's only a matter of time before they find me. I don't know why they're looking for me, but I know I'm the 'she' in question. They want to find me, and they're willing to hurt Beth to do it.

I hesitate for only a moment before stepping out of the room. On the other side of the hallway, I see Beth huddling on the floor, her arm held tightly by a black-garbed man. A dozen more men are standing around them, holding assault rifles and machine guns—which they point at me as soon as I come out.

"Are you looking for me?" I ask calmly. I've never been more terrified in my life, but my voice comes out steady, almost amused. I didn't know it was possible to be numb with fear, but that's how I feel right now—so terrified that I don't actually feel afraid anymore.

My mind is strangely clear, and I register several things at once. The men look Middle Eastern, with their olive-toned skin and dark hair. While a couple of them are clean-shaven, the majority seem to have thick black beards. At least two of them are wounded and bleeding. And for all their weapons, they seem quite anxious, as though they're expecting to be attacked any minute.

The man holding Beth barks out another order in a language I now realize is Arabic, and I recognize his voice as belonging to the man who'd spoken in English. He seems to be their leader. At his command, two of the men walk up to me and grab my arms, dragging me toward him. I manage not to stumble, though my stitches ache with a renewed ferocity.

"Is this her?" he hisses at Beth, shaking her roughly. "Is this Julian's little whore?"

"That would be me," I tell him before Beth can answer. My voice is still unnaturally calm. I don't think it's fully hit me yet, the danger that I'm in. All I want to do right now is stop him from hurting Beth. At the same time, at the back of my mind I'm processing the fact that they want me because I'm Julian's lover. That could only mean one thing: Julian is alive and they mean to use me against him. I suppress a shudder of relief at the thought.

The leader stares at me, apparently as surprised by my uncharacteristic bravery as I am. Letting go of Beth, he comes up to me, grasping my jaw with hard, cruel fingers. Leaning in, he studies me, his dark eyes gleaming coldly. He's short for a man, only about five-seven at most, and his breath washes over my face, bringing with it the fetid odor of garlic and stale tobacco. I fight the urge to gag, holding his gaze defiantly with my own.

After a few seconds, he lets go of me and says something in Arabic to his troops. Two of the men hurry over and grab Beth again. She screams and starts fighting them, and one of them backhands her, stunning her into silence. At the same time, the leader's hand closes around my upper arm, squeezing it painfully. "Let's go," he says sharply, and I let myself be led toward the door at the end of the hallway.

The door opens to a staircase, and I realize that we're on the second floor. The gunmen form a circle around me, the leader, and Beth, and we all go down the stairs and out through a door that leads to an unpaved open area outside. We pass one man's dead body in the staircase, and there are several more lying outside. I avert my eyes, swallowing convulsively to keep the bile from rising up in my throat. The sun is bright, and the air is hot and humid, but I can barely feel the warmth on my frozen skin. The reality of my situation is beginning to sink in, and I start to shiver, small shudders wracking my frame.

There are several black SUVs waiting for us, and the men drag me and Beth to one of them, forcing us into the back seat. Two of them climb in with us, forcing us to huddle together. I can feel Beth shaking, and I reach over to squeeze her cold hand with my own, drawing comfort from the human touch. She looks at me, and the terror in her eyes chills my blood. Her freckled face is pale, and her right cheek is swollen, with a massive bruise starting to form there. Her lower lip is split in two places, and there is a smear of blood on her chin. Whoever these men are, they have no compunction about hurting women.

I desperately want to ask her what she knows, but I keep quiet. I don't want to draw any more attention to ourselves than necessary. My mind flashes back to the dead bodies we'd just passed, and I fight the urge to throw up. I don't know what these people intend for us, but I strongly suspect our chances of getting out alive are minimal. Every minute that we survive, every minute that they leave us alone, is precious, and we need to do whatever it takes to extend those minutes for as long as possible.

The car starts up and pulls away. Still holding Beth's hand, I look out the window, seeing the white building of the clinic disappearing behind us. The road we're on is unpaved and bumpy, and the atmosphere in the car is tense. The two men in the backseat with us are gripping their weapons tightly, and I again get the sense that they're afraid of something . . . or someone.

I wonder if it's Julian. Does he know what happened? Is he even now on his way to the clinic? I stare out the window, my eyes dry and burning. It wasn't supposed to be like this. I should be going back to the island today, back to the placid life I've had for the past year. It's a life I crave now with a desperate intensity. I want to lie in Julian's embrace, to feel his touch and smell the warm, clean scent of his skin. I want him to own me and protect me, to keep me safe from everything and everyone except himself.

But he's not here. Instead the car is bumping along the road, taking us further and further away from safety. It's hot inside, and I can smell the spicy odor of unwashed male bodies and sweat; it permeates the car, making me feel like I'm suffocating. Beth seems to be in shock, her face blank and withdrawn. I want to hug her, but we're pressed too tightly together, so I just gently squeeze her hand instead. Her fingers are limp and clammy in my palm.

The ride seems to last forever, but it must be only about an hour, because the sun is still not all the way up in the sky when we arrive at our destination. It's an airstrip in the middle of nowhere, and there is a sizable plane sitting there. It looks vaguely military to me. The men force us out of the car and drag us toward the plane. I do my best to walk where they're leading me, not wanting to tear my stitches open. Beth doesn't put up a fight either, though she seems too shellshocked to walk straight, forcing them to practically carry her in.

Inside, the plane is far from luxurious. As I had suspected, the body of the plane is military in style, with seats along the walls, instead of arranged into rows. It's the kind of plane I've seen in movies, usually with Navy SEALs jumping out of it with parachutes. The men strap Beth and me into two of the seats and handcuff our hands before sitting down themselves.

The engines rev up, the plane begins to roll, and then we're airborne, the sun shining brightly in my eyes.

CHAPTER TWENTY-TWO

By the time we land a couple of hours later, I'm dying of thirst and desperately need to pee. Sneaking a glance at Beth, I see that she's in even worse discomfort, her eyes glazed and feverish-looking. The swelling on her face has turned into an ugly bruise, and her lips are crusted with blood. With my hands cuffed together, I can't even reach over to give her a comforting pat on the arm.

As soon as the plane touches down, they unbuckle us and drag us out of the plane with our hands still cuffed in front of us. The leader approaches us, giving us a quick once-over before pointing toward a black SUV parked a few yards away. He spits out some order at his men, and I understand it to mean that our journey is about to continue. Before they can force us into the vehicle, however, I speak up. "Hey," I say quietly, "I have to use the restroom."

Beth flashes me a panicked look, but I ignore her, focusing my attention on the leader. I'm pretty sure I'd sooner die than piss my pants—or my hospital gown, as the matter may be. He hesitates for a second, staring at me, then jerks his thumb toward the bushes. "Go, bitch," he says harshly. "You have one minute."

I scramble toward the bushes, ignoring the man with a machine gun who follows me there. Thankfully, he looks away as I hike up my gown and squat to relieve myself, my face flaming with embarrassment. Out of the corner of my eye, I see Beth following my example a dozen yards away.

Once we're both done, we get into another hot, stuffy car. This time, the ride is even longer, the road winding through what appears to be some kind of jungle. By the time we get to a nondescript warehouse-like building—our final destination—I'm soaked with sweat and badly dehydrated. I'm hungry too, but that need is secondary to the thirst that's consuming me right now.

When we get into the building, we are led toward two metal chairs standing in the corner. My handcuffs are unlocked, but before I have a chance to rejoice, the same man who guarded me at the bushes binds my wrists together behind my back. Then he ties my ankles to the chair, one to each leg, before wrapping a rope all around my body to secure me to the chair. His touch on my skin is indifferent, impersonal; I'm just a thing to him, not a woman. Turning my head to the side, I see that the same thing is done to Beth, except that her handler seems to enjoy causing her pain, yanking her legs roughly apart to tie them to the chair. She doesn't make a sound, but her face gets even paler and her cracked lips tremble slightly.

I watch it all with helpless anger, then turn away once the man leaves her alone, focusing my attention on our surroundings instead.

It seems that my initial impression was correct. We're inside some warehouse, with tall boxes and metal shelves forming a maze in the middle. Now that we're securely tied to the chairs, the men leave us alone, gathering around a long table in the other corner.

Beth and I finally have some privacy to talk.

"Are you okay?" I ask her, taking care to keep my voice pitched low. "Did they hurt you? Before I came out, I mean . . ."

She shakes her head, her mouth tightening. "Just smacked me around a bit," she says quietly. "It's nothing. You shouldn't have come out, Nora. That was stupid."

"They would've found me anyway. It was just a matter of time." I'm convinced of that. "Do you know who they are or what they want from us?"

"I'm not sure, but I can guess," she says, her hands clenching tightly in her lap. "I think they're part of the Jihadist terrorist group that Julian told me about a couple of months ago. Apparently, they're upset that he wouldn't sell them some weapon that his company recently developed."

"Why not?" I ask curiously. "Why wouldn't he sell it to them?"

She shrugs. "I don't know. Julian is very selective when it comes to his business partners, and it could be that he just didn't trust them enough."

"So they took us as leverage?"

"Yes, I think so," she says softly. "At least, that's what you're here for. Someone at the clinic must've been in their employ because they knew who you were and what you meant to Julian. I was sleeping in one of the rooms downstairs when they found me, and they immediately went up to the second floor, to the room where you were staying. I think they intend to use you to force Julian's hand when it comes to giving them this weapon."

I draw in a shaky breath. "I see." I can only imagine how men psychotic enough to kill innocent civilians would 'force Julian's hand.' Gruesome images of severed body parts dance through my mind, and I push them away with effort, not wanting to give in to the panic that threatens to swallow me whole.

"It's lucky that Julian wasn't at the clinic when they came," Beth says, interrupting my dark thoughts. "They killed everyone, all sixteen of Julian's men who were stationed there guarding us."

I swallow hard. "Sixteen men?"

Beth nods. "They had insane firepower, and they came with a good thirty or forty men of their own. You didn't see the worst of it, because they entered from the back. There were bodies piled six feet high in the other staircase, with many of the casualties coming from their side."

I stare at her, trying to control my breathing. *Shit. Shit, shit, shit.* For them to sacrifice so many of their comrades, whatever they want from Julian must be a hell of a weapon. Would he give it to them to save us? Does he care for me and Beth enough? I know he wants me—and is concerned about my well-being on some level—but I have no idea if he would put me ahead of his business interests.

Of course, even if he gives them what they want, there is no guarantee that they will let us live. I remember what Julian told me about Maria's death... about how she was killed to punish him for some warehouse raid. In Julian's world, actions have consequences. Very brutal consequences.

"Do you think he'll come for us?" I ask Beth quietly. The irony of it all doesn't escape me. I now regard Julian as my potential savior, my knight in shining armor. He's not the one I need rescuing from anymore.

She looks at me, her eyes dark in her pale face. "He will," she answers softly. "He'll come for us. I just don't know if it will matter to us by then."

* * *

The next couple of hours drag by. The men largely ignore us, though I've seen a couple of them looking at my bare legs when their leader wasn't paying attention. Thankfully, the hospital gown is generally shapeless and made of thick material—about the least sexy outfit I can imagine. The thought of one—or several—of them touching me makes my skin crawl.

They also don't give us anything to eat or drink. That's not a good sign; it means they don't care if we live or die. My thirst is getting so bad that all I can think about is water, and there is an empty, gnawing feeling in my stomach. The worst thing of all, however, is the cold fear that comes at me in waves and the dark images that flicker through my mind like a bad horror movie.

I try to talk to Beth to keep myself from freaking out, but after our initial conversation, she's become quiet and withdrawn, responding in monosyllables at best. It's like mentally, she's not even there. I envy her. I'd like to be able to escape like that, but I can't. For my mind to let go, I need Julian and his particular brand of erotic torture.

When I'm just about ready to scream from frustration, two more men enter the warehouse. To my surprise, one of them looks like a businessman; his pinstriped suit is sharp and tailored, and a stylish Strotter bag hangs messenger-style across his body. He's also relatively young, probably only in his thirties, and appears to be in good shape. Smoothly shaven, with olive complexion and glossy dark hair, he could've been on the cover of GQ—if it weren't for the fact that he's most likely a terrorist.

He exchanges a few words with the men on the other side of the warehouse, then heads toward Beth and me. As he approaches us, I notice the cold gleam in his eyes and the way his nostrils flare slightly. There's something vaguely reptilian in his unblinking stare, and I suppress a shudder when he stops a couple of feet away and studies me, his head cocked to the side.

I stare back at him, my heart pounding heavily in my chest. Objectively, he could be considered handsome, but I don't feel even the slightest tug of attraction. The only thing I feel is fear. It's actually a relief; some part of me has always wondered if I'm simply wired wrong—if I'm destined to desire the men who scare me. Now I see that it's a Julian-specific phenomenon for me. I'm frightened and repulsed by the criminal standing in front of me now—a perfectly normal reaction that I embrace.

"How long have you known Esguerra?" the man asks, addressing me. He has a British accent, mixed with a hint of something foreign and exotic. At the sound of his voice, Beth looks up, startled, and I see that she's back with us for the moment.

I hesitate for a second before answering. "About fifteen months," I finally say. I don't see the harm in revealing that much.

He lifts his eyebrows. "And he kept you hidden this whole time? Impressive . . ."

I suppress the sudden urge to snicker. Julian quite literally kept me hidden on his island, so this guy is more right than he realizes. My lips twitch involuntarily, and I see a flicker of surprise cross the man's face.

"Well, you're a brave little whore, aren't you?" he says slowly, watching me with his dark gaze. "Or do you think this is all a joke?"

I don't say anything in response. What can I say? *No, I don't think it's a joke. I know you're going to torture me and probably kill me to get back at Julian.* Somehow that just doesn't have the right ring to it.

His eyes narrow, and I realize I somehow managed to make him angry. He looks like a cobra about to strike. My heartbeat spikes, and I tense, bracing myself for a blow, but he simply reaches for his Strotter bag and opens it to reveal his iPad. Glancing down, he quickly types some email, then looks up at me. "Let's see if Esguerra thinks it's a joke," he says quietly, closing the bag. "For your sake, girl, I hope that's not the case."

Then he turns and walks away, heading back to where the other men are gathered.

* * *

Despite my terror and discomfort, I somehow manage to fall asleep in the chair. My body is still recovering from the operation, and I'm both physically and emotionally exhausted from the events of the past day.

I wake up to the sound of voices. The guy in the suit and the short one I had pegged as the leader are standing in front of me, setting up what looks like a large camera on a tall tripod.

I swallow, staring at them. My mouth feels as dry as the Sahara desert, and despite all the time that's passed, I don't have the least urge to pee. I'm guessing that means I'm badly dehydrated.

Seeing that I'm awake, the Suit—I decide to call him that in my mind—gives me a thin-lipped smile. "It's showtime. Let's see just how much Esguerra wants his little whore back."

Nausea roils my empty stomach, and I turn my head to look at Beth. She's staring straight ahead, her face white and her gaze vacant. I don't know if she slept at all, but she seems even more out of it than before.

They point the camera toward us, checking the angle a couple of times, and then the Suit comes over to stand next to me. As soon as the camera light goes on, he puts his hand on my head, roughly stroking my tangled hair. "You know what I want, Esguerra," he says evenly, looking at the camera. "You have until midnight tomorrow to get it to me. Do that, and your slut will remain unharmed. I'll even give her back to you. If not, well . . . you'll get her back anyway." He pauses, smiling cruelly. "Little by little."

I stare at the camera, bile rising in my throat. I haven't been harmed—yet—but I can sense the violence in these men. It's the same darkness that stains Julian's soul. Men like these are different. They don't abide by the social contract. They don't play by the same rules as everyone else.

The Suit's hand leaves my hair, and he takes a step toward Beth. "You may be doubting me, Esguerra," he says, still speaking to the camera. "You may be thinking that I lack resolve. Well, let me do a little demonstration of what will happen to your pretty whore if I don't get what I want. We'll start with the redhead and move on to that one"—he nods toward me—"tomorrow after midnight."

"No!" I scream, realizing what he means to do. "Don't touch her!" I struggle to get free, but the ropes are holding me too tightly. There is nothing I can do but watch helplessly as he wraps his hand around Beth's throat and begins to squeeze. "Don't you fucking touch her! Julian will kill you for this! He'll fucking murder you—"

Ignoring my screams, the Suit barks out an order in Arabic, and a man steps forward, cutting Beth's ropes with a sharp knife. I catch a glimpse of her terrified eyes, and then they throw her on the ground, face down. The Suit presses his knee against her back and yanks on her hair, forcing her head to arch back. I can see her legs drumming uselessly against the ground, and my screams grow louder as the Suit takes out a short, thin knife and begins cutting Beth's cheek.

She yells, struggling, and I can see blood spraying everywhere as he slices open her face, leaving behind a deep bloody gash. I gag, my stomach heaving, but he's far from done. Beth's other cheek is next, and then he presses the knife into her upper arm, cutting off a strip of flesh. Her agonized screams echo throughout the warehouse, joined by my own hysterical cries. I feel her pain as though it's my own, and I can't bear it. "Leave her alone!" I shriek. "You fucking bastard! Leave her alone!"

He doesn't, of course. He continues cutting her, his dark eyes shining with excitement. He's enjoying this, I realize with sick horror; he's not doing it just for the camera. Beth's struggles grow weaker, her cries turning into sobbing moans. There is blood everywhere; Beth is practically drowning in it. I don't know how she's able to remain conscious through this. Black spots swim in front of my vision, and I feel like the walls are closing in on me, my ribcage squeezing my lungs and preventing me from drawing in air.

Suddenly, Beth's body jerks, and she lets out a strange gurgle before falling silent. All I can hear now is the sound of my own harsh, sobbing breaths. Beth is lying there unmoving, a pool of blood spreading out from her neck area. The Suit gets up, wiping the knife on his pants, and faces the camera. "That was an expedited show for you, Esguerra," he says, smiling widely. "I didn't want to drag it out too much, since I know you'll need the time to get me what I asked for. Of course, if I don't receive it, the next show will be much, much longer." Taking a step toward me, he runs one bloody finger down my cheek. "Your little whore is so pretty, I might even let my men play with her before I start . . ."

This time I can't control myself. Hot vomit rushes into my throat, and I barely manage to turn my head to the side before the contents of my stomach empty out onto the floor in a series of violent heaves.

CHAPTER TWENTY-THREE

After the camera is turned off, they leave me alone again. Beth's body is dragged away, and the floor is carelessly mopped, leaving behind several reddish-brown streaks. I stare at them, my thoughts slow and sluggish, as if I'm in a stupor. I'm no longer shaking, though an occasional shudder still wracks my body. My stitches ache dully, and I wonder if I tore any of them during my struggles earlier. I don't see any blood seeping through my hospital gown, so maybe I didn't.

A little while later, they bring me some water. I greedily gulp down the whole cup, causing some of the men to laugh and say something in Arabic while rubbing their crotches suggestively. I almost think they are hoping that Julian doesn't come through, so they get to 'play' with me before the Suit goes to work.

For now, though, they mercifully leave me alone. I am even allowed outside for a minute to use the restroom, and the same guy as before—the impassive one—guards me while I go into the bushes. I think he's now my official bathroom companion, and I mentally start calling him Toilet Guy.

I name some of the others, too. The one with the black beard down to the middle of his chest—I call him Blackbeard. The one with the receding hairline is Baldie. The short guy who led the raid on the clinic—he's Garlic Breath.

I do this to distract myself from thoughts of Beth. I can't allow myself to think about her yet—not if I want to remain sane. If I get out of this alive, then I will mourn the woman who had become my friend. If I survive, then I will allow myself to cry and grieve, to rage at the senseless violence of her death. But right now, I can only exist from moment to moment, focusing on the most inconsequential, ridiculous things to keep myself from being crushed under the weight of brutal reality.

Time ticks by slowly. As darkness descends, I stare at the floor, the walls, the ceiling. I think I even nod off a couple of times, although I jerk awake at the least hint of any sound, my heart racing. They still haven't fed me, and the hunger pangs in my stomach are a gnawing ache. It doesn't matter, though. I'm just grateful to still be alive—a state of affairs I know will not continue for long, unless Julian comes through with the weapon.

Closing my eyes, I try to pretend that I'm home on the island, reading a book on the beach. I try to imagine that at any moment, I can go back to the house and find Beth there, prepping dinner for us. I try to convince myself that Julian is simply away on one of his business trips and I will see him again soon. I picture his smile, the way his dark hair curls around his face, framing the hard masculine perfection of his features, and I ache for him, for the warmth and safety of his strong embrace, even as my mind gradually drifts toward an uneasy sleep.

* * *

A large hand clamps tightly over my mouth, jerking me awake. My eyes fly open, adrenaline surging through my veins. Terrified, I begin to struggle . . . and then I hear a familiar voice whispering in my ear, "Shh, Nora. It's me. I need you to be quiet now, okay?"

I nod slightly, my body shaking with relief, and the hand leaves my mouth. Turning my head, I stare at Julian in disbelief.

Crouching beside me, he's dressed all in black. A bulletproof vest is covering his chest and shoulders, and his face is painted with black diagonal stripes. There is a machine gun hanging across his shoulder, and an entire array of weapons is clipped to his belt. He looks like a deadly stranger. Only his eyes are familiar, startlingly bright in his paint-darkened face.

For a second, I'm convinced that I'm dreaming. He can't be standing here, in this warehouse in the middle of nowhere, talking to me. Not when his enemies are less than thirty yards away. My heart racing, I cast a quick, frantic glance around the warehouse.

The men in the other corner appear to be asleep, stretched out on blankets on the floor. I count eight of them—which means that several of them are probably outside, guarding the building. I don't see the Suit anywhere; he must also be outside.

Turning my attention back to Julian, I see him cutting through the ropes at my ankles with a wicked-looking knife. "How did you get in here?" I whisper, staring at him in dazed wonder.

He pauses for a second, looking up at me. "Be quiet," he says, his words almost inaudible. "I need to get you out before they wake up."

I nod, falling silent as he resumes cutting my ropes. Despite our perilous situation, I am almost dizzy with joy. Julian is here, with me. He came for me. The surge of love and gratitude is so strong, I can barely contain it. I want to jump up and hug him, but I remain still as he finishes his task, getting rid of the remaining ropes.

As soon as I'm free, he pulls me to my feet and wraps his arms around me, holding me tightly against him. I can feel the fine trembling in his powerful body, and then he releases me, taking half a step back. Framing my face with his palms, he looks down at me, his blue gaze hard and fiercely possessive. A moment of wordless communication passes between us, and I know. I know what he can't say right now.

I know he would always come for me.

I know he would kill for me.

I know he would die for me.

Lowering his arms, he takes my hand. "Let's go," he says quietly, still looking at me. "We don't have much time."

I grip his hand tightly, letting him lead me toward the darkened area near the wall on the opposite side of where the men are sleeping. The maze of shelves and boxes in the middle of the warehouse quickly hides us from their view, and Julian stops there, crouching down again and letting go of my palm. I hear a fumbling sound, like his hand is searching for something along the floor, and then there is a quiet creak as he lifts a board off the floor and places it to the side.

On the floor in front of us is a large square opening.

I kneel down beside it, peering into the darkness below.

"Climb down," Julian whispers in my ear, putting his hand on my knee and squeezing it lightly. The familiar touch calms me a bit. "There is a ladder."

I swallow, reaching out with my hand to find said ladder. How does he know this?

"I hacked into their computer and found the blueprints of this building," he explains quietly, as though reading my mind. "There is a storage area below that has a drainpipe leading outside. Find it and crawl through it." His hand leaves my knee, and I feel bereft without his touch, the danger of our situation hitting me again.

My fingers touch the metal ladder, and I grab it, maneuvering myself toward it. Julian holds my arm as I find my footing and cautiously begin to descend. It's pitch-black down there, and under normal circumstances, I would be hesitant to go into an unknown basement, but there's nothing more frightening to me right now than the men we're escaping from.

I climb down a few rungs, then look up, seeing Julian still sitting there. The expression on his face is tense and alert, like he's listening for something.

And then I hear it—a murmur of voices, followed by shouts in Arabic.

My absence had been discovered.

Julian rises to his feet with one smooth motion and looks down at me, his hands gripping the machine gun. "Go," he orders, his voice low and hard. "Now, Nora. Get to the drainpipe and outside. I'll hold them back."

"What? No!" I stare at him in horrified shock. "Come with me—"

He gives me a furious glare. "Go," he hisses. "Now, or we're both dead. I can't worry about you and fight them off."

I hesitate for a second, feeling torn. I don't want to leave him behind, but I don't want to stand in his way either. "I love you," I say quietly, looking up at him, and see a quick flash of white teeth in response.

"Go, baby," he says, his tone much softer now. "I'll be with you soon."

My heart aching, I do as he says, climbing down the ladder as quickly as I can. The shouts are growing louder, and I know the men are searching the warehouse, starting with the maze in the middle. It's only a matter of time before they get to the darkened area along this wall. My entire body is shaking with a combination of nerves and adrenaline, and I focus on not falling as I descend further into the darkness.

Rat-tat-tat! The burst of gunfire above startles me, and I climb down even faster, my breathing hard and erratic. As soon as my feet touch the floor, I stretch out my hands in front of me and begin to grope in the darkness, searching for the wall with the drain pipe.

More gunfire. Yells. Screams. My heart is pounding so hard, it sounds like a drum in my ears.

Something squeaks underneath my feet, and tiny paws run over my bare toes. I ignore it, frantically searching for that drainpipe. Rats are nothing to me right now. Somewhere up there, Julian is in mortal danger. I don't know if he's by himself or if he brought reinforcements, but the thought of him being hurt or killed is so agonizing that I can't focus on it now. Not if I want to survive.

My hands touch the wall, but I can't find an opening. It's too dark. Panting, I make my way along the wall, sweeping my hands up and down the smooth surface. My stitches ache, but I barely register the pain. I need to find a way out. If they catch me again, I will not survive for long.

Another burst of gunfire, followed by more yells.

I continue searching, my terror and frustration growing with every moment. *Julian. Julian is up there.* I try not to think about it, but I can't. There's nothing I can do to help him; logically, I know that. I'm barefoot and dressed in a hospital gown, without so much as a fork to defend myself with. In the meantime, he's armed to the teeth and wearing a bulletproof vest.

Of course, logic has nothing to do with the agonizing fear I feel at the thought of losing him.

He will survive, I tell myself as I continue looking for the drainpipe. Julian knows what he's doing. This is his world, his area of expertise. This is the part of his life he was shielding me from on the island.

My hands touch something hard on the wall near my knees and then sink into the opening.

The drainpipe. I found it.

There is another high-pitched squeak, and something scrambles out of the pipe toward me. I jump back, startled, but then I get on all fours and determinedly crawl inside, steeling myself for more potential rodent encounters.

The drainpipe is large enough that I can be on my hands and knees, and I crawl as fast as I can, ignoring the stale smell of sewage and rust. Thankfully, it's only a little bit wet in there, and I try not to dwell on what that wetness might be.

Finally, I reach the other opening. Compressing myself into a little ball, I manage to turn around and climb out feet first.

Stepping away from the pipe, I gaze at my surroundings. The sky above me is covered with stars, and the air is thick with the scent of warm earth and jungle vegetation. I can see the warehouse building on the small hill above me, less than fifty yards away.

I stare at it, sick with fear for Julian. There is another burst of gunfire, accompanied by flashes of bright light. The gunfight is still going on—which is a good sign, I tell myself. If Julian was dead—if the terrorists had won—there would be no more shooting. He must've come with reinforcements after all.

Wrapping my arms around myself, I press my back against a tree, my legs trembling from the combination of terror and adrenaline.

And in that moment, the sky lights up as the building explodes . . . and a blast of scorching-hot air sends me flying into the bushes several feet away.

CHAPTER TWENTY-FOUR

The next twenty-four hours are a blur in my memory.

After I get to my feet, I am dizzy and disoriented, my head throbbing and my body feeling like one giant bruise. There is a din in my ears, and everything seems to be coming at me as though from a distance.

I must've passed out from the blast, but I am not sure. By the time I recover enough to walk, the fire consuming the building is almost over.

Dazed, I stumble up the hill and start searching through the smoldering ruins of the warehouse. Occasionally, I find something that looks like a charred limb, and a couple of times, I come across a body that's very nearly whole, with only a head or a leg missing. I register these findings on some level, but I don't fully process them. I feel oddly detached, like I'm not really there. Nothing touches me. Nothing bothers me. Even the physical sensations are dulled by shock.

I search for him for hours. By the time I stop, the sun is high up in the sky, and I'm dripping with sweat.

I have no choice but to face the truth now.

There are no survivors. It's as simple as that.

I should cry. I should scream. I should feel something.

But I don't.

I just feel numb instead.

Leaving the warehouse, I begin walking. I don't know where I am going, and I don't care. All I'm capable of doing is putting one foot in front of the other.

By the time it starts getting dark, I come across a cluster of tiny houses made of wooden poles and cardboard. There is a shallow creek running through the middle of the settlement, and I see a couple of women doing laundry there by hand.

Their shocked faces are the last thing I remember before I collapse a few feet away from them.

* * *

"Miss Leston, do you feel up to answering a few questions for me? I'm Agent Wilson, FBI, and this is Agent Bosovsky."

I look up at the plump middle-aged man standing next to my bed. He's not at all like I imagined FBI agents to be. His face is round, almost cherubic-looking, with rosy cheeks and dancing blue eyes. If Agent Wilson wore a red hat and had a white beard, he would've made a great Santa Claus. In contrast, his partner—Agent Bosovsky— is painfully thin, with deep frown lines etched into his narrow face.

For the past two days, I have been recuperating in a hospital in Bangkok. Apparently, one of the women at the creek had notified the local authorities about the girl that wandered into their village. I vaguely recall them questioning me, but I doubt I made any sense when I spoke to them. However, they understood enough to contact the American Embassy on my behalf, and the US officials took it from there.

"Your parents are on the way," Agent Bosovsky says when I continue to stare at them without saying a word. "Their flight lands in a few hours."

I blink, his words somehow penetrating the layer of ice that has kept me insulated from everyone and everything since the explosion. "My parents?" I croak, my throat feeling strangely swollen.

The thin agent nods. "Yes, Miss Leston. They were notified yesterday, and we got them on the earliest flight to Bangkok. They wanted to speak to you, but you were sedated at that point."

I process that information. The doctors already informed me that I have a mild concussion, along with first-degree burns and lacerations on my feet. Other than that, they were impressed by my overall good health—dehydration, recent surgery, and various bruises notwithstanding. Still, they must've sedated me to let me rest.

"Do you think you could answer some questions before your parents arrive?" Agent Wilson asks gently when I continue to remain silent.

I nod, almost imperceptibly, and he pulls up a chair. Agent Bosovsky does the same thing.

"Miss Leston, you were abducted in June of last year," Agent Wilson says, the expression on his round face warm and understanding. "Can you tell us anything about your abduction?"

I hesitate for a moment. Do I want to tell them anything about Julian? And then I remember that he's dead and that none of it matters. For a second, the agony is so sharp, it steals my breath away, but then the numbing wall of ice encases me again. "Sure," I say evenly. "What do you want to know?"

"Do you know his name?"

"Julian Esguerra. He is—" I swallow hard. "He *was* an arms dealer."

The FBI agent's eyes widen. "An arms dealer?"

I nod and tell them what I know about Julian's organization. Agent Bosovsky scribbles down notes as quickly as he can, while Agent Wilson continues asking me questions about Julian's activities and the terrorists who stole me from him. They seem disappointed that he's dead—and that I know so little—and I explain that I haven't been off the island since my abduction.

"He kept you there for the entire fifteen months?" Agent Bosovsky asks, the frown lines on his thin face deepening. "Just you and this woman, Beth?"

"Yes."

The agents exchange a look, and I stare at them, knowing what they're thinking. *Poor girl, kept like an animal in a cage for a criminal's amusement.* Once I felt that way too, but no longer. Now I would do anything to rewind the clock and go back to being Julian's captive.

Agent Wilson turns toward me and clears his throat. "Miss Leston, we'll have a sexual abuse counselor speak to you later this afternoon. She's very good—"

"There's no need," I interrupt. "I'm fine."

And I am. I don't feel victimized or abused. I just feel numb.

After a few more questions, they leave me alone. I don't tell them any details of my relationship with Julian, but I think they get the gist of it.

The FBI sketch artist comes to see me next, and I describe Julian to him. He keeps giving me funny looks as I correct his interpretation of my descriptions. "No, his eyebrows are a little thicker, a little straighter . . . His hair is a little wavier, yes, like that . . ."

He has particular trouble with Julian's mouth. It's hard to describe the beauty of that dark, angelic smile of his. "Make the upper lip a little fuller . . . No, that's too full—it should be more sensuous, almost pretty . . ."

Finally, we're done, and Julian's face stares at me from the white sheet of paper. A bolt of agony spears through me again, but the numbness comes to my rescue right away, as it did before.

"That's a handsome fellow," the artist comments, examining his handiwork. "You don't see men like that every day."

My hands clench tightly, my nails digging into my skin. "No, you don't."

The next person to visit my room is the sexual abuse counselor they mentioned to me before. She's a slightly overweight brunette who looks to be in her late forties, but something about her direct gaze reminds me of Beth.

"I'm Diane," she says, introducing herself to me as she pulls up a chair. "May I call you Nora?"

"That's fine," I say wearily. I don't particularly want to talk to this woman, but the determined look on her face tells me that she has no intention of leaving until I do.

"Nora, can you tell me about your time on the island?" she asks, looking at me.

"What do you want to know?"

"Whatever you feel comfortable telling me."

I think about it for a moment. The truth of the matter is that I'm not comfortable telling her anything. How can I describe the way Julian made me feel? How can I explain the highs and lows of our unorthodox relationship? I know what she's going to think—that I'm screwed up in the head for loving him. That my feelings aren't real, but a byproduct of my captivity.

And she would probably be right—but it doesn't matter to me anymore. There is right and wrong, and then there's what Julian and I had together. Nothing and no one will ever be able to fill the void left inside me. No amount of counseling would make the pain of losing him go away.

I give Diane a polite smile. "I'm sorry," I say quietly. "I'd rather not talk to you right now."

She nods, not the least bit surprised. "I understand. Often, as victims, we blame ourselves for what happened. We think we did something to cause this thing to happen to us."

"I don't think that," I say, frowning. Okay, maybe the thought did flit briefly through my mind when I was first taken, but getting to know Julian had quickly disabused me of that notion. He was a man who simply took what he wanted—and he had wanted me.

"I see," she says, looking slightly puzzled. Then her brow clears as she appears to solve the mystery in her mind. "He was a very good-looking man, wasn't he?" she guesses, staring at me.

I hold her gaze silently, not willing to admit anything. I can't talk about my feelings right now, not if I want to maintain that icy distance that keeps me sane.

She looks at me for a few seconds, then gets up, handing me her card. "If you're ever ready to talk, Nora, please call me," she says softly. "You can't keep it all bottled up inside. It will eventually consume you—"

"Okay, I will call you," I interrupt, taking the card and placing it on my bedside table. I'm lying through my teeth, and I'm sure she knows it.

The corners of her mouth tilt up in a faint smile, and then she exits the room, finally leaving me alone with my thoughts.

* * *

For my parents' arrival, I insist on getting up and putting on normal clothes. I don't want them to see me lying in a hospital bed. I'm sure they have already spent too much time worrying about me, and the last thing I want is to add to their anxiety.

One of the nurses gives me a pair of jeans and a T-shirt, and I gratefully put them on. They fit me well. The nurse is a petite Thai woman, and we're roughly the same size. It's strange to wear these types of clothes again. I had gotten so used to light summer dresses that jeans feel unusually rough and heavy against my skin. I don't put on any shoes, though, since my feet still have to heal from the burns I got wandering through the remnants of the warehouse.

When my parents finally enter the room, I am sitting in a chair, waiting for them. My mom comes in first. Her face crumples as soon as she sees me, and she rushes across the room, tears streaming down her face. My dad is right behind her, and soon they are both hugging me, chattering a mile a minute, and sobbing with joy.

I smile widely, hug them in return, and do my best to reassure them that I'm all right, that all of my injuries are minor and there's nothing to worry about. I don't cry, though. I can't. Everything feels dull and distant, and even my parents seem more like beloved memories than real people. Nonetheless, I make an effort to act normally; I already caused them far too much stress and anxiety.

After a little while, they calm down enough to sit and talk.

"He contacted you, right?" I ask, remembering Julian's promise. "He told you I was alive?"

My dad nods, his face drawn tight. "A couple of weeks after you disappeared, we got a deposit into our bank account," he says quietly. "A deposit in the amount of one million dollars from an untraceable offshore account. Supposedly it was a lottery that we won."

My mouth falls open. "What?" Julian gave my parents money?

"At the same time, we received an email," my dad continues, his voice shaking. "The subject was: 'From your daughter with love'. It had your picture. You were lying on a beach, reading a book. You looked so beautiful, so peaceful..." He swallows visibly. "The email said that you were well and that you were with someone who would take care of you—and that we should use the money to pay off our mortgage. It also said that we would be putting you in danger if we went to the police with this information."

I stare at him in bemusement, trying to imagine what they must've thought at that point. *A million dollars...*

"We didn't know what to do," my mom says, her hands anxiously twisting together. "We thought this could be a useful lead in the investigation, but at the same time, we didn't want to do anything to jeopardize you, wherever you were..."

"So what did you do?" I ask in fascination. The FBI didn't say anything about a million dollars, so my parents couldn't have spoken to them about this. At the same time, I can't imagine my parents simply taking the money and not pursuing this further.

"We used the money to hire a team of private investigators," my dad explains. "The best ones we could find. They were able to track the deposit to a shell corporation in the Cayman Islands, but the trail died there." He pauses, looking at me. "We've been using that money to look for you ever since."

"What happened, honey?" my mom asks, leaning forward in her chair. "Who took you? Where did this money come from? Where have you been this whole time?"

I smile and begin answering their questions. At the same time, I watch them, drinking in their familiar features. My parents are a handsome couple, both of them healthy and in good shape. They had me when they were both in their early twenties, so they are still relatively young. My dad has only traces of grey in his dark hair, though there is more grey now than I remember seeing before.

"So you really were swimming in the ocean and reading books on the beach?" My mom stares at me in disbelief as I describe my typical day on the island.

"Yes." I give her a huge smile. "In some ways, it was like a really long vacation. And he did take care of me, like he told you he would."

"But why did he take you?" my dad asks in frustration. "Why did he steal you away?"

I shrug, not wanting to go into detailed explanations about Maria and Julian's extreme possessiveness. "Because that's just the type of man he was, I guess," I say casually. "Because he couldn't really date me normally, given his profession."

"Did he hurt you, honey?" my mom asks, her dark eyes filled with sympathy. "Was he cruel to you?"

"No," I say softly. "He wasn't cruel to me at all."

I can't explain the complexity of my relationship with Julian to my parents, so I don't even try. Instead, I gloss over many aspects of my captivity, focusing only on the positive. I tell them about my early morning fishing expeditions with Beth and my newfound painting hobby. I describe the beauty of the island and how I got back into running. By the time I pause to catch my breath, they are both staring at me with strange looks on their faces.

"Nora, honey," my mom asks uncertainly, "are you . . . are you in love with this Julian?"

I laugh, but the sound comes out raw and empty. "Love? No, of course not!" I'm not sure what gave her that idea, since I have been trying to avoid talking about Julian at all. The more I think about him, the more I feel like the wall of ice around me might crack, letting the pain drown me.

"Of course not," my dad says, watching me closely, and I see that he doesn't believe me.

Somehow both of my parents can sense the truth—that I'm far more traumatized by my rescue than by my abduction.

CHAPTER TWENTY-FIVE

Over the next four months, I attempt to pick up the pieces of my life.

After another day in the Bangkok hospital, I'm deemed healthy enough to travel, and I go home, back to Illinois with my parents. We have two FBI escorts on our trip home—Agents Wilson and Bosovsky—who use the twenty-hour flight to ask me even more questions. Both of them seem frustrated because, according to their databases, Julian Esguerra simply doesn't exist.

"There are no other aliases you've heard him use?" Agent Bosovsky asks me for the third time, after their Interpol query comes back without any results.

"No," I say patiently. "I only knew him as Julian. The terrorists called him Esguerra."

Beth's guess about the identities of the men who stole us from Julian's clinic turned out to be correct. They were indeed part of a particularly dangerous Jihadist organization called Al-Quadar—that much the FBI had been able to find out.

"This just doesn't make sense," Agent Wilson says, his round cheeks quivering with frustration. "Anyone with that kind of clout should have been on our radar. If he was head of an illegal organization that manufactured and distributed cutting-edge weapons, how is it possible that not a single government agency is aware of his existence?"

I don't know what to tell him, so I just shrug in response. The private investigators my parents hired hadn't been able to find out anything about him either.

My parents and I had debated telling the FBI about Julian's money, but ultimately decided against it. Revealing this information so late in the game would only get my parents in trouble and could potentially cause the FBI to think that I had been Julian's accessory. After all, what kidnapper sends money to his victim's family?

By the time we get home, I am exhausted. I'm tired of my parents hovering over me all the time, and I'm sick of the FBI coming to me with a million questions that I can't answer. Most of all, I'm tired of being around so many people. After more than a year with minimal human contact, I feel overwhelmed by the airport crowds.

I find my old room in my parents' house virtually untouched. "We always hoped you'd be back," my mom explains, her face glowing with happiness. I smile and give her a hug before gently ushering her out of the room. More than anything, I need to be alone right now—because I don't know how long I can keep up my 'normal' facade.

That night, as I take a shower in my old childhood bathroom, I finally give in to my grief and cry.

* * *

Two weeks after my arrival home, I move out of my parents' house. They try to talk me out of it, but I convince them that I need this—that I have to be on my own and independent. The truth of the matter is, as much as I love my parents, I can't be around them twenty-four-seven. I'm no longer that carefree girl they remember, and I find it too draining to pretend to be her.

It's much easier to be myself in the tiny studio I rent nearby.

My parents try to give me what remains of Julian's gift to them—half a million with small change—but I refuse. The way I see it, that money had been for my parents' mortgage and I want it used for that purpose. After numerous arguments, we reach an agreement: they pay off most of their mortgage and refinance the rest, and the remaining money goes into my college fund.

Although I technically don't need to work for a while, I get a waitressing job anyway. It gets me out of the house, but is not particularly demanding—which is exactly what I need right now. There are nights when I don't sleep and days when getting out of bed is torture. The emptiness inside me is crushing, the grief almost suffocating, and it takes every bit of my strength to function at a semi-normal level.

When I do sleep, I have nightmares. My mind replays Beth's death and the warehouse explosion over and over again, until I wake up drenched in cold sweat. After those dreams, I lie awake, aching for Julian, for the warmth and safety of his embrace. I feel lost without him, like a rudderless ship at sea. His absence is a festering wound that refuses to heal.

I miss Beth, too. I miss her no-nonsense attitude, her matter-of-fact approach to life. If she was here, she would be the first one to tell me that shit happens and that I should just deal with it. She would want me to move on.

And I try . . . but the senseless violence of her death eats at me. Julian was right—I didn't know what real hatred was before. I didn't know what it was like to want to hurt someone, to crave their death. Now I do. If I could go back in time and kill the terrorist who murdered Beth so brutally, I would do it in a heartbeat. It's not enough for me that he died in that explosion. I wish I had been the one to end his life.

My parents insist that I see a therapist. To pacify them, I go a few times. It doesn't help. I'm not ready to bare my heart and soul to a stranger, and our sessions end up being a waste of time and money. I'm not in the right frame of mind to receive therapy—my loss is too fresh, my emotions too raw.

I start painting again, but I can't do the same sunny landscapes as before. My art is darker now, more chaotic. I paint the explosion over and over again, trying to get it out of my mind, and every time it comes out a little different, a little more abstract. I paint Julian's face, too. I do it from memory, and it bothers me that I can't quite capture the devastating perfection of his features. No matter how much I try, I can't seem to get it right.

All of my friends are away at college, so for the first couple of weeks, I only speak to them on the phone and via Skype. They don't quite know how to act around me, and I don't blame them. I try to keep our conversations light, focusing mostly on what's been happening in their lives since our graduation, but I know they feel strange talking about boyfriend troubles and exams to someone they see as a victim of a horrible crime. They look at me with pity and disturbing curiosity in their eyes, and I can't bring myself to talk to them about my experience on the island.

Still, when Leah comes home from the University of Michigan, we get together to hang out. After a few hugs, most of the initial awkwardness dissipates, and she's again the same girl who was my best friend all through middle school and beyond.

"I like your place," she says, walking around my studio and examining the paintings I have hanging on the walls. "That's some pretty cool art you've got there. Where did you get these from?"

"I painted them," I tell her, pulling on my boots. We're going out to a local Italian restaurant for dinner. I'm dressed in a pair of skinny jeans and a black top, and it feels just like old times.

"You did?" Leah gives me an astonished look. "Since when do you paint?"

"It's a recent development," I say, grabbing my trench coat. It's already fall, and it's starting to get chilly. I had gotten used to the tropical climate of the island, and even sixty degrees feels cold to me.

"Well, shit, Nora, this is really good stuff," she says, coming up to one of the explosion paintings to take a closer look. Those are the only ones I have up—my Julian portraits are private. "I didn't know you had it in you."

"Thanks." I grin at her. "Ready to go?"

* * *

We have a great dinner. Leah tells me about going to college at Michigan and about Jason, her new boyfriend. I listen attentively, and we joke about boys and their inexplicable need to do keg stands.

"When are you applying to college?" she asks when we're mid-way through dessert. "You were going to go local at first. Are you still planning to do that?"

I nod. "Yes, I think I'm going to apply for the spring semester." Although I can now afford to go to any university, I have no desire to change my plans. The money sitting in my bank account doesn't seem quite real to me, and I'm strangely reluctant to spend it.

"That's awesome," Leah says, grinning. She seems a little hyper, like she's overly excited about something.

I soon learn what that something is.

"Hey, Nora," a familiar voice says behind me, just as we're getting ready to pay our bill.

I jump up, startled. Turning, I stare at Jake—the boy I had been on the date with that fateful night when Julian took me.

The boy Julian had hurt to keep me in line.

He looks almost the same: shaggy sun-streaked hair, warm brown eyes, a great build. Only the expression on his face is different. It's drawn and tense, and the wariness in his gaze is like a kick to my stomach.

"Jake . . ." I feel like I'm confronting a ghost. "I didn't know you were in town. I thought you were away at Michigan—"

And then I realize the truth. Turning, I look accusingly at Leah, who gives me a huge smile in response. "I hope you don't mind, Nora," she says brightly. "I told Jake I was coming to see you this weekend, and he asked to join me. I wasn't sure how you'd feel about that, given everything"—her face reddens a bit—"so I just mentioned that we'd be here tonight."

I blink, my palms beginning to sweat. Leah doesn't know about the beating Jake received because of me. That little tidbit is something I disclosed only to the FBI. She's probably afraid that seeing Jake might bring back painful memories of my abduction, but she can't possibly guess at the nauseating swirl of guilt and anxiety I feel right now.

Jake knows I'm responsible for the assault, however. I can see it in the way he looks at me.

I force myself to smile. "Of course I don't mind," I lie smoothly. "Please, have a seat. Let's get some coffee." I motion toward the seat on the other side of our booth and sit down myself. "How have you been?"

He smiles back at me, his brown eyes crinkling at the corners in the way I found endearing once. He's still one of the cutest guys I've ever met, but I no longer feel any attraction to him. The crush I had on him before pales in comparison to my all-consuming Julian obsession—to the dark and desperate craving that makes me toss and turn at night.

When I can't sleep, I often think about the things Julian and I used to do together—the things he made me do . . . the things he trained me to want. In the dark of the night, I masturbate to forbidden fantasies. Fantasies of exquisite pain and forced pleasure, of violence and lust. I ache with the need to be taken and used, hurt and possessed. I long for Julian—the man who awakened this side of me.

The man who is now dead.

Pushing that excruciating thought aside, I focus on what Jake is telling me.

"—couldn't go into that park for months," he says, and I realize that he's talking about his experience after my abduction. "Every time I did, I thought about you and where you might be . . . The police said it was like you vanished off the face of the planet—"

I listen to him, shame and self-loathing coiling deep inside my chest. How can I feel this way about a man who did such a terrible thing and hurt so many people in the process? How sick am I to love someone capable of such evil? Julian was not a tortured, misunderstood hero forced to do bad things by circumstances beyond his control. He was a monster, pure and simple.

A monster that I miss with every fiber of my being.

"I'm so sorry, Nora," Jake says, distracting me from my self-flagellation. "I'm sorry I couldn't protect you that night—"

"Wait . . . What?" I stare at him in disbelief. "Are you crazy? Do you know what you were up against? There's no way you could've done anything—"

"I should've still tried." Jake's voice is heavy with guilt. "I should've done something, anything . . ."

I reach out across the table, impulsively covering his hand with my own. "No," I say firmly. "You're in no way to blame for this." I can see Leah out of the corner of my eye; she's twiddling with her phone and trying to pretend she's not here. I ignore her. I need to convince Jake that he didn't screw up, to help him move past this.

His skin is warm under my fingers, and I can feel the vibrating tension within him. "Jake," I say softly, holding his gaze, "nobody could've prevented this. Nobody. Julian has—*had*—the kind of resources that would make a SWAT team jealous. If it's anybody's fault, it's mine. You got dragged into this because of me, and I am truly sorry." I'm apologizing for more than that night in the park, and he knows it.

"No, Nora," he says quietly, his brown eyes filled with shadows. "You're right. It's *his* fault, not ours." And I realize that he's offering me absolution, too—that he also wants to free me from my guilt.

I smile and squeeze his hand, silently accepting his forgiveness.

I wish I could forgive myself so easily, but I can't.

Because even now, as I sit there holding Jake's hand, I can't stop loving Julian.

No matter what he had done.

CHAPTER TWENTY-SIX

"You know, I think he's still really into you," Leah says as she drives me home. "I'm surprised he didn't ask you out right then and there."

"Ask me out? Jake?" I give her an incredulous stare. "I'm the last girl he'd want to date."

"Oh, I wouldn't be too sure about that," she says thoughtfully. "You guys might've only been on one date, but he was seriously depressed when you disappeared. And the way he was looking at you tonight . . ."

I let out a nervous laugh. "Leah, please, that's just crazy. Jake and I have a complex history. He wanted closure tonight, that's all." The idea of dating Jake—of dating anyone—feels strange and foreign. In my mind, I still belong to Julian, and the thought of letting another man touch me makes me inexplicably anxious.

"Yeah, closure, right." Leah's voice is dripping with sarcasm. "The entire evening he was staring at you like you're the hottest thing he's ever seen. It's not closure he wants from you, I guarantee that."

"Oh, come on—"

"No, seriously," Leah says, glancing at me as she stops at a stoplight. "You should go out with him. He's a great guy, and I know you liked him before . . ."

I look at her, and the urge to make her understand wars with my deep-seated need to protect myself. "Leah, that was before," I say slowly, deciding to disclose some of the truth. "I'm not the same person now. I can't date a guy like Jake . . . not after Julian."

She falls silent, turning her attention back to the road as the light changes to green.

When she stops in front of my apartment building, she turns toward me. "I'm sorry," she says quietly. "That was stupid and inconsiderate of me. You seem so okay that I forgot for a moment . . ." She swallows, tears glistening in her eyes. "If you ever want to talk about it, I'm here for you—you know that, right?"

I nod, giving her a smile. I'm lucky to have a friend like her, and someday soon, I may take her up on her offer. But not yet—not while I feel so raw and shredded inside.

* * *

The next few weeks crawl by at a snail's pace. I exist moment to moment, taking it one day at a time. Every morning, I write out a list of tasks that I want to accomplish that day and diligently adhere to it, no matter how much I may want to crawl under my bed covers and never come out.

Most of the time, my lists include mundane activities, such as eating, running, going to work, doing grocery shopping, and calling my parents. Occasionally, I add more ambitious projects as well, such as applying to college for the spring semester—which I do, as I told Leah I would.

I also sign up for shooting lessons. To my surprise, I turn out to be pretty good at handling a gun. My instructor says I'm a natural, and I start doing research on what I need to do to acquire a firearms license in Illinois. I also tackle self-defense classes and start learning a few basic moves to protect myself. I will never be able to win against someone like Julian and the men who took me and Beth, but knowing how to shoot and fight makes me feel better, more in control of my life.

Between all those new activities, my work, and my art, I'm too busy to socialize, which suits me just fine. I'm not in the mood to make new friends, and all of my old ones are away.

Jake and Leah are both back at Michigan. He pings me on Facebook, and we chat a few times. He doesn't ask me out, though.

I'm glad. Even if he wasn't going to college three-and-a-half hours away, it would never work out between us. Jake is smart enough to realize that nothing good could ever come out of getting involved with someone like me—someone who, for all intents and purposes, is still Julian's captive.

I dream of him almost every night. Like an incubus, my former captor comes to me in the dark, when I'm at my most vulnerable. He invades my mind as ruthlessly as he once took my body. When I'm not reliving his death, my dreams are disturbingly sexual. I dream of his mouth, his cock, his hands. They're everywhere, all over me, inside me. I dream of his terrifyingly beautiful smile, of the way he used to hold and caress me.

Of the way he used to torture me until I forgot everything and lost myself in him.

I dream of him... and wake up wet and throbbing, my body empty and aching for his possession. Like an addict going through a withdrawal, I am desperate for a fix, for something to take the edge off my need.

I am not ready to date, but my body doesn't care about that—and finally, I decide to give in.

Dressing up, I grab my old fake ID and head to a local bar.

* * *

The men swarm around me like flies. It's easy, so fucking easy. A girl alone in a bar—that's all the encouragement they need. Like wolves scenting prey, they sense my desperation, my desire for something more than a cold, lonely bed tonight.

I let one of them buy me drinks. A shot of vodka, then one of tequila... By the time he asks me if I want to leave, everything around me is fuzzy. Nodding, I let him lead me to his car.

He's a good-looking man in his thirties, with sandy hair and blue-grey eyes. Not particularly tall, but reasonably well built. He's an attorney, he tells me as he drives us to a nearby motel.

I close my eyes as he continues talking. I don't care who he is or what he does. I just want him to fuck me, to fill that gaping void inside. To take away the chill that has seeped deep into my bones.

He rents a room at the front desk, and we go upstairs. When we get into the room, he takes off my coat and begins to kiss me. I can taste beer and a hint of tacos on his tongue. He presses me to him, his hands hot and eager as they begin to explore my body—and suddenly, I can't take it anymore.

"Stop." I shove him away as hard as I can. Taken by surprise, he stumbles back a couple of steps.

"What the fuck—" He gapes at me, mouth open in disbelief.

"I'm sorry," I say quickly, grabbing my coat. "It's not you, I promise."

And before he can say a word, I run out of the room.

Catching a taxi, I go home, sick from the alcohol and utterly miserable. There is no fix for my addiction, no way to quench my thirst.

Even drunk, I can't bear another man's touch.

CHAPTER TWENTY-SEVEN

It starts off as another erotic dream.

Strong, hard hands slide up my naked body, callused palms scratching my skin as he squeezes my breasts, his thumbs rubbing against my peaked, sensitive nipples. I arch against him, feeling the warmth of his skin, the heavy weight of his powerful body pressing me into the mattress. His muscular legs force my thighs apart, and his erection prods at my sex, the broad head sliding between the soft folds and exerting light pressure on my clit.

I moan, rubbing against him, my inner muscles clenching with the need to take him deep inside. I'm soaking wet and panting, and my hands grasp his tight, muscular ass, trying to force him in, to get him to fuck me.

He laughs, the sound a low, seductive rumble in his chest, and his big hands grasp my wrists, pinning them above my head. "Miss me, my pet?" he murmurs in my ear, his hot breath sending erotic chills down the side of my body.

My pet? Julian never talks in my dreams—

I gasp, my eyes popping open . . . and in the dim early morning light, I see *him*.

Julian.

Naked and aroused, he's sprawled on top of me, holding me down on my bed. His dark hair is cut shorter than before, and his magnificent face is taut with lust, his eyes glittering like blue jewels.

I freeze, staring up at him, my heart thudding heavily in my ribcage. For a moment, I think that I'm still dreaming—that my mind is playing cruel tricks on me. My vision dims, blurs, and I realize that I literally stopped breathing for a moment, that the shock has driven all air out of my lungs.

I inhale sharply, still frozen in place, and he lowers his head, his mouth descending on mine. His tongue slips between my parted lips, invading me, and the hauntingly familiar taste of him makes my head spin.

There is no longer any doubt in my mind.

It's really Julian—he's as alive and vital as ever.

Fury, sharp and sudden, spikes through me. He's alive—he's been alive all along! The entire time while I mourned him, while I tried to mend my shattered soul, he's been alive and well, undoubtedly laughing at my pathetic attempts to get on with my life.

I bite his lip, hard, filled with the savage need to hurt him—to rip his flesh as he ripped apart my heart. The coppery tang of blood fills my mouth, and he jerks back with a curse, his eyes darkening with anger.

I'm not afraid, however. Not anymore. "Let me go," I hiss furiously, struggling against his hold. "You fucking asshole! You bastard! You were never dead! You were never fucking dead . . ." To my complete humiliation, the last phrase escapes as a choked sob, my voice breaking at the end.

His jaw tightens as he stares at me, the sensuous perfection of his lips marred by the bloody mark from my teeth. He holds me effortlessly, his hard cock poised at the soft entrance to my body. Enraged, I twist to the side, trying to bite him again, and he transfers my wrists into his left palm, restraining me with one hand while grabbing my hair with the other. Now I can't move at all; all I can do is glare at him, tears of rage and bitter frustration burning my eyes.

Unexpectedly, his expression softens. "Looks like my little kitten grew some claws," he murmurs, his voice filled with dark amusement. "I think I like it."

I literally see red. "Fuck you!" I shriek, bucking against him, heedless of our naked bodies rubbing together. "Fuck you and what you like—"

His mouth swoops down on me, swallowing my angry words, and my teeth snap at him in another biting attempt. He jerks away at the last second, laughing softly. At the same time, the head of his cock begins to push inside me. Maddened beyond bearing, I scream—and his right hand releases my hair, slapping over my mouth instead. "Shhh," he whispers in my ear, ignoring my muffled cries. "We wouldn't want your neighbors to hear, now would we?"

At this moment, I couldn't care if the whole world heard us. I'm filled with the primitive need to lash out at him, to hurt him as he hurt me. If I had a gun with me, I would've gladly shot him for the agony he put me through.

But I don't have a gun. I don't have anything, and he slowly pushes deeper into my vulnerable opening, his thick cock stretching me, penetrating me with its heated hardness. I'm still wet from my earlier 'dream,' but I'm also tense with anger, and my body protests the intrusion, all of my muscles tightening to keep him out. It's like our first time again—except that the twister of emotions in my chest right now is far more complex than the fear I once felt. My struggles gradually dying down, I gaze up at him mutely, reeling from the shock of his return.

When he's all the way inside me, he stops, slowly lifting his hand from my mouth.

I remain silent, tears spilling out of the corners of my eyes.

Lowering his head, he kisses me gently, as though apologizing for taking me so ruthlessly. My lungs cease to work; as always, this peculiar mix of cruelty and tenderness turns me inside out, wreaking havoc on my already-conflicted mind.

"I'm sorry, baby," he murmurs, his lips brushing against my tear-wet cheek. "It wasn't supposed to happen like that. You were mine to protect and I fucked up. I fucked up so fucking bad . . ." He exhales softly. "I never meant to leave you, never meant to let you go—"

"But you did." My voice is small and hurt, like that of a wounded child. "You let me think you were dead—"

"No." He lets go of my wrists and props himself up on his elbows, framing my face with his big hands. His eyes burn into mine so intensely, I feel like he's consuming me with his gaze. "It wasn't like that. It wasn't like that at all."

My hands slowly lower to his shoulders. "What was it like then?" I ask bitterly. How could he have done this to me? How could he have stolen me, taken everything from me, only to abandon me so cruelly?

"I'll explain everything," he promises, his voice low and thick with lust. There's sweat beading up on his brow, and I can feel his cock throbbing deep within me. He's holding on to his control by a shred.

"But right now, I need you, Nora. I need this . . ." He thrusts his hips forward, and I moan as he hits my G-spot, sending a blast of sensation through my nerve endings.

"That's right," he whispers harshly, repeating the motion. "I need this. I want to feel your tight little pussy sheathing me like a glove. I want to fuck you, and I want to fucking *devour* you. Every single inch of you is mine, Nora, only mine . . ." He lowers his head again, taking my mouth in a deep, penetrating kiss as he continues thrusting into me with a slow, relentless rhythm.

My own breathing picks up, a rush of heat flooding my body. My fingers tighten on his shoulders, and my legs wrap around his muscular thighs, taking him deeper into me. After months of abstinence, it's almost too much, but I welcome the slight burn, the exquisite pleasure-pain of his possession. I can feel the tension growing inside me, the delicious prickling of pre-orgasmic bliss, and then I explode with a strangled cry, my inner muscles clamping tightly around his thick cock.

"Yes, baby, that's it," he groans hoarsely, his pace picking up, and then, with one last, powerful thrust, he finds his own peak, his shaft pulsing deep within me. I can feel the warmth of his seed releasing inside me, and I hold him close as he collapses on top of me, his large body heavy and covered with sweat.

* * *

"Do you want coffee or tea?" I ask, glancing at Julian as I putter around the tiny kitchen in the corner of my studio. He's sitting at the table by the wall, wearing a pair of jeans—the only thing he deigned to put on after his shower. His bronzed, rippled torso draws my eyes, and my hand shakes slightly as I reach for a cup. With his hair cut short, his cheekbones appear sharper, his features even more chiseled than before. Frowning, I take a closer look. He seems thinner than I recall him being, almost as if he lost some weight.

Ignoring my staring, Julian leans back in the flimsy chair I bought at IKEA, stretching out his long legs. His feet are bare and strikingly masculine. "Coffee would be great," he says lazily, watching me with a heavy-lidded gaze.

He reminds me of a panther patiently stalking its prey.

I swallow, placing the cup on the counter and reaching for the coffeemaker. Unlike him, I'm wearing jeans, thick socks, and a fleece sweater. Being fully dressed makes me feel less vulnerable, more in control.

The whole thing is surreal. If it weren't for the slight soreness between my thighs, I would've been convinced that I am hallucinating. But no, my captor—the man who had been the center of my existence for so long—is here in my tiny apartment, dominating it with his powerful presence.

After the coffee is ready, I pour each of us a cup and join him at the table. I feel off-balance, like I'm walking on a tightrope. One second I want to scream with joy that he's alive, and the next I want to kill him for putting me through this torture. And through it all, at the back of my mind is the knowledge that neither of those is an appropriate response for this situation. By all rights, I should be trying to escape and call the police.

Julian doesn't seem the least bit afraid of that possibility. He's as comfortable and self-assured in my studio as he was on his island. Picking up his cup, he takes a sip of the coffee and looks at me, a mesmerizing half-smile playing on his beautiful lips.

I curve my hands around my own cup, enjoying the warmth between my palms. "How did you survive the explosion?" I ask quietly, holding his gaze.

His mouth twists slightly. "I very nearly didn't. When they saw that they were losing, one of those suicidal motherfuckers set off a bomb. Two of my men and I happened to be near the ladder to the basement, and we dove into the opening at the last minute. A section of the floor collapsed on me, knocking me out and killing one of the men who was with me. Luckily for me, the other one—Lucas—survived and remained conscious. He managed to drag both of us into the drainpipe, and there was enough fresh air coming in from the outside that we didn't die of smoke inhalation."

I draw in a shaky breath. *The drainpipe . . .* That was the only place I hadn't looked that horrific day when I spent hours combing through the burning ruins of the building. I had been so dazed and shellshocked, it hadn't even occurred to me to check there for survivors.

"By the time Lucas got us both to a hospital, I was in pretty bad shape," Julian continues, looking at me. "I had a cracked skull and

189

several broken bones. The doctors put me in a medically induced coma to deal with the swelling in my brain, and I didn't regain consciousness until a few weeks ago." Lifting his hand, he touches his short hair, and I realize the reason for his new haircut. They must've shaved his head in the hospital.

My hand trembles as I lift my cup to take a sip. He had almost died after all—not that it makes his absence for the past few weeks any more forgivable. "Why didn't you contact me at that point? Why didn't you let me know you were alive?" How could he let my torture continue even a day longer than necessary?

He tilts his head to the side. "And then what?" he asks, his voice dangerously silky. "What would you have done, my pet? Rushed to my side to be with me in Thailand? Or would you have told your pals at the FBI where I could be found, so they could get me while I was weak and helpless?"

I inhale sharply. "I wouldn't have told them—"

"No?" He shoots me a sardonic look. "You think I don't know that you talked to them? That they now have my name and picture?"

"I only spoke to them because I thought you were dead!" I jump to my feet, nearly upending my coffee cup. All of my anger suddenly surfaces. Furious, I grip the edge of the table and glare at him. "I never betrayed you, even though I should have—"

He rises to his feet, unfolding his tall, muscular body with athletic grace. "Yes, you probably should have," he agrees softly, his gaze darkening as we stare at each other across the table. "You should've turned me in at that clinic in the Philippines and run as far and fast as you can, my pet."

I run my tongue over my dry lips. "Would that have helped?"

"No. I would've found you anywhere."

My stomach twists with excitement and a dollop of fear. He's not joking. I can see it on his face. He would've come for me, and no one could've stopped him.

"Who are you?" I breathe, staring at him incredulously. "Why was there no record of you in any of the government databases? If you're a big-time arms dealer, why hasn't the FBI heard about you before?"

He looks at me, his eyes strikingly blue in his darkly tanned face. "Because I have a wide network of connections, Nora," he says quietly. "And because, as part of my interactions with my clients, I occasionally come across some information that the United States government finds valuable—information that relates to the safety and security of the American public."

My jaw drops. "You're a spy?"

"No." He laughs. "Not in the traditional sense of the word. I'm not on anyone's payroll—we simply exchange favors. I help your government, and in return, they make me invisible to all. Only a few of the highest-level officials in the CIA know that I exist at all." He pauses, then adds softly, "Or at least, that was the case before the FBI got their hands on you, my pet. Now it's a bit more complicated, and I'll have to call in quite a few of those favors to get this information erased."

"I see," I say evenly. My head is spinning. The man who kidnapped me is working with my government. It's almost more than I can process right now.

He smiles, visibly enjoying my confusion. "Don't over-think it, my pet," he advises, his eyes gleaming with amusement. "Just because I help prevent an occasional terrorist attack doesn't make me a good guy."

"No," I agree. "It doesn't." Turning away, I walk over to the small window and gaze outside. The sun is just beginning to come up, and there is a light layer of snow on the ground.

The first snow of the season—it must've fallen overnight.

I don't hear him moving, but suddenly he's behind me, his large arms folding around me, pressing me against his body. I can smell the clean male scent of his skin, and some of the residual tension drains out of me. *Julian is alive.*

"So where do we go from here?" I ask, still staring at the snow. "Are you taking me back to the island?"

He's silent for a moment. "No," he says finally. "I can't. Not without Beth there." There is a tight note in his voice, and I realize that he's missing her too, that he feels her loss just as acutely.

I turn around in his embrace and look up at him, placing my hands on his chest. "I'm glad those motherfuckers are dead." The words come out in a low, fierce hiss. "I'm glad you killed them all."

"Yes," he says, and I see a reflection of my rage and pain in the hard glitter of his eyes. "The men who hurt her are dead, and I'm taking steps to wipe out their entire organization. By the time I'm done, Al-Quadar will be nothing more than a file in government archives."

I hold his gaze without blinking. "Good." I want them all destroyed. I want Julian to tear them apart and make them feel Beth's agony.

In this moment, we understand each other perfectly. He's a killer, and that's exactly what I need him to be. I don't want a sweet, gentle man with a conscience—I want a monster who will brutally avenge Beth's death.

A faint smile lifts the corners of his lips. Bending down, he kisses me lightly on the forehead, then releases me to walk over to the bed, where the rest of his clothes are.

Frowning, I watch as he pulls on a long-sleeved T-shirt, socks, and a pair of boots. "Are you leaving?" I ask, feeling like a cold fist is squeezing my heart at the thought.

"No," he replies, putting on his leather jacket and walking over to my closet. "*We* are leaving." Opening the closet door, he pulls out my winter coat and warm boots and tosses them to me.

I catch the coat on auto-pilot and put it on. "Are you kidnapping me again?" I ask, pulling on the boots.

"I don't know." Coming up to me, he cups my face in his hand, his thumb rubbing lightly against my lower lip. "Am I?"

I don't know either. For the first time in months, I feel alive. I feel emotions again, sharp and bright. Fear, excitement, exhilaration.

Love.

It's not the sweet, tender kind of love I always dreamed of, but it's love. Dark, twisted, and obsessive, it's both a compulsion and an addiction. I know the world will condemn me for my choices, but I need Julian as much as he needs me.

"What if I don't want to go with you?" I don't know why I feel the need to ask. I already know the answer.

He smiles. Dropping his hand from my face, he reaches into the pocket of his jacket and pulls out a small syringe, showing it to me.

"I see," I say calmly. He's come prepared for any eventuality.

He puts the syringe away and offers me his hand. I hesitate for a moment, then I put my hand in his large palm. He curls his fingers around mine, and his eyes look impossibly blue in that moment, almost radiant.

We walk out together, holding hands like a couple. He leads me to a car that's waiting for us—a black car with window glass that looks to be unusually thick. Likely bulletproof.

He opens the door for me, and I climb inside.

As the car takes off, he pulls me closer to him, and I bury my face in the crook of his neck, breathing in his familiar scent.

For the first time in months, I feel like I'm home.

Keep Me
Twist Me: Book 2

PART I: THE ARRIVAL

CHAPTER ONE

❖ JULIAN ❖

There are days when the urge to hurt, to kill, is too strong to be denied. Days when the thin cloak of civilization threatens to slip at the least provocation, revealing the monster inside.

Today is not one of those days.

Today I have her with me.

We're in the car on the way to the airport. She's sitting pressed against my side, her slim arms wrapped around me and her face buried in the crook of my neck.

Cradling her with one arm, I stroke her dark hair, delighting in its silky texture. It's long now, reaching all the way down to her narrow waist. She hasn't cut her hair in nineteen months.

Not since I kidnapped her for the first time.

Inhaling, I draw in her scent—light and flowery, deliciously feminine. It's a combination of some shampoo and her unique body chemistry, and it makes my mouth water. I want to strip her bare and follow that scent everywhere, to explore every curve and hollow of her body.

My cock twitches, and I remind myself that I just fucked her. It doesn't matter, though. My lust for her is constant. It used to bother me, this obsessive craving, but now I'm used to it. I've accepted my own madness.

She seems calm, content even. I like that. I like to feel her cuddled against me, all soft and trusting. She knows my true nature, yet she still feels safe with me. I have trained her to feel that way.

I have made her love me.

After a couple of minutes, she stirs in my arms, lifting her head to look at me. "Where are we going?" she asks, blinking, her long black lashes sweeping up and down like fans. She has the kind of eyes that could bring a man to his knees—soft, dark eyes that make me think of tangled sheets and naked flesh.

I force myself to focus. Those eyes fuck with my concentration like nothing else. "We're going to my home in Colombia," I say, answering her question. "The place where I grew up."

I haven't been there for years—not since my parents were murdered. However, my father's compound is a fortress, and that's precisely what we need right now. In the past few weeks, I've implemented additional security measures, making the place virtually impregnable. Nobody will take Nora from me again—I've made sure of that.

"Are you going to be there with me?" I can hear the hopeful note in her voice, and I nod, smiling.

"Yes, my pet, I'll be there." Now that I have her back, the compulsion to keep her near is too strong to deny. The island had once been the safest place for her, but no longer. Now they know of her existence—and they know she's my Achilles' heel. I need to have her with me, where I can protect her.

She licks her lips, and my eyes follow the path of her delicate pink tongue. I want to wrap her thick hair around my fist and force her head down to my lap, but I resist the urge. There will be plenty of time for that later, when we're in a more secure—and less public—location.

"Are you going to send my parents another million dollars?" Her eyes are wide and guileless as she looks at me, but I can hear the subtle challenge in her voice. She's testing me—testing the bounds of this new stage of our relationship.

My smile broadens, and I reach over to tuck a strand of hair behind her ear. "Do you want me to send it to them, my pet?"

She stares at me without blinking. "Not really," she says softly. "I would much rather call them instead."

I hold her gaze. "All right. You can call them once we get there."

Her eyes widen, and I see that I surprised her. She was expecting that I would keep her captive again, cut off from the outside world. What she doesn't realize is that it's no longer necessary.

I've succeeded in what I set out to do.

I've made her completely mine.

"Okay," she says slowly, "I'll do that."

She's looking at me like she can't quite figure me out—like I'm some exotic animal she's never seen before. She often looks at me like that, with a mixture of wariness and fascination. She's drawn to me— she's been drawn to me from the very beginning—yet she's still afraid of me on some level.

The predator in me likes that. Her fear, her reluctance—they add a certain edge to the whole thing. It makes it that much sweeter to possess her, to feel her curled up in my arms every night.

"Tell me about your time at home," I murmur, settling her more comfortably against my shoulder. Brushing back her hair with my fingers, I look down at her upturned face. "What have you been up to all these months?"

Her soft lips curve in a self-deprecating smile. "You mean, besides missing you?"

A warm sensation spreads through my chest. I don't want to acknowledge it. I don't want it to matter. I want her to love me because I have a sick compulsion to own all of her—not because I feel anything in return. "Yes, besides that," I say quietly, thinking of the many ways I'm going to fuck her when I get her alone again.

"Well, I met with some of my friends," she begins, and I listen as she gives me a general overview of her life over the past four months. I already know much of this, since Lucas had taken the initiative to put a discreet security detail on Nora while I had been in a coma. As soon as I woke up, he gave me a thorough report on everything, including Nora's daily activities.

I owe him for that—and for saving my life. Over the past few years, Lucas Kent has become an invaluable part of my organization. Few others would've had the balls to step up like that. Even without knowing the full truth about Nora, he had been smart enough to infer that she means something to me and take steps to ensure her safety.

Of course, the one thing he didn't do was restrict her activities in any way. "So did you see him?" I ask casually, lifting my hand to play with her earlobe. "Jake, I mean?"

Her body turns into stone in my arms. I can feel the rigid tension in each muscle. "I ran into him briefly, after dinner with my friend Leah," she says evenly, looking up at me. "We had some coffee together, the three of us, and that was the only time I saw him."

I hold her gaze for a second, then nod, satisfied. She didn't lie to me. The reports had mentioned that particular incident. When I first read about it, I wanted to kill the boy with my bare hands.

I still might do that, if he approaches Nora ever again.

The thought of another man near her fills me with white-hot fury. According to the reports, she didn't date during our time apart—with one notable exception. "How about that lawyer?" I ask softly, doing my best to control the rage boiling inside me. "Did the two of you have a good time?"

Her face turns pale underneath her golden skin tone. "I didn't do anything with him," she says, and I can hear the apprehension in her voice. "I went out that night because I was missing you, because I was tired of being alone, but nothing happened. I had a couple of drinks, but I still couldn't go through with it."

"No?" Much of the anger drains out of me. I can read her well enough to know when she's lying—and right now she's telling the truth. Still, I make a mental note to have this investigated further. If the lawyer touched her in any way, he'll pay.

She looks at me, and I can feel her own tension dissipating. She can discern my moods like no one else. It's as if she's attuned to me on some level. It's been that way with her from the very beginning. Unlike most women, she's always been able to sense the real me.

"No." Her mouth tightens. "I couldn't let him touch me. I'm too fucked up to be with a normal man now."

I lift my eyebrows, amused despite myself. She's no longer the frightened girl I brought to the island. Somewhere along the way, my little pet grew some sharp claws and was starting to learn how to use them.

"That's good." I run my fingers playfully across her cheek, then bend my head to inhale her sweet scent. "Nobody is allowed to touch you, baby. Nobody but me."

She doesn't respond, just continues looking at me. She doesn't need to say anything. We understand each other perfectly. I know I will kill any man who lays a finger on her, and she knows it too.

It's strange, but I've never felt possessive about a woman before. This is new territory for me. Before Nora, women were all interchangeable in my mind—just soft, pretty creatures passing through my life. They came to me willingly, wanting to be fucked, to be hurt, and I indulged them, satisfying my own physical needs in the process.

I fucked my first woman when I was fourteen, shortly after Maria's death. She was one of my father's whores; he sent her to me after I dispatched two of the men who murdered Maria by castrating them in their own homes. I think my father was hoping the lure of sex would be enough to distract me from my path of vengeance.

Needless to say, his plan didn't work out.

She came into my room wearing a tight black dress, her makeup perfectly done and her lush, full mouth painted a glossy red. When she began to strip in front of me, I reacted just like any teenage boy would—with instant, violent lust. But I wasn't any teenage boy at that point. I was a killer; I had been one since I was eight.

I took the whore roughly that night, partly because I was too inexperienced to control myself, partly because I wanted to lash out at her, at my father, at the whole fucking world. I took my frustrations out on her flesh, leaving behind bruises and bite marks—and she came back for more the next night, this time without my father's knowledge. We fucked like that for a month, with her stealing into my room every chance she got, teaching me what she liked . . . what she claimed many women liked. She didn't want sweet and gentle in bed; she wanted pain and force. She wanted someone to make her feel alive.

And I found that I liked that. I liked hearing her scream and beg as I hurt her and made her come. The violence crawling under my skin had found another outlet, and it was one I used every chance I got.

It wasn't enough, of course. The rage dwelling deep within me couldn't be pacified so easily. Maria's death changed something inside me. She had been the only pure, beautiful thing in my life, and she was gone. Her death accomplished more than my father's training ever could: it killed any remaining conscience I might've possessed. I was no longer a boy reluctantly following in my father's footsteps; I was a predator who craved blood and vengeance. Ignoring my father's orders to let the matter drop, I hunted down Maria's killers one by one and made them pay, drinking in their screams of agony, their pleas for mercy and for quicker death.

After that, there were retaliations and counter-retaliations. People died. My father's men. His rival's men. The violence kept escalating until my father decided to pacify his associates by removing me from the business. I was sent away, to Europe and Asia . . . and there I found dozens more women like the one who had introduced me to sex. Beautiful, willing women whose proclivities mirrored my own. I gave them their dark fantasies, and they gave me momentary pleasure—an arrangement that suited my life perfectly, especially after I came back to take up the reins of my father's organization.

It wasn't until nineteen months ago, during a business trip to Chicago, that I found *her*.

Nora.

My Maria reincarnated.

The girl I intend to keep forever.

CHAPTER TWO

❖ NORA ❖

Sitting there in Julian's embrace, I feel the familiar hum of excitement mixed with trepidation. Our separation hasn't changed him one bit. He's still the same man who almost killed Jake, who didn't hesitate to kidnap a girl he wanted.

He's also the man who nearly died rescuing me.

Now that I know what happened to him, I can see the physical signs of his ordeal. He's leaner than before, his tan skin stretched tightly over sharp cheekbones. There is a ragged pink scar on his left ear, and his dark hair is extra-short. On the left side of his skull, the growth pattern of that hair is a bit uneven, as though it's concealing a scar there as well.

Despite those tiny imperfections, he's still the most gorgeous man I've ever seen. I can't tear my eyes away from him.

He's alive. Julian is alive, and I'm with him again.

It still seems so surreal. Up until this morning, I thought he was dead. I was convinced he had died in the explosion. For four long, excruciating months, I had been forcing myself to be strong, to get on with my life and try to forget the man sitting next to me right now.

The man who stole my freedom.

The man I love.

Raising my left hand, I gently trace the outline of his lips with my index finger. He's got the most incredible mouth I have ever seen—a mouth made for sin. At my touch, his beautiful lips part, and he catches the tip of my finger with his sharp white teeth, biting down on it lightly, then sucking my finger into his mouth.

A tremor of arousal runs through me as his warm, wet tongue laves my finger. My inner muscles clench, and I can feel my underwear getting damp. God, I'm so easy when it comes to him. One look, one touch, and I want him. My sex feels swollen and slightly sore after the way he fucked me earlier, but my body aches for him to take me again.

Julian is alive, and he's taking me away again.

As that fact begins to sink in, I pull my finger away from his lips, a sudden chill feathering over my skin and cooling my desire. There's no turning back now, no possibility of changing my mind. Julian is again in charge of my life, and this time I'd willingly flown into the spider's web, placing myself at his mercy.

Of course, it wouldn't have mattered if I had been unwilling, I remind myself. I remember the syringe in Julian's pocket, and I know that the outcome would've been the same regardless. Conscious or sedated, I would've been accompanying him today. For some messed-up reason, that fact makes me feel better, and I place my head back on Julian's shoulder, letting myself relax against him.

It's futile to fight against one's destiny, and I'm starting to accept that fact.

* * *

With traffic, our ride to the airport takes a little over an hour. To my surprise, we don't go to O'Hare. Instead we end up at a small airstrip where a sizable plane awaits our arrival. I can make out the letters 'G650' on its tail.

"Is that yours?" I ask as Julian opens the car door for me.

"Yes." He doesn't look at me or elaborate further. Instead his gaze appears to be scanning our surroundings, as though looking for hidden threats. There is an alertness to his manner that I don't remember seeing before, and for the first time, I realize that the island was his sanctuary as well, a place where he could truly relax and let down his guard.

As soon as I climb out, Julian grips my elbow and ushers me toward the plane. The driver follows us. I didn't see him before, as a panel separated the backseat area of the car from the front, so now I sneak a glance at him as we walk toward the plane.

The guy must be one of Julian's Navy SEALs. His blond hair is cut short, and his pale eyes are ice-cold in his square-jawed face. He's even taller than Julian, and he moves with the same athletic, warrior-like grace, his every movement carefully controlled. There is a huge assault rifle in his hands, and I have no doubt that he knows exactly how to use it. Another dangerous man... one that many women would undoubtedly find attractive, with his regular features and muscular body. He doesn't appeal to me, but I'm spoiled. Few men can hold a candle to Julian's dark-angel allure.

"What kind of a plane is this?" I ask Julian as we walk up the steps and enter a luxurious cabin. I don't know anything about private jets, but this one looks fancy. I'm doing my best not to gawk at everything, but I'm failing miserably. The cream-colored leather seats inside are huge, and there is an actual couch with a coffee table in front of it. There is also an open door leading to the back of the airplane, and I catch a glimpse of a king-size bed sitting there.

My mouth falls open in shock. *The plane has a bedroom.*

"It's one of the higher-end Gulfstreams," he replies, turning me so he can help me take off my coat. His warm hands brush against my neck, sending a pleasant shiver through me. "An ultra-long-range business jet. It can take us directly to our destination without needing to make a fuel stop."

"It's very nice," I say, watching as Julian hangs my coat in the closet by the door and then takes off his own jacket. I can't take my eyes off him, and I realize that a part of me still fears that this is not real—that I'll wake up and find out that this was all just a dream... that Julian had truly died in the explosion.

The thought causes a shudder to run through me, and Julian notices my involuntary movement. "Are you cold?" he asks, stepping toward me. "I can have the temperature adjusted."

"No, I'm fine." Nevertheless, I enjoy Julian's warmth as he pulls me toward him and rubs my arms for a few seconds. I can feel the heat of his body seeping through my clothes, chasing away the memory of those awful months when I thought I'd lost him.

Wrapping my arms around Julian's waist, I hug him fiercely. He's alive, and I have him with me. That's all that matters now.

"We're ready for takeoff." An unfamiliar male voice startles me, and I let go of Julian, looking back to see the blond driver standing there, watching us with an unreadable expression on his hard face.

"Good." Julian keeps his arm around me, pressing me against his side when I try to step away. "Nora, this is Lucas. He's the one who dragged me out of the warehouse."

"Oh, I see." I beam at the man, my smile wide and genuine. This man had saved Julian's life. "It's very nice to meet you, Lucas. I can't even begin to thank you for what you did—"

His eyebrows arch a little, as though I said something that surprised him. "I was just doing my job," he says, his voice deep and slightly amused.

The corner of Julian's mouth lifts in a faint smile, but he doesn't respond to that. Instead he asks, "Is everything ready for us at the estate?"

Lucas nods. "All set." Then he looks at me, his face as expressionless as before. "It's nice to meet you too, Nora." And turning around, he disappears into the pilot's area at the front.

"He drives *and* flies planes for you?" I ask Julian after Lucas is gone.

"He's very versatile," Julian says, leading me toward the plush seats. "Most of my men are."

As soon as we sit down, a strikingly beautiful dark-haired woman comes into the cabin from somewhere in the front. Her white dress appears to have been poured on her curves, and with the full layer of makeup she has on, she looks as glamorous as a movie star—except for the tray with a champagne bottle and two glasses she's holding in her hands.

Her gaze lands on me briefly before sliding over to Julian. "Would you like anything else, Mr. Esguerra?" she asks as she bends down to place the tray on the table between our seats. Her voice is soft and melodic, and the hungry way she looks at Julian sets my teeth on edge.

"This should suffice for now. Thank you, Isabella," he says, giving her a brief smile, and I feel a sudden sharp stab of jealousy. Julian told me once that he hadn't fucked anyone else since meeting me, but I still can't help wondering if he had sex with this woman at some point in the past. She looks like a bombshell, and her manner makes it clear she would be more than willing to bring Julian anything he wants—including herself, naked on a silver platter.

Before my thoughts can travel any further down that road, I take a deep breath and force myself to look out the window at the slowly falling snow. A part of me knows that this whole thing is insane, that it's illogical to feel so possessive about Julian. Any rational woman would be overjoyed to have her kidnapper's attention deflected away from her, but I'm no longer rational when it comes to him.

Stockholm Syndrome. Capture-bonding. Traumatic bonding. My therapist had used all of these terms during our few brief sessions together. She had been trying to get me to talk about my feelings for Julian, but it had been too painful for me to discuss the man I'd thought I lost, so I stopped going to her. I did look up the terms later, though, and I can see why they would be applicable to my experience. I don't know if it's as simple as that, though, or if it even matters at this point. Naming something doesn't make it go away. Whatever the cause of my emotional attachment to Julian, I can't turn it off. I can't make myself love him any less.

By the time I turn back to face Julian, the flight attendant is gone from the main cabin. I can hear the jet engines roaring to life, and I automatically fasten my safety belt, as I'd been taught to do my whole life.

"Champagne?" he asks, reaching for the bottle at the table.

"Sure, why not," I say, and watch him deftly pour me a glass.

He hands it to me, and I sit back in my spacious seat, sipping the bubbly drink as the plane starts rolling.

My new life with Julian has begun.

CHAPTER THREE

❖ JULIAN ❖

Sipping from my own glass, I study Nora as she looks out the window at the rapidly shrinking ground below. She's wearing jeans and a blue fleece sweater, her small feet clad in a pair of chunky-looking black sheepskin boots. Uggs, I think they're called. Despite that off-putting footwear, she still looks sexy—though I far prefer seeing her in summer dresses, her smooth skin glowing in the sun.

Watching her calm expression, I wonder what she's thinking, if she has any regrets.

She shouldn't. I would've taken her regardless.

As though sensing my gaze on her, she turns toward me. "How did they find out about me?" she asks quietly. "The men who kidnapped me, I mean. How did they learn of my existence?"

At her question, my entire body tenses. My mind flashes back to those hellish hours after the attack on the clinic, and for a moment, I'm gripped by that same volatile mix of burning fury and paralyzing fear.

She could've died. She would've died, if I hadn't found her in time. Even if I'd given them what they wanted, they would've still killed her to punish me for not giving in to their demands sooner. I would've lost her, just like I lost Maria.

Just like we both lost Beth.

"It was the nursing assistant at the clinic." My voice comes out sounding cold and distant as I place my champagne glass back on the tray. "Angela. She was on Al-Quadar's payroll all along."

Nora's eyes glitter brightly. "That bitch," she whispers, and I can hear the pain and anger in her voice. Her hand shakes as she puts down her own glass on the table. "That fucking bitch."

I nod, trying to control my own rage as images from the video Majid sent me slide through my mind. They tortured Beth before killing her. They made her suffer. Beth, whose life had held nothing but suffering since her asshole of a father sold her to a brothel across the Mexican border at the age of thirteen. Who had been one of the very few people whose loyalty I never questioned.

They made her suffer . . . and now I will make them suffer worse.

"Where is she now?" Nora's question brings me out of a pleasurable reverie where I have each member of Al-Quadar strung up and at my mercy. When I look at her blankly, she clarifies, "Angela."

I smile at her naïve question. "You don't have to worry about her, my pet." All that remains of Angela are ashes, scattered on the lawn of the clinic in the Philippines. Peter's brand of questioning is brutal but effective, and he always disposes of the evidence afterwards. "She paid for her betrayal."

Nora swallows, and I know she understands exactly what I mean. She's no longer the same girl I met in that club in Chicago. I can see the shadows in her eyes, and I know I'm responsible for putting them there. Despite my best efforts to keep her sheltered on the island, the ugliness of my world touched her, tainted her innocence.

Al-Quadar will pay for that as well.

The scar on my head begins to throb, and I touch it lightly with my left hand. My head still aches occasionally, but other than that, I'm almost back to my normal self. Considering that I spent a good portion of the last four months as a vegetable, I'm quite content with this state of affairs.

"Are you all right?" There is a concerned expression on Nora's face as she reaches up to touch the area above my left ear. Her slender fingers are gentle on my scalp. "Does it still hurt?"

Her touch sends pleasure streaking down my spine. I want this from her. I want her to care about my well-being. I want her to love me even though I stole her freedom—even though, by all rights, she should hate me.

I have no illusions about myself. I'm one of those men they show on the news—the ones that everyone fears and despises. I took a young woman because I wanted her and for no other reason.

I took her, and I made her mine.

I make no excuses for my actions. I feel no guilt either. I wanted Nora, and now she's here with me, looking at me like I'm the most important person in her world.

And I am. I am exactly what she needs now . . . what she craves. I will give her everything, and I will take everything from her in return. Her body, her mind, her devotion—I want it all. I want her pain and her pleasure, her fear and her joy.

I want to be her entire life.

"No, it's fine," I say in response to her earlier question. "It's almost healed."

She pulls her fingers away, and I catch her hand, not ready to forego the pleasure of her touch. Her hand is slim and delicate in my grasp, her skin soft and warm. She tries to tug it away reflexively, but I don't let her, my fingers tightening around her small palm. Her strength is insignificant compared to mine; she can't make me release her unless I choose to let her go.

She doesn't really want me to let her go, anyway. I can feel the excitement rising within her, and my body hardens, a dark hunger awakening within me again. Reaching across the table, I slowly and purposefully unbuckle her safety belt.

Then I stand up, still holding her hand, and lead her to the bedroom at the back of the airplane.

* * *

She's silent as we enter the room and I close the door behind us. The area is not soundproof, but Isabella and Lucas are at the front of the plane, so we should have some privacy. I don't normally care if someone hears or sees me having sex, but what I do with Nora is different. She's mine, and I don't intend to share her. In any way.

Letting go of her hand, I walk over to the bed and sit down on it, leaning back and crossing my legs at the ankles. A casual pose, though there's nothing casual in the way I feel as I look at her.

The desire to possess her is violent, all-consuming. It's an obsession that goes beyond a simple sexual need, though my body burns for her. I don't just want to fuck her; I want to imprint myself on her, to mark her from the inside out, so that she will never belong to any man but me.

I want to own her completely.

"Take off your clothes," I order, holding her gaze. My dick is so hard, it's as though it's been months, instead of hours, since I had her. It takes all of my self-restraint not to rip off her clothes, bend her over the bed, and pound into her flesh until I explode.

I control myself because I don't want a quick fuck. I have other things in mind for today.

Taking a deep breath, I force myself to stay still, watching as she slowly begins to disrobe. Her face is flushed, her breathing coming faster, and I know she's already aroused, her pussy hot and slick, primed for me. At the same time, I can feel the hesitation in her movements, see the wariness in her eyes. There is a part of her that still fears me, that knows what I'm capable of.

She's right to be afraid. There is something within me that thrives on the pain of others, that wants to hurt them.

That wants to hurt *her*.

She takes off her fleece sweater first, revealing a black tank top underneath. Her pink bra straps peek through, and the innocent color excites me for some reason, sending a fresh surge of blood straight to my cock. The tank top comes off next, and by the time she's pulled off her boots and jeans, I'm all but ready to explode.

In her pink matching bra-and-panties set, she's the most delectable creature I have ever seen. Her petite body is fit and toned, the muscles in her arms and legs subtly defined. Despite her slenderness, she is undeniably feminine, her ass perfectly curved and her small breasts surprisingly round. With her long hair flowing down her back, she looks like a Victoria's Secret model in miniature. The only flaw is a small scar on the right side of her flat stomach—the reminder of her appendectomy.

I have to touch her.

"Come here," I say hoarsely, my cock straining painfully against the fly of my jeans.

Staring at me with her huge dark eyes, she approaches cautiously, uncertainly, as though I might attack her at any time.

I suck in another deep breath to prevent myself from doing exactly that. Instead, when she reaches me, I lean forward and firmly grip her waist, drawing her toward me so that she's standing between my legs. Her skin is cool and smooth to the touch, her ribcage so narrow that I can almost encircle her waist with my hands. It would be so easy to damage her, to break her. Her vulnerability turns me on almost as much as her beauty.

Reaching up, I find the clasp of her bra and release her breasts from their confinement.

As the bra slips down her arms, my mouth goes dry and my entire body tightens. Even though I've seen her naked hundreds of times, each time is a revelation. Her nipples are small, pinkish-brown in color, and her breasts are the same light golden hue as the rest of her body. Unable to resist, I cup those soft, round mounds in my hands, squeezing them, kneading them. Her flesh is sleek and firm, her nipples stiff against my palms. I can hear the catch in her breathing as my thumbs rub across those hardened peaks, and my hunger intensifies.

Releasing her breasts, I hook my fingers into the waistband of her underwear and push it down her legs, then cup her sex with my right hand. My middle finger pushes into her small opening, and the warm moisture I find there makes my cock jerk. She gasps as my callused thumb presses against her clit, and her hands reach up to grab my shoulders, her sharp little nails digging into my skin.

I can't wait any longer. I must have her.

"Get on the bed." My voice is thick with lust as I withdraw my hand from her pussy. "I want you on your stomach."

She scrambles to obey as I rise to my feet and begin to disrobe.

I've trained her well. By the time I've removed my own clothes, she's lying on her stomach fully naked, a pillow propping up her curvy little ass. Her arms are folded under her head, and her face is turned toward me. She's watching me with those thickly lashed eyes of hers, and I can sense her nervous anticipation. She both desires and fears me in this moment.

It turns me on, that look, but it also awakens another kind of hunger in me. A darker, more perverse need. Out of the corner of my eye, I spot the belt from my jeans lying on the floor. Picking it up, I wind the buckle end around my right hand and approach the bed.

Nora doesn't move, though I can see the anxious tension in her body. My lips twitch. *Such a good girl.* She knows it would go worse for her if she resists. Of course, by now she also knows that I will temper her pain with pleasure, that she will derive enjoyment from this too.

Pausing at the edge of the bed, I extend my free hand and trail my fingers along her spine. She trembles under my touch, a reaction that sends dark excitement surging through me. This is exactly what I want, what I need—this deep, twisted connection that exists between us. I want to drink in her fear, her pain. I want to hear her screams, feel her helpless struggles—and then have her melt in my arms as I bring her to ecstasy again and again.

For some reason, this small girl brings out the worst in me, makes me forget whatever shreds of morality I possess. She's the only woman I've ever forced into my bed, the only one I've wanted this much . . . and in such a wrong way. Having her here, at my mercy, is beyond heady—it's the most powerful drug I've ever tasted. I've never felt this way about another human being before, and the knowledge that she's mine, that I can do anything I want to her, is a rush unlike any other. With all those other women, it was a game we played, a way to scratch a mutual itch, but with Nora, it's different. With her, it's something more.

"Beautiful," I murmur, stroking the soft skin of her thighs and buttocks. Soon it will be marked, but for now I'm enjoying its smoothness. "So very, very beautiful . . ." Bending over her, I press a gentle kiss to the base of her spine, inhaling her warm female scent and letting the anticipation build. A shiver ripples through her, and I smile, adrenaline surging through my veins.

Straightening, I take a step back and swing the belt.

I don't use a lot of force, but she still jumps when the belt lands on the round globes of her ass, a soft whimper escaping her lips. She doesn't try to move or crawl away; instead her small fists grip the sheets tightly, and her eyes squeeze shut. I swing harder a second time, then again and again, my movements taking on a hypnotic, trance-like rhythm. With each stroke of the belt, I sink deeper and deeper into the blackness, my world narrowing until all I see, all I hear, all I feel is her. The reddening of her tender flesh, the pained gasps and sobs that issue from her throat, the way her body quivers and trembles under each stroke of my belt—I drink it all in, letting it feed my addiction, soothe the desperate hunger gnawing at my insides.

Time blurs and stretches. I don't know if it's been minutes or hours. When I finally stop, she's lying limp and unmoving, her buttocks and thighs covered with pink welts. There is a dazed, almost blissful expression on her tear-wet face, and her slender body is shaking, small tremors rippling over her skin.

Letting the belt drop to the floor, I carefully pick her up and sit down on the bed, holding her cradled on my lap. My own heart is hammering in my chest, my mind still reeling from the incredible rush I just experienced. She shudders, hiding her face against my shoulder, and begins to cry. I stroke her hair, slowly, soothingly, letting her come down from her endorphin-induced high as I come down from mine.

This is what I need now—to comfort her, to feel her in my arms. I want to be her everything: her protector and her tormentor, her joy and her sorrow. I want to bind her to me physically and emotionally, to brand myself so deeply on her mind and soul that she will never think about leaving me.

As her sobs begin to ease, my sexual hunger returns. My soothing caresses become more purposeful, my hands starting to roam over her body with an intent to arouse, not just to calm. My right hand slips between her thighs, my fingers pressing against her clit, and at the same time, my other hand grips her hair and pulls on it, forcing her to meet my gaze. She still looks dazed, her soft lips parted as she stares at me, and I lean down, taking her mouth in a deep, thorough kiss. She moans into my mouth, her hands clutching at my shoulders, and I can feel the heat rising between us. My balls draw up tightly against my body, my cock aching for her slick, warm flesh.

I stand up, still holding her in my arms, and place her on the bed. She winces, and I realize the sheets are rubbing against her welts, hurting her. "Turn over, baby," I whisper, wanting only her pleasure now. She obediently rolls over onto her stomach, in the same position as before, and I position her so that she's on her hands and knees, her elbows bent.

On all fours, with her ass tilted up and her back slightly arched, she's the hottest thing I've ever seen. I can see everything—the folds of her delicate pussy, the tiny hole of her anus, the delicious curves of her cheeks, pink with marks from the belt. My heart is pounding heavily in my chest, and my cock is throbbing painfully as I grasp her hips, line the head of my dick up against her opening, and push inside.

Hot, wet flesh envelops me, sheathing me in tight, slick perfection. She moans, arching toward me, trying to take me deeper, and I oblige, withdrawing partially and then slamming back in. A cry escapes her throat, and I repeat the move, my spine prickling with pleasure at the clinging grip of her tight channel. Waves of heat roll through me, and I begin to thrust with abandon, barely cognizant of my fingers digging into the soft skin of her hips. Her moans and cries increase in volume, and then I feel her peaking, her inner muscles contracting around my cock, milking it. Unable to hold on any longer, I explode, my vision blurring from the force of my release as my seed erupts into her warm depths.

Panting, I collapse onto my side, pulling her with me. Our skin is damp with sweat, gluing us together, and my heart is racing. She's breathing heavily too, and I can feel her pussy clenching around my softening cock as one last orgasmic shudder ripples through her.

We lie joined together as our breathing begins to ease. I'm holding her spooned against me, the soft curve of her ass pressing into my groin, and a sense of peace, of contentment, slowly steals over me. It's always like that with her. Something about her calms my demons, makes me feel almost normal. Almost . . . happy. It's not something I can explain or rationalize; it's just there. It's what makes my need for her so acute, so desperate.

So dangerously fucked up.

"Tell me you love me," I murmur, stroking her outer thigh. "Tell me you missed me, baby."

She shifts in my arms, turning over to face me. Her dark eyes are solemn as she meets my gaze. "I love you, Julian," she says softly, her delicate palm curving around my jaw. "I missed you more than life itself. You know that."

I do—but I still need this from her. In recent months, the emotional aspect has become as necessary to me as the physical. It amuses me, this strange quirk of mine. I want my little captive to love me, to care about me. I want to be more than just the monster of her nightmares.

Closing my eyes, I draw her deeper into my embrace and let myself relax.

In a few hours, she's going to be mine in every sense of the word.

CHAPTER FOUR

❖ NORA ❖

I must've fallen asleep in Julian's arms because I wake up when the plane begins to descend. Opening my eyes, I stare at the unfamiliar surroundings, my body sore and aching from the sex we just had.

I had forgotten what it was like with Julian, how devastating and cathartic the roller coaster ride of pain and ecstasy could be. I feel both empty and exhilarated at the same time, wrung out, yet invigorated by the maelstrom of emotions.

Sitting up gingerly, I wince as my bruised bottom touches the sheets. That had been one of the more intense belting sessions; I won't be surprised if these bruises last a while. Casting a glance around the room, I spot a door that I assume leads to the bathroom. Julian is not in the room, so I get up and go over there, feeling the need to wash up.

To my surprise, the bathroom contains a small shower, as well as a real sink and toilet. With all these amenities, Julian's jet seems more like a flying hotel than any commercial plane I've been on. There is even a plastic-wrapped toothbrush, toothpaste, and mouthwash tucked inside a little shelf on the wall. I use all three and follow up with a quick shower. Then, feeling infinitely more refreshed, I go back into the bedroom to get dressed.

When I enter the main cabin, I see Julian sitting on the couch, an open laptop on the table in front of him. The sleeves of his shirt are pushed up, exposing tan, muscular forearms, and there is a frown of concentration on his face. He looks serious—and so devastatingly beautiful that my breath catches for a moment.

As though sensing my presence, he looks up, his blue eyes gleaming. "How are you, my pet?" he asks, his voice low and intimate, and I feel a hot flush moving over my entire body in response.

"I'm fine." I don't know what else to say. My butt hurts because you whipped me, but that's okay because you trained me to enjoy it? Yeah, sure.

His lips curl in a slow smile. "Good. I'm glad to hear it. I was just about to come get you. You should get into your seat—we'll be landing soon."

"Okay." I follow his suggestion, trying not to flinch at the pain caused by the simple act of sitting down. I will definitely have bruises for the next few days.

Strapping myself in, I look out the window, curious about our destination. As the plane breaks through the cloud cover, I see a large city spread out below, with mountains looming on the edge of it. "What city is that?" I ask, turning towards Julian.

"Bogotá," he replies, closing his laptop. Picking it up, he walks over to sit down next to me. "We'll only be there for a few hours."

"You have business there?"

"You could say that." He looks vaguely amused. "There is something I'd like to get done before we fly to the estate."

"What?" I inquire warily. An amused Julian is rarely a good sign.

"You'll see." And opening the laptop again, he focuses on whatever he was doing before.

* * *

A black car similar to the one that dropped us off at the airport waits for us when we get off the plane. Lucas assumes the role of our driver again, while Julian continues working on his laptop, seemingly absorbed in his task.

I don't mind. I'm too busy staring at everything as we drive through the crowded streets. Bogotá has a certain 'Old World' vibe that I find fascinating. I can see traces of its Spanish heritage everywhere, mixed with a uniquely Latino flavor. It makes me crave arepas—corn cakes that I used to get from a Colombian food truck in downtown Chicago.

"Where are we going?" I ask Julian when the car pulls up in front of a stately old church in a wealthy-looking neighborhood. Somehow I hadn't pictured my captor as the church-going type.

Instead of answering, he climbs out of the car and extends his hand to me. "Come, Nora," he says. "We don't have a lot of time."

Time for what? I want to question him further, but I know it's futile. He's not going to answer me unless he feels like it. Placing my hand in Julian's large palm, I climb out of the car and let him lead me toward the church building. For all I know, we're meeting some of his associates here—though why he wants me with him for that is anyone's guess.

We enter through a little side door and find ourselves in a small, but beautifully decorated room. Old-fashioned wooden benches line the sides of it, and there is a pulpit with an intricate cross toward the front.

For some reason, the sight of it makes me nervous. An insane, improbable thought occurs to me, and my palms begin to sweat. "Um, Julian . . ." I look up to find him gazing at me with a strange smile. "Why are we here?"

"Can't you guess, my pet?" he says softly, turning to face me. "We're here to get married."

For a moment, all I can do is stare at him in mute shock. Then a nervous laugh escapes my throat. "You're joking, right?"

He lifts his eyebrows. "Joking? No, not at all." He reaches for my hand again, and I feel him sliding something onto my left ring finger.

My heart racing, I look down at my left hand in numb disbelief. The ring looks like something a Hollywood star might wear—a thin, diamond-encrusted band with a large, round stone sparkling in the center. It's both delicate and ostentatious, and the fit is utterly perfect, as though it had been made just for me.

The room fades in front of my eyes, spots of light dancing in the corners of my vision, and I realize that I literally stopped breathing for a few seconds. Desperately sucking in air, I look up at Julian, my entire body beginning to shake. "You . . . you want to marry me?" My voice comes out in a kind of horrified whisper.

"Of course I do." His eyes narrow slightly. "Why else would I bring you here?"

I have no response to that; all I can do is stand there and stare at him, feeling like I'm hyperventilating.

Marriage. Marriage to Julian.

It simply doesn't compute. Marriage and Julian are so far apart in my mind, they might as well be on opposite poles of the planet. When I think of marriage, it's in the context of a pleasant, yet distant future—a future that involves a doting husband and two noisy children. In that picture, there is a dog and a house in the suburbs, soccer games and school picnics. There is no killer with the face of a fallen angel, no beautiful monster to make me scream in his arms.

"I can't marry you." The words tumble out before I can think better of it. "I'm sorry, Julian, but I can't."

His face turns black. In a flash, he's on me, one arm wrapped around my waist, pressing me against him, and the other hand gripping my jaw. "You said you loved me." His voice is soft and even, but I can feel the dark rage underneath. "Was that a lie?"

"No!" Shaking, I hold Julian's furious gaze, my hands pushing helplessly against his powerful chest. I can feel the weight of the ring on my finger, and it adds to my panic. I don't know how to explain, how to make him understand something that I can barely comprehend myself. I want to be with Julian. I can't live without him, but marriage is something else entirely, something that doesn't belong in our twisted relationship. "I do love you! You know that—"

"So why would you refuse?" he demands, his eyes dark with fury. His grip on my jaw tightens, his fingers biting into my skin.

My eyes begin to burn. How can I explain my reluctance? How can I say that he's not someone I can picture as my husband? That he's part of a life I never imagined, never wanted, and that marrying him would mean giving up that vague, far-off dream of a normal future? "Why do you want to marry me?" I ask desperately. "Why do you want something so traditional? I'm already yours—"

"Yes, you are." He leans down until his face is mere inches from mine. "And I want a legal document to that effect. You will be my wife, and no one will be able to take you from me."

I stare at Julian, my chest tightening as I begin to understand. This is not a sweet, romantic gesture on his part. He's not doing this because he loves me and wants to start a family. That's not the way Julian operates. Marriage would legitimize his possession of me—it's as simple as that. It would be a different form of ownership, a more permanent one . . . and something within me shudders at the very idea.

"I'm sorry," I say evenly, gathering my courage. "I'm not ready for this. Can we discuss it again at some point later?"

His expression hardens, his eyes turning into chips of blue ice. Abruptly releasing me, he takes a step back. "All right." His voice is as cold as his gaze. "If that's how you want to play it, my pet, we'll do it your way."

Reaching into his pocket, he pulls out a smartphone and begins typing on it.

A sick sensation curls low in my stomach. "What are you doing?" When he doesn't answer, I repeat my question, trying not to sound as panicked as I feel. "Julian, what are you doing?"

"Something I should've done a long time ago," he finally replies, looking up at me as he pockets his phone. "You still dream of him, don't you? Of that boy you once wanted?"

My heart stops beating for a second. "What? No, I don't! Julian, I promise you, Jake has nothing to do with this—"

He interrupts with a curt, dismissive gesture. "I should've removed him from your life a long time ago. Now I will remedy that oversight. Maybe then you will accept that you are with me now, not him."

"I *am* with you!" I don't know what to say, how to convince Julian not to do it. Stepping toward him, I grip his hands, the heat of his skin burning my frozen fingers. "Listen to me, I love *you*, only you . . . He doesn't mean anything to me—he hasn't for a long time!"

"Good." His expression doesn't soften, though his fingers fold around mine, imprisoning them in his grasp. "Then you shouldn't care what happens to him."

"No, that's not how it works! I care because he's a human being, an innocent bystander in all of this, and for no other reason!" I'm shaking so hard now, my teeth are chattering. "He doesn't deserve to be punished for my sins—"

"It doesn't matter to me what he deserves." Julian's voice lashes at me like a whip as he uses his grip on my hands to pull me closer. Leaning down, he grits out, "I want him out of your mind and out of your life, do you understand me?"

The burning in my eyes intensifies, my vision blurring from unspilled tears. Through the haze of panic clouding my mind, I realize there's only one thing I can do to stop this—only one way I can prevent Jake's death.

"All right," I whisper in defeat, staring at the monster I'd fallen in love with. "I will do it. I will marry you."

* * *

The next hour feels surreal.

After calling off his henchmen, Julian introduces me to a wizened old man wearing a Catholic priest's robes. The man doesn't speak English, so I nod and pretend to follow along as he chatters at me in rapid-fire Spanish. It's embarrassing to admit, but the only Spanish I know is from my classes in high school. When I was growing up, my parents spoke English in the house, and I didn't spend enough time with my abuela to pick up anything more than a few basic phrases.

When my introduction to the priest is over, Julian leads me to another room—a small office that has a desk and two chairs. As soon as we get there, two young women enter the room. One of them brings in a long white dress, while the other one carries shoes and accessories. They're friendly and excited, chatting with me in a mix of Spanish and English as they start doing my hair, and I try to respond in kind. However, my answers come out awkward and wooden, the growing knot of dread in my chest preventing me from acting like the eager young bride they expect to see. Noticing my lack of enthusiasm, Julian shoots me a dark glare, then disappears, leaving the women to fuss over me.

By the time they're done prettifying me, I'm both mentally and physically exhausted. Even though Chicago and Bogotá are in the same time zone, I feel jet-lagged and utterly drained. A strange numbness steals over me, easing the churning tension in my stomach.

It's happening. It's really happening. Julian and I are getting married.

The panic that gripped me earlier is gone, having mellowed into a type of weary resignation. I don't know what I expected from a man who held me captive for fifteen months. A reasonable discussion on the pros and cons of getting married at this point in our relationship? I mentally snort. *Yeah, sure.* In hindsight, it's clear that our four-month separation had dulled my memories of those initial terrifying weeks on the island—that I had somehow managed to romanticize my abductor in my mind. I had foolishly begun to think that things could be different between us, to believe I had some say in my life.

"All done." The woman who was working on my hair gives me a beaming smile, interrupting my thoughts. "Beautiful, señorita, very beautiful. Now, please, the dress, and then we make your face nice."

They give me silk undergarments to go with the dress, and then tactfully turn away, giving me some privacy. Not wanting to drag it out, I swiftly change and pull on the dress—which, like the ring, fits me perfectly.

Now all that remains is makeup and accessories, and the two women make short work of that. Ten minutes later, I'm ready for my wedding.

"Come look," one of them says, leading me toward the corner of the room. There is a full-length mirror there that I hadn't noticed before, and I stare in stunned silence at my reflection, hardly recognizing the image I see.

The girl in the mirror is beautiful and sophisticated, with her hair styled in an artful updo and her makeup tastefully done. The mermaid-style dress is just right for her slim frame, with a sweetheart bodice exposing the graceful slope of her neck and shoulders. Teardrop-shaped diamond earrings decorate her small earlobes, and a matching necklace sparkles around her neck. She's everything a bride should be . . . especially if one ignores the shadows in her eyes.

My parents would've been so proud.

The thought pops out of nowhere, and I realize for the first time that I'm getting married without my family there, that my parents won't get to see their only child on that special day. A dull ache spreads through my chest at the thought. There will be no wedding-dress shopping with my mom, no cake-tasting with my dad.

No bachelorette party with my friends at an all-male strip club.

I try to imagine how Julian might react to something like that, and an unexpected snicker escapes my lips. I have a strong suspicion those poor strippers would leave the club in body bags if I so much as ventured near them.

A knock on the door interrupts my semi-hysterical musings. The women rush to answer it, and I hear Julian speaking to them in Spanish. Turning toward me, they wave goodbye and quickly leave.

As soon as they're gone, Julian enters the room.

Despite everything, I can't help staring at him. Dressed in a crisp black tuxedo that hugs his tall, powerful frame to perfection, my husband-to-be is simply breathtaking. My mind flashes to our sex session on the plane, and wet heat gathers between my thighs even as my bruises begin to throb at the reminder. He's studying me too, his gaze hot and proprietary as it moves over my body.

"Isn't it bad luck for the groom to see the bride before the ceremony?" I inject as much sarcasm into my voice as I can, trying to ignore the effect he has on my senses. At this moment, I hate him almost as much as I love him, and the fact that I want to jump his bones bothers me to no small degree. I should be used to it by now, but I still find it disturbing, the way my brain and my body don't communicate in his presence.

A small smile tugs at the corner of his sensual mouth. "It's okay, my pet. I think you and I are past such concerns. Are you ready?"

I nod and walk toward him. There's no point in delaying the inevitable; one way or another, we're getting married today. Julian offers me his arm, and I loop my hand through the crook of his elbow, letting him lead me back into the beautiful room with the pulpit.

The priest is already waiting for us, as is Lucas. There is also a sizable camera sitting on top of a tall tripod.

"Is that for wedding pictures?" I ask in surprise, stopping in the entryway.

"Of course." Julian's eyes gleam at me. "Memories and all that good stuff."

Uh-huh. I can't fathom why Julian wants this—the dress, the tux, the church. The entire thing is confusing to me. We're not entering into a loving union; he's simply binding me to him tighter, formalizing his ownership. All these accoutrements are meaningless, especially since Lucas is the only one who'll witness the event.

The thought makes my chest ache again. "Julian," I say quietly, looking up at him, "can I call my parents now? I want to tell them about this. I want to let them know I'm getting married." I'm almost certain he will refuse my request, but I feel compelled to ask regardless.

To my surprise, he smiles at me. "If you wish, my pet. In fact, after you talk to them, they can watch our ceremony on a live video feed. Lucas can set that up for us."

I gape at him in shock. He wants my parents to watch the wedding? To see *him*—the man who kidnapped their daughter? For a moment, I feel like I entered an alternate universe, but then the sheer genius of his plan dawns on me.

"You want me to introduce you to them, don't you?" I whisper, staring at him. "You want me to tell them that I came with you of my own free will, to show them how happy we are together. Then you won't have to worry about the authorities or anyone else coming after you. I'll be just another girl who fell for a handsome, wealthy man and ran off with him. These pictures . . . that video . . . it's all about staging a show . . ."

His smile widens. "How you act and what you say to them is entirely up to you, my pet," he says silkily. "They can witness a joyous occasion, or you can tell them you were abducted again. It's your choice, Nora. You can do whatever you wish."

CHAPTER FIVE

❖ JULIAN ❖

Her dark eyes are wide and unblinking as she stares at me, and I know exactly what her choice will be. As far as her parents are concerned, she'll be the happiest bride in the world.

She'll put on the best act of her life.

Anger and something else—something I don't care to examine closely—churns in my gut at the thought. Rationally I understand her hesitation. I know what I am, what I have done to her. A smart woman would run as fast as she could—and Nora has always been smarter, more perceptive than most.

She's also young. I forget that sometimes. In the comfortable world of middle-class America, few women get married at her age. It's possible that marriage is not something she thought about yet; in fact, it's likely, given that she had been in high school when I met her.

Rationally I understand all that . . . but rationality has nothing to do with the savage emotions seething under my skin. I want to string her up, whip her, and then fuck her until she's raw and begging for mercy—until she admits that she's mine, that she can't fucking live without me.

I don't do any of that, though. Instead I smile coolly and wait for her decision.

She inclines her head in a small nod. "All right." Her voice is barely audible. "I'll do it. I'll tell them all about our love affair."

I conceal my satisfaction. "As you wish, my pet. I'll have Lucas set up a secure connection for you."

And leaving her standing there, I walk over to Lucas to discuss the logistics of that specific operation.

* * *

I ask Padre Diaz to give us an hour before starting the ceremony and then sit down on one of the benches, giving Nora some privacy to talk to her parents. Of course, I'm monitoring her conversation through a little bluetooth device in my ear, but she doesn't need to know that.

Leaning back against the wall, I get comfortable and prepare to be entertained.

Her mother picks up on the first ring.

"Hi Mom... it's me." Nora's voice is cheerful and upbeat, practically brimming with excitement. I stifle a smile; she's going to be even better at this than I thought.

"Nora, honey!" Gabriela Leston's voice is filled with relief. "I'm so glad you called. I tried calling you five times today, but your phone kept going to voicemail. I was about to go over there in person—oh, wait, what number are you calling from?"

"Mom, don't freak out, but I'm not at home, okay?" Nora's tone is soothing, but I wince internally. I don't know much about normal parents, but I'm pretty sure saying the words 'don't freak out' ensures that they do exactly that.

"What do you mean?" Her mother's voice immediately sharpens. "Where are you?"

Nora clears her throat. "Um, I'm in Colombia, actually."

"WHAT?" I flinch at the earsplitting shout. "What do you mean, you're in Colombia?"

"Mom, you don't understand, it's great news..." And Nora launches into an explanation of how we had fallen in love on the island, how devastated she had been when she'd thought I was dead—and how ecstatic she was to learn that I'm alive.

After she's done, there is only silence on the phone. "Are you telling me that you're with him now?" her mother finally asks, her voice hoarse and strained. "That he came back for you?"

"Yes, exactly." Nora's tone is jubilant. "Don't you see, Mom? I couldn't really talk to you about any of this before because it was too difficult—because I thought I'd lost him. But now we're together again, and there's something . . . something *amazing* that I have to tell you."

"What is it?" Her mother sounds understandably wary.

"We're getting married!"

There is another long silence on the other end of the line. Then: "You're getting married . . . to *him*?"

I suppress another smile as Nora starts trying to convince her mother that I am not as bad as they think—that it was a combination of unfortunate circumstances that resulted in her kidnapping and that things are very different between us now. I'm not sure if Gabriela Leston is buying this, but she doesn't really need to. The recording of this conversation will be distributed to key individuals in certain government agencies, helping soothe their ruffled feathers. I'm too valuable for them to fuck with, but it still doesn't hurt to play along. Perception is everything, and Nora as my wife is much more palatable to them than Nora as my captive.

I could've married her earlier, but I was trying to keep her hidden, keep her safe. That's why I abducted her and took her to my island: so no one would find out about her existence and her importance to me. Now that the secret is out, however, I want the entire world to know that she's mine—that if they dare touch her, they will pay. News of my vendetta against Al-Quadar is starting to filter through the sewers of the underworld, and I've made sure that the rumors are even more brutal than the reality.

It's those rumors that will keep Nora's family safe—that and the security detail I put on her parents. It's unlikely anyone would try to get to me through my in-laws—I'm not exactly known as a family man—but I am not taking any chances. The last thing I want is for Nora to grieve for her parents the way she's still grieving for Beth.

By the time Nora is wrapping up her conversation, Padre Diaz starts getting impatient. I give him a warning look, and he immediately stops fidgeting, all visible traces of annoyance fading from his features. The good Padre has known me since I was a boy, and he knows when he should exercise caution.

When I glance in Nora's direction again, she waves to me, motioning for me to approach. I get up and walk over to her, turning off my bluetooth device on the way. As I get close, I hear her saying, "Listen, Mom, let me introduce you to him, okay? I'll ask him to put

ANNA ZAIRES

us on video—that way it'll be almost like we're all meeting in person . . . Yeah, we'll connect with you in a couple of minutes." And hanging up, she looks up at me expectantly.

"Lucas." I barely raise my voice, but he's already there, carrying a laptop with a secure connection. Placing it on a windowsill, he props it up so that the little camera points at us. A minute later, the video call is established, and Gabriela Leston's face fills the screen. Tony Leston—Nora's father—is behind her. Both pairs of dark eyes immediately turn toward me, studying me with a peculiar mix of hostility and curiosity.

"Mom, Dad, this is Julian," Nora says softly, and I incline my head with a small smile. Lucas walks back to the other end of the room, leaving us alone.

"It's very nice to meet you both." I purposefully keep my voice cool and steady. "I'm sure Nora has already filled you in on everything. I apologize for the speed with which this is happening, but I would love it if you could be a part of our wedding. I know it would mean a great deal to Nora to have her parents present, even if it is remotely." There is nothing I can say to the Lestons to justify my actions or make them like me, so I don't even try. Nora is mine now, and they will have to learn to accept that fact.

Nora's father opens his mouth to say something, but his wife elbows him sharply. "All right, Julian," she says slowly, staring at me with eyes eerily similar to her daughter's. "So you are marrying Nora. May I ask where you're going to be living after that, and whether we're going to see her again?"

I smile at her. Another smart, intuitive woman. "For the first few months, we'll probably be here, in Colombia," I explain, keeping my tone light and friendly. "There are certain business matters that I have to take care of. After that, however, we'd be more than happy to come for a visit—or to have you visit us."

Gabriela nods. "I see." The tension on her face remains, though relief briefly flickers in her eyes. "And what about Nora's future plans? What about college?"

"I will make sure she gets a good education and has a chance to pursue her art." I give the Lestons a level look. "Of course, I'm sure you realize that Nora doesn't need to worry about money anymore. Neither do you. I am more than comfortable, financially, and I always take care of my own."

Tony Leston's eyes narrow with anger. "You can't buy our daughter—" he starts saying, only to be elbowed into silence again by his wife. Nora's mother clearly has a better grasp on the situation; she realizes that this conversation could just as easily not be happening.

I lean closer to the camera. "Tony, Gabriela," I say quietly, "I understand your concern. However, in less than a half hour, Nora will be my wife—my responsibility. I can assure you that I will take care of her and do my best to ensure her happiness. You have nothing to worry about."

Tony's jaw tightens, but he remains silent this time. It's Gabriela who speaks next. "We would appreciate it if we could talk to her on a regular basis," she says evenly. "To make sure she's as happy as she seems today."

"Of course." I have no problem making that concession. "Now, the ceremony is starting in a few minutes, so we need to set up a better video feed for you. It was a pleasure meeting you both," I say politely, then close the laptop.

Turning, I see Nora watching me with some bemusement. In the long white dress and with her hair all done, she looks like a princess—which I suppose makes me the evil dragon stealing her away.

Inexplicably amused by the thought, I lift my hand and run my fingers down her baby-soft cheek. "Are you ready, my pet?"

"Yes, I think so," she murmurs, staring up at me. They did something to her eyes, those women I hired, making her eyes seem even larger and more mysterious. Her mouth also looks softer and shinier than usual, utterly fuckable. A sharp surge of lust catches me off-guard, and I force myself to take a step back before I do something sacrilegious at my own wedding.

"The video is all set up," Lucas informs me, coming up to us.

"Thank you, Lucas," I say. Then, turning toward Nora, I take her hand and lead her toward Padre Diaz.

CHAPTER SIX

❖ NORA ❖

The ceremony itself takes only about twenty minutes. Cognizant of the camera trained on us, I smile widely and do my best to look like a happy, glowing bride.

I still don't fully understand my own reluctance. After all, I'm marrying the man I love. When I thought he was dead, I wanted to die myself, and it took all of my strength to survive from one day to the next. I don't want to be with anyone but Julian . . . and yet I can't shake the chill deep inside.

He handled my parents smoothly, I will give him that. I'm not sure what I had been expecting, but the calm, almost civil conversation that took place hadn't been it. He had been in control the entire time, his matter-of-fact attitude leaving no room for tearful accusations and recriminations. He had apologized for the rushed wedding, but not for abducting me in the first place—and I know it's because he feels no guilt about that. In his mind, he has a right to me. It's as simple as that.

After a lengthy speech in Spanish, Padre Diaz begins speaking to Julian. I catch a few words—something about spouse, love, protection—and then I hear Julian's deep voice responding "Sí, quiero."

It's my turn next. Looking up at Julian, I meet his gaze. There is a warm smile on his lips, but his eyes tell a different story. His eyes reflect hunger and need, and underneath it all, a dark, all-consuming possessiveness.

"Sí, quiero," I say quietly, repeating Julian's words. *Yes, I do. Yes, I want.* My rudimentary Spanish is good enough to translate that at least.

Julian's smile deepens. Reaching into his pocket, he takes out another ring—a slim, diamond-studded band that matches my engagement ring—and slides it onto my nerveless finger. Then he presses a platinum band into my palm and extends his left hand to me.

His palm is almost twice the size of mine, his fingers long and masculine. He has a man's hands—strong and roughened with calluses. Hands that can pleasure or hurt with equal ease.

Taking a deep breath, I slide the wedding band onto Julian's left ring finger and look up at him again, only half-listening as Padre Diaz concludes the ceremony. Staring at Julian's beautiful features, all I can think about is that it's done.

The man who kidnapped me is now my husband.

* * *

After the ceremony, I say goodbye to my parents, assuring them that I will speak to them again soon. My mom is crying, and my dad is wearing a stony expression that usually means he's extremely upset.

"Mom, Dad, I promise I'll be in contact," I tell them, trying to hold back my own tears. "I won't disappear on you again. Everything is going to be fine. You have nothing to worry about . . ."

"I promise she will call you very soon," Julian adds, and after a few more tearful goodbyes, Lucas disconnects the video feed.

The next half hour is spent taking pictures all over the beautiful church. Then we change back into our regular clothes and head back to the airport.

At this point, it's evening and I'm completely exhausted. The stress of the past couple of hours, combined with all the travel, has made me nearly comatose, and I close my eyes, leaning back against the black leather seat as the car winds its way through the dark streets of Bogotá. I don't want to think about anything; I just want to empty my mind and relax. Shifting, I try to find a better position, one that doesn't place too much weight on my still-tender bottom.

"Tired, baby?" Julian murmurs, placing his hand on my leg. His fingers squeeze lightly, massaging my thigh, and I force my heavy eyelids to open.

"A bit," I admit, turning toward him. "I'm not used to this much flying—or marrying."

He grins at me, his teeth flashing white in the darkness. "Well, luckily you won't have to go through this experience again. The marrying, I mean. I can't promise anything about the flying."

Maybe I'm overly tired, but that strikes me as ridiculously funny for some reason. A giggle escapes my throat, first one, then another, until I'm laughing uncontrollably, all but rolling on the backseat of the car.

Julian watches me calmly, and when my laughter finally begins to quiet down, he pulls me into his lap and kisses me, claiming my mouth with a long, fierce kiss that literally steals my breath away. By the time he lets me come up for air, I can barely remember my own name, much less what I was laughing about before.

We're both panting, our breath intermingling as we stare at each other. There's hunger in his gaze, but there's also something more—an almost violent longing that goes deeper than simple lust. A strange tightness squeezes my chest, and I feel like I'm falling further, losing even more of myself. "What do you want from me, Julian?" I whisper, lifting my hand to cradle the hard contours of his jaw. "What do you need?"

He doesn't answer, but his large hand covers mine, holding it pressed against his face for a few moments. He closes his eyes, as though absorbing the sensation, and when he opens them, the moment is gone.

Shifting me off his lap, he drapes a heavy arm over my shoulders and settles me comfortably against his side. "Get some rest, my pet," he murmurs into my hair. "We still have a ways to go before we get home."

* * *

I fall asleep on the plane again, so I have no idea how long the flight is. Julian shakes me awake after we land, and I follow him sleepily off the plane.

Warm, humid air hits me as soon as we disembark, so thick it feels like a damp blanket. Bogotá had been much warmer than Chicago, with the temperature somewhere in the high sixties, but this . . . this feels like I stepped into a wet sauna. With my winter boots and a fleece sweater, I feel like I'm being cooked alive.

"Bogotá is at a much higher elevation," Julian says, as though reading my mind. "Down here, it's tierra caliente—the low-elevation hot zone."

"Where are we?" I ask, waking up a bit more. I can hear the chirping of insects, and the smell in the air is that of lush green vegetation, of the tropics. "Which part of the country, I mean?"

"The southeast," Julian replies, leading me toward an SUV waiting on the other side of the runway. "We're actually right on the edge of the Amazon rainforest."

I lift my hand to rub at the corner of my eye. I don't know much about Colombian geography, but that sounds very remote to me. "Are we near some villages or towns?"

"No," Julian says. "That's the beauty of this location, my pet. We're completely isolated and safe. Nobody will bother us here."

We reach the car, and he helps me inside. Lucas joins us a couple of minutes later, and then we're off, driving down an unpaved road through a heavily wooded area.

It's pitch-black outside, the headlights of the car our only source of illumination, and I peer curiously through the darkness, trying to discern our destination. All I can see, however, are trees and more trees.

Abandoning that futile effort, I decide to get more comfortable instead. It's cooler in the car with the air conditioning working full-blast, but I'm still too hot, so I take off my sweater. Thankfully, I'm wearing a tank top underneath. As the chilly air blows across my heated skin, I sigh with relief, fanning myself to accelerate the cooling process.

"I have clothes for you here that are more weather-appropriate," Julian says, observing my actions with a half-smile. "I probably should've thought to bring them with me, but I was far too eager to retrieve you."

"Oh?" I glance at him, absurdly pleased by his admission.

"I came after you as soon as I could," he murmurs, his eyes gleaming in the dark interior of the car. "You didn't think I'd leave you alone for long, did you?"

"No, I didn't," I say softly. And it's the truth. If there's one thing I've always been sure of, it's that Julian wants me. I'm not sure if he loves me—if he's capable of loving anyone—but I've never doubted the strength of his desire for me. He risked his life for me back at that warehouse, and I know he would do so again. It's a certainty that goes bone-deep and fills me with a peculiar sense of comfort.

Closing my eyes, I lean back against the seat with another sigh. The dichotomy of my emotions makes my head hurt. How can I be upset with Julian for forcing me to marry him and at the same time be glad that he couldn't wait to abduct me again? What sane person feels that way?

"We've arrived," Julian says, interrupting my musings, and I open my eyes, realizing that the car had stopped.

In front of us is a sprawling two-story mansion surrounded by several smaller structures. Bright outdoor lights illuminate everything in the vicinity, and I can see wide green lawns and lush, meticulously maintained landscaping. Julian wasn't exaggerating when he called this place an estate.

I can also see some of the security measures, and I gaze around curiously as Julian helps me out of the car and leads me toward the main building. On the far edges of the property, there are towers spaced a few dozen yards apart, with armed men visible at the top of each one.

It's almost as if we're in prison, except that these guards are meant to keep the bad people out, not in.

"You grew up here?" I ask Julian as we approach the house. It's a beautiful white building with stately columns at the front. It reminds me a bit of Scarlett O'Hara's plantation from *Gone with the Wind*.

"I did." He shoots me a sidelong glance. "I spent most of my time here until I was about seven or eight. After that, I was usually in the cities with my father, helping him with business."

After we walk up the porch steps, Julian stops at the doorway and bends down to lift me into his arms. Before I can say anything, he carries me over the threshold, setting me back on my feet once we're inside. "No reason why we can't observe this little tradition," he murmurs with a mischievous grin, maintaining his hold on my sides as he looks down at me.

My lips twitch in an answering smile. I can never resist Julian when he's being playful like this. "Ah, yes, I forgot that you're Mr. Traditional today," I tease, purposefully trying not to think about the forced nature of our marriage. It's important for my sanity to keep the good times separate from the bad, to live in the moment as much as possible. "And here I thought you just felt like picking me up."

"I did," he admits, his grin widening. "It's the first time my inclinations and tradition have coincided, though, so why don't we go with 'observing tradition'?"

"I'm game," I say softly, gazing up at him. In this moment, my mind is firmly in the 'good times' camp, and I would gladly go along with anything he wants, do anything he wants.

"Señor Esguerra?" An uncertain female voice interrupts us, and I turn to see a middle-aged woman standing there. She's wearing a black short-sleeved dress, with a white apron wrapped around her rounded frame. "Everything is ready, just as you requested," she says in accented English, watching us with barely restrained curiosity. "Should I serve you dinner?"

"No, thank you, Ana," Julian replies, his hand resting possessively on my hip. "Just bring a tray with some sandwiches to our room, please. Nora is tired from our travels." Then he looks down at me. "Nora, this is Ana, our housekeeper. Ana, this is Nora, my wife."

Ana's brown eyes widen. Apparently the 'wife' bit is as much of a shock to her as it had been to me. She recovers quickly, though. "Very pleased to meet you, Señora," she says, giving me a wide smile. "Welcome."

"Thank you, Ana. It's nice to meet you too." I smile back, ignoring the sharp pain squeezing my chest. This housekeeper is nothing like Beth, but I can't help thinking of the woman who had become my friend—and of her cruel, pointless death.

No, don't go there, Nora. The last thing I need is to wake up screaming from another nightmare.

"Please make sure we're not disturbed tonight," Julian instructs Ana, "unless it's something urgent."

"Yes, Señor," she murmurs, and disappears through the wide double doors leading out of the entryway area.

"Ana is one of the staff here," Julian explains as he guides me toward a wide, curved staircase. "She's been with my family in one capacity or another for most of her life."

"She seems very nice," I say, studying my new home as we walk up the stairs. I've never been inside such a lavish residence, and I can hardly believe I'm going to be living here. The decor is a tasteful mix of old-fashioned charm and modern elegance, with gleaming wooden floors and abstract art on the walls. I suspect the gilded picture frames alone are more expensive than anything I had in my studio apartment back home. "How many people are on the staff?"

"There are two who always take care of the house," Julian answers. "Ana, whom you've just met, and Rosa, who's the maid. You'll probably meet her tomorrow. There are also several gardeners, handymen, and others who oversee the property as a whole." Pausing in front of one of the doors upstairs, he opens it for me. "Here we are. Our bedroom."

Our bedroom. That has a very domestic ring to it. On the island, I had my own room, and even though Julian slept with me most nights, it still felt like my private space—something I apparently wouldn't have here.

Stepping inside, I cautiously survey the bedroom.

Like the rest of the house, it has an opulent, old-fashioned feel to it, despite several modern touches. There is a thick blue rug on the floor, and a massive four-poster bed in the center. Everything is done in shades of blue and cream, with some gold and bronze mixed in. The drapes covering the windows are thick and heavy, like in a luxury hotel, and there are a few more abstract paintings on the walls.

It's beautiful and intimidating, like the man who is now my husband.

"Why don't we take a bath?" Julian says softly, stepping up behind me. His powerful arms fold around me, his fingers reaching for my belt buckle. "I think we could both use one."

"Sure, that sounds good," I murmur, letting him undress me. It makes me feel like a doll—or maybe a princess, given our surroundings. As Julian tugs off my shirt and pushes down my jeans, his hands brush against my bare skin, causing tingles of heat to ripple down to my core.

Our wedding night. Tonight is our wedding night. My breathing quickens from a combination of arousal and nerves. I don't know what Julian has in store for me, but the hard ridge pressing against my lower back leaves no doubt that he intends to fuck me again.

When I am completely naked, I turn to face him and watch as he takes off his own clothes, his well-defined muscles gleaming in the soft light coming from the recessed ceiling. His body is slightly leaner than before, and there is a new scar near his ribcage. Still, he's the most striking man I have ever seen. He's already fully erect, his thick, long cock jutting out at me, and I swallow, my sex clenching at the sight. At the same time, I am cognizant of a faint soreness deep inside and the continued tenderness of my bruised bottom.

I want him, but I don't know if I can handle any more pain today.

"Julian . . ." I hesitate, unsure how to best phrase it. "Is there any way . . . Can we—?"

He steps toward me, framing my face with his large hands. His eyes glitter brightly as he looks down at me. "Yes," he whispers, understanding my unspoken question. "Yes, baby, we can. I will give you the wedding night of your dreams."

CHAPTER SEVEN

❖ JULIAN ❖

Bending down, I hook my arm under her knees and pick her up. She barely weighs anything, her small frame impossibly light as I carry her to the bathroom, where Ana prepared the jacuzzi for us.

My wife. Nora is now my wife. The fierce satisfaction I feel at the thought makes no sense, but I don't intend to dwell on it. She's mine, and that's all that matters. I will fuck her and pamper her, and she will fulfill my every need, no matter how dark and twisted. She will give me all of herself, and I will take it.

I will take it all, and then I'll demand more.

Tonight, though, I will give her what she wants. I will be sweet and gentle, as tender as any husband with his new bride. The sadist inside me is quiescent for now, content. There will be plenty of time later to punish her for her reluctance at the church. At this moment, I have no desire to hurt her—I just want to hold her, to stroke her silky skin and feel her shuddering with pleasure in my arms. My cock is hard, throbbing with need, but the hunger is different now, more controlled.

Reaching the large round jacuzzi, I step in and lower both of us into the bubbling water, sitting down with Nora ensconced on my lap. She lets out a blissful sigh and relaxes against me, closing her eyes and putting her head on my shoulder. Her glossy hair tickles my skin, the long ends floating in the water. I shift slightly, letting the strong jets pummel my back, and feel the tension gradually draining out of me despite my lingering arousal.

For a couple of minutes, I am content to just sit there, holding her cradled in my arms. Despite the sweltering heat outside, the temperature inside the house is cool, and the hot water feels good on my skin. Soothing. I imagine it feels good to Nora too, easing the soreness from the bruises I inflicted earlier.

Lifting my hand, I lazily stroke her back, marveling at the smoothness of her golden skin. My dick twitches, clamoring for more, but I'm in no rush this time. I want to prolong this moment, to heighten the anticipation for us both.

"This is nice," she murmurs after a while, tilting her head back to gaze at me. Her cheeks are flushed from the heat of the water and her lids are partially lowered, making her look like she's already been thoroughly fucked. "I wish I could take a bath like this every day."

"You can," I say softly, shifting her off my lap so she's facing me and reaching under the water to pick up her right foot. "You can do whatever you want here. It's your home now."

Applying light pressure to her sole, I begin to massage it the way she likes, enjoying the quiet moans that escape her lips at my touch. Her feet are small and pretty, like the rest of her. Sexy even, with the pink polish on her slender toes. Giving in to a sudden urge, I lift her foot to my mouth and suck on it lightly, swirling my tongue around each toe. She gasps, staring at me, and I can hear her breathing picking up, see her eyes darkening with arousal. This turns her on, I realize, and the knowledge makes my dick harden further.

Holding her gaze, I reach for Nora's other foot and give it the same treatment. Her toes curl at the touch of my tongue and her breathing becomes unsteady, her own tongue coming out to moisten her lips. The ache in my groin intensifying, I release her foot and slowly slide my hand up the inside of her leg, feeling her thigh muscles quivering with tension as I approach her sex. My fingers brush against her pussy, parting the soft folds. Then I push the tip of my middle finger into her small opening, using my thumb to press on her clit at the same time.

Inside, she's impossibly hot and slick, her inner walls gripping my finger so tightly that my cock jumps in response. She lets out a soft moan, lifting her hips toward me, and my finger slides deeper into her, causing a choked cry to issue from her throat. She scoots back reflexively, as though trying to pull away, but I wrap my free hand around her arm and pull her toward me, gathering her against my side. "Don't fight it, baby," I murmur, holding her still as I begin to fuck her with my finger, my thumb applying even, rhythmic pressure to her clit. "Just let yourself feel . . . Yes, that's it . . ."

Her head falls back and her eyes close, an expression of intense rapture appearing on her face as she lets out another moan.

Beautiful. She's so fucking beautiful. I can't tear my gaze away, drinking in the sight of her coming apart in my arms. Her slim body arches and tightens, and then she cries out as her flesh ripples around my finger in release, the squeezing motion making my dick throb in agonized need.

I can't take this much longer. Withdrawing my finger, I slide my hands under her body and pick her up as I rise to my feet. She opens her eyes and loops her arms around my neck, watching me intently as I step out of the jacuzzi and begin carrying her back to the bedroom. We're both dripping with water, but I can't bear to stop for even a moment. I don't give a fuck about getting our sheets wet right now—I don't give a fuck about anything except her.

Reaching the bed, I put her down, my hands shaking with violent lust. On any other night, I would already be inside her, pounding her tight little pussy until I explode, but not tonight. Tonight is for her. Tonight I will give her what she asked for—a wedding night with a lover, not a monster.

She watches me, her dark eyes slumberous with desire as I climb onto the bed between her legs and bend over her soft, tender flesh. Ignoring my aching cock, I begin with small kisses on the insides of her thighs and then move up until I reach my goal: her wet cleft, pink and swollen from her earlier orgasm.

Pulling her folds apart with my fingers, I lick the area directly around her clit, tasting her essence, then push my tongue inside, penetrating her as deeply as I can. She shudders, her hands finding their way down to my head, and I feel her nails digging into my skull. One of her fingers brushes against my scar, sending a bolt of pain through me, but I ignore that too, focusing solely on pleasuring her, on making her come. I revel in every drop of moisture I wring from her body, every gasp and moan that escapes her lips as my tongue works over the bundle of nerves at the peak of her sex. She begins to tremble, her thighs vibrating with tension, and I taste a spurt of salty-sweet moisture as she comes with a helpless cry, her hips lifting off the bed and her pussy grinding against my tongue.

When she finally goes limp, breathing heavily from her release, I crawl over her and kiss the delicate shell of her ear. I'm not done with her yet, not by a long shot.

"You're so sweet," I whisper, feeling her shiver at the heat of my breath. My cock throbs harder at her response, my balls full to bursting, and my next words come out low and rough, almost guttural. "So fucking sweet... I want to fuck you so badly, but I won't"—I tongue the underside of her earlobe, causing her hands to clutch convulsively at my sides—"not until you come for me again. You think you can come for me, baby?"

"I... I don't think so..." She gasps, twisting in my arms as my mouth moves down to the smooth column of her throat, leaving a warm, damp trail on her skin.

"Oh, I think you can," I murmur, my right hand slipping down her body to feel her soaking-wet pussy. As my lips travel over her shoulders and upper chest, I massage her swollen clit with my fingers, and she begins to pant again, her breathing becoming erratic as my mouth approaches her breasts. Her rosy nipples are hard, practically begging for my touch, and I close my lips over one taut bud, sucking on it strongly. She lets out a sound that's halfway between a moan and a whimper, and I turn my attention to the other nipple, sucking on it until she's trembling underneath me, the moisture from her sex inundating my hand. Before she can reach her peak, however, I slither down her body and taste her again, my tongue pushing inside her just as her contractions begin anew.

I lick her until her orgasm is fully over, then I move up over her again, supporting myself with my right elbow. Using my left hand, I grasp her jaw, forcing her to meet my gaze. Her eyes look unfocused, clouded with the aftermath of pleasure, and I lower my head, claiming her mouth with a deep, thorough kiss. I know she can taste herself on my lips, and the thought excites me, causing my pulse to spike. At the same time, her arms fold around my neck, embracing me, and I feel her breasts pushing against my chest, her nipples like hard little pebbles.

Holy fuck. I have to have her. Now.

My self-control fraying, I continue kissing her as I use my knees to spread open her thighs. Pressing the head of my cock against her opening, I slide my left hand into her hair to cradle the back of her skull.

Then I begin to push into her body.

She's small inside too, her pussy tighter than any I've known before. I can feel her wet flesh gradually engulfing me, stretching for me, and my spine tingles, my balls drawing up against my body. I'm not even fully inside her yet, and I'm about to explode from the mind-numbing pleasure. *Slow*, I harshly remind myself. *Go slow.*

She tears her mouth away from mine, her breath coming in soft little pants against my ear. "I want you," she whispers, her legs coming up to clasp my hips. The movement brings me deeper into her, making me groan in desperate need. "Please, Julian . . ."

Her words destroy whatever shreds of restraint I still possess. *To hell with going slow.* A low growl vibrates deep within my chest, and my hand fists in her hair as I begin to thrust into her, savagely, relentlessly. She cries out, and her arms tighten around my neck, her body eagerly welcoming my ruthless assault.

My mind explodes with sensations, with overwhelming ecstasy. This, right here, is what I want, what I need. Why I will never let her go. Our bodies strain together on the bed, wet sheets tangling around our limbs as I lose myself in her, in the sounds and smells of hot, no-holds-barred sex. Nora is like liquid fire in my arms, her slim body arching against me, her legs twining around my thighs. Each thrust brings me deeper into her until I feel like we're fusing together, melding into one another.

She reaches her peak first, her pussy squeezing me even tighter. I hear her strangled cry as she bites my shoulder in the throes of her orgasm, and then I'm there, shuddering over her as my seed shoots out in continuous heated spurts.

Breathing harshly, I sink down on top of her, my arms no longer able to support my weight. Every muscle in my body is shaking from the force of my release, and I'm covered with a thin veil of sweat. After a few moments, I muster the strength to roll over onto my back, pulling her to lie on top of me.

It shouldn't be this intense again, not after the way we fucked earlier, but it is. It always is. There's never a moment when I don't want her, when I don't think about her. If I ever lost her—

No. I refuse to think about that. It won't happen. I won't let it.

I will do whatever it takes to keep her safe.

Safe from everyone but me.

CHAPTER EIGHT

❖ NORA ❖

When I wake up in the morning, Julian is already gone.

Climbing out of bed, I head straight for the shower, feeling grimy and sticky after last night. We both fell asleep right after sex, too worn out to bother washing up or changing the wet sheets. Then, just before dawn, Julian woke me up by sliding inside me again, his skilled fingers bringing me to orgasm before I was fully awake. It's as if he can't get enough of me after our long separation, his already-strong libido going into overdrive.

Of course, I can't get enough of him either.

A smile curves my lips as I remember the searing passion of last night. Julian promised me the wedding night of my dreams, and he certainly delivered. I don't even know how many orgasms I've had over the past twenty-four hours. Of course, now I'm even more sore, my insides raw from so much fucking.

Still, I feel immeasurably better today, both physically and mentally. The bruises on my thighs are less tender to the touch, and I'm no longer feeling quite as overwhelmed. Even the idea of being married to Julian doesn't seem as frightening in the morning light. Nothing has truly changed, except that now there is a piece of paper joining us together, letting the world know that I belong to him. Captor, lover, or husband—it's all the same; the label doesn't alter the reality of our dysfunctional relationship.

Stepping under the shower spray, I tilt my head back, letting the hot water flow over my face. The shower is as luxurious as the rest of the house, the circular stall big enough to accommodate ten people. I wash and scrub every inch of my body until I begin to feel human again. Then I go back into the bedroom to get dressed.

I find an enormous closet in the back of the room, filled mostly with light summer clothes. Remembering the stifling heat outside, I select a simple blue sundress, then slide my feet into a pair of brown flip-flops. It's not the most sophisticated outfit, but it'll do.

I'm ready to explore my new home.

* * *

The estate is huge, much bigger than I thought yesterday. Besides the main house, there are also barracks for the two-hundred-plus guards who patrol the perimeter, and a number of houses occupied by other employees and their families. It's almost like a small town—or maybe some type of military compound.

I learn all this from Ana over breakfast. Apparently Julian left instructions that I was to be fed and shown around when I woke up. Julian himself is occupied with work, as usual.

"Señor Esguerra has an important meeting," Ana explains, serving me a dish she calls *Migas de Arepa*—scrambled eggs made with pieces of corn cakes and a tomato-onion sauce. "He asked me to look after you today, so please let me know if you need anything. After breakfast I can have Rosa give you a tour if you like."

"Thank you, Ana," I say, digging into my food. It's incredibly delicious, the sweetness of the arepas complementing the zesty flavor of the eggs. "A tour would be great."

We chat for a bit as I finish up my meal. In addition to learning about the estate, I find out that Ana has lived in this house most of her life, having started as a young maid working for Julian's father. "That's how I learned English," she says, pouring me a cup of frothy hot chocolate. "Señora Esguerra was American, like you, and she didn't speak any Spanish."

I nod, remembering Julian telling me about his mother. She had been a model in New York City before marrying Julian's father. "So you knew Julian when he was a child?" I ask, sipping the hot, rich drink. Like the eggs, it's unusually flavorful, with hints of clove, cinnamon, and vanilla.

"I did." Ana stops there, as though afraid of saying too much. I give her an encouraging smile, hoping to prod her into telling me more, but she begins to clear off the dishes instead, signaling an end to the conversation.

Sighing, I finish my hot chocolate and get up. I want to learn more about my husband, but I have a feeling Ana may be just as close-mouthed on this topic as Beth.

Beth. The familiar pain shoots through me again, bringing with it a burning rage. Memories of her violent death are never far from my mind, threatening to drown me in hate if I let them. When Julian first told me about what he did to Maria's attackers, I had been horrified . . . but now I understand it. I wish I could somehow lay my hands on the terrorist who killed Beth, make him pay for what he did to her. Even the knowledge that he's dead doesn't pacify my anger; it's always there, eating at me, poisoning me from within.

"Señora, this is Rosa," Ana says, and I turn toward the dining room entrance to see a young dark-haired woman standing there. She looks to be about my age, with a round face and a bright smile. Like Ana, she's wearing a short-sleeved black dress with a white apron. "Rosa, this is Señor Esguerra's new wife, Nora."

Rosa's smile brightens further. "Oh, hello, Señora Esguerra, it's a pleasure to meet you." Her English is even better than Ana's, her accent barely noticeable.

"Thank you, Rosa," I say, taking an immediate liking to the girl. "It's very nice to meet you too. And, please, call me Nora." I look toward the housekeeper. "You too, please, Ana, if you don't mind. I'm not used to the 'Señora' bit." And it's true. It's especially strange to hear myself addressed as Señora Esguerra. Does this mean that Julian's last name is now mine? We haven't discussed this yet, but I suspect Julian would want to follow tradition in this case as well.

Nora Esguerra. My heart beats faster at the thought, some of yesterday's irrational fear returning. For nineteen-and-a-half years, I have been Nora Leston. It's a name that I'm used to, that I'm comfortable with. The idea of changing it makes me deeply uneasy, as though I'm losing another part of myself. As though Julian is stripping me of everything that I used to be, transforming me into someone I barely recognize.

"Of course," Ana says, interrupting my anxious musings. "We're happy to call you anything you wish." Rosa nods vigorously in agreement, beaming at me, and I take a few deep breaths to calm my racing heartbeat.

"Thank you." I manage to give them a smile. "I appreciate it."

"Would you like to see the house before we go outside?" Rosa asks, smoothing her apron with her palms. "Or would you prefer to start outdoors?"

"We can start indoors, if that's okay with you," I tell her. Then I thank Ana for the breakfast, and we begin the tour.

Rosa shows me the downstairs first. There are over a dozen rooms, including a large library stocked with a variety of books, a home theater with a wall-sized TV, and a sizable gym filled with high-end exercise equipment. I'm also pleased to discover that Julian remembered my painting hobby; one of the rooms is set up as an art studio, with blank canvasses lined up in front of a huge south-facing window. "Señor Esguerra had all of this put in a couple of weeks before you came," Rosa tells me, leading me from room to room. "So everything is brand-new."

I blink, surprised to hear that. I had assumed that the art studio was new, since Julian is not into painting, but I didn't realize he'd redone the entire house. "He didn't have a pool put in too, did he?" I joke as we walk down the hall.

"No, the pool was already there," Rosa says in absolute seriousness. "But he did have it renovated." And leading me toward a screened back porch, she shows me an Olympic-sized pool surrounded by tropical greenery. In addition to the pool itself, there are lounge chairs that look amazingly comfortable, huge umbrellas that provide shade from the sun, and several outdoor tables with chairs.

"Nice," I murmur, feeling the hot, humid air on my skin. I have a feeling the pool will come in quite handy in this weather.

Going back indoors, we head upstairs. Besides the master suite, there are a number of bedrooms, each one bigger than my entire apartment back home. "Why is the house so big?" I ask Rosa after we view all the lavishly decorated rooms. "There are only a few people living here, right?"

"Yes, that's true," Rosa confirms. "But this house was built by the older Señor Esguerra, and from what I understand, he entertained a lot here, frequently inviting his business associates to stay over."

"How did you come to work here?" I give Rosa a curious look as we go down the curving staircase. "And learn to speak English so well?"

"Oh, I was born here, on the Esguerra estate," she says breezily. "My father was one of the older Señor's guards, and my mother and older brother also worked for him. Señor's wife—she was American, you see—taught me English when I was a child. I think she was maybe a bit bored here, so she gave lessons to the entire household staff and anyone else who wanted to learn the language. Then she insisted that we speak only English in the house, even among ourselves, so we could practice."

"I see." Rosa seems chattier than Ana, so I ask her the same question I posed to the housekeeper earlier. "If you grew up here, did you know Julian back then?"

"No, not really." She glances at me as we exit the house onto the front porch. "I was very young, only four years old when your husband left the country, so I don't remember much from when he was a boy. Up until a couple of weeks ago, I saw him here for only a short time after . . ." She swallows, looking down at the ground. "After it all happened."

"After his parents' death?" I ask quietly. I remember Julian telling me that his parents were killed, but he never explained how it happened. He just said it was one of his father's rivals.

"Yes," Rosa says somberly, her bright smile nowhere in sight. "A few years after Julian left, one of the North Coast cartels tried to take over the Esguerra organization. They struck at many of its key operations and even came here, to the estate. A lot of people died that day. My father and brother, too."

I stop in my tracks, staring at her. "Oh God, Rosa, I'm sorry . . ." I feel terrible that I brought up such a painful subject. For some reason, it hadn't occurred to me that people here might've been impacted by the same events that had shaped Julian. "I'm so sorry—"

"It's okay," she says, her expression still strained. "It happened almost twelve years ago."

"You must've been very young then," I say softly. "How old are you now?"

"Twenty-one," she replies as we begin walking down the porch steps. Then she shoots me a curious look, some of her somberness fading. "What about you, Nora, if you don't mind me asking? You seem young as well."

I grin at her. "Nineteen. Twenty in a few months." I'm glad she feels comfortable enough with me to ask personal questions. I don't want to be 'Señora' here, don't want to be treated like some lady of the manor.

She grins back, her former zest for life apparently restored. "I thought so," she says with evident satisfaction. "Ana thought you were even younger when she saw you last night, but she's almost fifty and everyone our age looks like a baby to her. My guess this morning was twenty, and I was right."

I laugh, charmed by her frankness. "You were, indeed."

During the rest of the tour, Rosa peppers me with questions about me and my life back in the States. She's apparently fascinated with America, having watched a number of American movies in an effort to improve her English. "I hope to go there someday," she says wistfully. "See New York City, walk in Times Square among all the bright lights . . ."

"You should definitely go," I tell her. "I only visited New York once, and it was great. Lots of things to do as a tourist."

As we talk, she shows me around the estate, pointing out the guards' barracks that Ana mentioned earlier, and the men's training area on the far side of the compound. The training area consists of an indoor fighting gym, an outdoor shooting range, and what appears to be an obstacle course on a large, grass-covered field. "The guards like to keep in top shape," Rosa explains as we pass by a group of hard-faced men practicing some type of martial arts. "Most of them are former military, and all are very good at what they do."

"Julian trains with them too, right?" I ask, watching in fascination as one man knocks out his opponent with a powerful kick to the head. I know a little self-defense from the lessons I took back home, but it's kid stuff compared to this.

"Oh, yes." Rosa's tone is somewhat reverential. "I've seen Señor Esguerra on the field, and he's as good as any of his men."

"Yes, I'm sure he is," I say, remembering Julian rescuing me from the warehouse. He had been completely in his element, arriving in the night like some angel of death. For a moment, the dark memories threaten to swamp me again, but I push them away, determined not to dwell on the past. Turning away from the fighters, I ask Rosa, "Do you know where he is today, by any chance? Ana said he's in a meeting."

She shrugs in response. "He's probably in his office, in that building over there." She points toward a small modern-looking structure near the main house. "He had it remodeled as well, and he's been spending a lot of time there since his return. I saw Lucas, Peter, and a few others go in there this morning, so I assume Julian is meeting with them."

"Who's Peter?" I ask. I already know Lucas, but I'm hearing Peter's name for the first time.

"He's one of Señor Esguerra's employees," Rosa replies as we walk back toward the house. "He came here a few weeks ago to oversee some of the security measures."

"Oh, I see."

By the time we arrive at the house, my clothes are sticking to my skin from the extreme humidity. It's a relief to be back indoors, where the air-conditioning keeps the temperature nice and cool. "That's Amazonia for you," Rosa says, smiling as I gulp down a glass of cold water I grab from the kitchen. "We're right next to the rainforest, and it's always like a steam bath outside."

"Yeah, no kidding," I mutter, feeling in dire need of another shower. It had been hot on the island as well, but the breeze coming from the ocean had made it tolerable, even pleasant. Here, however, the heat is almost smothering, the air still and thick with moisture.

Placing the empty glass on the table, I turn toward Rosa. "I think I might use that pool you showed me," I tell her, deciding to take advantage of the amenities. "Would you like to join me?"

Rosa's eyes widen. She's clearly surprised by my invitation. "Oh, I'd love to," she says sincerely, "but I need to help Ana prepare lunch and then clean the bedrooms upstairs . . ."

"Of course." I feel slightly embarrassed because, for a moment, I forgot that Rosa is not here solely to keep me company—that she has actual duties and responsibilities around the house. "Well, in that case, thank you for the tour. I really appreciate it."

She grins at me. "It was my pleasure, happy to do it anytime."

And as she busies herself in the kitchen, I head upstairs to change into a swimsuit.

CHAPTER NINE

❖ JULIAN ❖

I find Nora by the pool, lounging with a book under one of the umbrellas. Her slim legs are crossed at the ankles, and she's wearing a strapless white bikini, her golden skin gleaming with droplets of water. She must've been swimming recently.

Hearing my footsteps, she sits up and places her book on a side table. "Hi," she says softly when I approach her lounge chair. Her sunglasses are too big for her small face, making her look a bit like a dragonfly, and I make a mental note to buy her a more fitting pair on the next trip to Bogotá.

"Hello, my pet," I murmur, sitting down on her chair. Raising my hand, I pull the sunglasses off her nose and lean forward to take her mouth in a short, deep kiss. She tastes like sunlight, her lips soft and yielding, and my cock instantly stiffens, reacting to the proximity of her almost-naked body. Tonight, I promise myself as I reluctantly lift my head. I will have her again tonight.

"What was your meeting about this morning?" she asks, her breathing slightly uneven after the kiss. Her dark eyes hold curiosity and just a hint of caution as she looks at me. She's testing the waters again, trying to determine how much I'm willing to share with her now.

I consider that for a moment. It's tempting to continue keeping her in the dark. Despite everything, Nora is still so naïve, so ignorant of the real world. She got a small taste of it back in that warehouse, but it was nothing compared to the things I deal with every day. I want to continue shielding her from the brutal nature of my reality, but there is no safety in ignorance any longer—not when my enemies know about her. Besides, I have a feeling my young wife is tougher than her delicate appearance would suggest.

She has to be, to survive me.

Arriving at a decision, I give her a cool smile. "We just got intelligence on two Al-Quadar cells," I say, watching her reaction. "Now we're figuring out how we can wipe them out and capture some of their members in the process. The meeting was to coordinate the logistics of that operation."

Her eyes widen slightly, but she does a good job of controlling her shock at my revelations. "How many cells are there?" she asks, shifting forward in the chair. I can see her right palm curling into a fist next to her leg, though her voice remains calm. "How big is their organization?"

"Nobody knows, except their top leaders. That's why it's so hard to eradicate them—they're scattered all over the world, like vermin. They made a mistake, though, when they tried to play hardball with me. I am very good at exterminating vermin."

Nora swallows reflexively, but continues holding my gaze. *Brave girl.* "What did they want from you?" she asks. "Why did they decide to play hardball?"

I hesitate for a second, then decide to fill her in. She might as well know the full story at this point. "My company developed a new type of weapon—a powerful explosive that's almost impossible to detect," I explain. "A couple of kilos is all it would take to blow up a mid-sized airport, and a dozen kilos could take out a small city. It's got the explosive force of a nuclear bomb, but it's not radioactive, and the substance that it's made of resembles plastic, so it can be molded into nearly anything . . . even children's toys."

She stares at me, her face turning pale. She's beginning to understand the implications of this. "Is that why you didn't want to give it to them?" she asks. "Because you didn't want to place such a dangerous weapon in the hands of terrorists?"

"No, not really." I give her an amused look. It's sweet of her to ascribe noble motives to me, but she should know better at this point. "It's simply that the explosive is difficult to produce in large quantities, and I already have a long list of buyers waiting. Al-Quadar was at the very bottom of that list, so they would've had to wait years, if not decades, to get it from me."

To Nora's credit, her expression doesn't change. "So who is at the top of your list?" she says evenly. "Some other terrorist group?"

"No." I laugh softly. "Not even close. It's your government, my pet. They put in an order so large, it will keep my factories busy for years."

"Oh, I see." Initially she appears relieved, but then a puzzled frown creases her smooth forehead. "So legitimate governments buy things from you too? I thought the US military developed their own weapons . . ."

"They do." I grin at her naïveté. "But they would never pass up a chance to get their hands on something like this. And the more they buy, the less I can sell to others. It's an arrangement that works well for everyone."

"But why don't they just take it from you by force? Or simply shut down your factories?" She stares at me in confusion. "In general, if they know of your existence, why do they allow you to produce illegal weapons?"

"Because if I didn't do it, somebody else would—and that person might not be nearly as rational and pragmatic as I am." I can see the disbelieving look on Nora's face, and my grin widens. "Yes, my pet, believe it or not, the US government would rather deal with me, who bears America no particular ill will, than to have someone like Majid in charge of a similar operation."

"Majid?"

"The motherfucker who killed Beth." My voice hardens, my amusement disappearing without a trace. "The one responsible for stealing you at the clinic."

Nora tenses at the mention of Beth, and I see her hands balling into fists again. "The Suit—that's what I called him in my mind," she murmurs, her gaze appearing distant for a moment. "Because he was wearing a suit, you see . . ." She blinks, then focuses her attention on me again. "That was Majid?"

I nod, keeping my expression impassive despite the rage churning inside me. "Yes. That was him."

"I wish he hadn't died in the explosion," she says, surprising me for a moment. Her eyes glitter darkly in the sunlight. "He didn't deserve such an easy death."

"No, he didn't," I agree, now comprehending her meaning. Like me, she wishes that Majid had suffered. She hungers for revenge; I can hear it in her voice, see it on her face. It makes me wonder what would happen if she somehow ended up with Majid at her mercy. Would she be able to truly hurt him? To inflict such pain that he would beg for death?

It's an idea I find more than a little intriguing.

"Did you ever bring Beth here?" she asks, interrupting that train of thought. "To this compound, I mean?"

"No." I shake my head. "Before she came to stay on the island, Beth traveled with me, and I didn't come here for a long time."

"Why not?"

I shrug. "It wasn't my favorite place, I guess," I say casually, ignoring the dark memories that flood my mind at her innocent question. The estate was where I'd spent most of my childhood, where my father's belt and fists reigned supreme until I was old enough to fight back. It was where I killed my first man—and where I came to retrieve my mother's bloodied corpse twelve years ago. It wasn't until I renovated the house completely that I could stand the thought of coming to live here again, and even then, it's only Nora's presence that makes it bearable for me to be here.

She places her hand on my knee, bringing me back to the present. "Julian . . ." She pauses for a moment, as though unsure whether to proceed. Then she apparently decides to forge ahead. "There's something I would like to ask you," she says quietly, but firmly.

I lift my eyebrows. "What is it, my pet?"

"I took lessons back home," she says, her hand unconsciously tightening on my knee. "Self-defense and shooting, that sort of thing . . . and I'd like to resume them here, if possible."

"I see." A smile curves my mouth. My earlier speculations had been right, it seems. She's not the same frightened, helpless girl I brought to the island. This Nora is stronger, more resilient . . . and even more appealing. I remember reading about her lessons in Lucas's report, so her request is not totally unexpected. "You would like me to train you how to fight and use weapons?"

She nods. "Yes. Or maybe have someone else teach me, if you're busy."

"No." The thought of any one of my men laying his hands on her, even in a teaching capacity, makes me see red. "I will teach you myself."

* * *

I decide to start Nora's training that afternoon, after I catch up on a few business emails. For some reason, I like the idea of teaching her self-defense. I don't intend for her to ever be in a dangerous situation again, but I still want her to know how to protect herself if the need arises.

The irony of what I'm doing doesn't escape me. Most people would say I'm the one she needs protection from, and they would probably be right. I don't give a fuck, though. Nora is mine now, and I will do whatever it takes to keep her safe—even if it involves teaching her how to kill someone like me.

When I'm done with my emails, I go searching for her back at the house. This time I find her in the house gym, running on the treadmill at full speed. Judging by the sweat trickling down her slender back, she's been going at this pace for a while.

Making sure not to startle her, I come up to her from the side.

Spotting me, she reduces the speed on the treadmill, slowing down to a jog. "Hi," she says breathlessly, reaching for a small towel to wipe her face. "Is it time for the training?"

"Yes, I have a couple of hours now." My words come out low and husky as a familiar surge of arousal hardens my cock. I love seeing her like this, all out of breath, with her skin damp and glowing. It reminds me of how she looks after a particularly messy bout of sex. Of course, the fact that she's wearing only a pair of running shorts and a sports bra doesn't help. I want to lick the droplets of sweat off her smooth, flat belly, then throw her on the nearest mat for a quick fuck.

"Excellent." She gives me a huge smile and hits the 'Stop' button on the treadmill. Then she hops off the machine, grabbing her water bottle. "I'm ready."

She looks so excited that I decide to hold off on the mat fucking for now. Delayed gratification can be a good thing, and I did carve out this time specifically for her training.

"All right," I say. "Let's go." And taking her hand, I lead her out of the house.

We go to the field where I usually work out with my men. At this time of day, it's too hot for serious exercise, so the area is largely empty. Still, as we pass by, I see a few of the guards surreptitiously staring at Nora. It makes me want to rip their eyes out. I think they can tell—because they look away as soon as they glance at me. I know it's irrational to be this possessive of her, but I don't care. She belongs to me, and they all need to know that.

"What are we doing first?" she asks as we approach a storage shed in the corner of the training field.

"Shooting." I give her a sideways look. "I want to see how good you are with a gun."

She smiles, her eyes gleaming with eagerness. "I'm not bad," she says, and the confidence in her voice makes me grin. It seems that my pet learned a few things in my absence. I can't wait to see her demonstrate her new skills.

Inside the shed are some weapons and training gear. Going in, I select a few of the most commonly used guns—everything ranging from a 9mm handgun to an M16 assault rifle. I even grab an AK-47, although she might be too small to use it with ease.

Then we go outside to the shooting range.

There are a number of targets set up at different intervals. I have her begin with the closest target: a dozen empty beer cans propped on a wooden table some fifty feet away. Handing her the 9mm, I instruct her on how to use it and then have her aim at the cans.

To my shock, she hits ten of the twelve cans on her first try. "Dammit," she mutters, lowering the weapon. "I can't believe I missed those two."

Surprised and impressed, I have her try out the other guns. She's comfortable with most types of handguns and hunting rifles, hitting most of the targets again, but her arms shake when she tries to aim the AK-47.

"You would have to get stronger to use that one," I tell her, taking the assault rifle from her.

She nods in agreement, reaching for her water bottle. "Yes," she says between sips. "I want to get stronger. I want to be able to handle all these weapons, same as you."

I can't help laughing at that. Despite her generally easygoing nature, Nora has a strong competitive streak. I've noticed it before, when we did that three-mile race on the island.

"Okay," I say, still chuckling. Taking the bottle from her, I drink some water and then return it to her. "I can train you to get stronger as well."

After she practices shooting a few more times, we return the guns to the shed. Then I take her to the indoor training gym, to show her some basic fighting moves.

Lucas is there, sparring with three of the guards. Seeing us enter the room, he stops and respectfully nods at Nora, keeping his eyes fixed firmly on her face. He knows by now how I feel about her, and is smart enough not to display any interest in her slim, half-naked form. His sparring partners, however, are not that wise, and it takes a murderous glare from me for them to stop gaping at her.

"Hi Lucas," Nora says, ignoring this little interplay. "It's good to see you again."

Lucas gives her a carefully neutral smile. "You too, Mrs. Esguerra."

To my annoyance, Nora visibly flinches at the moniker, and my mild irritation with the guards morphs into sudden anger at her. Her reluctance to marry me earlier is like a festering splinter at the back of my brain, and it doesn't take much to bring back the way I felt at the church.

For all of her supposed love for me, she still refuses to accept our marriage, and I'm no longer inclined to be reasonable and forgiving.

"Out," I bark at Lucas and the guards, jerking my thumb toward the door. "We need this space."

They clear out within seconds, leaving me and Nora alone.

She takes a step back, suddenly looking wary. She knows me well, and I can tell she senses something amiss.

As usual, she can guess what it is. "Julian," she says cautiously, "I didn't mean to react like that. I'm just not used to being called that, that's all . . ."

"Is that right, my pet?" My voice is like brushed silk, reflecting none of the simmering fury inside. Stepping toward her, I lift my hand and slowly trace my fingers over her jawline. "Would you prefer *not* to be called that? Perhaps you wish I hadn't come back for you at all?"

Her huge eyes grow even larger. "No, of course not! I told you, I want to be here with you—"

"Don't lie to me." The words come out cold and sharp as I drop my hand. It infuriates me that I care about this at all, that I let something as insignificant as Nora's feelings bother me. What does it matter if she loves me? I shouldn't want that from her, shouldn't expect it. And yet I do—it's part of this fucked-up obsession I have with her.

"I'm not lying," she denies vehemently, taking a step back. Her face is pale in the dim light of the room, but her gaze is direct and unwavering as she stares at me. "I shouldn't want to be with you, but I do. Do you think I don't realize how wrong this is? How messed-up? You kidnapped me, Julian . . . You forced me."

The accusation hangs between us, stark and heavy. If I were a different man, a better man, I would look away. I would feel remorse for what I'd done.

But I don't.

I'm not into self-deception. I never have been. When I abducted Nora, I knew that I crossed a line, that I sank to a new low. I did it with the full knowledge of what that makes me: an irredeemable beast, a destroyer of innocence. It's a label I'm willing to live with to have her.

I would do anything to have her.

So instead of looking away, I hold her gaze. "Yes," I say quietly. "I did." My anger is gone, replaced by an emotion I don't want to analyze too closely. Taking a step toward her, I lift my hand again and stroke the plush softness of her lower lip with my thumb. Her lips part at my touch, and the hunger that I've been suppressing all day sharpens, clawing at my insides.

I want her.

I want her, and I'm going to take her.

After this, she will have no doubt that she belongs to me.

CHAPTER TEN

❖ NORA ❖

Staring up at my husband, I fight the urge to back away. I shouldn't have let Julian see my reaction to my new name, but I had been enjoying the shooting session—and Julian's company—so much that I had forgotten the reality of my new situation. Hearing 'Mrs. Esguerra' fall from Lucas's lips startled me, bringing back that disconcerting feeling of lost identity, and, for a moment, I had been unable to hide my dismay.

That moment was all it took to transform Julian from a laughing, teasing companion to the terrifying, unpredictable man who first brought me to his island.

I can feel the rapid beating of my pulse as his thumb caresses my lips, his touch gentle despite the darkness gleaming in his eyes. He doesn't seem upset by my reckless accusations; if anything, he looks calmer now, almost amused. I'm not sure what I thought would happen when I threw the words at him, but I hadn't expected him to admit his crimes so easily, without even a hint of guilt or regret. Most people try to justify their actions to themselves and others, twisting the facts to suit their purposes, but Julian is not most people. He sees things as they are; he's just not bothered by the idea of committing acts most people would cringe at. Instead of a deluded psycho who thinks he's doing the right thing, my new husband is simply a man without a conscience.

A man whom I both love and fear right now.

Without saying another word, Julian lowers his fingers and grips my upper arm, leading me toward one of the wide wrestling mats near the wall. As we walk, I catch a glimpse of the bulge in his shorts, and my breathing speeds up from a combination of anxiety and involuntary desire.

Julian intends to fuck me, right here and now, where anyone can walk in on us.

An uncomfortable mixture of lust and embarrassment makes my skin burn. Logic tells me this is not likely to be one of our more vanilla encounters, but my body doesn't know the difference between a punishment fuck and tender lovemaking. All it knows is Julian, and it's conditioned to crave his touch.

To my surprise, Julian doesn't fall on me right away. Instead he releases my arm and looks at me, his sensuous mouth twisted into a cold, slightly cruel smile. "Why don't you show me what you learned in those self-defense classes of yours, my pet?" he says softly. "Let's see some of the moves they taught you."

I stare at him, my heart climbing into my throat as I realize what Julian wants. He wants me to fight him, to resist—even though it won't change the outcome.

Even though it'll only make me feel helpless and defeated when I lose.

"Why?" I ask in desperation, trying to put off the inevitable. I know Julian is just toying with me, but I don't want to play this game, not after everything that has occurred between us. I want to forget those early days on the island, not relive them in this twisted way.

"Why not?" He begins to circle around me, causing my anxiety to spike. "Isn't that why you took those classes, so you could protect yourself from men like me? Men who want to take you, to abuse you?"

My breathing accelerates further, adrenaline flooding my system as an involuntary fight-or-flight response kicks in. Instinctively I turn, trying to keep him in sight at all times, as if he were a dangerous predator—because he is one right now.

A beautiful, deadly predator who is intent on me as his prey.

"Go ahead, Nora," he murmurs, stopping so that my back is against the wall. "Fight."

"No." I try not to flinch when he reaches for me, his hand closing around my wrist. "I'm not doing this, Julian. Not like this."

His nostrils flare. He's not used to me denying him anything, and I hold my breath, waiting to see what he will do. My heart is beating painfully in my chest, and a thin trickle of sweat slides down my back as I hold his gaze. By now I know Julian wouldn't truly harm me, but that doesn't mean he won't punish me for my defiance.

"All right," he says softly. "If that's how you want it." And using his grip on my wrist, he twists my arm upwards, forcing me down to my knees. With his free hand, he unzips his shorts, letting his erection spring free. Then he wraps my hair around his fist and pushes my mouth toward his cock. "Suck it," he orders roughly, staring down at me.

Relieved by the simple task, I gladly obey, closing my lips around the thick column of his sex. He tastes like salt and man, the tip of his shaft damp with pre-cum, and some of my anxiety fades, edged out by growing desire. I love pleasuring him like this, and as Julian's grip on my wrist slackens, I use both hands to cup his balls, kneading and massaging them with firm pressure.

He groans, closing his eyes, and I begin to move my mouth back and forth, using a sucking motion to bring him deeper into my throat each time. The way he holds my hair hurts my scalp, but the discomfort only enhances my arousal. Julian was right when he said I have masochistic tendencies. Whether by nature or by nurture, I get off on pain now, my body craving the intensity of these types of sensations.

Looking up at him, I drink in the tortured expression on his face, enjoying the small taste of power he allows me.

Today, though, he doesn't let me set the pace for long. Instead he pushes his hips forward, forcing his cock further into my throat, and I gag, spitting up some saliva. That seems to please him, and he mutters thickly, "Yes, that's it, baby," opening his eyes to watch me as he begins to fuck my face with a hard, relentless rhythm. I choke again, and more saliva dribbles out, coating my chin and his cock with viscous moisture.

He releases me then, but before I can catch my breath, he pushes me down on the mat, face first, causing me to fall onto my hands. Then he gets behind me, and I feel him pulling my shorts and underwear down to my knees. My sex clenches in hungry anticipation . . . but that's not where he wants me today. It's the other opening that holds his attention, and I tense instinctively as I feel the head of his cock pressing between my cheeks.

"Relax, my pet," he murmurs, grasping my hips to hold me in place as he begins to push in. "Just relax . . . Yes, there is a good girl . . ."

I take small, shallow breaths as I try to follow Julian's advice, fighting the urge to tighten up as he slowly begins to penetrate my ass. I know from experience this will hurt a lot less if I'm not so tense, but my body seems determined to fight this intrusion. After months of abstinence, it's almost as if I'm a virgin there again, and I feel a heavy, burning pressure as my sphincter is forcefully stretched open.

"Julian, please . . ." The words come out in a low, pleading whisper as he ruthlessly pushes deeper, the saliva coating his cock acting as makeshift lube. My insides twist, and sweat breaks out all over my body as the tight ring of muscle finally gives in, letting his massive cock slide all the way in. Now he's throbbing deep inside me, making me feel unbearably full, engulfed and overtaken.

"Please what?" he breathes, sliding one muscular arm under my hips to hold me in place. At the same time, his other hand grabs my hair again, forcing my body to arch backwards. The new angle deepens the penetration, and I cry out, beginning to shake. It's too much, I can't take it, but Julian is not giving me a choice. This is my punishment, being fucked like an animal on a dirty mat, with no care or preparation. It should make me feel sick, killing all traces of desire, but somehow I'm still turned on, my body eager for whatever sensations Julian chooses to dole out. "Please what?" he repeats, his voice low and rough. "Please fuck me? Please give me more?"

"I . . . I don't know . . ." I can hardly speak, my senses overwhelmed. He stills then, not moving, and I'm grateful for that small mercy, as it gives me a chance to adjust to the brutal hardness lodged within me. I try to steady my breathing, to relax, and the pain gradually begins to lessen, transforming into something else—a sizzling heat that permeates my nerve endings.

He starts to move again, his thrusts slow and deep, and the heat intensifies, centering low in my core. My nipples tighten, and a rush of wetness inundates my sex. Despite the discomfort, there is something perversely erotic about being taken like this, about being possessed in a way that's so dirty and forbidden. Closing my eyes, I begin to get into the primal rhythm of his movements, the thrust and drag that makes my insides churn with agony and pleasure. My clit swells, becoming more sensitive, and I know it will take only a few light touches to make me come, to relieve the tension building within me.

But he doesn't touch my clit. Instead his hand releases my hair and slides down to my neck. Then he grips my throat, forcing me to rise up so that I'm standing on my knees, my back slightly arched. My eyes pop open and my hands automatically fly up, clutching at his strangling fingers, but there's nothing I can do to loosen his hold. In this position, he's even deeper inside me, and I can barely breathe, my heart beginning to pound with a new, unfamiliar fear.

He leans forward then, and I can feel his lips brushing against my ear. "You are mine for the rest of your life," he whispers harshly, the warmth of his breath making my skin prickle with goosebumps. "Do you understand me, Nora? All of you—your pussy, your asshole, your fucking inner thoughts . . . It's all mine to use and abuse as I will. I own you, inside and out, in every way possible . . ." His sharp teeth sink into my earlobe, causing me to gasp at the sudden pain. "Do you understand me?" There is a dark note in his voice that scares me. This is new—he's never done this to me before—and my pulse soars sky-high as his fingers tighten around my throat, slowly but inexorably cutting off my air supply.

Rising panic sends adrenaline surging through my veins. "Yes . . ." I manage to rasp out, my fingers now clawing at his hand, trying to pry it away. To my horror, I start seeing stars, the room blurring and going dark in front of my eyes. *Surely he doesn't mean to kill me . . . Surely he doesn't mean to kill me . . .* I am terrified, yet for some strange reason, my sex throbs and electric shivers run over my skin as my arousal spirals inexorably higher.

"Good. Now tell me . . . whose wife are you?" His fingers tighten further, and the stars go supernova as my brain struggles to get enough oxygen. My body is on the brink of suffocation, yet it's more alive in this moment than it's ever been, every sensation sharpened and refined. The burning thickness of his cock inside my ass, the heat of his breath on my temple, the pulsing of my engorged clit—it's too much and not enough at the same time. I want to scream and struggle, but I can't move, can't breathe . . . and as if from far away, I hear Julian demanding again, "Whose?"

Right before I pass out, his grip on my throat eases, and I choke out, "Yours" . . . even as my body convulses in a paroxysm of agonized ecstasy, the orgasm sudden and startlingly intense as much-needed oxygen rushes into my lungs.

Frantically gulping in air, I slump against him, trembling all over. I can't believe I came like this, without Julian touching my sex at all.

I can't believe I came while being afraid of dying.

After a moment, I become conscious of his lips grazing my sweat-dampened cheek. "Yes," he murmurs, his hand now gently stroking my throat, "that's right, baby . . ." He's still buried inside me, his hard cock splitting me apart, invading me. "And what's your name?"

"Nora," I gasp out hoarsely, quivering as his fingers trail down from my neck to my breasts. I'm still wearing my sports bra, and his hand burrows under the tight material, cupping my breast.

"Nora what?" he persists, his fingers pinching my nipple. It's erect and sensitive from my orgasm, and his touch sends a fresh ripple of heat down to my core. "Nora what?"

"Nora Esguerra," I whisper, closing my eyes. It's a fact I will never forget now—and as Julian resumes fucking me again, I know that Nora Leston will never exist again.

She is gone for good.

PART II: THE ESTATE

CHAPTER ELEVEN

❖ NORA ❖

Over the next couple of weeks, I slowly acclimate to my new home. The estate is a fascinating place, and I spend much of my time exploring it and meeting its inhabitants.

Besides the guards, there are a few dozen people living here, some by themselves, others with their families. They all work for Julian in one capacity or another, from the oldest generation to the youngest. Some—like Ana and Rosa—take care of the house and the grounds, while others are involved in Julian's business. He may have only recently returned to the compound, but many of his employees have lived here since the time when Juan Esguerra—Julian's father— reigned as one of the most powerful drug lords in the country. To an American like myself, such loyalty to an employer is unfathomable.

"They're well paid, provided with free housing, and your husband even hired a teacher for their children a few years ago," Rosa explains when I ask her about this unusual phenomenon. "He might not have been here much in person, but he's always been good at taking care of his people. They're all free to leave if they want, but they know they're unlikely to find anything better. Besides, here they're protected, but out there, they and their families are fair game for nosy policemen or anyone else seeking information on the Esguerra organization." Giving me a wry smile, she adds, "My mother says that once you're a part of this life, you're always a part of this life. There's no going back."

"So why did they choose this life?" I ask, trying to understand what would make one move to a weapons dealer's isolated compound on the edge of the Amazon rainforest. I don't know many sane people who would do something like that willingly—particularly if they knew there was no easy way to return home.

Rosa shrugs. "Well, everybody has a different story. Some were wanted by the authorities; others made enemies of dangerous people. My parents came here to escape poverty and provide a better life for me and my brothers. They knew they were taking a risk, but they felt they had no other choice. To this day, my mother is convinced that they made the right decision for themselves and their children."

"Even after—?" I start asking, then shut my mouth when I realize that I'm about to bring up painful memories for Rosa again.

"Yes, even after," she says, understanding my half-spoken question. "There are no guarantees in life. They could've died anyway. My father and Eduardo—my oldest brother—were killed doing their jobs, but at least they had jobs. Back at my parents' village, there were no jobs, and the cities were even worse. My parents did whatever they could to keep food on the table, but it wasn't enough. When my mother became pregnant with me, Eduardo, who was twelve at the time, went to Medellín seeking to become a drug mule—just so that our family wouldn't starve. My father went after him to stop him, and that's when the two of them ran into Juan Esguerra, who was in the city for negotiations with the Medellín Cartel. He offered both my father and brother a job in his organization, and the rest is history." She stops and smiles at me before continuing, "So you see, Nora, working for Señor Esguerra was the best alternative for my family. As my mother says, at least I never had to sell myself for food, the way she did in her youth."

Rosa says that last part without any bitterness or self-pity. She's simply stating facts. Rosa genuinely considers herself lucky to have been born on the Esguerra estate. She's grateful to Julian and his father for providing her family with a good living, and, despite her longing to see America, she doesn't mind living in the middle of nowhere. To her, this compound is home.

I learn all of this during our walks. While Rosa doesn't like jogging, she's more than happy to take a brisk walk with me in the morning, before it gets too hot and muggy. It's something we started doing on my third day here, and it's quickly becoming part of my daily routine.

I like spending time with Rosa; she's bright and friendly, reminding me a bit of my friend Leah. And Rosa seems to enjoy my company as well—although I'm sure she would be nice to me regardless, given my position here. Everybody on the estate treats me with respect and politeness.

After all, I'm the Señor's wife.

After the incident at the gym, I have done my best to accept the fact that I'm married to Julian—that the beautiful, amoral man who abducted me is now my husband. It's an idea that still disturbs me on some level, but with each day that passes, I grow more and more accustomed to it. My life changed irrevocably when Julian stole me, and that far-off 'normal' future is a dream I should've given up a long time ago. Clinging to it while falling in love with my kidnapper had been as irrational as developing feelings for him in the first place.

Instead of a house in the suburbs and two-point-five kids, my future now holds a heavily guarded compound near the Amazon jungle and a man who both excites and terrifies me. It's impossible for me to imagine having children with Julian, and I dread the fact that in a few short months, the three-year birth control implant I got at seventeen will cease to be effective. At some point, I will need to bring up this issue with Julian, but for now I'm trying not to think about it. I'm no more ready to be a mother than I was to be a wife, and the possibility of having that choice forced on me makes me break out in a cold sweat. I love Julian, but raising children with a man who thinks nothing of kidnapping and killing? That's a whole other matter.

My parents and friends back home aren't helping. I spoke once with Leah, telling her about my hasty marriage, and her reaction had been shocked, to say the least.

"You married that arms dealer?" she exclaimed incredulously. "After everything he's done to you and Jake? Are you insane? You're only nineteen—and he should be in jail!" And no matter how much I tried to spin everything in a positive light, I could tell she got off the phone thinking that my abduction left me a few cards short of a full deck.

My parents are even worse. Every time I talk to them, I have to fend off their probing questions about my unexpected marriage and Julian's plans for our future. I don't blame them for adding to my anxiety; I know they're worried sick about me. The last time we had a video call, my mom's eyes were red and swollen, as though she'd been crying. It's obvious that the hastily concocted story I told them at my wedding has done little to alleviate their concerns. My parents know how my relationship with Julian began, and they're having a hard time believing I could be happy with a man they see as pure evil.

And yet I *am* happy, my fretting about the future aside. The icy emptiness inside me is gone, replaced by a dazzling abundance of emotions and sensations. It's as though the black-and-white movie of my life has been redone in technicolor.

When I'm with Julian, I'm complete and content in a way that I don't fully understand and can't quite come to terms with. It's not like I was miserable before I met him. I had great friends, a loving family, and the promise of a good, if unexceptional, life ahead of me. I even had a crush—Jake—who gave me the proverbial butterflies in my stomach. It makes no sense that I somehow needed something as perverse as this relationship with Julian to enrich my life and give me that which I was missing.

Of course, I'm no shrink. Perhaps there is an explanation for my feelings—some childhood trauma that I've repressed, or a chemical imbalance in my brain. Or maybe it's just Julian and the deliberate way he's been molding my physical and emotional responses since those early days on the island. I am cognizant of his conditioning methods, but my recognition of them doesn't alter their effectiveness. It's strange to know that you're being manipulated, and at the same time enjoy the results of that manipulation.

But enjoy them I do. Being with Julian is thrilling—both frightening and exhilarating, like riding a wild tiger. I never know which side of him I will see at any given moment: the charming lover or the cruel master. And as messed-up as it is, I want both—I am addicted to both. The light and the dark, the violence and the tenderness—it all goes together, forming a volatile, dizzying cocktail that plays havoc with my equilibrium and makes me fall even deeper under Julian's spell.

Of course, the fact that I see him now every day doesn't help. On the island, Julian's frequent absences gave me time to recover from the potent effect he has on my mind and body, enabling me to maintain some emotional balance. Here, however, there is no respite from the magnetic pull he exerts on me, no way to shield myself from his intoxicating allure. With each day that passes, I lose a little more of my soul to him, my need for him growing, rather than decreasing with time.

The only thing that keeps me from freaking out is the knowledge that Julian is drawn to me just as strongly. I don't know if it's my resemblance to Maria or just our inexplicable chemistry, but I know the addiction works both ways.

Julian's hunger for me knows no bounds. He takes me a couple of times every night—and often during the day as well—yet I get the sense he still wants more. It's there in the intensity of his gaze, in the way he always touches me, holds me. He can't keep his hands off me—and that makes me feel better about my own helpless attraction to him.

He also seems to enjoy spending time with me outside of the bedroom. True to his promise, Julian has begun training me, teaching me how to fight and use different weapons. After the initial rocky start, he turned out to be an excellent instructor—knowledgeable, patient, and surprisingly dedicated. We train together nearly every day, and I've already learned more in these couple of weeks than in the prior three months in my self-defense courses. Of course, it would be a misnomer to call what he teaches me self-defense; Julian's lessons have more in common with some kind of assassin bootcamp.

"You aim to kill every time," he instructs during one afternoon session where he makes me throw knives at a small target on the wall. "You don't have the size or the strength, so for you, it's all about speed, reflexes, and ruthlessness. You need to catch your opponents off-guard and eliminate them before they realize how skilled you are. Every strike has to be deadly; every move has to count."

"What if I don't want to kill them?" I ask, looking up at him. "What if I just want to wound them, so I can run away?"

"A wounded man can still hurt you. It doesn't take much strength to squeeze a trigger or stab you with a knife. Unless you have a good reason for wanting your enemy alive, you aim to kill, Nora. Do you understand me?"

I nod and throw a small, sharp knife at the wall. It thuds dully against the target, then falls down, having barely scratched the wood. Not my best attempt, but better than my prior five.

I don't know if I can do what Julian says, but I do know that I never want to feel defenseless again. If it means learning the skills of an assassin, I'm happy to do it. It doesn't mean I will ever use them, but just knowing that I can protect myself makes me feel stronger and more confident, helping me cope with the residual nightmares from my time with the terrorists.

To my relief, those have gotten better as well. It's like my subconscious knows that Julian is here—that I'm safe with him. Of course, it also helps that when I do wake up screaming, he's there to hold me and chase the nightmare away.

The first time it happens is the third night after my arrival at the estate. I dream of Beth's death again, of the ocean of blood that I'm drowning in, but this time, strong arms catch me, save me from the vicious rip current. This time, when I open my eyes, I'm not alone in the darkness. Julian has turned on the bedside lamp and is shaking me awake, a concerned expression on his beautiful face.

"I'm here now," he soothes, pulling me into his lap when I can't stop trembling, tears of remembered horror running down my face. "All is well, I promise..." He strokes my hair until my sobbing breaths begin to even out, and then he asks softly, "What's the matter, baby? Did you have a bad dream? You were screaming my name..."

I nod, clinging to him with all my strength. I can feel the warmth of his skin, hear the steady beating of his heart, and the nightmare slowly begins to recede, my mind coming back to the present. "It was Beth," I whisper when I can speak without my voice breaking. "He was torturing her... killing her."

Julian's arms tighten around me. He doesn't say anything, but I can feel his rage, his burning fury. Beth had been more than a housekeeper to him, though the precise nature of their relationship had always been something of a mystery to me.

Desperate to distract myself from the bloody images still filling my mind, I decide to satisfy the curiosity that had gnawed at me all through my time on the island. "How did you and Beth meet?" I ask, pulling back to look at Julian's face. "How did she come to be on the island with me?"

He looks at me, his eyes dark with memories. Before, whenever I would ask these types of questions, he would brush me off or change the topic, but things are different between us now. Julian seems more willing to talk to me, to let me more fully into his life.

"I was in Tijuana seven years ago for a meeting with one of the cartels," he begins speaking after a moment. "After my business was concluded, I went looking for entertainment in Zona Norte, the red-light district of the city. I was passing by one of the alleys when I saw it . . . a screaming, crying woman huddled over a small figure on the ground."

"Beth," I whisper, remembering what she told me about her daughter.

"Yes, Beth," he confirms. "It wasn't any of my business, but I'd had a couple of drinks and I was curious. So I came closer . . . and that's when I saw that the small figure on the ground was a child. A beautiful baby girl with red curly hair, a tiny replica of the woman crying over her." A savage, furious glint enters his eyes. "The child was lying in a pool of blood, with a gunshot wound in her small chest. She had apparently been killed to punish her mother, who didn't want to let her pimp offer the child to some clients with more *unique* tastes."

Nausea, sharp and strong, rises in my throat. Despite everything I've been through, it still horrifies me to know that there are such monsters out there. Monsters far worse than the man I've fallen in love with.

No wonder Beth saw the world in shades of black; her life had been overtaken by darkness.

"When I heard the full story, I took Beth and her daughter with me," Julian continues in a low, hard voice. "It still wasn't any of my business, but I couldn't let this type of thing slide—at least not after seeing that child's body. We buried the daughter in a cemetery just outside Tijuana. Then I took a couple of my men, and Beth and I came back to look for the pimp." A small, vicious smile appears on his lips as he says softly, "Beth killed him personally. Him and his two thugs—the ones who helped murder her daughter."

I inhale slowly, not wanting to start crying again. "And she came to work for you after that? After you helped her like that?"

Julian nods. "Yes. It wasn't safe for her to stay in Tijuana, so I offered her a job as my personal cook and maid. She accepted, of course—it was far better than being a streetwalker in Mexico—and she traveled with me everywhere after that. It wasn't until I decided to acquire you that I offered her the opportunity to stay permanently on the island and, well, you know the rest of the story."

"Yes, I do," I murmur, pushing against his chest to extricate myself from his embrace—an embrace that suddenly feels suffocating rather than comforting. The 'acquire you' part of the story is an unpleasant reminder of how I came to be here . . . of the fact that the man by my side ruthlessly planned and carried out my abduction. On the spectrum of evil, Julian may not be all the way on the black side, but he's not very far from it.

Still, as days go on, my nightmares slowly ease. As perverse as it is, now that I'm back with my kidnapper, I'm starting to heal from the ordeal of being stolen from him. Even my art has become more peaceful. I still feel compelled to paint the flames of the explosion, but I have begun to get interested in landscapes again, capturing on canvas the wild beauty of the rainforest that encroaches on the borders of the property.

As before, Julian encourages my hobby. In addition to setting up the studio for me, he retained an art instructor—a thin, elderly man from the south of France who speaks English with a thick accent. Monsieur Bernard had taught in all the best art schools in Europe before retiring in his late seventies. I have no idea how Julian persuaded him to come to the estate, but I'm thankful for his presence. The techniques he teaches me are far more advanced than what I had learned through my instructional videos before, and I'm already starting to see a new level of sophistication in my art—as does Monsieur Bernard.

"You have talent, Señora," he says with his heavy French accent, examining my latest attempt at painting a sunset in the jungle. The trees look dark against the glowing orange and pink of the setting sun, with the edges of the painting blurred out and out of focus. "This has a—how do you say it? An almost *sinister* feel to it?" He glances at me, his faded gaze suddenly sharp with curiosity. "Yes," he continues softly after studying me for a few moments. "You have talent and something more—something inside you that comes out through your art. A darkness I rarely see in one so young."

I don't know how to respond to that, so I simply smile at him. I am not sure whether Monsieur Bernard knows about my husband's profession, but I'm almost certain the elderly instructor has no idea how my relationship with Julian began.

As far as the world is concerned now, I'm the pampered young wife of a handsome, rich man, and that's all there is to it.

* * *

"I've enrolled you for the winter quarter at Stanford," Julian says casually over dinner one night. "They have a new online program. It's still in the experimental stages, but the early feedback is quite good. It's all the same professors; it's just that the lectures are recorded, instead of being live."

My jaw drops. I'm enrolled at *Stanford*? I had no idea college of any kind—much less a top ten university—was even on the table. "What?" I say incredulously, putting down my fork. Ana had prepared a delicious meal for us, but I no longer have any interest in the food on my plate, all my attention focused on Julian.

He smiles at me calmly. "I promised your parents you would get a good education, and I'm delivering on that promise. You don't like Stanford?"

Stunned, I stare at him. I don't have an opinion about Stanford because I had never even entertained the possibility of going there. My grades in school had been good, but my SAT scores weren't sky-high, and my parents couldn't have afforded such an expensive school anyway. Community college followed by a transfer to one of the state colleges was going to be my path to getting a degree, so I never looked at Stanford or any school of its caliber. "How did you get me in?" I finally manage to ask. "Isn't their admission rate in the single digits? Or is the online program less competitive?"

"No, it's even more competitive, I believe," Julian says, filling his plate with a second serving of chicken. "I think they're only taking a hundred students for the program this year, and there were about ten thousand applicants."

"Then how did you—" I begin saying, then shut up as I realize that getting me into an elite school is child's play to someone with Julian's wealth and connections. "So I start in January?" I ask instead, excitement trickling through my veins as the shock begins to wear off. *Stanford. Oh my God, I will be going to Stanford.* I should probably feel guilty that I didn't get in on my own merit—or at least be outraged at Julian's high-handedness—but all I can think about is my parents' reaction when I tell them the news. *I will be going to freaking Stanford!*

Julian nods, reaching for more rice. "Yes, that's when the winter quarter begins. They should email you an orientation packet in the next couple of days, so you'll be able to order your textbooks once you find out the class requirements. I'll make sure they're delivered to you here in time."

"Wow, okay." I know it's not an appropriate response for something of this magnitude, but I can't think of anything more clever to say. In less than two weeks, I will be a student at one of the most prestigious universities in the world—the last thing I expected when Julian came for me again. Granted, it will be an online program, but it's still far better than anything I could've dreamed of.

A number of questions occur to me. "What about my major? What will I be studying?" I ask, wondering if Julian made that decision for me too. The fact that he took the matter of my college education into his own hands doesn't surprise me; after all, this is the man who abducted me and forced me to marry him. He's not exactly big on giving me choices.

Julian gives me an indulgent smile. "Whatever you want, my pet. I believe there is a common set of subjects you'll need to take, so you won't need to decide your major for a year or two. Do you have some ideas of what you want to study?"

"No, not really." I had been planning to take classes in different areas to figure out what I wanted to do, and I'm glad that Julian left me this option. In high school I had done equally well in most subjects, which made it hard to narrow down my career options.

"Well, you still have time to figure it out," Julian says, sounding for all the world like a guidance counselor. "There is no rush."

"Right, uh-huh." A part of me can't believe we're having this conversation. Less than two hours ago, Julian cornered me by the pool and fucked my brains out on one of the lounge chairs. Less than five hours ago, he taught me how to disable a man by stabbing him in the eye with my fingers. Two nights ago, he tied me to our bed and whipped me with a flogger. And now we're discussing my potential major in college? Trying to wrap my mind around such a strange turn of events, I ask Julian on autopilot, "So what did *you* study in college?"

As soon as the words leave my mouth, I realize that I have no idea if Julian even went to college—that I still know very little about the man I sleep with every night. Frowning, I do some quick mental math. According to Rosa, Julian's parents were killed twelve years ago, at which point he took over his father's business. Given that about twenty months had passed since Beth told me that Julian was twenty-nine, he had to be somewhere around thirty-one today—which meant he took over his father's business at nineteen.

For the first time, it dawns on me that Julian had been right around my age when he took his father's place as the head of an illegal drug operation and transformed it into a cutting-edge—though equally illegal—weapons empire.

To my surprise, Julian says, "I studied electrical engineering."

"What?" I can't hide my shock. "But I thought you took over your father's business really young—"

"I did." Julian gives me an amused look. "I dropped out of Caltech after a year and a half. But while I was there, I studied electrical engineering through an accelerated program."

Caltech? I stare at Julian with newfound respect. I've always known that he's smart, but engineering at Caltech is a whole different level of brilliance. "Is that why you chose to go into arms dealing? Because you had a background in engineering?"

"Yes, partly. And partly because I saw more opportunities there than in the drug trade."

"More opportunities?" Picking up my fork, I twirl it between my fingers as I study Julian, trying to understand what would make one abandon one criminal enterprise for another. Surely someone with his level of intelligence and drive could've chosen to do something better—something less dangerous and immoral. "Why didn't you just get your degree from Caltech and do something legitimate with it?" I ask after a few moments. "I'm sure you could've gotten any job you wanted—or maybe started your own business if you didn't like the corporate world."

He looks at me, his expression unreadable. "I thought about it," he says, shocking me yet again. "When I left Colombia after Maria's death, I wanted to be done with that world. For the rest of my teenage years, I tried my hardest to forget the lessons my father taught me, to keep the violence within me under control. That's why I enrolled in Caltech—because I thought I could take a different path . . . become someone other than who I was meant to be."

I stare at him, my pulse quickening. This is the first time I've heard Julian admit to ever wanting something different than the life he's currently leading. "So why didn't you? Surely there was nothing tying you to that world once your father was dead . . ."

"You're right." Julian gives me a thin smile. "I could've ignored my father's death and let the other cartel take over his organization. It would've been easy. They had no idea where I was or what name I was using at that point, so I could've started fresh, finishing college and getting a job with one of the Silicon Valley start-ups. And I probably would've done that—if they hadn't also killed my mother."

"Your mother?"

"Yes." His beautiful features twist with hatred. "They gunned her down right here on the estate, along with dozens of others. I couldn't ignore that."

No, of course he couldn't. Not somebody like Julian, who had already killed for revenge. Remembering the story he told me about the men who murdered Maria, I feel a chill rippling over my skin. "So you came back and killed them?"

"Yes. I gathered all of my father's remaining men and hired some new ones. We attacked in the middle of the night, striking at the cartel leaders right in their homes. They weren't expecting such fast retaliation, and we caught them off-guard." His lips curl into a dark smile. "By the time the morning came, there were no survivors—and I knew I had been foolish to think that I could ignore what I am . . . to imagine that I could be something other than the killer I was born to be."

The chill running over my skin transforms into full-on goosebumps. This side of Julian terrifies me, and I clasp my hands together under the table to prevent them from shaking. "You told me you saw a therapist after your parents' death. Because you wanted to kill more."

"Yes, my pet." There is a savage gleam in his blue eyes. "I killed the cartel leaders and their families, and when it was all over, I thirsted for more blood . . . more death. The craving inside me only intensified during the years that I'd been away; leading a so-called 'normal' life made it worse, not better." He pauses, and I shudder at the black shadows I see in his gaze. "Seeing a therapist was a last-ditch attempt to fight against my nature, and it didn't take me long to realize that it was futile—that the only way to move forward was to embrace it and accept my fate."

"And you did that by going into arms dealing." I try to keep my voice steady. "By becoming a criminal."

At that moment, Ana comes into the dining room and begins to clear the dishes off the table. Watching her, I slowly rub my arms, trying to dispel the coldness within me. In a way, it makes it worse, the fact that Julian had a choice and that he consciously chose to embrace the darkest part of himself. It tells me there is no hope for redemption, no chance of making him see the error of his ways. It's not that he never knew there was an alternative to a life of crime; on the contrary, he had experienced such an alternative and decided to reject it.

"Would you like anything else?" Ana asks us, and I shake my head mutely, too disturbed to think about dessert. Julian, however, asks for a cup of hot chocolate, sounding as unruffled as ever.

When Ana exits the room, Julian smiles at me, as though sensing the direction of my thoughts. "I was always a criminal, Nora," he says softly. "I killed for the first time when I was eight, and I knew then that there would be no going back. I tried to bury that knowledge for a while, but it was always there, waiting for me to come to my senses." He leans back in his seat, his posture indolent, yet predatory, like the lazy sprawl of a jungle cat. "The truth of the matter is I need this kind of life, my pet. The danger, the violence—and the power that comes with it all—they suit me in a way that a boring corporate job could never have." He pauses, then adds, his eyes glittering, "They make me feel alive."

* * *

When we get to the bedroom that evening, I go to take a quick shower while Julian responds to a couple of urgent work emails on his iPad. By the time I come out of the bathroom with a towel wrapped around my damp body, he's put the tablet away and is beginning to undress. As he pulls off his shirt, I sense an unusual excitement within him, a pent-up energy in his movements that hadn't been there before.

"What happened?" I ask warily, our earlier conversation fresh in my mind. Things that excite Julian are, more often than not, something that would make me shudder. Pausing by the bed, I adjust the towel, strangely reluctant to bare myself to his gaze quite yet.

He gives me a brilliant smile as he sits down on the bed to take off his socks. "Do you remember when I told you we had some intelligence on two Al-Quadar cells?" When I nod, he says, "Well, we succeeded in destroying them and even captured three terrorists in the process. Lucas is having them brought here for questioning, so they'll be arriving in the morning."

"Oh." I stare at him, my stomach churning with an unsettling mix of emotions. I understand what 'questioning' implies in Julian's world. I should be horrified and disgusted by the idea that my husband will most likely torture those men—and I am—but deep inside, I also feel a kind of sick, vengeful joy. It's an emotion that disturbs me a lot more than the thought of Julian interrogating them tomorrow. I know these men are not the same ones who murdered Beth, but that doesn't change the way I feel about them. There is a part of me that wants them to pay for Beth's death . . . to suffer for what Majid did.

Apparently misinterpreting my reaction, Julian rises to his feet and says softly, "Don't worry, my pet. They won't hurt you—I'll make sure of that." And before I can respond, he pushes down his jeans to reveal a growing erection.

At the sight of his naked body, a wave of desire washes over me, heating me from the inside out despite my mental turmoil. Over the past couple of weeks, Julian has regained some of the muscle he lost during his coma, and he's even more stunning than before, his shoulders impossibly broad and his skin darkly tanned from the hot sun. Raising my eyes to his face, I wonder for the hundredth time how someone so beautiful can carry such evil inside—and whether some of that evil is beginning to rub off on me.

"I know they won't hurt me here," I say quietly as he reaches for me. "I'm not afraid of them."

A sardonic half-smile appears on his lips as he tugs the towel off my body, dropping it carelessly on the floor. "Are you afraid of *me*?" he murmurs, stepping closer to me. Lifting his hands, he cups my breasts in his large palms and squeezes them, his thumbs playing with my nipples. As he gazes down at me, I notice an amused, yet slightly cruel glint in his blue eyes.

"Should I be?" My heartbeat picks up, my core clenching at the feel of his hard cock brushing against my stomach. His hands are hot and rough on the sensitive skin of my bare breasts, and I inhale sharply as my nipples tighten under his touch. "Are you going to hurt me tonight?"

"Is that what you want, my pet?" He pinches my nipples forcefully, then rolls them between his fingers, causing me to bite back a moan of pleasure tinged with pain. His voice deepens, turning dark and seductive. "Do you want me to hurt you . . . to mark your soft skin and make you scream?"

I lick my lips, tremors of heat and anxious excitement running through my body. I should be frightened, particularly after our conversation tonight, but I'm desperately aroused instead. As perverse as it is, I want this too—I want the ferocity of his desire, the cruelty of his affection. I want to lose myself in the twisted rapture of his embrace, to forget about right and wrong and simply feel. "Yes," I whisper, for the first time admitting to my own dark needs—to the aberrant craving he has instilled in me. "Yes, I do . . ."

Heat flares in his eyes, savage and volcanic, and then we're tumbling to the bed in a primal tangle of limbs and flesh. There's no trace of the deceptively gentle lover now, or of the sophisticated sadist who manipulates my mind and body every night. No, this Julian is pure male lust, untamed and uncontrolled.

His hands roam over my body, and his mouth is on me, licking, sucking, and biting every inch of my flesh. His left hand finds its way between my thighs, and one big finger pushes into me, making me gasp as he ruthlessly drives it in and out of my wet, quivering sex. He's rough, but the heat inside me only intensifies, and I rake my nails down his back, desperate for more as we roll on the bed, going at each other like animals.

I end up on my back, pinned by his muscled body, my arms stretched above my head and my wrists caught in the iron grip of his right hand. It's the position of the conquered, yet my heart pounds with anticipation rather than fear at the look of predatory hunger on his face.

"I'm going to fuck you," he says harshly, his knees wedging between my thighs and spreading them wide. There's no seduction in his voice now, only raw, aggressive need. "I'm going to fuck you until you beg for mercy—and then I'm going to fuck you more. Do you understand me?"

I manage a tiny nod, my chest heaving as I stare up at him. My breathing is coming fast and hard, and my skin burns where his body touches me. For a moment, I can feel the throbbing length of his erection brushing against the inside of my thigh, the broad head smooth and velvety, and then he grasps his cock with his free hand and guides it to my entrance.

I'm wet, but nowhere near ready for the brutal thrust with which he joins our bodies, and a shock of pain lashes at my nerve endings as he slams into me, nearly splitting me in half. A cry escapes my throat and my inner muscles tighten, resisting the vicious penetration, but he doesn't give me any time to adjust. Instead he sets a hard, bruising pace, claiming me with a violence that leaves me shaken and breathless, helpless to do anything but accept the relentless pounding of my body.

I don't know how long he fucks me like this—or how many times I come from the battering force of his thrusts. All I know is that by the time he reaches his peak, shuddering over me, I'm hoarse from screaming and so sore that it hurts when he pulls out of me, the wetness of his semen stinging my abraded flesh.

I'm also too worn out to move, so he gets up and goes to the bathroom, returning with a cool, wet towel. Pressing it against my swollen sex, he gently cleans me, then goes down on me, his lips and tongue forcing my exhausted body into another orgasm.

And then we sleep, entwined in each other's arms.

CHAPTER TWELVE

❖ JULIAN ❖

The next morning I wake up when the sunlight touches my face. I deliberately left the drapes open last night, wanting to get an early start on the day. Light works better than any alarm with me, and it's far less disruptive to Nora, who's sleeping draped across my chest.

For a few minutes, I just lie there, luxuriating in the feel of her warm skin pressed against mine, in the soft exhalations of her breath and the way her long lashes lie like dark crescents on her cheeks. I had never wanted to sleep with a woman before her, had never understood the appeal of having another person in your bed for anything but fucking. It was only when I acquired my captive that I learned the simple pleasure of drifting off to sleep while holding her sleek little body . . . of feeling her next to me throughout the night.

Taking a deep breath, I gently shift Nora off me. I need to get up, though the temptation to lie there and do nothing is strong. She doesn't wake up when I sit up, just rolls onto her side and continues sleeping, the blanket sliding off her body and leaving her back largely exposed to my gaze. Unable to resist, I lean over to kiss one slender shoulder and notice a few scratches and bruises marring her smooth skin—marks that I must've inflicted on her last night.

It turns me on, seeing them on her. I like the idea of branding her in some way, of leaving signs of my possession on her delicate flesh. She already wears my ring, but it's not enough. I want more. With each passing day, my need for her grows, my obsession with her intensifying rather than lessening with time.

It disturbs me, this development. I had been hoping that seeing Nora every day and having her as my wife would quell this desperate hunger I feel for her all the time, but just the opposite seems to be happening. I resent every minute that I spend away from her, every moment that I'm not touching her. Just like with any addiction, I seem to require larger and larger doses of my chosen drug, my dependence on her increasing until I'm constantly craving my next fix.

I don't know what I would do if I ever lost her. It's a fear that makes me wake up in a cold sweat at night and assaults my mind at random times throughout the day. I know that she's safe here on the estate—nothing short of a direct attack by a full-fledged army can penetrate my security—but I still can't help worrying, can't help fearing that she'll be taken from me somehow. It's insane, but I'm tempted to keep her chained to my side at all times, so I would know she's okay.

Casting one last look at her sleeping form, I get up as quietly as I can and head into the shower, forcing my thoughts away from my obsession. I will see Nora again this evening, but first, there is an overnight delivery that requires my attention. As my mind turns to the upcoming task, I smile with grim anticipation.

My Al-Quadar prisoners are waiting.

* * *

Lucas had them brought to a storage shed on the far edge of the property. The first thing I notice as I walk in is the stench. It's an acrid combination of sweat, blood, urine, and desperation. It tells me that Peter has already been hard at work this morning.

As my eyes adjust to the dim light inside the shed, I see that two of the men are tied to metal chairs, while the third is hanging from a hook in the ceiling, strung up by a rope binding his wrists above his head. All three of them are covered in dirt and blood, making it difficult to tell their age or nationality.

I approach one of the seated ones first. His left eye is swollen shut, and his lips are puffy and encrusted with blood. His right eye, though, is glaring at me with fury and defiance. A young man, I decide, studying him closer. Early twenties or late teens, with a straggly attempt at a beard and close-trimmed black hair. I doubt he's anything more than a foot soldier, but I still intend to question him. Even small fish can occasionally swallow useful bits of information—and then regurgitate them if prompted properly.

"His name is Ahmed," a deep, faintly accented voice says behind me. Turning, I see Peter standing there, his face as expressionless as always. The fact that I didn't spot him right away doesn't surprise me; Peter Sokolov excels at lurking in the shadows. "He was recruited six months ago in Pakistan."

An even smaller fish than I expected, then. I'm disappointed, but not surprised.

"What about this one?" I ask, walking to the other man in a chair. He appears a bit older, closer to thirty, his thin face clean-shaven. Like Ahmed, he's been roughed up a bit, but there is no fury in his gaze as he looks at me. There is only icy hatred.

"John, also known as Yusuf. Born in America to Palestinian immigrants, recruited by Al-Quadar five years ago. That's all I got out of that one thus far," Peter says, pointing at the man hanging on the hook. "John himself hasn't talked to me yet."

"Of course." I stare at John, inwardly pleased by this development. If he's trained to withstand a significant amount of pain and torture, then he's at least a mid-level operative. If we manage to crack him, I'm certain we'll be able to get some valuable insights.

"And this one is Abdul." Peter gestures toward the hanging man. "He's Ahmed's cousin. Supposedly, he joined Al-Quadar last week."

Last week? If that's true, the man is all but useless. Frowning, I walk up to him to take a closer look. At my approach, he tenses, and I see that his face is one massive, swollen bruise. He also reeks of urine. As I pause in front of him, he begins to babble in Arabic, his voice filled with fear and desperation.

"He says he told us all he knows." Peter comes to stand next to me. "Claims he only joined his cousin because they promised to give his family two goats. Swears he's not a terrorist, never wanted to hurt anyone in his life, has nothing against America, et cetera, et cetera."

I nod, having gathered that much myself. I don't speak Arabic, but I understand some of it. A cold smile stretches my lips as I take a Swiss army knife out of my back pocket and pull out a small blade. At the sight of the knife, Abdul yanks frantically at the ropes holding him up, and his pleas grow in volume. He's clearly as green as they come—which makes me inclined to believe that he's telling the truth about not knowing anything.

It doesn't matter, though. All I need from him is information, and if he can't provide it, he's a dead man. "Are you sure you don't know anything else?" I ask him, slowly twirling the knife between my fingers. "Perhaps something you might've seen, heard, come across? Any names, faces, anything of that sort?"

Peter translates my question, and Abdul shakes his head, tears and snot running down his battered, bloodied face. He babbles some more, something about knowing only John, Ahmed, and the men who were killed during their capture yesterday. Out of the corner of my eye, I see Ahmed glaring at him, no doubt wishing that his cousin would keep his mouth shut, but John doesn't seem alarmed by Abdul's verbal diarrhea. John's lack of concern only confirms what my instincts are telling me: that Abdul is telling the truth about not knowing anything else.

As though reading my mind, Peter steps next to me. "Do you want to do the honors, or should I?" His tone is casual, like he's offering me a cup of coffee.

"I'll do it," I reply in the same manner. There is no room for softness in my business, no place for sentimentality. Abdul's guilt or innocence doesn't matter; he allied himself with my enemies and, by doing so, signed his own death warrant. The only mercy I will grant him is that of a swift end to the misery of his existence.

Ignoring the man's terrified pleas, I slice my blade across Abdul's throat, then step back, watching as he bleeds out. When it's over, I wipe the knife on the dead man's shirt and turn to the two remaining prisoners.

"All right," I say, giving them a placid smile. "Who's next?"

* * *

To my annoyance, it takes most of the morning to break Ahmed. For a new recruit, he's surprisingly resilient. He ultimately gives in, of course—they all do—and I learn the name of the man who acts as an intermediary between their cell and another one that's run by a more senior leader. I also learn of a plan to blow up a tour bus in Tel-

Aviv—information that my contacts in the Israeli government will find quite useful.

I let John watch the whole process, up until the moment Ahmed takes his last breath. Even though John may be trained to withstand torture, I doubt he's psychologically prepared to see his colleague taken apart piece by piece, all the while knowing that he, John, will be next. Few people are capable of maintaining their cool in a situation like that—and I know that John is not one of them when I catch his gaze dropping to the floor during a particularly gruesome moment. Still, I know it will take us at least a few hours to extract anything from him, and I can't neglect my business for the rest of the day. John will have to wait until this afternoon, after I've had lunch and caught up on some work.

"I can start if you'd like," Peter says when I tell him this. "You know I can do this on my own."

I do know that. In the year that he's worked for me, Peter has proven himself more than capable in this area. However, I prefer to be hands-on whenever possible; in my line of work, micromanaging often pays off.

"No, that's okay," I say. "Why don't you take a lunch break as well? We'll resume this at three."

Peter nods, then slips out of the shed, not even bothering to wash the blood off his hands. I'm more fastidious about these matters, so I walk over to a bucket of water sitting by the wall and rinse the worst of the gory residue off my hands and face. At least I don't need to worry about my clothes; I deliberately wore a black T-shirt and shorts today, so the stains wouldn't be visible. This way, if I run into Nora before I have a chance to change, I won't give her nightmares. She knows what I'm capable of, but knowing and seeing are two very different things. My little wife is still innocent in some ways, and I want her to keep as much of that innocence as possible.

I don't see her on my way home, which is probably for the best. I always feel more feral immediately after a kill, edgy and excited at the same time. It used to bother me, this enjoyment I get out of things that would horrify most people, but I no longer worry about it. It's who I am, who I was trained to be. Self-doubt leads to guilt and regret, and I refuse to entertain those useless emotions.

Once inside the house, I take a thorough shower and change into fresh clothes. Then, feeling much cleaner and calmer, I go down to the kitchen to grab a quick lunch.

Ana isn't there when I walk in, so I make myself a sandwich and sit down to eat at the kitchen table. I have my iPad with me, and for the next half hour, I deal with manufacturing issues at my factory in Malaysia, catch up with my Hong Kong-based supplier, and shoot an email to my contact in Israel about the upcoming bombing.

When I'm done with lunch, I still have a number of phone calls to make, so I head to my office, where I have secure lines of communication set up.

I run into Nora on the porch as I exit the house.

She's coming up the stairs, talking and laughing with Rosa. Dressed in a patterned yellow dress, with her hair loose and streaming down her back, she looks like a ray of sunshine, her smile wide and radiant.

Spotting me, she stops in the middle of the stairs, her smile turning a bit shy. I wonder if she's thinking about last night; my own thoughts certainly turned in that direction as soon as I saw her.

"Hi," she says softly, looking at me. Rosa stops too, inclining her head at me respectfully. I give her a curt nod of acknowledgment before focusing on Nora.

"Hello, my pet." The words come out unintentionally husky. Apparently sensing that she's in the way, Rosa mumbles something about needing to help out in the kitchen and escapes into the house, leaving Nora and me alone on the porch.

Nora grins at her friend's prompt departure, then walks up the remaining steps to stand next to me. "I got the orientation packet from Stanford this morning and already registered for all the classes," she says, her voice filled with barely suppressed excitement. "I have to say, they work *fast*."

I smile at her, pleased to see her so happy. "Yes, they do." And they should—given the generous donation one of my shell corporations made to their alumni fund. For three million dollars, I expect the Stanford admissions office to bend over backwards to accommodate my wife.

"I'm going to call my parents tonight." Her eyes are shining. "Oh, they're going to be so surprised . . ."

"Yes, I'm sure," I say dryly, picturing Tony and Gabriela's reaction to this. I've listened to a few more of Nora's conversations with them, and I know they didn't believe me when I said that Nora would get a good education. It will be useful for my new in-laws to learn that I keep my promises—that I'm serious when it comes to taking care of their daughter. It won't change their opinion of me, of course, but at least they'll be a bit calmer about Nora's future.

Nora grins again, likely picturing the same thing, but then her expression turns unexpectedly somber. "So did they already arrive?" she asks, and I hear a trace of hesitation in her voice. "The Al-Quadar men you've captured?"

"Yes." I don't bother to sugarcoat it. I don't want to traumatize her by letting her see that side of my business, but I'm not going to hide its existence from her either. "I've begun interrogating them."

She stares at me, her earlier excitement nowhere in sight. "Oh, I see." Her eyes travel over my body, lingering on my clean clothes, and I'm glad that I took the precaution to shower and change earlier.

When she lifts her eyes to meet my gaze, there is a peculiar look on her face. "So did you learn anything useful?" she asks softly. "By interrogating them, I mean?"

"Yes, I did," I say slowly. It surprises me that she's curious about this, that she's not acting as appalled as I would've expected. I know she hates Al-Quadar for what they did to Beth, but I still would've expected her to cringe at the thought of torture. A smile tugs at my lips as I wonder just how dark my pet is willing to go these days. "Do you want me to tell you about it?"

She surprises me again by nodding. "Yes," she says quietly, holding my gaze. "Tell me, Julian. I want to know."

CHAPTER THIRTEEN

❖ NORA ❖

I don't know what demon prompted me to say that, and I hold my breath, waiting for Julian to laugh at me and refuse. He has never been keen on telling me much about his business, and though he has opened up to me since his return, I get the sense that he's still trying to shield me from the uglier parts of his world.

To my shock, he doesn't refuse or mock me in any way. Instead he offers me his hand. "All right, my pet," he says, an enigmatic smile playing on his lips. "If you'd like to learn, come with me. I have some calls to make."

My heart pounding, I tentatively put my hand in his and let him lead me down the stairs. As we walk toward the small building that serves as Julian's office, I can't help wondering if I'm making a mistake. Am I ready to give up the questionable comfort of ignorance and dive head first into the murky cesspool of Julian's empire? Truthfully, I have no idea.

Yet I don't stop, don't tell Julian that I changed my mind . . . because I haven't. Because deep inside, I know that burying my head in the sand changes nothing. My husband is a dangerous, powerful criminal, and my lack of knowledge about his activities doesn't alter the fact that I'm dirty by association. By willingly going into his arms every night—by loving him despite everything he's done—I am implicitly condoning his actions, and I'm not naïve enough to think otherwise. I might have started off as Julian's victim, but I don't know if I can claim that dubious distinction anymore. Syringe or not, I went with him knowing full well what he was and what kind of life I was signing up for.

Besides, a dark curiosity is riding me now. I want to know what he learned this morning, what kind of information his brutal methods availed him. I want to know what phone calls he's planning to make and to whom he's planning to speak. I want to know everything there is to know about Julian, no matter how much the reality of his life horrifies me.

When we come up to the office building, I see that the door is made of metal. Just like on the island, Julian opens it by submitting to a retina scan—a security measure that no longer surprises me. Given what I now know about the types of weapons Julian's company produces, his paranoia appears quite justified.

We go inside, and I see that it's all one big room, with a large oval table near the entrance and a wide desk with a bunch of computer screens at the back. Flatscreen TV monitors line the walls, and there are comfortable-looking leather chairs around the table. Everything seems very high-tech and luxurious. To me, Julian's office looks like a cross between an executive conference room and some place I imagine the CIA might meet to strategize.

As I stand there, gaping at everything, Julian places his hands on my shoulders from behind. "Welcome to my lair," he murmurs, his fingers tightening for a brief moment. Then he lets go of me and walks over to sit down behind the desk.

I follow him there, driven by burning curiosity.

There are six computer monitors sitting on the table. Three of them are showing what appears to be a live feed from various surveillance cameras, and two are filled with different charts and blinking numbers. The last computer is the one closest to Julian, and it's displaying some type of unusual-looking email program.

Intrigued, I take a closer look, trying to figure out what I'm seeing. "Are you monitoring your investments?" I ask, peering at the two computers with the blinking numbers. I'm far from a stock guru, but I've seen a couple of movies about Wall Street, and Julian's setup reminds me of the traders' desks they had there.

"You could say that." When I turn to look at him, Julian leans back in his chair and smiles at me. "One of my subsidiaries is a hedge fund of sorts. It dabbles in everything from currencies to oil, with a focus on special situations and geopolitical events. I have some very qualified people running it, but I find that stuff quite interesting and occasionally like to play with it myself."

"Oh, I see . . ." I stare at him, fascinated. This is yet another side of Julian I knew nothing about before. It makes me wonder how many more layers I'm going to uncover with time. "So who are you planning to call?" I ask, remembering the phone calls he mentioned earlier.

Julian's smile widens. "Come here, baby, have a seat," he says, reaching out to grab my wrist. Before I know it, he's got me sitting on his lap, his arms effectively caging me between his chest and the edge of the desk. "Just sit here and be quiet," he whispers in my ear, and quickly types something on his keyboard while I sit there, breathing in his warm scent and feeling his hard body all around me.

I hear a few beeps, then a man's voice comes from the computer. "Esguerra. I was wondering when you would be in touch." The speaker has an American accent and sounds well educated, if a bit stuffy. I immediately picture a middle-aged man in a suit. A bureaucrat of some kind, but a senior one, judging from the confidence in his voice. One of Julian's government contacts, perhaps?

"I assume our Israeli friends filled you in already," Julian says.

Holding my breath, I listen intently, not wanting to miss anything. I don't know why Julian decided to let me learn this way, but I'm not about to quibble.

"I don't have much to add," Julian continues. "As you already know, the operation was a success, and I now have a couple of detainees that I'm milking for information."

"Yes, so we've heard." There is silence for a second, then the man says, "We would appreciate hearing this kind of news first next time. It would've been nice if the Israelis had heard about the bus from us, rather than the other way around."

"Oh, Frank . . ." Julian sighs, wrapping his arm around my waist and shifting me slightly to the left. Feeling off-balance, I clutch at Julian's arm, trying not to make any sounds as he settles me more comfortably on his leg. "You know how these things work. If you'd like to be the one spoon-feeding the Israelis, I need a little something to sweeten the deal."

"We already wiped away all traces of your misadventure with the girl," Frank says evenly, and I tense, realizing he's referring to my abduction.

A misadventure? Really? For a second, irrational fury spikes through me, but then I take a calming breath and remind myself that I don't actually want Julian punished for what he did to me—not if it means being separated from him again. Still, it would've been nice if they had at least acknowledged that Julian committed a crime instead of calling it a fucking 'misadventure.' It's stupid, but I feel disrespected somehow—like I don't even matter.

Oblivious to my stewing over his word choice, Frank continues, "There's nothing more we can give you at this point—"

"Actually, you can," Julian interrupts. Still holding me tightly, he strokes my arm in a proprietary, soothing gesture. As usual, his touch warms me from within, takes away some of my tension. He probably understands why I'm upset; no matter how you slice it, it's insulting to have your kidnapping talked about so casually.

"How about a little tit for tat?" Julian continues softly, addressing Frank. "I let you be the heroes next time, and you let me in on some back-channel action with Syria. I'm sure there are a few tidbits you'd like to leak . . . and I'd love to be the one to help you out."

There is another moment of silence, then Frank says gruffly, "Fine. Consider it done."

"Excellent. Until next time then," Julian says and, reaching forward, clicks on the corner of the screen to disconnect the call.

As soon as he's done, I twist around in Julian's arms to look at him. "Who was that man?"

"Frank is one of my contacts at the CIA," Julian replies, confirming my earlier supposition. "A paper pusher, but one who's quite good at his job."

"Ah, I thought so." Beginning to feel restless, I push at Julian's chest, needing to get up. He releases me, watching with a faint smile as I back up a couple of steps, then prop my hip against the desk and give him a questioning look. "What was that about Israelis and the bus? And Syria?"

"According to one of my Al-Quadar guests, there is an attack planned on a tour bus in Tel-Aviv," Julian explains, leaning back in his chair. "I notified the Mossad—the Israeli intelligence agency—about it earlier today."

"Oh." I frown. "So why did Frank object to that?"

"Because the Americans have a savior complex—or would like the Israelis to think they do. They want this information to be coming from them instead of me, so that the Mossad owes *them* a favor."

"Ah, I see." And I do. I'm beginning to understand how this game works. In the shadowy world of intelligence agencies and off-the-record politics, favors are like currency—and my husband is rich in more ways than one. Rich enough to ensure that he would never be prosecuted for petty crimes like kidnapping or illegal arms dealing. "And you want Frank to give you some info to leak to Syria, so they owe *you* a favor, right?"

Julian grins at me, white teeth flashing. "Yes, indeed. You're a quick study, my pet."

"Why did you decide to let me listen in today?" I ask, eyeing him curiously. "Why today of all days?"

Instead of responding, he rises to his feet and comes toward me. Stopping next to me, he bends forward and places his hands on the desk on both sides of my body, trapping me again. "Why do you think, Nora?" he murmurs, leaning closer. His breath is warm against my cheek, and his arms are like steel beams surrounding me. It makes me feel like a small animal caught in a hunter's snare—an unsettling sensation that nonetheless turns me on.

"Because we're married?" I guess in an uneven voice. His face is mere inches from mine, and my lower belly tightens with a strong surge of arousal as he nudges his hips forward, letting me feel his hardening erection.

"Yes, baby, because we're married," he says huskily, his eyes darkening with lust as my peaked nipples brush against his chest, "and because I think you're no longer as fragile as you seem . . ."

And lowering his head, he captures my mouth in a hungry, possessive kiss, his hands sliding up my thighs with familiar intent.

* * *

Over the next few days, I learn more about Julian's dark empire, and I begin to understand how little most people know about what goes on behind the scenes. None of what I hear in Julian's office ever shows up on the news . . . because if it did, heads would roll, and some very important people would end up in jail.

Amused by my continued interest, Julian lets me listen in on more conversations. Once I even get to watch a video conference from the back of the room, where I can't be seen by the camera. To my shock, I recognize one of the men on the video feed. It's a prominent US general—someone I've seen a couple of times on popular talk shows. He wants Julian to move his manufacturing operations from Thailand out of fear that political instability in the region could derail the next shipment of the new explosive—the shipment that's supposed to go to the US government.

My former captor hadn't been lying when he said he has connections; if anything, he'd understated the extent of his reach.

Of course, politicians, military leaders, and others of their ilk are but a small fraction of the people Julian deals with on a daily basis. The majority of his interactions are with clients, suppliers, and various intermediaries—shady and usually frightening individuals from all over the world. His acquaintances range from Russian mafia and Libyan rebels to dictators in obscure African countries. When it comes to selling weapons, my husband is very egalitarian. Terrorists, drug lords, legitimate governments—he does business with them all.

It turns my stomach, but I can't bring myself to stay out of Julian's office. Every day I follow him there, driven by morbid curiosity. It's like watching some kind of undercover exposé; the things I learn are both fascinating and disturbing.

It takes Julian three days, but he manages to break the last Al-Quadar prisoner. How, he doesn't tell me and I don't ask. I know it's through torture, but I don't know the particulars. I just know that the information he extracts results in Julian locating two more Al-Quadar cells—and the CIA owing him another favor.

Now that Julian has decided to let me into that portion of his life, we spend even more time together. He likes having me in his office. Not only is it convenient for when he wants sex—which is at least once during the day—but he also seems to enjoy the speed with which I'm learning. I'm sharp, he says. Intuitive. I see things as they are instead of as I want them to be—a rare gift, according to Julian.

"Most people wear blinders," he tells me over lunch one day, "but not you, my pet. You face reality head-on . . . and that's what lets you see beneath the surface."

I thank him for the compliment, but inwardly I wonder if it's necessarily a good thing, seeing beneath the surface like that. If I could pretend to myself that at the core, Julian is a good man—that he is simply misunderstood and can ultimately be reformed—it would be so much easier for me. If I were blind to my husband's nature, I wouldn't feel so conflicted about my feelings for him.

I wouldn't worry that I'm in love with the devil.

But I do see him for what he is—a demon in a handsome man's disguise, a monster wearing a beautiful mask. And I wonder if that means that I'm a monster too . . . that I'm evil for loving him.

I wish I had Beth to talk to about this. I know she wasn't exactly an expert on normal, but I still miss her unorthodox views on things, the way she could turn everything on its head and have it make some kind of twisted sense. I'm pretty sure I know what she would say in regard to my situation. She would tell me I'm lucky to have someone like Julian—that we are meant to be together and everything else is bullshit.

And she would probably be right. When I think back to those lonely, empty months before Julian's return—when I had my freedom and normal life, but didn't have *him*—all my doubts fade away. No matter what he is or what he does, I would sooner die than go through that soul-crushing misery again.

For better or worse, I'm no longer complete without Julian, and no amount of self-flagellation can alter that fact.

* * *

A week after Julian's conversation with Frank, I knock on the heavy metal door and wait for him to let me in. I had spent the morning walking with Rosa and preparing for my upcoming classes, while Julian went in without me to do some paperwork for his offshore accounts. Apparently, even crime lords have to deal with taxes and legal matters; it appears to be a universal evil that no one can avoid.

When the door swings open, I'm surprised to see a tall, dark-haired man sitting across the large oval table from Julian. He looks to be in his mid-thirties, just a few years older than my husband. I have seen him walking around the estate before, but I've never had an occasion to interact with him in person. From a distance, he'd reminded me of a sleek, dark predator—an impression that's only strengthened by the way he's looking at me now, his gray eyes tracking my every move with a peculiar mix of watchfulness and indifference.

"Come in, Nora," Julian says, gesturing for me to join them. "This is Peter Sokolov, our security consultant."

"Oh, hi. It's very nice to meet you." Walking over to the table, I give Peter a cautious smile as I sit down next to Julian. Peter is a good-looking man, with a strong jaw and high, exotically slanted cheekbones, but for some reason, he makes the fine hair at the back of my neck stand up. It's not what he says or does—he nods at me politely while sitting there, his pose deceptively calm and relaxed—it's what I see in his steel-colored eyes.

Rage. Pure, undiluted rage. I sense it within Peter, feel it emanating from his pores. It's not anger or a momentary flare-up of temper. No, this emotion goes deeper than that. It's a part of him, like his hard-muscled body or the white scar that bisects his left eyebrow.

For all his cold, carefully controlled demeanor, the man is a deadly volcano waiting to explode.

"We were just finishing up," Julian says, and I catch a note of displeasure in his voice. Tearing my eyes away from Peter, I see a tiny muscle flexing in Julian's jaw. I must've stared at Peter for too long without realizing it, and my husband misinterpreted my involuntary fascination as interest.

Shit. A jealous Julian is never a good thing. In fact, it's a very, very bad thing.

As I rack my brain trying to figure out how to diffuse the situation, Peter rises to his feet. "We can resume this tomorrow if you'd like," he says calmly, addressing Julian. I can't help noticing that unlike most on the estate, Peter doesn't defer to my husband. Instead he speaks to Julian as an equal, his demeanor respectful, yet utterly self-assured. I catch a faint Eastern European accent in his speech, and I wonder where he's from. Poland? Russia? Ukraine?

"Yes," Julian says, getting up as well. His expression is still dark, but his voice is now smooth and even. "I'll see you tomorrow."

Peter disappears, leaving us alone, and I slowly rise to my feet, my palms beginning to sweat. I didn't do anything wrong, but convincing Julian of that won't be easy. His possessiveness borders on the obsessive; sometimes I'm surprised he doesn't keep me locked away in his bedroom, so that other men will never see me.

Sure enough, as soon as the door closes behind Peter, Julian steps toward me. "Did you like Peter, my pet?" he says softly, crowding me with his powerful body until I'm forced to back up against the table. "Do you have a thing for Russian men?"

"No." I shake my head, holding Julian's gaze. I'm hoping he can see the truth on my face. Peter might be handsome, but he's also scary— and the only scary man I want is the one glaring at me right now. "Not even a little bit. That's not why I was looking at him."

"No?" Julian's eyes narrow as he grasps my chin. "Why then?"

"He frightened me," I admit, figuring that honesty is the best policy here. "There's something about him that I found disturbing."

Julian studies me intently for a second, then releases my chin and steps back, causing me to let out a relieved breath. *Storm averted.*

"As insightful as always," he murmurs, his voice holding a note of rueful amusement. "Yes, you're right, Nora. There is indeed something disturbing about Peter."

"What is his deal?" I ask, my curiosity reawakening now that Julian is no longer angry with me. I know Julian doesn't employ choirboys, but what I sensed in Peter is different, more volatile. "Who is he?"

Julian gives me a small, grim smile and walks over to sit down behind his desk. "He's former Spetsnaz—Russian Special Forces. He was one of the best until his wife and son were killed. Now he wants revenge, and he came to me hoping that I can help him."

I feel a flicker of pity. It's not only rage then; Peter is also filled with grief and pain.

"Help him how?" I ask, leaning back against the table. Julian's security consultant didn't strike me as someone who'd need help with many things.

"By using my connections to get him a list of names. Apparently, there were some NATO soldiers involved, and the cover-up is a mile deep."

"Oh." I stare at Julian, feeling uneasy. I can only imagine what Peter intends to do with those soldiers. "So did you give him this list?"

"Not yet. I'm working on it. A lot of this information seems to be classified, so it's not easy."

"Can't you ask your contact at the CIA to help you?"

"I did ask him. Frank is dragging his feet because there are some Americans on that list." Julian looks annoyed for a brief second. "He'll come through eventually, though. He always does. I just need to have something the CIA wants badly enough."

"Right, of course," I murmur. "A favor for a favor . . . Is that why Peter is working for you? Because you promised him this list?"

"Yes, that's our deal." Julian smiles sharply. "Three years of loyal service in exchange for getting him those names at the end. I also pay him, of course—but Peter doesn't care about money."

"What about Lucas?" I ask, my thoughts turning to Julian's right-hand man. "Does he also have a story?"

"Everybody has a story," Julian says, but he sounds distracted now, his attention straying to the computer screen. "Even you, my pet."

And before I can pry further, he busies himself with emails, putting an end to our discussion for the day.

CHAPTER FOURTEEN

❖ JULIAN ❖

The next few weeks come as close to domestic bliss as I have ever experienced. Other than one day trip to Mexico for a negotiation with the Juarez cartel, I spend all my time on the estate with Nora.

With her classes having started, Nora's days are filled with textbooks, papers, and tests. She's so busy that she often studies late into the evening—a practice that I dislike, but don't put a stop to. She seems determined to prove that she can hold her own with the students who got into the Stanford program on their own merit, and I don't want to discourage her. I know she's doing this partly for her parents—who continue to worry about her future with me—and partly because she's enjoying the challenge. Despite the added stress, my pet seems to be thriving these days, her eyes bright with excitement and her movements filled with purposeful energy.

I like that development. I like seeing her happy and confident, content with her life with me. Though the monster inside me still gets off on her pain and fear, her growing strength and resilience appeal to me. I never wanted to break her, only to make her mine—and it pleases me to see her becoming my match in more ways than one.

Although schoolwork consumes much of her time, Nora continues her tutelage with Monsieur Bernard, saying that she finds it relaxing to draw and paint. She also insists that I continue giving her self-defense and shooting lessons twice a week—a request that I'm more than happy to fulfill, as it gives us more time together. As the training progresses, I see that she's better with guns than with knives, though she's surprisingly decent with both. She's also becoming quite good at certain fighting moves, her small body slowly but surely turning into a lethal weapon. She even manages to bloody my nose one time, her sharp elbow connecting with my face before I have a chance to block her lightning-fast strike.

It's an achievement she should be proud of, but, of course, being the good girl that she is, Nora is immediately horrified and remorseful.

"Oh my God, I'm so sorry!" She rushes to me, grabbing a towel to stop the bleeding. She appears so distraught that I burst out laughing, though my nose throbs like a son of a bitch. This is what I get for being distracted during training. She'd managed to catch me off-guard at a moment when I was looking at her breasts and fantasizing about pulling up her sports bra.

"Julian! Why are you laughing?" Nora's voice rises in pitch as she presses the towel to my face. "You should see a doctor! It could be broken—"

"It's fine, baby," I reassure her between bouts of laughter, taking the towel from her shaking hands. "I can promise you I've had worse. If it were broken, I'd know it." My voice sounds nasal due to the towel pressed against my nose, but I can feel the cartilage with my fingers, and it's straight, undamaged. I'll have a black eye, but that's about it. If I hadn't deflected to the right at the last second, though, her move could've crushed my nose completely, forcing fragments of bone into my brain and killing me on the spot.

"It's not fine!" Nora steps away, still looking extremely upset. "I could've seriously hurt you!"

"Wouldn't I have deserved it?" I say, only half-teasing. I know there is a part of her that still resents me for the way I took her—that will always resent me for that. If I were her, I wouldn't apologize for causing me pain. I'd look for opportunities to kick my ass any chance I got.

She glares at me, but I see that she's beginning to calm down now that the immediate shock is over. "Probably," she says in a more level tone of voice. "But that doesn't mean I want you to suffer. I'm stupid and irrational like that, you see."

I grin at her, lowering the towel. The bleeding is almost over; as I had suspected, it was only a mild hit. "You're not stupid," I say softly, stepping closer to her. Though my nose still hurts, there is a new, growing ache in a much lower region of my body. "You're exactly as I want you to be."

"Brainwashed and in love with my kidnapper?" she asks drily as I reach for her, dropping the bloodied towel on the floor.

"Yes, exactly," I murmur, pulling off her sports bra to bare her small, perfectly shaped breasts. "And very, very fuckable . . ."

And as I tug her down to the mat, my injury is the last thing on my mind.

* * *

As Nora's semester progresses, we develop a routine. I usually wake up before her and go for a training session with my men. When I return, she's awake, so we eat breakfast, and then I head into the office while Nora goes for a walk with Rosa and listens to the online lectures. After a few hours, I come back to the house, and we have lunch together. Then I go back to my office, and Nora either meets Monsieur Bernard for her art lesson or joins me in the office, where she studies quietly while I work or conduct meetings. Even though she appears not to be paying attention at those times, I know that she does—because she often asks me follow-up questions about the business at dinner.

I don't mind her curiosity, even though I know she silently condemns what I do. The idea that I supply weapons to criminals and the often-brutal methods I use to maintain control over the business are anathema to Nora. She doesn't understand that if I didn't do this, someone else would, and the world would not necessarily be safer or better. Drug lords and dictators would get their weapons one way or another. The only question is who would profit from it—and I would prefer that person to be me.

I know Nora doesn't agree with that reasoning, but it doesn't matter. I don't need her approval—all I need is her.

And I have her. She's with me so much that I'm beginning to forget what it feels like not to have her by my side. We're rarely apart for more than a few hours at a time, and when we are, I miss her so intensely, it's like a physical ache in my chest. I have no idea how I had been able to leave her alone on the island for days or even weeks at a time. Now I don't even like to see Nora go for a run without me, so I do my best to accompany her when she sprints around the estate in late afternoon.

I do that because I want my wife's company, but also to make sure that she's safe. Though my enemies can't steal her here, there are snakes, spiders, and poisonous frogs in the area. And in the nearby rainforest, there are jaguars and other jungle predators. The chances of her getting stung or seriously hurt by a wild animal are small, but I'm not willing to risk it. I can't bear the thought of any harm coming to her. When Nora had her appendicitis attack, I'd nearly gone out of my mind with panic—and that was before my addiction to her reached this new, utterly insane level.

My fear of losing her is starting to border on the pathological. I recognize that, but I don't know how to control it. It's a sickness that seems to have no cure. I worry about Nora constantly, obsessively. I want to know where she is at every moment of every day. She's rarely out of my sight, but when she is, I can't concentrate, my mind conjuring up deadly accidents that could befall her and other frightening scenarios.

"I want you to put two guards on Nora," I tell Lucas one morning. "I want them to tail her whenever she walks around the estate, so they can make sure nothing happens to her."

"All right." Lucas doesn't blink at my unusual request. "I'll work with Peter to free up two of our best men."

"Good. And I want them to text me a report on her every hour on the dot."

"Consider it done."

The guards' hourly reports keep my fears at bay for a couple of weeks—until I get an email that turns my world upside down.

* * *

"Majid is alive," I tell Nora at dinner, carefully watching her reaction. "I just heard from one of Peter's contacts in Moscow. He's been spotted in Tajikistan."

Her eyes widen in shock and dismay. "What? But he died in the explosion!"

"No, unfortunately he didn't." I do my best to keep my rage under control. The fact that Beth's murderer is alive makes my blood boil with pure acid. "It turns out he and four others left the warehouse two hours before I got there. You didn't see him there when I came for you, right?"

"No, I didn't." Nora frowns. "I assumed he was outside, guarding the building or something . . ."

"That's what I thought, too. But he wasn't. He was nowhere near the warehouse when the explosion occurred."

"How do you know this?"

"The Russians captured one of the four men who left with Majid that night. They caught him in Moscow, plotting to blow up the subway." Despite my best efforts, fury seeps into my voice, and I can see the corresponding tension in Nora. If there's any topic that can move my pet to anger, it's that of Beth's murderers. "They interrogated him and learned that he's been in hiding in Eastern Europe and Central Asia for the past few months, along with Majid and the three others."

Before Nora can respond, Ana walks into the dining room.

"Would you like some dessert?" the housekeeper asks us, and Nora shakes her head, her soft mouth drawn in a tight line.

"None for me, thanks," I say curtly, and Ana disappears, leaving us alone once again.

"So what now?" Nora asks. "Are you going to track him down?"

"Yes." And when I do, I'm going to take him apart, one piece of flesh and bone at a time—but I don't tell Nora that. Instead I explain, "His cohort admitted to last seeing Majid in Tajikistan, so that's where we'll start our search. Apparently, he's managed to gather a sizable group of new followers in the last few months, injecting fresh blood into Al-Quadar."

That last tidbit worries me quite a bit. Though we've done serious damage to the terrorist group over the past couple of months, the Al-Quadar organization is so spread out that there could still be a dozen functional cells throughout the world. Combined with the new recruits, these cells could be just powerful enough to be dangerous—and, according to the intelligence Peter got from his contacts, Majid is getting ready for something big . . . something in Latin America.

He's preparing to strike back at me.

He won't penetrate the security of the estate, of course, but just the possibility of these motherfuckers coming within a hundred miles of Nora makes me livid with rage and awakens the fear that I can't quite shake.

The stark, irrational fear of losing her.

There are two-hundred-plus highly trained men guarding the compound and dozens of military-grade drones sweeping the area. Nobody can touch her here, but that doesn't change the way I feel, doesn't quell the primitive panic gnawing at my insides. All I want to do is grab Nora and carry her as far away as possible, to a place where no one will ever find her . . . where she will be mine and mine alone.

But there is no place like that anymore. My enemies know about her, and they know that she's important to me. I've proven that by coming after her before. If they still want the explosive—and I am certain that they do—they will try to get her, again and again, until they are completely wiped out.

Overkill or not, given this new information, I need to take additional precautions to ensure Nora's safety.

I need to make sure I always have a connection to her.

"What are you thinking?" Nora asks, a concerned expression on her face, and I realize that I've been staring at her for a couple of minutes without saying anything.

I force myself to smile. "Nothing much, my pet. I just want to make sure you're safe, that's all."

"Why wouldn't I be safe?" She looks more puzzled than worried.

"Because there is a rumor Majid may be planning something in Latin America," I explain as calmly as I can. I don't want to frighten her, but I do want her to understand why I have to take these precautions.

Why I have to do what I'm about to do to her.

"You think they're coming here?" Her face pales a bit, but her voice remains steady. "You think they're going to try to attack the estate?"

"They might. It doesn't mean they will succeed, but they will most likely try." Reaching across the table, I close my fingers around her delicate hand, wanting to reassure her with my touch. Her skin is chilled, betraying her agitation, and I massage her palm lightly to warm it up. "That's why I want to make sure that I can always find you, baby—that I can always know where you are."

She frowns, and I feel her hand growing even colder before she pulls it out of my grasp. "What do you mean?" Her voice is even, but I can see the pulse at the base of her throat beginning to quicken. As I had anticipated, she's not overjoyed with the idea.

"I want to put some trackers on you," I explain, holding her gaze. "They will be embedded in a couple of places on your body, so if you're ever stolen from me, I would be able to locate you right away."

"Trackers? You mean ... like GPS chips or something? Like something you would use to tag cattle?"

My lips tighten. She's going to be difficult about this, I can already tell. "No, not like that," I say evenly. "These trackers are currently classified and intended specifically for human use. They will have GPS chips, yes, but they will also have sensors that measure your heart rate and body temperature. This way I will always know if you're alive."

"And you will always know where I am," she says quietly, her eyes dark in her pale face.

"Yes. I will always know where you are." The thought fills me with immense relief and satisfaction. I should've done this weeks ago, as soon as I retrieved her from Illinois. "It's for your own safety, Nora," I add, wanting to emphasize that point. "If you had these trackers when you and Beth were taken, I would've found you right away."

And Beth would still be alive. I don't say that last part, but I don't need to. At my words, Nora flinches, like I just struck her a blow, and pain flashes across her face.

She recovers her composure a second later, however. "So let me get this straight . . ." She leans forward, placing her forearms on the table, and I see that her fingers are tightly laced together, her knuckles white with tension. "You want to implant some chips *inside my body* that will tell you where I am *all the time*—just so I'll be safe on a remote compound that has more security than the White House?"

Her tone is heavy with sarcasm, and I feel my temper rising in response. I indulge her in many things, but I will not take risks with her safety. It would've been easier if she'd chosen to cooperate, but I'm not about to let her reluctance deter me from doing the right thing.

"Why, yes, my pet, that's right," I say silkily, getting up from my chair. "That's exactly what I want. You're getting these trackers today. Now, in fact."

CHAPTER FIFTEEN

❖ NORA ❖

Stunned, I stare at Julian, my heartbeat roaring in my ears. A part of me can't believe he's going to do this to me against my will—tag me like some dumb animal, depriving me of any semblance of privacy and freedom—while the rest of me is screaming that I'm an idiot, that I should've known that a tiger doesn't change his stripes.

It's just that the last few weeks had been so different from anything we've had together before. I'd begun to imagine that Julian was opening up to me, that he was truly letting me into his life. Despite his dominance in the bedroom and the control he exerts over all aspects of my life, I'd started to feel less like his sex toy and more like his partner. I let myself believe that we were becoming something like a normal couple, that he was beginning to genuinely care for me . . . to respect me.

Like a fool, I bought into the delusion of a happy life with my kidnapper—with a man utterly lacking in conscience or morals.

How stupid, how gullible of me. I want to kick myself and cry at the same time. I've always known what kind of man Julian is, but I still let myself get taken in by his charm, by the way he seemed to want me, need me.

I allowed myself to think I could be something more than a possession to him.

Realizing that I'm still sitting there, reeling from the painful disillusionment, I push back my chair and get up to face Julian from across the table. The kicked-in-the-stomach sensation is still there, but now so is anger. Pure and intense, it's spreading through my body, sweeping out the remnants of shock and hurt.

These trackers have nothing to do with my safety. I know the extent of the security measures on the estate, and I know that the chances of anyone being able to take me again are beyond minuscule. No, the renewed terrorist threat is just a pretext, a convenient excuse for Julian to do what he's probably been planning to do all along. It gives him a reason to increase his control over me, to bind me to him so tightly that I will never so much as take a breath without his knowledge.

The trackers will make me his prisoner for the rest of my life... and as much as I love Julian, that is not a fate I'm willing to accept.

"No," I say, and I'm surprised at how calm and steady my voice sounds. "I'm not getting these implants."

Julian raises his eyebrows. "Oh?" His eyes glint with anger and a faint hint of amusement. "And how would you prevent it, my pet?"

I lift my chin, my heartbeat accelerating further. Despite all the hours of training in the gym, I'm still no match for Julian in a fight. He can subdue me in thirty seconds flat—not to mention he has all these guards under his command. If he's set on forcing these trackers on me, I won't be able to stop him.

But that doesn't mean I won't try.

"Fuck you," I say, clearly enunciating each word. "Fuck you and these chips of yours." And operating on pure adrenaline-driven instinct, I shove the dinner plates across the table at Julian and bolt for the door.

The plates crash to the floor with a shattering noise, and I hear Julian cursing as he jumps back to avoid getting splattered with food. He's distracted for a moment, and that's all the time I need as I sprint to the door and out into the foyer. I don't know where I'm going, nor do I have anything resembling a plan. All I know is that I can't stay there and meekly go along with this new violation.

I can't be Julian's submissive little victim again.

I hear him chasing after me as I run through the house, and I have a sudden flashback to my first day on the island. I ran then too, trying to escape from the man who would become my entire life. I remember how terrified I felt, how woozy from the drugs he'd given me. That was the day Julian had first introduced me to the devastating pleasure-pain of his touch, the day I first realized I was no longer in charge of my life.

I don't know why I let this tracker thing surprise me. Julian has never once expressed regret over taking away any of my choices, has never apologized for kidnapping me or forcing me to marry him. He treats me well because he wants to, not because there are any adverse consequences to doing otherwise. There's no one to stop him from doing anything he wants with me, no safe word that I can use to enforce my limits.

I may be his wife, but I'm still his captive in every way that counts.

I'm at the front door now, and I grab the handle, pulling it open. Out of the corner of my eye, I see Ana standing near the wall, gaping at me as I fly out the door with Julian hot on my heels. I'm running so fast that I feel only a flash of embarrassment at the notion of her seeing us like this. I think our housekeeper suspects the BDSM-y nature of our relationship—my summer clothes don't always hide the marks Julian leaves on my skin—and I hope she chalks this up to nothing more than a kinky game.

I have no idea where I'm heading as I sprint down the front steps, but that doesn't matter. All I want is to evade Julian for a few moments, to buy myself some time. I don't know what it will gain me, but I know that I need this—that I need to feel like I did *something* to defy him, that I didn't bow down to the inevitable without a fight.

I'm halfway across the wide green lawn when I feel Julian gaining on me. I can hear his harsh breathing—he must be going at his top speed as well—and then his hand closes around my left upper arm, spinning me around and yanking me into his hard body.

The impact stuns me for a moment, knocking the breath out of my lungs, but my body reacts on autopilot, my self-defense training kicking in. Instead of attempting to pull away, I drop down like a stone, trying to pull Julian off-balance. At the same time, my knee comes up, aiming for his balls, and my right fist flies straight at his chin.

Anticipating my move, he twists at the last moment, turning so that my fist misses his face and my knee connects with his thigh instead. Before I get a chance to try anything else, he drops me, letting my back hit the grass, and immediately pins me down with his full weight, using his legs to control mine and catching my wrists to stretch my arms up above my head.

I'm now completely incapacitated, as helpless as ever, and Julian knows it.

A soft chuckle escapes his throat as he meets my furious gaze. "Dangerous little thing, aren't you?" he murmurs, settling more comfortably on top of me. To my annoyance, his breathing is already beginning to return to normal, and his blue eyes are glowing with unconcealed amusement and delight. "You know, if I hadn't been the one to teach you that move, my pet, it might've actually worked."

My chest heaving, I glare up at him, seething with an urge to do something violent to him. The fact that he's enjoying this only intensifies my fury, and I buck upward with all my strength, trying to throw him off me. It's futile, of course; he's more than twice my size, every inch of his powerful body packed with steely muscle. All I succeed in doing is amusing him further.

Well, that, and arousing him—as evidenced by the hardening bulge against my leg.

"Let go of me," I hiss between clenched teeth, sharply cognizant of my body's automatic response to that hardness—to his body pressing against me this way. Being held down like this is something I associate with sex these days, and I hate that I'm turned on right now, my core pulsing with heated need despite my anger and resentment. It's yet another thing I have no control over; my body is conditioned to respond to Julian's dominance no matter what.

His sensuous lips curl into a satisfied half-smile. The bastard is undoubtedly aware of my involuntary arousal. "Or what, my pet?" he breathes, staring at me as he pries my tense legs apart with his knees. "What are you going to do?"

I glare at him defiantly, doing my best to ignore the threat of his rock-hard erection pressing against my entrance. Only his jeans and my flimsy underwear separate us now, and I know Julian can get rid of these barriers in a heartbeat. The only obstacle to him fucking me right now—and the one I'm counting on—is the fact that we're in full view of all the guards and whoever else happens to be strolling by the house at this particular moment. Exhibitionism is not Julian's thing— he's too possessive for that—and I feel reasonably certain he won't take me out in the open like this.

He may do other things to me, but I'm safe from sexual punishment for now.

That fact and my anger spur my reckless reply. "Actually, the real question is what are *you* going to do, Julian?" I say, my voice low and bitter. "Are you going to drag me kicking and screaming to get these trackers put in? Because that's what you'll have to do, you know—I'm not going to go along with this like some good little captive. I'm done playing that role."

His smile disappears, replaced by a look of ruthless determination. "I'm going to do whatever it takes to keep you safe, Nora," he says harshly and rises to his feet, hauling me up with him.

I struggle, but it's pointless; within a second, he has me lifted up in his arms, one of his hands restraining my wrists and the other arm tightly hooked under my knees, essentially immobilizing my legs. Incensed, I arch my spine, trying to break his grip, but he's holding me too securely for that. All I succeed in doing is tiring myself out, and after a couple of minutes, I stop, panting in frustrated exhaustion as Julian begins walking back toward the house, carrying me like a helpless child.

"You can scream if you want," he informs me as we approach the porch steps. His voice is calm and detached, and his face is empty of all emotion as he glances down at me. "It won't change anything, but you're welcome to try."

I know he's probably using reverse psychology on me, but I remain silent as he pushes open the front door with his back and enters the house. My earlier anger is fading, a kind of weary resignation taking its place. I've always known that fighting Julian is pointless, and what happened today only confirms that fact. I can resist all I want, but it will avail me nothing.

As Julian carries me into the foyer, I see Ana still standing there, staring at us in shock and fascination. She must've stayed to watch the conclusion of the chase through the window, and I can feel her gaze following us as Julian walks past her without a word.

Now that the immediate rush of adrenaline has passed, I am aware of a deep flush of embarrassment. It's one thing for Ana to notice a few faint bruises on my thighs, but it's another thing entirely for her to see us like this. I'm sure she's seen worse—after all, she works for a crime lord—but I still can't help feeling uncomfortably exposed. I don't want people on the estate to know the truth about my relationship with Julian; I don't want them to look at me with pity in their eyes. I had plenty of that back home in Oak Lawn, and I'm not eager to repeat the experience.

"Are you just going to shove the trackers in?" I ask Julian as he brings me into our bedroom. "With no anesthesia or anything?" My tone is deeply sarcastic, but I am genuinely wondering about that. I know my husband enjoys inflicting pain on me sometimes, so it's not entirely out of the question that this will be some type of a sexual thing for him.

Julian's jaw flexes as he lowers me to my feet. "No," he says curtly, releasing me and stepping back. My eyes immediately stray to the door, but Julian is between me and the exit as he walks over to a small commode and rummages through the drawers. "I'll make sure you don't feel a thing." And as I watch, he pulls out a small, very familiar-looking syringe.

My insides grow cold. I recognize that syringe—it's the one he had in his pocket when he came back for me, the one he would've used on me if I hadn't gone with him of my own volition.

"Is that how you drugged me when you stole me from the park?" My voice is even, betraying little of the fact that I'm crumbling inside. "What kind of drug is that?"

Julian sighs, looking inexplicably weary as he comes toward me. "It has a long, complicated name that I don't remember off the top of my head—and yes, it's what I used to bring you to the island. It's one of the best drugs of its kind, with very few side effects."

"Few side effects? How lovely." Taking a step back, I cast a frantic glance around the room, looking for something I can use to defend myself. There's nothing, though. Other than a jar of hand creme and a box of tissues on the bed stand, the room is immaculately neat, free of clutter. I keep backing away until my knees hit the bed, and then I know I have nowhere else to go.

I'm trapped.

"Nora . . ." Julian is less than a foot from me now, the syringe in his right hand. "Don't make this harder than it has to be."

Harder than it has to be? Is he fucking serious? A fresh spurt of fury gives me renewed strength. I throw myself on the bed and roll across it, hoping to make it to the other side so I can dash for the door. Before I get to the edge, however, Julian is on top of me, his muscular body pressing me into the mattress. With my face buried in the fluffy blanket, I can hardly breathe, but before I get a chance to panic, Julian shifts most of his weight off me, enabling me to turn my head to the side. As I suck in air, I feel him moving—he's uncapping the syringe, I realize with an icy shudder—and I know I have only seconds before he drugs me again.

"Don't do this, Julian." The words come out in a desperate, broken plea. I know begging him is futile, but there is nothing else I can do at this point. My heart pounds heavily in my chest as I play my last card. "Please, if you care for me at all—*if you love me*—please don't do this . . ."

I can hear his breath catching, and for a moment, I feel a spark of hope—a spark that's immediately extinguished as he gently moves my tangled hair off my neck, exposing my skin. "It's really not going to be that bad, baby," he murmurs, and then I feel a sharp prick in the side of my neck.

Immediately my limbs grow heavy, my vision dimming as the drug kicks in. "I hate you," I manage to whisper, and then the darkness claims me again.

CHAPTER SIXTEEN

❖ JULIAN ❖

I hate you . . . If you love me, don't do this . . .

As I pick up her unconscious body, Nora's words echo in my mind, repeating over and over like a glitchy record. I know it shouldn't hurt this much, but it does. With just a couple of sentences, she somehow managed to flay me open, to break through the wall that has encased me since Maria's death—the wall that has enabled me to keep a distance from everyone and everything except her.

She doesn't truly hate me. I know that. She wants me. She loves me or, at the very least, thinks she does. Once all of this is over, we're going to go back to the life we've had for the past couple of months, except I will feel better, more secure.

Less afraid of losing her.

If you love me, don't do this . . .

Fuck. I don't know why I care that she said that. I certainly don't love her. I can't. Love is for those who are noble and selfless, for people who still have some semblance of a heart.

That's not me. It's never been me. What I feel for Nora is nothing like the soft, flowery emotion depicted in all the books and movies. It's deeper, far more visceral than that. I need her with a violence that twists my guts, with a longing that both demolishes and uplifts me. I need her like I need air, and I would do whatever it takes to keep her with me.

I would die for her, but I would never let her go.

315

Cradling her small, limp body in my arms, I carry her out of the bedroom to the living room. David Goldberg, our resident doctor, is already there, waiting with his medical bag and supplies on the couch. I'd asked him to stop by earlier today, so he can do the procedure as soon as possible after dinner, and I'm glad that he's on time. I only gave Nora a quarter of the drug that was in the syringe, and I want to make sure everything is done before she wakes up.

"She's already under?" Goldberg asks, getting up to greet us. A short, balding man in his forties, he's one of the most talented surgeons I've ever met. I pay him an arm and a leg to treat minor injuries, but I consider it worth it. In my line of work, one never knows when a good doctor will come in handy.

"Yes." I carefully put Nora down on the couch. Her left arm hangs off the edge, so I gently arrange her in a more comfortable pose, making sure that her dress covers her slim thighs. Goldberg won't care either way—he's far more likely to get a hard-on for me than for my wife—but I still don't like the idea of exposing her unnecessarily, even to a man who's openly gay.

"You know, I could've just numbed the area," he says, pulling out the tools he needs. All of his movements are practiced and efficient; he's a master at what he does. "It's a simple procedure—nothing that requires the patient to be unconscious."

"It's better this way." I don't explain further, but I think Goldberg gets it, because he doesn't say anything else. Instead he puts on his gloves, takes out a large syringe with a thick hypodermic needle, and approaches Nora.

I step back to give him some room.

"How many trackers would you like? One or more?" he asks, glancing in my direction.

"Three." I've thought about this before, and that's what makes the most sense to me. If she's ever stolen, my enemies might think to look for a locator chip on her body, but they're unlikely to look for three of them.

"Okay. I will put one in her upper arm, one in her hip, and one in her inner thigh."

"That should work." The trackers are tiny, about the size of a grain of rice, so Nora won't even feel them there after a few days. I'm also planning to have her wear a special wristband as a decoy; it will have a fourth tracker in it. This way, if her abductors find the wristband tracker, they might be foolish enough to get rid of it and not look for any on her body.

"Then that's what I'll do," Goldberg says and, swabbing Nora's upper arm with a disinfecting solution, presses the needle to her skin. A small droplet of blood wells up as the needle goes in, depositing the tracker; then he disinfects the area again and tapes a small bandage over it.

The implant in her hip is next, followed by one in her inner thigh. It takes less than six minutes between the start and the end of the procedure, and Nora sleeps peacefully through it all.

"All done," Goldberg says, pulling off his gloves and packing up his bag. "You can take off the bandages in an hour, once the bleeding stops, and put on regular Band-Aids. Those areas might be tender for a couple of days, but there shouldn't be any scarring, particularly if you keep the insertion points clean in the meantime. If anything, call me, but I don't anticipate any problems."

"Excellent, thank you."

"My pleasure." And with that, Goldberg packs up his bag and exits the room.

* * *

Nora regains consciousness around three in the morning.

I'm sleeping lightly, so I wake up as soon as she begins to stir. I know she'll have a headache and some nausea from the drug, and I have a water bottle prepared in case she's thirsty. I expect the side effects to be mild, since I gave her a small dose. When I took her from the park, I had to give her a lot more to make sure she stayed under for the full twenty-hour-plus trip to the island, so she should recover much faster today.

I hate you.

Fuck, not again. I push away the memory of her small, accusing whisper and focus on the present. I can feel her stirring next to me, a small sound of discomfort escaping her throat as the mattress rubs against the tender spot in her upper arm. That sound does something to me, gets under my skin for some reason. I don't want Nora in pain—not from this, at least—and I reach for her, pulling her closer to me so I can hug her from the back.

She stiffens at my touch, rigid tension spreading through her body, and I know that she's awake now, that she remembers what happened.

"How are you feeling?" I ask, keeping my voice low and soothing as I stroke the smooth curve of her outer thigh with my hand. "Do you want some water or anything?"

She doesn't say anything, but I feel her head moving slightly, and I interpret that as a nod.

"All right then." Reaching back with my hand, I grab the water bottle, fumbling a bit in the dark. Propping myself up on one elbow, I turn on the bedside lamp, so I can see, and hand the bottle to Nora.

She blinks a few times, squinting at the light, and takes the water from me, her slender fingers curving around the bottle as she sits up. The movement causes the blanket to slide down, exposing her upper body. I undressed her before putting her in bed, so she's naked now, with only her thick hair hiding her pretty, pink-tipped breasts from my gaze. Familiar lust stirs within me, but I push it down, wanting to make sure she's okay first.

I let her take a few sips of the water before asking again, "How are you feeling?"

She shrugs, her eyes not meeting mine. "Fine, I guess." Her hand lifts across her body to her upper arm, touching the Band-Aid there, and I see her shiver slightly, as though she's cold. "I have to use the bathroom," she says suddenly and, not waiting for my response, climbs out of bed. I catch a brief glimpse of her rounded little ass before she disappears through the bathroom door, and my dick jumps, ignoring my mind's directive to be still for once.

Sighing, I lie back on the pillow to wait for her. Who am I kidding? My pet always has that effect on me. I can no more ignore seeing her naked than I can stop breathing. Almost involuntarily, my hand slips under the blanket, my fingers curling around my hard shaft as I close my eyes and imagine her hot, velvety inner walls gripping my cock, her pussy wet and deliciously tight . . .

I hate you.

Fuck. My eyes fly open, some of the heat inside me cooling. I'm still hard, but now the lust is intermixed with a strange heaviness in my chest. I don't know where this is coming from. I should feel happier now that the trackers are in, but I don't. Instead I feel like I lost something . . . something I didn't even know I had.

Annoyed, I close my eyes again, this time purposefully focusing on the growing ache in my balls as I pump my fist up and down my dick, letting the hunger build. Even if she does hate me, so what? She probably *should* hate me, given everything I've done to her. I've never let such concerns stop me from doing what I wanted, and I'm not about to start now. Nora will get used to the trackers just as she got used to being mine, and if the compound security is ever breached, she'll thank her lucky stars for my foresight.

Hearing the door open, I open my eyes and see her emerging from the bathroom. She still doesn't look at me directly. Instead she keeps her eyes on the floor as she scurries to the bed and climbs under the covers, pulling the blanket up to her chin. Then she stares blankly at the ceiling, as if I don't even exist.

She might as well have slapped my face with her indifference.

The lust inside me turns sharper, darker. I won't stand for this kind of behavior, and she knows it. The urge to punish her is strong, nearly irresistible, and it's only the knowledge that she's already hurt that prevents me from tying her up and giving in to my sadistic inclinations.

Still, I'm not going to let her get away with this. Not tonight, not ever.

Throwing off my blanket, I sit up and command sharply, "Come here."

She doesn't move for a moment, but then her eyes lift to my face. There's no fear in her gaze, no emotion of any kind, in fact. Her huge dark eyes are lifeless, like those of a beautiful doll.

The heaviness in my chest region grows. "Come here," I repeat, the harshness of my tone masking the intensifying turmoil within me. "Now."

She obeys, her conditioning finally kicking in. Pushing away her blanket, she comes to me on all fours, crawling across the bed with her back arched and her ass slightly raised. It's exactly the way I like her to move in the bedroom, and my breathing quickens, my cock swelling to an almost painful thickness. I've trained her well; even distressed, my pet knows how to please me.

"Good girl," I murmur, reaching for her as soon as she's within my grasp. Sliding my left hand into her hair, I wrap my right arm around her waist and pull her into my lap, gathering her against me. Then I slant my mouth across hers, kissing her with a hunger that seems to emanate from the very core of my being.

She tastes like minty toothpaste and herself, her lips soft and receptive as I plunder the silky depths of her mouth. As the kiss goes on, her eyes close, and her hands come up to rest tentatively at my sides. I can feel her nipples pebbling against my chest, and the realization that she's responding the same as always sends a wave of relief through me, alleviating much of my uncharacteristic unease.

Whatever strange mood she's in, she's still mine in all the ways that matter.

Still kissing her, I lean forward until we're both lying flat on the bed, with me covering her. I'm careful to handle her gently, so I don't put any pressure on the Band-Aid-covered areas. The monster inside me may crave her pain and tears, but that desire pales in comparison to my overwhelming need to comfort her, to take away that lifeless look in her eyes.

Reining in my own lust, I set about caring for her the only way I know how. I kiss her all over, tasting her soft, warm skin as I make my way from the delicate curve of her ear down to her little toes. I massage her hands, arms, feet, legs, and back, enjoying her quiet moans of pleasure as I rub out all stiffness in her muscles. Then I bring her to orgasm with my mouth and my fingers, delaying my own release until my balls almost turn blue.

When I finally enter her body, it's like coming home. Her hot, slick sheath welcomes me, squeezes me so tightly that I nearly explode on the spot. As I begin to move inside her, her arms close around my back, embracing me, holding me close—and then we detonate together at the end, our bodies straining together in violent, mind-shattering bliss.

CHAPTER SEVENTEEN

❖ NORA ❖

I wake up later than usual, my head and mouth feeling like they've been stuffed with cotton. For a moment, I struggle to remember what happened—*did I somehow have too much to drink?*—but then memories of last night seep into my mind, twisting my stomach into knots and flooding me with confused despair.

Julian made love to me last night. He made love to me after violating me—after drugging me and forcing the trackers on me against my will—and I let him. No, I didn't just let him; I reveled in his touch, allowing the blazing heat of his caresses to burn away the frozen hurt inside me, to make me forget, if only for a moment, about the ragged wound he inflicted on my heart.

I don't know why this, out of all the horrible things Julian has done, affects me so strongly. In the grand scheme of things, putting the trackers under my skin—allegedly to keep me safe—is nothing compared to kidnapping me, beating up Jake, or blackmailing me into marriage. These trackers are not even necessarily forever. Theoretically, if I ever make it off the estate, I can go to a doctor and have the implants removed, so I may not even be stuck with them for the rest of my life. My fear yesterday definitely had an irrational component to it; I was reacting on instinct and not thinking things through.

Nonetheless, it felt like a part of me died last evening—like the prick of that syringe killed something inside me. Maybe it's because I had begun to feel that Julian and I were growing closer, that we were becoming more like a regular couple. Or maybe because my Stockholm Syndrome—or whatever psychological issue I have—made me imagine rainbows and unicorns where there were none. Whatever the reason, Julian's actions felt like the most agonizing betrayal. When I regained consciousness last night, I felt so devastated that I wanted to crawl into a hole and disappear.

But Julian didn't let me. He made love to me. He made love to me when I thought he would whip me—when I expected him to punish me for not being his compliant little pet. He gave me tenderness when I expected cruelty; instead of taking me apart, he made me feel whole again, even if it was only for a few hours.

And now... now I miss him. Without him by my side, the coldness within me is beginning to creep back, the pain slowly returning to choke me from the inside. The fact that Julian did this to me against my objections—that he did this even though I *begged him not to*—is almost more than I can handle. It tells me that he doesn't love me—that he may never love me.

It tells me that the man I'm married to may never be anything more than my captor.

* * *

At breakfast Julian is not there, a fact that contributes to my growing depression. I've gotten so used to having most of my meals with him that his absence feels like a rejection—though how I can still crave his company after everything is beyond my comprehension.

"Señor Esguerra grabbed a quick snack earlier," Ana explains, serving me eggs mixed with refried beans and avocado. "He received some news that he had to deal with right away, so he's not able to join you this morning. He apologized for that and told me that you can come to the office whenever you're ready." Her voice is unusually warm and kind, and there is sympathy on her face as she looks at me. I don't know if she knows all the details about what happened last night, but I have a feeling she overheard the gist of it.

Embarrassed, I lower my gaze to my plate. "Okay, thank you, Ana," I murmur, staring at the food. It looks as delicious as usual, but I have no appetite this morning. I know I'm not sick, but I feel that way, with my stomach churning and my chest aching. The fresh implants in my thigh, hip, and upper arm throb with a nagging pain. All I want to do is crawl under the covers and sleep the day away, but unfortunately, that's not an option. I have a paper to do for my English Literature class, and I'm two lectures behind for my Calculus class. I did cancel my morning walk with Rosa, though; I have no desire to see my friend while I'm feeling this way.

"Would you like some hot chocolate or anything? Maybe coffee or tea?" Ana asks, still hovering by the table. Normally, when Julian and I are eating together, she makes herself scarce, but for some reason, she seems reluctant to leave me alone this morning.

I look up from my plate and force myself to give her a smile. "No, I'm okay, Ana, thanks." Picking up my fork, I spear some eggs and bring them to my mouth, determined to eat something to alleviate the concern I see on the housekeeper's softly rounded face.

As I chew, I see Ana hesitating for a moment, as though she wants to say something else, but then she disappears into the kitchen, leaving me to my breakfast. For the next few minutes, I make a serious attempt to eat, but everything tastes like sand and I finally give up.

Getting up, I head to the porch, wanting to feel the sun on my skin. The coldness inside me seems to be spreading with each moment, my depression deepening as the morning wears on.

Stepping out the front door, I walk over to the edge of the porch and lean on the railing, breathing in the hot, humid air. As I gaze out onto the wide green lawn and the guards in the distance, I feel my vision blurring, hot tears welling up and beginning to slide down my cheeks.

I don't know why I'm crying. Nobody died; nothing truly terrible has happened. I've been through so much worse in the past two years, and I've coped with it—I've adjusted and survived. This relatively minor thing shouldn't make me feel like my heart has been ripped out.

My growing conviction that Julian is not capable of love shouldn't destroy me like this.

A hand gently touches my shoulder, startling me out of my misery. Swiftly wiping my cheeks with the back of my hand, I turn around and am surprised to see Ana standing there, an uncertain expression on her face.

"Señora Esguerra... I mean, Nora..." She stumbles over my name, her accent thicker than usual. "I'm sorry to interrupt, but I was wondering if you had a minute to talk?"

Taken aback by the unusual request, I nod. "Of course, what is it?" Ana and I are not particularly close; she's always been somewhat reserved around me, polite but not overly friendly. Rosa told me that Ana is like that because that's what Julian's father demanded of his staff, and the habit is difficult for her to break.

Looking relieved by my response, Ana smiles and walks up to join me at the railing, placing her forearms on the painted white wood. I give her a questioning look, wondering what she wants to discuss, but she seems content to just stand there for a moment, her gaze trained on the jungle in the distance.

When she finally turns her head to look at me and speaks, her words catch me off-guard. "I don't know if you know this, Nora, but your husband lost everybody he's ever cared about," she says softly, no trace of her customary reserve in sight. "Maria, his parents... Not to mention many others he knew both here on the estate and out in the cities."

"Yes, he told me," I say slowly, eyeing her with some caution. I don't know why she's suddenly decided to talk to me about Julian, but I'm more than happy to listen. Maybe if I understand my husband better, it will be easier for me to maintain my emotional distance from him.

Maybe if he's not such a puzzle, I won't be drawn to him as strongly.

"Good," Ana says quietly. "Then I hope you understand that Julian didn't mean to hurt you last night... that whatever he did was because he cares for you."

"Cares for me?" The laugh that escapes my throat is sharp and bitter. I don't know why I'm talking about this with Ana, but now that the floodgates have been opened, I can't seem to close them again. "Julian doesn't care about anyone but himself."

"No." She shakes her head. "You're wrong, Nora. He does. He cares about you very much. I can see it. He's different with you than with others. Very different."

I stare at her. "What do you mean?"

She sighs, then turns to face me fully. "Your husband was always a dark child," she says, and I see a deep sadness in her gaze. "A beautiful boy, with his mother's eyes and her features, but so hard inside . . . It was his father's fault, I think. The older Señor never treated him like a child. From the time Julian was old enough to walk, his father would push him, make him do things that no child should do . . ."

I listen raptly, hardly daring to breathe as she continues.

"When Julian was little, he was afraid of spiders. We have big ones here, very scary ones. Some poisonous ones. When Juan Esguerra found out, he led his five-year-old son into the forest and made him catch a dozen large spiders with his bare hands. Then he made the boy kill them slowly with his fingers, so Julian would see what it's like to conquer his fears and make his enemies suffer." She pauses, her mouth tight-lipped with anger. "Julian didn't sleep for two nights after that. When his mother found out, she cried, but there was nothing she could do. Señor's word here was law, and everyone had to obey."

I swallow the bile rising in my throat and look away. What I just learned only adds to my despair. How can I expect Julian to love someone after being raised that way? The fact that my husband is a stone-cold killer with sadistic tendencies is not surprising; the only wonder is that he's not even worse.

It's hopeless. Utterly hopeless.

Sensing my distress, Ana lays her hand on my arm, her touch warm and comforting, like that of my mom.

"For the longest time, I thought Julian would grow up to be just like his father," she says when I turn to look at her. "Cruel and uncaring, incapable of any softer emotion. I thought that until I saw him with a kitten one day when he was twelve. It was a tiny creature, all fluffy white fur and big eyes, barely old enough to eat on its own. Something happened to its mother, and Julian found the kitten outside and brought it in. When I saw him, he was trying to coax it to drink milk, and the expression on his face—" She blinks, her eyes looking suspiciously wet. "It was so . . . so tender. He was so patient with the kitten, so gentle. And I knew then that his father hadn't succeeded in breaking Julian completely, that the boy could still feel."

"What happened to that kitten?" I ask, bracing myself. I'm prepared to hear another horror story, but Ana just shrugs in response.

"It grew up in the house," she says, gently squeezing my arm before taking her hand away. "Julian kept it as his pet, named it Lola. He and his father had a fight about that—the older Señor hated animals—but by then Julian was old enough, and tough enough, to stand up to his father. Nobody dared to touch the little creature for as long as it was under Julian's protection. When he left for America, he took the cat with him. As far as I know, it lived a nice long life and passed away from old age."

"Oh." Some of my tension fades. "That's good. Not good that Julian lost his pet, I mean, but that it lived for a long time."

"Yes. It's good indeed. And you know, Nora, the way he looked at that kitten . . ." She trails off, gazing at me with a strange smile.

"What?" I ask warily.

"He looks at you like that sometimes. With that same kind of tenderness. He might not always show it, but he treasures you, Nora. In his own way, he loves you. I truly believe that."

I press my lips together, trying to hold back the tears that threaten to flood my eyes again. "Why are you telling me this, Ana?" I ask when I'm certain I can speak without breaking down. "Why did you come out here?"

"Because Julian is the closest thing I have to a son," she says softly. "And because I want him to be happy. I want both of you to be happy. I don't know if this changes anything for you, but I thought you should know a little more about your husband." Reaching out, she squeezes my hand and then walks back inside the house, leaving me standing by the railing, even more confused and heartsick than before.

* * *

I don't join Julian in the office that afternoon. Instead I lock myself in the library and work on the paper, trying not to think about my husband and how much I want to be sitting by his side. I know that just being near him would make me feel better, that his presence alone would help with my hurt and anger, but some masochistic impulse keeps me away. I don't know what I'm trying to prove to myself, but I'm determined to keep my distance for at least a few hours.

Of course, there's no avoiding him at dinner.

"You didn't come today," he observes, watching me as Ana ladles us some mushroom soup for an appetizer. "Why not?"

I shrug, ignoring the imploring look Ana gives me before going back to the kitchen. "I wasn't feeling well."

Julian frowns. "You're sick?"

"No, just a bit under the weather. Plus I had a paper to finish and some lectures to catch up on."

"Is that right?" He stares at me, his eyebrows drawn together. Leaning forward, he asks softly, "Are you sulking, my pet?"

"No, Julian," I reply as sweetly as I can, dipping my spoon in the soup. "Sulking would imply that I'm mad at something you did. But I don't get to be mad, do I? You can do whatever you want to me, and I'm supposed to just accept it, right?" And taking a sip of the richly flavored soup, I give him a saccharine smile, enjoying the way his eyes narrow at my response. I know I'm tugging on a tiger's tail, but I don't want a sweet, gentle Julian tonight. It's too misleading, too unsettling for my peace of mind.

To my frustration, he doesn't take the bait. Whatever anger I managed to provoke is short-lived, and in the next moment, he leans back, a slow, sexy smile teasing at the corners of his lips. "Are you trying to guilt me, baby? Surely you know by now that I'm beyond that kind of emotion."

"Of course you are." I meant the words to sound bitter, but they come out breathless instead. Even now, he has the power to make my senses whirl and spin with nothing more than a smile.

He grins, knowing full well how he affects me, and dips his own spoon into the soup. "Just eat, Nora. You can show me how mad you are in the bedroom, I promise." And with that tantalizing threat, he begins consuming his soup, leaving me no choice but to follow his lead.

As we eat, Julian peppers me with questions about my classes and how my online program is going so far. He seems genuinely interested in what I have to say, and I soon find myself talking to him about my difficulties with Calculus—*has a more boring subject ever been invented?*—and discussing the pros and cons of taking a Humanities course next semester. I'm sure he must find my concerns amusing—after all, it's just school—but if he does, he doesn't show it. Instead he makes me feel like I'm talking to a friend, or maybe a trusted advisor.

That's one of the things that make Julian so irresistible: his ability to listen, to make me feel important to him. I don't know if he does it on purpose, but there are few things more seductive than having someone's undivided attention—and I always have that with Julian. I've had it since day one. Evil kidnapper or not, he's always made me feel wanted and desired, like I'm the center of his world.

Like I genuinely matter.

As the dinner continues, Ana's story plays over and over in my mind, making me viciously glad that Juan Esguerra is dead. How could a father do that to his son? What kind of monster would purposefully try to mold his child into a killer? I picture twelve-year-old Julian standing up to that brute for a defenseless kitten, and I feel an unwitting flash of pride at my husband's courage. I have a feeling keeping that pet against his father's wishes had been far from easy.

I'm still nowhere near ready to forgive Julian, but as we make our way through the second course, I consider the possibility that something other than Julian's stalker tendencies was behind his desire to implant those trackers in me. Could it be that instead of not caring for me, he cares too much? Could his love be that dark and obsessive? That twisted? I'd known, of course, about Maria's death and that of his parents, but I never put the two events together, never thought of it as Julian losing everyone he's ever cared about. If Ana is right—if I truly am that special to Julian—then it's not particularly surprising that he'd go to such lengths to ensure my safety, especially since he almost lost me once.

It's insane and scary, but not particularly surprising.

"So what was so urgent this morning?" I ask, finishing my second serving of the baked salmon dish Ana prepared as the main course. My appetite is back with a vengeance, all traces of my earlier malaise gone. It's amazing what even a little bit of Julian's company does to me; his proximity is better than any mood-boosting drug on the market. "When you couldn't join me for breakfast, I mean?"

"Oh, yes, I've been meaning to tell you about that," Julian says, and I see a gleam of dark excitement in his eyes. "Peter's contacts in Moscow got us permission to move in with an operation to extract Majid and the rest of the Al-Quadar fighters from Tajikistan. As soon as we're ready—hopefully in a week or so—we'll be making our move."

"Oh, wow." I stare at him, both excited and disturbed by the news. "When you say 'we,' you mean your men, right?"

"Well, yes." Julian appears puzzled by my question. "I'm going to take a group of about fifty of our best soldiers and leave the rest to guard the compound."

"You're going to go on this operation yourself?" My heart skips a beat as I wait anxiously for his answer.

"Of course." He looks surprised that I would think otherwise. "I always go on these types of missions myself if I can. Besides, I have some business in Ukraine that's best handled in person, so I'll deal with that on the way back."

"Julian . . ." I feel sick all of a sudden, all the food I've eaten sitting in my stomach like a rock. "This sounds really dangerous . . . Why do you have to go?"

"Dangerous?" He laughs softly. "Are you worried about me, my pet? I can assure you, there's no need. The enemy is going to be outnumbered and outgunned. They don't stand a chance, believe me."

"You don't know that! What if they set off a bomb or something?" My voice rises as I remember the horror of the warehouse explosion. "What if they trick you in some way? You know they want to kill you—"

"Well, technically, they want to force me to give them the explosive," he corrects me, a dark smile curving his lips, "and *then* they want to kill me. But you have nothing to worry about, baby. We'll scan their quarters for any signs of bombs before we go in, and we'll all be wearing full-body armor that can withstand all but a rocket blast."

I push my plate away, not the least bit reassured. "So let me get this straight . . . You're forcing me to wear trackers here, where nobody can touch a single hair on my head, and you're planning to traipse off to Tajikistan to play 'capture the terrorist'?"

Julian's smile disappears, his expression hardening. "I'm not playing, Nora. Al-Quadar represents a very real threat, and it's one that I need to eliminate as quickly as possible. We need to strike at them before they come after us, and this is the perfect opportunity to do that."

I glare at him, the sheer unfairness of the whole thing making my blood pressure rise. "But why do you have to go in person? You have all these soldiers and mercenaries at your command—surely they don't need you there—"

"Nora . . ." His voice is gentle, but his eyes are hard and cold, like icicles. "This is not up for debate. The day I start fearing my own shadow is the day I need to leave this business for good—because it will mean that I have grown soft. Soft and lazy, like the man whose factory I took when I was first starting out . . ." He smiles again at my look of shock. "Oh, yes, my pet, how do you think I switched from drugs to weapons? I took over someone's existing operation and built on it. My predecessor also had soldiers and mercenaries at his command, but he was little more than a glorified paper pusher and everyone knew it. He didn't keep tight reins on his organization, and it was a simple matter to bribe a few people and overthrow him, taking his rocket factory for my own." Julian pauses to let me digest that for a second, then adds, "I'm not going to be that man, Nora. This mission is important to me, and I have every intention of overseeing it myself. Majid will not survive this time—I will make sure of that."

CHAPTER EIGHTEEN

❖ JULIAN ❖

After dinner is over, I lead Nora to our bedroom, my hand resting on the small of her back as we walk up the stairs. She's quiet, like she's been ever since I explained to her about the upcoming mission, and I know that she's still upset with me, both about the trackers and the trip itself.

I find her concern touching, even sweet, but I have no intention of passing up this opportunity to lay my hands on Majid. My pet doesn't understand the dark thrill of being in the middle of action, of feeling the jolt of adrenaline and hearing the whizzing of bullets. She doesn't realize that to someone like me the sight of blood and the sound of my enemies' screams are a turn-on, that I crave them almost as much as sex. This trait of mine is why one shrink thought I might be borderline sociopathic . . . well, this and my general lack of remorse. It's a label that's never particularly bothered me—at least not once I got past my youthful delusion that I could someday lead a 'normal' life.

As we enter the bedroom, the hunger that I've been restraining since yesterday intensifies, the monster inside me demanding his due. The distance I'm sensing from Nora only makes it worse. I can feel the barriers she's trying to erect between us, the way she's trying to shut me out of her thoughts, and it maddens me, feeding the sadistic yearning coiling within.

I am going to smash those barriers tonight. I am going to tear them down until she has no defenses left—until I own her mind fully again.

She excuses herself to go take a quick shower, and I let her, walking over to the bed to wait for her return. I am already semi-hard, my cock stirring in anticipation of what I'm going to do to her, and my pants are starting to feel uncomfortably tight. Hearing the water turn on, I undress, then reach into the bedside drawer and pull out an assortment of tools I plan to use on her tonight.

True to her word, Nora doesn't take long. Five minutes, and she's coming out of the bathroom, a plush white towel wrapped around her petite body. Her hair is piled on top of her head in a messy bun, and her golden skin is damp, droplets of water still clinging to her neck and shoulders. She must've taken off the Band-Aids in order to shower, because I can see a tiny scab and some bruising on her arm where the tracker went in. The sight of it fills me with an odd mixture of emotions—relief that I can now always keep an eye on her and something that tastes strangely like regret.

Her gaze flicks toward the bed, and she stops dead in her tracks, her eyes widening as she takes in the objects I laid out.

I smile, enjoying the startled expression on her face. We haven't played with toys in a while—at least not to this extent. "Drop the towel and get on the bed," I command, getting up and reaching for the blindfold.

She looks up at me, her lips parted and her skin softly flushed, and I know that she's excited by this too—that her needs now mirror mine. There's only a hint of hesitation in her movements as she unwraps the towel and lets it fall to the floor, leaving her standing there fully naked.

As I feast my eyes on her slim, shapely body, my balls tighten and my heartbeat picks up. Rationally I know there must be women more beautiful than Nora out there, but if there are, I can't think of any. From the top of her head down to her dainty toes, she fits my preferences to a tee. My body craves her with an intensity that seems to be growing stronger every day, with a desperation that almost consumes me.

She climbs onto the bed, getting into a kneeling position with her feet tucked underneath her tight, round ass. Her movements are fluid and graceful, like those of a sleek little cat.

Getting on my knees behind her, I move her hair off her shoulder and gently kiss her neck, enjoying the way her breathing changes in response. She smells like warm female skin and flower-scented body wash, a mixture that makes my head spin and my dick throb with need. Some nights this is all I want from her—the sweetness of her response, the feel of her in my arms. Some nights I want to treat her like the fragile, breakable creature she is.

Tonight, however, I want something different.

Pulling back, I tie the blindfold around her eyes, making sure she can't see anything. I want her to focus solely on the sensations she'll be experiencing, to feel everything as acutely as possible. Next, I pick up a pair of padded handcuffs and snap them around her wrists, securing her hands behind her back.

"Um, Julian . . ." Her tongue comes out to moisten her lower lip. "What are you going to do to me?"

I smile, the tiny hint of fear in her voice turning me on even more. "What do you think I'm going to do to you, my pet?"

"Flog me?" she guesses, her voice low and a bit husky. I can see her nipples growing taut as she speaks, and I know the idea is not exactly repellent to her.

"No, baby," I murmur, reaching for one of the other items I have prepared—a pair of nipple clamps connected by a thin metal chain. "You're not healed enough for that yet. I have other things in mind for you today." And picking up the clamps, I wrap my arms around her from the back and pinch her left nipple between my fingers. Then I apply one of the clamps to the hard bud, tightening the screw until her breath hisses out between her teeth.

"How does it feel?" I ask softly, leaning down to kiss the top of her ear as I reach for her right nipple. Her bound hands, curled tightly into fists, press into my stomach, reminding me of her helplessness. "I want to hear you describe it . . ."

She draws in a shuddering breath, her chest heaving. "It hurts—" she begins to say, then cries out sharply as I apply the second clamp to her nipple and tighten it the same way.

"Good . . ." I lightly bite her earlobe. My erection brushes against her lower back, the contact sending vibrations of pleasure down to my balls. "And now?"

"It—it hurts even more . . ." Her words come out in a ragged whisper. Her back is tense against me, and I know that she's telling the truth, that her sensitive nipples are likely in agony from the vicious bite of the toy. I've used nipple clamps on her before, on the island, but those were a gentler version, capable of applying only light pressure. These are much more hardcore, and I smile darkly as I imagine how much they'll hurt when they come off.

Cupping the undersides of her breasts with my hands, I squeeze them lightly, molding the soft flesh with my fingers. "Yes, it hurts, doesn't it?" I murmur as she jerks in pain, the movement of my hands pulling on the chain between her nipples. "My poor baby, so sweet, yet so abused . . ."

Releasing her breasts, I run my hand down her smooth, flat stomach until I reach the soft folds between her legs. As I had suspected, despite the pain—or more likely, because of it—she's soaking wet, her pussy already liquid with need. My cock throbs in response. The sight of her restrained, with her delicate nipples clamped and hurting, appeals to me in a way that my old shrink would've undoubtedly found disturbing. Doing my best to control my hunger, I touch her small clit with my thumb, pressing on it lightly, and she moans, leaning back against my chest, her hips lifting up in a silent plea for more.

"Tell me what you're feeling now." I deliberately keep the pressure on her clit feather-light. "Tell me, Nora."

"I . . . I don't know . . ."

"Tell me how those little nipples feel. I want to hear you say it." I accompany the demand with a firm pinch of her clit, causing her to cry out and buck against me from the sudden pain.

"They—they still hurt," she gasps when she recovers, "but it's different now, less sharp and more like a steady throb . . ."

"Good girl . . ." I stroke her swollen clit gently as a reward. "And what does it feel like when I touch you like this?"

Her small pink tongue comes out again, flicking over her bottom lip. "It feels good," she whispers, "really good . . . Please, Julian . . ."

"Please what?" I prod, wanting to hear her beg. She has the perfect voice for begging, sweet and innocently sexy. Her pleading affects me in a way that's just the opposite of what she intends—it makes me want to torment her more.

"Please touch me . . ." She lifts her hips again, trying to intensify the pressure on her sex.

"Touch you where?" I move my hand, depriving her of my touch altogether. "Tell me exactly where you want me to touch you, my pet."

"My . . . my clit . . ." The words come out on a breathless moan. I can see the sheen of sweat on her forehead, and I know that my torture is having an effect on her, that the sensations she's feeling are as intense as I intended.

"All right, baby." I touch her again, pressing my fingers into her slick folds to stimulate the bundle of nerves with light, even strokes. "Like that?"

"Yes." She's breathing faster now, her chest rising and falling as her orgasm approaches. "Yes, just like that . . ." Her voice trails off, her body tightening like a string, and then she cries out, jerking in my arms as she reaches her peak. I hold her through it, keeping the pressure on her clit steady until her contractions abate, and then I reach for another item I have prepared.

It's a dildo this time, one that's roughly the size of my own dick. Made of a special blend of silicone and plastic, it's designed to imitate the feel of human flesh, right down to the skin-like texture on the outside. It's as close as I will let Nora get to experiencing another man's cock.

Holding her against me with one arm, I bring the dildo to her sex and position the broad head at her slick, quivering opening. "Tell me what you're feeling now," I order her, and begin to push the object in.

She gasps, her breathing quickening again, and I feel her squirming as the large toy slowly enters her pussy. Her fingers clench and unclench against my stomach in an agitated tempo, her nails scratching my skin. "I—I don't . . ."

"You don't what?" My tone sharpens as her sentence trails off. "Tell me how it feels to you."

"It feels . . . thick and hard." The tremor in her voice stiffens my cock further, making it pulse with hungry need.

"And?" I prompt, pushing the object deeper. The dildo looks almost too big for her delicate body to accept, and the sight of her tight sheath gradually engulfing it is almost painfully erotic.

"And"—she exhales sharply, her head falling back against my shoulder—"and it feels like it's stretching me and filling me . . ."

"Yes, baby, that's right." By now the dildo is all the way inside her, with only the end sticking out. I reward her for her honesty by rubbing her clit with my fingers, spreading wetness from her dripping opening all around her soft folds. When she's panting again, her hips undulating against my hand, I stop before she can come and release her from my hold, moving back a bit. Then I push her forward, pressing her face against the mattress, and pull her legs out from underneath her, making her lie flat on her belly.

As much as I want to continue playing with her, I can no longer wait to fuck her.

Deprived of my touch and with her clamped nipples rubbing painfully against the sheets, she whimpers, trying to roll over onto her side. I don't let her, holding her down with one hand as I shove a pillow under her hips with another. Then I grab lube and squirt it directly on the small, puckered opening between her ass cheeks, right above where the edge of the dildo is protruding from her stretched, glistening pussy.

She tenses, now realizing my intentions, and I slap her ass with one hand, quelling any protest she might've been trying to make. "Easy now. You need to tell me how it feels, do you understand me, my pet?"

She whimpers as I straddle her and press the tip of my cock to her tight little asshole, but I feel her trying to relax underneath me, just like I taught her. Anal sex is something she's still not entirely comfortable with, and her reluctance pleases me in some perverse way. It shows me both how far I've come with her training and how far I still have to go.

"Do you understand?" I repeat in a harsher tone when she remains silent, breathing heavily into the mattress, her bound hands tightly clenched behind her back. I desperately want to shove my cock in all the way, but I settle for just nudging her with it, smearing the lube all around her back opening. Tonight I want to get inside her mind just as much as I want to get inside her body, and I won't settle for anything less.

"Yes . . ." Her words are muffled by the blanket as I press forward and begin to penetrate her ass, ignoring her attempts to squirm away. "It feels . . . oh God . . . I can't . . . Julian, please, it's too much—"

"Tell me," I order, continuing to press in, pushing past the resistance of her sphincter. With her pussy already filled with the dildo, her ass is so tight around my cock that I'm shaking from the effort it's taking to control myself. My voice is thick with lust when I rasp out, "I want to hear everything."

"It—it burns . . ." She's panting, and I can see droplets of sweat gathering between her shoulder blades, strands of her long hair sticking to her damp skin. "Oh fuck . . . I'm too full . . . It's too intense . . ."

"Yes, that's good . . . Continue talking . . ." I'm now almost all the way in, and I can feel my dick rubbing against the dildo as only a thin wall separates it from the toy. She's trembling underneath me now, her body overwhelmed by the sensations, and I stroke her back in a soothing motion as I press forward one last inch, bottoming out deep within her body.

She makes an incoherent noise, her shoulders beginning to shake, and her muscles tighten around my cock in a futile effort to push me out. The movement shifts the dildo within her, and she cries out, her shaking intensifying. "I can't . . . Julian, please, I can't . . ."

I groan, explosive pleasure zinging through my balls as her ass squeezes my dick. My control dissolving, I withdraw from her halfway and then plunge back in, reveling in the feel of her body's resistance, in the almost agonizing tightness of her hot, smooth passage around my shaft.

She screams into the blanket as I begin to drive into her in earnest, a mix of sobs and gasping pleas escaping her throat as I set a hard, rhythmic pace. Leaning forward, I brace myself over her with one hand and slide the other under her hips, finding her sex. Now every thrust of my hips presses her clit against my fingers, and her screams take on a different note, that of unwilling pleasure, of ecstasy mixed with pain. I can feel the dildo shifting and moving as I fuck her, and my orgasm boils up with sudden intensity, my spine tightening as my balls draw up flush against my body. Just as I'm about to erupt, her ass clamps down on me, and I realize with dark pleasure that she's coming too, that her muscles are spasming around my cock as she cries out underneath me. And then the orgasm hits me, a shockwave of pleasure ripping through my body as jets of my seed spurt out into her hot depths, leaving me stunned and breathless from the force of my release.

When my heart no longer feels like it's about to explode, I carefully withdraw from her ass and pull the dildo from her pussy. She lies there limp and pliant, small sobs still shaking her frame as I unlock the handcuffs and massage her delicate wrists. Next, I untie the blindfold, sliding it out from under her. The silky piece of cloth is drenched from Nora's tears, and as I gently turn her over, I see wet streaks on her blanket-creased cheeks. She blinks at me, squinting against the bright light, and I reach for her nipples, releasing first one, then the other from the clamps. She doesn't react for a moment, but then her entire body jolts as blood rushes back to the abused buds. A moan escapes her throat, and fresh tears well up in her eyes as her hands go up to cover her breasts, cradling them protectively against the pain.

"Shh," I soothe, leaning down to kiss her. Her lips taste salty from her tears, and a tiny flame of arousal reignites within me. My cock, now flaccid, twitches, her pain and tears turning me on despite my extreme satiation. I'm not up for round two quite yet, though, and instead of deepening the kiss, I reluctantly lift my head and gaze down at her.

She stares up at me, her eyes slightly unfocused, and I know she's still recovering from the intensity of the experience I put her through. In this moment, she's utterly defenseless, both mind and body unshielded, and I use her weakened state to press my advantage. "Tell me how you feel now," I murmur, raising one hand to tenderly caress her jaw. "Tell me, baby."

She closes her eyes, and I see a single tear roll down her cheek. "I feel . . . empty and full at the same time, destroyed, yet replenished," she whispers, her words barely audible. "I feel like you shredded me into pieces and then remade those pieces into something else, something that's no longer me . . . something that belongs to you . . ."

"Yes." I absorb her words hungrily. "And what else?"

She opens her eyes, meeting my gaze, and I see a strange sort of hopelessness etched into her face. "And I love you," she says quietly. "I love you even though I see you for what you are—even though I know what you're doing to me. I love you because I'm no longer capable of *not* loving you . . . because you're now part of me, for better or for worse."

I hold her gaze, the dark empty corners of my soul sucking in her words like a desert plant takes in water. Her love may not be freely given, but it's mine. It will always be mine. "And you are part of *me*, Nora," I admit, my voice low and unusually hoarse. This is the closest I can come to telling her how much she means to me, how deep my longing for her runs. "I hope you know that, my pet."

And before she can respond, I kiss her again, then slide my arms under her body, pick her up, and carry her to the bathroom to wash up.

CHAPTER NINETEEN

❖ NORA ❖

The week before Julian's departure is bittersweet. I still have not entirely forgiven him for the forced tracker implants—or for the bracelet embedded with yet another tracker he made me start wearing a couple of days later. Nevertheless, ever since Julian's words that evening, I've been feeling infinitely better.

I know what he said is not exactly a declaration of undying love, but from a man like Julian, it might as well be. Ana is right: Julian lost everyone who has ever mattered to him. Everyone except me, that is. The fact that he clings to me with such brutal possessiveness may be overwhelming at times, but it's also an indication of his feelings.

His love for me is wrong and perverse in many ways, but it's no less real because of that.

Of course, knowing this makes my fear for Julian's safety on the upcoming trip even more intense. As his departure time approaches, my joy over his confession fades, and anxiety takes its place.

I don't want Julian to leave. Every time I think of him going on this mission, I'm gripped by a suffocating sense of dread. I know there is an irrational component to my fear, but that doesn't lessen it in any way. Aside from the very real danger Julian will face, I'm simply afraid to be alone. We've spent so little time apart in the past couple of months that the thought of being without him for even a few days makes me feel deeply stressed and uneasy.

It doesn't help that I have exams and papers galore, or that my parents have been steadily pressuring me to come for a visit—something that Julian won't allow until the Al-Quadar threat is fully contained.

"You can't leave the estate, but they can come visit us here if you'd like," he tells me during shooting practice one afternoon. "I would advise against it, though. Right now your parents are more or less off the radar, but the more contact I appear to have with your family, the more danger they'll be in. It's up to you, though. Just say the word, and I'll send a plane for them."

"No, that's okay," I say hastily. "I don't want to draw any unnecessary attention to them." And raising my gun, I start shooting at the beer cans on the far edge of the field, letting the now-familiar jolt of the weapon take away some of my frustration.

I realized that my parents are in danger a couple of days after we came to the estate. To my relief, Julian told me that he'd already put a discreet security detail on them—highly trained bodyguards whose job is to protect my family while letting them go about their lives. The alternative, he explained, is to bring them to the estate with us—a solution that my parents rejected as soon as I brought it up.

"What? We're not moving to Colombia to live with an illegal arms dealer!" my dad exclaimed when I told him about the potential danger. "Who does that bastard think he is? I just got a new job—not to mention, we can't leave all of our friends and relatives!"

And that was as far as that got. I can't say I blame my parents for not wanting to move halfway across the world to be with me in my abductor's compound. They're still young, both in their early forties, and they've always led active, busy lives. My dad plays lacrosse nearly every weekend, and my mom has a group of girlfriends who get together for wine and gossip on a regular basis. My parents are also still very much in love with each other, with my dad constantly surprising my mom with little gifts of flowers, chocolate, or a dinner out. Growing up, I had no doubt that they both loved me, but I also knew that I wasn't the absolute epicenter of their lives.

No, if what Julian says is true—and I'm inclined to trust him on this—it's best if my parents don't appear to have too close of a connection to the Esguerra organization.

Their ability to lead a normal life depends on it.

* * *

On the night before Julian is scheduled to leave, I ask Ana to prepare a special dinner for us. I recently discovered that Julian has a weakness for tiramisu, so that is our dessert for tonight. For the main course, Ana makes lasagna the same way that Julian's mother used to make it. The housekeeper told me it was his favorite dish when he was a boy.

I don't know why I'm doing this. It's not like a good meal will suddenly convince Julian to forego the cruel pleasure of getting his hands on Majid. I know my husband well enough to understand that nothing can dissuade him from that. Julian is used to danger. I think he even craves it to some extent. I'm not foolish enough to think that I can domesticate him with one dinner.

Still, I want this evening to be special. I need it to be special. I don't want to think about terrorists and torture, abduction and mind fuckery. For just one night, I want to pretend that we're a regular couple, that I'm simply a wife who wants to do something nice for her husband.

Before dinner, I take a shower and blow-dry my long brown hair until it's smooth and shiny. I even apply a little eyeshadow and lipgloss. I don't normally put this much effort into my appearance, since Julian is already insatiable as is, but tonight I want to look extra pretty for him. My dress for the evening is a strapless little number, ivory with a black trim at the waist, and my shoes are sexy black peep-toe pumps. Underneath, I'm wearing a black strapless pushup bra and a matching thong, the most wicked lingerie set I have in my wardrobe.

I'm going to seduce Julian tonight, for no other reason other than because I want to.

He gets delayed by some last-minute logistics, so I end up waiting for him at the candle-lit dinner table for a few minutes, anxiety and excitement battling for supremacy in my chest. Anxiety because I feel sick thinking about tomorrow, and excitement because I can't wait to spend time with Julian.

When he finally walks into the room, I stand up to greet him, and his gaze fastens on me with breathtaking intensity. Stopping a few feet away, he runs his eyes over my body. When he lifts his eyes back to my face, the fire that burns in the blue depths sends an electric tingle straight to my core. A slow, sensual smile curls his lips as he says softly, "You look gorgeous, my pet . . . Absolutely gorgeous."

A flush of pleasure warms my skin at the compliment. "Thank you," I whisper, my eyes glued to his face. He changed for dinner as well, putting on a light blue polo shirt and a pair of gray khaki pants that fit his tall, broad-shouldered body like they were made for him. With his dark, lustrous hair back to its former length, Julian can easily pass for a model or a movie star vacationing on a golf resort. My voice sounds breathless as I say, "You look pretty amazing yourself."

His smile widens as he approaches the table and stops in front of me. "Thank you, baby," he murmurs, his strong fingers curving around my bare shoulders as he lowers his head and captures my mouth in a deep, yet incredibly tender kiss. I melt on the spot, my neck arching back under the hungry pressure of his lips, and it's not until Ana pointedly clears her throat behind us that I regain my senses enough to realize that we're not in our own bedroom. Embarrassed, I push him away, and Julian lets me, releasing me and stepping back with a smile.

"Dinner first, I guess," he says wryly and, walking around the table, takes a seat across from me.

Ana, her cheeks slightly red, serves us lasagna, pours us each a glass of wine, and disappears before I have a chance to do more than say a quick thank-you.

"Lasagna . . ." Julian sniffs appreciatively at the food. "I can't remember the last time I had this."

"Ana told me your mother used to make it for you when you were little," I say softly, watching as he takes the first bite. "I hope you still like it."

His eyes lift from his plate, his gaze locking on mine as he chews the food. "You arranged this?" he asks after he swallows, and there is a strange note in his voice. He gestures toward the wine and the candles burning on the outer edges of the table. "It wasn't Ana who set all of this up?"

"Well, she did all the work," I admit. "I merely asked her for a few things. I hope you don't mind."

"Mind? No, of course not." His voice still sounds a bit odd, but he doesn't question me further. Instead he begins to eat in earnest, and the conversation turns to my upcoming exams.

After we're done with the lasagna, Ana brings out the dessert. It looks as rich and scrumptious as any I've seen in an Italian restaurant, and I watch Julian's reaction as Ana places it on the table in front of him.

If he's surprised, he doesn't show it. Instead he gives Ana a warm smile and thanks her for the efforts. It's not until she leaves the room that he turns to look at me. "A tiramisu?" he says softly, his eyes reflecting the dancing light from the candles. "Why, Nora?"

I shrug. "Why not?"

He studies me for a moment, his gaze unusually thoughtful as it lingers on my face, and I wait for him to press further. But he doesn't. Instead he picks up his fork. "Why not indeed," he murmurs and turns his attention to the mouthwatering dessert.

I follow his lead, and soon our plates are all but licked clean.

* * *

When we get upstairs, Julian leads me to the bed. Instead of undressing me right away, however, he captures my face between his palms. "Thank you for a wonderful evening, baby," he whispers, his eyes dark with some indefinable emotion.

I smile up at him, my hands coming up to rest on his waist. "Of course . . ." My heart feels like it's about to overflow with happiness. "It's my pleasure."

He looks as though he's about to say something else, but then he just slants his mouth across mine and begins to kiss me with deep, almost desperate passion. My eyes drift shut as pleasure spirals through me. His lips are unbelievably soft, his tongue skillfully caressing mine, and the rich, dark taste of him makes my head spin. As we kiss, his hands slide around my back, pressing me closer to him. The hardness of his erection against my belly sends a spear of heat straight to the center of my sex, and I clutch at his sides, my knees weakening as his lips wander from my mouth to my earlobe and then down to my neck.

"You are so fucking hot," he mutters thickly. His breath almost burns my sensitive skin, and I moan, my head falling back as he arches me over his arm to nibble at the tender area just above my collarbone. My nipples tighten, and my sex begins to ache with the familiar pulsing tension as Julian licks my skin, then blows cool air over the wet spot, sending erotic chills all over my body.

Before I can recover, he tugs me upright, spinning me around so that I'm standing with my back to him. Then his hands are on the back of my dress, pulling down the zipper. The little dress falls to the floor, leaving me wearing nothing but my black heels, push-up bra, and thong.

Julian sucks in an audible breath, and I turn around, giving him a slow, teasing smile. "You like?" I murmur, taking a couple of steps back to give him a better view. The expression on his face makes my pulse quicken with excitement. He's looking at me like a starving man looks at a piece of cake, with agonized longing and naked lust. His eyes say that he wants to devour me and savor me at the same time . . . that I'm the hottest woman he's ever seen in his life.

Instead of answering, he steps toward me and reaches behind my back to unhook my bra. As soon as my breasts are free, he covers them with his warm palms, his thumbs rasping across my hardened nipples. "You are fucking exquisite," he whispers roughly, staring down at me, and I draw in a shaky breath, his words and the touch of his hands making my insides quiver. "You're all I can think about, Nora . . . all I can focus on . . ."

His confession turns my bones to jelly. The knowledge that I have this effect on him—that this powerful, dangerous man is just as consumed by me as I am by him—makes my heart pound in a wild, erratic rhythm. Regardless of how it all began, Julian is now mine, and I want him as much as he wants me.

Emboldened, I wrap my arms around his neck and pull his head down toward me. As our lips meet, I put everything I have into that kiss, letting him feel how much I need him, how much I love him. My hands slide into his thick, silky hair as his arms close around my back, pressing me against him, and my peaked nipples rub against the ribbed cotton of his shirt, reminding me of the tantalizing contrast between my near-nakedness and his clothed state. His hard erection pushes into my belly, and the heat within me spikes as our mouths mesh in a symphony of lust, coming together with explosive yearning.

I'm not sure how we end up on the bed, but I find myself there, my hands frantically tearing at Julian's clothes as he rains hot kisses on my chest and stomach. His hand closes around my thong, ripping it off with a single motion, and then his fingers push into my opening, two big fingers penetrating me with a roughness that makes me gasp and arch against him. "You're so fucking wet," he growls, thrusting his fingers deeper into me before pulling them out and bringing them to my face. "Taste how much you want me."

Unbearably aroused, I close my lips around his fingers, sucking them into my mouth. They're coated with my moisture, but the taste doesn't repel me. If anything, it turns me on, makes me burn even hotter. Julian groans as I suck on his fingers, swirling my tongue around them as if they were his cock, and then he pulls his hand away. Rearing up, he pulls his shirt over his head with a single motion, exposing the rippling muscles underneath. His pants are next, and I catch a brief glimpse of his erection before he climbs on top of me, his powerful hands grabbing my wrists and pinning them next to my shoulders. Then his eyes lock on mine, and he pushes my thighs apart with his knees, pressing the head of his cock against my opening.

My heart thrumming with anticipation, I hold his gaze. His face is taut with lust, his jaw clenched tight as he slowly penetrates me. I expected him to take me roughly, but he's careful tonight, working his thick cock into me with a deliberateness that's both arousing and frustrating. There's no pain as my body stretches to accept him, only pleasurable fullness, but some sick part of me now wants the roughness, the violence.

"Julian . . ." I run my tongue over my lips. "I want you to fuck me. *Really* fuck me." To emphasize my request, I wrap my legs around his hips, pulling him all the way into me. We both groan at the intense sensation, and I see his pupils dilating until only a thin rim of blue remains around the black circle.

"You want me to fuck you?" His voice is guttural, so filled with hunger that I can barely make out the words. His hands tighten on my wrists, almost cutting off my circulation. "To really fuck you?"

I nod, my pulse somewhere in the stratosphere. It still feels wrong to admit this about myself, to acknowledge that I need something I once dreaded.

To know that I'm *asking* my kidnapper to abuse me.

Julian inhales sharply, and I can feel the dam of his control cracking. His mouth descends on mine, his lips and tongue now savage, almost vicious. This kiss devours me, steals my breath and soul. At the same time, his cock withdraws from me nearly all the way and then slams back in with a hard, brutal thrust that splits me in half—and sets my nerve endings on fire.

I cry out into his mouth, my legs wrapping tighter around his firm, muscled ass as he begins to fuck me without restraint. It's a possession as violent as any rape, but I revel in it, my body loving the ferocious assault. It's what I want now, what I need. I may have bruises tomorrow, but for the moment, all I can feel is the massive tension gathering within me, the pressure coiling deep within my sex. Each ruthless thrust winds me tighter and tighter, until I feel like I will shatter . . . and then I do, an explosion of pleasure rocketing through my body as I fly apart in Julian's arms, utterly swamped by the dark bliss.

He comes then too, his head thrown back in pained ecstasy, each muscle in his neck tightly corded as he grinds his cock deeper into me with a harsh cry. The pressure of his groin against my clit prolongs my contractions, wringing every drop of sensation from my body, leaching all remnants of strength from my muscles.

In the aftermath, he rolls off me and gathers me against him, cradling me from behind. And as our breathing begins to slow, we drift off into a deep and dreamless sleep.

CHAPTER TWENTY

❖ JULIAN ❖

The next morning I wake up before Nora, as usual. She's sleeping in her favorite position: draped across my chest, one of her legs resting on top of mine. Quietly extricating myself from her, I head into the shower, trying not to think of the temptation of her sexy little body lying there, all soft and warm from sleep. It's unfortunate, but I don't have time to sate myself with her this morning; the plane is already waiting for me on the landing strip.

She managed to surprise me last night. All week long I'd sensed a slight, almost imperceptible distance from her. I may have broken through her barriers that night, but she rebuilt them to a small degree. She hadn't been pouting or giving me the silent treatment, but I could tell that she hadn't fully forgiven me either.

Until last evening.

I thought I didn't need her forgiveness, but the light, almost euphoric feeling in my chest today says otherwise.

My shower takes less than five minutes. Once I'm dressed and ready to go, I walk over to the bed to give Nora a kiss before I leave. Leaning over her, I brush my lips against her cheek, and in that moment, her eyes flutter open.

Her lips curve upward in a sleepy smile. "Hi . . ."

"Hi yourself," I say huskily, reaching over with my hand to brush a tangled strand of hair off her face. Fuck, she does things to me. Things that no small girl should be able to do. I'm about to finally get revenge on the man who killed Beth and stole Nora from me, and all I can think about is climbing back into bed with her.

She blinks a few times, and I see her smile fading as she remembers that today is not just any morning. All traces of sleepiness disappear from her face as she sits up and stares at me, heedless of the blanket falling down and exposing her naked torso.

"You're leaving already?"

"Yes, baby." Trying to keep my eyes off her round, perky breasts, I sit down on the bed next to her and clasp her hand between both of my palms, rubbing it softly. "The plane is already fueled up and waiting for me."

She swallows. "When are you going to be back?"

"If all goes well, in about a week. I have to meet with a couple of officials in Russia first, so I won't get to Tajikistan right away."

"Russia? Why?" A small frown bisects her forehead. "I thought you were going to take care of some business in Ukraine on your way back."

"I was, but things changed. Yesterday afternoon I received a call from one of Peter's contacts in Moscow. They want me to meet with them first, or else they won't let us get to Tajikistan."

"Oh." Nora looks even more concerned now, her frown deepening. "Do you know why?"

I have some suspicions, but none that I want to share with her at the moment. She's far too worried as is. Russians have always been unpredictable, and the increasingly volatile situation in that region doesn't help matters.

"I've had some interactions with them in the past," I say noncommittally, and get up before she has a chance to question me further. "I have to go now, baby, but I'll see you in a few days. Good luck with your tests, okay?"

She nods, her eyes suspiciously bright as she looks at me, and unable to resist, I bend down and kiss her one last time before walking out of the room.

* * *

Moscow in March is colder than a witch's tit. The cold seeps through my thick layers of clothing and settles deep within my bones, making me feel as if I'll never get warm again. I have never particularly liked Russia, and this visit only solidifies my negative opinion of the place.

Freezing. Dirty. Corrupt.

I can deal with the last two, but all three combined is too much. No wonder Peter was glad to remain behind to watch the compound. The bastard knew exactly what I would be getting into. I could see the smirk on his face as he watched the plane take off. After the tropical heat of the jungle, the bone-chilling temperatures of Moscow in the last grip of winter feel downright painful—as do my negotiations with the Russian government.

It takes nearly an hour, ten different appetizers, and half a bottle of vodka before Buschekov gets to the point of the meeting. The only reason I tolerate this is because it takes about this long for my feet to defrost from the sub-zero chill outside. The traffic on the way to the restaurant was so bad that Lucas and I ended up getting out of the car and walking eight blocks, freezing our asses off in the process.

Now, however, I'm finally able to move my toes—and Buschekov seems ready to talk business. He's one of the unofficial officials here: a person who wields significant influence in the Kremlin, but whose name never comes up on the news.

"I have a delicate matter I'd like to discuss with you," Buschekov says after the waiter clears off some of the empty platters. Or, rather, our interpreter says that after Buschekov says something in Russian. Since neither Lucas nor I understand more than a few words of the language, Buschekov hired a young woman to translate for us. Pretty, blond, and blue-eyed, Yulia Tzakova looks to be only a couple of years older than my Nora, but the Russian official assured me that the girl knows how to be discreet.

"Go on," I say in response to Buschekov's statement. Lucas sits next to me, silently consuming his second serving of caviar-stuffed blinis. He's the only one I brought with me to this meeting. The rest of my men are stationed nearby in case of any difficulties. I doubt the Russians will try anything at the moment, but one can never be too cautious.

Buschekov gives me a thin-lipped smile and responds in Russian.

"I'm sure you are aware of the difficulties in our region," Yulia translates. "We would like you to assist us in resolving this matter."

"Assist you how?" I have a good idea of what the Russians want, but I still want to hear him lay it all out.

"There are certain parts of Ukraine that need our help," Yulia says in English after Buschekov answers. "But, world opinion being what it is right now, it would be problematic if we went in and actually gave that help."

"So you would like me to do it instead."

He nods, his colorless eyes trained on my face as Yulia translates my statement. "Yes," he says, "we would like a sizable shipment of weapons and other supplies to reach the freedom fighters in Donetsk. It cannot be traced back to us. In return, you would be paid your usual fee and granted safe passage to Tajikistan."

I smile at him blandly. "Is that all?"

"We would also prefer it if you avoided any dealings with Ukraine at this time," he says without blinking. "Two chairs and one ass and all that."

I assume that last statement makes more sense in Russian, but I understand the gist of what he's saying. Buschekov is not the first client to demand this from me, and he won't be the last. "I'm afraid I will require additional compensation for that," I say calmly. "As you know, I don't usually take sides in these types of conflicts."

"Yes, so we've heard." Buschekov picks up a piece of salted fish with his fork and chews it slowly as he looks at me. "Perhaps you might reconsider that position in our case. The Soviet Union may be gone, but our influence in this region is still quite substantial."

"Yes, I'm aware. Why do you think I'm here right now?" The smile that I give him now has a sharper edge. "But neutrality is an expensive commodity to give up. I'm sure you understand."

Something icy flickers in Buschekov's gaze. "I do. I'm authorized to offer you twenty percent more than the usual payment for your cooperation in this matter."

"Twenty percent? When you're cutting my potential profits in half?" I laugh softly. "I don't think so."

He pours himself another shot of vodka and swirls it around the glass, regarding me thoughtfully. "Twenty percent more and the captured Al-Quadar terrorist remitted into your custody," he says after a few moments. "This is our final offer."

I study him while I pour myself some vodka as well. Truthfully, this is better than I had been hoping to get out of him, and I know better than to push too far with the Russians. "We have a deal then," I say and, lifting my glass in an ironic toast, knock back the shot.

* * *

My car is waiting for us on the street when we exit the restaurant. The driver finally made it through the traffic, which means we won't freeze on our way to the hotel.

"Would you mind giving me a lift to the nearest subway?" Yulia asks as Lucas and I approach the car. I can see her already beginning to shiver. "It should be about ten blocks from here."

I give her a considering look, then motion Lucas over with a short gesture. "Frisk her."

Lucas walks over and pats her down. "She's clean."

"Okay, then," I say, opening the car door for her. "Hop in."

She climbs in and settles next to me in the back, while Lucas joins the driver in the front. "Thank you," she says with a pretty smile. "I really appreciate it. This is one of the worst winters in recent years."

"No problem." I'm not in the mood to make small talk, so I pull out my phone and begin answering emails. There's one from Nora, which makes me grin. She wants to know if I landed safely. *Yes*, I write back. *Now just trying not to get frostbite in Moscow.*

"Are you staying here for long?" Yulia's soft voice interrupts me as I'm about to pull up a report detailing Nora's movements around the estate in my absence. When I glance up at her, the Russian girl smiles and crosses her long legs. "I could show you around town if you'd like."

Her invitation couldn't be more blatant if she'd palmed my cock right then and there. I can see the hungry gleam in her eyes as she looks at me, and I realize that she's one of those: a woman turned on by power and danger. She wants me because of what I represent— because of the thrill it gives her to play with fire. I have no doubt that she would let me do whatever I want to her, no matter how sadistic or depraved, and then she would beg for more.

She's exactly the type of woman I would've gladly fucked before meeting Nora. Unfortunately for Yulia, her pale beauty does nothing for me now. The only woman I want in my bed is the dark-haired girl who's currently several thousand miles away.

"Thanks for the invitation," I say, giving Yulia a cool smile. "But we'll be leaving soon, and I'm afraid I'm too exhausted to do your town justice tonight."

"Of course." Yulia smiles back, unfazed by my rejection. She clearly has enough self-confidence not to be offended. "If you change your mind, you know where to find me." And as the car rolls to a halt in front of the subway stop, she gracefully climbs out, leaving behind a faint trail of expensive perfume.

As the car begins moving again, Lucas turns around to face me. "If you don't want her, I'd be happy to entertain her tonight," he offers casually. "If that's all right with you, of course."

I grin. Hot blondes have always been Lucas's weakness. "Why not," I say. "She's all yours if you want her." We don't fly out until tomorrow morning, and I have plenty of security in place. If Lucas wants to spend the night fucking our interpreter, I'm not about to deny him that pleasure.

As for me, I plan to use my fist in the shower while thinking of Nora, and then get a good night's rest.

Tomorrow is going to be an eventful day.

* * *

The flight to Tajikistan from Moscow is supposed to take a little over six hours in my Boeing C-17. It's one of the three military airplanes that I own, and it's big enough for this mission, easily fitting in all of my men and our equipment.

Everyone, myself included, is dressed in the latest combat gear. Our suits are bulletproof and flame-retardant, and we're fully armed with assault rifles, grenades, and explosives. It may be overkill, but I'm not taking chances with my men's lives. I enjoy danger, but I'm not suicidal, and all the risks I take in my business are carefully calculated. Nora's rescue in Thailand was probably the most perilous operation I've been involved with in recent years, and I wouldn't have done it for anyone else.

Only for her.

I spend the majority of the flight going through the manufacturing specifications for a new factory in Malaysia. If all goes well, I may shift missile production there from its current location in Indonesia. The local officials in the latter region are getting too greedy, demanding higher bribes each month, and I'm not inclined to indulge them for much longer. I also answer a few questions from my Chicago-based portfolio manager; he's working on setting up a fund-of-funds through one of my subsidiaries and needs me to give him some investment parameters.

We're flying over Uzbekistan, just a few hundred miles from our destination, when I decide to check in with Lucas, who's piloting the plane.

He turns toward me as soon as I enter the cabin. "We're on track to get there in about an hour and a half," he says without my asking. "There is some ice on the landing strip, so they're de-icing it for us right now. The helicopters are already fueled up and ready to go."

"Excellent." The plan calls for us to land about a dozen miles from the suspected terrorist hideout in the Pamir Mountains and fly by helicopters the rest of the way. "Any unusual activities in that area?"

He shakes his head. "No, everything is quiet."

"Good." Entering the cabin, I sit down next to Lucas in the copilot's seat and strap myself in. "How was the Russian girl last night?"

A rare smile flashes across his stony face. "Quite satisfying. You missed out."

"Yes, I'm sure," I say, though I don't feel even the slightest flicker of regret. There's no way some one-night stand can approximate the intensity of my connection with Nora, and I have no desire to settle for anything less than that.

Lucas grins—an expression that's even more uncommon on his hard features. "I have to say, I never expected to see you as a happily married man."

I raise my eyebrows. "Is that right?" This is probably the most personal observation he's ever made to me. In all the years he's been with my organization, Lucas has never before bridged the distance from loyal employee to friend—not that I've encouraged him to do so. Trust has never come easy to me, and there have been only a handful of individuals I've been able to call 'friend.'

He shrugs, his face smoothing out into his usual impassive mask, though a hint of amusement still lurks in his eyes. "Sure. People like us aren't generally considered good husband material."

An involuntary chuckle escapes my throat. "Well, I don't know if, strictly speaking, Nora considers me 'good husband material.'" A monster who abducted her and fucked with her head, sure. But a good husband? Somehow I doubt it.

"Well, if she doesn't, then she should," Lucas says, turning his attention back to the controls. "You don't cheat, you take good care of her, and you've risked your life to save her before. If that's not being a good husband, then I don't know what is." As he speaks, I see a small frown appearing on his face as he peers at something on the radar screen.

"What is it?" I ask sharply, all of my instincts suddenly on alert.

"I'm not sure," Lucas begins saying, and at that moment, the plane bucks so violently that I'm nearly thrown out of my seat. It's only the seatbelt I'd strapped on out of habit that prevents me from hitting the ceiling as the plane takes a sudden nosedive.

Lucas grabs the controls, a steady stream of obscenities coming out of his mouth as he frantically tries to correct our course. "Shit, fuck, shit, shit, motherfucking shit—"

"What hit us?" My voice is steady, my mind strangely calm as I assess the situation. There is a grinding, sputtering noise coming from the engines. I can smell smoke and hear screams in the back, so I know there's a fire. It had to be an explosion. That means someone either shot at us from another plane or a surface-to-air missile exploded in close vicinity, damaging one or more of the engines. It couldn't have been a direct missile hit because the Boeing is equipped with an anti-missile defense that's designed to repel all but the most advanced weapons—and because we are still alive and not blown into pieces.

"I'm not sure," Lucas manages to say as he wrestles with the controls. The plane evens out for a brief second and then nosedives again. "Does it fucking matter?"

I'm not sure, to be honest. The analytical part of me wants to know what—or who—is going to be responsible for my death. I doubt it's Al-Quadar; according to my sources, they don't have weapons this sophisticated. That leaves the possibility of error by some trigger-happy Uzbekistani soldier or an intentional strike by someone else. The Russians, perhaps, though why they would do this is anyone's guess.

Still, Lucas is right. I don't know why I care. Knowing the truth won't change the outcome. I can see the snowy peaks of Pamir in the distance, and I know we're not going to make it there.

Lucas resumes his cursing as he fights with the controls, and I grip the edge of my seat, my eyes trained on the ground rushing toward us at a terrifyingly rapid pace. There is a roaring sound in my ears, and I realize that it's my own heartbeat—that I can actually hear the blood coursing through my veins as surging adrenaline sharpens all of my senses.

The plane makes a few more attempts to come out of the nosedive, each one slowing our fall by a few seconds, but nothing seems able to arrest the lethal descent.

As I watch us plummeting to our deaths, I have only one regret.

I will never get to hold Nora again.

PART III: THE CAPTIVE

CHAPTER TWENTY-ONE

❖ NORA ❖

Two days without Julian.

I can't believe it's been two entire days without Julian. I've been going about my usual routine, but without him here, everything feels different.

Emptier. Darker.

It's like the sun has hidden behind a cloud, leaving my world in shadow.

It's crazy. Utterly insane. I've been without Julian before. When I was on the island, he would leave on these trips all the time. In fact, he spent more time *off* the island than *on* it, and somehow I still managed to function. This time around, however, I have to constantly fight off a horrible feeling of unease, of anxiety that seems to worsen with every hour.

"I really don't know what's wrong with me," I tell Rosa during our morning walk. "I lived for eighteen years without him, and now all of a sudden, I can't go for two days?"

She grins at me. "Well, of course. The two of you are all but inseparable, so this doesn't surprise me in the least. I've never seen a couple this much in love before."

I sigh, ruefully shaking my head. For all her seeming practicality, Rosa has a romantic streak as wide as the sea. A couple of weeks ago, I finally confided in her, telling her how Julian and I met and about my time on the island. She had been shocked, but not nearly as much as I would've been in her place. In fact, she seemed to think the whole thing was rather poetic.

"He stole you because he couldn't live without you," she said dreamily when I tried to explain to her why I still have reservations about Julian. "It's like the kind of thing you read about in books or see in movies..." And when I stared at her, hardly able to believe my ears, she added wistfully, "I wish someone wanted *me* enough to steal me away."

So yes, Rosa is definitely not the person to knock some sense into me. She thinks my withering away without Julian is a natural result of our grand love affair, instead of something that likely requires psychiatric help.

Of course, Ana is not much better either.

"It's normal to miss your husband," the housekeeper tells me when I can barely force myself to eat at dinner. "I'm sure Julian misses you just as much."

"I don't know, Ana," I say doubtfully, pushing the rice around on my plate. "I haven't heard from him all day. He responded to my email yesterday, but I sent him two emails today—and nothing." This, more than anything, is what upsets me, I think. Julian either doesn't care about the fact that I'm worried—or he's not in a position to respond to me, being knee-deep in fighting terrorists.

Either possibility makes me queasy.

"He could be flying somewhere," Ana says reasonably, taking my plate away. "Or be someplace with no signal. Truly, you shouldn't worry. I know Julian, and he can take care of himself."

"Yes, I'm sure he can, but he's still human." He can still be killed by a stray bullet or an untimely bomb.

"I know, Nora," Ana says soothingly, patting my arm, and I see the same worry reflected in the depths of her brown eyes. "I know, but you can't let yourself think bad thoughts. I'm sure you'll hear from him in a few hours. He'll contact you by morning at the latest."

* * *

I sleep fitfully, waking up every couple of hours to check my email and phone. By morning, there's still no word from Julian, and I stumble wearily out of bed, bleary-eyed but determined.

If Julian isn't contacting me, I'm going to take matters into my own hands.

The first thing I do is hunt down Peter Sokolov. He's talking with a few guards on the far edge of the estate when I find him, and he seems surprised when I approach him and ask to speak to him privately. Nevertheless, he accommodates my request right away.

As soon as we're out of earshot of the others, I ask, "Have you heard from Julian?" I still find the Russian man intimidating, but he's the only one I know who may have answers.

"No," he responds in his accented voice. "Not since their plane took off from Moscow yesterday." There is a hint of tension around his eyes as he speaks, and my anxiety triples as I realize that Peter is concerned too.

"They were supposed to check in, weren't they?" I say, staring up at his exotically handsome features. My chest feels like I can't get enough air. "Something went wrong, didn't it?"

"We can't assume that yet." His tone is carefully neutral. "It's possible they're not responding to our calls because of security reasons—because they don't want anyone to intercept their communications."

"You don't really believe that."

"It's unlikely," Peter admits, his gray eyes cool on my face. "This is not the usual procedure in these types of cases."

"Right, of course." Doing my best to battle the nauseating fear spreading through me, I ask evenly, "So what's Plan B? Are you going to send in a rescue team? Do you have more men standing by that can act as backup?"

Peter shakes his head. "There's nothing to be done until we know more," he explains. "I've already put out feelers in Russia and Tajikistan, so we should have a better idea of what happened soon. So far, all we know is that their plane took off from Moscow without any problems."

"When do you think you'll hear back from your sources?" I'm trying to contain my panic, but some of it seeps through in my voice. "Today? Tomorrow?"

"I don't know, Mrs. Esguerra," he says, and I see a hint of pity in those merciless gray eyes. "It could be at any time. I will let you know as soon as I hear something."

"Thanks, Peter," I say and, not knowing what else to do, walk back to the house.

* * *

The next six hours go by at a crawl. I pace around the house, going from room to room, unable to focus on any specific activity. Whenever I sit down to study or try to paint, a dozen different scenarios, each one more horrible than the next, start playing in my head. I want to believe that everything will be okay, that Julian's plane disappeared off the grid for some innocuous reason, but I know better than that.

There are no fairy tales in the world Julian and I live in, only savage reality.

I haven't been able to eat anything all day, though Ana has tried tempting me with everything from steak to dessert. To pacify her, I eat a few bites of papaya around lunchtime and resume my aimless pacing around the house.

By early afternoon, I'm literally sick from anxiety. My head is pounding, and my stomach feels like it's eating itself, the acid burning a hole in my insides.

"Let's go for a swim," Rosa offers when she finds me in the library. I can see the concern on her face, and I know Ana probably sent her to distract me. Rosa is usually too busy with her duties to take off in the middle of the day, but she's obviously making an exception today.

The last thing I feel like doing is swimming, but I agree. Rosa's company is better than driving myself insane with worry.

As we exit the library together, I see Peter walking in our direction, a grave expression on his face.

My heart stops for a moment, then begins slamming furiously against my ribcage.

"What is it?" My tongue can barely form the words. "Did you hear anything?"

"The plane went down in Uzbekistan, a couple of hundred miles from the Tajikistan border," he says quietly, stopping in front of me. "It looks like there was a miscommunication, and the Uzbekistani military shot them down."

Blackness creeps in at the edges of my vision. "Shot them down?" My voice sounds like it's coming from a distance, like the words belong to someone else. I am vaguely aware of Rosa placing a supportive arm around my back, but her touch does nothing to arrest the iciness spreading through me.

"We're looking for the wreckage right now," Peter says, almost gently. "I'm sorry, Mrs. Esguerra, but I doubt they could've survived."

CHAPTER TWENTY-TWO

❖ NORA ❖

I'm not sure how I get to the bedroom, but I find myself there, curled up in a ball of silent agony on the bed that Julian and I shared.

I can feel soft hands on my hair, hear voices murmuring in Spanish, and I know both Ana and Rosa are there with me. The housekeeper sounds like she's crying. I want to cry too, but I can't. The pain is too raw, too deep to allow the comfort of tears.

I thought I knew what it feels like to have your heart ripped out. When I mistakenly thought that Julian was dead, I had been devastated, destroyed. Those months without him had been the worst ones of my life. I thought I knew what it was like to feel loss, to know that I would never see his smile again or feel the warmth of his embrace.

It's only now that I realize that there are degrees of agony. That pain can range from devastating to soul-shattering. When I lost Julian before, he had been the center of my world. Now, however, he is my entire world, and I don't know how to exist without him.

"Oh, Nora..." Ana's voice is thick with tears as she strokes my hair. "I'm sorry, child... I'm so sorry..."

I want to tell her that I'm sorry too, that I know Julian mattered to her as well, but I can't. I can't speak. Even breathing seems to require exorbitant effort, as though my lungs have forgotten how to function. One tiny breath in, one tiny breath out—that's all I seem capable of doing at the moment.

Just breathing. Just not dying.

After a while, the quiet murmurs and soothing touches stop, and I realize that I'm alone. They must've covered me with a blanket before they left, because I can feel its soft fluffy weight on top of me. It should make me feel warm, but it doesn't.

All I feel is a frozen, aching void where my heart used to be.

* * *

"Nora, child . . . Come, drink something . . ."

Ana and Rosa are back, their soft hands pulling me to a sitting position. A cup of hot chocolate is offered to me, and I accept it on autopilot, cradling it between my cold palms.

"Just a sip," Ana urges. "You haven't eaten all day. Julian wouldn't want this, you know that."

The jolt of agony at the mention of his name is so strong that the cup almost slips out of my grip. Rosa grabs for it, steadying my hands, and gently, but inexorably pushes the cup toward my lips. "Come on, Nora," she whispers, her gaze filled with sympathy. "Just drink some."

I force myself to take a few sips. The rich, warm liquid trickles down my throat, the combined rush of sugar and caffeine chasing away some of my numb exhaustion. Feeling a fraction more alive, I glance at the window and realize with shock that it's already dark—that I must've lain there for a few hours without registering the passage of time.

"Any word from Peter?" I ask, looking back at Ana and Rosa. "Did they find the wreckage?"

Rosa looks relieved that I'm talking again. "We haven't seen him since the afternoon," she says, and Ana nods, her eyes red-rimmed and swollen.

"Okay." I take a few more sips of the hot chocolate and then hand the cup back to Ana. "Thank you."

"Can I get you something to eat?" Ana asks hopefully. "A sandwich perhaps, or some fruit?"

My stomach roils at the thought of food, but I know that I need to eat something. I can't die alongside Julian, no matter how appealing that option seems at the moment. "Yes, please." My voice sounds strained. "Just a piece of toast with cheese, if you don't mind."

Jumping off the bed, Rosa gives me a huge, approving smile. "There we go. See, Ana, I told you she's a fighter." And before I can change my mind about the meal, she runs out of the room to grab the food.

"I'm going to shower," I tell Ana, getting up as well. All of a sudden, I have a strong urge to be alone—to be away from the smothering concern I see on Ana's face. My body feels cold and brittle, like an icicle that might shatter at any moment, and my eyes are burning with unshed tears.

Just focus on breathing. Just one tiny breath after another.

"Of course, child." Ana gives me a kind, weary smile. "You go right ahead. The food will be waiting for you when you come out."

And as I make my escape into the bathroom, I see her quietly slipping out of the room.

* * *

"Nora! Oh my God, Nora!"

Rosa's screams and frantic knocking on the bathroom door startle me out of my numb, almost catatonic state. I have no idea how long I've been standing under the hot spray, but I immediately jump out. Then, wrapping a towel around myself, I race to the door, my wet feet sliding on cold tiles.

My heart hammering in my throat, I yank open the door. "What is it?"

"He's alive!" Rosa's scream nearly deafens me with its high-pitched volume. "Nora, Julian is alive!"

"Alive?" For a moment, I can't process what she's saying, my brain sluggish from hunger and grief. "Julian is alive?"

"Yes!" she squeals, grabbing my hands and jumping up and down. "Peter just got word that they found him and a few of his men alive. They're being taken to the hospital as we speak!"

My knees buckle, and I sway on my feet. "To the hospital?" My voice is barely above a whisper. "He's really alive?"

"Yes!" Rosa pulls me into a bone-crushing hug, then releases me, stepping back with a giant grin on her face. "Isn't that amazing?"

"Yes, of course . . ." My head is spinning with joy and disbelief, my pulse racing a mile a minute. "You said he's being taken to a hospital?"

"Yes, that's what Peter said." Rosa's expression sobers a bit. "He's talking to Ana downstairs. I didn't stay to listen—I wanted to give you the news as soon as possible."

"Of course, thank you!" I'm electrified all of a sudden, all traces of my mental fog and despair falling away. *Julian is alive and being taken to a hospital!*

Running to the closet, I pull out the first dress I find and throw it on, dropping the towel on the floor. Then I dash to the door and fly down the stairs, with Rosa hurrying after me.

Peter is in the kitchen next to Ana. The housekeeper's eyes widen as she sees me barreling toward them, my feet bare and my hair dripping-wet from the shower. I probably look like a crazy woman, but I don't give a damn. All I care about is finding out more about Julian.

"How is he?" I pant, skidding to a stop a foot away from the two of them. "What kind of condition is he in?"

An expression shockingly similar to a smile flickers across Peter's hard face as he looks at me. "They're going to run some tests at the hospital, but right now it looks like your husband survived a plane crash with nothing worse than a broken arm, a couple of cracked ribs, and a nasty gash on his forehead. He's unconscious, but that appears to be mostly due to blood loss from his head wound."

And as I stare at Peter in open-mouthed incredulity, he explains, "The plane fell in a heavily wooded area, so the trees cushioned much of the impact. The pilot's cabin—where Esguerra and Kent were sitting—got ripped off by the force of the impact, and that seems to have saved their lives." The smile disappears then, and his metallic eyes darken. "Most of the others died, though. The fuel was in the back, and it exploded, destroying that portion of the plane. Only three of the soldiers back there survived, and they're badly burned. If it weren't for the combat gear they were all wearing, they would not have survived either."

"Oh my God." A wave of horror washes over me. Julian is alive, but nearly fifty of his men perished. I've had minimal interaction with most of the guards, but I've seen many of them around the estate. I know them, if only by sight. They were all strong, seemingly indestructible men. And now they're dead. Gone—just as Julian would've been if he hadn't been up front.

"What about Lucas?" I ask, starting to shake with delayed reaction. It's beginning to hit me that Julian was in a plane crash and *survived*. That, like a cat with nine lives, he beat the odds yet again.

"Kent has a broken leg and a severe concussion. He was also unconscious when they were found."

Relief spirals through me, and my eyes, burning with dryness before, fill with sudden tears. Tears of gratitude, of joy so intense that it's impossible to contain. I want to laugh and sob at the same time.

Julian is alive, and so is the man who once saved his life.

"Oh, Nora, child . . ." Ana's plump arms close around me as my tears overflow. "It will be all right now . . . Everything will be all right . . ."

Shaking with repressed sobs, I let her hold me for a moment in a motherly embrace. Then I pull away, smiling through the tears. For the first time, I believe that it *will* be all right. That the worst is now over.

"How soon can we fly out?" I ask Peter, wiping at the wetness on my cheeks. "Can the plane be ready in an hour?"

"Fly out?" He gives me a strange look. "We can't fly out, Mrs. Esguerra. I'm under strict orders to remain on the estate and make sure that you are safe here."

"What?" I stare at him incredulously. "But Julian is hurt! He's in the hospital, and I'm his wife—"

"Yes, I understand." Peter's expression doesn't change, his eyes cool and veiled as he looks at me. "But I'm afraid Esguerra will quite literally murder me if I allow you to be in danger."

"Are you telling me that I can't go see my husband who was just in a plane crash?" My voice rises as a wave of sudden fury sweeps through me. "That I'm supposed to sit here and do nothing while Julian is lying injured half a world away?"

Peter doesn't appear impressed with my outburst. "I will do my best to arrange a secure phone call and perhaps a video connection for you," he says calmly. "I will also keep you informed of any developments in regards to his health. Beyond that, I'm afraid there is nothing I can do at the moment. I am currently working to tighten security around the hospital where Esguerra and the others are being taken, so hopefully he will return here safe and sound, and you will see him shortly."

I want to scream, yell, and argue, but I know it won't do any good. I have about as much leverage over Peter as I do over Julian—which is none at all. "Fine," I say, taking a deep breath to calm myself. "You do that—and I want to know as soon as he regains consciousness."

Peter inclines his head. "Of course, Mrs. Esguerra. You will be informed right away."

CHAPTER TWENTY-THREE

❖ JULIAN ❖

I first become aware of the noises. Low feminine murmurs intermingled with rhythmic beeping. A hum of electricity in the background. All of this overlaid with a throbbing pain in the front of my skull and a strong antiseptic odor in my nostrils.

A hospital. I'm in a hospital of some kind.

My body hurts, the pain seemingly everywhere. My first instinct is to open my eyes and seek answers, but I lie still, letting the recollections come to me.

Nora. The mission. Flying to Tajikistan. I relive it all, the remembered sensations sharp and vivid. I see myself talking to Lucas in the cabin, feel the plane bucking underneath us. I hear the sputtering whine of the engines and experience the gut-churning sensation of falling from the sky. I endure the paralysis of fear in those last few moments as Lucas tries to level out the plane above the tree line to buy us precious seconds—and then I feel the bone-jarring impact of the crash.

Beyond that, there is nothing else, just darkness.

It should've been the permanent darkness of death, yet I'm alive. The pain in my battered body tells me so.

Continuing to lie still, I assess my new situation. The voices around me—they're speaking in a foreign language. It sounds like a mixture of Russian and Turkish. Likely Uzbek, given where we were flying at the time of the crash.

It's two women speaking, their tone casual, almost gossipy. Logic tells me they are probably nurses at this hospital. I can hear them moving about as they chat with one another, and I carefully crack open one eye to look at my surroundings.

I'm in a drab room with pale green walls and a small window on the far wall. Fluorescent lights on the ceiling emit a low buzzing sound—the hum of electricity I'd noticed earlier. A monitor is hooked up to me, with an IV line connected to my wrist. I can see the nurses on the other side of the room. They're changing the sheets on an empty bed that's standing there. A thin curtain separates my area from that bed, but it's drawn open, enabling me to see the room fully.

Other than the two nurses, I'm alone. There's no sign of any of my men. My pulse jumps at the realization, and I do my best to steady my breathing before they notice. I want them to continue thinking that I'm unconscious. There doesn't seem to be any overt threat, but until I know what happened to the plane and how I ended up here, I don't dare drop my guard.

Cautiously flexing my fingers and toes, I close my eyes and take mental stock of my injuries. I feel weak, like I lost a lot of blood. My head throbs, and I can feel a heavy bandage over my forehead. My left arm—which aches mercilessly—is immobilized, as if it's in a cast. My right one seems fine, however. It hurts to breathe, so I assume my ribs are damaged in some way. Beyond that, I can feel all of my appendages, and the pain in the rest of my body feels more like scrapes and bruises than broken bones.

After a few minutes, one of the nurses leaves while the other one walks over to my bed. I remain still and quiet, feigning unconsciousness. She adjusts the sheet covering me, then checks the bandage on my head. I can hear her humming softly under her breath as she turns to leave as well, and at that moment, heavier footsteps enter the room.

A man's voice, deep and authoritative, asks a question in Uzbek.

I crack open my eyes again to steal a glance at the doorway. The new arrival is a lean middle-aged man wearing a military officer's uniform. Judging by the insignia on his chest, he must be fairly high up.

The nurse answers him, her voice soft and uncertain, and then the man approaches my bed. I tense, prepared to defend myself if necessary despite the weakness in my muscles. However, the man doesn't reach for a weapon or make any threatening moves. Instead he studies me, his expression oddly curious.

Going on instinct, I open my eyes fully and look at him, my body still coiled for a potential strike. "Who are you?" I ask bluntly, figuring that the direct approach is best at this point. "Where is this place?"

He looks startled, but recovers his composure almost right away. "I'm Colonel Sharipov, and you are in Tashkent, Uzbekistan," he answers, taking half a step back. "Your airplane crashed, and you were brought here." He has a thick accent, but his English is surprisingly good. "The Russian embassy has been in contact about you. Your people are sending another plane to pick you up."

He knows who I am then. "Where are my men? What happened to my plane?"

"We're still investigating the cause of the crash," Sharipov says, his eyes shifting slightly to the side. "It's unclear at this point—"

"Bullshit." My voice is deadly quiet. I can tell when someone is lying, and this fucker is definitely trying to blow smoke up my ass. "You know what happened."

He hesitates. "I'm not authorized to discuss the investigation—"

"Did your military fire a missile at us?" I use my right arm to prop myself up into a sitting position. My ribs protest the movement, but I ignore the pain. I may feel as weak as an infant, but it's never a good idea to seem that way in front of an enemy. "You might as well tell me now because I will learn the truth one way or another."

His face tightens at my implied threat. "No, it was not us. Right now, it appears that one of our missile launchers was used, but nobody issued the order to shoot down your plane. We received word from Russia that you would be passing through our airspace, and we were told to let you through."

"You have an idea of who is responsible, though," I observe coldly. Now that I'm sitting up, I don't feel quite as vulnerable—though I would feel even better if I had a gun or a knife. "You know who used the launcher."

Sharipov hesitates again, then reluctantly admits, "It's possible that one of our officers may have been bribed by the Ukrainian government. We're looking into that possibility now."

"I see." It all finally makes sense. Somehow Ukraine got word of my cooperation with the Russians and decided to eliminate me before

I became a threat. *Those fucking bastards.* This is why I try not to take sides in these petty conflicts—it's too costly, in more ways than one.

"We have stationed a few soldiers on this floor," Sharipov says, changing the topic. "You will be safe here until the Russian envoy arrives to bring you to Moscow."

"Where are my men?" I repeat my earlier question, my eyes narrowing as I see Sharipov's gaze slide away again. "Are they here?"

"Four of them," he admits quietly, looking back at me. "I am afraid the rest didn't make it."

I keep my expression impassive, though it feels like a sharp blade is twisting in my insides. I should be used to it by now—to people dying around me—but somehow it still weighs on me. "Who are the survivors?" I ask, keeping my voice level. "Do you have their names?"

He nods and rattles off a list of names. To my relief, Lucas Kent is among them. "He regained consciousness briefly," Sharipov explains, "and helped identify the others. Besides you, he's the only one who wasn't burned by the explosion."

"I see." My relief is replaced by slowly building rage. Nearly fifty of my best men are dead. Men I've trained with. Men I've gotten to know. As I process that fact, it occurs to me that there is only one way the Ukrainian government would've known about my negotiations with the Russians.

The pretty Russian interpreter. She was the only outsider privy to that conversation.

"I need a phone," I tell Sharipov, swinging my feet to the floor and standing up. My knees shake a bit, but my legs are able to hold my weight. This is good. It means I'm capable of walking out of here under my own steam.

"I need it right now," I add when he just gapes at me as I pull the IV needle out of my arm with my teeth and peel the monitor sensors off my chest. My hospital gown and bare feet undoubtedly look ridiculous, but I don't give a fuck. I have a traitor to deal with.

"Of course," he says, recovering from his shock. Reaching into his pocket, he pulls out a cell phone and hands it to me. "Peter Sokolov wanted to talk to you as soon you woke up."

"Good. Thanks." Placing the phone in my left hand, which protrudes from the cast, I begin to punch in numbers with my right. It's a secure line that moves through so many relays, it would take a world-class hacker to trace it to its destination. As I hear the familiar clicks and beeps of the connection, I reclaim the phone with my right hand and tell Sharipov, "Please ask one of the nurses to get me some regular clothes. I'm tired of wearing this."

The colonel nods and walks out of the room. A second after he leaves, Peter's voice comes on the line: "Esguerra?"

"Yes, it's me." My grip on the phone tightens. "I assume you heard the news."

"Yes, I heard." A pause on the line. "I had Yulia Tzakova detained in Moscow. It seems like she's got some connections that our Kremlin friends overlooked."

So Peter is already on top of this. "Yes, it seems like it." My voice is even, though anger boils within me. "Needless to say, we're scrapping the mission. When are we getting picked up?"

"The plane is on its way. It should be there in a few hours. I sent Goldberg along in case you could use a doctor."

"Good thinking. We'll be waiting. How is Nora?"

There is a brief moment of silence. "She's better now that she knows you're alive. She wanted to fly out there as soon as she heard."

"You didn't let her, though." It's a statement, not a question. Peter knows better than to fuck up like that.

"No, of course not. Do you wish to see her? I may be able to set up a video connection with the hospital."

"Yes, please set it up." What I really want is to see her and hold her in person, but the video will have to do for now. "In the meantime, I'm going to check on Lucas and the others."

* * *

Because of the bulky cast on my arm, it's a struggle to put on the clothes the nurse brings me. The pants go on without any issues, but I end up having to rip out the left sleeve to get the cast through the armhole. My ribs hurt like hell, and every movement requires tremendous effort as my body wants nothing more than to lie back down on the bed and rest. I persist, though, and after a few tries, finally succeed in clothing myself.

Thankfully, walking is easier. I can maintain a regular stride. As I exit the room, I see the soldiers Sharipov mentioned earlier. There are five of them, all dressed in army fatigues and toting Uzis. Seeing me emerge into the hallway, they silently fall into step behind me, following me as I head over to the Intensive Care Unit. Their expressionless faces make me wonder if they're there to protect me or to protect others *from* me. I can't imagine the Uzbekistani government is thrilled to have an illegal arms dealer in their civilian hospital.

Lucas is not there, so I check on the others first. As Sharipov told me, they are all badly burned, with bandages covering most of their bodies. They're also heavily sedated. I make a mental note to transfer a huge bonus into each of their bank accounts to compensate them for this, and to have them seen by the best plastic surgeons. These men knew the risks when they came to work for me, but I still want to make sure they're taken care of.

"Where is the fourth man?" I ask one of the soldiers accompanying me, and he directs me to another room.

When I get there, I see that Lucas is asleep. He doesn't look nearly as bad as the others, which is a relief. He'll be able to return with me to Colombia once the plane arrives, whereas the burned men will have to stay here for at least a few more days.

Coming back to my room, I find Sharipov there, placing a laptop on the bed. "I was asked to give this to you," he explains, handing me the computer.

"Excellent, thank you." Taking the laptop from him with my right hand, I sit down on the bed. Or, more appropriately, collapse on the bed, my legs shaking from the strain of walking all over the hospital. Thankfully, Sharipov doesn't see my ungainly maneuver, as he's already heading out the door.

As soon as he's gone, I go on the internet and download a program designed to conceal my online activities. Then I go to a special website and put in my code. That brings up a video chat window, and I put in yet another code there, connecting to a computer back at the compound.

Peter's image appears first. "Finally, there you are," he says, and I see the living room of my house in the background. "Nora is coming down."

A moment later, Nora's small face shows up on the screen. "Julian! Oh my God, I thought I would never see you again!" Her voice is filled with barely contained tears, and there are wet tracks on her cheeks. Her smile, however, radiates pure joy.

I grin at her, all my anger and physical discomfort forgotten in a sudden surge of happiness. "Hi baby, how are you?"

She gapes at me. "How am *I*? What kind of question is that? You're the one who was just in a plane crash! How are *you*? Is that a cast on your arm?"

"It appears to be." I lift my right shoulder in a brief shrug. "It's my left arm, though, and I'm right-handed, so it's not a big deal."

"What about your head?"

"Oh, this?" I touch the thick bandage around my forehead. "I'm not sure, but since I'm walking and talking, I assume it's something minor."

She shakes her head, staring at me with disbelief, and my grin broadens. Nora probably thinks I'm trying to be all macho in front of her. My pet doesn't realize that these kinds of injuries truly are minor for me; I've had worse from my father's fists as a child.

"When are you coming home?" she asks, bringing her face closer to the camera. Her eyes look enormous this way, her long lashes spiky with residual wetness. "You *are* coming home now, right?"

"Yes, of course. I can't exactly go after Al-Quadar like this." I wave my right hand toward the cast. "The plane is already on its way to get me and Lucas, so I'll be seeing you very soon."

"I can't wait," she says softly, and my chest tightens at the raw emotion I see on her face. A feeling very much like tenderness winds through me, intensifying my longing for her until I ache with it.

"Nora—" I begin saying, only to be interrupted by a sharp *crack* outside. It's followed by several more, a rapid-fire burst of noise that I recognize right away.

Gunshots. The guns are using silencers, but nothing can quiet the deafening bang of a machine gun going off.

Immediately, there are screams and answering gunfire. Unsilenced this time. The soldiers stationed on the floor must be responding to whatever threat is out there.

In a millisecond, I'm off the bed, the laptop sliding to the floor. Adrenaline rockets through me, speeding up everything and at the same time slowing my perception of time. It feels like things are happening in slow motion, but I know that it's just an illusion—that it's my brain's attempt to deal with intense danger.

I operate on instinct honed by a lifetime of training. In an instant, I assess the room and see that there's no place to hide. The window on the opposite wall is too small for me to fit through, even if I were inclined to risk falling from the third floor. That leaves only the door and the hallway—which is where the gunshots are coming from.

I don't bother trying to figure out who's attacking. It's immaterial at the moment. The only thing that matters is survival.

More gunfire, followed by a scream right outside. I hear the heavy *thump* of a body falling nearby, and I choose that moment to make my move.

Pushing open the door, I dive in the direction of the thumping sound, using the momentum of the dive to slide on the linoleum floor. My cast knocks against the wall as I bump into the dead soldier, but I don't even register the pain. Instead I pull him over me, using his body as a shield as bullets begin flying all around me. Spotting his weapon on the floor, I grasp it with my right hand and begin firing shots into the other end of the hallway, where I see masked men with guns crouched behind a hospital gurney.

Too many. I can already see that. There are too fucking many of them and not enough bullets in my gun. I can see the bodies littering the hallway—the five Uzbekistani soldiers have been mowed down, as well as a few of the masked attackers—and I know it's futile. They will get me too. In fact, it's surprising that I'm not already riddled with holes, human shield or not.

They don't want to kill me.

I realize that fact just as my gun bucks one last time, discharging the last round of bullets. The floor and walls around me are destroyed from their bullets, but I'm unscathed. Since I don't believe in miracles, that means the attackers are not aiming *at* me.

They're aiming all around me, to keep me contained in one spot.

Rolling the dead man off me, I slowly get to my feet, keeping my gaze trained on the armed figures at the far end of the hallway. The gunfire stops as I begin to move, the silence deafening after all the noise.

"What do you want?" I raise my voice just enough to be heard on the other end of the hallway. "Why are you here?"

A man rises up from behind the gurney, his weapon trained on me as he begins to walk in my direction. He's masked like all the others, but something about him seems familiar. As he stops a few feet away, I see the dark glitter of his eyes above the mask, and recognition spears through me.

Majid.

Al-Quadar must've heard that I'm here, within their reach.

I move without thinking. I'm still holding the now-empty machine gun, and I lunge at him, swinging the gun as I would a bat, arching it deceptively high before jabbing it low. Even with my injuries, my reflexes are excellent, and the butt of the weapon makes contact with Majid's ribs before I'm thrown back against the wall, my left shoulder exploding in agony. My ears are ringing from the blast as I slide down the wall, and I realize that I've been shot—that he managed to fire his weapon before I could inflict real damage.

I can hear yelling in Arabic, and then rough hands grab me, dragging me along the floor. I struggle with all of my remaining strength, but I can feel my body beginning to shut down, my heart laboring to pump its dwindling supply of blood. Something presses down on my shoulder, exacerbating the fiery pain, and black spots cover my vision.

My last thought before I lose consciousness is that death will likely be preferable to what awaits me if I survive.

CHAPTER TWENTY-FOUR

❖ NORA ❖

I don't realize that I'm screaming until a hand slaps over my mouth, muffling my hysterical shrieks.

"Nora. Nora, stop it." Peter's steady voice pulls me out of the vortex of horror, dragging me back to reality. "Calm down and tell me exactly what you saw. Can you calm down enough to talk?"

I manage a small nod, and he releases me, stepping back. Out of the corner of my eye, I see Rosa and Ana standing a few feet away. Ana's hands are clamped over her mouth, tears running down her cheeks again, and Rosa looks scared and distraught.

"I didn't"—I can barely force the words through my swollen throat—"I didn't *see* anything. I just heard it. We were talking, and then all of a sudden, there were gunshots and—and screaming, and then more gunshots. Julian—" My voice breaks as I speak his name. "Julian must've dropped the computer because everything went topsy-turvy on the screen, and then all I could see was the wall, but I heard it—the gunfire, the screams, more gunfire . . ." I am not conscious of sobbing uncontrollably until Peter's hands close around my shoulders and gently guide me toward the couch.

He forces me to sit down as I begin to shake, the terror of what I just witnessed combining with memories from a few months earlier, when I had been taken by Al-Quadar in the Philippines. For a few horrifying moments, the past and the present merge, and I'm again in that clinic, hearing those gunshots and feeling fear so intense that my mind can't register it. Only now it's not Beth and I who are in danger.

It's Julian.

They came for him—and I know exactly who *they* are.

"It's Al-Quadar." My voice is hoarse as I get up, ignoring the tremors that continue to rack my body. "Peter—it's Al-Quadar."

He nods in agreement, and I see that he's already on his phone. "Da. Da, eto ya," he says, and I realize that he's speaking Russian. "V gospitale problema. Da, seychas-zhe." Lowering the phone, he tells me, "I just notified the Uzbekistani police of the events in the hospital. They're on their way, as are more soldiers. They'll be there within minutes."

"It will be too late." I don't know where my certainty comes from, but I can feel it deep within my bones. "They have him, Peter. If he's not dead yet, he will be very shortly."

He looks at me, and I can see that he knows it too—that he knows how hopeless the whole thing is. We're dealing with one of the most dangerous terrorist organizations in the world, and they have the man who's been hunting them down and decimating their ranks.

"We're going to track them down, Nora," Peter says quietly. "If they haven't killed him yet, there's a chance we may be able to retrieve him."

"You don't really believe that." I can see it on his face. He's just saying it to placate me. Majid's people have been able to evade detection for months, and it's only the lucky capture of that terrorist in Moscow that led to the discovery of their whereabouts. They will disappear again, hiding somewhere else now that they know their location in Tajikistan has been compromised.

They will disappear, and so will Julian.

Peter gives me an indecipherable look. "It doesn't matter what I believe. The fact is that they want something from your husband: the explosive. They wanted it before, and I'm certain that they want it now. It would be very foolish of them to kill him right away."

"You think they're going to torture him first." Bile rises in my throat as I remember Beth's screams, the blood spreading everywhere as Majid systematically cut off bits and pieces of her body. "Oh my God, you think they're going to torture him until he breaks and gives them this explosive."

"Yes," Peter says, his gray eyes steady on my face as Ana begins to sob quietly into Rosa's shoulder. "I do. And that gives us time to find them."

"Not enough time." I stare at him, sick with terror. "Not nearly enough time. Peter, they're going to torture him and kill him while we look for them."

"We don't know that for sure," he says, pulling out his phone again. "I'm going to throw all of our resources at this. If Al-Quadar so much as blips on the radar someplace, we'll know it."

"But that could take weeks—even months!" My voice rises as hysteria grabs hold of me again. I can feel my grip on sanity slipping as the roller coaster of grief, joy, and terror I've been riding for the past couple of days plunges me into a bottomless pit of despair. It was only yesterday that I thought I'd lost Julian again, only to learn that he's alive. And now, just when it seemed like the worst was over, fate has dealt us the cruelest blow of all.

The monsters who murdered Beth are going to take Julian from me too.

"It's the only option we have, Nora." Peter's voice is soothing, like he's talking to a fractious child. "There is no other way. Esguerra is tough. He may be able to hang on for a while, no matter what they do to him."

I take a deep breath to regain control of myself. I can break down later, when I'm alone. "Nobody is tough enough to withstand nonstop torture." My voice is almost even. "You know that."

Peter inclines his head, conceding my point. From what I heard about his unique skills, he knows better than anyone how effective torture can be. As I look at him, an idea enters my head—an idea that I never would've entertained before.

"The terrorist they captured," I say slowly, holding Peter's gaze. "Where is he now?"

"He's supposed to be remitted into our custody, but for now he's still in Moscow."

"Do you think he might know something?" My hands twist in the skirt of my dress as I stare at Julian's torturer-in-chief. A part of me can't believe I'm about to ask him to do this, but my voice is steady as I say, "Do you think you could make him talk?"

"Yes, I'm sure I could," Peter says slowly, looking at me with something resembling respect. "I don't know if he'll know where they might go next, but it's worth a shot. I will fly out to Moscow immediately and see what I can find out."

"I'm coming with you."

His reaction is immediate. "No, you're not," he says, frowning at me. "I'm under explicit orders to keep you safe here, Nora."

"Your boss has just been captured and is about to be tortured and killed." My voice is sharp and biting as I enunciate every word. "And you think *my* safety is a priority right now? Your orders no longer apply because they have Julian. They no longer need me for leverage over him."

"Well, actually, they would love to have you for leverage over him. They could break him much faster if they had you as well." Peter shakes his head, his expression regretful but determined. "I'm sorry, Nora, but you need to stay here. If we do end up rescuing your husband, he would be very displeased to learn that I allowed you to be in danger."

I turn away, shaking, terror and frustration mingling together and feeding on each other until it feels like I will burst from it all. I feel helpless. Utterly and completely useless. When I had been taken, Julian came for me. He rescued me—but I can't do the same for him.

I can't even get off the estate.

"Nora . . ." It's Rosa. I can feel her hand on my arm as I blindly stare out the window, my mind running through all the dead ends like a rat in a maze. "Nora, please . . . Come, let's get you a bite to eat . . ."

I shake my head in curt denial and pull my arm away, keeping my gaze trained on the green lawn outside. There's something nibbling at the edge of my brain, some errant, half-formed thought that I can't quite grasp. It has to do with something Peter said, something he mentioned in passing . . . I hear him leaving the room, his footsteps quiet in the hallway, and suddenly it hits me.

Spinning around, I sprint after him, ignoring the shock on Rosa's face as I push her out of the way. "Peter! Peter, wait!"

He stops in the hallway, giving me a cool look as I skid to a stop next to him. "What is it?"

"I know," I gasp out. "Peter, I know exactly what to do. I know how to get Julian back."

His expression doesn't change. "What are you talking about?"

I draw in a gulping breath and begin to explain my plan, speaking so fast I'm tripping over the words. I can see him shaking his head as I speak, but I persist anyway, driven by a sense of urgency more intense than anything I've ever experienced. I need to convince Peter that I'm right. Julian's life depends on it.

"No," he says when I'm done. "This is insane. Julian would kill me—"

"But he might be *alive* to kill you," I interrupt. "There's no other option. You know that as well as I do."

He shakes his head, and the look he gives me is genuinely regretful. "I'm sorry, Nora—"

"I will give you the list," I blurt out, grasping at the only straw I can think of. "I will give you the list of names before your three years are up if you do this. Julian will hand it over as soon as he gets it into his hands."

Peter stares at me, his expression changing for the first time. "You know about the list?" he asks, his voice pulsing with such anger that I have to fight the urge to step back. "The list Esguerra promised me?"

I nod. "I do." Under any other circumstances, I would be terrified to provoke this man, but I'm beyond fear at the moment. A recklessness born of desperation drives me now, giving me uncharacteristic courage. "And I know that you won't get it if Julian dies," I continue, pressing my point. "All this time you've been working for him will be in vain. You'll never be able to get revenge on the people who killed your family."

His impassive look disappears completely, his face transforming into a mask of blazing fury. "You don't know shit about my family," he roars, and this time I do take a step back, my self-preservation instinct belatedly kicking in as I see his hands tightening into fists. "You fucking dare taunt me with them?"

He takes a step toward me as I back away, my heart hammering in my chest. Then, with a sharp, violent motion, he twists and punches the wall, his fist breaking through the drywall. I flinch, jumping back, and he punches the wall again, taking his rage out on it as he undoubtedly wants to do on me.

"Peter . . ." My voice is low and soothing, like I'm talking to a wild animal. I can see Rosa and Ana in the doorway, looking terrified, and I try to diffuse the situation. "Peter, I'm not taunting you—I'm just pointing out the facts. I want to help you, but first you need to help me."

He glares at me, his chest heaving with rage, and I see him struggling to regain control. I'm shaking on the inside, but I keep my gaze steady on his face. *Don't show fear. Whatever you do, don't show fear.* To my intense relief, his breathing gradually begins to slow, the fury twisting his features ebbing as he brings himself back from whatever dark place his mind was in.

"I'm sorry," he says after a few moments, his voice strained. "I shouldn't have reacted like that." He takes one deep breath, then another, and I see his usual controlled mask sliding into place. "How do I know you'll be able to keep your promise about the list?" he says in a more normal tone of voice, his anger seemingly gone. "You're asking me to do something that Esguerra will hate. How do I know he'll come through with the list if I do this?"

"I will make him give it to you." I have no idea how I can *make* Julian do anything, but I don't let any of my doubts show. "I swear to you, Peter. Help me with this, and you can have your revenge before your three years here are up."

He stares at me, and I can practically feel his internal debate. He knows my arguments are sound. If he does what I ask, he stands a chance of getting that list of names sooner. If Julian dies, he won't get the list at all.

"Fine," he says, apparently reaching a decision. "Get ready then. We're leaving in an hour."

* * *

When we land in a small airport near Chicago, there is a thick layer of snow on the ground, making me grateful that I decided to wear my old Uggs. It's already evening, and the wind is bitterly cold, biting through my winter coat. I barely register the discomfort, however, all my thoughts consumed by the ordeal to come.

There is no bulletproof car waiting for us. Nothing to draw attention to our arrival. Peter calls a taxi for me, and I get into the back of the car by myself, while he heads back to the plane.

The driver, a kindly middle-aged man, tries to chat me up, likely in the hopes of figuring out who I am. I'm sure he thinks I'm a celebrity of some kind, arriving on a private jet like that. I give monosyllabic responses to all his questions, and he quickly catches on to my desire to be left alone. The rest of the drive passes in silence as I stare out the window at the night-darkened roads. My head pounds from stress and jet lag, and my stomach roils with nausea. If I hadn't forced myself to eat a sandwich on the plane, I would probably be passing out from exhaustion.

When we get to Oak Lawn, I direct the taxi to my parents' house. They're not expecting me, but that's for the best. It makes the whole thing look more authentic, less like a setup.

The driver helps me unload a small suitcase I packed for the occasion, and I pay him, tipping him an extra twenty bucks for my earlier rudeness. He drives off, and I wheel my suitcase to the door of my childhood home.

Stopping in front of the familiar brown door, I ring the doorbell. I know my parents are home because I see the lights in the living room. It takes them a couple of minutes to get to the door—a couple of minutes that feel like an hour in my exhausted state.

My mom opens the door, and her jaw goes slack with astonishment as she sees me standing there, my hand resting on the handle of the suitcase.

"Hi Mom," I say, my voice shaking. "Can I come in?"

CHAPTER TWENTY-FIVE

❖ JULIAN ❖

At first, there is only darkness and pain. Pain that tears at me. Pain that shreds me from within. The darkness is easier. There is no pain in that, only oblivion. Still, I hate the nothingness that consumes me when I'm in that dark void. Hate the blankness of non-existence. As time passes, I come to crave the pain because it's the opposite of that blankness—because feeling something is better than feeling nothing.

Gradually, the dark void recedes, lessens its hold on me. Now, alongside the pain, there are memories. Some good, some bad—they come at me in waves. My mother's gentle smile as she reads me a bedtime story. My father's hard voice and harder fists. Running through the jungle after a colorful butterfly, as happy and carefree as only a child can be. Killing my first man in that jungle. Playing with my cat Lola, then fishing and laughing with a bright-eyed, twelve-year-old girl . . . with Maria.

Maria's body broken and violated, her light and innocence forever destroyed.

Blood on my hands, the satisfaction of hearing her murderers' screams. Eating sushi in the best restaurant in Tokyo. Flies buzzing over my mother's corpse. The thrill of closing my first deal, the lure of money pouring in. More death and violence. Death I cause, death I revel in.

And then there is *her*.

My Nora. The girl I stole because she reminded me of Maria.

The girl who is now my reason for existing.

I hold the image of her in my mind, letting all the other memories fade into the background. She's all I want to think about, all I want to focus on. She makes the hurt go away, makes the darkness disappear. I may have brought her suffering, but she's brought me the only happiness I've known since my early years.

As time crawls by, I become aware of other things. Besides the pain, there are sounds and sensations. I hear voices and feel a cold breeze on my face. My left shoulder burns, my broken arm throbs, and I'm dying of thirst. Still, I seem to be alive.

I twitch my fingers to verify that fact. Yes, alive. Almost too weak to move, but alive.

Fuck. The rest of the memories flood in, and before I even open my eyes, I know where I am, and I know I probably shouldn't have fought the darkness. Oblivion would've been better than this.

"Welcome back," a man's voice says softly, and I open my eyes to see Majid's smiling face hovering over me. "You've been under long enough. It's time for us to begin."

* * *

They drag me along a hard cement floor of what appears to be some kind of a construction site. From the looks of it, it's going to be an industrial building, and the room they haul me into has no windows, only a doorway. I think about fighting, but I'm too weak from my injuries to have any chance of success, so I decide to bide my time and conserve what little strength I have left. I'm guessing I will need it to cope with what they have in store for me.

They begin by stripping me naked and stringing me up with a rope that they loop over a beam in the unfinished ceiling. They're not gentle about it, and the cast on my left arm breaks as they tie my wrists together and draw my bound arms up over my head. The agonizing pain in my injured arm and shoulder makes me pass out, and it's not until they throw ice-cold water on my face that I regain consciousness again.

In a way, I admire their methods. They know what they're doing. Take away a man's clothes, and he immediately feels more vulnerable. Keep him cold, weak, and injured, and he's already at a disadvantage, his psyche as battered as his body. They are starting off on the right foot. If I hadn't put others through this myself, I would've been begging and pleading right about now.

As it is, my body is in a complete fight-or-flight mode. The knowledge that I'm so close to death—or at least to excruciating pain—makes my heart pound with a sickeningly fast rhythm. I don't want to give them the satisfaction of seeing me shake, but I can feel small tremors running over my skin, both from the cold water they poured on me in an already-freezing room and from a surfeit of adrenaline. They've strung me up so high that only the tips of my toes touch the ground, and with the majority of my weight being supported by my tied wrists, my wounded arm and shoulder are already screaming in agony.

As I hang there, trying to breathe through the pain, Majid approaches me, a smug smile creasing his face. "Well, if it isn't Esguerra himself," he drawls, his British accent making him sound like some Middle Eastern version of James Bond. "How nice of you to pay our corner of the world a visit."

I don't say anything, just gaze at him contemptuously, knowing that will irritate him more than anything. I know what he's going to demand, and I have no intention of giving it to him—not when he's going to kill me in the most painful way possible anyway.

Sure enough, my lack of response provokes him. I can see the flare of rage in his eyes. Majid Ben-Harid thrives on the fear and misery of others. I understand that about him because I'm the same way. And because we're such kindred souls, I know how to spoil the fun for him. He's going to destroy my body, but he won't enjoy it quite as much as he'd like.

I won't let him.

It's small consolation for the fact that I'm going to die a torturous death, but it's all I've got at the moment.

His smug smile gone, Majid steps toward me. "I see you're not up for chitchat," he says, bringing a large butcher knife up to my face. "Let's cut to the chase then." He runs the tip of the blade down my cheek, cutting just deep enough for blood to run down my chin in a thin trickle. "You give me the location of your explosive factory, as well as all the security details, and I"—he leans so close that I can see the black of his pupils in the mud-brown irises of his eyes—"I will make your death quick. If you don't . . . well, I'm sure I don't need to elaborate on the alternative. What do you say? Do you want to make it easy for us or hard? Because the outcome will be the same either way."

I don't respond, and I don't flinch away, not even when that blade continues its painful, cutting journey down my neck, chest, and stomach, leaving a bloody trail wherever it touches my skin.

It doesn't matter what I choose because Majid has no intention of honoring any promises he makes to me. He'll never give me a quick death—not even if I hand-deliver the explosive to him tomorrow. I've caused too much damage to Al-Quadar over the past few months, foiled too many of their plans. As soon as I give him what he wants, he'll take me apart in the most excruciating manner possible, just to show his troops how he metes out punishment to those who cross him.

That's what I would do in his place, at least.

The knife stops just below my ribs, the sharp point digging into my flesh, and I can see Majid's eyes gleaming with vicious pleasure. "Well?" he whispers, pressing it in a fraction of an inch. "Play or no play, Esguerra? It's really up to you. I can begin by harvesting some organs, just to make it extra profitable for us—or if you'd prefer, I can start lower, with your wife's favorite part . . ."

I suppress an instinctive male urge to shudder at that last bit and keep my expression calm, almost amused. I know he won't do anything too damaging at first—because if he did, I would bleed out right away. I've already lost too much blood, so it won't take much to send me under. The last thing Majid would want is to deprive himself of a conscious victim. If he's serious about getting that explosive, he'll have to start small and work up to the brutality he just threatened me with.

"Go ahead," I say coolly. "Do your best."

And giving him a mocking smile, I wait for the torture to begin.

CHAPTER TWENTY-SIX

❖ NORA ❖

The evening of my arrival home is a nonstop stream of crying, hugs, and questions about what happened and how I managed to come back.

I tell my parents as much of the truth as I can, explaining about the plane crash in Uzbekistan and Julian's subsequent capture by the terrorist group he's been fighting. As I speak, I can see them battling shock and disbelief. Terrorists and planes downed by missiles are so far outside of the normal paradigm of their lives that I know it's hard for them to process. It was difficult for me once, too.

"Oh, Nora, honey . . ." My mom's voice is soft and sympathetic. "I'm so sorry—I know you loved him, despite everything. Do you know what's going to happen now?"

I shake my head, trying to avoid looking at my dad. He thinks this is a good development; I can see it on his face. He's relieved that I'm most likely rid of the man he considers to be my abuser. I'm certain both of my parents think Julian deserves this, but my mom is at least attempting to be sensitive to my feelings. My dad, though, can hardly hide his satisfaction at this turn of events.

"Well, whatever happens, I'm glad you came home." My mom reaches out to take my hand. Her dark eyes are swimming with fresh tears as she gazes at me. "We're here for you, honey, you know that, right?"

"I do, Mom," I whisper, my throat tight with emotion. "That's why I came back. Because I missed you . . . and because I couldn't be alone on that estate."

That much is true, but that's not the real reason I'm here. I can't tell my parents the real reason.

If they knew I came home to get kidnapped by Al-Quadar, they would never forgive me for that.

* * *

Despite my exhaustion, I barely sleep that night. I know it'll take some time for Al-Quadar to respond to my presence in town, but I'm still consumed by dread and nervous anticipation. Every time I drift off, I have nightmares, only in these dreams it's not Beth who's being cut into pieces—it's Julian. The bloody images are so vivid that I wake up nauseated and shaking, my bedsheets drenched with sweat. Finally, I give up on sleep altogether and pull out the art supplies I brought with me in my suitcase. I'm hoping that painting will prevent me from dwelling on the fact that my nightmares may be playing out at this very moment in some Al-Quadar hideout thousands of miles away.

As the light of the rising sun filters into the room, I stop to examine what I painted. It looks abstract at first—just swirls of red, black, and brown—but a closer inspection reveals something different. All the swirls are faces and bodies, people tangled together in a paroxysm of violent ecstasy. The faces reveal both agony and pleasure, lust and torment.

It's probably my best work to date, and I hate it.

I hate it because it shows me how much I've changed. How little of the old me remains.

"Wow, honey, this is amazing . . ." My mom's voice startles me out of my musings, and I turn around to see her standing in the doorway, gazing at the painting with genuine admiration. "That French instructor of yours must be really good."

"Yes, Monsieur Bernard is excellent," I agree, trying to keep the weariness out of my voice. I'm so tired that I just want to collapse, but that's not an option at the moment.

"You didn't sleep well, did you?" My mom furrows her forehead, looking worried, and I know I didn't succeed in hiding my tiredness from her. "Were you thinking about him?"

"Of course I was." A sudden swell of anger sharpens my voice. "He's my husband, you know."

She blinks, clearly taken aback, and I immediately regret my harsh tone. This situation is not my mom's fault; if anyone is blameless in all this, it's my parents. My temper is the last thing they deserve... particularly since my desperate plan will likely cause them even more anguish.

"I'm sorry, Mom," I say, going over to give her a hug. "I didn't mean it like that."

"It's okay, honey." She strokes my hair, her touch so gentle and comforting that I want to weep. "I understand."

I nod, even though I know she can't possibly comprehend the extent of my stress. She can't—because she doesn't know that I'm waiting.

Waiting to be taken by the same monsters who have Julian.

Waiting for Al-Quadar to snap at the bait.

* * *

The morning drags by. It's a Saturday, so both of my parents are home. They're happy about that, but I'm not. I wish they were at work today. I want to be alone if—no, *when*—Majid's goons come for me. It had been relatively safe to spend the night, since Al-Quadar would need time to put whatever plan they have into action, but now that it's morning, I don't want my parents near me. The security detail Julian put in place around my family would ensure their safety, but those same bodyguards may also interfere with my abduction—and that's the last thing I want.

"Shopping?" My dad gives me a strange look when I announce my intention to hit the stores after breakfast. "Are you sure, honey? You just got home, and with everything going on—"

"Dad, I've been in the middle of nowhere for months." I give him my best men-just-don't-get-it look. "You have no idea what that's like for a girl." Seeing that he's unconvinced, I add, "Seriously, Dad, I could use the distraction."

"She's got a point," my mom chimes in. Turning toward me, she gives me a conspiratorial wink and tells my dad, "There's nothing like shopping to take a woman's mind off things. I'll go with Nora—it'll be just like the old times."

My heart sinks. I can't have my mom coming along if the point is to have my parents away from potential danger. "Oh, I'm sorry, Mom," I say regretfully, "but I already promised Leah I'd meet her. It's spring break, you know, and she's home." I had seen an update to that effect on Facebook earlier this morning, so I'm only partially lying. My friend is indeed in town—I just hadn't made any plans to see her today.

"Oh, okay." My mom looks hurt for a moment, but then she shakes it off and gives me a bright smile. "No worries, honey. We'll see you after you catch up with your friends. I'm glad you're distracting yourself like that. It's for the best, really . . ."

My dad still looks suspicious, but there is nothing he can do. I'm an adult, and I'm not exactly asking for their permission.

As soon as breakfast is over, I give them each a kiss and a hug and walk over to the bus stop on 95th street to get on the bus going to the Chicago Ridge Mall.

* * *

Come on, take me already. Fucking take me already.

I have been wandering through the mall for hours, and to my frustration, there is still no sign of Al-Quadar. They either don't know that I'm here, or they don't care about me now that they have Julian.

I refuse to entertain the latter possibility because if it's true, Julian is as good as dead.

The plan has to work. There is no other alternative. Majid simply needs more time. Time to sniff out that I'm here alone and unprotected—a convenient tool that they can use to force Julian to give them what they want.

"Nora? Holy shit, Nora, is that you?" A familiar voice yanks me out of my thoughts, and I turn around to see my friend Leah gaping at me with astonishment.

"Leah!" For a second, I forget all about the danger and rush forward to embrace the girl who had been my best friend for ages. "I had no idea you would be here!" And it's true—despite my lie to my parents this morning, I had not expected to run into Leah like that. In hindsight, though, I probably should have, since we used to hang out at this mall nearly every weekend when we were younger.

"What are you doing here?" she asks when we get the hug out of the way. "I thought you were in Colombia!"

"I was—I mean, I am." Now that the initial excitement is over, I'm realizing that running into Leah could be problematic. The last thing I want is for my friend to suffer because of me. "I'm just here for a brief visit," I explain hurriedly, casting a worried look around. All seems to be normal, so I continue, "I'm sorry I didn't tell you I was home, but things were kind of hectic and, well, you know how it is . . ."

"Right, you must be busy with your new husband and stuff," she says slowly, and I can feel the distance between us growing even though we haven't moved an inch. We haven't spoken since I told her about my marriage—just exchanged a few brief emails—and I see now that she still questions my sanity . . . that she no longer understands the person I've become.

I don't blame her for that. Sometimes I don't understand that person either.

"Leah, babe, there you are!" A man's voice interrupts our conversation, and my heart jumps as a familiar male figure approaches Leah from behind me.

It's Jake—the boy I once had a crush on.

The boy Julian stole me from that fateful night in the park.

Only he's not a boy anymore. His shoulders are heavier now; his face is leaner and harder. At some point in the past few months, he's become a man—a man who only has eyes for Leah. Stopping next to her, he bends down to give her a kiss and says in a low, teasing voice, "Babe, I got you that present . . ."

Leah's pale cheeks turn beet-red. "Um, Jake," she mumbles, tugging on his arm to draw his attention to my presence, "look who I just ran into."

He turns toward me, and his brown eyes go round with shock. "Nora? What—what are you doing here?"

"Oh, you know . . . just—just some shopping . . ." I hope I don't sound as dumbfounded as I feel. *Leah and Jake? My best friend Leah and my former crush Jake?* It's as if my world just tilted on its axis. I had no idea they were dating. I knew Leah broke up with her boyfriend a couple of months ago because she mentioned it in an email, but she never told me she'd hooked up with Jake.

As I look at them, standing next to each other with identical uncomfortable expressions on their faces, I realize it's not altogether illogical. They both go to the University of Michigan, and they have an overlapping circle of friends and acquaintances from our high school. They even have a traumatic experience in common—having their friend/date abducted—that could've brought them closer together.

I also realize in that moment that all I feel when I look at them is relief.

Relief that they seem happy together, that the darkness from my life didn't leave a permanent stain on Jake's. There's no regret for what might have been, no jealousy—only an anxiety that grows with every minute Julian spends in Al-Quadar's hands.

"I'm sorry, Nora," Leah says, giving me a wary look. "I should've told you about us earlier. It's just that—"

"Leah, please." Pushing aside my stress and exhaustion, I manage to give her a reassuring smile. "You don't have to explain. Really. I'm married, and Jake and I only had one date. You don't owe me any explanations . . . I was just surprised, that's all."

"Do you want to, um, grab some coffee with us?" Jake offers, sliding his arm around Leah's waist in a gesture that strikes me as unusually protective. I wonder if it's me he's protecting her from. If so, he's even smarter than I thought.

"We could catch up since you're in town and all," he continues, and I shake my head in refusal.

"I'd love to, but I can't," I say, and the regret in my voice is genuine. I desperately want to catch up with them, but I can't have them near me in case Al-Quadar chooses this particular moment to strike. I have no idea how the terrorists would get to me in the middle of a crowded mall, but I'm certain they'll find a way. Glancing down at my phone, I pretend to be dismayed at the time and say apologetically, "I'm afraid I'm already running late . . ."

"Is your husband here with you?" Leah asks, frowning, and I see Jake's face turning white. He probably didn't consider the possibility of Julian being nearby when he extended his invitation to me.

I shake my head, my throat tightening as the horrible reality of the situation threatens to choke me again. "No," I say, hoping I sound halfway normal. "He couldn't make it."

"Oh, okay." Leah's frown deepens, a puzzled look entering her eyes, but Jake regains some of his color. He's obviously relieved that he won't be confronted by the ruthless criminal who's caused him so much grief.

"I really have to run," I say, and Jake nods, his grip on Leah's waist tightening to keep her close.

"Good luck," he says to me, and I can tell he's glad I'm leaving. He's been raised to be polite, however, so he adds, "It was good seeing you," though his eyes say something different.

I give him an understanding smile. "You too," I say and, waving goodbye to Leah, I head for the mall exit.

* * *

I forget about Jake and Leah as soon as I step out into the parking lot. Painfully alert, I scan the area before reluctantly pulling out my phone and calling for a cab. I would hang out at the mall longer, but I don't want to chance running into my friends again. My next stop will be Michigan Avenue in Chicago, where I can browse some high-end stores while praying that I get taken before I completely lose my mind.

The cold wind bites through my clothes as I stand there waiting, my thigh-length peacoat and thin cashmere sweater offering little protection from the chilly temperature outside. It takes a solid half hour before the cab finally pulls up to the curb. By that time, I'm half-frozen, and my nerves are stretched so tightly I'm ready to scream.

Yanking the door open, I climb into the back of the car. It's a clean-looking cab, with a thick glass partition separating the front seat from the back and the windows in the back lightly tinted. "The city, please." My voice is sharper than it needs to be. "The stores on Michigan Avenue."

"Sure thing, miss," the driver says softly, and my head snaps up at the hint of accent in his voice. My eyes lock with his in the front mirror, and I freeze as a bolt of pure terror shoots down my spine.

He could've been one of a thousand immigrants driving a cab for a living, but he's not.

He's Al-Quadar. I can see it in the cold malevolence of his gaze.

They have finally come for me.

It's what I have been waiting for, but now that the moment is here, I find myself paralyzed by a fear so intense, it chokes me from within. My mind flashes into the past, and the memories are so vivid, it's almost as if I'm there again. I feel the pain of barely healed stitches in my side, see the dead bodies of the guards at the clinic, hear Beth's screams . . . and then I taste vomit at the back of my throat as Majid touches my face with a blood-covered finger.

I must've gone as pale as a sheet because the driver's gaze hardens, and I hear the faint click of car door locks being activated.

The sound galvanizes me into action. Adrenaline pumping in my veins, I dive for the door and jerk at the handle while screaming at the top of my lungs. I know it's useless, but I need to try—and, more importantly, I need to give the appearance of trying. I can't sit calmly while they take me back to hell.

I can't let them find out that this time I want to go back there.

As the car begins moving, I continue wrestling with the door and banging on the window. The driver ignores me as he peels out of the parking lot at top speed, and none of the mall visitors seem to notice anything wrong, the tinted windows of the car hiding me from their gaze.

We don't go far. Instead of getting out onto the highway, the car swings around to the back of the building. I see a beige van waiting for us, and I struggle harder, my nails breaking as I claw at the door with a desperation that's only partially feigned. In my rush to rescue Julian, I hadn't fully considered what it would mean to be taken by the monsters of my nightmares—to go through something so horrific again—and the terror that swamps me is only slightly lessened by the fact that this situation is of my own doing.

The driver pulls up next to the van, and the locks click open. Pushing open the door, I scramble out on all fours, scraping my palms on rough asphalt, but before I can get to my feet, a hard arm clamps around my waist and a gloved hand slaps over my mouth, muffling my screams.

I hear orders being barked out in Arabic as I'm carried to the van, kicking and struggling, and then I see a fist flying toward my face.

There's an explosion of pain in my skull, and then there's nothing else.

CHAPTER TWENTY-SEVEN

❖ JULIAN ❖

I drift in and out of consciousness, the periods of wakeful agony interspersed with short stretches of soothing darkness. I don't know if it's been hours, days, or weeks, but it feels like I've been here forever, at the mercy of Majid and the pain.

I haven't slept. They don't let me sleep. I gain respite only when my mind shuts down from the torment, and they have ways of bringing me back when I'm under for too long.

They waterboard me first. I find it funny, in a kind of perverse way. I wonder if they're doing it because they know I'm part-American, or if they just think it's an efficient method of breaking someone without inflicting severe damage.

They do it a few dozen times, pushing me to the brink of death and then bringing me back. It feels like I'm drowning over and over again, and my body fights for air with a desperation that seems out of place given the situation. It wouldn't be such a bad thing if they accidentally drowned me; my mind knows that, but my body struggles to live. Every second with that wet rag on my face feels like an eternity, the trickle of water somehow more terrifying than the sharpest blade.

They pause every once in a while and throw questions at me, promising to stop if only I would answer. And when my lungs feel like they're bursting, I want to give in. I want to put an end to this—yet something inside me won't let me. I refuse to give them the satisfaction of winning, of letting them kill me while knowing that they achieved what they wanted.

As my body strains for air, my father's voice comes to me.

"Are you going to cry? Are you going to cry like your mama's pretty boy or face me like a man?"

I'm four years old again, cowering in the corner as my father kicks me repeatedly in the ribs. I know the right answer to his question—I know I need to face him—but I'm scared. I'm so scared. I can feel the wetness on my face, and I know it will make him angry. I don't mean to cry. I haven't truly cried since I was a baby, but the pain in my ribs makes my eyes water. If my mother were here, she'd hold me and kiss me, but she doesn't come near me when my father is in this kind of mood. She's too afraid of him.

I hate my father. I hate him, and I want to be like him all at once. I don't want to be scared. I want to be the one with the power, the one everyone's afraid of.

Rolling up into a little ball, I use the bottom of my shirt to wipe the betraying moisture off my face, and then I get to my feet, ignoring my fear and the ache in my bruised ribs.

"I'm not going to cry." Swallowing the knot in my throat, I look up to meet my father's angry gaze. "I'm never going to cry."

Curses in Arabic. More wetness on my face.

My mind is violently wrenched back to the present as I convulse, gagging and sucking in air when the soaked rag is removed. My lungs expand greedily, and through the ringing in my ears, I hear Majid yelling at the man who almost killed me.

Well, fuck. Looks like this portion of the fun is over.

They start with the needles next. Long, thick needles that they drive under my toenails and fingernails. I'm able to bear this better, my mind divorcing itself from my tortured body and taking me back to the past.

I'm nine now. My father brought me to the city for negotiations with his suppliers. I'm sitting on the steps, guarding the entrance to the building, a gun tucked into my belt underneath my T-shirt. I know how to use this gun; I already killed two men with it. I threw up after the first one, earning myself a beating, but the second kill had been easier. I didn't even flinch when I pulled the trigger.

A few teenage boys walk out onto the street. I recognize their tattoos; they're part of a local gang. My father probably used them at some point to distribute his product, but right now they appear to be bored and at loose ends.

I watch as they meander up and down the street, kicking at some broken bottles and ribbing each other. A part of me envies their easy camaraderie. I don't have a lot of friends, and the boys I occasionally play with all seem to be afraid of me. I don't know if it's because I'm the Señor's son, or if they've heard things about me. I don't usually mind their fear—I encourage it, in fact—but sometimes I wish I could just play like a regular kid.

These teenage boys haven't heard about me, though. I can tell because when they spot me sitting there, they smirk and walk toward me, thinking they've found easy prey to bully.

"Hey," one of them calls out. "What's a little boy like you doing here? This is our neighborhood. You lost, kid?"

"No," I say, replicating their smirks. "I'm about as lost as you . . . kid."

The boy who spoke to me swells up with anger. "Why you little shit—" He starts toward me, and immediately freezes when I point my gun at him without blinking.

"Try it," I invite him softly. "Come closer, why don't you?"

The boys begin to back away. They're not completely dumb; they see that I know how to handle the weapon.

My father and his men come out at that moment, and the boys scatter like a pack of rats.

When I tell my father what happened, he nods approvingly. "Good. You don't back down, son. Remember that—you take what you want, and you never back down."

Cold water in my face, followed by a brutal slap, and I'm back in the present. They have me tied to a chair now, my wrists bound behind my back and my ankles tied to the chair legs. My fingers and toes throb with agony, but I'm still alive—and for now unbroken.

I can see the frustrated fury on Majid's face. He's not happy with the progress thus far, and I have a feeling he's about to amp up his efforts.

Sure enough, he approaches me, his knife clutched in his fist. "Last chance, Esguerra . . ." He stops in front of me. "I'm giving you one last chance before I start cutting off some useful body parts. Where is the fucking factory, and how do we get in?"

Instead of answering, I gather whatever little saliva remains in my mouth and spit at him. The red-tinted spittle splatters all over his nose and cheeks, and I watch with satisfaction as he wipes it off with his sleeve, his body vibrating with rage at the insult.

I don't have a chance to enjoy his reaction for long, though, because he fists his hand in my hair and yanks on it, causing my neck to bend painfully backwards.

"Let me tell you what's about to happen, you piece of shit," he hisses, pressing the blade against my jaw. "I'm going to start with your eyes. I'm going to cut your left eyeball in half—and then I'm going to do the same with your right. And when you're blind, I'm going to start trimming your dick, inch by inch, until there's only a tiny stub left . . . Do you understand me? If you don't start talking now, you will never see or fuck again."

Fighting the urge to throw up, I remain silent as he pushes the knife upward, toward the thin skin under my left eye. The blade cuts through my cheek on the way, and I feel the warmth of the blood trickling down my cold skin. I know he's not bluffing, but I also know that giving in will not change the outcome. Majid will torture me to get answers—and once he gets them, he will torture me even more.

Glaring at my lack of reaction, Majid presses the knife deeper into my skin. "Last fucking chance, Esguerra. Do you want to keep your eye or not?"

I don't respond, and he drags the knife higher, causing my eyelids to squeeze shut reflexively.

"All right then," he whispers, enjoying my body's involuntarily panic as I try to jerk out of his reach . . . and then I feel a nauseating explosion of pain as the blade punctures through my eyelid and penetrates deep into my eye.

* * *

I must've lost consciousness again because there's more cold water being thrown at me. I'm shivering, my body going into shock from the excruciating agony. I can't see anything out of my left eye—all I feel there is a burning, leaking emptiness. My stomach roils with bile, and it takes all of my effort not to vomit all over myself.

"How about the second eye, Esguerra, hmm?" Majid smiles at me, his bloodied knife held tightly in his fist. "Would you like to be blind while we take your dick off, or would you rather see it all? Of course, it's not too late to stop all this . . . Just tell us what we want to know, and we might even let you live—since you're so brave and all."

He's lying. I can hear it in the gloating tone of his voice. He thinks he's got me nearly broken, so desperate to stop the pain that I will believe anything he says.

"Fuck you," I whisper with my remaining strength. *You don't back down. You never back down.* "Fuck you and your pathetic little threats."

His eyes narrow with rage, and the knife flashes toward my face. I squeeze my remaining eye shut, preparing for the agony . . . but it never comes.

Surprised, I peel open my uninjured eyelid and see that Majid got distracted by one of his minions. The man seems excited, pointing toward me as he chatters in rapid Arabic. I strain to make out some of the words I know, but he's speaking too fast. Judging by the smile spreading across Majid's face, however, whatever he's saying is good news for Majid—which means it's probably bad news for me.

My supposition is confirmed when Majid turns toward me and says with a cruel smirk, "Your other eye is safe for now, Esguerra. There is something I *really* want you to see in a few hours."

I glare at him, unable to hide my hatred. I don't know what he's talking about, but the pit of my stomach tightens as the terrorists file out of the windowless room. There's only one thing that would persuade me to give in—and she is safe and sound in my compound. They can't possibly be talking about Nora, not with all the security I have around her. It's some new mind game they're playing with me, trying to make me think they have something worse in store for me than what I've already suffered. It's a delay tactic, a way to prolong my suffering—nothing more.

I have no intention of falling for their trick, but as I wait there, bound and in the worst pain of my life, I'm not strong enough to stop the anxiety from creeping up on me. I should be grateful for this respite from torture, but I'm not.

I would gladly let Majid cut off every one of my limbs if only I could be certain that Nora is safe.

I don't know how much time passes while I wait in torment, but finally I hear voices outside. The door opens, and Majid drags in a small figure dressed in a pair of Uggs and a man's shirt that hangs down to her knees. Her hands are bound behind her back, and there is a bloody stain on the underside of her left arm.

My stomach drops and cold horror spreads through my veins as Nora's dark eyes lock on my face.

My worst fear has come to pass.

They have the only person who matters to me in the whole fucking world.

They have my Nora—and this time, I can't rescue her.

CHAPTER TWENTY-EIGHT

❖ NORA ❖

Trembling from head to toe, I stare at Julian, my chest squeezing with agony at the sight. There is a rough, dirty-looking bandage on his shoulder, with blood seeping out of it, and his naked body is a mass of cuts, bruises, and scrapes. His face is even worse. Below the old bandage on his forehead, there isn't a spot left that isn't discolored or swollen. The most horrifying thing of all, however, is the huge bleeding gash running through his left cheek and all the way up into his eyebrow—a mess of ragged flesh where his eye used to be.

Where his eye *used* to be.

They cut out his eye.

I can't even begin to process that at the moment, so I don't try. For now, Julian is alive, and that's all that matters.

He's tied to a metal chair, his legs bound apart and his arms restrained behind his back. I can see the shock and horror on his bloodied face as he takes in my presence, and I want to tell him that everything will be all right—that this time I am saving *him*—but I can't. Not yet.

Not until Peter has a chance to get here with the reinforcements.

My bruised cheekbone is throbbing where they hit me, and the underside of my left arm is burning with pain from the open wound there. They stripped off my clothes and cut out my birth control implant while I was knocked out, probably fearing that it was a tracker of some kind. I hadn't expected that—I figured, if anything, they would find one of the real trackers—but it worked out even better than I'd hoped. After cutting out the implant and seeing that it was nothing more than a simple plastic rod, they must've dismissed me as a threat, thinking that I am exactly what I was pretending to be: a naïve girl who went to see her parents, oblivious of any remaining danger. It makes me glad that I had the foresight to leave the bracelet tracker at the estate, so as not to arouse their suspicions.

To my relief, it doesn't seem like they touched me much in other ways. At least, if they did anything more than cop a feel while I was unconscious, I feel no evidence of it. There is no soreness or stickiness between my legs, no pain of any kind. My skin is crawling at the knowledge that they had me naked, but it could've easily been much worse. When I woke up, I was already wearing someone's shirt and my own Ugg boots. They must be saving all the drama for when I'm in front of Julian.

This was the part of my plan that Peter found most risky: that time from my capture until my arrival at their hideout.

"You know that they can search every inch of you and find all three of the tracking devices Julian placed on you," he told me before we left the estate. "And then you'll both be lost to us. You do understand what they will do to you to make Julian talk, right?"

"Yes, I do, Peter." I gave him a grim smile. "I understand perfectly. There is no other choice, though, and the trackers are tiny, the insertion wounds nearly invisible at this point. They may find one or two, but I doubt they'll find all three—and if they do, by the time they do, you may have a fix on their location."

"Maybe," he said, his eyes speaking volumes about his opinion on my sanity, "or maybe not. There are a hundred things that can go wrong between the time you get taken and when they bring you to Julian."

"It's a risk I'll have to take," I told him, bringing the discussion to an end. I knew how dangerous it would be for me to act as a human tracking device to locate the terrorists, but I couldn't see any other way to get to Julian in time—and judging by his current state, I was nearly too late as is.

I see Julian attempting to compose himself, to hide his visceral reaction to my presence, but he's not entirely successful. After the initial shock passes, his jaw tightens, and his undamaged eye begins to glitter with violent rage as he takes in my semi-dressed state. His powerful muscles bunch, straining against the restraints. He looks like he wants to rip apart everyone in the room, and I know that the ropes tying him to the chair are the only thing preventing him from launching a suicidal attack on our captors. The other terrorists must be thinking the same thing, because two of them step closer to Julian, clutching their weapons just in case.

Looking delighted with this turn of events, Majid laughs and drags me to the middle of the room, his grip on my arm excruciatingly tight. "You know, your dumb little whore all but fell into my lap," he says conversationally, fisting his hand in my hair and forcing me down to my knees. "We found her shopping in your absence, like all those greedy American bitches. Figured we'd bring her here, so you can see her pretty little face before I carve it up . . . Unless you want to start talking?"

Julian remains silent, glaring at Majid with murderous hatred, while I take small, shallow breaths to cope with my terror. My eyes are watering from the pain in my scalp, and the fear pulsing through me feels almost like a living thing. With my hands restrained behind my back, there's nothing I can do to prevent Majid from hurting me. I have no idea how long it's going to take Peter to arrive, but there's every chance he might not make it in time. I can see the rust-colored stains on the blade hanging loosely from Majid's belt, and nausea rises in my throat as I realize that it's Julian's blood.

If we're not rescued soon, it will be my blood, too.

To my horror, Majid reaches for that blade, still holding my hair in that painful grip. "Oh, yes," he whispers, pressing the flat edge against my neck, "I think her head will make a nice little trophy—after I cut it up a bit, of course . . ." He pushes the knife upward, and I freeze in terror as I feel the blade cutting into the soft skin under my chin, followed by the stomach-churning sensation of warm liquid trickling down my neck.

The growl that emanates from Julian doesn't resemble anything human. Before I can do more than gasp, he surges forward, using the balls of his feet to propel himself and the chair off the floor. His action is so sudden and violent that the two men standing next to him don't react in time. Julian literally crashes into one of them, bringing the armed terrorist down to the floor, and, with one twist of his body, drives the metal leg of the chair into the man's throat.

The next few seconds are a blur of blood and screams in Arabic. Majid releases his hold on me and yells out some orders, galvanizing the others into action as he springs into the fray himself.

Still tied to the chair, Julian is dragged off the injured man's body, and I watch in horrified fascination as the man Julian attacked writhes on the floor, clutching his throat as rattling, gurgling sounds escape from his mouth. He's dying—I can see it in the weakening spurts of blood coming from the ragged wound in his neck—yet his agony doesn't seem to touch me. It's as though I'm watching a movie instead of observing a human being bleeding to death in front of my eyes.

Majid and the other terrorists rush to his aid, trying to staunch the flow of blood, but it's too late. The man's frantic grip on his throat eases, his eyes glazing over, and the stench of death—of evacuated bowels and violence—fills the room.

He's dead.

Julian killed him.

I should be disgusted and appalled, but I'm not. Maybe those emotions will hit me later, but for now, all I feel is a strange mixture of gladness and pride: gladness that one of these murderers is dead, and pride that Julian was the one to kill him. Even tied up and weakened by torture, my husband managed to take down one of his enemies— an armed man who was stupid enough to stand within Julian's lethal reach.

My lack of empathy disturbs me on some level, but I don't have time to dwell on it. Whether Julian intended to create a distraction or not, the end result is that nobody is paying attention to me at the moment—and as soon as I realize it, I spring into action.

Jumping to my feet, I cast a frantic glance around the room. My gaze lands on a small knife on a table near the wall, and I leap toward it, my pulse racing. The terrorists are all gathered around Julian on the other side of the room, and I hear grunts, curses, and the sickening sound of fists hitting flesh.

They're punishing Julian for this murder—and, for now, ignoring me.

Turning my back to the table, I manage to palm the knife and wedge the blade underneath the duct tape they wrapped around my wrists. My hands are trembling, causing the sharp blade to nick my skin, but I ignore the pain, trying to saw through the thick tape before they realize what's happening. My grip is slippery with sweat and blood, but I persist, and finally, my hands are free.

Shaking, I survey the room again, and spot an assault rifle leaning negligently against the wall. One of the terrorists must've left it there in the confusion resulting from Julian's unexpected attack.

My heart throbbing in my throat, I inch along the wall toward the weapon, desperately hoping that the terrorists won't glance in my direction. I have no idea what I'm going to do with one gun against a roomful of men armed to their teeth, but I have to do something.

I can't stand by and watch them beat Julian to death.

My hands close around the weapon before anyone notices anything, and I suck in a shaking breath of relief. It's an AK-47, one of the assault rifles I practiced with during my training with Julian. Gripping the heavy weapon, I lift it and point in the direction of the terrorists, trying to control the adrenaline-induced trembling in my arms. I've never shot at a person before—only at beer cans and paper targets—and I don't know if I have what it takes to pull the trigger.

And as I'm trying to work up the courage to act, a blinding explosion rocks the room, knocking me off my feet and onto the floor.

* * *

I don't know if I hit my head or was merely dazed by the explosion, but the next thing I'm aware of is the sound of gunfire outside the walls. The entire room is filled with smoke, and I cough as I instinctively attempt to get to my feet.

"Nora! Stay down!" It's Julian, his voice hoarse from the smoke. "Stay down, baby, do you hear me?"

"Yes!" I yell back, intense joy filling every cell of my body as I realize that he's alive—and in a good enough condition to speak. Keeping low to the ground, I peer out from behind the table that fell next to me, and see Julian lying on his side on the other end of the room, still tied to the metal chair.

I also see that the smoke is coming in from the vent in the ceiling, and that the room is empty except for the two of us. The battle, or whatever is happening, is taking place outside.

Peter and the guards must have arrived.

Almost crying with relief, I grab the AK-47 lying next to me, lower myself onto my stomach, and begin to belly-crawl toward Julian, holding my breath to avoid inhaling too much smoke.

At that moment, the door swings open, and a familiar figure steps into the room.

It's Majid—and in his right hand, he's holding a gun.

He must've realized that Al-Quadar were losing and came back to kill Julian.

A surge of hatred rises in my throat, choking me with bitter bile. This is the man who murdered Beth... who tortured Julian and would've done the same thing to me. A vicious, psychotic terrorist who had undoubtedly murdered dozens of innocent people.

He doesn't see me there, all his attention on Julian as he lifts his gun and points it at my husband. "Goodbye, Esguerra," he says quietly... and I squeeze the trigger of my own weapon.

Despite my prone position, my aim is accurate. Julian had me practice shooting sitting, lying down, and even running at some point. The assault rifle bucks in my shaking arms, slamming painfully against my shoulder, but the two bullets hit Majid exactly where I intended—in his right wrist and elbow.

The shots throw him back against the wall and knock the gun out of his grasp. Screaming, he clutches at his bleeding arm, and I get up, heedless of the danger posed by the bullets flying outside. I can hear Julian yelling something at me, but his exact words don't register through the ringing in my ears.

In this moment, it's as though the entire world fades away, leaving me alone with Majid.

Our eyes meet, and for the first time, I see fear in his dark, reptilian gaze. He knows that I am the one who shot him, and he can read the cold intent on my face.

"Please, don't—" he begins saying, and I squeeze the trigger again, discharging five more bullets into his stomach and chest.

In the brief silence that follows, I watch as Majid's body slides down the wall, almost in slow motion. His face is slack with shock, blood dribbling out of the corner of his mouth, and his eyes are open, staring at me with a kind of numb disbelief. He moves his lips, as though to say something, and a rattling gurgle escapes his throat as more blood bubbles up out of his mouth.

Lowering the gun, I step closer to him, drawn by a strange compulsion to see what I have wrought. Majid's eyes plead with mine, begging for mercy without words. I hold his gaze, stretching out the moment . . . and then I aim the AK-47 at his forehead and pull the trigger again.

The back of his head explodes, blood and bits of brain tissue splattering against the wall. His eyes glaze over, the whites around the irises turning crimson as blood vessels burst in his eyes. His body goes limp, and the smell of death, sharp and pungent, permeates the room for the second time today.

Except it's not Julian who's the killer this time.

It's me.

My hands are steady as I lower the weapon again, watching the blood trickle down the wall behind Majid. Then I walk toward Julian, kneel down beside him, and carefully place the gun on the floor as I begin to work on untying his ropes.

Julian is silent as I free him from his bonds, and so am I. The sounds of gunfire outside are beginning to die down, and I'm hoping that means Peter's forces are winning. Either way, though, I'm ready for whatever may come, a strange calm engulfing me despite our still-precarious situation.

When Julian's arms and legs are free, he kicks the chair away and rolls onto his back, his right hand closing around my wrist. His left arm, still partially in a cast, is immobile at his side, and there's more blood on his face and body from the beating he just received. His grip on my wrist, however, is surprisingly strong as he pulls me closer, forcing me down on the floor next to him.

"Stay down, baby," he whispers through swollen lips. "It's almost over . . . Please, stay down."

I nod and stretch out next to him on the right, being careful not to aggravate his injuries. With the door open, some of the smoke in the room is beginning to clear out, and I can breathe freely for the first time since the explosion.

Julian releases my wrist and slides his arm under my neck, gathering me against him in a protective embrace. My hand accidentally brushes against his ribs, causing him to hiss in pain, but when I try to scoot back, he merely holds me tighter.

When Peter and the guards step through the door a few minutes later, they find us lying in each other's arms, with Julian pointing the AK-47 at the door.

CHAPTER TWENTY-NINE

❖ JULIAN ❖

"How is she?" Lucas asks, sitting down on the chair next to my bed. There is a thick bandage on his head, and he has to use crutches for his broken leg. Other than that, he's already on the mend. He was unconscious in another room when Al-Quadar attacked the Uzbekistani hospital and thus missed all the fun.

"She's . . . okay, I think." I press a button to get the bed into a half-sitting position. My ribs ache at the motion, but I ignore the discomfort. Pain has been my constant companion since the crash, and I'm more or less used to it at this point.

Ever since our rescue from that construction site in Tajikistan five days ago, Nora and I have been recuperating in a special facility in Switzerland. It's a private clinic staffed with top doctors from all over the world, and I've had Lucas personally supervise the security here. Of course, with the most dangerous cells of Al-Quadar eliminated, there's less of an immediate threat, but it still pays to be cautious. I've had all of my injured men transferred here as well, so they could recover faster and in a nicer environment.

The room Nora and I share is state-of-the-art, equipped with everything from video games to a private shower. There are two adjustable beds—one for me and one for Nora—with Egyptian cotton sheets and memory foam mattresses on each. Even the heart-rate monitors and IV drips positioned around the beds look sleek, more decorative than medical. The whole setup is so luxurious, I can almost forget I'm in yet another hospital.

Almost, but not quite.

If I never set foot inside a hospital again, I will die a happy man.

To my tremendous relief, all of Nora's injuries turned out to be minor. The wound on her arm needed a few stitches, but the blow to her face left only a nasty bruise on her cheekbone. The doctors also confirmed that she hadn't been sexually assaulted, despite her state of undress. Within a few hours of our arrival here, Nora was pronounced healthy and ready to go home.

I, on the other hand, am a bit worse off, though not nearly as fucked up as I could've been.

They've already performed two operations on me—one to minimize the scarring on my face, and the second one to put a prosthetic eye into the vacant eye socket, so I don't resemble a cyclops. I will never be able to see out of my left eye again—at least not until bionic eye technology advances further—but the surgeons have assured me that I'm going to look nearly normal once everything is healed.

My other injuries aren't too bad either. They had to reset my broken arm and wrap it in a new cast, but the gunshot wound in my left shoulder is healing nicely, as are my cracked ribs. I still have some crusted blood under my fingernails and toenails from the needle torture, but it's gradually getting better. The beating Majid's men gave me at the end bruised my kidneys a bit. However, thanks to Peter's prompt arrival, I escaped other internal injuries and more broken bones. When all is said and done, I will have a few more scars—and potentially some weakness in my left arm—but my appearance won't scare little children.

I'm grateful for that. I've never been particularly vain about my looks, but I want to make sure that Nora still finds me attractive, that I don't disgust her with my touch. She's assured me that my scars and bruises don't bother her, but I don't know if she really means it. Because of my injuries, we haven't had sex since our rescue, and I won't know how she truly feels until I have her in my bed again.

In general, I'm not sure how Nora has been feeling for the past five days. With all the surgeries and doctors in the way, we haven't had a chance to talk about what happened. Whenever I bring it up, she changes the topic, as though she wants to forget the whole thing. I would let her—except she's also been unusually quiet. Withdrawn in some way. It's as if the trauma she's gone through has caused her to retreat within herself . . . to shut down her emotions in some manner.

"So she's handling it?" Lucas asks, and I know he's talking about Majid's death. All of my men know about the way Nora gunned him down, and about her role in my rescue. They admire her for being so brave, whereas I'm battling a daily urge to throttle her for risking her life. And Peter—well, that's a whole other matter. If he hadn't disappeared promptly after bringing us to the clinic, I would've torn his head off for placing her in that kind of danger.

"She is," I say in response to Lucas's question. My concerns about Nora's mental state are not something I want to share with him. "She's handling it about as well as can be expected. The first kill is never easy, of course, but she's tough. She'll get through it."

"Yes, I'm sure she will." Reaching for his crutches, Lucas gets up and asks, "How soon do you want to head back to Colombia?"

"Goldberg says we can leave tomorrow. He wants me to stay here one more night, to make sure everything is healing properly, and then he'll oversee my care back at the compound."

"Excellent," Lucas says. "I will make the arrangements then."

He hobbles out of the room, and I reach for my laptop to check on Nora's whereabouts. She went to get a snack from the cafe on the first floor of the clinic, but she's already been gone longer than ten minutes, and I am beginning to get worried.

Logging in, I pull up the report from the trackers and see that she's standing in the hallway, about fifty feet away from the room. The dot showing her location is stationary; she must be chatting with someone there.

Relieved, I close the laptop and place it back on the bedstand.

I know my fear for her is excessive, but I can't control it. Seeing Majid's knife at Nora's throat had been the worst experience of my life. I had never been so terrified as when I saw the blood trickling down her smooth skin. I literally saw a wall of red at that moment, the rage pumping through me giving me a surge of strength I hadn't known I possessed. Killing that terrorist hadn't been a conscious decision; the need to protect Nora had overwhelmed both my instinct for self-preservation and common sense.

If I had been thinking more clearly, I would've come up with some other way to get Majid's attention away from Nora until the reinforcements could arrive.

I had begun to suspect the rescue plan as soon as Majid mentioned shopping. It made a terrible kind of sense: Nora knew that my enemies would want her as leverage, and she knew that she had the trackers. I couldn't believe that she would put herself out there like that—or that Peter would let her—but it was the only thing that could explain how Al-Quadar were able to lay their hands on her in my absence.

Instead of staying safe at the estate, Nora risked her life to save mine.

Knowing what Majid was capable of, she faced her nightmares to rescue *me*—the man she has every reason to hate.

I don't know if I believed that she truly loved me until that moment . . . until I saw her standing there, scared, yet determined, her small body swathed in a man's shirt ten sizes too big for her. Nobody had ever done anything like that for me before; even when I was a child, my mother would slink away at the first sign of my father's temper, leaving me to his tender mercies. Other than the guards I hired, nobody had ever protected me. I had always been on my own.

Until her.

Until Nora.

As I'm remembering how fierce she looked with her gun pointed at Majid, the door to the room opens, and the subject of my musings walks in.

She's wearing a pair of jeans and a brown long-sleeved top, her thick hair caught in a ponytail behind her back and her feet clad in ballet-type flats. The bruise on her cheekbone is still there, but she covered it up with some makeup today, probably so she could video-chat with her parents without worrying them. She's been talking to them almost daily since our arrival at the clinic. I think she feels guilty about scaring them with her disappearance again.

She's also munching on an apple, her white teeth biting into the juicy fruit with evident enjoyment.

My heart begins to thump heavily in my ribcage as my chest expands with joy and relief. It's like that every time I see her now, my reaction the same whether she's been gone fifteen minutes or several hours.

"Hi." She walks over and gracefully perches on the right side of my bed. Leaning down, she presses her soft lips to my cheek in a brief kiss, then lifts her head to smile at me. "Want some apple?"

"No, thanks, baby." My voice turns husky as her touch makes me painfully aware of the fact that I haven't fucked her since leaving the estate. "It's all yours."

"All right." She bites into the apple. "I ran into Dr. Goldberg in the hallway," she says after swallowing. "He said you're getting better, and we can go home tomorrow."

"Yes, that's right." I watch her tongue flick out to clean up a tiny piece of fruit from her lower lip, and a bolt of heat tightens my balls. I am definitely getting better—or at least my cock believes that I am. "We'll leave as soon as he okays it."

Nora bites off another piece of apple and chews it slowly, studying me with a peculiar expression.

"What is it, baby?" Reaching for her free hand, I bring her delicate palm up to my face and rub the back of her hand against my cheek. I know I'm probably scratching her soft skin with my stubble—I haven't shaved in over a week—but I can't resist the lure of her touch. "Tell me what's on your mind."

She puts the apple core down on a napkin on the bedstand. "We should talk about Peter," she says quietly. "And about the promise I made to him."

I tense, my grip on her palm tightening. "What promise?"

"The list." Her fingers twitch in my grasp. "The list of names you promised him for the three years of service. I told him I'd give it to him as soon as you had it—if he helped me rescue you."

"Fuck." I stare at her in disbelief. I had been wondering how she'd persuaded Peter to disobey a direct order, and here is my answer. "You promised you'd help him get revenge if he assisted you in that insanity?"

Nora nods, her eyes trained on mine. "Yes. It was the only thing I could think of at the time. He knew that if you died, he wouldn't get the list at all—and I told him he'd get it earlier if he helped me."

My eyebrows snap together as a wave of fury rolls through me. That Russian motherfucker put my wife in mortal danger, and that's not something I can ever forgive or forget. He might've saved my life, but he had risked Nora's in order to do it. If he hadn't disappeared after carrying out the rescue, I would've killed him for that. And now Nora wants me to give him that list?

Not fucking likely.

"Julian, I promised him," she insists, apparently sensing my unvoiced reply. Her gaze is filled with uncharacteristic determination as she adds, "I know you're mad at him, but the whole plan was my idea—and he didn't want to do it at first."

"Right. Because he knew your safety should've been his top priority." Realizing I'm still squeezing her palm, I release her hand and say harshly, "The bastard's lucky he's still alive."

"I understand that." Nora gives me a level look. "So does Peter, believe me. He knew you'd react like this—which is why he left after dropping us off here."

I inhale, trying to hang on to my temper. "And good riddance to him. He knows I'll never trust him now. I ordered him to keep you safe on the estate, and what did he do?" I glare at her as the memory of her getting dragged into that windowless room, bloodied and scared, scrapes at my brain. "He fucking hand-delivered you to Majid!"

"Yes, and by doing so, saved your life—"

"I don't care about my fucking life!" I sit up all the way, ignoring the jolt of pain in my ribs. "Don't you get it, Nora? *You* are the only person I care about. *You*—not me, not anyone else!"

She stares at me, and I see her large eyes beginning to glisten with moisture. "I know, Julian," she whispers, blinking. "I know that."

I look at her, and the anger drains out of me, replaced by an inexplicable need to make her understand. "I don't know if you do, my pet." My voice is quiet as I reach for her hand again, needing its fragile warmth. "You are everything to me. If something happened to you, I wouldn't want to survive—I wouldn't want a life that doesn't have you in it."

Her lips tremble, the tears pooling in her eyes before spilling over. "I know, Julian . . ." Her fingers curl around my palm, squeezing it tightly. "I know, because it's the same for me. When I thought your plane went down"—she swallows, her voice breaking—"and then afterwards, when I heard the gunshots during our call . . ."

I draw in a breath, her distress making my chest hurt. "Don't, baby . . ." I bring her hand up to my lips and kiss the inside of her palm. "Don't think about it anymore. It's over—there's nothing more to fear. Majid is gone, and we're on the verge of completely eradicating Al-Quadar . . ."

As I speak, I see her expression flattening, her gaze growing strangely shuttered. It's as if she's trying to pull back her emotions, to build some kind of a mental wall to protect herself. "I know," she says, and her lips stretch into the kind of empty smile I've often seen her wear since our rescue. "It's done. He's dead."

"Are you sorry about that?" I ask, lowering her hand. I need to understand the source of her withdrawal, to get to the bottom of whatever is causing her to shut down like this. "Are you sorry you killed him, baby? Is that why you've been upset the last few days?"

She blinks, as if startled by my question. "I'm not upset."

"Don't lie to me, my pet." Releasing her hand, I gently grasp her chin and look into her shadowed eyes. "Do you think I don't know you by now? I can see that you've been different since Tajikistan, and I want to understand why."

"Julian . . ." Her voice holds a pleading note. "Please, I don't want to talk about this."

"Why not? Do you think I don't get it? Do you think I don't know what it's like to kill for the first time and live with the knowledge that you took a human life?" I pause, watching for a reaction. When I see none, I continue, "We both know that Majid deserved it, but it's normal to feel like shit afterwards. You need to talk about it, so you can begin to come to terms with everything that happened—"

"No, Julian," she interrupts, the careful blankness of her gaze giving way to a sudden flare of anger. "You *don't* get it. I know Majid deserved to die, and I'm not sorry that I killed him. I have no doubt that the world is a better place without him."

"So what is it then?" I'm beginning to suspect where this is heading, but I want to hear her say it.

"I killed him," she says quietly, looking at me. "I stood next to him, looked him in the eye, and pulled the trigger. I didn't kill him to protect you, or because I had no other choice. I killed him because I wanted to." She pauses, then adds, her eyes glittering, "I killed him because I wanted to see him die."

CHAPTER THIRTY

❖ NORA ❖

Julian stares at me, the expression on his bandaged face unchanged at my revelation. I want to look away, but I can't, his grip on my chin forcing me to hold his gaze as I lay bare the awful secret that's been eating at me since our rescue.

His lack of reaction makes me think he doesn't fully understand what I'm saying.

"I killed him, Julian," I repeat, determined to make him comprehend now that he forced me to talk about this. "I murdered Majid in cold blood. When I saw him step into the room, I knew what I wanted to do, and I did it. I shot the weapon out of his hand—and when he was unarmed, I shot him again in the stomach and chest, making sure not to hit him in the heart, so he'd live a couple of minutes longer. I could've killed him right away, but I didn't." My hands squeeze into fists on my lap, my nails digging painfully into my skin as I confess, "I kept him alive because I wanted to look him in the face when I took his life."

Julian's unbandaged eye gleams a deeper blue, and I feel a wave of burning shame. I know it doesn't make sense—I know I'm talking to a man who's committed crimes far worse than this—but I don't have the excuse of his fucked-up upbringing. Nobody forced me to become a killer. When I shot Majid that day, I did it of my own initiative.

I killed a man because I hated him and wanted to see him die.

I wait for Julian to respond, to say something either dismissive or condemning, but he asks softly instead, "And how did you feel when it was over, my pet? When he lay there dead?" His hand releases my chin and moves down to rest on my leg, his large palm covering most of my thigh. "Were you glad to see him like that?"

I nod, dropping my gaze to escape his penetrating stare. "Yes," I admit, a shudder rippling through me as I remember the almost-euphoric high of seeing the bullets from my gun tearing through Majid's flesh. "When I saw the life leave his eyes, I felt strong. Invincible. I knew he could no longer hurt us, and I was glad." Gathering my courage, I look up at him again. "Julian... I blew a man's brains out—and the scary thing is I don't regret it at all."

"Ah, I see." A smile tugs at his partially healed lips. "You think you're a bad person because you feel no guilt over killing a murderous terrorist—and you believe you should."

"Of course I should." I frown at the inappropriate amusement in his voice. "I killed a man—and you yourself said that it's normal to feel shitty about it. You felt bad after your first kill, right?"

"Yes." Julian's smile takes on a bitter edge. "I did. I was a child, and I didn't know the man I was forced to shoot. He was someone who had double-crossed my father, and to this day, I have no idea what kind of person he was... whether he was a hardened criminal or just someone who got mixed-up with bad company. I didn't hate him—I had no opinion about him, really. I killed him to prove that I could do it, to make my father proud of me." He pauses, then continues, his expression softening, "So you see, my pet, it was different. When you killed Majid, you rid the world of evil, whereas I... well, that's a whole other story. You have no reason to feel bad about what you did, and you're smart enough to know it."

I look at him, my throat tightening as I imagine eight-year-old Julian pulling that trigger. I don't know what to say, how to assuage his guilt over that long-ago event, and anger at Juan Esguerra fills my chest. "You know, if your father were alive, I would shoot him too," I say savagely, causing Julian to let out a delighted chuckle.

"Oh, yes, I'm sure you would," he says, grinning at me. The expression should've looked grotesque on his bruised and swollen face, but somehow it looks sexy instead. Even beat-up, bandaged like a mummy, and with several days' worth of dark stubble on his jaw, my husband radiates an animal magnetism that transcends mere looks.

The doctors told us that his face will be nearly normal once everything is healed, but even if it isn't, I strongly suspect Julian will be just as seductive with an eye patch and some scars.

As though in response to my thoughts, his hand on my thigh moves higher, toward the juncture between my legs. "My fierce little darling," he murmurs, his grin fading as a familiar heated gleam appears in his uncovered eye. "So delicate, yet so ferocious . . . I wish you could've seen yourself that day, baby. You were magnificent when you faced Majid, so brave and beautiful . . ." His fingers press roughly on my clit through my jeans, and I suck in a startled breath, my nipples hardening as a surge of liquid need dampens my sex.

"Yes, that's right, baby," he whispers, his fingers moving upward to my zipper. "You with that weapon was the sexiest thing I've ever seen. I couldn't take my eyes off you." The zipper slides down with a metallic hiss, the sound strangely erotic, and my core clenches with a sudden desperate ache.

"Um, Julian . . ." My breathing is uneven, my heartbeat speeding up as Julian's hand delves into the open fly of my jeans. "What—what are you doing?"

His lips curve in a wicked half-smile. "What does it look like I'm doing?"

"But . . . but you can't . . ." The sentence devolves into a moan as his fingers boldly push into my underwear and cup my sex, his middle finger slipping between my wet folds to massage my throbbing clit. The heat that blasts through my nerve endings feels almost like an electric spark, every hair on my body standing up in response to the zing of pleasure. I gasp, feeling the tension gathering inside me, but before I can reach my peak, Julian's fingers withdraw, leaving me hovering on the edge.

"Take off your clothes, then climb on top," he orders hoarsely, pulling back the blanket to reveal a hospital gown tented with a massive erection. "I need to fuck you. Now."

I hesitate for a moment, worried about his injuries, and Julian's jaw tightens in displeasure.

"I mean it, Nora. Take those clothes off."

Gulping, I jump off the bed, unable to believe that I feel the compulsion to obey him even now. His left arm is in a cast, he can barely move without pain, and yet my instinctive response is to fear him—to want him and fear him at the same time.

"And lock the door," he commands as I begin to pull my shirt up. "I don't want to be interrupted."

"Okay."

Leaving my shirt on, I hurry over to the door to turn the lock that gives us privacy. Every step I take reminds me of the pulsing heat between my legs, my tight jeans rubbing against my sensitized clit and adding to my arousal.

When I return, Julian is in a semi-reclining position on the bed, his gown untied at the front and his hand stroking his erect cock. There is a stiff bandage around his ribs, but it does nothing to detract from the raw power of his muscular body. Even wounded, he manages to dominate the room, his appeal as magnetic as ever.

"Good girl," he murmurs, watching me with a heavy-lidded stare. "Now strip for me, baby. I want to see your sexy little ass wriggling out of those jeans."

I sink my teeth into my lower lip, the heat in his gaze turning me on even more. "All right," I whisper, and turning my back to him, I bend forward and slowly pull down my jeans, making sure to sway my hips from side to side as I expose my thong-clad ass to his eyes.

When the jeans are all the way down to my ankles, I turn back to face him and kick off my shoes, then step out of my jeans, leaving them lying on the floor. Julian watches my movements with undisguised lust, his breathing becoming heavy as the tip of his cock starts to glisten with moisture. He's no longer touching himself, his hands clutching the sheets instead, and I know it's because he's close to coming, the hard column of his sex jutting up in defiance of gravity.

Keeping my eyes trained on him, I proceed to take off my shirt, pulling it up over my head in a slow, teasing motion. Underneath, I'm wearing a silky white bra that matches my thong. I bought several outfits online earlier in the week, and I'm glad I decided to get a few nicer underwear sets. I love to see that look of uncontrollable hunger on Julian's face—the expression that says he would move mountains to have me at that moment.

As the shirt falls to the floor, he says roughly, "Come here, Nora." His gaze devours me, consumes me. "I need to touch you."

I inhale, my sex flooding with wetness as I take a couple of steps toward the bed, pausing in front of him. He reaches for me, smoothing his palm over my ribcage, and then moves his hand higher, toward my bra. His fingers close around my left breast, kneading it through the silky material, and I gasp as he pinches my nipple, causing it to stiffen further.

"Take the rest of your clothes off." His hand leaves my body, making me feel bereft for a moment, and I hurriedly unclasp my bra and push the thong down my legs before stepping out of it.

"Good. Now straddle me."

Biting my lip, I climb onto the bed, straddling Julian's hips. His cock brushes against the inside of my thighs, and I grasp it in my right hand, guiding it toward my aching entrance.

"Yes, that's it," he mutters, reaching out to grip my hip as I begin to lower myself onto his shaft. Releasing his cock, I use my palms to brace myself on the bed, and he groans, "Yes, take me in, my pet . . . All the way . . ." Using his grip on my hip, he pushes me lower, forcing his cock deeper into me, and I moan at the exquisite stretching sensation, my body adjusting to being filled and penetrated by his thick length.

It feels like the sweetest of reliefs, the pleasure-pain of his possession acute and achingly familiar all at once. As I watch him, drinking in the look of tormented pleasure on his face, it suddenly dawns on me that this could just as easily not be happening—that instead of lying underneath me, Julian could be six feet underground, his powerful body mangled and destroyed.

I am not cognizant of having made any sounds, but I must have, because Julian's eye narrows, his hand tightening on my hip. "What is it, baby?" he asks sharply, and I realize that I've begun to shake, chills wracking my body at the image of him lying there cold and broken. My desire evaporates, replaced by remembered terror and dread. It's as if I've been doused with ice water, the horror of what we've been through bubbling up and choking me from within.

"Nora, what is it?" Julian's hand slides up to my throat, gripping the nape of my neck to bring my face closer to his. His eye bores into me as my hands clutch convulsively at the sheets on each side of his chest. "What is it? Tell me!"

I want to explain, but I can't speak, my throat closing up as my heartbeat spikes, cold sweat drenching my body. All of a sudden, I can't breathe, toxic panic clawing at my chest and constricting my lungs, and I begin to hyperventilate as black dots encroach on the edges of my vision.

"Nora!" Julian's voice reaches me as if from afar. "Fuck . . . Nora!"

A stinging blow across my face snaps my head to the side, and I gasp, my hand flying up to cradle my left cheek. The shock of pain startles me out of my panic, and my lungs finally begin working, my chest expanding to let in much-needed air. Panting, I turn my head to stare incredulously at Julian, the darkness in my mind receding as reality pushes back in.

"Nora, baby . . ." He's gently rubbing my cheek now, soothing the pain he inflicted. "I'm so sorry, my pet. I didn't want to slap you, but you looked like you were having a panic attack. What happened? Do you want me to call for a nurse?"

"No—" My voice breaks as sobs rise up, bursting out of my throat. Tears begin to flow down my face as I realize that I completely freaked out—and that it happened during sex. Julian's cock is still buried inside me, only slightly softer than before, and yet I am shaking and crying, like a crazy person. "No," I repeat in a choked voice. "I'm all right . . . Really, I'll be fine . . ."

"Yes, you will be." His voice takes on a hard, commanding tone as his hand moves down to grip my throat. "Look at me, Nora. Now."

Unable to do anything else, I obey, meeting his gaze with my own. His eye glitters a bright, fierce blue. As I look at him, my breathing begins to slow, my sobs easing and my desperate panic fading. I am still crying, but silently now, more as a reflex than anything else.

"Okay, good," Julian says in that same harsh tone. "Now you're going to ride me—and you will not think of whatever got you so upset. Do you understand me?"

I nod, his instructions calming me further. As my anxiety melts away, other sensations start to creep in. I become aware of the clean, familiar scent of his body, the crisp feel of his leg hair pressing against my calves . . .

The way his cock feels inside me, warm, thick, and hard.

My body responds again, further distracting me from my panic. Taking a deep breath, I begin to move, rising up and then lowering myself onto his shaft, my core growing wet and soft as pleasure starts to curl low in my belly.

"Yes, just like that, baby," Julian murmurs, his hand sliding down my body to press against my clit, intensifying the tension growing inside me. "Fuck me. Ride me. Use me to forget your demons."

"Yes," I whisper. "I will." And keeping my eyes on his face, I pick up the pace, letting the physical pleasure carry me away from all the darkness, the inferno of our passion burning away the memories of icy horror within.

When we come, it's within seconds of each other, our bodies as attuned to each other as our souls.

* * *

That evening I go to sleep in Julian's bed, not my own. The doctors okayed it after cautioning me not to jostle his ribs or face during the night.

I lie on his right, my head pillowed on his uninjured shoulder. I should be asleep, but I'm not. My mind is buzzing, humming like a beehive. A million thoughts are running through my head, my emotions oscillating from elation to sadness.

We're both alive and more or less intact. We're together again, having both survived against all odds. I no longer have any doubts that in some fucked-up way, we're meant to be. For better or worse, we fit each other now, our twisted, damaged parts locking together like a jigsaw puzzle.

I have no idea what the future holds, whether things can ever truly be all right again. I still need to convince Julian to honor my promise to Peter—and I need to ask the doctors for a morning-after pill, given the fact that neither one of us remembered to use protection earlier today. I don't know if it's possible to get pregnant so quickly after losing the implant, but it's not a risk I'm willing to take. The possibility of a child—of a helpless baby subjected to our kind of life— horrifies me now more than ever.

Maybe I will change my mind with time. Maybe in a few years, I will feel differently. Less scared. For now, though, I am sharply cognizant of the fact that our life will never be a fairy tale. Julian is not a good man—and I'm no longer a good woman.

That should worry me . . . and maybe tomorrow it will. At this moment, however, feeling his warmth surrounding me, I am only aware of a deepening sense of peace, of a certainty that this is right.

That this is where I belong.

Raising my hand, I trace my fingers across his half-healed lips, feeling the sensual shape of them in the darkness.

"Will you ever let me go?" I murmur, remembering our long-ago conversation.

His lips twitch in a faint smile. He remembers too. "No," he replies softly. "Never."

We lie in silence for a few moments, and then he asks quietly, "Do you want me to let you go?"

"No, Julian." I close my eyes, a smile curving my own lips. "Never."

Hold Me

Twist Me: Book 3

PART I: THE RETURN

CHAPTER ONE

❖ JULIAN ❖

A gasping cry wakes me up, dragging me out of restless sleep. My uninjured eye flies open on a rush of adrenaline, and I jackknife to a sitting position, the sudden movement causing my cracked ribs to scream in protest. The cast on my left arm bangs into the heart-rate monitor next to the bed, and the wave of agony is so intense that the room spins around me in a sickening swirl. My pulse is pounding, and it takes a moment to realize what woke me.

Nora.

She must be in the grip of another nightmare.

My body, coiled for combat, relaxes slightly. There's no danger, nobody coming after us right now. I'm lying next to Nora in my luxurious hospital bed, and we're both safe, the clinic in Switzerland as secure as Lucas can make it.

The pain in my ribs and arm is better now, more tolerable. Moving more carefully, I place my right hand on Nora's shoulder and try to gently shake her awake. She's turned away from me, facing in the opposite direction, so I can't see her face to check if she's crying. Her skin, however, is cold and damp from sweat. She must've been having the nightmare for a while. She's also shivering.

"Wake up, baby," I murmur, stroking her slender arm. I can see the light filtering through the blinds on the window, and I know it must be morning. "It's just a dream. Wake up, my pet . . ."

She stiffens under my touch, and I know she's not fully awake, the nightmare still holding her captive. Her breathing is coming in audible, gasping bursts, and I can feel the tremors running through her body. Her distress claws at me, hurting me worse than any injury, and the knowledge that I'm again responsible for this—that I failed to keep her safe—makes my insides burn with acidic fury.

Fury at myself and at Peter Sokolov—the man who allowed Nora to risk her life to rescue me.

Before my cursed trip to Tajikistan, she had been slowly getting over Beth's death, her nightmares becoming less frequent as the months wore on. Now, however, the bad dreams are back—and Nora is worse off than before, judging by the panic attack she had during sex yesterday.

I want to kill Peter for this—and I might, if he ever crosses my path again. The Russian saved my life, but he endangered Nora's in the process, and that's not something I will ever forgive. And his fucking list of names? Forget it. There is no way I'm going to reward him for betraying me like this, no matter what Nora promised him.

"Come on, baby, wake up," I urge her again, using my right arm to lower myself back down on the bed. My ribs ache at the movement, but less fiercely this time. I carefully shift closer to Nora, pressing my body against hers from the back. "You're okay. It's all over, I promise."

She draws in a deep, hiccuping breath, and I feel the tension within her easing as she realizes where she is. "Julian?" she whispers, turning around to face me, and I see that she's been crying after all, her cheeks coated with moisture from her tears.

"Yes. You're safe now. Everything is fine." I reach over with my right hand and trail my fingers over her jaw, marveling at the fragile beauty of her facial structure. My hand looks huge and rough against her delicate face, my nails ragged and bruised from the needles Majid used on me. The contrast between us is glaring—though Nora is not entirely unscathed either. The purity of her golden skin is marred by a bruise on the left side of her face, where those Al-Quadar motherfuckers hit her to knock her out.

If they weren't already dead, I would've ripped them apart with my bare hands for hurting her.

"What did you dream about?" I ask softly. "Was it Beth?"

"No." She shakes her head, and I see that her breathing is beginning to return to normal. Her voice, however, still holds echoes of horror as she says hoarsely, "It was you this time. Majid was cutting out your eyes, and I couldn't stop him."

I try not to react, but it's impossible. Her words hurl me back to that cold, windowless room, to the nauseating sensations I've been trying to forget for the past several days. My head begins to throb with remembered agony, my half-healed eye socket burning with emptiness once again. I feel blood and other fluids dripping down my face, and my stomach heaves at the recollection. I'm no stranger to pain, or even to torture—my father believed that his son should be able to withstand anything—but losing my eye had been by far the most excruciating experience of my life.

Physically, at least.

Emotionally, Nora's appearance in that room probably holds that honor.

It takes all of my willpower to wrench my thoughts back to the present, away from the mind-numbing terror of seeing her dragged in by Majid's men.

"You did stop him, Nora." It kills me to admit this, but if it weren't for her bravery, I would probably be decomposing in some dumpster in Tajikistan. "You came for me, and you saved me."

I still have trouble believing that she did that—that she voluntarily placed herself in the hands of psychotic terrorists to save my life. She didn't do it out of some naïve conviction that they wouldn't harm her. No, my pet knew exactly what they were capable of, and she still had the courage to act.

I owe my life to the girl I abducted, and I don't quite know how to deal with that.

"Why did you do it?" I ask, stroking the edge of her lower lip with my thumb. Deep down, I know, but I want to hear her admit it.

She gazes at me, her eyes filled with shadows from her dream. "Because I can't survive without you," she says quietly. "You know that, Julian. You wanted me to love you, and I do. I love you so much I would walk through hell for you."

I take in her words with greedy, shameless pleasure. I can't get enough of her love. I can't get enough of her. I wanted her initially because of her resemblance to Maria, but my childhood friend had never evoked even a fraction of the emotions Nora makes me feel. My affection for Maria had been innocent and pure, just like Maria herself.

My obsession with Nora is anything but.

"Listen to me, my pet . . ." My hand leaves her face to rest on her shoulder. "I need you to promise me that you will never do something like that again. I'm obviously glad to be alive, but I would sooner have died than had you in that kind of danger. You are *never* to risk your life for me again. Do you understand me?"

The nod she gives me is faint, almost imperceptible, and I see a mutinous gleam in her eyes. She doesn't want to make me mad, so she's not disagreeing, but I have a strong suspicion she's going to do what she thinks is right regardless of what she says right now.

This obviously calls for more heavy-handed measures.

"Good," I say silkily. "Because next time—if there is ever a next time—I will kill anyone who helps you against my orders, and I will do it slowly and painfully. Do you understand me, Nora? If anyone so much as endangers a hair on your head, whether it's to save *me* or for any other reason, that person will die a very unpleasant death. Do I make myself clear?"

"Yes." She looks pale now, her lips pressed together as if to contain a protest. She's angry with me, but she's also scared. Not for herself— she's beyond that fear now—but for others. My pet knows I mean what I say.

She knows I'm a conscienceless killer with only one weakness.

Her.

Gripping her shoulder tighter, I lean forward and kiss her closed mouth. Her lips are stiff for a moment, resisting me, but as I slide my hand under her neck and cup her nape, she exhales and her lips soften, letting me in. The surge of heat in my body is strong and immediate, her taste causing my cock to harden uncontrollably.

"Um, excuse me, Mr. Esguerra . . ." The sound of a woman's voice is accompanied by a timid knock on the door, and I realize it's the nurses making their morning rounds.

Fuck. I'm tempted to ignore them, but I have a feeling they'll just come back again in a bit—possibly when I'm balls-deep inside Nora's tight pussy.

Reluctantly releasing Nora, I roll over onto my back, sucking in my breath at the jolt of pain, and watch as Nora jumps off the bed and hurriedly pulls on a robe.

"Do you want me to open the door for them?" she asks, and I nod, resigned. The nurses have to change my bandages and make sure I'm well enough to travel today, and I have every intention of cooperating with their plans.

The sooner they're done, the faster I can get out of this fucking hospital.

As soon as Nora opens the door, two female nurses come in, accompanied by David Goldberg—a short, balding man who's my personal doctor at the estate. He's an excellent trauma surgeon, so I had him oversee the repairs on my face, to make sure the plastic surgeons at the clinic didn't fuck anything up.

I don't want to repel Nora with my scars if I can help it.

"The plane is already waiting," Goldberg says as the nurses begin to unwrap the bandages on my head. "If there are no signs of infection, we should be able to head home."

"Excellent." I lie still, ignoring the pain resulting from the nurses' ministrations. In the meantime, Nora grabs some clothes from the closet and disappears into the bathroom that adjoins our room. I hear the water running and realize she must've decided to use this time to take a shower. It's probably her way of avoiding me for a bit, since she's still upset over my threat. My pet is sensitive to violence being doled out to those she views as innocent—like that stupid boy Jake she kissed the night I took her.

I still want to rip out his insides for touching her . . . and someday I probably will.

"No sign of infection," Goldberg tells me when the nurses are done removing the bandages. "You're healing well."

"Good." I take slow, deep breaths to control the pain as the two nurses clean the sutures and rebind my ribs. I've been taking half of my prescribed dose of painkillers for the past two days, and I'm definitely feeling it. In another couple of days, I'll go off the painkillers completely to avoid becoming dependent on them.

One addiction is plenty for anyone.

As the nurses are wrapping up, Nora comes out of the bathroom, freshly showered and dressed in a pair of jeans and a short-sleeved blouse. "All clear?" she asks, glancing at Goldberg.

"He's good to go," he replies, giving her a warm smile. I think he likes her—which is fine with me, given his homosexual orientation. "How are you feeling?"

"I'm fine, thanks." She lifts her arm to show a large Band-Aid over the area where the terrorists cut out her birth control implant by mistake. "I'll be happy when the stitches are out, but it doesn't bother me much."

"Great, glad to hear it." Turning toward me, Goldberg asks, "When should we plan to head out?"

"Have Lucas get the car ready in twenty minutes," I tell him, carefully swinging my feet to the floor as the nurses exit the room. "I'll get dressed, and we'll go."

"Will do," Goldberg says, turning to leave the room.

"Wait, Dr. Goldberg, I'll walk out with you," Nora says quickly, and there's something in her voice that catches my attention. "I need something from downstairs," she explains.

Goldberg looks surprised. "Oh, sure."

"What is it, my pet?" I stand up, ignoring my nakedness. Goldberg politely averts his eyes as I catch Nora's arm, preventing her from walking out. "What do you need?"

She looks uncomfortable, her gaze shifting to the side.

"What is it, Nora?" I demand, my curiosity piqued. My grip on her arm tightens as I pull her closer.

She looks up at me. Her cheeks are tinged with color, and there is a defiant set to her jaw. "I need the morning-after pill, okay? I want to make sure I get it before we leave."

"Oh." My mind goes blank for a second. Somehow I hadn't thought about the fact that with her implant gone, Nora can get pregnant. I've had her in my bed for almost two years, and during that entire time, she's been protected by the implant. I'm so used to that, it hadn't even occurred to me that we need to take precautions now.

But it had clearly occurred to Nora.

"You want the morning-after pill?" I repeat slowly, still trying to process the idea that Nora—my Nora—could be pregnant.

Pregnant with my child.

A child that she clearly doesn't want.

"Yes." Her dark eyes are huge in her face as she stares up at me. "It's unlikely from just one time, of course, but I don't want to risk it."

She doesn't want to risk being pregnant with my child. My chest feels oddly tight as I look at her, seeing the fear she's trying so hard to conceal. She's worried about my reaction to this, afraid I'll prevent her from taking this pill.

Afraid I'll force an unwanted child on her.

"I'll be right outside," Goldberg says, apparently sensing the rising tension in the room, and before I can say a word, he slips out the door, leaving us alone.

Nora lifts her chin, meeting my gaze head on. I can see the determination on her face as she says, "Julian, I know we never talked about this, but—"

"But you're not ready," I interrupt, the tightness in my chest intensifying. "You don't want a baby right now."

She nods, her eyes wide. "Right," she says warily. "I'm not even done with school yet, and you've been injured—"

"And you're not sure if you want to have a child with a man like me."

She swallows nervously, but doesn't deny it or look away. Her silence is damning, and the tightness in my chest morphs into a strange aching pain.

Releasing her arm, I step back. "You can tell Goldberg to get you the pill and whatever birth control he thinks is best." My voice sounds unusually cold and distant. "I'll wash up and get dressed."

And before she can say anything else, I go into the bathroom and close the door.

I don't want to see the look of relief on her face.

I don't want to think about how that would feel.

CHAPTER TWO

❖ NORA ❖

Stunned, I watch Julian's naked form disappear into the bathroom. He's hampered by his injuries, his movements stiffer than usual. Still, there is a certain grace to the way he walks. Even after his hellish ordeal, his muscular body is strong and athletic, the white bandage around his ribs emphasizing the width of his shoulders and the bronzed hue of his skin.

He didn't object to the morning-after pill.

As that fact sinks in, my knees go weak with relief, the adrenaline-induced tension draining out in a sudden whoosh. I had been almost certain he would deny me this; the expression on his face as we spoke had been shuttered, unreadable . . . dangerous in its opaqueness. He had seen right through my flimsy excuses about my school and his injuries, his undamaged eye gleaming with a cold blue light that made my stomach knot in dread.

But he didn't deny me the pill. On the contrary, he suggested I get a new method of birth control from Dr. Goldberg.

I feel almost light-headed with joy. Julian must be on board with the no-kids bit, his strange reaction notwithstanding.

Not wanting to question my good fortune, I hurry out of the room to grab Dr. Goldberg. I want to make sure I get what I need before we leave the clinic.

Birth control implants aren't easy to come by in our jungle compound.

* * *

"I took the pill," I tell Julian when we're comfortably ensconced on his private jet—the same plane that took us from Chicago to Colombia after Julian returned for me in December. "And I got this." I raise my right arm to show him a tiny bandage where the new implant went in. My arm aches dully, but I'm so happy to have the implant that I don't mind the discomfort.

Julian looks up from his laptop, his expression still closed off. "Good," he says curtly, and resumes working on the email to one of his engineers. He's outlining the exact specifications of a new drone he wants designed. I know this because I asked him about it a few minutes ago, and he explained what he's doing. He's been much more open with me in the past couple of months—which is why I find it odd that he seems to want to avoid the topic of birth control.

I wonder if he doesn't want to discuss it because of Dr. Goldberg's presence. The short man is sitting at the front of the jet, more than a dozen feet from us, but we don't have total privacy. Either way, I decide to let it go for now and bring it up again at a more opportune moment.

As the plane ascends, I entertain myself by watching the Swiss Alps until we get above the clouds. Then I lean back and wait for the beautiful flight attendant—Isabella—to come around with our breakfast. We left the hospital so quickly this morning that I only managed to grab a cup of coffee.

Isabella comes into the cabin a few minutes later, her bombshell body squeezed into a tight red dress. She's holding a tray with coffee and a platter of pastries. Goldberg appears to have fallen asleep, so she heads toward us, her lips curved in a seductive smile.

The first time I saw her, when Julian came back for me in December, I was insanely jealous. Since then I've learned that Isabella has never had a relationship with Julian and is actually married to one of the guards at the estate—two facts that have gone a long way toward soothing the green-eyed monster within me. I've only seen the woman once or twice in the past couple of months; unlike most of Julian's employees, she spends the majority of her time outside the compound, working as his eyes and ears at several high-end private jet companies.

"You'd be surprised how loose-lipped people get after a couple of drinks at thirty thousand feet," Julian explained once. "Executives, politicians, cartel bosses . . . They all like having Isabella around, and they don't always watch what they say in her presence. Thanks to her, I've gotten everything from insider trading tips to intel about drug deals in the area."

So yeah, I'm no longer quite as jealous of Isabella, but I still can't help feeling that her manner with Julian is a little too flirtatious for a married woman. Then again, I'm probably not the best judge of appropriate married-woman behavior. If I were to stare at any man longer than a second, I would be signing his death warrant.

Julian takes possessiveness to a whole new level.

"Would you like some coffee?" Isabella asks, stopping next to his seat. She's more circumspect in her staring today, but I still feel the urge to slap her pretty face for the come-hither smile she gives my husband.

Okay, so Julian is not the only one with possessiveness issues. As messed up as it is, I feel proprietary about the man who abducted me. It makes no sense, but I gave up trying to make sense of my crazy relationship with Julian a long time ago.

It's easier to just accept it.

At Isabella's question, Julian looks up from his laptop. "Sure," he says before glancing in my direction. "Nora?"

"Yes, please," I say politely. "And a couple of those croissants."

Isabella pours us each a cup, sets the pastry platter on my table, and sashays back to the front of the plane, her lushly curved hips swaying from side to side. I experience a moment of envy before reminding myself that Julian wants *me*.

He wants me too much, in fact, but that's a whole other issue.

For the next half hour, I read quietly as I eat my croissants and sip my coffee. Julian appears to be concentrating on his drone design email, so I don't bother him; instead, I do my best to focus on my book, a sci-fi thriller I bought at the clinic. My attention, however, keeps wandering, my thoughts straying every couple of pages.

It feels odd to be sitting here reading. Surreal, in a way. It's as if nothing had happened. As if we hadn't just survived terror and torture.

As if I hadn't blown a man's brains out in cold blood.

As if I hadn't almost lost Julian again.

My heart starts beating faster, the images from this morning's nightmare invading my mind with startling clarity. *Blood ... Julian's body cut and mangled ... His beautiful face with vacant eye sockets ...* The book slips out of my shaking hands, falling to the floor as I attempt to suck in air through a suddenly constricted throat.

"Nora?" Strong, warm fingers close around my wrist, and through the panicked haze veiling my vision, I see Julian's bandaged face in front of me. He's gripping me tightly, his laptop forgotten on the table next to him. "Nora, can you hear me?"

I manage to nod, my tongue coming out to wet my lips. My mouth is dry with fear, and my blouse is sticking to my back from perspiration. My hands are clutching the edge of the seat, my nails digging into the soft leather. A part of me knows that my mind is playing tricks on me—that this extreme anxiety is unfounded—but my body is reacting as if the threat is real.

As if we're back at that construction site in Tajikistan, at the mercy of Majid and the other terrorists.

"Breathe, baby." Julian's voice is soothing as his hand comes up to gently cradle my jaw. "Breathe slowly, deeply ... There's a good girl ..."

I do as he says, keeping my eyes on his face as I take deep breaths to manage my panic. After a minute, my heartbeat slows, and my hands uncurl from the edge of my seat. I'm still shaking, but the suffocating fear is gone.

Feeling embarrassed, I wrap my fingers around Julian's palm and pull his hand away from my face. "I'm okay," I manage to say in a relatively steady voice. "I'm sorry. I don't know what came over me."

He stares at me, his eye glittering, and I see a mixture of rage and frustration in his gaze. His fingers are still gripping mine, as if reluctant to let go. "You're not okay, Nora," he says harshly. "You're anything but okay."

He's right. I don't want to admit it, but he's right. I haven't been okay since Julian left the estate to hunt down the terrorists. I've been a mess since his departure—and I seem to be even more of a mess now that he's back.

"I'm fine," I say, not wanting him to think me weak. Julian was tortured, and he seems to be handling it, whereas I'm falling apart for no good reason.

"Fine?" His eyebrows snap together. "In the past twenty-four hours, you've had two panic attacks and a nightmare. That's not fine, Nora."

I swallow and look down at my lap, where his hand is holding mine in a tight, possessive grip. I hate the fact that I can't just brush this stuff off, the way Julian seems to. Sure, he still has some nightmares about Maria, but this ordeal with the terrorists appears to have hardly fazed him. By all rights, he should be the one freaking out, not me. I was barely touched, whereas he'd undergone days of torment.

I'm weak, and I hate it.

"Nora, baby, listen to me."

I look up, drawn by the softer note in Julian's voice, and find myself captured by his gaze.

"This is not your fault," he says quietly. "Any of it. You've been through a lot, and you're traumatized. You don't need to pretend with me. If you start to panic, tell me, and I'll help you through it. Do you understand me?"

"Yes," I whisper, strangely relieved by his words. I know it's ironic that the man who brought all the darkness into my life is helping me cope with it, but it's been that way from the beginning.

I've always found solace in my captor's arms.

"Good. Remember that." He leans over to kiss me, and I meet him halfway, cognizant of his injured ribs. His lips are unusually tender as they touch mine, and I close my eyes, my remaining anxiety fading as heated need warms my core. My hands find themselves on the back of his neck, and a moan vibrates low in my throat as his tongue invades my mouth, his taste familiar and darkly seductive at the same time.

He groans as I kiss him back, my tongue curling around his. His right arm wraps around my back, bringing me closer to him, and I feel the growing tension in his powerful body. His breathing speeds up, and his kiss turns hard, devouring, making my body throb in response.

"Bedroom. Now." His words are more of a growl as he tears his mouth away and rises to his feet, dragging me up off my seat. Before I can say anything, he wraps his fingers around my wrist and marches me toward the back of the plane. I give mental thanks that Dr. Goldberg is sound asleep and Isabella went back to the front of the plane; nobody's there to see Julian dragging me off to bed.

As we enter the small room, he kicks the door shut behind us and pulls me toward the bed. Even injured, he's incredibly strong. His strength both arouses and intimidates me. Not because I'm afraid he'll hurt me—I know he will, and I know I'll enjoy it—but because I've seen what he can do.

I've seen him kill a man with nothing more than a leg of a chair.

The memory should disgust me, but somehow it's exciting as well as scary. Then again, Julian is not the only one who's taken a life this week.

We're both killers now.

"Strip," he commands, stopping a couple of feet from the bed and releasing my wrist. The sleeves of his button-down shirt are ripped out to accommodate the cast on his left arm, and with the bandage across his face, he looks wounded and dangerous at the same time—like a modern-day pirate after a raid. His right arm is bulging with muscle, and his uncovered eye is startlingly blue in his tanned face.

I love him so much it hurts.

Taking a step back, I begin to undress. My blouse is first, followed by my jeans. When I'm wearing only a white thong and a matching bra, Julian says hoarsely, "Climb on the bed. I want you on all fours, with your ass toward me."

Heat slithers down my spine, intensifying the growing ache between my legs. Turning, I do as he says, my heart pounding with nervous anticipation. I remember the last time we had sex on this plane—and the bruises that decorated my thighs for days afterwards. I know Julian is not well enough for anything that strenuous, but that knowledge doesn't diminish my trepidation or my hunger.

With my husband, fear and desire go hand in hand.

When I'm positioned to Julian's satisfaction, with my ass at the height of his groin, he steps closer to me and hooks his fingers in the waistband of my underwear, pulling it down to my knees. I quiver at his touch, my sex clenching, and he groans, his hand trailing up my thigh to delve between my folds. "Your pussy is so fucking wet," he whispers roughly as he pushes two large fingers into me. "So wet for me, and so tight... You want this, don't you, baby? You want me to take you, to fuck you..."

I gasp as he curls those fingers, hitting a spot that makes my whole body go taut. "Yes...." I can barely speak as waves of heat wash over me, clouding my mind. "Yes, please..."

He chuckles, the sound low and filled with dark delight. His fingers withdraw, leaving me empty and pulsing with need. Before I can object, I hear the sound of a zipper being pulled down and feel the smooth, broad head of his cock brushing against my thighs.

"Oh, I will," he murmurs thickly, guiding himself toward my opening. "I will please you so fucking well"—the tip of his cock penetrates me, making my breath catch in my throat—"you'll scream for me. Won't you, baby?"

And not waiting for my response, he grips my right hip and pushes in all the way, startling a gasping cry out of my throat. As always, his entry batters my senses, his thickness stretching me nearly to the point of pain. If I hadn't been so turned on, he would've hurt me. As it is, his roughness only adds a delicious edge, intensifying my arousal and inundating my sex with more moisture. With my underwear down around my knees, I can't open my legs any wider, and he feels enormous inside me, every inch of him hard and burning hot.

I expect him to set a brutal pace to match that first thrust, but now that he's in, he moves slowly. Slowly and deliberately, his every movement calculated to maximize my pleasure. *In and out, in and out* . . . It feels like he's stroking me from the inside, teasing out every bit of sensation my body is capable of producing. *In and out, in and out* . . . I'm close to orgasm, but I can't get there, not with him moving at this snail's pace. *In and out* . . .

"Julian," I groan, and he slows his pace even more, causing me to whimper in frustration.

"Tell me what you want, baby," he murmurs, withdrawing almost all the way. "Tell me exactly what you want."

"Fuck me," I breathe out, my hands fisting in the sheets. "Please, just make me come."

He chuckles again, but the sound is strained, his breathing turning heavy and uneven. I feel his cock thickening further inside me, and I squeeze my inner muscles around it, willing him to move just a little faster, to give me that extra bit I need . . .

And he finally does.

Holding my hip, he picks up the pace, fucking me harder and faster. His thrusts reverberate through me, sending shockwaves of pleasure radiating out from my core. My hands clutch at the sheets, my cries growing in volume as the tension inside me becomes unbearable, intolerable . . . and then I splinter into a million pieces, my body pulsing helplessly around his massive shaft. He groans, his fingers digging into my flesh as his grip on my hip tightens, and I feel him grinding against my ass, his cock jerking inside me as he finds his release.

When it's all over, he withdraws from me and takes a step back. Shaking from the intensity of my orgasm, I collapse onto my side and turn my head to look at him.

He's standing there with his jeans unzipped, his chest rising and falling with heavy breaths. His gaze is filled with lingering desire as he stares at me, his eye glued to my thighs, where his seed is slowly leaking out of my opening.

I flush and glance around the room, searching for a tissue. Thankfully, there is a box on a shelf near the bed. I reach for it and use a tissue to wipe away the evidence of our joining.

Julian observes my actions silently. Then he steps back, his expression growing shuttered again as he tucks his softening cock back inside his jeans and pulls up the zipper.

Grabbing the blanket, I draw it up to cover my naked body. I feel cold and exposed all of a sudden, the heat inside me dissipating. Normally, Julian would hold me after sex, reinforcing our closeness and using tenderness to balance out the roughness. Today, however, he doesn't seem inclined to do that.

"Is everything okay?" I ask hesitantly. "Did I do something wrong?"

He gives me a cool smile and sits down on the bed next to me. "What could you have done wrong, my pet?" Looking at me, he lifts his hand and picks up a lock of my hair, rubbing it between his fingers. Despite the playfulness of his gesture, there is a hard gleam in his eye that deepens my unease.

I experience a sudden flash of intuition. "It's the morning-after pill, isn't it? Are you upset because I took it?"

"Upset? Because you don't want a child with me?" He laughs, but there is a harshness to the sound that twists my stomach into knots. "No, my pet, I'm not upset. I would make an awful father, and I know it."

I stare at him, trying to understand why his words are making me feel guilty. He's a killer and a sadist, a man who ruthlessly abducted me and kept me captive, and yet I feel bad—as if I inadvertently hurt him.

As if I truly did something wrong.

"Julian . . ." I don't know what to say. I can't lie that he would make a good father. He would see right through me. So instead I ask cautiously, "Do you *want* to have children?"

Then I hold my breath, waiting for his answer.

He looks at me, his expression unreadable once more. "No, Nora," he says quietly. "The last thing you and I need are children. You can have all the birth control implants you want. I won't force you to get pregnant."

I exhale in sharp relief. "Okay, good. So then why—"

Before I can conclude the question, Julian rises to his feet, signaling an end to our discussion. "I'll be in the main cabin," he says evenly. "I have some work to do. Come join me when you get dressed."

And with that, he disappears from the room, leaving me lying in bed naked and confused.

CHAPTER THREE

❖ JULIAN ❖

I'm in the middle of reviewing my portfolio manager's write-up on a potential investment when Nora quietly takes her seat next to me. Unable to resist the lure of her presence, I turn to look at her, watching as she begins reading her book.

Now that I've had a few minutes apart from her, the irrational need to lash out and hurt her is gone. In its place is an inexplicable sadness . . . an odd and unexpected sense of loss.

I don't understand this. I didn't lie to Nora when I said I don't want children. I've never given the subject much thought, but now that I'm considering it, I can't even imagine being a father. What would I do with a child? It would be just one more weakness for my enemies to exploit. I have no interest in babies, nor do I know how to raise them. My parents certainly weren't role models in that regard. I should've been glad that Nora doesn't want kids, but instead, when she brought up the morning-after pill, it felt like a kick to the gut.

Like a rejection of the worst kind.

I had been trying not to think about it, but seeing her wipe my seed off her thighs brought back those unwelcome emotions, reminded me that she doesn't want this from me.

That she'll never want this from me.

I don't understand why that matters. I never planned to start a family with Nora. Marriage had been a way to cement our bond, nothing more. She's my pet . . . my obsession and my possession. She loves me because I've made her love me, and I want her because she's necessary to my existence. Children are not a part of this dynamic.

They can't be.

Catching me looking at her, Nora gives me a tentative smile. "What are you working on?" she asks, placing her book face down on her lap. "Still the drone design?"

"No, baby." I force myself to focus on the fact that she came for me in Tajikistan—that she loves me enough to do something so insane—and my mood begins to lift, the lingering tightness in my chest fading.

"What is it then?" she persists, and I smile involuntarily, amused by her inquisitiveness. Nora is no longer content to be on the fringes of my life; she wants to know everything, and she's growing bolder in her quest for answers.

If this were anyone else, I'd be annoyed. With Nora, however, I don't mind. I enjoy her curiosity. "I'm going over a prospective investment," I explain.

She looks intrigued, so I tell her that I'm reading about a biotech startup that specializes in brain chemistry drugs. If I decide to proceed, I would be a so-called angel investor—one of the first to fund the company. Venture capital is something that's always interested me; I like to stay on top of innovation in all kinds of fields and profit from it to the best of my ability.

She listens to my explanation with evident fascination, those dark eyes of hers focused on my face the entire time. I like it, the way she absorbs knowledge like a sponge. It makes it fun for me to teach her, to show her different parts of my world. The few questions she asks are insightful, showing me that she understands exactly what I'm talking about.

"If that drug can erase memories, couldn't it be used to treat PTSD and such?" she asks after I describe to her one of the startup's more promising products, and I agree, having arrived at the same conclusion just minutes earlier.

I hadn't anticipated this when I kidnapped her—the sheer enjoyment I would get out of spending time with her. When I first took her, I saw her solely as a sexual object, a beautiful girl who obsessed me so much I couldn't get her out of my thoughts. I didn't expect her to become my companion as well as my bedmate, didn't realize I would enjoy simply *being* with her.

I didn't know she would come to own me as much as I own her.

It really is for the best that she remembered to take the pill. Once we're both healed, our life can go back to normal.

Our normal, at least.

I will have Nora with me, and I won't let her out of my sight ever again.

* * *

It's dark when we land. I lead a sleepy Nora off the plane, and we get in the car to drive home.

Home. It's strange thinking of this place as home again. It was my home when I was a child, and I hated it. I hated everything about it, from the humid heat to the pungent smell of moist jungle vegetation. Yet when I got older, I found myself drawn to places just like this—to tropical locations that reminded me of the jungle where I grew up.

It took Nora's presence here to make me realize I didn't hate the estate after all. This place was never the object of my hatred—it was always the person it belonged to.

My father.

Nora nestles closer to me in the backseat, interrupting my musings, and yawns delicately into my shoulder. The sound is so kitten-like that I laugh and wrap my right arm around her waist, pulling her closer to me. "Sleepy?"

"Hmm-mm." She rubs her face against my neck. "You smell good," she mumbles.

And just like that, my cock turns rock-hard, reacting to the feel of her lips brushing against my skin.

Fuck. I blow out a frustrated breath as the car stops in front of the house. Ana and Rosa are standing on the front porch, ready to greet us, and my dick is bursting out of my pants. I shift to the side, trying to ease Nora away from me so my erection can subside. Her elbow brushes against my ribs, and I tense in pain, mentally cursing Majid to hell and back.

I can't fucking wait to heal. Even sex earlier today hurt, especially when I set a harder pace at the end. Not that it lessened the pleasure much—I'm pretty sure I could fuck Nora on my deathbed and enjoy it—but it still annoyed me. I like pain with sex, but only when I'm the one doling it out.

On the plus side, my erection is no longer quite as visible.

"We're there," I tell Nora as she rubs her eyes and yawns again. "I'd carry you over the threshold, but I'm afraid I might not make it this time."

She blinks, looking confused for a moment, but then a wide smile spreads across her face. She remembers too. "I'm no longer a new bride," she says, grinning. "So you're off the hook."

I grin back at her, unusual contentment filling my chest, and open the car door.

As soon as we climb out, we're attacked by two crying women. Or, more precisely, Nora is attacked. I just watch in bemusement as Ana and Rosa hug her, laughing and sobbing at the same time. After they're done with Nora, they turn toward me, and Ana sobs harder as she catches a glimpse of my bandaged face. "Oh, pobrecito . . ." She lapses into Spanish like she sometimes does when she's upset, and Nora and Rosa try to soothe her, saying that I'll recover, that the important thing is that I'm alive.

The housekeeper's concern is both touching and disconcerting. I've always been vaguely aware that the older woman cares about me, but I didn't realize her feelings are this strong. For as long as I can recall, Ana has been a warm, comforting presence at the estate— someone who fed me, cleaned after me, and bandaged my childhood scrapes and bruises. I've never let her get too close, though, and for the first time I feel a twinge of regret about that. Neither she nor Rosa, the maid who's Nora's friend, try to hug me like they did my wife. They think I wouldn't welcome it, and they're probably right.

The only person I want affection from—no, *crave* affection from— is Nora, and that's a recent development.

After the three women are done with their emotional reunion, we all head into the house. Despite the late hour, Nora and I are hungry, and we devour the meal Ana prepared for us with record speed. Then, replete and exhausted, we go upstairs to our bedroom.

A quick shower and an equally quick fuck later, I drift off to sleep with Nora's head pillowed on my uninjured shoulder.

I'm ready for our normal life to resume.

* * *

The scream that wakes me up is bloodcurdling. Full of desperation and terror, it bounces off the walls and floods my veins with adrenaline.

I'm on my feet and off the bed before I even realize what's happening. As the sound dies down, I grab the gun hidden in my nightstand and simultaneously hit the light switch with the back of my hand.

The nightstand lamp turns on, illuminating the room, and I see Nora huddled in the middle of the bed, shaking under the blanket.

There's no one else in the room, no visible threat.

My racing heartbeat begins to slow. We didn't get attacked. The scream must've come from Nora.

She's having yet another nightmare.

Fuck. The urge to do violence is almost too strong to be contained. It fills every cell of my body until I'm shaking with rage, with the need to kill and destroy every motherfucker responsible for this.

Starting potentially with myself.

Turning away, I draw in several deep breaths, trying to hold back the churning fury within me. There's no one I can lash out at here, no enemy I can crush to take the edge off my temper.

There's only Nora, who needs me to be calm and rational.

After a few seconds pass and I'm certain I won't hurt her, I turn back to face her and put the gun back into the nightstand drawer. Then I climb back on the bed. My ribs and shoulder ache dully, and my head throbs from my sudden movements, but that pain is nothing compared to the heaviness in my chest.

"Nora, baby . . ." Leaning over her, I pull the blanket off her naked body and place my right hand on her shoulder to shake her awake. "Wake up, my pet. It's just a dream." Her skin is clammy to the touch, and the whimpering noises she's making pain me more than any of Majid's torture. Fresh rage wells up, but I suppress it, keeping my voice low and even. "Wake up, baby. You're dreaming. It's not real."

She rolls over onto her back, still shaking, and I see that her eyes are open.

Open and unseeing as she gasps for air, her chest heaving and her hands clutching at the sheets in desperation.

She's not having a dream—she's in the middle of a full-blown panic attack, likely one caused by her nightmare.

I want to throw my head back and roar out my rage, but I don't. She needs me now, and I won't let her down.

Not ever again.

Rising to my knees, I straddle her hips and bend down to grasp her jaw in my right hand. "Nora, look at me." I make the words a command, my tone harsh and demanding. "Look at me, my pet. Now."

Despite her panic, she obeys, her conditioning too strong to be denied. Her eyes flick up to meet my gaze, and I see that her pupils are dilated, her irises nearly black. She's also hyperventilating, her mouth open as she tries to draw in enough air.

Fuck and double fuck. My first instinct is to hold her against me, to be gentle and calming, but I remember her panic attack during sex the night before and the way nothing seemed to help her then.

Nothing except violence.

So instead of murmuring useless endearments, I lean down, propping myself up on my right elbow, and take her mouth in a hard, brutal kiss, using my grip on her jaw to keep her still. My lips smash against hers, and my teeth sink into her lower lip as I roughly push my tongue inside, invading her, hurting her. The sadistic monster inside me thrills with delight at the metallic taste of her blood, while the rest of me aches at her mind's agony.

She gasps into my mouth, but the sound is different now, more startled than desperate. I can feel her chest expanding as she draws in a full breath, and I realize that my crude method of reaching her is working, that she's now focusing on the physical rather than the mental pain. Her fists uncurl, her hands no longer grasping at the sheets, and she stills underneath me, her body tensing with a different sort of fear.

A fear that arouses the darkest, most predatory part of me—the part that wants to subjugate and devour her.

The rage that still simmers within me adds to this hunger, mingling with it and feeding upon it until I become this need, this mindless, terrible craving. My focus narrows, sharpens, until all I'm aware of is the silky feel of her lips, flavored with blood, and the curves of her naked body, small and helpless underneath mine. My cock stiffens to a painful hardness as she grabs my right forearm with both of her hands and makes a soft, agonized sound in the back of her throat.

Suddenly, the kiss is no longer enough. I have to have all of her.

Letting go of her jaw, I push myself up with one arm, rising onto my knees. She stares up at me, her lips swollen and tinged with red. She's still panting, her chest rising and falling in rapid tempo, but the unseeing look in her eyes is gone. She's with me—she's fully present—and that's all my inner demon requires at the moment.

I climb off her in one swift motion, ignoring the pang of pain in my ribs, and reach into the bedside drawer again. Only this time, instead of a gun, I pull out a braided leather flogger.

Nora's eyes widen. "Julian?" Her voice is breathless with remnants of her panic.

"Turn over." The words come out rough, betraying the violent need raging inside me. "Now."

She hesitates for a moment, then rolls over onto her stomach.

"On your knees."

She gets on all fours and turns her head to look at me, awaiting further instructions.

Such a well-trained pet. Her obedience heightens my lust, my desperate hunger to possess her. The position showcases her ass and exposes her pussy, causing my dick to swell up even more. I want to swallow her whole, lay claim to every inch of her. My muscles tense, and almost without thinking, I swing the flogger, letting the leather threads bite into the smooth skin of her buttocks.

She cries out, her eyes closing as her body stiffens, and the darkness inside me takes over, obliterating all remnants of rational thought. I watch, almost as if from a distance, as the flogger kisses her skin again and again, leaving pink marks and reddening streaks on her back, ass, and thighs. She flinches at the first few strokes, crying out in pain, but as I find a rhythm, her body begins to relax into the strokes, anticipating rather than resisting the sting. Her cries soften, and her pussy folds begin to glisten with moisture.

She's responding to the flogging as if to a sensual caress.

My balls tighten as I drop the flogger and crawl up behind her, looping my right forearm under her hips to drag her toward me. My cock presses against her entrance, and I groan as I feel her slick heat rubbing against the tip, coating it with creamy moisture. She moans, arching her back, and I push into her, forcing her flesh to engulf me, to take me in.

Her pussy is unbelievably tight, her inner muscles squeezing me like a fist. It doesn't matter how often I fuck her; each time, it's new in some way, the sensations sharper and richer than in my memory. I could stay inside her forever, feeling her softness, her moist heat. Except I can't—the primitive urge to move, to thrust into her, is too strong to be denied. My heartbeat drums loudly in my ears, my body pulsing with savage need.

I hold still for as long as I can, and then I begin to move, each thrust causing my groin to press against her pink, freshly flogged ass. She moans with every stroke, her body tightening around my invading cock, and the sensations build upon each other, intensifying to an unbearable degree. My skin prickles from my impending orgasm, and I begin to drive into her faster, harder, until I feel her contractions begin, her pussy rippling around me as she screams out my name.

It's the last straw. The orgasm I've been holding off overtakes me with explosive force, and I erupt deep inside her with a hoarse groan, stunning pleasure rocketing through my body. It's a bliss unlike any other—an ecstasy that goes far beyond physical satisfaction. It's something I've experienced only with Nora.

Will ever experience only with Nora.

Breathing heavily, I withdraw from her body, letting her collapse on the bed. Then I lower myself onto my right side and gather her against me, knowing she needs tenderness after brutality.

And in a way, I need it too. I need to comfort her, to soothe her. To bind her to me when she's at her most vulnerable, so I can ensure her love.

It might be cold-blooded, but I don't leave important things like that to chance.

She turns around to face me and buries her face in the crook of my neck, her shoulders shaking with quiet sobs. "Hold me, Julian," she whispers, and I do.

I will always hold her, no matter what.

PART II: THE HEALING

CHAPTER FOUR

❖ NORA ❖

"Julian, do you have a minute?"

Entering my husband's office, I walk over to his desk. He looks up to greet me, and I marvel yet again at the tremendous progress he's made in his recovery over the past six weeks.

His arm cast is gone now, as are all the bandages. Julian tackled healing the same way as he approaches any goal: with single-minded ruthlessness and determination. As soon as Dr. Goldberg approved removal of the cast, Julian dove headfirst into physical therapy, spending hours each day on exercises designed to restore mobility and function to the left side of his body. With his scars beginning to fade, there are days when I almost forget that he was so badly injured—that he had gone through hell and emerged relatively unscathed.

Even his eye implant doesn't seem jarring to me anymore. Our stay at the clinic in Switzerland and all the procedures cost Julian millions—I saw the bill in his inbox—but the doctors did a phenomenal job with his face. The implant matches Julian's real eye so perfectly that when he looks at me straight on, it's almost impossible to tell that it's fake. I have no idea how they managed to make it that exact shade of blue, but they did, right down to every striation and natural color variation. The fake pupil even shrinks in bright light and dilates when Julian is excited or aroused, thanks to a biofeedback device Julian wears as a watch. The watch measures his pulse and skin conductance and sends the information to the implant, allowing for the most natural-looking responses. The only thing the implant doesn't do is replicate normal eye motion ... or allow Julian to see from it.

"That part—the connection to the brain—will take a few more years," Julian told me a couple of weeks ago. "They're working on it now in a lab in Israel."

So yeah, the implant is remarkably lifelike. And Julian is learning to minimize the weirdness of only one eye moving by turning his entire head to look at something straight on—like the way he's looking at me now.

"What is it, my pet?" he asks, smiling. His beautiful lips are fully healed now, and the fading scars on his left cheek add a dangerous, yet appealing edge to his looks. It's as if a bit of his inner darkness is visible on his face now, but instead of repelling me, it draws me to him even more.

Probably because I need that darkness now—it's the only thing keeping me sane these days.

"Monsieur Bernard just told me that he has a friend who'd be interested in displaying my paintings," I say, trying to sound like world-class art instructors give me those kinds of news all the time. "He apparently owns an art gallery in Paris."

Julian's eyebrows rise. "Is that right?"

I nod, barely able to contain my excitement. "Yes, can you believe it? Monsieur Bernard sent him photos of my latest works, and the gallery owner said they're exactly what he's been looking for."

"That's wonderful, baby." Julian's smile widens, and he reaches over to pull me down into his lap. "I'm so proud of you."

"Thank you." I want to jump up and down, but I settle for looping my arms around his neck and planting an excited kiss on his mouth. Of course, as soon as our lips touch, Julian takes over the kiss, turning my spontaneous expression of gratitude into a prolonged sensual assault that leaves me breathless and dazed.

When he finally lets me come up for air, it takes me a second to remember how I ended up on his lap.

"I'm so proud of you," Julian repeats, his voice soft as he looks at me. I can feel the bulge of his erection, but he doesn't take it further. Instead, he gives me a warm smile and says, "I will have to thank Monsieur Bernard for taking those photos. If the gallery owner does end up displaying your work, perhaps we'll take a little trip to Paris."

"Really?" I gape at him. This is the first time Julian's indicated that we might not be staying on the estate all the time. And to go to Paris? I can hardly believe my ears.

He nods, still smiling. "Sure. Al-Quadar is no longer a threat. It's as safe as it's ever likely to be, so with sufficient security, I don't see why we can't visit Paris in a bit—especially if there's a compelling reason to do so."

I grin at him, trying not to think about how Al-Quadar stopped being a threat. Julian hasn't told me much about that operation, but the little I do know is enough. When our rescuers raided the construction site in Tajikistan, they uncovered a tremendous amount of valuable information. After our return to the estate, every person even remotely connected to the terrorist organization was eliminated, some quickly and others slowly and painfully. I don't know how many deaths took place in recent weeks, but I wouldn't be surprised if the body count is well into the triple digits.

The man who's holding me right now is responsible for what amounts to a mass slaughter—and I still love him with all my heart.

"A trip to Paris would be amazing," I say, pushing aside all thoughts of Al-Quadar. Instead, I focus on the mind-boggling possibility that my paintings might be displayed in an actual art gallery. *My* paintings. It's so hard to believe that I ask Julian cautiously, "You didn't tell Monsieur Bernard to do this, right? Or somehow bribe this friend of his?" Since Julian used his financial clout to get me into the highly selective online program at Stanford University, I wouldn't put anything past him.

"No, baby." Julian's smile broadens. "I didn't have anything to do with this, I promise. You have a genuine talent, and your instructor knows it."

I believe him, if only because Monsieur Bernard has been raving about my paintings in recent weeks. The darkness and complexity that he saw in my art early on is even more visible now. Painting is one of the ways I've been dealing with my nightmares and panic attacks. Sexual pain is another—but that's a whole other matter.

Not wanting to dwell on my fucked-up mental state, I jump off Julian's lap. "I'm going to tell my parents," I say brightly as I head for the door. "They'll be very excited."

"I'm sure they will be." And giving me one last smile, he turns his attention back to his computer screen.

* * *

My video chat with my parents takes close to an hour. As always, I have to spend a solid twenty minutes assuring my mom that I'm safe, that I'm still at the estate in Colombia, and that no one is coming after us. After I disappeared from the Chicago Ridge Mall, my parents have become convinced that Julian's enemies are everywhere, ready to strike at a moment's notice. If I don't call or email my parents daily nowadays, they go into complete panic mode.

Not that they think I'm safe with Julian, of course. In their minds, he's no different than the terrorists who kidnapped me. In fact, I think my dad believes Julian is worse—given that my husband stole me away not once, but twice.

"A gallery in Paris? Why, that's wonderful, honey!" my mom exclaims when I finally get around to sharing my news with her. "We're so happy for you!"

"Are you still focusing on your classes?" my dad asks, frowning. He's less enthusiastic about my painting. I think he's afraid I will abandon all thoughts of college and become a starving artist—a fear that's beyond illogical, given the circumstances. If there's one thing I don't need to worry about these days, it's money. Julian recently told me that he set up a trust fund in my name and also named me as the sole beneficiary in his will. This way, if anything happens to him, I'll still be taken care of—by which he means I'll have enough money to run a small country.

"Yes, Dad," I say patiently. "Don't worry—I'm still focusing on school. I told you, I'm just taking a lighter load this quarter. I'll make up for it by taking a couple of classes in the summer."

The lighter load is something Julian insisted on when we returned, and despite my initial objections, I'm glad he did. For some reason, everything feels harder this quarter. My papers take me forever to write, and studying for exams is exhausting. Even with the lighter load, I've been feeling overwhelmed, but that's not something I want to tell my parents. It's bad enough that Julian is worried.

So worried, in fact, that he brought a shrink to the estate for me.

"Are you sure, honey?" my mom asks, peering at me with concern. "Maybe you should take the summer off, relax for a couple of months. You look really tired."

Shit. I was hoping the dark circles under my eyes wouldn't be as noticeable on video.

"I'm fine, Mom," I say. "I just stayed up late studying and painting, that's all."

I also woke up in the middle of the night screaming and couldn't fall back asleep until Julian whipped and fucked me, but my parents don't need to know that. They wouldn't understand that pain is therapeutic for me now, that I've grown to need something I once dreaded.

That the cruel side of Julian is something I've wholeheartedly embraced.

As we wrap up the conversation, I remember something Julian promised me once: that he'd take me to visit my family when the danger from Al-Quadar subsided. My heart jumps in excitement at the thought, but I decide to keep quiet until I have a chance to ask Julian about it at dinner. For now, I just tell my parents that we'll speak again soon, and log off from the secure connection.

There are now two things I need to discuss with Julian tonight . . . and both will be somewhat tricky.

* * *

"A trip to Chicago?" Julian looks vaguely surprised when I bring it up. "But you saw your parents less than two months ago."

"Right, for all of one evening before Al-Quadar kidnapped me." I blow on my cream-of-mushroom soup before dipping my spoon into the hot liquid. "I was also worried sick about you, so I'm not sure that evening counts as quality time with my family."

Julian studies me for a second before murmuring, "All right. You may have a point." Then he starts eating his own soup while I stare at him, hardly able to believe he would agree so easily.

"So we'll go?" I want to make sure there's no misunderstanding.

He shrugs. "If you want. After your exams are over, I'll take you there. We'll have to beef up the security around your parents, of course, and take a few extra precautions, but it should be possible."

I begin to smile, but then I remember something he told me once. "Do you think our going there would put my parents in danger?" I ask, my stomach twisting with sudden nausea. "Could they become a target if you're seen as being in close contact with them?"

Julian gives me an even look. "It's a possibility. A remote possibility, but it's not completely out of the question. There was obviously much greater danger when the terrorists were out for blood, but I do have other enemies. None so determined—at least as far as I know—but there are plenty of individuals and organizations who'd love to get their hands on me."

"Right." I swallow a spoonful of soup and immediately regret it, as the creamy liquid makes me feel even more nauseated. "And you think they might use my parents as leverage?"

"It's unlikely, but I can't completely rule it out. This is why I've had the security detail on your family from the start. It's a precaution, nothing more—but it's a necessary precaution, in my opinion."

I take a deep breath, doing my best to ignore the churning in my belly. "So would our going to Chicago increase the danger to them or not?"

"I don't know, my pet." Julian looks faintly regretful. "My best guess is no, but there are no guarantees."

I pick up a glass and take a sip of water, trying to get rid of the sickeningly fatty taste of soup on my tongue. "What if I go by myself?" I suggest without much thought. "Then nobody will think you're in any way close to your in-laws."

Julian's face darkens in an instant. "By yourself?"

I nod, instinctively tensing at the shift in his mood. Even though I know Julian wouldn't harm me, I can't help being wary of his temper. I may be with him willingly now, but he still has absolute control over my life—just as he did when I was his captive on the island.

In all the ways that count, he's still my dangerous, amoral kidnapper.

"You're not going anywhere by yourself." Julian's voice is soft, but the look in his eyes is hard, like steel. "If you want me to take you to Chicago, I'll do it—but you're not stepping a foot off this estate without me. Do you understand me, Nora?"

"Yes." I take a few more sips of water, still feeling the aftertaste of soup in my throat. What the hell did Ana put in it this evening? Even the smell of it is unpleasant. "I understand." My words come out sounding calm rather than resentful—mostly because I'm feeling too sick to get angry at Julian's autocratic attitude. Downing the rest of my water, I say, "It was just a suggestion."

Julian stares at me for a few moments, then gives a minute nod. "All right."

Before he has a chance to say anything more, Ana walks into the room, carrying our next course—fish with rice and beans. Seeing my nearly untouched soup, she frowns. "You don't like the soup, Nora?"

"No, it's delicious," I lie. "I'm just not that hungry and wanted to save room for the main course."

Ana gives me a concerned look, but clears off our dishes without further comment. My appetite has been unpredictable since our return, so this is not the first time I've left a meal untouched. I haven't weighed myself, but I think I've lost at least a couple of pounds in recent weeks—which is not necessarily a good thing in my case.

Julian frowns also, but doesn't say anything as I start playing with the rice on my plate. I really, really don't want food right now, but I force myself to pick up a forkful and put it in my mouth. The rice also tastes too rich, but I determinedly chew and swallow, not wanting to have Julian focus on my lack of eating.

I have something more important to discuss with him.

As soon as Ana leaves the room, I put my fork down and look at my husband. "I got another message," I say quietly.

Julian's jaw tightens. "I know."

"You're monitoring my email now?" My stomach roils again, this time with a mix of nausea and anger. I guess I shouldn't be surprised, given the trackers still implanted in my body, but something about this casual invasion of privacy really upsets me.

"Of course." He doesn't look the least bit apologetic or remorseful. "I figured he might contact you again."

I inhale slowly, reminding myself that arguing about this is futile. "Then you know Peter won't leave us alone until you give him that list," I say, as calmly as I can manage. "Somehow he knows that you got it from Frank last week. His message said, 'It's time to remember your promise.' He won't go away, Julian."

"If he keeps harassing you via email, I'll make sure he goes away for good." Julian's tone hardens. "He knows better than to try to get to me through you."

"He saved your life and my life," I remind him for the dozenth time. "I know you're mad that he disobeyed your orders, but if he hadn't, you'd be dead."

"And you wouldn't be having these nightmares and panic attacks." Julian's sensuous lips flatten. "It's been six weeks, Nora, and you haven't gotten any better. You barely sleep, hardly eat, and I can't remember the last time you went for a run. He should've *never* put you in that kind of danger—"

"He did what was necessary!" Slapping my palms on the table, I rise to my feet, no longer able to sit still. "You think I'd be feeling better if you died? You think I wouldn't have nightmares if Majid mailed us your body in pieces? My fucked-up head is not Peter's fault, so stop blaming him for this mess! I promised him that list, and I want to give it to him!" By the time I get to the last sentence, I'm full-on yelling, too angry to care about Julian's temper.

He stares at me, his eyes narrowed. "Sit down, Nora." His voice is dangerously soft. "Now."

"Or what?" I challenge, feeling uncharacteristically reckless. "Or what, Julian?"

"Do you really want to go there, my pet?" he asks in that same soft tone. When I don't respond, he points at my chair. "Sit down and finish the meal Ana prepared for you."

I hold his gaze for a few more seconds, not wanting to give in, but then I lower myself back into my chair. The surge of defiant anger that came upon me so suddenly is gone, leaving me drained and wanting to cry. I hate the fact that Julian can win a fight so easily, that I'm still not fearless enough to test his limits.

Not over something as minor as finishing a meal, at least.

If I'm going to defy him, it will be over something that matters.

Dropping my gaze to my plate, I pick up my fork and spear a piece of fish, trying to ignore my growing queasiness. My stomach churns with every bite, but I persist until I finish nearly half of my portion. Julian, in the meantime, polishes off everything on his plate, his appetite obviously unaffected by our argument.

"Dessert? Tea? Coffee?" Ana asks when she comes back to clear off our plates, and I mutely shake my head, not wanting to prolong the ordeal of this tense meal.

"I'll pass too, thanks, Ana," Julian says politely. "Everything was wonderful, as usual."

Ana beams at him, clearly pleased. I've noticed that Julian has made it a point to praise her more often since our return—that in general, his manner toward her is slightly warmer these days. I don't know what caused the change, but I know Ana appreciates it. Rosa told me the housekeeper has been all but dancing on air in recent weeks.

As Ana begins clearing off the table, Julian gets up and walks around to offer me his arm. I loop my hand through the crook of his elbow, and we head upstairs in silence. As we walk, my heart starts beating faster and my queasiness intensifies.

Tonight's argument only confirms what I have known for a while: Julian is never going to see reason on the issue of Peter's list. If I'm to keep my promise, I will have to take matters into my own hands and brave the consequences of my husband's displeasure.

Even if the thought of that literally makes me sick.

CHAPTER FIVE

❖ JULIAN ❖

As soon we enter the bedroom, Nora excuses herself to freshen up.

She disappears into the bathroom, and I undress, enjoying the freedom of having both arms unencumbered by a cast. My left shoulder still aches during exercise, but I'm regaining my strength and range of motion. Even the loss of my eye doesn't bother me that much; the headaches and eye strain are lessening by the day, and I've learned to compensate for the blind spot to my left by turning my head more frequently.

All in all, I'm pretty much back to normal—but I can't say the same about Nora.

Every time I wake up to her screams, every time she starts hyperventilating out of nowhere, a toxic mixture of rage and guilt blankets my chest. I've never been prone to dwelling on the past, but I can't help wishing that I could somehow rewind the clock, undo the unintended consequences of my fucked-up choices.

That I could have Nora—my Nora—back.

She slips out of the bathroom a few minutes later, already showered and wearing a white fleece robe. Her smooth skin is glowing from the hot water, and her long, dark hair is piled haphazardly on top of her head, exposing her slender neck.

A neck that's beginning to look far too delicate, almost frail from her weight loss.

"Come here, baby," I murmur, patting the bed next to me. I had contemplated punishing her for her outburst at dinner, but all I want to do now is hold her. Well, fuck her and hold her, but the fucking can wait.

She walks toward me, and I reach for her as soon as she's within arm's length. She feels disturbingly light as I tug her down to my lap, the shadows under her eyes betraying her exhaustion.

She's completely worn out, and I don't know what to do. The therapist I brought to the estate three weeks ago appears to be useless, and Nora refuses to take the anti-anxiety meds the doctor prescribed for her. I could force her, of course, but I distrust those pills myself. The last thing I want is to get Nora hooked on them.

The only thing that seems to help her—temporarily, at least—is an emotional release achieved through sexual pain. It's something she requires now, something she begs for nearly every night.

My pet has become as addicted to receiving pain as I am to giving it—and that development both pleases and devastates me.

"You barely ate again," I say softly, settling her more comfortably on my knees. Reaching up, I free her hair from the clip holding it up, and watch the dark mass spill down her back in a thick, glossy stream. "Why, baby? Is there something wrong with Ana's cooking?"

"What? No—" she begins saying, but then she corrects herself. "Well, maybe. I just didn't like the soup today. It was too rich."

"I'll ask Ana not to make it in the future, then." I distinctly remember Nora eating the soup and loving it before, but I decide against reminding her of that. I don't care what she eats, as long as she stays healthy.

"Just please don't tell her that I complained." Nora's gaze fills with worry. "I wouldn't want her to be offended."

"Of course." A smile tugs at my lips. "I'll take your secret to the grave, I promise."

An answering smile appears on her face, lighting up her features, and I feel much of the lingering tension between us dissipating. "Thank you," she whispers, staring at me. Then, placing one small hand on my shoulder and another on the back of my neck, she closes her eyes and presses her soft lips to mine.

I inhale sharply, my body tightening with instant lust. Her breath is sweet and minty, her slight weight warm in my arms. I can feel her slender fingers on my skin, smell her delicate scent, and my spine prickles with growing hunger, my cock hardening against the curve of her ass.

This time, though, the hunger doesn't come with the need to hurt her. Instead, it's tinged with tenderness. The darker impulses are there, but they're overshadowed by my stark awareness of her fragility. Tonight, more than ever, I want to protect her, heal her from the wounds she should've never sustained. I want to be her hero, her savior.

For just one night, I want to be the husband of her dreams.

Closing my eyes, I focus on her taste, on the way her breathing changes as I deepen the kiss. The way her head falls back and her body melts against mine, her fingernails gently scratching at my scalp as her hand slides into my hair. She's my world, my everything, and I want her so much I ache with it.

She's still bundled in her fleecy robe, the material soft on my bare thighs and cock. As good as it feels, however, I know her naked flesh will feel even better, so I grasp the tie at her waist, pulling on it. At the same time, I lift my head and open my eyes to look at her.

As the tie unravels, her robe parts, exposing a V of smooth, tan skin. I can see the inside curves of her breasts and the taut flatness of her belly, but her nipples and lower body are still covered, as if by design.

It's an erotic visual, made even more sensual by the way she's breathing, her ribcage moving up and down in a fast, panting rhythm. Her lips are reddened from the kiss, and her skin is softly flushed.

My little pet is turned on.

As if sensing my gaze on her, she opens her eyes, her long lashes sweeping up. We look at each other, and the aching need inside me grows. It's a feeling that's somehow different from the lust surging through my body, a complex want that's layered on top of my usual obsessive craving.

A yearning that terrifies me with its intensity.

"Tell me you love me." All of a sudden, I need this from her. "Tell me, Nora."

She doesn't blink. "I love you."

My arms tighten around her. "Again."

"I love you, Julian." She holds my gaze, her eyes soft and dark. "More than anything else in the world."

Fuck. My chest constricts, the ache intensifying rather than easing. It's too much, yet somehow not enough.

Bending my head, I claim her lips again, putting all the things I can't express in words into that kiss. I feel her breathing growing shallow, and I know I'm holding her too tightly, but I can't help it. Mixed with the overwhelming longing is a strange, irrational fear.

Fear that I might lose her. That she might slip away, like some beautiful, ephemeral dream.

No. I angle my head to delve deeper into her mouth, letting her taste, her scent, absorb me, chasing away the shadows. She won't slip away. I won't let her. She's real, and she's mine. I kiss her until we're both gasping for air, until the fear inside me abates, burned away by the scorching heat.

Then I make love to her, as tenderly as I can.

When I drift off to sleep some time later, it's with Nora cocooned safely in my embrace.

CHAPTER SIX

❖ NORA ❖

It takes all of my willpower to remain awake as I hear Julian's breathing take on the even rhythm of sleep. My own eyelids feel heavy, my body lethargic from exhaustion and sexual satiation. All I want to do is close my eyes and let the comforting darkness swallow me, but I can't.

There's something I must do first.

I wait until I'm certain Julian is asleep, and then I carefully wriggle out of his hold. To my relief, he doesn't stir, so I get up and find the robe that had fallen on the floor during sex.

Quietly putting it on, I pad barefoot into the bathroom. My stomach, still unsettled from dinner, roils with nausea again, and I have to swallow several times to keep the food from coming back up.

It's probably not the best idea to do this when I'm feeling sick. I know that—but I also know that if I don't do this now, I may not have the courage to attempt it later. And I need to do this. I need to fulfill my promise, to repay the debt I owe Peter. It's important to me. I don't want to be the girl who can't take any action on her own, the wife who always lives in her husband's shadow.

I don't want to be Julian's helpless little pet for the rest of my life.

Splashing cold water on my face, I take several deep breaths to quell my nausea and walk back into the bedroom. The shades are open just a sliver, but the moon is full tonight, and there's enough light for me to see where I'm going.

My destination is the dresser, on top of which Julian's laptop is sitting. He doesn't always bring the computer into the bedroom, but he did tonight—which is another reason why I don't want to wait to implement my plan.

·The plan itself is beyond simple. I'm going to take the laptop, access Julian's email, and send the list to Peter. If everything goes well, Julian won't find out about this for a while. And by the time he does, it will be too late. I will have repaid my debt to Julian's former security consultant, and my conscience will be clear.

Well, as clear as it can be knowing that Peter will likely kill the people on that list in horrifying ways.

No, don't think about it. I remind myself that those people are responsible for the deaths of Peter's wife and son. They're not innocent civilians, and I shouldn't think of them as such.

The only thing I should worry about at the moment is getting the list to Peter without waking up Julian.

I walk across the room as quietly as I can, my heart thumping heavily in my chest. When I reach the dresser, I stop and listen.

All is quiet. Julian must still be asleep.

Biting my lip, I reach for the laptop and pick it up. Then I pause to listen again.

The room is still silent.

Exhaling slowly, I walk back toward the bathroom, cradling the laptop against my chest. When I get there, I slip inside, lock the door behind me, and sit down on the edge of the Jacuzzi.

So far, so good. Ignoring the churning in my stomach, I open the laptop.

A password request box pops up.

I take another deep breath, fighting my worsening nausea. I expected this. Julian is paranoid about security and changes his password at least once a week. However, the last time he changed it was the day after Frank, Julian's CIA contact, emailed him the list.

Julian changed it when I was already hatching my plan—and I made sure I was nearby when he did so. I didn't stare at his laptop, of course. That would've been suspicious. Instead, I quietly filmed him with my smartphone while pretending to be checking my email.

Now if only I interpreted the recorded keystrokes correctly . . .

Holding my breath, I put in "NML_#042160" and hit "enter."

The computer screen blinks . . . and I'm in.

My breath whooshes out in relief. Now all I need to do is find the email from Frank, open the attachment, log into my own email, and send the list to the same email address that Peter has been contacting me from.

Should be easy enough, especially if I can keep my dinner down.

"Nora?" A knock startles me so much that I almost drop the computer. My lungs seize with panic, and I freeze, staring at the door.

Julian knocks again. "Nora, baby, are you all right?"

He doesn't know I have his computer. The realization causes me to start breathing again.

"Just using the bathroom," I call out, hoping Julian doesn't hear the adrenaline-induced shakiness in my voice. At the same time, I open Julian's email program and begin searching for Frank's name. "I'll be out soon."

"Of course, baby, take your time." The words are accompanied by the fading sound of footsteps.

I let out a relieved breath. I have a few more minutes.

I begin scanning through the emails containing the word "Frank." There are over a dozen from last week, but the one I want should have a little attachment icon next to it . . . Aha! There. Quickly, I open it.

It's a spreadsheet containing names and addresses. Automatically, I glance through them. There are over a dozen rows, and the addresses run the gamut from cities in Europe to various towns in the United States. One in particular jumps out at me: Homer Glen, Illinois.

It's a place near Oak Lawn, my hometown. Less than a forty-minute drive from my parents' house.

Stunned, I read the name next to the address.

George Cobakis.

Thank God. It's nobody I know.

"Nora?" Julian's voice is back, and the tense note in it makes my heart jump into my throat. His next words confirm my fear. "Nora, do you have my computer?"

"What? Why?" I hope I don't sound as guilty as I feel. *Shit. Shit, shit, shit.* Frantically, I save the list to the desktop and open a new browser.

"Because my laptop is missing." His voice is tight with the beginnings of fury. "Are you in there with it?"

"What? No!" Even I can hear the lie in my voice. My hands are beginning to shake, but I get to the Gmail page and begin putting in my username and password.

The doorknob rattles. "Nora, open the door. Right now."

I don't respond. My hands are shaking so much that I mistype the password and have to put it in again.

"Nora!" Julian bangs on the door. "Open this fucking door before I break it down!"

I'm finally in my Gmail. My heart hammering in my chest, I search for the last email from Peter.

Bang. The door shakes from a hard kick.

My nausea intensifies, my pulse racing as I find the email.

Bang. Bang. More kicks against the door as I click "reply" and attach the list.

Bang. Bang. Bang.

I hit "Send"—and the door flies off the hinges, crashing to the floor in front of me.

Julian is standing there naked, his eyes like icy blue slits in his beautiful face. His powerful hands are clenched into fists, and his nostrils are flared, spots of color burning high on his cheekbones.

He's magnificent and terrifying, like an enraged archangel.

"Give me the laptop, Nora." His voice is frighteningly calm. "Now."

Bile rises in my throat, forcing me to swallow convulsively. Standing up, I walk over to him on trembling legs and hand over the computer.

He takes it from me with one hand and, before I can back away, wraps the other one around my right wrist, shackling me to him.

Then he looks at the screen.

I see the exact moment when he realizes what I did.

"You sent it to him?" Setting the computer down on the bathroom counter, he grabs my other arm and drags me closer to him. His eyes burn with fury. "You fucking sent it to him?" He gives me a hard shake, his fingers biting into my skin.

My stomach somersaults, nausea washing over me in sickening wave. "Julian, let go—"

And jerking out of his hold with desperation-fueled strength, I dive for the toilet bowl, just barely reaching it before I throw up.

* * *

"How long have you had this nausea?" Dr. Goldberg takes my pulse as I lie on the bed, with Julian pacing around the room like a caged jaguar.

"I don't know," I say, my eyes tracking Julian's movements. He's wearing a T-shirt and jeans now, but his feet are still bare. He's making circles in front of the bed, every muscle in his body taut and his jaw tightly clenched.

He's either still mad at me, or madly worried about me. I'm guessing it's a combination of the two. Within minutes of my throwing up, he had the doctor in our room and me bundled comfortably on the bed.

It reminds me of how quickly he acted when I got appendicitis on the island.

"I think I just ate something bad or maybe caught a virus," I say, turning my attention back to the doctor. "I started feeling sick at dinner."

"Uh-huh." Dr. Goldberg takes out a plastic-wrapped needle with a tube attached to a vial. "May I?"

"Okay." I don't particularly want him to take my blood, but I have a feeling Julian won't let me refuse. "Go ahead."

The doctor finds a vein in my arm and slides the needle in while I look away. I'm still slightly nauseous and don't want to test my stomach's fortitude with the sight of blood.

"All done," he says after a moment, removing the needle and swabbing my skin with an alcohol-scented cotton ball. "I'll run the tests and let you know what I find."

"She's also constantly tired," Julian says in a low voice, stopping next to the bed. He's not looking at me, which annoys me a bit. "And she's sleeping poorly, with the nightmares and all."

"Right." The doctor rises to his feet, clutching the vial. "I need to run this to my lab. I'll be back within the hour."

He hurries out of the room, and Julian sits down on the bed, looking at me. His face is unusually pale, a frown etched into his forehead. "Why didn't you tell me you were feeling sick, Nora?" he asks quietly, reaching out to pick up my hand. His fingers are warm on my palm, his grip gentle despite the turmoil I sense within him.

I blink in surprise. I thought he would question me about Peter's list, not this. "It wasn't too bad at dinner," I say carefully. "I felt better after I took a shower and we . . . well, you know." I wave my free hand in a gesture meant to encompass the bed.

"We fucked?" Julian's tense expression eases slightly, unexpected amusement flickering in his eyes.

"Right." Heat crawls up my body at the mental images his words bring up. Apparently, I'm not too sick to be turned on. "That made me feel better."

"I see." Julian regards me speculatively, stroking the inside of my wrist with his thumb. "And you decided that since you were feeling so well, you were going to hack into my computer."

And there it is. The reckoning I anticipated. Except Julian doesn't seem as angry as before, his touch on me soothing rather than punishing.

It looks like food poisoning—or whatever I've got—has its perks.

I offer him a cautious smile. "Well, yeah. I figured it was as good of an opportunity as any." I don't bother apologizing or denying my actions. There's no point. It's done. I paid my debt to Peter.

"How did you know my password?" Julian's thumb continues moving over my wrist in a circular motion. "I never told you what it was."

"I filmed you when you were changing it a few days ago. After I found out that Frank came through on the list."

The corners of Julian's mouth twitch, almost imperceptibly. "That's what I thought. I was wondering why you were on your phone so much that day."

I lick my lips. "Are you going to punish me?" Julian seems more amused than angry at the moment, but I can't imagine he'll let me off scot-free.

"Of course, my pet." There's no trace of hesitation in his voice.

My pulse jumps. "When?"

"When I choose." His eyes gleam as he releases my hand. "Now, would you like some water or anything?"

"Some crackers and chamomile tea would be nice," I say on autopilot, staring at him. I'd expected this, of course, but I still can't help feeling anxious.

"I'll get that for you." Julian gets up. "Be back in a few."

He disappears through the door, and I close my eyes, my earlier tiredness returning now that the adrenaline rush is over. Maybe I'll just catch a quick nap before Julian comes back . . .

A knock on the door startles me again, causing me to jerk to a sitting position. "Yes?"

"Nora, this is David Goldberg. May I come in?"

"Oh, sure." I lie back down, my heart still beating too fast. "Did you already run the tests?" I ask as the doctor enters the room.

"Yes." There is an odd expression on his face as he stops next to the bed. "Nora, you've been fatigued lately, right? And unusually stressed?"

"Yes." I frown, starting to feel uneasy. "Why?"

"Have you noticed anything else? Mood swings? Atypical food cravings or dislikes? Maybe some tenderness in your breasts?"

I stare at him, a cold fist seizing my chest. "What are you saying?" The symptoms he's listing—surely he can't mean . . .

"Nora, the blood tests I ran showed a strong presence of the hCG hormone," Dr. Goldberg says gently. "You're pregnant." He pauses, then adds quietly, "Given the timing of the implant removal, my best guess is you're about six weeks along."

CHAPTER SEVEN

❖ JULIAN ❖

Carrying the tray with tea and crackers, I walk up the stairs toward the bedroom. I should be furious with Nora, but instead, my worry for her is tinged with reluctant admiration.

She defied me. She locked herself in the bathroom and hacked into my computer to pay a debt that she believed was owed. She had to know that she would be caught, but she did it anyway—and I can't help respecting her for it.

I would've done the same thing in her shoes.

In hindsight, I should've expected this. She's been adamant about wanting to get the list to Peter, so it's not all that surprising that she decided to act on her own. From the very beginning, I've sensed a quiet, stubborn strength within her, a steel core that belies her delicate appearance.

My pet might be compliant much of the time, but that's only because she's smart enough to choose her battles—and I should've known she'd choose to fight this one.

As I approach the bedroom, I hear voices and recognize Goldberg's slightly nasal pitch.

He's back with the test results, and Nora sounds upset.

Fuck. Fear, icy and sharp, bites at me. If it's something serious, if she's truly sick... Picking up my pace, I reach the door in two long steps. Tea sloshes over the rim of the cup, but I barely notice, all my focus on Nora.

Gripping the tray with one hand, I push open the door and step in.

She's sitting on the bed, her eyes huge in her colorless face as Goldberg says, "I'm afraid it *is* possible—"

My heart freezes. "What's possible?" I ask sharply. "What's wrong?"

Goldberg turns to look at me. "Oh, there you are." He sounds relieved. "I was just explaining to your wife that the morning-after pill is only ninety-five-percent effective when taken within twenty-four hours, and even though the likelihood of conception was low given the timing of the implant removal, there was still a small chance of pregnancy—"

"Pregnancy?" I feel like he's speaking a foreign language. "What are you talking about?"

Goldberg sighs, looking tired. "Nora is six weeks pregnant, Julian. It looks like the morning-after pill didn't work."

I stare at him, stunned, and he says, "Listen, I know it's a lot to take in. Why don't I leave the two of you to discuss this, and I'll answer any questions you might have in the morning? For now, the best thing for Nora would be to get some rest. Stress is not good in her condition."

I nod, still mute with shock, and he swiftly departs, leaving me alone with Nora.

Nora, who's sitting there like a wax doll, her face nearly as white as the robe she's wearing.

Hot liquid spills over my hand, burning me, and I realize that I forgot about the tray I'm holding. The pain clears my mind, and I finally process the meaning of Goldberg's words.

Nora is pregnant.

Not sick. Pregnant.

The icy fear eases, replaced by a new, entirely foreign emotion.

Placing the tray with the half-full cup of tea on the nightstand, I sit down next to my wife and wrap my hands around her small palms. "Nora." I pull on her hands to get her to face me, and see that she's still shellshocked, her gaze blank and distant. "Nora, baby, talk to me."

She blinks, as if coming back to herself, and her hands jerk in my grasp. I release her and watch as she scoots back, drawing her knees up and wrapping her arms around herself. Her eyes lock with mine, and we stare at each other in silence as seconds tick by.

"Did you do this?" she finally asks, her voice a strained whisper. "Did you ask Dr. Goldberg to give me a placebo instead of the morning-after pill? Is the new implant in my arm a fake?"

"No." I don't bother being outraged at her accusation. If I'd wanted her pregnant, I might've considered doing something along those lines, and Nora is smart enough to know that. "No, my pet. This is as much of a shock to me as it is to you."

She nods, and I know she believes me. There is no reason for me to lie. She's mine to do with as I please. If I had impregnated her on purpose, I wouldn't deny it.

"Come here," I murmur, reaching for her. She's stiff as I pull her closer, but I ignore her resistance. I need to hold her, to feel her in my arms. Her hair tickles my chin as I pull her onto my lap and inhale deeply, closing my eyes.

Nora is not sick.

She's carrying my baby.

It seems surreal, unnatural. She's tiny in my embrace, barely bigger than a child herself. Yet she's going to be a mother—and I'm going to be a father.

A father, like the man who gave me life and molded me into what I am today.

Unbidden, an old memory comes to me.

"Catch!" He throws the ball at me, laughing. I jump for it, and my five-year-old hands close around it, snatching it from mid-air.

"I got it!" I feel so proud of myself, so full of joy. "Father, I caught it on the first try!"

"Good job, son." He grins at me, and in that moment, I love him. His approval matters to me more than anything else in the world. I forget about the frequent bite of his belt, about all the times he yelled at me and called me worthless.

He's my father, and in that moment, I love him.

My eyes fly open, and I stare blankly at the wall, still holding Nora. I can't believe I ever loved that man. He's been the subject of my hatred for so long, I'd forgotten there were those kinds of moments.

I'd forgotten there were times he made me happy.

Would I make my child happy? Or would he or she hate me? I told Nora I would make an awful father, but I have no idea if that's the truth. For the first time, I try to imagine myself holding a newborn baby, playing with a chubby-cheeked toddler, teaching a five-year-old how to swim . . . The pictures come to me with surprising ease, filling me with an unsettling mixture of fear and longing.

With a desire for something I've never known.

A stifled sob startles me, and I realize that it's Nora.

She's crying, her slim body shaking in my arms. I can feel the wetness from her tears on my neck, and it burns me like acid.

For a moment, I had forgotten how much she doesn't want this child.

How much she doesn't want a child with *me*.

"Hush, my pet." The words come out harsher than I intended, but I can't help it. The unpleasant tightness in my chest is back, and with it, the irrational urge to hurt her. Fighting it, I say in a softer tone, "This is not the end of the world, believe me."

She stills, falling silent for a moment, but then another sob racks her body. And another.

I can't take it anymore. Her misery is like a hot knife plunging into my side—agonizing and maddening at the same time.

Thrusting my hand into her hair, I close my fist around the silky strands and pull her head back, forcing her to look up at me. Her eyes, wide and shocked, meet mine. I can see the tears sparkling on her lashes, and the sight enrages me further, awakening the beast inside.

Her lips tremble, parting as if she would speak, but I lower my head, swallowing her words with a deep, hard kiss. Lust, sharp and strong, kindles in my veins, hardening my cock and clouding my brain. I want her, and I want to punish her at the same time. I can feel her struggling against me, taste the salt from her tears, and it spurs me on, heightening the twisted hunger.

I'm not sure how we end up on the bed, with her stretched helplessly beneath me, but the clothes we're wearing seem like an intolerable barrier, so I tear them off, feeling more animal than man. My fingers close around her wrists, transferring both of them into my left hand, and my knees push between her thighs, parting them roughly.

I can hear Nora pleading, begging me to stop, but I can't. The need to possess her is like a fire under my skin, burning away all rational thought. Grasping my cock with my free hand, I guide it to her opening and penetrate her in one deep thrust, taking her body as I long to claim her heart and soul.

She's small and tight around me, her muscles clenching desperately to keep me out, but the squeezing pressure only intensifies my violent urge to fuck her. Her resistance maddens me, drives me to take her harder, to batter her with my cock as I hold her pinned under my body. Every thrust is a merciless claim, a brutal conquest of that which already belongs to me. I fuck her for what feels like hours, cognizant of nothing but the ferocious hunger seething under my skin.

It's not until I collapse on top of her, breathing heavily from an explosive orgasm, that the fog of lust clears from my mind, and I realize what I've done.

Releasing her wrists, I push up onto my elbows and gaze down at her, my cock still buried inside her body. She's lying underneath me, her eyes squeezed shut and her face pale. I can see a smear of blood on her lower lip. I either cut it with my teeth or she bit it in pain.

As I stare at her, she slowly opens her eyes, meeting my gaze . . . and for the first time in decades, I taste the bitter ashes of remorse.

CHAPTER EIGHT

❖ NORA ❖

My mind is blank, emptied of all thought as I look at Julian. I'm vaguely aware that he's still inside me, but that's all I can process at the moment. I feel broken, destroyed, the raw soreness of my body amplified by the deep, stabbing pain in my soul.

I don't know why this bout of rough sex felt so much like a violation. Why it reminded me of those early days on the island, when Julian was my cruel captor instead of the man I love. Only a couple of days ago, he tortured me with a flogger and nipple clamps, and I reveled in it, begging for more.

I begged today too, but it wasn't for more. Sex wasn't what I wanted—not with my heart breaking for the tiny life growing inside me.

For the innocent child conceived by two killers.

"Nora . . ." Julian's voice is an aching whisper. The pain in it tugs at what remains of my heart. I want to hate him for hurting me, but I can't. It's part of his nature. It's who he is.

It's why any child of ours is doomed.

I hold his gaze, feeling like I'm crumbling into pieces. "Let me go, Julian. Please."

"I can't." His face twists, the scars around his eye standing out in stark relief. "I can't, Nora."

I swallow painfully, knowing he's not talking about our physical position. "I'm not asking that of you. Please, I just— I just need a moment."

He withdraws from me, rolling over onto his back, and I turn away onto my side, gathering my knees to my chest. The nausea that plagued me earlier is gone, but I feel weak. Exhausted. My body aches from Julian's hard use, and a sense of hopelessness engulfs me, adding to my growing despair.

I'm barely cognizant of Julian getting up. It's only when he presses a warm washcloth between my legs that I realize he must've gone to the bathroom and returned. I don't have the energy to move, so I lie still and let him clean the residue of sex off my thighs.

Afterwards, he pulls me into his embrace and covers us both with a blanket. As the familiar warmth of his body seeps into me, lulling me to sleep, I dream that I feel the brush of his lips against my temple and hear a whispered, "I'm sorry."

* * *

"As I began to explain last night, this pregnancy was improbable, but not impossible," Dr. Goldberg says as I sit down on the couch next to Julian. "The morning-after pill is ineffective about five percent of the time, and your probability of being able to conceive a few days after the removal of the old implant was also somewhere in the five-percent range, so if you do the math . . ." He shrugs, giving me a sheepish smile.

"What about the fact that Nora is still on birth control?" Julian asks, frowning. "She has a new implant in her arm—she's had it for weeks."

"Right." The doctor nods. "We'll have to remove that as soon as possible and have Nora start taking prenatal vitamins." He pauses, then adds delicately, "That is, if you want to keep the baby."

"We do," Julian responds before I can process the question. "And we want to make sure the child is healthy." He reaches for my hand and wraps his fingers around my palm, squeezing it possessively. "And Nora, of course."

Finally comprehending Dr. Goldberg's words, I glance at Julian. His jaw is set in hard, uncompromising lines. Abortion hadn't occurred to me as an option, but I'm surprised Julian is so vehemently against it. He claimed not to want children, and I can't imagine he'd be hypocritical enough to have moral or religious objections to the procedure.

"Of course," the doctor says. "Obstetrics is not my specialty, but I can examine Nora and remove the implant, and prescribe her the appropriate vitamins. I can also recommend an excellent obstetrician who might agree to oversee Nora's pregnancy here. I already emailed you her contact info."

"Good." Releasing my hand, Julian gets up, looking restless and tense. "I want the absolute best care for Nora."

"You'll have it," Dr. Goldberg promises, rising to his feet as well. Turning toward me, he says, "At least this explains something."

"Explains what?" I stand up too, uncomfortable being the only one sitting.

"Your persistent nightmares and panic attacks." The doctor gives me a sympathetic look. "It's not uncommon for pregnancy hormones to amplify anxiety, particularly in the wake of traumatic events."

"Oh." I stare at him. "So I'm not just overreacting to what happened?"

"You're not," Dr. Goldberg assures me. "Depression and anxiety can happen to pregnant women with much less provocation. You do need to take it easy and relax as much as possible, though, both for your sake and that of the baby. Acute stress during pregnancy can lead to all sorts of complications, including a miscarriage."

"I will make sure she rests and doesn't stress." Julian reaches for me again, intertwining his fingers with mine. It's as if he can't bear not to touch me today. "What about food, drinks?"

"I'll give you a list of what to avoid," Dr. Goldberg says. "You probably know about alcohol and caffeine, but there are a few more things, like sushi and seafood high in mercury."

"All right." Julian turns his head to look at me. "Baby, would you be okay with the doctor examining you now and removing the implant?" His voice is unusually soft, his gaze filled with indefinable emotion.

"Um, sure." I see no reason to procrastinate, and I like that Julian asked, instead of just ordering the examination in his usual autocratic manner.

"Good." He lifts my hand—the one he's holding—and presses a kiss to the back of my wrist before letting it go. "I'll be back in a bit."

I nod, and Julian quietly exits the room, closing the door behind him.

"All right, Nora." Dr. Goldberg smiles at me, reaching for his bag and pulling out latex gloves. "Shall we begin?"

* * *

After the doctor leaves, I change into a swimsuit and go to the back porch, grabbing my Psychology textbook on the way. Pregnancy or not, I have an exam to study for, and I'm determined to do so—if for no other reason than to distract myself from the situation. My arm once again sports a tiny, Band-Aid-covered wound, and I try to ignore the faint ache there, not wanting to focus on the fact that my birth control implant is gone . . . and the reason why.

It's strange, but the broken feeling of last night is no longer there. It's been replaced by a kind of distant hurt. I should probably be traumatized and angry at Julian, but I'm not. Like the days right after my abduction, last night feels like it belongs to a different era, to a time before we became who we are. I know I'm playing that game with myself again—the one where I exist solely in the moment and push all the bad stuff into a separate corner of my brain—but I need that game to stay sane.

I need that game because I can't stop loving my captor, no matter what he does.

It doesn't help that the Julian of this morning is a far cry from the brutal savage of last night. From the moment I woke up, he's been treating me like I'm made of crystal. Breakfast in bed followed by a foot rub, constant little kisses and affectionate gestures—if I didn't know better, I'd think he's feeling guilty.

Of course, I do know better. Only a thin line separates the monster of last night from the tender lover of this morning. Guilt is an emotion that's as foreign to my husband as pity for his enemies.

When I get to the back porch, I grab a lounge chair under an umbrella and make myself comfortable. As always, the air outside is hot and humid, so thick it's almost smothering. I don't mind, though. I'm used to it. If it gets unbearable, I'll jump into the pool. For now, I open my textbook and begin re-reading the chapter on neurotransmitters.

I'm only halfway through when a moving shadow makes me look up.

It's Julian. Dressed in a pair of black swim trunks, he's standing next to my chair, his gaze traveling over me with unabashed hunger.

I lick my lips, staring up at him. In the bright sunlight, he's almost unbearably beautiful, the new scars somehow only adding to his stark masculinity. From his shoulders to his calves, every inch of his body is packed with lean, hard muscle. His powerful chest is dusted with dark hair, and his abs are clearly defined, with a line of hair trailing down from his navel into his shorts.

He's stunning, more gorgeous than any man I've known—and I want him.

I want him despite last night, despite everything.

"How are you feeling, baby?" he asks, his voice low and husky. "Any nausea? Tiredness?"

"No." I sit up, swinging my feet to the ground, and put down the textbook. "I'm okay today."

Julian sits down next to me and tucks a strand of my hair behind my ear. "Good," he says softly. "I'm glad."

"Did you come out for a swim?" I try to ignore the warmth pooling between my thighs at his touch. "I thought you would go to your office."

"I did, just for a few minutes, but I'm taking the rest of the day off."

"Really?" Julian's days off are so rare they're practically nonexistent. "Why?"

He gives me a wry smile. "I couldn't focus."

"Oh." I regard him cautiously. "Do you want to go for a swim then? I was thinking of diving in after I finished this chapter, but I can go now."

"Sure." Julian rises to his feet and offers me his hand. "Let's go."

I place my hand in his and let him lead me to the pool. As we approach the water, he suddenly bends down, slides his arm under my knees, and picks me up.

Startled, I laugh, wrapping my arms around his neck. "Julian! Don't throw me in! I like to walk in slowly—"

"I wouldn't throw you in, my pet," he murmurs, holding me as he descends into the pool. His eyes gleam with unexpected humor. "What kind of monster do you think I am?"

"Um, do I have to answer that?" I can't believe I'm in the mood to tease him, but I feel ridiculously lighthearted all of a sudden. Some weird hormonal fluctuation, no doubt, but I don't mind. I'll take lighthearted over depressed any day of the week.

"You do have to answer," he says, a wicked grin appearing on his face. The water is now up to his waist, and he stops, holding me against his chest. "Or else . . ."

"Or else what?"

"This." Julian lowers me a few inches, letting my dangling feet touch the water. He tries for a menacing scowl, but I can see the corners of his mouth twitching with a suppressed smile.

"Are you threatening me with a dunking, sir?" Wiggling my right foot in the water, I give him a look of mock reproof. "I thought we just established that you wouldn't throw me in?"

"Who said anything about throwing?" He steps further into the pool, letting the water creep higher up my calves. His fake scowl disappears, edged out by a darkly sensual smile. "There are other ways to deal with naughty girls."

"Oh, do tell . . ." My inner muscles clench at the images flooding my mind. "What kind of ways?"

"Well, for starters"—he bends his head, his lips nearly touching mine as I hold my breath in anticipation—"some cooling off is required."

And before I can react, he sinks down, lowering us both into the water—which immediately engulfs me up to my chin.

"Julian!" Laughing in outrage, I release my grip on his neck and push at his shoulders. The pool is heated, but the water is still cool compared to my sun-warmed skin. "You said you wouldn't!"

"I said I wouldn't throw you," he corrects, his wicked grin returning. "I didn't say anything about carrying you in."

"Okay, that's it." I succeed at slipping out of his hold and putting a couple of feet of distance between us. "You want war? You have it, mister!" Scooping up water with my palm, I throw it at him and watch, laughing, as it hits him square in the face.

He wipes the water away, blinking in stunned disbelief, and I back away, laughing even harder.

Recovering from his shock, he begins to advance toward me. "Did you just splash me?" His voice is low and threatening. "Did you just throw water in my face, my pet?"

"What? No!" I mockingly bat my eyelashes as I attempt to retreat to the deeper end of the pool. "I wouldn't dare—" My words end in a squeal as Julian lunges for me, closing the distance between us in a blink of an eye. At the last moment, I manage to jump out of his reach and start swimming away, still laughing hysterically.

I'm a good swimmer, but less than two seconds pass before Julian's steely fingers close around my ankle. "Gotcha," he says, dragging me toward him. When I'm close enough, he grabs my arm to bring me to a vertical position and wraps his muscular arms around my back, grinning at my ineffective attempts to push him away.

"Okay, you got me," I concede, laughing. "Now what?"

"Now this." Bending his head, he kisses me, the warmth from his large body counteracting the coolness of the water.

As his tongue invades my mouth, I tense involuntarily, memories of last night surfacing with sudden clarity. For a few dark moments, I relive the terrible feeling of helplessness, of painful betrayal, and I know I wasn't entirely successful at compartmentalizing the good and the bad. As much as I'd like to pretend that today is a day like any other, it's not, and no amount of playful laughter changes the fact that the evil in Julian's soul will never be completely eradicated.

That the monster will always lie in wait.

And yet, as he continues kissing me, the heat of desire grows within me, luring me under its spell. He's tender with me now, and my body softens, basking in that tenderness, in the insidious warmth of his embrace. I want to believe in the illusion of his caring, in the mirage of his twisted love, and so I let the dark memories fade, leaving me in the brighter present.

Leaving me with the man I love.

CHAPTER NINE

❖ JULIAN ❖

Nora and I end up swimming and playing in the pool until Ana comes looking for us, saying that lunch is ready. By then I'm starving, and I'm guessing Nora must be hungry as well. I'm also suffering from blue balls from all that making out, but that's something that will have to wait until later.

I want Nora to eat even more than I want to fuck her.

Seeing my pet like this—so happy, vibrant, and carefree—has gone a long way toward easing the heavy pressure in my chest, but it hasn't removed it completely. The look on her face after I took her . . . It haunts me, invading my thoughts despite my best efforts to put it out of my mind. I know I've done worse to her in the past, but something about last night *felt* worse.

It felt like I wronged her.

Perhaps it's because she's now completely mine. I no longer have to condition her, to mold her into what I need her to be. She loves me enough to risk her life for me, enough to want to be with me of her own free will. Everything I've done to her in the past was calculated to a certain extent, but last night I hurt her without meaning to.

I hurt her when all I wanted was to hold her, heal her.

I hurt the woman who's carrying my child—and even if Nora seems to have forgiven me for that, I can't forgive myself.

"What can I get for you, Nora?" Ana asks when we're seated at the dining room table. The older woman is beaming at my wife, as happy as I've ever seen her. "Some toast? Maybe a little plain rice?"

Nora's eyes widen at the housekeeper's words, but she manages to say calmly, "I'll have whatever you prepared, Ana. I'm better today, really."

Despite my earlier thoughts, I can't help smiling. Goldberg must've let something slip, or else Ana overheard us talking this morning. That's why Ana's smile is wide enough to swallow up her whole face: she knows about Nora's pregnancy and is overjoyed at the news.

At Nora's reassurance, Ana's expression brightens even more. "Oh, good. I realize now that you must've been baby-sick yesterday. It happens, you know," she says in a conspiratorial tone. "Right around six weeks is when they say it starts."

"Oh, great." Nora tries to keep the glumness out of her voice, but she's not entirely successful. "Looking forward to it."

"I'll make sure you have the best care, baby," I murmur, reaching across the table to cover Nora's delicate hand with mine. "I'll get you whatever you need to feel well."

I already contacted the obstetrician Goldberg recommended, emailing her while Nora was having her examination. I might not have planned to have this child, but now that it's here, the thought of something happening to it is unbearable. When Goldberg hinted at the possibility of abortion today, it was all I could do not to rip his throat out.

Planned or not, this child is my flesh and blood, and I'll kill anyone who tries to harm it.

Nora gives me a small smile. "I'm sure it will be fine. Women have children all the time." Despite her reassuring words, her voice sounds strained, and I know she's still uneasy with this development.

Uneasy with the fact that she's carrying my baby.

Taking a deep breath, I suppress the instinctive swell of anger. On a rational level, I understand her fear. Nora loves me, but she's not blind to my nature.

She can't be, especially after last night.

"Yes, it will be fine," I say evenly, giving her hand a gentle squeeze before releasing it. "I'll make sure of it."

And for the remainder of the meal, we avoid the topic, both of us more than happy to focus on something else.

* * *

I spend the rest of the day with Nora, completely ignoring the work that's waiting for me. For the first time in ages, I can't bring myself to care about manufacturing issues in Malaysia or the fact that the Mexican cartel is demanding lower prices on customized machine guns. The Ukrainians are trying to make amends and bribe me out of my alliance with the Russians, Interpol is up in arms about the CIA sending me Peter Sokolov's list, a new terrorist group in Iraq wants to get on the waiting list for the explosive, and I don't give a fuck about any of that.

All that matters to me today is Nora.

After lunch, we go for a walk around the estate, and I show her some of my favorite boyhood haunts, including a small lake on the edge of the property where I once encountered a jaguar.

"Really? A jaguar?" Nora's eyes are wide as we exit the forested area and emerge onto a small, grassy clearing in front of the lake. The tall trees surrounding it provide both shade and privacy from the guards—which is why I frequently spent time there as a child.

"They come out of the jungle sometimes," I say in response to Nora's question. "It's rare, but it happens."

"How did you get away from it?" She gives me a concerned look. "You said you were only nine."

"I had a gun with me."

"So you killed it?"

"No. I shot a tree next to it and scared it off." I could've killed it—my aim was excellent by then—but the thought of harming the fierce creature had been repellent for some reason. It wasn't the jaguar's fault it had been born a predator, and I didn't want to punish it for having the misfortune of wandering into human territory.

"What did your parents say when you told them about it?" Nora sits down on a broken tree trunk and looks up at me. Her smooth shoulders gleam with the light reflected off the lake. "Mine would've been terrified for me."

"I didn't tell them." I sit down next to her and, unable to resist, bend my head to press a kiss to her right shoulder. Her skin smells delicious, and the hunger ignited by our play at the pool returns, my body hardening at her proximity once more.

"Why not?" she asks huskily, turning to look at me as I lift my head. "Why didn't you tell them?"

"My mother was already frightened of the jungle, and my father would've been upset that I didn't bring him the jaguar's pelt. So there was no point in telling either of them," I explain. Reaching for her hair, I thread my fingers through the thick, silky mass, enjoying the sensuous feel of it sliding through my hands. My cock is stiff with need, but this is as far as I intend to take it for now.

There won't be sex until tonight, when she's comfortable in our bed and I can be sure I won't hurt her.

"Oh." Nora tilts her head, moving it closer to my hands, and regards me through half-closed eyelids. Her expression is reminiscent of a cat being petted. "What about your friends? Did you tell them what happened?"

"No," I murmur, my arousal growing despite my good intentions. "I didn't tell anyone."

"Why not?" Nora all but purrs as I slide my fingers through her hair again, lightly massaging her scalp in the process. "You didn't think they would believe you?"

"No, I knew they would believe me." I withdraw my hands from her hair as my need intensifies, threatening my self-control. "I just didn't have close friends, that's all."

Something uncomfortably close to pity flickers in her gaze, but she doesn't say anything or ask any follow-up questions. Instead, she leans closer and presses her lips to mine, her small hands coming up to rest on both sides of my face.

Her touch is strangely innocent and uncertain, as if she's kissing me for the first time. Her lips just barely graze mine, each touch a hint, a promise of more to come. I can almost taste her, almost feel her, and the urge to fuck her is so strong I shudder with it. It's only the memory of last night—of the wounded, betrayed look in her eyes—that enables me to stay still and accept her not-quite-kisses, my hands resting on her shoulders. I know I should stop her, push her away, but I can't.

Her hesitant kisses are the sweetest thing I've ever felt.

When I think I can't bear much more, her hot little mouth moves to my jaw and then trails down my neck, kissing and nibbling with the same torturous gentleness. Her hands release my face and slide down my body, her fingers closing around the bottom edge of my shirt. She begins to lift the shirt, and I groan as her knuckles brush against my naked sides, her touch leaving my skin burning in its wake.

"Nora..." I suck in my breath as she scoots down and kneels between my spread legs, her face at the level of my navel. "Nora, baby, you need to stop teasing me."

She ignores my directive, keeping my shirt bunched up. "Who's teasing?" she whispers, looking up at me. And before I can respond, she leans in and places a warm, damp kiss on my stomach.

Fuck. My entire body jerks, my balls tightening on a savage surge of lust. The sight of her kneeling there pushes my buttons in all the wrong ways, calling to my darkest desires. My hands knot into fists, and I take short, deep breaths, reminding myself that she's fragile right now.

That she's pregnant with my child, and I can't take her like an animal again.

Except she's licking my stomach now. *Fucking licking it.* Tracing each muscle indentation with her tongue, like she's trying to imprint it on her memory.

"Nora." My voice is hoarse. "Baby, that's enough."

She pulls back, looking up at me through those long, thick lashes of hers. "Are you sure?" she murmurs, still not letting go of my shirt. "Because I think I want more." And leaning in again, she scrapes her teeth over my lower abs, then sucks on the spot, her mouth hot and wet on my bare skin.

Skin that's right next to the throbbing cock still confined in my shorts.

Fucking hell.

"Nora..." I can barely form the words, my fingers digging into the bark of the tree in an effort not to grab her. "You don't want this, baby, stop it—"

"Who said that I don't want it?" Moving back, she looks up at me again, her gaze dark and heated. "I do want it, Julian... You made me want it."

I suck in a hard breath, my cock jerking as she releases my shirt and reaches for my belt buckle instead. "I don't want to hurt you."

Her lips curve up. "Yes, Julian, you do." She succeeds in undoing the belt, and her hand delves into my shorts, her slender fingers closing around my swollen length and squeezing lightly. "Don't you?"

I nearly explode, my hands reaching for her before I even realize what I'm doing. "Yes..." My voice is closer to a growl as I drag her onto my lap, forcing her to straddle my legs. "I want to hurt you, fuck you, take you in every way possible and then some. I want to mark your pretty skin and hear you scream as I drive deep into your pussy and make you come all over my cock. Is that what you want to hear, my pet?" Gripping her arms tightly, I glare at her. "Is that what you want?"

She runs her tongue over her lips, her eyes gleaming with a peculiar darkness. "Yes." Her voice is whisper-soft. "Yes, Julian. That's exactly what I want."

Fuck. I close my eyes, literally shaking with lust. With the way she's straddling my lap in her dress, only a tiny thong separates her pussy from my dick. If I shift her up a few inches, I could be inside her, pounding her tight little body . . .

The temptation is unbearable.

One, one thousand. Two, one thousand. Three, one thousand. I force myself to do the mental count until I regain a modicum of control.

Then I open my eyes and meet her gaze again.

"No, Nora." My voice is almost steady as I let go of her arms and move my hands up to cup her face in my palms instead. "That's not how this is going to go."

She blinks, looking taken aback. "What—"

I bend my head, cutting her off with a kiss. Slowly and deeply, I invade her mouth, tasting her, stroking her with my tongue. Then I fist my hand in her hair and push her down between my legs, enjoying the look of shock on her small face.

"You're going to suck my cock," I say harshly. "And then, if you're a good girl, you'll get your reward. Understand?"

Nora's eyes widen, but she complies right away. Pulling my dick out of my shorts, she closes her lips around it and begins to stroke it rhythmically with her hand. The interior of her mouth is hot, silky, and wet, almost as delicious as her pussy, and the pressure of her hand is nothing short of perfect. I'm so near the edge all it takes is a couple of minutes, and the orgasm boils out of my balls, blasting ecstasy through my nerve endings. Groaning, I grip her hair and push deeper into her throat, forcing her to swallow every drop.

Then I pull out, kneel on the ground next to her, and make her lie down on the grass. "Spread open your legs," I order, tugging her dress up to expose her lower body.

She does as I instruct, her gaze filled with anticipation and a hint of wariness. I place my hands on her sleek, tan thighs and stroke them, enjoying the delicate texture of her skin. Then I bend down, hook my fingers into her pink thong, and pull it aside, exposing her glistening pussy lips.

"You have such a sexy pussy, baby." The words come out low and raspy as my hunger, just barely quelled, returns with a vengeance. Bending lower, I inhale her sweet, musky scent. "Such a beautiful, wet little pussy."

Her breathing hitches, a moan vibrating in her throat as I press my lips to her folds, kissing them lightly. "Julian, please." She sounds tortured. "Please, I—I need you."

"Yes." I let my breath wash over her sensitive flesh. "I know you do." I give her slit a long, slow lick. "You'll always need me, won't you?"

"Yes." She pushes her hips up, begging. "Always."

"Then, my pet, here's your reward."

Pressing my tongue to her clit, I begin pleasuring her in earnest, drinking in her pleas and moans. When she finally shudders and cries out in release, I lap at her a few more times, drawing out her orgasm, and then I move up to lie beside her on the grass, folding my left arm under my head as a pillow and arranging her head on my right shoulder.

We lie like that for a while, gazing out at the shimmering water of the lake and listening to the quiet chirping of insects. I still want her, but the desire is more mellow now. More controlled. I didn't hurt her this time, but the heaviness in my chest is still there, still weighing on me.

Finally, I can no longer remain silent.

"Nora, last night . . . it wasn't because of Peter's list." I don't know why I feel compelled to tell her this, but I do. I want her to understand that I didn't intend to punish her at that moment, that the pain I inflicted was not part of some cruel design. I don't know why that would matter to her, coming from her kidnapper, or what the distinction really is, but I need her to know this. "It was a mistake. It shouldn't have happened."

She doesn't respond, doesn't acknowledge my words in any way, but after a few moments, she turns in my arms and rests her right hand on my chest, directly over my heart.

CHAPTER TEN

❖ NORA ❖

Over the next two weeks, I do my best to manage the new reality of my situation. Or, more precisely, to go about my life and pretend that nothing's happening.

The nausea comes and goes. I've found that eating small, frequent meals helps, as does sticking to plainer foods. Under Ana's and Julian's watchful eyes, I dutifully take prenatal vitamins and avoid the foods on Dr. Goldberg's list, but I try not to dwell on those things. Until the baby bump shows up, I intend to act as if everything's normal.

Thankfully, my body is cooperating for now. My breasts have gotten a little bigger, and they're more sensitive, but that's the only change I've detected. My stomach is still flat, and I haven't gained any weight. If anything, because of my unsettled tummy, I lost a couple of pounds—a fact that worries Julian, who's doing his best to coddle me into madness.

"I don't need to rest," I protest in exasperation as he once again tries to make me nap in the middle of the day. "Really, I'm fine. I slept ten hours last night. How much sleep does a person need?"

And it's true. For the past couple of weeks, I've been sleeping much better. As strange as it is, knowing that my anxiety has a hormonal cause has alleviated it to a large extent, significantly reducing my nightmares and panic attacks.

My shrink tells me it's because I'm less worried about my head being messed up from everything that's happened. Apparently, stressing about being overly stressed is particularly bad for the psyche, whereas less convoluted stress factors—like having a child with a sadistic arms dealer—are less anxiety-provoking.

"The human brain is highly unpredictable," Dr. Wessex says, looking at me through her trendy Prada glasses. "What you *think* scares you might not be what weighs on your subconscious at all. You may worry about this baby, but it doesn't frighten you as much as the thought that you might never get a grip on your anxiety. If your panic attacks stem from pregnancy, then you know it's a temporary issue—and that helps you feel less anxious about it."

I nod and smile, as if that makes perfect sense. I do that a lot when I talk to her. If Julian didn't insist that I continue my twice-weekly therapy sessions, I would've already stopped them. It's not that I dislike Dr. Wessex—a tall, stylish woman in her mid-forties, she's quite competent and seemingly nonjudgmental—but I find that talking to her just highlights the insanity that is my relationship with Julian.

Why, yes, Doctor, my husband—you know, the man who hired you and insisted you come out to the middle of nowhere—kept me captive on his island for fifteen months, and now I'm so brainwashed I can't live without him and crave abusive sex. Oh, and we're having a baby. Nothing fucked up about that, of course. Just your regular, run-of-the-mill crime family.

Yeah, sure.

In any case, trying to get me to take naps is the least egregious example of Julian's excessive coddling. He also monitors my diet, makes sure that the exercise routine I resumed is fully doctor-approved, and worst of all, treats me with kid gloves in bed. No matter how much I try to provoke him, he won't do more than hold me down in bed. It's as if he's afraid to unleash the brutality within himself, to lose control again.

"I told you, the obstetrician said rougher sex is okay as long as there's no spotting or leaking of amniotic fluid," I tell Julian after he takes me gently yet again. "I'm healthy, everything's normal, so there's really no harm."

"I'm not taking any chances," he replies, kissing the outer rim of my ear, and I know he has no intention of listening to me on the topic.

A part of me still can't believe that I want this from him, that I miss the dark edge to our lovemaking. It's not that I'm ever left unsatisfied—Julian makes sure I have at least a couple of orgasms every night—but something within me craves the intoxicating blend of pleasure-pain, the endorphin rush I get from truly intense sex. Even the fear he makes me feel is addictive in some way, whether I want to admit it or not.

It's sick, but the night we learned about my pregnancy—the night he forced me—has featured in my fantasies more than once in recent days.

What Dr. Wessex would say about that I don't know, and I don't care to find out. It's enough that the memory of that trauma, just like the recollections of my time on the island, have somehow taken on an erotic overtone in my mind.

It's enough to know that I'm completely twisted.

Of course, Julian's uncharacteristic gentleness in bed is not the only issue. Another casualty of his smothering concern for me is my self-defense training. It's particularly frustrating because for the first time in weeks, I have energy. Sleeping well has reduced my fatigue, and schoolwork no longer tires me as much. I've even been able to resume running—after first pre-clearing the activity with the doctor, of course—but Julian refuses to let me do anything that could possibly result in bruises. Shooting is also out of the question; apparently, firing a gun releases lead particles that could, in some unknown quantity, harm the unborn baby.

There are so many restrictions it makes me want to scream.

"You know this is only temporary, Nora," Ana says when I make the mistake of expressing my frustration to her at breakfast. "Just a few more months, and you'll have a baby in your arms—and then it will all be worth it."

I nod and paste a smile on my face, but the housekeeper's words don't cheer me up.

They fill me with dread.

In a little over seven months, I will be responsible for a child—and the idea terrifies me more than ever.

* * *

"You still haven't told your parents about the baby?" Rosa gives me an astonished look as we leave the house to go for our morning walk.

"No," I say, sipping a fruit smoothie with powdered vitamins. "I haven't gotten around to it yet."

"But I thought you talk to them every day."

"I do, but the subject hasn't come up." I probably sound defensive, but I can't help it. In terms of things I dread, telling my parents about my pregnancy is right up there with childbirth.

"Nora . . ." Rosa stops under a thick, vine-draped tree. "Are you worried they won't be happy for you?"

I picture my dad's probable reaction to learning that his not-quite-twenty-year-old daughter is pregnant with her kidnapper's child. "You could say that."

"But why wouldn't they be happy?" My friend looks genuinely confused. "You're married to a wealthy man who loves you and who'll take good care of you and the child. What more could they want?"

"Well, for one thing, for me not to be married to said man at all," I say drily. "Rosa, I told you our story. My parents aren't exactly Julian's biggest fans."

Rosa waves a dismissive hand. "All that is—how do you say it?— water under the bridge. Who cares how it all began? What matters is the present, not the past."

"Oh, sure. Seize the day and all that."

"There's no need to be sarcastic," Rosa says as we resume our walk. "You should talk to your parents, Nora. It's their grandchild. They deserve to know."

"Yeah, I'll probably tell them soon." I take another sip of my smoothie. "I'll have no choice."

We walk in silence for a couple of minutes. Then Rosa asks quietly, "You really don't want this child, do you, Nora?"

I stop and look at her. "Rosa . . ." How do I explain my concerns to a girl who grew up on the estate and who thinks that this kind of life is normal? That my relationship with Julian is romantic? "It's not that I don't want a baby. It's just that Julian's world—*our* world—is too fucked up to bring a child into it. How could somebody like Julian make a good father? How could I make a good mother?"

"What do you mean?" Rosa frowns at me. "Why wouldn't you make a good mother?"

"I'm in love with a crime lord who abducted me, and who kills and tortures people as part of his business," I say gently. "That hardly qualifies me to be a good parent. A case study for one of Dr. Wessex's papers, maybe, but not a good parent."

"Oh, please." Rosa rolls her eyes. "A lot of men do bad things. You Americans are so sensitive. Señor Esguerra is far from the worst there is, and you shouldn't blame yourself for caring about him. That doesn't make *you* bad in any way."

"Rosa, it's not just that." I hesitate, but then decide to just say it. "When we were in Tajikistan, I killed a man." I exhale slowly, reliving the dark thrill of pulling the trigger and watching Majid's brains splatter all over the wall. "I shot him in cold blood."

"So what?" She hardly blinks. "I've killed too."

I gape at her, stunned into silence, and she explains, "It was when the estate was attacked. I found a gun, hid in the bushes, and shot at the men attacking us. I wounded one and killed another. I later learned that the wounded one died too."

"But you were only a child." I can't get over my shock. "You're telling me you killed two people when you were what—ten, eleven?"

"Almost eleven," she says, shrugging. "And yes, I did."

"But . . . but you seem so—"

"Normal?" she supplies, looking at me with a strange smile. "Nice? Of course, why wouldn't I be? I killed to protect those I care about. I killed men who came here to bring us death and destruction. It's no different from cutting off the head of the snake that wants to bite you. If I hadn't killed them, more of our people would've died. Maybe they would've killed my mother, as well as my father and brother."

I don't know what to say to that. I could never have imagined that Rosa—cheerful, round-cheeked Rosa—was capable of something like that. I've always thought that evil leaves a trace. I see it in Julian, etched so deeply into his soul that it's a part of him. I see it in myself now, too. But I don't see it in Rosa. Not at all.

"How do you not let it affect you?" I ask. *How do you retain your innocence?*

She looks at me, and for the first time, she appears older than her twenty-one years. "You can choose to let the black stuff tarnish you, Nora, or you can brush it off," she says quietly. "I chose the latter. I killed, but that's not who I am. I don't let that act define me. It happened, and it's done. It's in the past. I can't change the past, so I'm not going to dwell on it. And neither should you. Your present, your future—that's what matters."

I bite my lip, my eyes beginning to burn with incipient tears. "But what kind of future can this child have with parents like us, Rosa? Look at what's happened to me and Julian over the past two years. How can I be sure my baby won't be kidnapped or tortured by Julian's enemies?"

"You can't be sure." Rosa's gaze is unflinching. "Nobody can be sure of anything. Bad things can happen to anyone, anywhere. There are soldiers who live to a ripe old age, and office workers who die young. There's no rhyme or reason to life, Nora. You can choose to live every moment in fear, or you can enjoy life. Enjoy what you have with Julian. Enjoy this baby you have growing inside you. It's a gift, not a curse, to bring forth life. You might not have chosen to bring a child into this world, but it's here now, and all you can do is love it. Treasure it. Don't let your fears spoil it for you." She pauses, and then adds softly, "Don't let your soul get tarnished by what you can't change."

CHAPTER ELEVEN

❖ JULIAN ❖

"So what's the damage?" I ask Lucas as we leave the training area. I'm breathing hard, my muscles are sore, and my left shoulder is aching, but I feel satisfied.

I'm nearly back to my former fighting shape—as the three guards limping away can testify.

"There was another hit in France, and two more in Germany." Lucas wipes the sweat off his face with a balled-up towel. "He's not wasting any time."

"I didn't think he would." Given Peter Sokolov's singular focus on revenge, I know it's only a matter of time before he eliminates the rest of the men on that list. "How did he do it this time?"

"The French guy was found floating in a river, with marks of torture and strangulation, so I'm guessing Sokolov must've kidnapped him first. For the Germans, one hit was a car bomb, and the other one a sniper rifle." Lucas grins darkly. "They must not have pissed him off as much."

"Or he went for expediency."

"Or that," Lucas agrees. "He probably knows Interpol is on his tail."

"I'm sure he does." I try to imagine what I would do if someone hurt my family, and a shudder of fury ripples through me. I can't even imagine what Peter must be feeling—not that it excuses his endangering Nora to get this fucking list.

I still want to kill him for that.

"By the way," Lucas says casually, "I'm having Yulia Tzakova brought here from Moscow."

I stop dead in my tracks. "The interpreter who betrayed us to the Ukrainians? Why?"

"I want to personally interrogate her," Lucas says, draping the towel around his neck. "I don't trust the Russians to do a thorough job." His expression is as impassive as ever, but I see a hint of excitement in his pale gaze.

He's looking forward to this.

I narrow my eyes, studying him. "Is it because you fucked her that night in Moscow?" The Russian girl came on to me first, but I passed on her invitation—and then Lucas expressed an interest in her. "Is that what this is about?"

His mouth hardens. "She fucked me over. Literally. So yeah, I want to get my hands on the little bitch. But I also think she might have some useful info for us."

I consider that for a moment, then nod. "In that case, go for it." It would be hypocritical of me to deny Lucas some fun with the pretty blonde. If he wants to personally make her pay for the plane crash, I see no harm in that.

She would've been dead before long in Moscow anyway.

"Did you already negotiate this with the Russians?" I ask as we resume walking.

Lucas nods. "Initially, they tried to say they'd only deal with Sokolov, but I convinced them it wouldn't be wise to get on your bad side. Buschekov saw the light when I reminded him of the recent troubles at Al-Quadar."

"Good." If even the Russians are inclined to accommodate me, then my vendetta against the terrorist organization achieved its intended effect. Not only is Al-Quadar utterly decimated, but my reputation is substantially enhanced. Few of my clients are likely to double-cross me now—a development that promises to be good for business.

"Yes, it's helpful," Lucas echoes my thoughts. "She'll be arriving here tomorrow."

I raise my eyebrows, but decide against commenting on the speed of this development. If he wants to play with the Russian girl this badly, it's his business. "Where are you going to keep her?" I ask instead.

"In my quarters. I'll be interrogating her there."

I grin, picturing the interrogation in question. "All right. Enjoy."

"Oh, I will," he says grimly. "You can bet on it."

* * *

After I take a shower, I go looking for Nora. Or, rather, I check my computer for the location of her embedded trackers and go directly to the library, where she must be studying for her finals.

I find her sitting at a desk facing away from me, typing furiously on her laptop. Her hair is tied up in a loose ponytail, and she's wearing a huge T-shirt that falls down to her knees.

My T-shirt, from the looks of it.

She's started doing that lately when she has to study. Claims my T-shirts are more comfortable than her dresses. I don't mind in the least. Seeing her dressed in my clothes only emphasizes the fact that she's mine.

Both she and the baby she's carrying.

She doesn't react as I step into the room and walk up to her. When I reach her, I see why.

She's wearing headphones, her smooth forehead wrinkled in concentration as she pounds at the keyboard, her fingers flying over the keys with startling speed. For a second, I consider leaving her to it, but it's too late. Nora must've seen me out of the corner of her eye, because she looks up and gives me a dazzling smile, removing her headphones.

"Hi." Her voice is soft and a little husky. "Is it dinnertime already?"

"Not quite." I smile back and place my hands on the nape of her neck. Her muscles feel tight, so I begin kneading them with my thumbs. "I just did a few rounds with my men and came here to take a shower before I go back to my office. Figured I'd check on you on the way."

"Oh." She arches into my touch, closing her eyes. "Oh, yeah, right there . . . Oh, that's so good . . ."

She sounds like I'm fucking her, and my response is instantaneous.

I get hard. Very hard.

Fuck.

Drawing in a breath, I rein in my lust, like I've been doing for the past two weeks. When I take her tonight, it will again be in a careful and controlled manner. Regardless of the provocation, I will not risk damaging the baby.

"Is that your Psychology paper?" I keep my tone even as I continue to massage her neck. "You seem to be really into it."

"Oh, yeah." She opens her eyes and tilts her head to look at me. "It's on Stockholm Syndrome."

My hands still. "Is that right?"

She nods, a dark little smile curving her lips. "Yes. Interesting subject, don't you think?"

"Yes, fascinating," I say drily. My pet is definitely getting bolder. Taunting me—likely in the hopes that I'll punish her.

And I want to. My hands itch to bend her over my knee, hike up that giant T-shirt, and spank her perfectly shaped ass until it's pink and red. My cock throbs at the image, especially when I imagine spreading open her cheeks afterwards and penetrating her tight little asshole—

Fucking stop thinking about it. I see Nora's smile deepen as her eyes flick down to the bulge in my jeans. The little witch knows exactly what she's doing to me, what kind of effect she's having on my body.

"Yes, I'm loving it," she murmurs, her gaze returning to my face. "I'm learning so much about the topic."

I inhale slowly and resume rubbing her neck. "Then you'll have to educate me, my pet," I say calmly, as if my body isn't raging with the need to fuck her. "I'm afraid I skipped Psychology at Caltech."

Nora's smile turns sardonic. "You're just a natural then, aren't you?"

I hold her gaze silently, not bothering to reply. There's no need for words. I saw her, I wanted her, and I took her. It's as simple as that. If she wants to label our relationship, to make it fit some psychobabble definition, she's free to do so.

She'll just never be free of me.

After a few moments, she sighs and closes her eyes, leaning into my touch again. I can feel her muscles slowly relaxing as I massage her shoulders and neck. The challenging expression fades from her face, leaving her looking peculiarly young and defenseless. With her eyelashes fanning over her smooth cheeks, she seems as innocent as a newborn fawn, untouched by anything bad in life.

Untouched by me.

For a moment, I wonder what it would be like if things were different. If I were just a boy she met in school, like that Jake I took her from. Would she love me more? Would she love me at all? If I didn't take her the way I did, would she have been mine?

It's foolish to wonder about that, of course. I might as well speculate about time travel or what I'd do if the world came to an end. My reality doesn't allow for what-ifs. What if my parents didn't die and I finished Caltech? What if I'd refused to kill that man when I was eight? What if I'd been able to protect Maria? If I think about all that, I'll go insane, and I refuse to let that happen.

I am what I am, and I can't change.

Not even for her.

* * *

"I talked to my parents this afternoon," Nora says as we sit down to dinner that evening. "They asked me again about visiting them."

"Did they now?" I give her a sardonic look. "And is that all you talked to them about?"

Nora looks down at her salad plate. "I'm going to tell them soon."

"When?" It pisses me off that she keeps acting like the baby doesn't exist. "When you deliver?"

"No, of course not." She looks up and frowns at me. "How do you know I didn't tell them yet, anyway? Are you listening in on my conversations?"

"Of course." I don't listen in on everything, but I've eavesdropped a few times. Just enough to know that her parents remain in blissful ignorance of the latest development in their daughter's life. Still, it wouldn't hurt to have Nora think all her conversations are monitored. "Did you expect me not to?"

Her lips tighten. "Yes, perhaps. Privacy being a basic human right and all that."

"There's no such thing as a basic human right, my pet." I want to laugh at her naïveté. "That's a made-up construct. Nobody owes you anything. If you want something in life, you have to fight for it. You have to make it happen."

"Like you made my captivity happen?"

I give her a cool smile. "Precisely. I wanted you, so I took you. I didn't sit around pining and wishing."

"Or dwelling on the construct of human rights, apparently." Her voice holds just the faintest edge of sarcasm. "Is that how you will raise our child? Just take what you want and don't worry about hurting people?"

I inhale slowly, noting the tension in her features. "Is that what worries you, my pet?"

"A lot of things worry me," she says evenly. "And yes, raising a child with a man who lacks a conscience is fairly high on the list."

For some reason, her words sting. I want to reassure her, tell her that she's wrong to worry, but I can't lie to her any more than I can lie to myself.

I have no idea how I'm going to raise this child, what kind of lessons I'm going to impart. Men like me—men like my father—aren't meant to have children. She knows it, and I know it too.

As though sensing my thoughts, Nora asks quietly, "Why do you even want this baby, Julian? Why is it so important to you?"

I look at her silently, unsure how to answer the question. There's no good reason for this child to be as important to me as it is. No reason for me to want it as badly as I do. I should've been upset—or at the very least, annoyed—by Nora's pregnancy, but instead, when Goldberg gave us the news, the emotion I felt was so foreign that I didn't recognize it at first.

It was joy.

Pure, unadulterated joy.

For a brief, blissful moment, I was truly happy.

When I don't respond, Nora exhales and looks down at her plate again. I watch as she cuts a piece of tomato and begins to eat her salad. Her face is pale and strained, yet each of her movements is so graceful and feminine that I'm hypnotized, completely absorbed by the sight of her.

I can watch her for hours.

When I first brought her to the island, the mealtimes were my favorite part of the day. I loved interacting with her, seeing her battle her fear and try to maintain her composure. Her stoic, fragile bravery had delighted me almost as much as her delicious body. She'd been terrified, yet I could see the calculation behind her timid smiles and shy flirting.

In her own quiet way, my pet has always been a fighter.

"Nora..." I want to take away her stress, her understandable worry, but I can't lie to her. I can't pretend to be someone I'm not. So when she looks up, I say only, "This baby is part you, part me. That's reason enough for me to care." And when she continues to look at me, her expression unchanging, I add quietly, "I'm going to do the best I can for our child, my pet. That much I can promise you."

The corners of her lips lift in a fleeting smile. "Of course you will, Julian. And so will I. But will that be enough?"

"We'll just have to wait and see, won't we?" I respond, and as Ana brings out the next course, we focus on the food and let the topic rest.

CHAPTER TWELVE

❖ NORA ❖

"Did you see the girl who was brought here this morning?" Rosa asks during our usual walk. "Ana said she was handcuffed and everything."

"What?" I give Rosa a startled look. "What girl? I went for a quick run before breakfast, and I didn't see anything."

"I didn't see anything either. Ana told me she spotted her, and she's really blond and beautiful. Apparently, Lucas Kent is keeping her in his quarters." Rosa is clearly relishing imparting this bit of gossip. "Ana thinks she might've betrayed Señor Esguerra in some way."

"Really?" I frown. "I don't know anything about any of this. Julian didn't mention it to me." In general, since I hacked into Julian's computer, he's been telling me less about his business. I don't know if that's because he now distrusts me or because he's trying to keep me as calm as possible in light of the pregnancy. I suspect it's the latter, given how overprotective he is these days.

"Do you want to walk by Kent's house to see?" Rosa's eyes glitter with excitement. "Maybe we can peek in his window."

I gape at her. "Rosa!" This is the last thing I would've expected from her. "We can't do that."

"Come on," my friend cajoles. "It'll be fun. Don't you want to see who this blond girl is and why Kent's got her?"

"I can just ask Julian about it. He'll tell me."

Rosa gives me a pleading look. "Yes, but I might die of curiosity before he does. I just want to see what Kent's doing with her, that's all."

"Why?" I have no desire to see Julian's right-hand man torture some unfortunate woman, and I have no idea why Rosa wants to witness something so disturbing. "If she betrayed Julian, it won't be pretty." My stomach lurches at the thought. Today is not one of my better days, nausea-wise.

Rosa flushes. "Just because. Come on, Nora." Grabbing my wrist, she begins to tug me in the direction of the guards' quarters. "Let's just go over there. You're pregnant, so no one will get mad at you for snooping."

I let myself get towed behind her, flabbergasted by her inexplicable desire to play spy. Normally, Rosa displays little interest in matters concerning my husband's criminal activities. I can't fathom what's behind her unusual behavior, unless . . .

"Are you interested in Lucas?" I blurt out, stopping and bringing us both to a halt. "Is that what this is all about?"

"What? No!" Rosa's voice takes on a higher pitch. "I'm just curious, that's all."

I stare at her, noting the brighter blush staining her cheeks. "Oh my God, you *are* interested."

Rosa huffs and lets go of my wrist, crossing her arms over her chest. "I'm not."

I hold up my palms in a conciliatory gesture. "Okay, okay. If you say so."

Rosa glares at me for a moment, but then her shoulders slump and her arms drop to her sides. "Okay, fine," she says glumly. "So maybe I do find him attractive. Just a little bit, okay?"

"Okay, of course," I say with a reassuring smile. With his blond hair and fierce, square-jawed face, Lucas Kent reminds me of a Viking warrior—or at least Hollywood's depiction of one. "He's a good-looking man."

Rosa nods. "He is. He doesn't know that I exist, of course, but that's to be expected."

"What do you mean?" I frown at her. "Have you ever tried talking to him?"

"Talking about what? I'm just the maid who cleans the main house and occasionally brings the guards some treats from Ana."

"You can ask him what his favorite food is," I suggest. "Or how his day went. It doesn't have to be anything complicated. Just a simple hello would probably put you on his radar." As I say this, I realize that being on the radar of a man like Lucas Kent may not be the best thing for Rosa—or any woman, really.

Before I can take back my suggestion, Rosa sighs and says, "I've said hello to him before. I just don't think he *sees* me, Nora. Not like that. And why would he? I mean, look at me." She gestures derisively toward herself.

"What are you talking about?" I still don't think getting Lucas's attention would be a positive development in Rosa's life, but I can't let that comment slide. "You're very attractive."

"Oh, please." Rosa gives me an incredulous look. "I'm average at best. Someone like Kent is used to supermodels—like that blond girl he's got with him now. I'm not his type."

"Well, if you're not his type, then he's a fool," I say firmly, and mean it. With her pleasantly round face, warm brown eyes, and bright smile, Rosa is quite pretty. She also has the kind of figure I've always envied: lush and curvy, with a nipped-in waist and full breasts. "You're a beautiful girl—a guy would have to be blind not to see that."

She snorts. "Right. That's why my love life is so great."

"Your love life is limited by the borders of this estate," I remind her. "Besides, didn't you tell me you dated a couple of the guards?"

"Oh, sure." She waves her hand dismissively. "Eduardo and Nick—but that doesn't mean anything. Guards are limited in their selection too, and they're not that picky. They'll fuck anything that moves."

"Rosa." I give her a reproving look. "Now you're just exaggerating."

She grins. "Okay, maybe. I should probably say 'anything *female* that moves'—though I hear Dr. Goldberg gets some action, too. Rumor has it tattooed guys are his fave." She waggles her eyebrows suggestively.

I shake my head, involuntarily grinning back, and we both burst into laughter at the image of the staid doctor getting it on with one of the big, tatted-up guards.

"Okay, now that we've established you're crushing on Mr. Blond and Dangerous," I say a couple of minutes later when we stop laughing and resume walking toward the guards' housing, "can you please tell me again why you want to spy on him with this chick?"

"I don't know," Rosa admits. "I just do. It's sick, I know, but I just want to see what he's like with another woman."

"Rosa . . ." I still don't get it. "If she arrived here in handcuffs, they're not exactly having a romantic date. You know that, right?"

"Yes, of course." She sounds remarkably flippant. "He's probably doing something horrible to her."

"And you want to see that why?"

She shrugs. "I don't know. Maybe I'm hoping that seeing him like that will help me get over this silly crush. Or maybe I'm just morbidly curious. Does it really matter?"

"No, I guess not." I hurry to keep up with her fast stride. "But I can tell you right now that Dr. Wessex would have a lot of fun with you."

"Oh, I'm sure," she says and grins at me again. "It's a good thing you're the one in therapy then, isn't it?"

* * *

The guards' barracks are on the very edge of the compound, right next to the jungle. Mixed in with the cluster of small, boxy buildings are a few regular-sized houses. From my earlier explorations, I know that they're occupied by some of the higher-ranked employees in Julian's organization and guards who have families.

As we approach, Rosa makes a beeline for one of those larger homes, and I follow her, half-running to keep up. My stomach is beginning to feel unsettled, and I'm already regretting that I gave in to this insanity.

"This is it," she says in a hushed tone as we go around the side of the house. "His bedroom is here."

"And you know this how?"

She grins at me. "I might've been out here a time or two before."

"Rosa . . ." I'm discovering a whole new side to my friend. "You've spied on the poor man before?"

"Just once or twice," she whispers, crouching under a window as I hang back a few feet and observe. "Now, shhh." She presses her finger to her lips in a silencing gesture.

I lean against a tree trunk, cross my arms, and watch as she slowly rises and peeks into the window. I'm astounded that she's bold enough to do this in broad daylight. Even though this side of Lucas's house faces the forest, there are plenty of guards in the area, and they could theoretically spot us hanging around.

Before I can voice that concern to Rosa, she turns toward me with a disappointed look on her face. "They're not there," she says in a low voice. "I wonder where they could be."

"Maybe he took her elsewhere," I say, relieved by this development. "Let's go."

"Hold on, let me just check something." Still crouching, she moves toward a window further to the left.

I reluctantly trail after her, increasingly nauseous and uncomfortable with the situation. Another minute, I promise myself, and I'll head back.

Just as I'm about to tell her that I'm leaving, Rosa lets out a soft gasp and waves for me to come closer. "There," she says in an excited whisper, pointing at the window. "He's got her right there."

Now my own curiosity kicks in. Bending down, I make my way to where Rosa is hiding and crouch next to her. "What is he doing?" I whisper, almost afraid to know.

"I don't know," she whispers back, turning to look at me. "He's not in the room. She's alone there."

"What is *she* doing then?"

"See for yourself. She's not looking this way."

I hesitate for a moment, but the temptation proves to be too much. Holding my breath, I rise just enough to see over the lower rim of the window, barely cognizant of Rosa peeking in next to me.

As I feared, the view inside makes my stomach flip.

The room I'm looking at is large and sparsely furnished. Judging by the black leather sofa near the wall and the TV on the opposite side, it must be Lucas's living room. The walls are painted white, and the carpet is gray. It's a starkly masculine room, functional and uncompromising, but it's not the decor that catches my attention.

It's the young woman in the middle.

Completely naked, she's tied to a sturdy wooden chair, her feet spread apart and her hands bound behind her back. Her head is lowered, her tangled blond hair concealing her face and much of her upper body. All I can see of her are narrow feet and long pale limbs covered with bruises.

Limbs that appear far too thin for a girl of her height.

As I stare in horrified fascination, she lifts her head in a sudden jerky movement and looks directly at me, her blue eyes sharp and clear in her delicately featured face.

I instantly duck, my pulse racing from a burst of adrenaline. Rosa, however, is still looking in the window, her expression that of avid curiosity.

"Rosa," I hiss, grabbing her arm. "She saw us. Let's go."

"Okay, okay," my friend concedes, letting me tug her away. "Let's go."

We head back toward our usual path in silence. Rosa appears to be deep in thought, and I can't bring myself to speak, my nausea intensifying with every step. As we pass by a set of rose bushes, I kneel down and throw up while Rosa holds my hair and repeatedly apologizes for causing me distress in my condition.

I wave her apologies away, shakily getting back on my feet. What disturbs me the most is not the fact that I saw a woman bound and likely about to be tortured.

It's that the sight didn't shock me as it should have.

* * *

Julian doesn't join me for dinner that night. According to Ana, he has an emergency call with one of his Hong Kong associates. I consider going to his office to listen in, but decide to use the time to call my parents instead.

"Nora, honey, when are we going to see you again?" my mom asks for the dozenth time after I give her a quick update on my classes. My dad is traveling for business, so it's just the two of us on video chat today. "I miss you so much."

"I know, Mom. I miss you too." I bite the inside of my cheek, my eyes suddenly burning with tears. *Fucking pregnancy hormones.* "I told you, Julian said we'll be able to come at some point soon."

"When?" my mom asks in frustration. "Why can't you just give us a date?"

Because I'm pregnant, and my overprotective kidnapper/husband refuses to even talk about going anywhere right now. "Mom..." I take a breath, trying to gather my courage. "I think there's something you should know."

My mom leans closer to the camera, instant worry creasing her forehead. "What is it, honey?"

"I'm eight weeks pregnant. Julian and I are having a baby." As soon as the words are out, I feel like a slab of granite was lifted off my shoulders. I hadn't realized until this moment how heavily this secret weighed on me.

My mom blinks. "What? Already?"

"Um, yeah." This is not the reaction I was expecting. Frowning, I lean closer to the camera. "What do you mean, *already*?"

"Well, your dad and I figured that with the two of you being married and all . . ." She shrugs. "I mean, we were hoping it wouldn't happen for a while, and you'd get to finish school first—"

"You figured I'd have children with Julian?" I feel like I'm in an alternate universe. "And you're okay with that?"

My mom sighs and leans back, regarding me with a weary expression. "Of course we're not okay with that. But we can't live our lives in denial, no matter how much your dad might want to try. Obviously, this is not what we wanted for you, but—" She stops and heaves another sigh before saying, "Look, honey, if this is what you want, if he really does make you as happy as you say, then it's not our place to interfere. We just want you happy and healthy. You know that, right?"

"I do, Mom." I blink rapidly, trying to contain a fresh influx of emotional tears. "I do."

"Good." She smiles, and I'm pretty sure I see her eyes glistening with tears of her own. "Now tell me all about it. Have you been sick? Have you been tired? How did you find out? Was it an accident?"

And for the next hour, my mom and I talk about babies and pregnancy. She tells me all about her own experience—I was an oops baby for her and Dad, conceived during their honeymoon—and I explain that I hurt my arm when I was abducted by the terrorists and had to have the implant out for a short time. It's the closest I can come to the truth: that Al-Quadar cut the implant out of my arm because they mistook it for a tracking device. My parents know about my abduction from the mall—I had to explain my disappearance to them somehow—but I didn't tell them the full story.

They have no idea that their daughter acted as bait to save her abductor's life and killed a man in cold blood.

By the time we finally wrap up our conversation, it's dark outside, and I'm beginning to feel tired. As soon as we disconnect, I shower, brush my teeth, and get in bed to wait for Julian.

After a while, my eyelids grow heavy, and I feel the lethargy of sleep stealing over me. As my mind begins to drift, an image appears in front of my eyes: that of a girl bound and helpless, tied to a chair in the middle of a large, white-walled room. Her hair, however, is not blond.

It's dark . . . and her belly is swollen with child.

CHAPTER THIRTEEN

❖ JULIAN ❖

It's nearly midnight by the time I finish work and get to our bedroom. Entering the room, I turn on the bedside lamp and see that Nora is already asleep, curled up under the blanket. I shower and join her there, pulling her naked body to me as soon as I get under the sheets. She fits me perfectly, her curvy little ass nestling against my groin and her neck pillowed on my outstretched arm. My other arm, bent, rests on her side, my hand cupping one small, firm breast.

A breast that feels a little plumper than before, reminding me that her body is changing.

It's bizarre how erotic I find that knowledge, how the thought of Nora growing round with child turns me on. I've never thought of pregnant women as being sexy, but with my wife, I find myself obsessed with her still-slim body, fascinated by its possibilities. My sex drive, always strong, is through the roof these days, and it's all I can do not to attack her constantly.

If not for my twice-daily jerk-off sessions, I wouldn't be able to restrain myself.

Even now, after I just masturbated in the shower, lying wrapped around her like this is torture. I'm not willing to move away, though. I need to feel her against me, even if all I'm going to do is cuddle her. She needs rest, and I have every intention of letting her sleep. However, as I settle more comfortably on the pillow, she stirs in my arms and says sleepily, "Julian?"

"Of course, baby." I give in to temptation and nuzzle the soft skin behind her ear as I slide my hand from her breast to the warm folds between her legs. "Who else could it be?"

"I—I don't know . . ." Her breathing catches as I find her clit and press on it. "What time is it?"

"It's late." I push one finger into her to test her readiness, and my dick throbs at the slickness I feel in her tight, hot channel. "I should let you go back to sleep."

"No." She gasps as I curve my finger inside her, hitting her G-spot. "I'm okay, really."

"Are you?" I can't resist tormenting her a little. I have to rein in my sadistic urges these days, but hearing her beg is not something I can pass up. Lowering my voice, I murmur, "I'm not so sure. I think I should stop."

"No, please don't." She moans as I circle her clit with my thumb and simultaneously rub my hard-on on her ass. "Please don't stop."

"Tell me what you want me to do to you then." I continue circling her clit. She feels like live fire in my arms, her body warm and sleek. Her hair smells flowery from her shampoo, and her inner walls flex around my finger, as if trying to suck it deeper into her pussy. "Tell me exactly what you want, my pet."

"You know what I want." She's panting now, her hips shimmying as she tries to force my fingers into a steady rhythm. "I want you to fuck me. Hard."

"How hard?" My voice roughens as dark, depraved images invade my mind. There are so many dirty things I want to do to her, so many ways I want to take her. Even after all this time, there is an innocence to her that makes me want to corrupt her. Makes me want to push her to the limits. "Tell me, Nora. I want to hear every detail."

"Why?" she asks breathlessly, grinding her pelvis against my hand. Her pussy is dripping now, coating my fingers with her wetness. "You won't do what I want."

"You don't get to ask why." Stilling my hand, I let some of the darker craving seep into my voice. "Now tell me."

"I—" She sucks in her breath as I resume playing with her clit. "I want you to fuck me so hard it hurts." Her voice quavers as I push a second finger into her, stretching her small opening. "I want you to tie me up and make me do what you want."

"Do you want me to fuck your ass?"

Her pussy clenches around my fingers as a shudder ripples through her body. "I—" Her voice breaks. "I don't know."

If my balls didn't feel like they're about to explode, I'd find her evasiveness amusing. One of these days I'm going to make her admit that she's grown to like anal sex, that she enjoys being taken that way. In fact, I'm going to make her *beg* for my cock in her little asshole. For now, though, all this talk is just that: talk. As much as I'd love to fuck every one of her tight holes, I can't. I won't risk the baby for momentary pleasure.

This verbal interlude will have to be enough until Nora gives birth.

Withdrawing my fingers from her body, I grip my dick and guide it to her warm, wet pussy. She moans as I begin to push into her. With both of us lying on our sides and with her legs closed, the fit is even tighter than usual, and I go slowly, ignoring the savage lust pounding through my veins.

Do not hurt her. Do not hurt her. The words are like a mantra in my brain. She arches her back, curving her spine to better accommodate me, and I slide my hand to the front of her sex, seeking out the small bud peeking through her folds. As my fingers make contact with her clit, she gasps out my name, and I feel her spasming around me, her inner muscles contracting as she finds her release.

My heart thumping heavily in my chest, I take deep breaths and hold still, trying to contain my own impending explosion. When the urge to come abates slightly, I begin to thrust into her, rubbing her engorged clit at the same time. She lets out an incoherent noise, something between a moan and a gasp, and her body tenses in my embrace. As I continue to fuck her in short, shallow strokes, she tenses even more, crying out, and I feel her swollen flesh clamping down on me as she reaches her second peak.

The sensation of her milking my cock is indescribable, the pleasure sharp and electric. It zings through me, hurling me into a sudden climax. Groaning harshly, I grind my pelvis against her, burrowing deep into her pussy as my seed bursts out with violent, orgasmic force.

Afterwards, we lie there trying to catch our breath, our bodies glued together with sweat. As my heart rate slowly returns to normal, a feeling of satiation, of relaxed contentment, spreads through me. I know I should get up and bring Nora to the shower for a quick rinse, but it feels too good to just lie there, holding her as my cock softens inside her body. Closing my eyes, I let myself luxuriate in the moment, my thoughts drifting as I start to sink into the heavy nothingness of sleep.

"Julian?" Nora's soft voice jolts me out of my near-slumber, sending my heartbeat spiking.

"What is it, baby?" My tone is sharp with sudden worry. "Are you okay?"

She lets out a heavy sigh and turns around in my arms, moving back to look at me. "Of course I'm okay. Why wouldn't I be?"

I exhale slowly, too relieved—and sexually replete—to get annoyed at her exasperated tone. "What is it then?" I ask more calmly, bringing the blanket up to cover her. The room is cool from air conditioning, and I know Nora gets chilly when she's tired.

She sighs again as I tuck the blanket around her. "You know I'm not made of glass, right?"

I don't bother replying to that. Instead, I stare at her, eyes narrowed, until she blows out a breath and says, "I just wanted to let you know that I talked to my parents, that's all."

"About the baby?"

"Yes." A pleased smile curves her lips. "Mom reacted surprisingly well."

"She's a smart woman, your mother. What about your father?"

"He wasn't on the call, but Mom said she'll talk to him."

"Good." I find it strangely satisfying, knowing that Nora finally took this step. It means she's that much closer to acceptance, to finally admitting that the baby is a fact of our lives. "Now you can stop worrying about it."

"Right." Her eyes gleam black in the soft light of the bedside lamp. "The hard part is over. Now all I need to do is give birth and raise the child."

Her tone is light, but I can hear the fear underneath the sarcasm. She's terrified about the future, and as much as I want to reassure her, I can't tell her that everything will be all right.

Because deep inside, I'm just as terrified as she is.

* * *

Given the late night in the office, I sleep longer than usual, and when I wake up, Nora is already stirring.

Hearing my movements, she rolls over in bed and gives me a sleepy smile. "You're still here."

"I am." Giving in to a momentary impulse, I pull her close, wrapping my arms tightly around her. Sometimes it feels like the time we have together is not enough. Even though I see her every day, I want more.

I constantly want more with her.

She drapes her leg over my thigh and burrows even closer, rubbing her nose against my chest. My body reacts predictably, my morning erection stiffening to a painful hardness. Before I can do anything, however, she distracts me by speaking. "Julian..." Her voice is muffled. "Who's the woman in Lucas's house?"

Surprised, I pull back to look at her. "How do you know about that?"

"Rosa and I saw her yesterday." Nora seems reluctant to meet my gaze. "We were, um... passing by." She glances up at me through her lashes.

"Were you now?" Propping myself up on my elbow, I study her, noting the flush on her face. "And why were you passing by? You don't normally walk in that area."

"We did yesterday." Pulling the blanket around herself, Nora sits up and gives me a determined look. "So who is she? What did she do?"

I sigh. I didn't want Nora exposed to that drama, but it looks like I can't avoid it. "The girl is the Russian interpreter who sold us out to the Ukrainians," I explain, carefully watching Nora's reaction. My pet is just getting over her nightmares, and the last thing I want is to trigger a relapse.

As I speak, Nora's eyes grow wide. "She's responsible for the plane crash?"

"Not directly, but the information she gave to the Ukrainians led to it, yes." If Lucas hadn't decided to take charge of the situation, I would've sent someone to Moscow to take care of the traitor—if the Russians hadn't done it for me first, that is.

As Nora digests that information, I see her expression changing, darkening. It's fascinating to observe. Her soft lips stiffen, and her gaze fills with pure hatred. "She almost killed you," she says in a choked voice. "Julian, that bitch almost killed you."

"Yes, and she killed nearly fifty of my men." It's that loss that eats at me more than anything—and I know it eats at Lucas as well. Whatever punishment he decides to dole out to his prisoner will be no less than she deserves, and I see that Nora is reaching the same realization.

As I watch, she jumps off the bed, leaving the blanket there. Grabbing her robe, she pulls it on before starting to pace around the room, visibly agitated. The brief glimpse of her naked body arouses me again, but I keep my gaze focused on her face as I get up.

"Does it bother you, my pet?" I ask. Nora stops pacing, her eyes straying to my lower body before she looks up at me. "Is that why you want to know about her?"

"Of course it bothers me." Nora's voice is filled with a tension I can't quite define. "There's a woman tied up on our compound."

"A female traitor," I correct. "She's hardly an innocent victim."

"Why couldn't you let the Russian authorities take care of it?" Nora steps closer. "Why did you need to bring her here?"

"Lucas wanted this. He has a bit of a . . . personal . . . relationship with her."

Nora's eyes widen with comprehension. "He had an affair with her?"

"More of a one-night stand, but yes." I walk toward the bathroom, and Nora follows me there. When I turn on the shower and begin brushing my teeth, she picks up her own toothbrush and does the same. I can see that she still looks agitated, so after I rinse out the toothpaste, I say, "If this really bothers you, I can have him take her away somewhere."

Nora puts down her toothbrush and gives me a sarcastic look. "So he could torture her with no one the wiser? How would that make it better?"

I shrug, walking over to the shower stall. "You wouldn't see it." I leave the stall door open, so I can talk to her. The shower is spacious enough that no water will get out.

"Right, of course." She stares at me as I begin to lather up. "So if I don't see it, it's not happening."

I let out another sigh. "Come here, baby." Ignoring the soap covering my hands, I reach for her and tug her into the stall with me. Then I take off her robe and throw it on the floor outside the stall.

She doesn't resist as I bring her under the hot spray with me. Instead, she closes her eyes and stands still as I pour shampoo into my palm and begin massaging it into her scalp. Even wet, her hair feels good to the touch, thick and silky around my fingers.

It's strange how much I enjoy taking care of her like this. How the simple act of washing her hair both soothes me and turns me on. At moments like these, it's easier to forget the violence within me, to quell the cravings I can't give in to for months to come.

"What difference does it make whether Lucas is the one to mete out punishment, or if it's the Russians?" I ask when I'm done lathering her hair. Nora's not saying anything, but I know she's still thinking about the interpreter, obsessing about her fate. "The outcome would be the same. You know that, my pet, right?"

She nods silently, then tilts her head back to rinse off the shampoo.

"So why are you dwelling on it?" I reach for the hair conditioner as she wipes the water off her face and opens her eyes to look at me. "Do you want her to walk free?"

"I should." She stares at me as I begin working the conditioner into her hair. "I shouldn't want her to suffer like this."

My lips curl with savage amusement. "But you do, don't you? You want revenge just as much as I do." Her agitation makes sense to me now. As with the man she killed, Nora's middle-class sensibilities are clashing with her instincts. She knows what society dictates she *should* feel, and it bothers her that the actual emotions she's experiencing are quite different.

It's not human nature to turn the other cheek, and my pet is starting to realize that.

Nora closes her eyes again and moves her head under the spray. The water cascades down her face, turning her lashes into long, dark spikes. "I wanted to die when I thought you were dead," she says, her voice barely audible through the running water. "It was even worse than when I lost you that first time. When I saw the girl, I figured she did *something* to harm your business, but I didn't realize she'd caused the crash."

I picture how Nora must've felt that day, and an acute ache spreads through my chest. I'd go insane if I ever thought I'd lost her. "Baby . . ." Stepping closer, I use my back to shield her from the spray and cup her face in my palms, staring down at her. "It's over. That episode in our lives is over, okay? It's in the past."

She doesn't reply, so I bend my head and take her mouth in a deep, slow kiss, comforting her the only way I know how.

CHAPTER FOURTEEN

❖ NORA ❖

I'm losing myself. Slowly and surely, I'm being drawn into Julian's dark orbit, sucked in by the twisted morass that is this estate.

I've known this for a while, of course. I've been observing my own transformation with a kind of distant horror and curiosity. Things that once seemed abhorrent to me are now part of my everyday life. Murder, torture, illegal arms dealing—intellectually, I still condemn it all, but it no longer bothers me as it once did. My moral compass has been gradually tilting off-course, and I've been letting it happen.

I've been letting Julian's world change me without so much as putting up a fight.

Even before I knew what the blond girl had done, her plight didn't affect me on any kind of deep emotional level. Like Rosa, I had been morbidly curious rather than appalled. And now that I know she's the interpreter who nearly killed Julian, the hatred surging through my veins leaves little room for pity. I understand that it's wrong to let Lucas punish her in this manner, but I don't *feel* the wrongness of it.

I want her to suffer, to pay for the agony she put us through.

The fact that I can think at all right now, much less analyze my disconcerting emotions, is bizarre. I'm in the shower, and Julian is kissing me, drugging my senses with his touch. His hands are cradling my face, and my body is responding to him as always, the warm water sluicing over my skin adding to the burning heat within me. My thoughts, however, are cold and clear. There's only one solution I can see, only one way I can attempt to salvage what remains of my soul.

I have to get away.

Not permanently. Not forever. But I have to leave, even if it's just for a couple of weeks. I need to regain my sense of perspective, re-immerse myself in the world outside our compound.

If not for my own sake, then for the tiny life I'm carrying.

"Julian . . ." My voice shakes when he finally releases my lips and slides one hand down my back, making my sex pulse with need. "Julian, I want to go home."

He stops abruptly and lifts his head, still holding me against him. His gaze hardens, the heat of desire morphing into something cold and menacing. "You *are* home."

"I want to see my parents," I insist, my heart beating rapidly in my chest. With Julian's powerful body surrounding me and the steam from the shower fogging up the stall, I feel like I'm trapped in a bubble of naked flesh and lust. My body clamors for his touch, but my mind screams that I can't give in. Not with so much at stake.

A muscle starts ticking in his jaw. "I told you I'll take you at some point. But not now. Not in your condition."

"Then when?" I force myself to hold his gaze. "When I have an infant to care for? Or a toddler? How about when the child is full-grown? Do you think it'll be safe for me to go then?"

Julian's lips thin into a hard, dangerous line. Backing me up against the shower wall, he grasps my wrists and pins them above my head. "Don't push me, my pet," he murmurs, his erection pressing into my stomach. "You won't like the consequences."

Despite my determination, a tendril of fear coils in my chest. I know Julian won't hurt me right now, but physical punishment is not the only weapon in my husband's arsenal. Images of Jake's brutal beating flash through my mind, bringing with them a sickening chill.

"Don't," I whisper as he leans down and brushes his lips against my ear, the tender gesture a stark contrast to the threat of his body looming over me. "Julian, don't do this."

He straightens, his eyes like hard blue gems. "Don't do what?" Transferring my wrists into one of his large palms, he trails his free hand over my breasts and down my belly, his fingers grazing over my burning skin.

"Don't—" My voice breaks, his touch making my core throb with need despite the lingering chill. "Don't let it be like this."

His hand comes up, his fingers catching my jaw in an inescapable grip. "Like what?" he asks, his tone deceptively even. "Like you're mine?"

My breath catches. "I'm your wife, not your slave—"

"You're whatever I wish you to be, my pet. I own you." The casual cruelty of his words hits me like a blow, knocking all air out of my lungs. Something of my reaction must've shown because his grip on me eases, his tone softening slightly as he says, "This is your home, Nora. Here. With me. Not out there."

"They're my parents, Julian. My family. Just like *you* are my family now. I can't spend my whole life locked in a cage for my safety. I'll go crazy." I can feel tears gathering behind my eyelids, and I blink rapidly, trying to hold them back. The last thing I want is to show what an emotional mess I am these days.

Stupid pregnancy hormones.

Julian stares at me, his eyes glittering with frustration, and then, with an abrupt movement, he releases me, stepping back. Turning off the water, he steps out of the stall, grabbing a towel with barely controlled violence. His cock is still hard, and the fact that he's not already on me is surprising, even considering his new, treat-Nora-like-glass approach.

Moving cautiously, I follow him out of the shower, my wet feet sinking into the plush softness of the bathroom mat. "Can you please—" I begin, but Julian is already stepping toward me with the towel. Wrapping it around me, he pats me dry before stepping back to grab another towel for himself.

"What does all this have to do with Yulia Tzakova?" His words stop me in my tracks as I'm about to leave the bathroom. When I turn toward him in confusion, he clarifies, "The Russian interpreter you saw yesterday. Does she have anything to do with your sudden desire to see your parents?"

I consider denying it for a second, but Julian can tell when I'm lying. "In a way," I say carefully. "I just need some time away from here, a change of scenery. I need a breather, Julian." I swallow, holding his gaze. "I need it badly."

He stares at me, and then, without saying another word, goes into the bedroom to get dressed.

* * *

At breakfast, Julian is silent, seemingly absorbed with emails on his iPad. I feel ignored—an unfamiliar sensation for me. Usually, when we have meals together, I have Julian's undivided attention, and the fact that he's focusing on something else bothers me far more than is reasonable.

I debate trying to break the silence, but I don't want to make things worse. As it is, this morning's argument probably killed my chances of getting off the estate. I should've waited until a more appropriate time to bring up the visit to my parents; blurting it out in the middle of a make-out session hadn't been the smartest move.

Of course, there's no guarantee that a different approach would've altered the outcome. Once Julian makes a decision, I have little chance of changing his mind, especially if the matter concerns my safety. I fought him on the trackers, and they're still embedded in my body. Julian will never let me remove them, just as he might never let me off the compound. For all intents and purposes, he does own me, and there's nothing I can do about that fact.

Trying not to give in to the dull despair pressing down on me, I finish my eggs and get up, not wanting to linger in the tense atmosphere. Before I can step away from the table, however, Julian looks up from his iPad and gives me a sharp look. "Where are you going?"

"To study for my exams," I reply cautiously.

"Sit." He gestures imperiously toward my chair. "We're not done yet."

Suppressing a flare of anger, I return to my seat and cross my arms. "I really have to study, Julian."

"When is your last final?"

I stare at him, my pulse accelerating as a tiny bubble of hope forms in my chest. "It's flexible with the online program. If I finish all the lectures early, I can take the exams right away."

"So early June?" he presses.

"No, sooner." I place my sweaty palms on the table. "I can potentially be done in the next week and a half."

"Okay." He looks down at the iPad again and types something as I watch him, hardly daring to breathe. After a minute, he looks up again, pinning me with a hard blue gaze. "I'm only going to tell you this once, Nora," he says evenly. "If you disobey me, or do anything to endanger yourself while we're in Chicago, I *will* punish you. Do you understand me?"

Before he even finishes speaking, I'm halfway around the table, nearly knocking over his chair as I leap on him. "Yes!" I don't even know how I end up on his lap, but somehow I'm there, my arms wrapped around his neck as I rain kisses all over his face. "Thank you! Thank you! Thank you!"

He lets me kiss him until I run out of breath, and then he frames my face with his big hands, gazing at me intently. I can see the gleam of desire in his eyes, feel the hard bulge pressing into my thighs, and I know we're going to continue what we started this morning. My body begins to pulse in anticipation, my nipples tightening under the fabric of my dress.

As if sensing my growing arousal, Julian smiles darkly and rises to his feet, holding me against his chest. "Don't make me regret this, my pet," he murmurs as he carries me toward the stairs. "You don't want to disappoint me, believe me."

"I won't," I vow fervently, winding my arms around his neck. "I promise you, Julian, I won't."

PART III: THE TRIP

CHAPTER FIFTEEN

❖ NORA ❖

I'm going home. Oh my God, I'm going home.

Even now, as I look out the window of the plane at the clouds below, I can hardly believe this is happening. Only two weeks have passed since our conversation at breakfast, and here we are, on our way to Oak Lawn.

"This plane is nothing like what I've seen on TV," Rosa says, gazing around the luxurious interior of the cabin. "I mean, I knew we wouldn't be flying on a regular airline, but this is *really* nice, Nora."

I grin at her. "Yes, I know. The first time I saw it, I had the same reaction." I sneak a quick glance at Julian, who's sitting on the couch with his laptop, seemingly ignoring our conversation. He told me he's planning to meet with his portfolio manager while we're in Chicago, so I'm guessing he's going over prospective investments in preparation. It's either that or the latest drone design modification from his engineers; that project has been taking up a lot of his time this week.

"My first time flying, and it's on a private jet. Can you believe it? The only way this could be better is if we were going to New York," Rosa says, bringing my attention back to her. Her brown eyes are bright with excitement, and she's practically bouncing in her plush leather seat. She's been like this for several days, ever since I got Julian to agree to have her come with us to America—something my friend has been dreaming about for years.

"Chicago is pretty nice too," I say, amused at her unintentional snobbery. "It's a cool city, you'll see."

"Oh, of course." Realizing she insulted my home, Rosa flushes. "I'm sure it's great, and I don't want you to think I'm ungrateful," she says quickly, looking distraught. "I know you're only bringing me along because you're nice, and I'm ecstatic to be going—"

"Rosa, you're coming along because I need you," I interrupt, not wanting her to go into this in front of Julian. "You're the only one Ana trusts to make my morning smoothies, and you know I need those vitamins."

Or at least that's what I told my obsessively protective husband when I asked to have Rosa come with us. I'm fairly certain I could've made the smoothies myself—or just swallowed the vitamin pills—but I wanted to make sure he'd allow my friend to join us. To this day, I'm not sure if he agreed because he believed me, or because he didn't have any objections to begin with. Either way, I don't want Rosa to inadvertently rock the boat . . . or the private jet, as the case may be.

It still doesn't feel entirely real, the fact that we're on our way to see my parents. The past two weeks have simply flown by. With all the exams and papers, I barely had time to think about the upcoming trip. It wasn't until three days ago that I was able to catch my breath and realize that the trip was, in fact, happening, and Julian had already made all the necessary preparations, beefing up the security around my parents to White House levels.

"Oh, yes, the smoothies," Rosa says, shooting a cautious look in Julian's direction. She finally caught on. "Of course, I forgot. And I'll be helping to unpack all the art supplies, so you don't overtire yourself."

"Right, exactly." I give her a conspiratorial grin. "Can't have me lifting heavy canvases and all that."

At that moment, the plane shakes, and Rosa's face turns white, her excitement evaporating. "What—what is that?"

"Just turbulence," I say, breathing slowly to combat an immediate swell of nausea. I'm still not entirely out of the morning-sickness phase, and the plane's jerky motion is not helpful.

"We won't crash, will we?" Rosa asks fearfully, and I shake my head to reassure her. When I glance over at Julian, however, I see that he's looking at me, his face unusually tense and his knuckles white as he grips the computer.

Without thinking, I unbuckle my seatbelt and get up, wanting to go over to him. If Rosa is afraid of crashing, I can only imagine how Julian must feel, having experienced a crash less than three months ago.

"What are you doing?" Julian's voice is sharp as he stands up, dropping the computer on the couch. "Sit down, Nora. It's not safe."

"I just—"

Before I finish speaking, he's already next to me, forcing me back into the seat and strapping me in. "Sit," he barks, glaring at me. "Did you not promise to behave?"

"Yes, but I just—" At the expression on Julian's face, I fall silent before muttering, "Never mind."

Still glaring at me, he steps back and takes a seat across from me and Rosa. She looks uncomfortable, her hands twisting in her lap as she gazes out the window. I feel bad for her; I'm sure it's awkward to see her friend being treated like a disobedient child.

"I don't want you to fall if the plane hits an air pocket," Julian says in a calmer tone when I show no further signs of trying to get up. "It's not safe to be walking around the cabin during turbulence."

I nod and focus on breathing slowly. It helps with both nausea and anger. Sometimes I forget the facts and start thinking that we have a normal marriage, a partnership of equals, instead of . . . well, whatever it is we have. On paper, I might be Julian's wife, but in reality, I'm far closer to his sex slave.

A sex slave who's desperately in love with her owner.

Closing my eyes, I find a comfortable position in the middle of the spacious leather seat and try to relax.

It's going to be a long flight.

* * *

"Wake up, baby." Warm lips brush against my forehead as my seatbelt is unbuckled. "We're here."

I open my eyes, blinking slowly. "What?"

Julian smiles at me, his blue gaze filled with amusement as he stands in front of me. "You slept the entire way. You must've been exhausted."

I had been a bit tired—the aftermath of all the studying and packing—but an eight-hour nap is a new record for me. Must be those pregnancy hormones again.

Covering a yawn with my hand, I get up and see Rosa already standing by the exit, holding her backpack. "We landed," she says brightly. "I barely felt the plane touch down. Lucas must be an amazing pilot."

"He is good," Julian agrees, wrapping a cashmere shawl around my shoulders. When I give him a questioning look, he explains, "It's only sixty-eight degrees outside. I don't want you to get cold."

I suppress the urge to snicker. Only someone from the tropics would consider sixty-eight degrees "cold"—though, to be fair, it probably is a bit chilly for the short-sleeved dress I'm wearing. Chicago weather in late May is unpredictable, with cool spring days interspersed with summer-like heat. Julian himself is dressed in a pair of jeans and a long-sleeved, button-up shirt.

"Thank you," I say, looking at him. On some level, I do find his concern touching, even if he takes it too far these days. Of course, it doesn't hurt that the feel of his large hands on my shoulders makes me want to melt against him, even with Rosa standing only a few feet away.

"You're welcome, baby," he says huskily, holding my gaze, and I know he feels it too—this deep, inexplicable pull we have toward one another. I don't know if it's chemistry or something else, but it ties us together more securely than any rope.

The clanging of the plane door opening snaps me out of whatever spell I was under. Startled, I step back, grabbing the shawl so it doesn't fall. Julian gives me a look that promises a continuation of what we started, and a shiver of anticipation runs through me.

"Is it okay for me to go down?" Rosa asks, and I turn to see her waiting impatiently by the open door.

"Sure," Julian says. "Go ahead, Rosa. We'll be right there."

She disappears through the exit, and Julian steps closer to me, making my breath catch in my throat. "Are you ready?" he asks softly, and I nod, mesmerized by the warm look in his eyes.

"In that case, let's go," he murmurs, taking my hand. His big, masculine palm engulfs my fingers completely. "Your parents await."

* * *

The car that takes us from the airport to my parents' house is a long, modern-looking limo with unusually thick glass.

"Bulletproof?" I ask when we get in, and Julian nods, confirming my guess. He's sitting in the back with me and Rosa, while Lucas is driving, as usual.

I wonder if the blond man resents this trip for taking him away from his Russian toy. The last I heard, the interpreter was still alive—and still held prisoner in Lucas's quarters. Julian told me that Lucas assigned two guards to watch over her in his absence and make sure she's all right. Apparently, he doesn't want anyone else to have the privilege of torturing the girl.

That whole situation makes me sick, so I try not to think about it. The only reason I even know as much as I know is because Rosa refuses to leave it alone, constantly begging me to ask Julian for updates. Her strange obsession with Julian's right-hand man worries me, even though I'm coming to the conclusion that Rosa was right about Lucas having zero interest in her. Still, as much as I don't want her to get involved with him, I also don't want her to be heartbroken—and I'm afraid things are trending in that direction.

"Are you sure your parents don't mind us coming so late?" Rosa asks, interrupting my thoughts. "It's almost nine in the evening."

"No, they're really anxious to see me." I glance down at my phone, which pings with yet another text from Mom. Picking it up, I skim the message and tell Rosa, "My mom already has the table set."

"And they don't mind me tagging along?" She chews on her lower lip. "I mean, you're their daughter, so of course they want to see you, but I'm just the maid—"

"You're my friend." Impulsively, I reach across the limo aisle and squeeze Rosa's hand. "Please stop worrying about it. You're not imposing."

Rosa smiles, looking relieved, and I glance at Julian to see his reaction. His face is impassive, but I catch a glimmer of amusement in his gaze. My husband is clearly not worried about imposing on my parents so late in the evening. And that makes perfect sense. Why would something like that faze him when he unapologetically abducted their daughter?

This should be an interesting dinner indeed.

* * *

"Nora, honey!" As soon as my parents' door swings open, I'm enveloped in a soft, perfumed embrace. Laughing, I hug my mom and then my dad, who's standing right behind her. He holds me tightly for a few moments, and I feel his heart beating rapidly in his chest.

When he pulls back to look at me, there is a sheen of moisture in his eyes. "We are so glad to see you," he says in a low, deep voice, and I smile up at him through my own veil of tears.

"Me too, Dad. Me too. I really missed you and Mom."

As soon as I say that, I remember that I'm not alone. Turning, I see that my mom is looking at Rosa and Julian, her smile now stiff and unnatural.

I take a deep breath to prepare myself. "Mom, Dad, you already know Julian. And this is Rosa Martinez. She's my best friend on the estate." I invited Lucas to join us for dinner as well, but he refused, explaining that he's part of the security detail tonight and needs to remain outside.

My mom nods cautiously at Julian. Then her smile warms a fraction as she looks at my friend. "It's nice to meet you, Rosa. Nora told us all about you. Please, come in."

She steps back to welcome them, and Rosa walks in, smiling uncertainly. She's followed by Julian, who strolls in looking as cool and confident as ever.

"Gabriela. It's so good to see you." Giving my mom a dazzling smile, my former captor leans down to brush his lips against her cheek in a European gesture. When he straightens, she looks flushed, like a schoolgirl with her first crush. Leaving her to recover, Julian turns his attention to my dad. "It's a pleasure meeting you in person, Tony," he says, extending his hand.

"Likewise," my dad says, his jaw tight as he takes Julian's proffered hand in a white-knuckled handshake. "I'm glad you were finally able to make it out here."

"Yes, so am I," Julian says smoothly, releasing my dad's hand. I notice red finger marks on his hand where my dad purposefully squeezed too hard, and my heart skips a beat. However, when I sneak a glance at my dad's hand, I realize with relief that there's no corresponding damage there.

Julian must've forgiven my dad this small act of aggression—or at least I'm hoping that's the case.

As we walk toward the dining room, I steal covert looks at my husband's handsome profile. Having my former captor in my childhood home is beyond strange. I'm used to being with him in exotic, foreign locations, not Oak Lawn, Illinois. Seeing Julian in my parents' house is a bit like encountering a wild tiger in a suburban mall—it's bizarre in a scary way.

"Oh, honey, you're so thin," my mom exclaims, eyeing me critically as we enter the dining room. "I knew you wouldn't start rounding out with the baby yet, but you look like you've lost weight."

"I know," Julian says, placing a hand on my lower back. His touch both warms and discomfits me, coming as it does in front of my parents. "With the nausea, it's been tough getting her to eat well. At least she stopped losing weight. You should've seen her four weeks ago."

"Was it really bad, honey?" my mom asks sympathetically when we stop in front of the table. She's keeping her eyes on my face, clearly determined to ignore Julian's possessive gesture. My dad, however, grits his teeth so hard I can practically hear the grinding noise.

"It got better once we learned that I'm pregnant. I started eating plainer foods at regular intervals, and it seemed to help," I explain, flushing. It's odd to talk about my pregnancy in front of my dad. We had danced around the issue during our video chats, with Dad gruffly asking after my health and me brushing off his inquiries. I know he hates the fact that I'm pregnant at my age, and despises the whole situation with Julian. My mom probably feels the same, but she's much more diplomatic about it.

"I hope you can eat tonight," my mom says worriedly. "Your dad and I prepared a lot of food."

"I'm sure I'll manage, Mom." Smiling, I sit down in the chair Julian pulls out for me. "Everything looks delicious."

And it's true. My parents have outdone themselves. The table has everything from my dad's rosemary chicken—a recipe he only uses for special occasions—to my grandmother's tamales and my favorite dish of roasted lamb chops. It's a feast, and my stomach growls in appreciation at the delicious smells emanating from the glass-covered platters.

Julian takes a seat to the left of me, and Mom and Dad sit down across from us.

"Come, sit next to me on this side," I tell Rosa, patting the empty chair to my right. I can see my friend still doesn't feel comfortable, convinced she's somehow imposing. Her usual bright smile is uncertain and a bit shy as she sits down next to me, smoothing her palms over the front of her blue dress.

"This table is amazing, Mrs. Leston," she says in her softly accented voice.

"Oh, thank you, sweetheart." My mom beams at her. "Your English is so good. Where did you learn to speak like that? Nora told me you've never been to the US before."

"No, I haven't." Looking pleased at the compliment, Rosa explains how Julian's mother taught her American English when she was a child. My parents listen to her story with interest, asking a number of follow-up questions, and I use this opportunity to excuse myself to visit the restroom.

When I return a few minutes later, the atmosphere at the table is thick with tension. The only person who appears at ease is Julian, who's leaning back in his chair and regarding my parents with an inscrutable gaze. My dad is visibly bristling, and my mom has her hand on his elbow in a classic calming gesture. Poor Rosa looks like she'd rather be anywhere else.

I sit down and debate asking what happened, but I have a feeling it would stir up the hornet's nest even more. "How's the new job going, Dad?" I ask brightly instead.

My dad takes a deep breath, then another, and attempts something that's supposed to be a smile. It looks more like a grimace, but I give him credit for trying.

Before he can answer my question, Julian leans forward, placing his forearms on the table, and says, "Tony, you may not be aware of this, but your daughter is now one of the wealthiest women in the world. She will want for nothing, regardless of her choice of profession or lack thereof. I understand that having a child during college is not optimal, but I would hardly call it 'destroying her life,' particularly in this situation."

My dad's chest swells with fury. "You think the child is the only problem? You stole—"

"Tony." My mom's voice is soft, but the inflection in it makes Dad stop mid-sentence. She then turns toward Julian. "I apologize for my husband's bad manners," she says evenly. "Obviously, we're well aware of your ability to provide for Nora financially."

"Good." Julian gives her a cool smile. "And are you also aware that Nora is becoming a sought-after artist?"

I pause in the middle of reaching for a lamb chop and gape at Julian. A sought-after artist? Me?

"I know that a gallery in Paris expressed some interest in her paintings," my mom says cautiously. "Is that what you mean?"

"Yes." Julian's smile sharpens. "What you may not know, however, is that the owner of that gallery is one of the leading art collectors in Europe. And he's very intrigued by Nora's work. So intrigued, in fact, that he just sent me an offer to purchase five of her paintings for his personal collection."

"Really?" I can't hide the eagerness in my voice. "He wants to buy them? For how much?"

"Fifty thousand euros—ten per painting. Though I'm sure we can negotiate for more."

I stop breathing for a moment. "Fifty *thousand*?" I would've been ecstatic to get five hundred dollars. Hell, I would've taken fifty bucks. Just the fact that someone wants my doodles is beyond belief. "Did you say *fifty thousand euros*?"

"Yes, baby." Julian's gaze warms as he looks at me. "Congratulations. You're about to make your first big sale."

"Oh my God," I breathe out. "Oh. My. God."

I can see the same shock reflected on my parents' faces. They, too, are stunned by this turn of events. Only Rosa seems to take this development in stride. "Congratulations, Nora," she exclaims, grinning. "I told you those paintings are amazing."

"When did you get this offer?" I ask Julian when I can speak again.

"Right before we got here." Julian reaches over to give my hand a gentle squeeze. "I was going to tell you later tonight, but I figured your parents might want to know too."

"Yes, we definitely do," my mom says, finally recovering from her shock. "That's . . . that's incredible, honey. We're so proud of you."

My dad nods, still mute, but I can see that he's just as impressed. And possibly beginning to change his mind about the potential of my hobby.

"Dad," I say softly, looking at him, "I don't intend to drop out of college. Even with the baby on the way, okay? Please, don't worry about me. Truly, I'm all right."

My dad stares at me, then at Julian, and then at me again. I wait for him to say something, but he doesn't. Instead, he reaches for the platter with the lamb chops and pushes them toward me. "Go ahead, honey," he says quietly. "You must be hungry after the long trip."

I gladly take the offering, and everyone else begins loading their plates.

The rest of the dinner goes about as well as could be expected. While there are a few tense silences, the majority of the meal is spent in relatively civil conversation. My mom asks about life on the estate, and Rosa and I show her some photos on Rosa's phone. In the meantime, my dad gets into a political discussion with Julian. To everyone's surprise, the two of them turn out to have the same cynical views on the situation in the Middle East, though Julian's knowledge of geopolitics far exceeds that of my dad's. Unlike my parents, who get their news from the media, Julian is part of the news.

He shapes the news, in fact, though few outside the intelligence community know that.

I have to give my parents their due. For people who believe that Julian belongs behind bars, they are surprisingly gracious hosts. I suspect it's because they're afraid of losing me if they alienate Julian. My mom would dine with the devil himself if that would ensure continued contact with her only daughter, and my dad tends to follow her lead when it comes to difficult situations.

Still, they watch Julian during the meal, eying him as warily as they would observe a savage creature. He's smiling, his potent charm turned on full-blast, but I know they can sense his ever-present aura of danger, the shadow of violence that clings to him like a dark cloak.

When we get to coffee and dessert, Julian gets an urgent text from Lucas and excuses himself to step outside for a few minutes. "It's nothing serious," he tells me when I give him a worried look. "Just a small business matter that needs my attention."

He walks out of the house, and Rosa chooses that moment to visit the restroom, leaving me alone with my parents for the first time since our arrival.

"A business matter?" my dad asks incredulously as soon as Rosa is out of earshot. "At ten-thirty at night?"

I shrug. "Julian deals with people in different timezones. It's ten in the morning somewhere."

I can see that my dad wants to question me further, but thankfully, my mom jumps in. "Your friend is really nice," she says, nodding toward the hallway where Rosa went. "It's hard to believe she grew up like that." She lowers her voice. "With criminals, I mean."

"Yes, I know." I wonder what my parents would think if they knew that Rosa had killed two men. "She's wonderful."

"Nora, honey..." My mom casts a furtive glance around the empty room, then leans forward, lowering her voice further. "I know we don't have much time right now, but tell us one thing. Are you truly happy with him? Because now that you're both on US soil, the FBI might be able to—"

"Mom, I can't live without him. If anything happened to him, I'd want to die." The stark truth escapes my lips before I can think of a gentler way to say it. I soften my tone. "I don't expect you to understand, but he's everything to me now. I truly love him."

"And does he love you back?" my dad asks quietly. He looks older in this moment, aged by the sorrowful pity I see in his eyes. "Is someone like that even capable of loving you, honey?"

I open my mouth to reassure him, but for some reason, I can't bring myself to say the words. I want to believe that in his own way Julian does love me, but there is a tiny kernel of doubt that's always present with me.

My dad hit the nail on the head.

Is Julian capable of love?

Truthfully, I still don't know.

CHAPTER SIXTEEN

❖ JULIAN ❖

The black Lincoln is already waiting when I step outside.

"I told them you were busy, but they insisted on this meeting," Lucas says, melting out of the shadows near the house. "I figured it was best to let you know."

I nod and walk over to the car.

The window in the back rolls down. "Let's take a ride," Frank says, unlocking the door. "We need to talk."

I give him a hard look. "I don't think so. If you want to talk, we're going to do it right here."

Frank studies me, likely wondering how much he can push me, and I see the exact moment he decides not to annoy me further.

"All right." He climbs out of the car, his gray suit stretching across his round stomach. "If you don't mind the nosy neighbors, sure."

I scope out our surroundings with a practiced glance. Unfortunately, he's right. There's already a curtain twitching across the street.

We're beginning to attract attention.

"There is a small park around the block," I say, reaching a decision. "Why don't we walk in that direction? You have exactly fifteen minutes."

Frank nods, and the black Lincoln pulls away, likely to circle the block. I have no doubt there is additional security staying out of sight, just like my men. There is no way the CIA would leave one of their own with me without protection.

"All right, talk," I say as we start in the direction of the park. I gesture for Lucas to follow at some distance. "Why are you here?"

"The better question is: why are you?" Frank's voice is edged with frustration. "Do you know how much trouble your presence is causing us? The FBI knows you're in their jurisdiction, and they're going apeshit—"

"I thought you took care of that."

"I did, but Wilson refuses to let it drop. He and Bosovsky are sniffing around, trying to dig up a cover-up. It's a fucking mess, and your visit isn't helping."

"How is this my problem?"

"We don't want you in this country, Esguerra," Frank says as we round the corner. "You have no reason to be here."

"No?" I quirk an eyebrow. "My wife's parents are here."

"Your wife?" Frank snorts. "You mean that eighteen-year-old you kidnapped?"

Nora is twenty now—or will be in a couple of days—but I don't correct him. Her age is hardly the main issue. "That's the one," I say coolly. "As you know full well, since you dragged me from dinner with her parents . . . my in-laws."

Frank gives me an incredulous stare. "Are you fucking serious? Where do you get the balls to look these people in the eye? You abducted their daughter—"

"Who is now my wife." My tone sharpens. "My relationship with her parents is none of your fucking business, so stay out of it."

"I will—if you stay out of this country." Frank stops, breathing heavily from keeping up with my longer stride. "I'm not kidding about this, Esguerra. We can delete files and records, but we can't erase people. Not in this matter."

"You're telling me the CIA can't silence two nosy FBI agents?" I give him a cold look. "Because if they're the only issue—"

"They're not," Frank interrupts, quickly realizing where I'm going with this. "It's not just the FBI, Esguerra." He reaches up to wipe the sweat off his forehead. "There are higher-ups who are nervous about your presence here. They don't know what to expect."

"Tell them to expect me to visit with my in-laws and leave." For once, I'm being entirely truthful with Frank. "I'm not here to conduct business, so your higher-ups don't need to worry."

Frank doesn't look like he believes me, but I don't give a fuck. If the CIA knows what's good for them, they'll keep the FBI off my back.

I'm here for Nora, and anyone who doesn't like it can go straight to hell.

* * *

When I return to the house, I find Nora arguing with Rosa about cleaning up the table.

"Rosa, please, today you're the guest," Nora says, reaching for the platter with the remnants of the lamb. "Please, just sit, and I'll help my mom—"

"No, no, no," Rosa objects, walking around the table and picking up dirty dishes. "You have the baby to worry about. Please, this is my job. Let me help."

"I'm ten weeks along, not nine months—"

"She's right, baby," I say, stepping up to Nora and plucking the platter from her hands. "It's been a long day, and I don't want you overtiring yourself."

Nora starts to argue, but I'm already carrying the platter to the kitchen, where Nora's parents are packing away the leftovers. As I walk in, Gabriela's eyes widen, but she accepts the platter from me with a quiet "thank you."

I smile at her and walk back to the dining room for more dishes.

It takes a few more trips for Rosa and me to clear off the table and bring everything to the kitchen. Nora sits on the living room couch, watching us work with a mixture of exasperation and curiosity.

Finally, the table is clean, and the Lestons come out of the kitchen to join us. I take a seat next to Nora on the couch and pick up her hand, bringing it to my lap so I can play with her fingers.

"Gabriela, Tony, thank you for a wonderful dinner," I say when Nora's parents sit down next to Rosa on the second couch. "I apologize that I had to step out and missed dessert."

"I saved you a slice of cake," Nora says as I massage her palm. "Mom packed it for us to go."

I give her mother a warm smile. "Thank you for that, Gabriela. I appreciate it."

Gabriela inclines her head. "Of course. It's unfortunate that your business took you away so late in the evening."

"Yes, it is," I agree, pretending not to notice the inquiry implicit in her statement. "And you're right, it *is* getting late . . ." I glance down at Nora, who's covering a yawn with her free hand.

"Nora says you're staying at a house in Palos Park," Tony says, watching us with an unreadable expression. "Is that where you're sleeping tonight?"

"Yes, that's right." The house is on the far edge of the community, with enough empty acreage surrounding it that Lucas was able to implement the required security features. "That's where we'll be staying for the duration of our visit."

"The two of you are welcome to use Nora's room if you wish," Gabriela offers, sounding uncertain.

"Thank you, but we wouldn't want to impose. It would be better if we had our own space for these two weeks." Still holding Nora's hand, I get up and give the Lestons a polite smile. "Speaking of which, I believe it's time for us to go. Nora needs her rest."

"*Nora* is fine," the subject of my concern mutters as I usher her toward the exit. "I'm capable of staying up past ten, you know."

I stifle a grin at the grumpy note in her voice. My pet doesn't like to admit that she tires easily these days. "Yes, I'm aware. But your parents need their rest too. Tomorrow is Thursday, isn't it?"

"Oh, right, of course." Stopping before we reach the front door, Nora turns to her parents. "I forgot that the two of you have work tomorrow," she says contritely. "I'm sorry. We probably should've left earlier—"

"Oh, no, honey," her mother protests. "We're so happy to have you here, and we told you to come this evening. When are we seeing you next?"

Nora looks up at me, and I say, "Tomorrow evening, if that works for the two of you. This time dinner will be at our house."

"We'll be there," Tony says, and I watch both Lestons hug and kiss Nora as they say their goodbyes.

CHAPTER SEVENTEEN

❖ NORA ❖

When we get into the limo, I realize that I *am* tired, the tense excitement of the evening dissipating and leaving me drained. Rosa again takes a seat across the aisle from us, and Julian pulls me close to him, draping his arm over my shoulders. As his warm masculine scent surrounds me, I relax against his side, letting my thoughts drift.

My former captor and I just had dinner with my parents. Like a family. It's so absurd I still can't believe it happened. I'm not sure what I imagined when Julian agreed to take me for a visit, but this wasn't it.

I guess on some level, I had simply refused to think about how something like this might go—my kidnapper sitting down to a civilized meal with my family. It was like a wall I'd put up in my mind, so I wouldn't have to worry. When I had thought of going back home, I had pictured myself with my parents . . . just the three of us, as though Julian would stay in the background, remaining part of my other, darker life.

It was ridiculous to think that way, of course. Julian never stays in the background. He dominates whatever situation he's in, bends it to his will. And even in this—in my relationship with my parents—he's taken charge, inserting himself into our family on his own terms, perfectly comfortable where other men would cringe in shame.

Apparently, a conscience is a useful thing to lack.

"How are you feeling, my pet?"

At Julian's murmured question, I tilt my head to look up at him, realizing I've been silent for the past few minutes. "I'm okay," I say, cognizant of Rosa's presence a couple of feet away. "Just digesting everything."

"Oh?" Julian gives me an amused look, loosening his grip on me so I can sit more comfortably. "Food-wise or thought-wise?"

"Both, I guess." I smile, realizing my unintentional joke. "It was a good meal."

"Yes, it was." Even in the dim interior of the car, I can see the sensuous curve of his mouth. "Your parents did a good job."

I nod. "They definitely did." I wonder what it must've been like for them, having dinner with the man who abducted their daughter.

With the criminal who's now their son-in-law and father of their grandchild.

Sighing, I snuggle back against Julian's side and close my eyes.

The insanity of my life has reached a whole new level.

* * *

It takes less than twenty minutes to reach the wealthy community of Palos Park. Growing up, I've always known of its existence, driving past it on the way to the Tampier Lake preserve. The residents of Palos Park tend to be lawyers and doctors, and I've never heard of anyone renting a house there for a couple of weeks.

Of course, Julian isn't just anyone.

The house he chose is on the very edge of the community, isolated by a tall, wrought-iron fence. Once we get past the electronic gates, we drive down a winding driveway for another couple of hundred yards before reaching the house itself.

Inside, the house is luxuriously appointed, nearly as nice as our mansion at the estate. From gleaming parquet floors to modern art on the walls, everything about our vacation residence screams "extreme wealth."

"How much did you pay for this?" I ask as we walk through an enormous dining area. "I didn't realize a house like this could be for rent."

"It's not," Julian says casually. "I bought it."

My jaw falls open. "What? When? You said you rented it."

"I said I got a house for our visit," he corrects. "I never said how I got it."

"Oh." I feel foolish at my assumption. "So when did you have a chance to buy it?"

"I began making the arrangements right after we agreed on this trip. It took almost a week for the prior owner to move out, but the house is now ours."

Ours. The word rolls so easily off his tongue that it doesn't register for a second. Then I process what he said. "*We* own this house?" I ask carefully. "As in, both of us?"

"Technically, one of our shell corporations owns it, but I made you a fifty-percent shareholder in that corporation, so yes, *we* own it," Julian says as we enter a spacious bedroom with a four-poster bed.

"Julian . . ." Stopping in front of the bed, I look up at him. "Why did you do this? I mean, the trust fund was more than enough—"

"Because you belong to me." He steps closer, a familiar heat igniting in his gaze as he reaches for the buttons of my dress. His fingers brush against my naked skin, making my nipples pebble with need. "Because I want to take care of you, spoil you, make sure you'll never want for anything in your life . . ." Despite his tender words, his eyes gleam darker as he finishes unbuttoning the dress and lets it fall to the floor. "Any other questions, my pet?"

I shake my head, staring up at him. I'm now wearing only a blue thong and a matching bra, and the way he's looking at me reminds me of a hungry lion about to pounce on a gazelle. He may want to take care of me, but at this particular moment, he also wants to devour me.

"Good." His voice is a deep, menacing purr. "Now turn around."

My pulse quickening in nervous anticipation, I do as he says. Even though I crave the darkness now, there is a tiny, instinctual curl of fear in my belly. Julian has always been unpredictable. For all I know, the domesticity of this evening reawakened his sadistic desires, unleashing the demon he's kept in check these recent weeks.

A warm, treacherous throb begins between my thighs at the thought.

As I stand there, I hear a quiet rustling, and then a soft cloth covers my eyes.

A blindfold, I realize, holding my breath. Deprived of my vision, I feel infinitely more vulnerable. My right hand twitches with the sudden urge to lift my arm and tear off the piece of cloth.

"Oh, no, you don't." Julian catches my arm, his fingers like steel cuffs on my wrist. Leaning down, he whispers in my ear, "Who said you could do that, my pet?"

I shiver at the heat of his breath. "I just—"

"Quiet." His command vibrates through me, adding to the heated pulsing between my legs. "I will tell you when to speak." Releasing my wrist, he pushes me forward, causing me to stumble and land face down on the bed. "Don't move," he orders, stepping closer.

I obey, hardly breathing as he runs his hands over me, starting with my shoulders and ending with my thighs. His touch is gentle, yet somehow invasive, like that of a stranger. Or maybe it just feels that way because of the blindfold. I can sense him behind me, but I can't see anything, and he's touching me like he would an object . . . doing with me whatever he pleases. I can feel the calluses on his large, warm palms, and the memory of our first time together flashes through my mind, making my belly tighten with anxiety and dark need.

When he's done stroking me, he rolls me over onto my back and rearranges me on the bed, placing a pillow under my head. Then he grabs my arm, and I feel him looping a rough-textured rope around my wrist. He secures the other end of that rope to what I can only assume is one of the bed posts.

After that, he walks around the bed and does the same with my other arm.

I'm left lying there like some kind of a sexual sacrifice, my arms stretched out diagonally and the blindfold still covering my eyes. I'm even more helpless than usual, and that fact both alarms and thrills me, like most of my interactions with Julian. For other couples, this is only pretend. But for us, it's as real as it gets. I don't have the option to say no. Julian will take me whether I want it or not, and perversely, that knowledge deepens the needy ache in my sex.

"You're beautiful." His harsh whisper is accompanied by a feather-light brush of his fingers over the sensitive skin of my stomach. "And all mine. Aren't you, my pet?"

"Yes." My breathing turns uneven as his fingers approach the top of my thong. "Yes, all yours."

The mattress dips as he climbs onto the bed and straddles my legs. The material of his jeans feels rough on my naked thighs, reminding me that he's still fully clothed. "That's right . . ." He leans down, the buttons of his shirt pressing into my stomach as he covers me with his hard, broad chest. His teeth graze over my earlobe, causing gooseflesh to rise over my arms as he murmurs into my ear, "Nobody will ever have you but me."

I suppress a shudder even as my core floods with liquid heat. From a different man, this would be just possessive pillow talk, but from Julian, it's both a threat and a statement of fact. If I were ever so foolish as to allow another man to touch me, Julian would kill him without a second thought.

"I don't want anyone but you." It's true, yet my voice shakes as Julian kisses my neck, then sucks on the tender flesh under my ear. "You know that."

He chuckles softly, the deep, masculine sound reverberating through me. "Yes, my pet. I do."

He climbs off me, and I sense him moving to the foot of the bed. When he catches my right ankle, I know why.

He's going to tie my legs as well.

The rope is looped around my ankle as I lie there, my heart racing. Julian rarely restrains me so thoroughly. He doesn't have to. Even if I were inclined to fight, he's strong enough to control me without ropes and chains.

Of course, I'm not inclined to fight. Not when I know what he's capable of, what he's willing to do to possess me.

When my right leg is secured, he reaches for my left. His hands are strong and sure as he wraps the rope around my ankle and ties the other end to the remaining bedpost, leaving me lying there with my legs spread open. It's a disconcerting position, and as soon as Julian moves back, I instinctively try to bring my legs together. I can't close them more than an inch, of course. Like the ropes around my wrists, the ankle restraints hold me tightly in place without cutting off my circulation.

My kidnapper may not be into traditional BDSM, but he certainly knows how to tie someone up.

"Julian?" It occurs to me that I'm still wearing my underwear, both the bra and the thong. "What are you going to do to me?"

He doesn't respond. Instead, I feel the mattress dip again as he gets up, and then I hear his footsteps and the sound of the door closing.

He walked out of the room, leaving me tied to the bed.

My heart starts beating faster.

I flex my arms, testing the rope again even though I know it's futile. As expected, there's almost no give in the restraints; the rope bites painfully into my skin when I try to pull on it. I'm nearly naked and alone, blindfolded and tied up in this unfamiliar house. And even though I know Julian won't let anything bad happen to me, I can't help the tension that invades my body as seconds tick by with no sign of his return.

After a couple of minutes, I test the rope again. Still no give in it . . . and still no sign of Julian.

I force myself to take a breath and slowly let it out. Nothing terrible is going on; nobody is hurting me. I don't know what game Julian is playing, but it doesn't seem particularly brutal.

But you want brutal, a small, insidious voice inside my head reminds me. *You want pain and violence.*

I quiet that voice and focus on remaining calm. Julian's mercurial approach to lovemaking may excite me, but it also frightens me. The sane part of me, at least. I want pain, yet I dread it in equal measures. It's always that way nowadays. It's as if I've been split in two, the remnants of the person I used to be warring with who I am now.

Another few minutes crawl by.

"Julian?" I can no longer remain silent. "Julian, where are you?"

Nothing. No response of any kind.

I rub the back of my head against the sheets, trying to dislodge the blindfold, but it doesn't budge more than an inch. Frustrated, I yank at the restraints with all my strength, but all I succeed in doing is hurting myself. Finally, I give up and try to relax, ignoring the anxiety creeping through me.

A few more minutes pass. Just when I think I might go out of my mind, the door creaks open, and I hear the soft sound of footsteps.

"Julian, is that you?" I can't hide the relief in my voice. "What happened? Where did you go?"

"Shhh." The sound is followed by a tickling sensation across my lips. "Who told you that you could speak, my pet?"

My pulse jumps at the cold note in his voice. Is he punishing me for something? "What—"

"Hush." His fingers press on my lips, silencing me. "Not another word."

I swallow, my throat suddenly feeling dry. He's not touching me anywhere but my lips, yet my body ignites, my earlier arousal returning despite my growing nervousness.

Or maybe because of it. It's impossible to tell.

"Suck on my fingers." His whispered command is accompanied by increasing pressure on the seam of my lips. "Now."

Obediently, I open my mouth and suck two of his large fingers in. They taste clean and slightly salty, the edges of his short nails rough against the tender roof of my mouth. I swirl my tongue around his fingers as I would over his cock, and his hand jerks, as though the sensation is just as intense for him.

Just as I'm starting to get into it, Julian withdraws his fingers and runs them down the front of my body, leaving a cool, damp trail on my skin. I shiver in response, my inner muscles tensing as his fingers circle my navel, his nails scraping lightly over my belly. *Lower*, I will him silently, *please, just go a bit lower*, but he lifts his hand instead, depriving me of his touch.

I open my mouth to plead with him, but then I remember that he doesn't want me to speak. Swallowing, I suppress the words, not wanting to displease him when he's in this unpredictable mood.

If Julian is indeed punishing me for something, I don't want to provoke him further.

So instead of begging, I lie still, waiting, my breathing fast and shallow as I try to listen to his movements. I can't hear anything. Is he just standing there watching me? Staring at my semi-naked body stretched out and restrained on the bed?

Finally, I hear something. A scraping noise, as if he picked up something from the nightstand.

I wait, listening tensely, and then I feel it.

Something cold and hard sliding under the tight band of my bra, pressing between my breasts.

I almost flinch in shock, but manage to remain still, my heart beating frantically.

Snip. The noise is unmistakeable.

It's the sound of metal cutting through thick fabric. Julian just used scissors on the front of my bra.

I allow myself a small exhalation of relief, but then I tense again as I feel the cold scissors sliding down my body.

Snip. Snip. Both sides of my thong are cut, the dull edge of the scissors pressing into my hipbones. I feel the warmth of Julian's hand as he pulls the mangled scrap of fabric off my body, and then I hear him suck in a breath. He's looking at me. I know it. I picture what he's seeing as I lie there naked, with my legs wide open, and a flush heats up my skin at the pornographic image in my mind.

"You're already wet." His voice, low and thick with lust, makes me burn even more. "Your pussy is dripping for me." He accompanies the words with a butterfly-soft touch on my aching clit. His fingertips feel rough on my sensitive flesh, yet fire rockets through my veins, filling me with desperate need. Unbidden, a moan escapes my throat, and I lift my hips toward him, silently begging for more.

This time, he answers my plea.

I feel the mattress dip again as he climbs onto the bed, settling between my legs. His hands, large and strong, grip the top of my thighs, and then he lowers his head to my sex. I feel his hot breath wash over my open folds. I almost whimper in anticipation, but I hold back at the last second, not wanting to do anything to cause Julian to change his mind. I want his touch. I need it. It's agonizing to be without it.

And then I feel it—the soft, wet pressure of his tongue between my folds, the pressure that both quenches and intensifies the ache. He doesn't lick me; he just holds his tongue against my clit, but it's enough. It's more than enough. I rock my hips in small, spasmodic movements, creating the exact rhythm I need, and the tension within me grows, the pleasure gathering in a hot, pulsing ball within my core. His tongue moves then, his lips closing around my clit in a strong sucking motion, and the ball bursts, shards of ecstasy blasting through my nerve endings as I cry out, no longer able to stay silent.

Before my orgasm is completely over, he starts licking me. Just soft, gentle licks that extend the pleasurable aftershocks coursing through my body. It feels good, even with my clit swollen and sensitized, so I lie there, enjoying it, limp and content from my release. It's not until a minute later that I realize that the pleasure is sharpening again, growing stronger, transforming into that aching tension.

I gasp, arching toward his mouth, needing more pressure to bring me over the edge, but he keeps touching me with those light licks, his tongue just barely grazing over my clit.

"Please, Julian . . ." The words escape before I can remember the restriction on speaking, but to my relief, he doesn't stop. Instead, he keeps licking me, his tongue moving in a rhythm that slowly and torturously winds me tighter, pushing me closer but not letting me get what I need. I try to push my hips higher, but I can't gain much leverage, stretched and spread as I am.

All I can do is endure, utterly at the mercy of whatever pleasure-torment Julian chooses to dole out.

Just when I think I can't bear much more, he shifts to the side, moving his right hand from my thigh to my throbbing sex. His large, blunt fingers probe my entrance, and I moan as he pushes two of them in, penetrating me with startling swiftness. I'm almost there, it's nearly what I need . . . and then his thumb presses hard on my clit.

I fly apart, acute pleasure rippling through my body as I convulse, gasping and crying out.

"Yes, that's it, baby," he murmurs. His hand leaves me, and I hear the sound of a zipper coming down. I register it only dimly. I feel drunk on orgasms, worn out by the brutal intensity of it all. My heart is pounding as if I ran a race, and my bones feel like they've turned to jelly.

There's no way I could possibly want more, yet when he covers me with his large body, a tiny twitch of renewed sensation makes my belly tighten. He's naked, having already removed his clothes, and I can feel his heat, his hardness. His raw male power. Even if I weren't restrained, I'd feel helpless and small, surrounded as I am by him, but with the rope on my ankles and wrists, that feeling is magnified. I can hardly breathe under his weight, but it doesn't matter. Even air feels optional at the moment.

All I need is Julian.

He shifts on top of me, propping himself up on his elbows. The hard, smooth tip of his erection brushes against my inner thigh as he lowers his head to kiss me, and I tense with anticipation as I feel him beginning to press in.

I'm wet and slick from the orgasms, my body primed for his possession, yet I still feel the stretch as his thick cock forces apart my inner walls, the sensation stopping just short of pain. His tongue invades my mouth at the same time, and I can't even moan as he begins to move, his thrusts deep and rhythmic. It's overwhelming, the feel of him, the taste of him, the way his body completely dominates and claims mine. I can't see, can't move. I'm drowning, and he's my only salvation.

I don't know how long it takes before the pulsing tension coils in my core once more. All I know is when Julian comes, I come with him, shuddering and crying out in his embrace.

Afterwards, he removes the blindfold and the ropes and carries me to the shower. I'm so exhausted I can barely stand, so Julian washes me, taking care of me as if I were a child. When he brings me back to bed, he pulls me into his arms, and as I fall asleep, I hear him say softly, "I will give you the world, my pet. The whole fucking world—just as long as you're mine."

CHAPTER EIGHTEEN

❖ JULIAN ❖

I wake up the next morning to the familiar feel of Nora sprawled on top of me. As usual, she's sleeping with her head pillowed on my chest and one of her slim legs draped across my thighs. I can feel the soft, plump weight of her breasts against my side, hear her even breathing, and my cock stiffens as recollections of last night invade my mind in graphic detail.

I don't know why I occasionally feel this urge to torment her, to hear her beg and plead. Why the sight of her bound to my bed gives me such satisfaction. When we were driving from her parents last night, I planned to take her gently and have her go to sleep, but when I saw her standing next to that four-poster bed, my good intentions went up in smoke. Something about the way she had been looking at me sharpened the dangerous hunger inside, bringing the darkness to the surface. What I wanted to do to her only began with ropes, and if I hadn't made myself walk out of the room after tying her up, I would've broken the vow I made to myself the night I hurt her.

The vow to keep violence out of our bedroom for the next few months.

Thankfully, leaving her for a bit and taking a cold shower in one of the guest rooms seemed to do the trick, taking the edge off the craving. When I came back, I was more in control, able to settle for torturing her with pleasure instead of pain.

A change in Nora's breathing brings my attention back to her. She shifts on top of me, making a soft noise, and rubs her cheek against my chest. "You didn't get up yet," she murmurs sleepily, and I smile, a peculiar sense of wellbeing spreading through me at the pleased note in her voice.

"No, not yet," I confirm, stroking her smooth, naked back. "I will in a few moments, though."

"Do you have to?" Her words are muffled. "You make a nice pillow."

"I'm glad I can be of use."

At my dry tone, she moves her head, looking up at me through her long, dark lashes. "Does it bother you? That I sleep on top of you like this?"

"No." I grin at her question. "Do you think I'd let you if it did?"

She blinks. "No. Of course you wouldn't." Moving off me, she sits up, pulling the blanket up around her. "We should probably get up. I wanted to go for a run before breakfast."

I sit up too. "A run?"

"Yes. It's safe here, isn't it?"

"Not as safe as at the compound." The idea of her running out there makes me uneasy, even with all the security measures and no obvious threat in sight. If anything were to happen to her . . .

"Julian, please." Nora begins to look upset. "I'm just going to run here, in Palos Park. I won't go far, but I can't stay cooped up in this house for two weeks—"

"I'll go with you." I get up and walk over to the closet to find a pair of running shorts. "Get dressed. We should hurry. I'm guessing Rosa is already preparing breakfast."

* * *

We start the run with an easy jog to warm up. It's a brisk sixty degrees out, but moving keeps me from feeling the chill, even though I'm not wearing a shirt. I debate having Nora put on more layers, but she looks comfortable in her cropped leggings and a T-shirt, so I decide to let it slide.

As we exit our driveway and turn onto the street, I keep a careful eye on neighbors' cars pulling out of their garages and people stepping out for their own morning run. Being around so many strangers makes me uneasy. My men are strategically positioned all around the community, so I know we're safe, but I can't help watching for signs of danger.

"You know nobody's going to jump at us from the bushes, right?" Nora says, obviously noticing my preoccupation with our surroundings. "It's not that kind of neighborhood."

I glance at her. "I know. I vetted it."

She smiles and picks up speed. "Of course you did."

I match her pace, and we run at a fast clip for the next several blocks. A light sheen of perspiration appears on Nora's face, making her golden skin glow, and I find myself increasingly distracted by the sight of her. She always looks sexy when she runs, her petite body athletic and feminine at the same time. The tight, round muscles of her ass bunch and flex with every step she takes, and I can't help picturing my hands squeezing those globes as I slam my cock into her.

Fuck. At this rate, I'm going to need another cold shower.

"What are you doing after breakfast?" Nora asks breathlessly as we pass a jogging couple. "Do you have some work to do?"

"I have that meeting with my portfolio manager in the city," I reply, trying to control the urge to turn and glare at the male jogger. The fucker eyed Nora a bit too appreciatively when we ran past him. "I'll be back before dinner."

"Oh, that's good." She's beginning to pant as she speaks. "I want to get a haircut today, and maybe meet with Leah and Jennie."

"What?" I turn my head to stare at her as we round the corner. "Where exactly are you planning to do these things?"

"At the Chicago Ridge Mall. I messaged Leah and Jennie last week, letting them know I'd be in town, and they said they were going to come in today and stay for the long Memorial Day weekend." She says it all in one long breath, then gulps in more air and gives me an imploring look. "You don't mind if I see them, right? I haven't seen Jennie in two years, and Leah—" She abruptly falls silent, and I know it's because she was going to say she saw Leah the last time she was in that cursed mall, when Peter let her act as bait for Al-Quadar. My pet doesn't realize I already know about that meeting—and about Jake's presence that day.

"You're not going to that mall." I know I sound harsh, but I can't help it. Just the thought of her wandering around that place by herself is enough to make me see red. "It's too crowded to be safe."

"But—"

"If you want to meet with your friends, you can do so here at the house or at some restaurant in Oak Lawn—*after* I make sure it's secure."

Nora's lips tighten, but she wisely doesn't voice any objections. She knows this is as far as she can push me. "Okay, I'll ask them to meet me at Fish-of-the-Sea," she says after a minute. "What about my haircut?"

I eye the long, thick ponytail hanging down her back. It looks beautiful to me, especially with the end swinging back and forth over her shapely ass. "Why do you need one?"

"Because"—she pants as we pick up the pace—"I haven't had so much as a trim in two years."

"So?" I still don't see the problem. "I like your hair long."

"You are such a *guy*." She can barely speak but somehow manages to roll her eyes. "I need to shape this mess. It's driving me crazy."

"I don't want you cutting it short." I don't know why I care all of a sudden, but I do. "If you trim it, don't take off more than a couple of inches."

Nora gives me an incredulous look as we stop to let a car pull out of the driveway in front of us. "Really? Why?"

"I told you. I like it long."

She rolls her eyes again as we resume running. "Yeah, okay. I wasn't going to shave it off or anything. I just want to get some layers put in."

"No more than a couple of inches," I repeat, giving her a hard look.

"Uh-huh, sure." I get the impression she's doing a third eye-roll in her head. "So I'll go for the haircut then?"

"Not at the Chicago Ridge Mall. Find a quiet place nearby, and I'll have my men secure it."

"Okay," she gasps as we begin a full-out sprint. "It's a deal."

* * *

Before I leave for the city, I make sure Nora is fully set with her plans for the day. I assign a dozen of my best men to be her security detail and give them orders to be as unobtrusive as possible. She probably won't even notice their presence, but they'll make sure nobody suspicious gets within three hundred feet of her.

"I'll be fine," she says when I hesitate in the hallway before leaving the house. "Really, Julian. It's just a haircut and lunch with the girls. I promise everything will be all right."

I take a deep breath and release it. She's right. I'm being paranoid at this point. The precautions I'm taking are the best way to keep her safe outside the compound. Of course, I could always keep her *inside* the compound for the rest of her life—that would be optimal for my peace of mind—but Nora wouldn't be happy that way, and her happiness matters to me.

It matters far more than I would've ever expected.

"How are you feeling?" I ask, still reluctant to go for some reason. "Any nausea? Tiredness?" I glance at her stomach—a stomach that's still flat in the tight jeans she's wearing.

"No, nothing." She gives me a reassuring smile when I look up to meet her gaze. "Not even a hint of nausea. I'm as healthy as a horse."

"All right then." Stepping toward her, I lift my hand to lightly stroke her cheek. "Be careful, baby, okay?"

"Okay," she whispers, looking up at me. "You too, Julian. Stay safe, and I'll see you soon."

And before I can step away, she rises up on her tiptoes and plants a brief, burning kiss on my lips.

CHAPTER NINETEEN

❖ NORA ❖

"Rosa, are you sure you don't want to go with me?"

"No, no, I told you—I have a lot to do before dinner. Señor Esguerra is trusting me to impress your family with this meal, and I don't want to disappoint him. You go ahead, have fun catching up with your friends." Rosa practically shoos me out of the enormous kitchen. "Go, or you'll be late for your hair appointment."

"All right, if you're sure." Shaking my head at Rosa's stubborn sense of duty, I head to the main entrance, where a car is already waiting for me. Thankfully, it's not the limo, but a regular-sized black Mercedes. I won't stand out too much, though this car, like the limo, also looks to be equipped with bulletproof glass.

The driver is a tall, thin man I've seen around the estate, but never spoken to. Julian told me this morning that his name is Thomas. Thomas doesn't introduce himself or say much this time either, all his attention focused on the road. As we leave the driveway, I see two black SUVs pull out behind us and follow us at some distance. It makes me feel like I'm the First Lady—or maybe a mafia princess.

The latter is probably a better comparison.

It takes less than a half hour to get to the hair salon. It's not an upscale place, but it has a good reputation in the area, and most importantly, Julian deemed its location easy to secure. I hadn't expected to get an appointment so easily, but they'd had a cancellation this morning and were thus able to fit me in at eleven.

"Just a little trim, please," I request after a tattooed, purple-haired lady shampoos my hair and leads me to one of the cutting stations. "No more than a couple of inches."

"Are you sure?" she asks. "Look at how thick it is. You should at least get some layers put in."

I frown, studying my reflection in the mirror. "Will it still be long?"

"Of course. You won't lose any of the length—it'll just be shaped nicely. The shortest layers, those around your face, will be well below your shoulders."

"In that case, go for it." I try to sound decisive, even though I feel nothing of the kind. It's hard to disobey Julian, even in this small thing, and that makes me determined to do so. "Let's layer up this mess."

As the hairstylist bustles around me, tugging and snipping at my hair, I watch the other people in the salon. After weeks of isolation on the estate, it feels odd to be among so many strangers. Nobody is paying me much attention, but I still feel uncomfortably exposed, as though everyone is staring at me. I'm also somewhat anxious. I know nobody here means me any harm, so the feeling is illogical, but some of Julian's paranoia is rubbing off on me.

Still, being here on my own is exciting. I know Julian's men are outside, so I don't truly have any freedom, but it feels like I do.

It feels like I'm a regular girl, out for a day of grooming and hanging out with her friends.

"All done," the stylist announces after a few minutes. "Now we just blow-dry, and you'll be all set."

I nod, trying to avoid looking at the long locks scattered all over the floor. It seems like a lot of hair, though the wet strands I see in the mirror don't appear particularly short.

"So, what do you think?" she asks after my hair is dry. She hands me a mirror. "How do you like it?"

I turn in the swiveling chair, studying my new hairstyle from all angles. It looks like a shampoo ad—long, dark, and sleek, with the shorter layers around my face adding some flattering volume.

"Perfect." I hand back the mirror with a smile. "Thank you so much."

Disobeying Julian seems to agree with me. Looks-wise, at least.

* * *

I still have some time to kill before meeting Leah and Jennie, so I go all out and get a mani-pedi at the same salon. In the middle of the pedi, my phone dings with an incoming message from Julian.

You're still there? he texts. Thomas says it's been almost two hours.

Getting nails painted, I respond. How are things with you?

Probably not as colorful as with you.

I grin and put my phone away. This all feels so wonderfully normal, even with the oversight from Thomas. It's like we're just a couple, with nothing dark and messed up in our lives.

Impulsively, I fish my phone out of my purse again.

Love you, I text, adding a smiley face at the end for emphasis.

There's no answer, but I didn't expect any. Julian would never acknowledge his feelings for me—whatever those may be—in a text. Still, my heart feels just a bit heavier as I put the phone away and pick up a gossip magazine instead.

Half an hour later, I'm as polished and shiny as the models in the magazine. My hair streams down my back in a smooth, glossy curtain, and my nails are prettier than they've been in months. Adding a generous tip, I pay and exit the salon, ready for the continuation of my day.

As expected, Thomas is waiting for me outside. I don't see any of the others from the security team, but I know they're there, guarding me from out of sight. Still, their lack of visible presence adds to the illusion of normality, and my spirits lift again as we drive to the seafood restaurant where Leah and Jennie agreed to meet me for lunch.

They're already there when I walk in, and the first few minutes are filled with hugs and excited exclamations over how long it's been since we've seen each other. I had been afraid that things might be tense with Leah after our last run-in at the mall, but my worries appear to have been unfounded. With the three of us together, it's like our high school days all over again.

"Oh gosh, Nora, I'd forgotten how beautiful you are," Jennie exclaims when we're all seated. "Either that, or living in the jungle is agreeing with you."

"Why, thank you," I say, laughing. "You look pretty great yourself. When did you decide to go red? I love that color on you."

Jennie grins, her green eyes sparkling. "When I started college. I decided it was time for a change, and it was either red or blue."

"I convinced her to go red," Leah says with a mischievous smile. "Blue wouldn't have matched her Irish complexion."

"Oh, I don't know," I say with a straight face. "I hear smurfs are all the rage lately."

Leah bursts into laughter, and Jennie and I join in. It feels so good to be back with the two of them. I've hung out with Leah a couple of times since my abduction, but I haven't seen Jennie in almost two years. She was studying abroad when I was home for those four months after the warehouse explosion, so we've never gotten a chance to reconnect beyond a few Facebook messages.

"Okay, Nora, spill," Jennie says after the waiter takes our orders. "What's it like being married to a modern-day Pablo Escobar? The rumors I hear are beyond bizarre."

Leah chokes on her water, and I burst out laughing again. I'd forgotten Jennie's propensity for shocking people.

"Well," I say when I calm down enough to speak, "Julian deals in weapons, not drugs, but otherwise, being married to him is quite nice."

"Oh, come on. Quite nice?" Jennie gives me an exaggerated frown. "I want all the gory details. Does he sleep with a machine gun under his pillow? Eat puppies for breakfast? I mean, the dude kidnapped you, for Pete's sake! Give us all the juicy—"

"Jennie," Leah cuts in sharply. She doesn't look the least bit amused. "I don't think this is a joking matter."

"It's okay," I reassure her. "Really, Leah, it's fine. Julian and I *are* married now, and we're happy together. We truly are."

"Happy?" Leah stares at me like I've grown horns. "Nora, you know what he's capable of, what he's done. How can you be happy with a man like that?"

I look back at her, not knowing how to respond. I want to say that Julian is not that bad, but the words stick in my throat. My husband *is* that bad. In fact, he's probably worse than Leah thinks. She doesn't know about the mass eradication of Al-Quadar in recent months or the fact that Julian has been a killer since childhood.

Of course, she also doesn't know that *I'm* a killer. If she did, she'd probably think Julian and I deserve each other.

To my relief, Jennie comes to my rescue. "Stop being such a party pooper," she says, poking Leah in the ribs. "So she's happy with him. That's better than being miserable, right?"

Leah's fair complexion reddens. "Of course. Sorry, Nora." She attempts a weak smile. "I guess I just have a hard time understanding it all. I mean, here you are, finally back in the US, and you're planning to go back to Colombia with him."

"That's what happens when people marry," Jennie says before I can respond. "They live together. Like you and Jake. It's only natural that Nora would go back with her husband—"

"You and Jake are living together?" I interrupt, looking at Leah in shock. "Since when?"

"Since two weeks ago," Jennie says gleefully. "Leah didn't tell you?"

"I was going to tell you today," Leah says to me. She looks uncomfortable. "I wanted to tell you in person."

"Why? They just had one date," Jennie says reasonably. "It's not like they were boyfriend-girlfriend."

"Jennie's right," I say. "Really, Leah, I'm happy for the two of you. You don't have to be afraid to tell me stuff like that. I won't flip out, I promise." I give her a big smile before asking, "Are you renting an apartment off-campus?"

"We are," Leah says, looking relieved at my question. "We both had roommate issues, so we decided living together might be the best option."

"Makes sense to me," Jennie says, and for the next few minutes, we discuss the pros and cons of living with boyfriends versus roommates.

"What about you, Jennie?" I ask after the waiter brings our appetizers. "Any boyfriends on the horizon for you?"

"Ugh, no." Jennie makes a disgusted face. "There are barely a dozen okay-looking guys at Grinnell, and they're all taken. The two of you should've talked some sense into me when I decided to go to college in the middle of nowhere. Seriously, it's worse than being in high school."

"No!" I widen my eyes in mock horror. "Worse than being in high school?"

"Nothing's worse than being in high school," Leah says, and the two of them begin to argue about the comparative availability of guys in a suburban high school versus a tiny liberal arts college.

As the meal proceeds, we talk about anything and everything except my relationship with Julian. Leah tells us about an internship she got at a Chicago law firm, and Jennie shares amusing stories about her recent vacation in Curaçao. "They had an oil-processing plant right next to our hotel. Can you believe it?" she complains, and Leah and I agree that even a salt-water infinity pool—a cool feature of Jennie's hotel—can't make up for something as atrocious as an oil refinery in a vacation spot.

Eventually, the conversation turns to my life on the estate, and I tell them all about my online classes at Stanford, the art lessons I'm getting from Monsieur Bernard, and my growing friendship with Rosa. "I wanted her to join us today, but she couldn't," I explain, feeling slightly guilty about that. "My parents are coming over for dinner, and Julian asked Rosa to help with the meal." As I say that, I realize how spoiled I sound—and from the envious looks on Jennie and Leah's faces, they realize it too.

"Wow," Jennie says, shaking her head. "No wonder you're happy with this guy. He treats you like a freaking princess. If someone gave me Stanford, servants, and a huge estate, I wouldn't mind getting kidnapped either."

"Jennie!" Leah gives her an appalled look. "You don't mean that."

"No, I probably don't," Jennie agrees, grinning. "Still, Nora, you have to admit, the whole thing is kind of cool."

I shrug, smiling. "Kind of cool" is one way to describe it. Messed up and complicated is another—but I'm happy to stick with Jennie's description for now.

"Wait, did you say your parents are coming over for dinner?" Leah asks, as if just now processing that part of my statement. "Like, to have dinner with you and him?"

"Yes," I say, enjoying the expressions on both of my friends' faces. "We had dinner at my parents' house last night, so today they're coming over to our place." And as Leah and Jennie continue to stare at me in shock, I explain that Julian purchased a house in Palos Park, so we'd have someplace secure to stay during our visits.

"Girl, I have to say, you live in a whole other world now," Jennie says, shaking her head. "Private island, an estate in Columbia, now this . . ."

"None of that makes up for the fact that he's a psychopath," Leah says, giving Jennie a sharp look before turning to me. "Nora, how are your parents dealing with him?"

"They're . . . dealing." I don't know how else to describe the wary acceptance on my parents' part. "It's obviously not easy for them."

"Yeah, I can imagine," Jennie says. "They're troopers, your parents. Mine would've gone nuts."

"I don't think 'going nuts' would've helped matters," Leah says astutely. "I'm sure Nora's parents are just happy to have her back."

I start to reply, but at that moment, both Jennie and Leah look up, gaping at something behind me. Instinctively, I turn, my heartbeat spiking—and look up straight into my former captor's blue gaze.

He's standing over me, his hand resting casually on the back of my chair and his lips curved in a dangerously sexy smile. "Mind if I join you, ladies?" he asks, looking amused.

"Julian." I jump in my seat, startled and more than a little flustered. "What are you doing here?"

"My meeting ended early, so I figured I'd swing by and see if you're ready to go home," he says. "But I see you're not done yet."

"Um, no. We were just about to get dessert." I cast an uncertain glance at Leah and Jennie, and see that they're both staring at Julian. Leah looks like she's ready to bolt, while Jennie's expression is a mixture of fascination and awe.

Shit. So much for a normal lunch with my friends. Turning my attention back to Julian, I say reluctantly, "I mean, I could be done if—"

"No, no, please join us if you have time," Jennie jumps in, apparently recovering from her shock. "They have great cheesecake here."

"Well, in that case, I must stay," Julian says smoothly, taking a seat next to me. "I wouldn't want to deprive Nora of such a delicacy." He smiles at me. "Your hair looks great, by the way, baby. You were right about the layers."

"Oh." Remembering my small act of rebellion, I touch my hair, feeling the shorter strands. His approval is both a disappointment and a relief. "Thanks."

"It does look nice on her," Leah says hoarsely, and I see that her eyes look less panicked now. Clearing her throat, she adds unnecessarily, "The new haircut, I mean."

Julian's smile broadens. "Yes. She looks gorgeous, doesn't she?"

"Yes, gorgeous," Jennie echoes, except she's looking at Julian instead of me. She seems mesmerized, and I can't blame her. With the scars on his face nearly gone and his eye implant indistinguishable from the real thing, Julian is as magnificent as ever, his masculine beauty dark and striking.

Finally gathering my scattered wits, I say, "Sorry, I've forgotten to introduce everyone. Julian—these are my friends Leah and Jennie. Leah, Jennie—this is Julian, my husband."

"It's nice to meet you both," Julian says with easy charm. "Nora's told me quite a bit about you."

"Oh?" Leah frowns. Unlike Jennie, she doesn't seem dazzled by his looks. "Like what?"

"Like the fact that the two of you have been friends since middle school," Julian says. "Or that you, Jennie, were Nora's date to the sophomore homecoming dance."

I blink, surprised. I had mentioned this to Julian at some point, but I didn't expect him to remember such trivia.

"Oh, wow," Jennie breathes, her eyes still glued to Julian's face. "I can't believe she's told you all that."

Leah's mouth tightens, and she motions at the waiter. "A slice of cheesecake, please, and then the check," she requests when he comes over. "Their portions are huge," she explains, even though nobody objected to the size of her order. "We can all split it."

"That's fine with me," I say. I'm surprised Leah is willing to stay long enough to eat the cheesecake. I wouldn't have blamed her if she'd walked out right then and there. I know she's aware of what happened to Jake, and the fact that she's willing to be somewhat civil to Julian speaks volumes about her commitment to our friendship.

"So tell me," Julian says when the waiter departs, "how was your lunch so far? Did Nora already tell you the big news?"

I freeze, horrified that he's outing me like this. Telling my friends about the baby was something I'd planned to do much later, when it was inevitable. Not today, when I could still pretend to be a carefree college girl.

"What big news?" Jennie asks eagerly, leaning forward. Her eyes are wide with curiosity. "Nora didn't tell us anything."

"She didn't tell you about the gallery owner in Paris?" Julian gives me a sidelong look. "The one who put in an offer to buy her paintings?"

"What?" Leah exclaims. "When did this happen, Nora?"

"Um, just yesterday," I mumble, a wave of relief sweeping away the sick feeling in my stomach. "Julian told me about it, but I haven't seen the offer yet."

"Wow, congratulations." Jennie beams at me. "So you're about to be a famous artist, huh?"

"I don't know about famous—" I begin, but Julian cuts me off.

"She is," he says firmly. "The gallery owner is offering ten thousand euros for each of the five paintings." And amidst my friends' exclamations of excitement, he explains that the gallery owner is a known art collector, and that my paintings are already gaining notoriety in Paris due to Monsieur Bernard's connections.

In the middle of all this, our cheesecake slice arrives. Leah had been right to order only one; the slice is nearly the size of my head. The waiter brings out four little plates, and we split the cake as Julian answers Jennie's questions about the Paris art scene and France in general.

"Wow, Nora, what an exciting life you're about to start," Jennie says, reaching for the check that the waiter brought. "You'll tell us when you have your first show, right?"

"I've got this," Julian says, picking up the check before Jennie can touch it. And before my friends can utter a word of protest, he hands two one-hundred-dollar bills to the waiter, saying, "Keep the change."

"Oh, thank you," Jennie says as the ecstatic-looking waiter hurries away. "You didn't have to do that. You just had a bite of the cheesecake, not any of the food."

"Please let us pay you for our portion," Leah says stiffly, reaching for her wallet, but Julian waves her off.

"Please, don't worry. It's the least I can do for Nora's friends." Rising to his feet, he extends his palm toward me. "Ready, baby?"

"Yes," I say, placing my hand in his. My few hours of freedom are over, but somehow I don't mind. As exciting as the day had been, it feels comforting to be claimed by Julian again.

To be back where I belong.

CHAPTER TWENTY

❖ JULIAN ❖

"Why did you come to meet me?" Nora asks as we get into the car after saying goodbye to her friends. "Were you afraid I might run away?"

"You wouldn't have gotten far if you tried." Turning to face her, I run my fingers through her hair. It's a bit shorter at the front, but still long and even silkier than usual.

"I wasn't going to run." Nora frowns up at me. "I don't want to run away from you. Not anymore."

"I know that, my pet." I force myself to stop touching her hair before I develop a fetish. "I wouldn't have brought you to America otherwise."

"So why did you come get me? I would've been home in an hour anyway."

I shrug, not wanting to admit how much I missed her. My addiction is completely out of control. No matter what I'm doing, I'm constantly thinking about her. Even a few hours apart are intolerable these days, as ridiculous as that may be.

"Okay, well, I'm glad Leah didn't freak out too much," Nora says when I remain silent. "I thought she'd run or call the police when you first showed up." She looks down, then glances up. "If you hadn't mentioned the big news, things would've been very awkward."

"Really?" I say silkily. "Maybe I should've told them the *really* big news." It was what I'd originally intended—to ask if Nora had already told them about the baby—but the horrified expression on her face gave away the truth before any of her friends could speak.

Nora reaches for my hand, her slender fingers curving around my palm. "I'm glad you didn't." She gives my hand a gentle squeeze. "Thank you for that."

"Why didn't you tell them?" I ask, placing my other palm over her small hand. "They're your friends—I would've expected you to share such things with them."

"I'm going to tell them." She looks uncomfortable. "Just not yet."

"Are you afraid they'll judge you?" I frown at her, trying to understand. "We're married. This is only natural. You know that, right?"

"They *will* judge me, Julian." Her soft lips twist. "I'll be a mother at twenty. Girls my age don't do marriage and babies. At least most that I know don't."

"I see." I study her thoughtfully. "What do they do? Parties? Clubs? Boyfriends?"

She lowers her gaze. "I'm sure you think it's silly."

It is, yet it isn't. It still catches me off-guard sometimes, how young she is. How limited her experience has been. I can't remember ever being that young. By the time I was twenty, I was already at the helm of my father's organization, having seen most of the world and done things that would make hardened mobsters shudder. Youth had skipped me by, and I keep forgetting that Nora still retains some of hers.

"Is that what you want?" I ask when she looks up at me again. "To go out? To have fun?"

"No—I mean, that would be nice, but I know it's not realistic." She draws in a deep breath, her hand twitching in my grasp. "It's fine, Julian. Really. I'm going to tell them soon. I just didn't want our lunch today to be all about that."

"Okay." Releasing her hand, I drape my arm over her shoulders and draw her closer. "Whatever you think best, my pet."

* * *

To my satisfaction, the second dinner with Nora's parents goes smoothly. Nora gives them a tour of the house while I catch up on some work, and by the time I join everyone for dinner, the Lestons seem much less tense than before.

"Wow, look at this table," Gabriela says when we all sit down. "Rosa, you prepared all this?"

Rosa nods, smiling proudly. "I did. I hope you all enjoy it."

"I'm sure we will," I say. The table is covered with dishes ranging from a white asparagus salad to the traditional Colombian recipe of *Arroz con Pollo.* "Thank you, Rosa."

"I'm still stuffed from that cheesecake," Nora says, grinning, "but I'll try to do this meal justice. Everything looks delicious."

As we dig into the food, the conversation revolves around Nora's day with her friends and the latest local gossip. Apparently, one of the Leston's divorced neighbors started dating a woman ten years his senior, while the man's miniature Chihuahua got into an altercation with another neighbor's Persian cat. "Can you believe it?" Tony Leston says, chuckling. "That cat outweighs the dog by a good ten pounds."

Nora and Rosa laugh while I observe the Lestons with bemusement. For the first time, I understand why Nora wanted to visit here so badly, what she meant when she said she needed a breather from the estate. The life Nora's parents lead—the life she used to lead before she met me—is so different I might as well be visiting another planet.

A planet populated by people blissfully ignorant of the realities of the world.

"What are you doing on Saturday, honey?" Gabriela asks, smiling warmly at her daughter. "Do you already have plans?"

Nora looks puzzled. "Saturday? No, not yet." And then her eyes widen. "Oh, Saturday. You mean my birthday?"

I suppress a flare of annoyance. I'd been hoping to surprise Nora again—preferably with a better outcome this time. Oh, well. Nothing to be done now. Leaning back in my chair, I say, "We do have something planned for the evening, but not during the day."

"Wonderful." Nora's mother beams at her. "Why don't you come over for lunch then? I'll make all of your favorite dishes."

Nora glances at me, and I give her a small nod. "We'd be happy to, Mom," she says.

Gabriela's smile dims slightly at the "we," so I lean forward and say to Nora, "I'm afraid I have some work to do, baby. Why don't you spend some time with your parents by yourself?"

"Oh, sure." Nora blinks. "Okay."

Tony and Gabriela look ecstatic, and I resume eating, tuning out the rest of their conversation. As much as I dislike the idea of being away from Nora, I want her to have some tension-free time with her parents—something that can only be achieved without my presence.

I want my pet to be happy on her birthday, no matter what it takes.

* * *

After the Lestons leave, Nora heads into the shower, and I pull out my phone to check my messages. To my surprise, there is an email from Lucas. It's just one line:

Yulia Tzakova escaped.

Sighing, I put the phone away. I know I should be furious, but for some reason, I'm only mildly annoyed. The Russian girl won't get far; Lucas will hunt her down and bring her back as soon as we return. For now, though, I picture his rage—the rage I can sense in the terse words of the email—and chuckle.

If the plane crash hadn't killed so many of my men, I'd almost feel sorry for the girl.

CHAPTER TWENTY-ONE

❖ NORA ❖

"*An eye for an eye.*" *Majid's eyes burn with hatred as he comes toward me, stepping over Beth's mangled body. The blood is ankle-deep as he walks, the dark liquid sloshing around his feet in a malevolent swirl. "A life for a life."*

"No." *I'm standing there shaking, the fear pulsing inside me in a sickening beat. "Not this. Please, not this."*

It's too late, though. He's already there, pressing his knife against my stomach. Smiling cruelly, he looks behind me and says, "The head will make a nice little trophy—after I cut it up a bit, of course . . ."

"Julian!"

My scream echoes through the room as I jump off the bed, trembling with icy terror.

"Baby, are you okay?" Strong arms close around me in the darkness, pulling me into a hard, warm embrace. "Shh . . ." Julian soothes as I begin to sob, clinging to him with all my strength. "Did you have another dream?"

I manage a small nod.

"What kind of dream, my pet?" Sitting down on the bed, Julian pulls me into his lap and strokes my hair. "The old one about me and Beth?"

I bury my face against his neck. "Sort of," I whisper when I can speak. "Except Majid was threatening *me* this time." I swallow the bile rising in my throat. "Threatening the baby inside me."

I can feel Julian's muscles tensing. "He's dead, Nora. He can't hurt you anymore."

"I know." I can't stop crying. "Believe me, I know."

One of Julian's hands moves down to my belly, warming my chilled skin. "It'll be okay," he murmurs, gently rocking me back and forth. "Everything will be okay."

I hold onto him tightly, trying to quiet my sobs. I want to believe him so badly. I want the last few weeks to be the norm, not the exception, in our lives.

Shifting on Julian's lap, I feel a growing hardness pressing into my hip, and for some reason, it eases my fear. If there's anything I can be sure of, it's our bodies' desperate, burning need for one another. And suddenly, I know exactly what I need.

"Make me forget," I whisper, pressing a kiss to the side of his neck. "Please, just make me forget."

Julian's breathing alters, his body tensing in a different way. "Gladly," he murmurs, turning to place me on the mattress.

And as he drives into me, I wrap my legs around his hips, letting the power of his thrusts push the nightmare out of my mind.

* * *

I wake up late on Friday morning, my eyes gritty from my middle-of-the-night crying bout. Dragging myself out of bed, I brush my teeth and take a long, hot shower. Then, feeling infinitely better, I go back into the bedroom to get dressed.

"How are you doing, my pet?" Julian steps into the room just as I zip up my shorts in front of the mirror. He's already dressed, his tall, muscular frame making the dark jeans and T-shirt he's wearing look like something out of GQ.

"I'm fine." Turning, I give him a sheepish smile. "I don't know why I had that dream last night. I haven't had one in weeks."

"Right." Leaning against the wall, Julian crosses his arms and gives me a penetrating look. "Did anything happen yesterday? Anything that could've triggered a relapse?"

"No," I say quickly. The last thing I want is for Julian to think I can't be on my own for a few hours. "Yesterday was an awesome day. I think it's just one of those things. Maybe I ate too much at dinner or something."

"Uh-huh." Julian stares at me. "Sure."

"I'm fine," I repeat, turning back toward the mirror to brush my hair. "It was just a stupid dream."

Julian doesn't say anything, but I know I haven't managed to allay his concerns. All through breakfast, he watches me like a hawk, undoubtedly looking for signs of an incipient panic attack. I do my best to act normal—a task greatly helped by Rosa's easy chatter—and when we're done eating, I suggest we go for a walk in the park.

"Which park?" Julian frowns.

"Any local park," I say. "Whichever one you think is most secure. I just want to get out of the house, get some fresh air."

Julian looks thoughtful for a second; then he types something on his phone. "All right," he says. "Give my men a half hour to prepare, and we'll head out."

"Will you come with us, Rosa?" I ask, not wanting to exclude my friend again, but to my surprise, she shakes her head.

"No. I'm going to the city," she explains. "Señor Esguerra"—she glances at Julian—"said he's fine with that as long as I take one of the guards with me. I don't need as much security as the two of you, so I figured I'd use the day to explore Chicago." She pauses and gives me a concerned look. "You don't mind, do you? Because I don't have to go—"

"No, no, you should definitely go. Chicago is a great city. You'll have fun." I give her a big smile, ignoring the sudden wash of envy. I want Rosa to have this kind of freedom; there's no reason for her to be stuck in the suburbs.

There's no reason for her to be confined like me.

* * *

The drive to the park takes less than thirty minutes. As we approach, I realize where we're going, and my stomach tightens.

I know this park.

It's the one where I was walking with Jake the night Julian kidnapped me.

The memories that come are sharp and vivid. In a dark flash, I relive the terror of seeing Jake unconscious on the ground and feeling the cruel prick of the needle on my skin.

"Are you okay?" Julian asks, and I realize I must've gone pale. His eyebrows come together. "Nora?"

"I'm fine." I attempt to smile as the car comes to a stop at the curb. "It's nothing."

"It's not nothing." His blue eyes narrow. "If you're not feeling well, we're going back to the house."

"No." I grab the door handle and tug at it frantically. The atmosphere in the car feels heavy all of a sudden, thick with memories. "Please, I just want some fresh air."

"All right." Apparently sensing my state, Julian motions to the driver, and the door locks click open. "Go ahead."

I scramble out of the car, the anxious feeling in my chest easing as soon as I step outside. Taking a deep breath, I turn to see Julian climb out of the car behind me, his face taut with worry.

"Why did you choose this park?" I ask, trying to keep my voice even. "There are others in the area."

He looks puzzled for a second; then understanding displaces worry on his face. "Because I had already scoped out this place," he says, stepping toward me. His hands close around my upper arms as he gazes down at me. "Is that what's bothering you, my pet? My choice of location?"

"Yes, somewhat." I take another deep breath. "It brings back certain . . . memories."

"Ah, of course." Julian's eyes gleam with sudden amusement. "I guess I should've been more cognizant of that. This just happened to be the easiest park to secure, since I had all the schematics from before."

"From when you stole me." I stare up at him. Sometimes his total lack of repentance still catches me off-guard. "You scoped out the park two years ago for my kidnapping."

"Yes." His beautiful lips curl in a smile as he releases my arms and steps back. "Now, are you feeling better, or should we go back?"

"No, let's take a walk," I say, determined to enjoy the day. "I'm fine now."

Julian takes my hand, lacing my fingers through his, and we enter the park. To my relief, in the daylight everything looks different than it did on that fateful evening, and it's not long before the dark memories recede, retreating back to that forbidden, closed corner of my brain.

I want to keep them there, so I focus on the bright sunlight and the warm spring breeze.

"I love this weather," I say to Julian as we pass by a playground. "I'm glad we came out."

He smiles and brings my hand up to brush a kiss across my knuckles. "Me too, baby. Me too."

As we walk, I see that the park is unusually busy for a Friday. There are older couples, moms and nannies with their charges, and a good number of people my age. I'm guessing they're college students, home for the long weekend. Here and there, I also spot a few military-looking types doing their best to blend in.

Julian's men. They're here to protect us, but their presence is also a stark reminder that I'm still a prisoner in a way.

"How were you able to find me?" I ask when we sit down on a bench. I know I should stop dwelling on the past, but for some reason, I can't stop thinking of those early days. "After our first meeting at the club, I mean?"

Julian turns to look at me, his expression unreadable. "I sent a guard to follow you home."

"Oh." So simple, yet so diabolical. "You already knew you wanted to steal me?"

"No." He clasps both of my hands between his palms. "I hadn't come to that decision yet. I told myself I just wanted to know who you were, to make sure you got home safely."

I stare at him, both fascinated and disturbed. "So when did you decide to abduct me?"

His eyes gleam a bright blue. "It was later, when I couldn't stop thinking about you. I went to your graduation because I told myself you couldn't possibly be the way I remembered you, the way you appeared in the pictures I had my guards take. I told myself that if I saw you in person again, this obsession would disappear ... but of course it didn't." His lips curl with irony. "It got worse. It's still getting worse."

I swallow, unable to look away from the dark intensity in his gaze. "Do you ever regret it? Taking me the way you did?"

"Regret that you're mine?" He lifts his eyebrows. "No, my pet. Why would I?"

Why, indeed. I don't know what other answer I expected. That he fell in love with me and now regrets having caused me suffering? That

I came to mean so much to him that he now sees his actions as wrong?

"No reason," I say quietly, pulling my hands out of his grasp. "I was just wondering, that's all."

His expression softens slightly. "Nora..."

I lean in, but before he can continue, we're interrupted by a burst of childish laughter. A tiny girl with blond pigtails waddles toward us, a large green ball clutched tightly in her chubby hands.

"Catch!" she shrieks, launching the ball at Julian, and I watch in amazement as Julian extends his hand to the side and deftly catches the awkwardly thrown object.

The toddler laughs in joy and waddles toward us faster, her short legs pumping as she runs. Before I can say anything, she's already at our bench, grabbing Julian's legs as casually as if he were a tree.

"Hi," she drawls, giving Julian a dimpled smile. "Can I please have my ball back?" She pronounces each word with a clarity that would do an older child proud. "I want to play more."

"Here you go." Julian smiles as he hands it back to her. "You can definitely have it back."

"Lisette!" A harried-looking blond woman jogs up to us, her face flushed. "There you are. Don't bother these strangers." Grabbing the child by the arm, she gives us an apologetic look. "I'm so sorry. She ran off before I could—"

"No worries," I reassure her, grinning. "She's adorable. How old is she?"

"Two-and-a-half going on twenty," the woman says with visible pride. "I don't know where she gets it from; God knows her dad and I barely finished high school."

"I can read," Lisette announces, staring at Julian. "What about you?"

Julian moves off the bench and crouches down on one knee in front of the girl. "I can too," he says gravely. "But not everybody can, so you're definitely ahead of the game."

The toddler beams at him. "I can also count to a hundred."

"Really?" Julian cocks his head to the side. "What else can you do?"

Seeing that we don't mind the child's presence, the blond woman visibly relaxes and lets go of her daughter's arm. "She knows all the words to that *Frozen* song," she says, smoothing the child's hair. "And can actually sing along."

"Can you really?" Julian asks the little girl with apparent seriousness, and she enthusiastically nods before belting out the song in a high-pitched, childish voice.

I grin, expecting Julian to stop her at any moment, but he doesn't. Instead, he listens attentively, his expression approving without being patronizing. When Lisette finishes with the song, he applauds and asks her about her favorite Disney movies, prompting the child to launch into excited chatter about *Cinderella* and *The Little Mermaid*.

"I'm sorry," her mother apologizes to me again when Lisette shows no signs of stopping. "I don't know what's come over her today. She's never this chatty with strangers."

"It's okay," Julian says, rising fluidly to his feet when Lisette pauses to catch her breath. "We don't mind. You have a wonderful daughter."

"Do you have any children of your own?" Lisette's mother asks, smiling at him with the same adoring expression as her daughter. "You're so good with her."

"No"—Julian's gaze flicks down to my stomach—"not yet."

"Oh!" The woman gasps, giving us a huge, delighted smile. "Congratulations. The two of you will have beautiful babies, I just know it."

"Thank you," I say, feeling my face turn hot. "We're looking forward to it."

"Well, we must be off," Lisette's mother says, grabbing her daughter's arm again. "Come, Lisette, sweetie, say goodbye to the nice young couple. They have things to do, and we need to go eat lunch."

"Goodbye." The toddler giggles, waving at Julian with her free hand. "Have a nice day."

Smiling, Julian waves back at her, and then turns to face me. "That lunch doesn't sound like a bad idea. What do you think, my pet? Ready to go home?"

"Yes." I step closer to Julian and loop my hand through the crook of his elbow. My chest aches strangely. "Let's go home."

On our drive back, for the first time ever, I allow myself a small daydream. A fantasy in which Julian and I are a normal family. Closing my eyes, I picture my former captor as he was in the park today: a dangerous, darkly beautiful man kneeling next to a precocious little girl.

Kneeling next to *our* child.

A child that, for the duration of this fantasy, I crave with all my being.

CHAPTER TWENTY-TWO

❖ JULIAN ❖

On Saturday morning, I get up early and make my way down to the kitchen. Rosa is already there, and after I verify that she has everything under control, I go back upstairs to Nora.

She's still sleeping when I enter the bedroom. Approaching the bed, I carefully pull the blanket off her, doing my best not to wake her up. She mumbles something, rolling over onto her back, but doesn't open her eyes. She looks unbelievably sexy, lying there naked like that, and I try to ignore the hard-on in my pants as I pick up the bottle of warm massage oil I brought from the kitchen and pour the liquid into my palm.

I begin with her feet, since I know how much my pet enjoys a foot rub. As soon as I touch her sole, her toes curl, and a sleepy moan escapes her lips. The sound makes me even harder, but I resist the urge to climb on the bed and bury myself in her tight, delicious body.

This morning, her pleasure is all that matters.

I rub one foot first, giving equal attention to each toe, then switch my focus to the other foot before working my way up to her slim calves and thighs. By then, Nora is all but purring, and I know she's awake even though her eyes are still closed.

"Happy birthday, baby," I murmur, leaning over her to massage the oil into her smooth, taut belly. "Did you sleep well?"

"Mmm." The inarticulate sound seems to be all she's capable of as I move my hands to her breasts. Her peaked nipples press into my palms, all but begging me to suck them. Unable to resist the temptation, I bend down and take one into my mouth, pulling on it with a strong sucking motion. Gasping, she arches up, her eyes flying open, and I turn my attention to her other breast, my oil-slick fingers slipping down her body to stimulate her clit.

"Julian," she moans, her breathing coming faster as I push two fingers into her tight, hot channel and curl them inside her. "Oh my God, Julian!" Her words end on a soft cry as her body goes taut, and then I feel her pulsing in release.

When her contractions ease, I withdraw my fingers from her swollen flesh and trail them up her ribcage. "Turn over, baby," I say softly. "I'm not done with you yet."

She obeys, and I reach for the massage oil again. Pouring a generous amount into my hand, I massage it into her neck, arms, and back, enjoying her continued moans of pleasure. By the time I get to the firm curves of her ass, I'm breathing heavily myself, my cock like an iron spike in my pants. Climbing onto the bed, I straddle her thighs and lean forward, covering her with my body.

"I want to fuck you," I whisper in her ear, knowing she can feel the hard pressure of my erection against her ass. "Do you want that, baby? Do you want me to take you and make you come again?"

She shudders underneath me. "Yes. Please, yes."

A dark smile forms on my lips. "Your wish is my command." Unzipping my pants, I pull out my cock and slide my left arm under her hips, elevating her ass for a better angle. On a different day, I'd pour the oil over her tiny asshole and take her there, reveling in her reluctance, but not today. Today, I'm going to give her only what she wants.

Pressing my cock to her small, slick entrance, I begin to push in.

Soft, wet heat engulfs me as I work my way deeper into her body. Despite the lust pounding through me, I move slowly, letting her adjust to my size. When I'm all the way in, she moans, clenching around me, and I nearly combust at the squeezing sensation, my balls tightening against my body.

"Julian..." She's panting again, squirming underneath me as I begin to thrust in slow, controlled movements. "Julian, please, let me come..."

Her begging pushes me over the edge, and with a low growl, I begin to fuck her harder, pounding into her tight, silky flesh. I can hear her cries, feel her body squeezing me even more, and when her contractions begin anew, I explode with a hoarse groan, my seed spurting into her spasming pussy.

Afterwards, I stretch out beside her and gather her into my arms.

"Happy twentieth birthday, baby," I murmur into her tangled hair, and she laughs softly, the sound full of delight.

* * *

"Oh, Julian, you really shouldn't have," Nora protests as I lock the delicate diamond pendant in place around her neck. "It's gorgeous, but—"

"But what?" I step back, admiring how the crescent-shaped stone looks against her golden skin in the mirror.

She turns away from the mirror to face me, her eyes dark and serious. "You already made the day so special for me, with the massage and the pancakes Rosa made for breakfast. You didn't need to get me such an expensive gift as well. Especially since I've never had a chance to get you anything for *your* birthday."

"My birthday is in November," I say, amused. "Last November you didn't even know that I survived the explosion, so there's no way you could've gotten anything for me. And the year before, well . . ." I smile, remembering how much she resented me her first few months on the island.

"Right." Nora's gaze is unblinking. "The year before, I had other things on my mind."

I laugh. "I'm sure. In any case, don't worry about it. I don't celebrate my birthday."

"Why not?" Her eyebrows pull together in a puzzled frown. "You don't like birthdays?"

"Not my own, no." My parents routinely forgot it when I was a child, and I'd learned to forget it as well. "In any case, that has nothing to do with this gift. If you don't like it, I can get you something else."

"No." Nora clutches the necklace possessively. "I love it."

"Then it's yours." Stepping toward her, I tilt her chin up with my fingers and press a brief kiss to her lips before stepping back. "Now you should get ready. Your parents are waiting to have lunch with you."

She blinks, staring at me. "What are we doing tonight? You told them we already have plans."

"We do. I'm taking you to a restaurant in the city." I pause, looking at her. "Unless you want to do something else? It's your choice."

"Really?" Her face lights up with excitement. "In that case, can we do something crazy?"

"Such as?"

"Can we go to a nightclub after dinner?"

My first inclination is to say no, but I bite back the words. "Why?" I ask instead.

She shrugs, looking slightly embarrassed. "I don't know. I just think it would be fun. I haven't been to a club since—" She falls silent, biting her lip.

"Since you met me."

She nods, and I recall the conversation we had after lunch with her friends. There had been a certain wistfulness in Nora's voice when she spoke of going out and having fun, a longing for things she thought she'd never experience.

"Which club do you want to go to?" I ask, unable to believe I'm even entertaining the idea.

Nora's eyes brighten. "Any club," she says quickly. "Whichever one you think is safest. I don't care where we go, just as long as there's music and dancing."

"How about the one where we met?" I suggest reluctantly. "My men are familiar with it from before, so it'll be easier—"

"Yes, perfect," she interrupts, beaming at me. "Can we take Rosa with us? I know she would love it too." My expression must reflect my thoughts because she swiftly clarifies, "Just to the club, not dinner. I also want the dinner to be just the two of us."

I sigh. "Sure. I'll have one of the guards drive her, so she can meet us at the club after dinner."

Nora squeals and throws her arms around my neck. "Thank you! Oh, I can't wait. This is going to be so great."

And as she heads out for lunch with her parents, I get together with Lucas to figure out how to secure a popular Chicago nightclub on a Saturday night.

* * *

584

"Wow, Julian, this is amazing," Nora exclaims as we walk into the high-end French restaurant I chose for our dinner. "How did you get a reservation? I heard people have to wait for months..." Then she stops and rolls her eyes. "Oh, never mind. What am I saying? Of course you of all people can get a reservation."

I smile at her obvious excitement. "I'm glad you like it. Let's hope the food is as good as the ambience."

The waiter leads us to our table, which is in a private nook at the back of the restaurant. Instead of wine, I order sparkling water for both of us, and also request the tasting menu after first explaining the restrictions associated with Nora's pregnancy.

"Very good, sir," the waiter says, bowing slightly, and before we know it, the first course is on our table.

As we nibble on asparagus risotto and langoustine ravioli, Nora tells me about her lunch and how happy her parents were to celebrate this birthday with her. "They got me a new set of paint brushes," she says, grinning. "I'm guessing that means my dad's no longer as skeptical about my hobby."

"That's good, baby. He shouldn't be. You have an amazing talent."

"Thank you." She gives me a glowing smile and reaches for her water glass.

As we talk, I find myself unable to look away from her. She's radiant tonight, more beautiful than I've ever seen her. Her strapless blue dress is sexy and elegant at the same time—though much too short for my peace of mind. When I saw her coming down the stairs tonight, in that dress and her silvery high-heeled shoes, it was all I could do not to drag her back upstairs and fuck her for three days straight. It doesn't help that she used some kind of make-up that makes her lips shiny and extra-lush. Every time she wraps those lips around a fork, I picture her sucking my cock and my pants get uncomfortably tight.

"You know, you never told me what you were doing in that club when we first met," she says when we're halfway through the third course. "Why were you in Chicago, in general? Most of your business is outside the US, isn't it?"

"Yes," I say, nodding. "I wasn't here for business in that sense. An acquaintance of mine recommended this hedge fund analyst to me, so I was interviewing him for the position of my personal portfolio manager."

"Oh." Nora's eyes widen. "Is that the guy you were meeting with the other day?"

"Yes. I liked what I saw two years ago, so I hired him. And then I decided to go out and see a bit of the city—which is how I ended up in that club."

"You weren't worried about security back then?"

"I had a few of my men with me, but no, Al-Quadar wasn't yet a major threat, and besides, I didn't have you to worry about." It wasn't until I acquired Nora that I became this paranoid about safety. My pet doesn't know how vulnerable she makes me, doesn't realize the lengths to which I would go to protect her. If I had been certain that Majid would let her go unharmed, I would've given him the explosive and whatever else Al-Quadar demanded.

I would've done anything to get her back.

"Were you planning to hook up with some woman that night?" Nora asks, taking a sip from her glass. Her tone is casual, but the look in her eyes is anything but.

I smile, pleased by her apparent jealousy. "Perhaps," I tease. "That's why most men go to clubs, you know. It's not for the dancing, I assure you."

"So did you?" She leans forward, her small hand tightening around her fork. "Did you pick up someone after I left?"

I'm tempted to tease her some more, but I can't bring myself to be that cruel. "No, my pet. I returned to my hotel room alone that night, unable to think of anything but this beautiful, petite girl I met." I also dreamed of her. Of her face that was so much like Maria's . . . of her silky skin and delicate curves.

Of the dark, twisted things I wanted to do to her.

"I see." Nora relaxes, a smile appearing on her face. "And the next day? Did you go out again?"

"No." I reach for a crab-stuffed fig. "I didn't see the point." Not when I was so obsessed I spent hours looking through the pictures my guards took of her.

Not when I already knew I'd never want any woman this much again.

CHAPTER TWENTY-THREE

❖ NORA ❖

By the time we walk out of the restaurant, I feel like I'm in seventh heaven. Our dinner tonight was the closest thing we've had to a real date, and for the first time in months, I'm feeling hopeful about the future.

We may never be "normal," but that doesn't mean we can't be happy.

As we drive to the club, I allow myself that daydream again, the one where Julian and I are a family. It feels more real now, more substantial. For the first time, I can picture us raising our child together. It wouldn't be easy, and we'd constantly be surrounded by guards, but we could do it. We could make it work. We'd live on the estate most of the time, but we'd travel too. We'd visit my parents and friends, and we'd go to places in Europe and Asia. I would have a career as an artist, and Julian's business would be something that's in the background of our lives, instead of front and center.

It wouldn't be the kind of life I dreamed of when I was younger, but it would be a good life nonetheless.

It takes us half an hour to get to the club in downtown traffic. When we exit the car, Rosa is already standing there, waiting for us. Seeing me, she grins and runs up to the car.

"Nora, you look gorgeous," she exclaims before turning to Julian. "And you too, Señor." She gives us a huge, beaming smile. "Thank you so much for taking me with you tonight. I've been dying to go to a real American nightclub."

"I'm glad you were able to come," I tell her, smiling. "You look amazing." And she does. In sexy red heels and a short yellow dress that plays up her curves, Rosa looks hot enough to be a pinup girl.

"Do you really think so?" she says eagerly. "I got this dress in the city on Thursday. I was worried it might be too much."

"There's no such thing," I say firmly. "You look absolutely phenomenal. Now, come, let's go dance." And grabbing her arm, I lead her to the club entrance, with an amused-looking Julian following on our heels.

Despite the club's location in an older, seedier part of downtown Chicago, there is a long line of people waiting by the door. The place must be even more popular now than it was two years ago. As we walk by, the men eye both me and Rosa, while the women gawk at Julian. I don't blame those women, even though some dark part of me wants to gouge their eyes out. My husband dressed up tonight, putting on a sharply tailored blazer and dark designer jeans, and he looks effortlessly hot, like a movie star coming out of a film premiere. Of course, movie stars don't usually conceal guns and knives under their stylish jackets, but I'm trying not to think about that.

One word from Julian to the bouncer, and we're inside, bypassing the waiting crowd. Nobody checks our IDs, not even at the bar where Julian buys Rosa a drink. I wonder if it's because Julian's men already warned the club management about us.

Either way, it's pretty neat.

It's only ten o'clock, but the club is already hopping, the latest pop and dance hits blaring from the speakers. Even though I've had no alcohol, I feel high, drunk with excitement. Laughing, I grab Rosa and Julian and drag them both to the dance floor, where tons of people are already grinding against one another.

When we get to the middle of the dance floor, Julian spins me around and pulls me against him, holding me from the back as we begin moving to the music. I instantly realize what he's doing. With the way he's holding me, I'm facing Rosa, and the three of us are sort of dancing together, but it's Julian's big body that surrounds me. Nobody can touch me, either on purpose or by accident, not without going through him first.

Even in the middle of a crowded dance floor, I belong to Julian and Julian alone.

Rosa grins, apparently also realizing Julian's agenda. She's even more excited than me, her eyes sparkling as she shakes her booty to the latest Lady Gaga song. Before long, a couple of good-looking young guys sidle up to her, and I watch, grinning, as she begins to flirt with them and gradually moves away from me and Julian.

As soon as she's occupied, Julian turns me around to face him. "How are you feeling, baby?" he asks, his deep voice cutting through the blasting music. The colored lights flicker over his face, making him look surreally handsome. "Any tiredness? Nausea?"

"No." Smiling, I vigorously shake my head. "I'm perfect. Better than perfect, in fact."

"Yes, you are," he murmurs, pulling me tighter against him, and I flush all over as I feel the hard bulge in his pants. He wants me, and my body responds immediately, the pulsing beat of the music echoing the sudden ache in my core. We're surrounded by people, but all of them seem to fade away as we stare at one another, our bodies beginning to move together in a primal, sexual rhythm. My breasts swell, my nipples pebbling as I press my chest against his, and even through the layers of clothing we're wearing, I can feel the heat coming off his large body . . . the same kind of heat that's building within myself.

"Fuck, baby," he breathes, staring down at me. His hips rock back and forth as we sway together, driven as much by our need for each other as the music's beat. "You can't wear this fucking dress ever again."

"The dress?" I stare up at him, my body burning. "You think it's the dress?"

He closes his eyes and takes a deep breath before opening them to meet my gaze. "No," he says hoarsely. "It's not the dress, Nora. It's you. It's always fucking you."

I half-expect him to drag me away then, but he doesn't. Instead, he loosens his grip on me, putting a couple of inches of space between us. I can still feel his body against mine, but the raw sexuality of the moment is reduced, enabling me to breathe again. We dance like that for a few more songs, and then I begin to feel thirsty.

"Can I please get some water?" I ask, raising my voice to be heard above the music, and Julian nods, leading me toward the bar. As we pass by Rosa, I see that she's still dancing with those two guys, seemingly content to be sandwiched between them. I give her a wink and a discreet thumbs-up, and then we're out of the dancing, writhing crowd.

Julian gets me a glass filled with ice water, and I gratefully chug it down, feeling parched. He smiles as he watches me drink, and I know he's remembering it too—our first meeting, right here by this bar.

As we turn to go back to the dance floor, I see Rosa walking toward the back, where the bathrooms are. She waves at me, grinning, and I wave back before turning to Julian.

"Let's dance some more," I say, grabbing his hand, and we dive back into the crowd just as a new song begins.

A few minutes later, I start to feel it—the familiar sensation of an overly full bladder.

"I have to pee," I tell Julian, and he grins, leading me off the dance floor again. We walk together to the back of the club, and I get in line to the girls' bathroom while Julian leans against the wall, watching as I wait my turn in the shadowed, circular hallway leading to the restrooms. I wonder if he's guarding me even here and almost snicker at the idea of him being worried enough to accompany me to the ladies' room.

Thankfully, he doesn't. Instead, he stays by the entrance to the narrow hallway, his arms crossed over his chest.

The line is long, and it takes almost fifteen minutes to get to my destination. When my turn finally comes, I step into the small three-stall room and do my business. It's only when I'm washing my hands that it occurs to me that Rosa disappeared in this direction, and I haven't seen her come out since.

Pulling out my phone from my tiny purse, I text Julian: *Did Rosa walk by you? Do you see her anywhere?*

There's no immediate answer, so I step out of the bathroom, about to head back, when a flash of something red a dozen feet away catches my attention. Frowning, I walk deeper into the circular hallway, past the restrooms, and then I see it.

A red, high-heeled shoe lying discarded on the floor.

My heart skips a beat.

Bending down, I pick it up, and a chill skitters down my spine.

There's no doubt now. It's Rosa's shoe.

My pulse speeding up, I straighten, looking around, but I don't see her anywhere. With the way the hallway curves, even the bathroom line is out of sight now.

Dropping the shoe, I pull out my phone again. There is a text from Julian in response to mine: *No, I don't see her.*

I begin to type out a reply, but at that moment, a door I hadn't noticed before swings open a few feet away.

A short, skinny guy steps out, closing the door behind him, and leans against the door frame.

A young guy, I realize, looking at him. More like a boy in his teens, his pale, freckled face unmarred by the slightest hint of stubble. His posture is casual, almost lazy, but something about the way he glances at me gives me pause.

"Excuse me." I approach him carefully, wrinkling my nose at the strong smell of alcohol and cigarettes coming off him. "Have you seen my friend? She's wearing a yellow dress—"

He spits on the floor in front of me. "Get the fuck outta here, bitch."

I'm so startled I step back. Then anger blasts through me, mixing with adrenaline. "Excuse me?" My hands curl into fists. "What did you just call me?"

The teenager's posture changes, becoming more combative. "I said—"

And at that moment, I hear it.

A woman's scream behind the door, followed by the sound of something falling.

My adrenaline levels surge. Without thinking, I step forward and swing upward with my right fist, just as Julian taught me. The momentum of my move adds to the force of the blow, and the guy gasps as my fist slams into his solar plexus. He starts to double over, and at that moment, my knee comes up, crushing his balls.

He bends over with a high-pitched scream, clutching his crotch, and I grab the back of his neck, using the momentum to pull him forward as I stick my right foot out.

It works even better than in training.

He pitches forward, arms flailing, and his head hits the wall on the opposite side of the hallway. Then he slides to the floor, his body limp and unmoving in front of me.

Shaking, I gape at it. I can't believe I just did that.

I can't believe I took down a guy in a fight—even if that guy was a drunk teenage boy.

Another scream behind the door snaps me out of my daze.

I recognize that voice now, and a fresh burst of adrenaline sends my heartbeat soaring. Operating solely on instinct, I jump over the young guy's fallen body and push open the door.

The room inside is long and narrow, with another door at the far end. A stained couch is by that door—and on that couch is my friend, struggling and sobbing under a man.

For a second, I'm too frozen to react, and then I notice streaks of red on the bright yellow of Rosa's torn dress.

A hot, dark rage explodes in my chest, sweeping away all remnants of caution.

"Let her go!" I yell, rushing into the room. Startled, the guy jumps off Rosa, and then, as if recalling his vile agenda, grabs her by the hair and drags her off the couch.

"Nora!" Rosa screams hysterically, pointing at something behind me.

Horrified, I spin around, but it's too late.

The other man is already on me, the back of his hand flying toward my face.

The blow knocks me into the wall, the impact of the hit jarring every bone in my back.

Dazed, I sink down to the floor, and through the ringing in my ears, I hear a man's voice say, "You can fuck that one if you want. I'll take my turn with this one in the car."

And as rough hands start tearing at my clothes, I see Rosa's attacker dragging her toward the door on the far side of the room.

CHAPTER TWENTY-FOUR

❖ JULIAN ❖

Bored, I step away from the wall and peer into the hallway. Nora is already at the front of the line, so I lean back against the wall and prepare to wait some more. I also make a mental note never to return to this club. These lines must be a regular occurrence here, and I find it ridiculous that they haven't put in a bigger restroom for the women.

Taking out my phone, I check my email for the third time. As expected, nothing's happened since three minutes ago, so I put the phone away again and consider walking over to the bar to get myself a drink. I've been abstaining all night to keep my reflexes sharp in case of danger, but one beer shouldn't impact anything.

Still, I decide against it. Even though several of my guards are sprinkled throughout the club, I don't feel comfortable having Nora out of sight for more than a couple of minutes. I would've even waited in that line with her, but the curving hallway is so narrow that there's only room for the women and the occasional man pushing his way through.

So I wait, amusing myself by watching the dancers on the floor. With all the grinding bodies, the atmosphere is heavily sexual, but the flickering lights and pulsing beat do nothing for me. Without Nora in my arms to excite me, I might as well be standing on a street corner watching grass grow.

My phone vibrates in my pocket, distracting me from my thoughts. Pulling it out, I look at Nora's message and frown.

Did Rosa walk by you? Do you see her anywhere?

Stepping away from the wall again, I glance into the hallway. I don't see either Rosa or Nora there, but the girl who was behind Nora in line is still waiting her turn.

Satisfied that Nora must be inside the bathroom, I turn to survey the club, searching for a yellow dress in the crowd. It's hard to see, with all the people and the dim lighting, but Rosa's dress is bright enough that I should be able to spot her.

I don't see anything, though. Not by the bar and not on the dance floor.

Starting to feel uneasy, I push through the crowd to get to the other side of the bar and look again.

Nothing. No yellow dress anywhere.

My unease morphs into full-blown alarm. Grabbing the phone again, I check the location of Nora's trackers.

She's still in the bathroom or right next to it.

Feeling marginally calmer, I message Lucas to put the men on alert and text Nora my response before pushing my way back toward the restrooms. Maybe I'm being paranoid, but I need to have Nora with me. Right now. My instincts are screaming that something's wrong, and I won't relax until I have her securely by my side.

When I get to the hallway, I see that the line of women is even longer now, and there's even a line to the men's room. The narrow hallway is completely blocked, so I begin to shove people aside, ignoring their shouts of outrage.

Nora is not in this line, though the trackers indicate she's nearby. She's also not in the women's bathroom, I realize as I pass by it. According to my tracking app, she's about thirty feet ahead, a bit to the left of the curving hallway. The crowd clears out past this point, and I pick up the pace, my worry intensifying.

A second later, I see it.

A man's body on the floor, next to a closed door.

My blood turns to ice, the fear sharp and acrid on my tongue. If somebody took Nora, if she's been harmed in any way—

No. I can't allow myself to go there, not when she needs me.

An icy calm engulfs me, blocking out the fear. Crouching down, I grab the knife from my ankle holster and slide it into my belt buckle for easy access. Then, rising to my feet, I take out my gun and step over the body, ignoring the blood trickling from the man's forehead.

According to the app, Nora is only a few feet to the left of me—which means she's behind that door.

Taking a deep breath, I push open the door and step into the room.

Immediately, a muffled cry to my right catches my attention. Spinning, I see two figures struggling by the wall . . . and all traces of calm flee.

Nora—my Nora—is fighting with a man twice her size. He's on top of her, one of his hands muffling her screams and the other hand tearing at her clothes. Her eyes are wild and furious, her fingers curved into claws as she rakes at his face and neck, leaving bloody streaks across his skin.

A red fog descends on me, a rage more violent than anything I've known.

One leap, and I'm on top of them, dragging the man off Nora. I don't shoot—too risky with her near—but the knife is in my hand as I pin him to the floor, my left forearm crushing his throat. He's choking, his eyes bulging as I raise the knife and plunge it into his side, again and again. Hot blood spurts out, spraying all over me, and I smell his terror, his knowledge of impending death. His hands beat at me, but I don't feel the blows. Instead, I watch his eyes as I stab him again and again, reveling in his dying struggles.

"Julian!" Nora's cry snaps me out of my bloodlust, and I spring to my feet, leaving her attacker's twitching body on the floor.

She's shaking, mascara and tears streaming down her face as she tries to stand up, holding the wall for support.

Fuck. Sickening fear fills my chest. I rush to her and gather her against me, frantically patting her down in search of injuries. Nothing feels broken, but her lower lip is split and puffy, and her dress has a small rip at the top. And the child— No, I can't think about that now.

"Baby, are you hurt?" My voice is barely recognizable as my own. "Did he hurt you?"

She shakes her head, her eyes still wild. "No!" She twists in my arms, pushing at me with surprising strength. "Let me go! We have to go after her!"

"What? Who?" Startled, I move back, holding her by one arm so she wouldn't fall.

"Rosa! He's got her, Julian! He grabbed her and dragged her out that way." Nora jabs her free hand in the direction of the door in the back. "We must go after her!" She sounds hysterical.

"Another man took her?"

"Yes! He said—" Nora's voice catches on a sob. "He said he was going to take his turn in the car. There were two of them here, and one took Rosa!"

I stare at her, a new fury building inside me. I may not be close to Rosa, but I like the girl and she's under my protection. The idea that someone dared to do this, to assault her and Nora this way—

"Hurry!" Nora implores, frantically tugging on the arm I'm holding to pull me toward the door. "Come on, Julian, we have to hurry! He *just* dragged her out that way, so we can still catch up!"

Fuck. I grit my teeth, every muscle in my body vibrating with tension. I've never been so torn in my life. Nora is hurt, and everything inside me screams that she's my first priority, that I should grab her and rush her to safety as quickly as possible. But if what she says is true, then the only way to save Rosa is to act immediately—and it'll take my men at least a few minutes to get to where we are.

"Please, Julian!" Nora begs, sobbing, and the panic in her eyes decides it for me.

"Stay here." My voice is cold and sharp as I release her arm and step back. "Do not move."

"I'm coming with you—"

"Like hell you are." Pulling out my gun, I thrust it into her hands. "Wait for me here, and shoot anyone you don't recognize."

And before she can argue with me, I stride swiftly toward the back door, messaging Lucas about the situation on the way.

CHAPTER TWENTY-FIVE

❖ NORA ❖

As soon as Julian disappears through the door, I sink to the floor, clutching the gun he gave me. My legs are trembling and my head is spinning, waves of nausea rolling through me. I feel like I'm hanging on to my sanity by a thread. Only the knowledge that Julian is on his way to rescue Rosa keeps me from slipping into complete hysteria. Drawing in a shuddering breath, I wipe at the moisture on my face with the back of my hand, and as I lower my arm, a streak of red catches my attention.

Blood.

There's blood on me.

I stare at it, repulsed yet fascinated. It has to be from the man Julian killed. Julian was covered in blood when he touched me, and it's all over me now, the streaks of red on my arms and chest reminiscent of one of my paintings. Strangely, the analogy calms me a bit. Drawing in another breath, I look up, turning my attention to the dead man lying a few feet away.

Now that he's not attacking me, I realize with shock that I recognize him. He's one of the two young men Rosa was dancing with. Does that mean that the second attacker is the other man? I frown, trying to remember the second man's features, but he's just a blur in my mind. I also don't recall ever seeing the teenage guy who was guarding the entrance to this room. Was he with Rosa's dancing companions? If so, why? None of this makes any sense. Even if the three of them are serial rapists, how could they have thought they'd get away with such a brutal assault in a club?

Of course, the motivations of the dead man don't matter anymore. I know he's dead because his body is no longer twitching. His eyes are open and his mouth is slack, a trickle of blood running down his cheek. He stinks of death too, I realize—of blood, feces, and fear. As the sickening smell registers, I scoot away, crawling a few feet to huddle closer to the couch.

Another man was killed in front of me. I wait for horror and disgust, but they don't come. Instead, all I feel is a kind of vicious joy. As if on a movie screen, I see Julian's knife rising and falling, sinking into the man's side again and again, and all I can think is that I'm glad the man is dead.

I'm glad Julian gutted him.

It's odd, but my lack of empathy doesn't bother me this time. I can still feel the man's hands on my body, his nails scraping my skin as he ripped at my clothes. He'd managed to pin me down while I was dazed from his blow, and even though I struggled as hard as I could, I knew I was losing. If Julian hadn't come when he did—

No. I shut that down mid-thought. Julian did come, so there's no need to dwell on the worst. All things considered, I've gotten off with minimal damage. My split lip throbs and my back feels like one giant bruise, but it's nothing irreparable. My body will heal. I've been hit before and survived.

The real question is: will Rosa?

The thought of her hurt, broken and violated, fills me with rage. I want Julian to slaughter the other man as savagely as he killed this one. In fact, I want to do it myself. I would've insisted on coming along, but arguing with Julian would've only slowed down Rosa's rescue.

For now, all I can do is wait and hope that Julian brings her back.

Spotting my little purse on the floor, I crawl over to pick it up. Every movement hurts, but I want that purse with me. It has my phone, which means I can reach Julian. And that's important—because it suddenly dawns on me that Rosa is not the only one in danger at the moment.

So is my husband.

No. I push that thought away too. I know what Julian is capable of. If anyone is equipped to handle this, it's the man who kidnapped me.

Julian's life has been steeped in violence from childhood; killing a scumbag or two must be like cutting grass for him.

Unless said scumbag is armed or has buddies.

No. I squeeze my eyes shut, refusing to entertain such thoughts. Julian will return with Rosa, and all will be well. It has to be. We're going to be a family, build a life together . . .

A family.

My eyes pop open, my hand flying to my stomach as I gasp out loud. For the first time, it strikes me that without Julian's intervention, Rosa and I might not have been the rapists' only victims. If I had been brutalized, knocked around some more, there's no telling what might've happened to the baby.

The terrifying thought steals my breath away.

I begin to shake again, fresh tears forming in my eyes. I don't even know why I'm crying. Everything is fine. It has to be.

Clutching my purse, I focus on the door in the back. Any second now, Julian will walk through it with Rosa, and our lives will go back to normal.

Any second now.

The seconds tick by slowly. So slowly that it's all I can do not to scream. I stare at the door until the tears stop and my eyes begin to burn from dryness. No matter how much I try, I can't keep the dark imaginings away, and the fear inside me feels like it's going to swallow me from within, eat away at me until there's nothing left.

Finally, the door starts to creak open.

I jump to my feet, aches and pains forgotten, but then I recall Julian's parting words.

He's not the only one who might walk through that door.

Lifting the gun he gave me, I take aim with trembling hands and wait.

CHAPTER TWENTY-SIX

❖ JULIAN ❖

As soon as I send my message to Lucas, I open the door and step out into the alley behind the club. Immediately, the smell of garbage hits my nostrils, mixing with the pungent odor of urine. It must've rained while we were inside because the pothole-ridden asphalt is wet, the light from a distant street lamp reflecting in the oily-looking puddles.

Reining in my violent rage and worry, I methodically scan my surroundings. Later I will let myself think about Nora's tear-streaked face and how badly I fucked up, but for now I need to focus on saving Rosa.

I owe her and Nora that much.

I don't see anyone nearby, so I wind my way through the dumpsters, heading toward the street. A few rats scurry away at my approach. I wonder if they can sense the thrum of violence in my veins, the lust for blood that intensifies with every step I take.

One death was not enough. Not nearly enough.

My footsteps echo wetly as I round the corner, turning onto a narrow side street, and then I see it.

Two figures struggling by a white SUV some thirty yards away.

I can see the yellow of Rosa's dress as the man tries to drag her into the car, and black rage surges through me again.

Pulling out my knife, I sprint toward them.

I know the exact moment Rosa's attacker sees me. His eyes widen, his face twisting with fear, and before I can react, he shoves Rosa at me and scrambles into the car.

I put on a burst of speed, managing to catch Rosa before she falls, and she clutches at me, sobbing hysterically. I try to soothe her while extricating myself from her clinging grip, but it's too late.

The car starts up with a roar, and the tires squeal as Rosa's assailant slams on the gas, escaping like the coward that he is.

Fuck. I stare after the disappearing car, panting. I know my men are stationed at the intersection ahead, but a public shootout would draw too much attention. Holding Rosa with one arm, I pull out my phone and tell Lucas to follow the white car.

Then I turn my attention to the sobbing woman in my arms.

"Rosa." Ignoring the adrenaline pumping through me, I gently pull her away from me to view the extent of her injuries. One side of her face is swollen and crusted with blood, and there are scratches and bruises all over her body, but to my relief, I don't see any broken bones. She looks so shaken, though, that I pitch my voice low, speaking to her as I would to a child. "How badly are you hurt, sweetheart?"

"He ... they ..." She seems to be incoherent as she stands there trembling, her dress ripped open, and I grit my teeth, fighting a fresh swell of fury. I can already see that whatever happened to her is not something she'll easily get over.

"Come, sweetheart, let me take you back to Nora." I keep my voice soft and soothing as I bend down to pick her up. Her shaking intensifies as I swing her up into my arms, and I clench my jaw tighter, walking back toward the alley as quickly as I can.

When we're in front of the door to the club, I lower Rosa to her feet. Then, holding her elbow for support, I carefully usher her through the doorway.

We're greeted by the sight of Nora pointing the gun in our direction. The second she spots us, however, her face lights up and she lowers the weapon.

"Rosa!" She drops the gun and runs across the room to us. "You got her, Julian! Oh, thank God, you got her!" Reaching us, she rises on her tiptoes and hugs me fiercely before wrapping her arms around Rosa and guiding her to the couch. I can hear her murmuring reassurances as Rosa clings to her, crying, and I use the opportunity to call for our car to come around to the alley.

A couple of minutes later, the car is ready.

"Come, baby. We have to go, get you both to the hospital," I say softly, approaching the couch, and Nora nods, her arms still wrapped around Rosa's shaking frame. My wife seems much calmer now, her earlier hysteria nowhere in sight. Still, I have to fight the urge to grab her and make sure she's as all right as she seems. The only thing that stops me is the knowledge that Rosa will fall apart without Nora's help.

Thankfully, my pet seems up to the task of dealing with her traumatized friend. That steel core I've always sensed within her has never been more evident than it is now. Even with the rage scorching my insides, I feel a flash of pride as I watch Nora get Rosa off the couch and lead her toward the exit into the alley.

Lucas is leaning against the car, waiting for us. As his gaze falls on Rosa, I can see his face changing, his impassive expression transforming into something dark and frightening.

"Those fuckers," he mutters thickly, walking around the car to open the door for us. "Those motherfucking fuckers." He can't seem to stop staring at Rosa. "They're going to fucking die."

"Yes, they will," I agree, watching with some surprise as he carefully separates Rosa from my wife and guides the crying girl into the car. His manner is so uncharacteristically caring that I can't help wondering if there's something between the two of them. That would be odd, given his fixation on the Russian interpreter, but weirder things have happened.

Shrugging mentally, I turn to Nora, who's standing by the open car door, her left hand gripping the top of the door frame. She seems lost in her own world, her gaze strangely distant as she lifts her right hand and places it on her belly.

"Nora?" I step toward her, a sudden fear gripping my chest, and at that moment, I see her face go chalk-white.

CHAPTER TWENTY-SEVEN

❖ NORA ❖

The cramping sensation I began to feel a few seconds ago suddenly intensifies, turns into a sharp pain. It lances across my stomach, stealing my breath just as Julian steps toward me, his face tight with worry. Gasping, I double over, and instantly I feel his strong hands on me, lifting me off my feet.

"Hospital, now!" he barks at Lucas, and before I can blink, I find myself inside the car, cradled on Julian's lap as we screech out of the alley.

"Nora? Nora, are you all right?" Rosa's voice is filled with panic, but I can't reassure her at the moment, not with my insides cramping and twisting. All I can do is take short, gasping breaths, my hands digging convulsively into Julian's shoulders as he rocks me back and forth, his big body tense underneath me.

"Julian." I can't help crying out as a particularly vicious cramp rips through my belly. I can feel a hot, slippery wetness on my thighs, and I know if I look down, I'll see blood. "Julian, the child . . ."

"I know, baby." He presses his lips to my forehead, rocking me faster. "Hang on. Please, hang on."

We fly through the dark streets, the streetlights and traffic lights blurring in front of my eyes. I can hear Rosa talking to me, her soft hands smoothing over my hair, and I'm aware of a vague sense of guilt that she has to deal with this after everything she's been through.

Mostly, though, what I feel is fear.

A hideous fear that it's too late, that nothing will ever be all right again.

* * *

"I'm so sorry, Mrs. Esguerra." The young doctor stops next to my bed, her hazel eyes filled with sympathy. "As you might've guessed, you miscarried. The good news—if there can be any at a time like this—is that you were still in your first trimester, and the bleeding has already stopped. There might be some spotting and discharge for the next few days, but your body should return to normal fairly quickly. There's no reason why you wouldn't be able to try for another child soon . . . if you wish to do so, of course."

I stare at her, my eyes feeling like they've been scraped with sandpaper. I can't cry anymore. I've cried all the tears within me. I'm aware of Julian's hand holding mine as he sits on the edge of the bed, of the continued dull cramping in my belly, and all I can think is that I lost the baby.

I lost our baby, and it's all my fault.

"Where's Rosa?" My throat is so swollen I have to force the words out. "Is she all right?"

"She's in the room next to you," the doctor says softly. She's unusually pretty, with a pale, heart-shaped face framed by wavy chestnut hair. "Would you like to speak to her?"

"Are they done with her examination?" Julian's voice is as hard as I've ever heard it. His face and hands are clean now—he used bottled water to wipe most of the blood off us before we got out of the car–but his gray jacket is stained brown. I wonder what the doctors think of our appearance, whether they realize that not all of the blood on us is mine.

"Yes, they're done." The doctor hesitates for a second. "Mr. Esguerra, your friend said she doesn't want to press charges or speak to the police, but that's something we strongly recommend in cases like these. At the very least, she should let our sexual assault nurse examiner collect the evidence. Perhaps you can talk to Ms. Martinez, help us convince her—"

"Do any of her injuries require hospitalization?" Julian interrupts, his hand tightening around my fingers. "Or can she go home with us?"

The doctor frowns. "She can go home, but—"

"And my wife?" He gives the young woman a piercing look. "You're certain there are no injuries beyond the bruises?"

"Yes, as I explained to you earlier, Mr. Esguerra, all the tests came back normal." The doctor meets his gaze without flinching. "There's no concussion or any kind of internal injuries, and there's no need for a D&C—dilation and curettage—procedure when the loss happens so early in the pregnancy. I recommend that Mrs. Esguerra take it easy for the next few days, but after that she can return to her normal activities."

Julian glances down at me. "Baby?" His tone softens a fraction. "Do you want to stay here until morning just in case, or would you rather go home?"

"Home." I swallow painfully. "I want to go home."

"Mrs. Esguerra . . ." The doctor places her hand on my forearm, her slender fingers warm on my skin. When I look up at her, she says gently, "I know it's little consolation for your loss, but I want you to know that the vast majority of miscarriages cannot be prevented. It's possible that the incident with you and your friend was a factor in this unfortunate event, but it's just as likely that there was some kind of chromosomal abnormality that would've caused this to happen regardless. Statistically speaking, some twenty percent of known pregnancies end in miscarriage, and up to seventy percent of first-trimester miscarriages occur because of those abnormalities—not something the mother did or didn't do."

I take in her words dully, my gaze slipping from her face to the name tag pinned to her chest. *Dr. Cobakis.* Something about that seems familiar, but I'm too tired to figure out what.

Listlessly, I look up again. "Thank you," I murmur, hoping she leaves the topic alone. I understand what she's trying to do. The doctor's probably run into this before—a woman's automatic tendency to blame herself when something goes wrong with her pregnancy. What she doesn't realize is that in my case, I *am* to blame.

I insisted on going to that club. What happened to Rosa and the baby is my fault and no one else's.

The doctor gives my forearm a gentle squeeze and steps back. "I'll get your friend ready for discharge while you get dressed," she says, and walks out of the room, leaving me alone with Julian for the first time since our arrival at the hospital.

As soon as the doctor is gone, he releases my hand and leans over me. "Nora . . ." In his gaze, I see the same agony that's tearing me up inside. "Baby, are you still in pain?"

I shake my head. The physical discomfort is nothing to me now. "I want to go home," I say hoarsely. "Please, Julian, just take me home."

"I will." He strokes the uninjured side of my face, his touch warm and gentle. "I promise you, I will."

CHAPTER TWENTY-EIGHT

❖ JULIAN ❖

I've never known an emptiness like this before, a burning void that pulses with raw pain. When I lost Maria and my parents, there had been rage and grief, but not this.

Not this awful emptiness mixed with the strongest bloodlust I've ever known.

Nora is still and silent as I carry her up the stairs to our bedroom. Her eyes are closed, her lashes forming dark crescents on her colorless cheeks. She's been like that—all but catatonic from blood loss and exhaustion—since we left the hospital.

As I lay her on the bed, I catch sight of her bruised cheekbone and split lip, and have to turn away to regain control. The violence seething within me feels so toxic, so corrosive, that I can't touch Nora right now—not without it marking her in some way.

After a few moments, I feel calm enough to face the bed. Nora hasn't moved, still lying where I placed her, and I realize she's fallen asleep. Inhaling slowly, I bend over her and begin to undress her. I could let her sleep until morning, but there are traces of dried blood on her clothes, and I don't want her to wake up like that.

She'll have enough to deal with in the morning.

When she's naked, I take off my own clothes and scoop her up, cradling her small, limp body against my chest as I walk to the bathroom. Entering the shower stall, I turn on the water, still holding her tightly.

She wakes up when the warm spray hits her skin, her eyes flying open as she convulsively clutches at my biceps. "Julian?" She sounds alarmed.

"Shh," I soothe. "It's okay. We're home." She looks a bit calmer, so I place her on her feet and ask softly, "Can you stand on your own for a minute, baby?"

She nods, and I make quick work of washing her and then myself. By the time I'm done, she's swaying on her feet, and I see that it's taking all her strength to remain upright. Swiftly, I bundle her into a large towel and carry her back to bed.

She passes out before her head touches the pillow. I tuck a blanket around her and sit next to her for a few moments, watching her chest rise and fall with her breathing.

Then I get up and get dressed to go downstairs.

* * *

Entering the living room, I see that Lucas is already waiting for me.

"Where's Rosa?" I ask, keeping my voice level. Later I will think about our child, about Nora lying there so hurt and vulnerable, but for now I push it all out of my mind. I can't afford to give in to my grief and fury, not when there is so much to be done.

"She's asleep," Lucas responds, rising from the couch. "I gave her Ambien and made sure she took a shower."

"Good. Thank you." I cross the room to stand next to him. "Now tell me everything."

"The clean-up crew took care of the body and captured the kid Nora knocked out in the hallway. They're holding him in a warehouse I rented on the South Side."

"Good." My chest fills with savage anticipation. "What about the white car?"

"The men were able to follow it to one of the residential high-rises downtown. At that point, it disappeared into a parking garage, and they decided against pursuing it there. I've already run the license plate number."

He pauses at that point, prompting me to say impatiently, "And?"

"And it seems like we might have a problem," Lucas says grimly. "Does the name Patrick Sullivan mean anything to you?"

I frown, trying to think where I've heard it before. "It's familiar, but I can't place it."

"The Sullivans own half of this town. Prostitution, drugs, weapons—you name it, they have their fingers in it. Patrick Sullivan heads up the family, and he's got just about every local politician and police chief in his pocket."

"Ah." It makes sense now. I haven't had dealings with the Sullivan organization, but I'd made it my business to know potential clients in the US and elsewhere. Sullivan's name must've come up in my research—which means we might indeed have a problem. "What does Patrick Sullivan have to do with this?"

"He has two sons," Lucas says. "Or rather, he *had* two sons. Brian and Sean. Brian is currently marinating in lye at our rented warehouse, and Sean is the owner of the white SUV."

"I see." So the fuckers who attacked Rosa and my wife are connected. More than connected, in fact—which explains their idiotic arrogance in assaulting two women at a public club. With their daddy running this town, they must be used to being the biggest sharks in the pool.

"Also," Lucas continues, "the kid we've got strung up in that warehouse is their seventeen-year-old cousin, Sullivan's nephew. His name is Jimmy. Apparently, he and the two brothers are close. Or *were* close, I should say."

My eyes narrow in sudden suspicion. "Do they have any idea who we are? Could they have singled out Rosa to get at me?"

"No, I don't think so." Lucas's face tightens. "The Sullivan brothers have a nasty history with women. Date-rape drugs, sexual assault, gang bangs of sorority girls—the list goes on and on. If it weren't for their father, they'd be rotting in prison right now."

"I see." My mouth twists. "Well, by the time we're done with them, they'll wish they were."

Lucas nods grimly. "Should I organize a strike team?"

"No," I say. "Not yet." I turn and walk over to stand by the window, gazing out into the dark, tree-lined yard. It's four in the morning, and the only light visible through the trees comes from the half-moon hanging in the sky.

This community is a quiet, peaceful place, but it won't stay that way for long. Once Sullivan figures out who killed his sons and nephew, these neat, landscaped streets will run red with blood.

"I want Nora and her parents taken to the estate before we do anything," I say, turning back to face Lucas. "Sean Sullivan will have to wait. For now, we'll focus on the nephew."

"All right." Lucas inclines his head. "I'll begin making the arrangements."

He walks out of the room, and I turn to look out the window again.

Despite the half-moon, all I see out there is the darkness.

CHAPTER TWENTY-NINE

❖ NORA ❖

"Nora, honey..." A familiar gentle touch pulls me out of my restless slumber. Forcing my heavy eyelids open, I stare uncomprehendingly at my mom, who's sitting on the edge of the bed and stroking my hair. My head aches so much that it takes me a few moments to process her presence in our bedroom—and notice her red-rimmed, swollen eyes.

"Mom?" Holding the blanket, I sit up, suppressing a groan at the pain caused by the movement. My back feels stiff and sore, and my lower abdomen is cramping dully. "What are you doing here?"

"Julian called us this morning," she says, her voice shaking. "He said you and Rosa were attacked at a club last night."

"Oh." A flash of anger wakes me fully. How dare Julian worry my parents like this? I would've come up with something less frightening to tell them, some gentler way to explain the loss of the baby.

The loss of the baby.

The agony is so sharp and sudden that I can't hold it in. A raw, jagged sob bursts out of my throat, bringing with it a flood of burning tears. Shaking, I clamp my hand over my mouth, but it's too late. The pain wells up and spills out, the tears like acid on my skin. I can feel my mom's arms around me, hear her crying, and I know I have to stop, but I can't. It's too much, the grief, the knowledge that I did this.

Suddenly, it's no longer my mom who holds me. Instead, I'm bundled in the blanket on Julian's lap, his strong arms wrapped around me as he cradles me against him, rocking me like a child. I can hear my dad's voice, the timbre low and soothing, and I know Dad is consoling Mom, trying to calm her in *her* pain. At some point, he and Julian must've come into the room, but I don't know how or when it happened.

Eventually, Julian carries me to the shower. It's there, away from my parents' eyes, that I'm finally able to regain control. "I'm sorry," I whisper as Julian towels me off and dresses me in a thick, terrycloth robe. "I'm so sorry. Where's Rosa? How is she?"

"She's all right," he says quietly. His eyes are bloodshot, making me suspect he didn't sleep much last night. "Well, as all right as can be expected. She's still in her room, but Lucas spoke to her and said she's doing better. And you have nothing to be sorry for, baby. Nothing."

I shake my head, the awful guilt seizing me again. "I need to go see her—"

"Wait, Nora." He grabs my arm just as I'm about to rush back into the bedroom. "Before you do, there's something you and I need to discuss with your parents."

"My parents?"

He nods, looking down at me. "Yes. That's why I called them here. We all need to talk."

* * *

"The Sullivan crime family?" My dad's voice rises incredulously. "You're telling me that the men who attacked my daughter are part of the mob?"

"Yes," Julian says, his face hard and expressionless. He's sitting next to me on the couch, his left hand resting on my knee. "It's something I discovered last night, after we returned from the hospital."

"We need to go to the police right away." My mom leans forward, her hands clenched tightly in her lap. "Those monsters need to pay for this. If you know who they are—"

"They'll pay, Gabriela." Julian's gaze turns to steel. "You don't have to worry about that."

"It's because of you, isn't it?" my dad says savagely, getting up in a sharp motion. "They came after you—"

"No," I interrupt, shaking my head. I'm still reeling from what I just learned, but if there's one thing I'm sure of, it's that for once, Julian's business is not at fault. "It was random, Dad. They had no idea who Rosa and I were. They were just"—I shudder, remembering—"just doing it for fun."

"Fun?" My dad stares at me, his features tense with anger as he sits down again. "Those assholes thought hurting two women would be fun?"

"Well, technically, they wanted only Rosa," I say dully. "I just happened to intervene."

Julian's hand tightens on my knee as he glances in my direction. For the first time this morning, I see a flash of fury behind his emotionless facade. I have no doubt that he blames me for this—for using my birthday to manipulate him into going to that club, for trying to rescue Rosa on my own.

For losing our child . . . the one I didn't even know I wanted until it was too late.

I have no idea what my punishment will be, but whatever it is, it'll be more than deserved.

"We have to go to the police," my mom says again. "We need to report—"

"No." This time, it's Julian who rises to his feet and begins to pace in front of the couch. "That wouldn't be wise."

"Why?" my dad asks sharply. "This is what civilized people do in this country. They go to the authorities—"

"The authorities are in Sullivan's pocket." Julian stops to give my dad a harsh look. "And even if they weren't, we might as well send Sullivan an email saying who we are."

"Right." I jump to my feet, ignoring the pain in my sore muscles. Finally, my sluggish brain connects all the dots, and I realize why Julian brought my parents here. If the man Julian gutted last night is indeed the head mobster's son, then my husband isn't the only dangerous criminal out for vengeance. "Mom, Dad, we can't do that."

My mom looks startled. "But, Nora—"

"It will be best if the two of you come visit us for a bit," Julian says, walking over to stand next to me. "Just until we get this situation sorted out."

"What?" My mom gapes at us. "What do you mean? Why? Oh." She abruptly falls silent. "You did something to one of those men last night, didn't you?" she says slowly, looking at Julian. "You don't want them to know who we are because . . . because—"

"Because one of Sullivan's sons is dead, yes." Julian might as well be corroborating the weather report. "They'll be looking for us, and when they figure out who we are, they'll come after you and Tony."

My mom visibly blanches, and my dad rises to his feet. "You're saying the mob is after us?" His voice is filled with angry disbelief. "That they might attack us because . . . because you—"

"Killed one of Sullivan's sons for trying to hurt Nora, yes." Julian's voice is the coldest I've ever heard it. "We can worry about casting blame later. For now, since I don't want Nora grieving for her parents, I suggest you notify your employers of your upcoming vacation and start packing."

"When are we leaving?" my mom asks, her face pale as she stands up as well. "And how long will this vacation be?"

"Gabs, you're not seriously thinking—" my dad begins, but my mom places her hand on his arm.

"I am." My mom's voice is steady now, her gaze filled with resolve. "I don't want this any more than you do, but you've heard about the Sullivans. They're bad news, and if Julian says we're in danger—"

"You trust this murderer?" My dad turns to glare at her. "You think we'll be safer with *him*?"

"Than here with the mob seeking vengeance? Yes, I think we will be," my mom retorts. "We don't exactly have many options, do we?"

"We can go to the police or the FBI—"

"No, Tony, we can't, not if what Julian says is true."

"Well, obviously *he* would be against going to the police—"

As they argue, I feel my headache intensifying. Finally, I can't take it anymore. "Mom, Dad, please." I step forward, ignoring the pounding in my temples. "Just come with us for a while. It doesn't have to be forever. Right, Julian?" I glance at my husband for confirmation.

Julian nods coolly. "Like I said, just until I get this situation straightened out. Hopefully no more than a month or two."

"A month or two? How exactly will you straighten this out in just a month or two?" my mom asks while my dad stands there, vibrating with tense anger.

"Do you really want to know, Gabriela?" Julian asks softly, and my mom turns even paler.

"No, that's okay." She sounds slightly hoarse. Clearing her throat, she asks, "So what do we tell our work? How do we explain such a long vacation on short notice? I mean, it's really more of a leave of absence—"

"You can tell them the truth: that your daughter suffered a miscarriage and needs you for the next few weeks." Julian's harsh words make me flinch. Noticing my reaction, he reaches for me, his fingers curving around my palm as he says to my mom in a softer tone, "Or you can come up with some other story. It's really up to you."

"Okay, we'll do that," my mom says quietly, looking at us, and when I glance at my dad, I see that the anger has left his face. Instead, he seems to be holding back tears. Catching my gaze, he steps toward me.

"I'm sorry, honey," he says quietly, his deep voice filled with sorrow. "I didn't have a chance to say it yet, but I'm so, so sorry for your loss."

"Thank you, Dad," I whisper, and then I have to turn away so I don't start crying again.

Immediately, Julian's arms close around me, bringing me into his embrace. "Tony, Gabriela," I hear him say softly. His hand rubs soothing circles on my back as I stand there, fighting tears, my face pressed against his chest. "I think it's best if Nora rests for now. Why don't the two of you discuss this, and we can talk some more later today? Ideally, I want you and Nora to fly out tomorrow, before Sullivan figures out who we are."

"Of course," my mom says quietly. "Come, Tony, we have a lot to do." And before I can turn around, I hear their footsteps heading out of the room.

When they're gone, Julian loosens his hold and pulls back to gaze at me. "Nora, baby—"

"I'm okay," I interrupt, not wanting his pity. The guilt that I managed to push aside for the past hour is back, stronger than ever. "I'm going to go talk to Rosa now."

Julian studies me for a moment and then steps back, letting me go. "All right, my pet," he says softly. "Go ahead."

CHAPTER THIRTY

❖ JULIAN ❖

As I watch Nora exit the room, I'm cognizant of a thick, heavy pressure in my chest. She's trying to hide her pain, to be strong, but I can tell that what happened is ripping her apart. Her breakdown this morning was just the tip of the iceberg, and the knowledge that I'm to blame for this—that I'm to blame for everything—adds to the violent rage churning in my gut.

This is all my fault. If I hadn't been so fucking eager to please her, to make her happy by giving in to her every whim, none of this would've happened. I should've listened to my instincts and kept her on the estate, where nobody could've touched her. At the very least, I should've denied her request to go to that accursed club.

But I didn't. I let myself get soft. I let my obsession with her cloud my judgment, and now she's paying the price. If only I hadn't let her go alone to that restroom, if only I'd chosen a different club . . . The poisonous regrets swirl in my brain until I feel like my head will explode.

I need to find an outlet for my fury, and I need to do so now.

Turning, I head for the front door.

"I brought the cousin here," Lucas says as soon as I step out onto the driveway. "I figured you might not want to go all the way to Chicago today."

"Excellent." Lucas knows me too well. "Where is he?"

"In that van over there." He points at a black van parked strategically behind the trees farthest from the neighbors.

Filled with dark anticipation, I walk toward it, with Lucas accompanying me. "Has he given us any info yet?" I ask.

"He gave us access codes to his cousin's parking garage and building elevators," Lucas says. "It wasn't difficult to get him to talk. I figured I'd leave the rest of the interrogation to you, in case you wanted to speak to him in person."

"That's good thinking. I definitely do." Approaching the van, I open the back doors and peer into the dark interior.

A skinny young man is lying on the floor, gagged. His ankles are tied to his wrists behind his back, contorting him into an unnatural position, and his face is bloodied and swollen. A strong scent of piss, fear, and sweat wafts toward me. Lucas and my guards did a solid job of working him over.

Ignoring the stench, I climb into the van and turn around. "Are the walls soundproof?" I ask Lucas, who remains on the ground.

He nods. "About ninety percent."

"Good. That should suffice." I close the doors behind me, locking me in with the boy—who immediately begins to writhe on the floor, making frantic noises behind the gag.

Pulling out my knife, I crouch next to him. His struggles intensify, panicked noises growing in volume. Ignoring the terrified look in his eyes, I grab his neck to hold him still and wedge the knife between the gag and his cheek, slicing through the piece of cloth. A trickle of blood runs down his cheek where the knife cut him, and I watch it, relishing the sight. I want more of his blood. I want to see this van covered with it.

As if sensing my thoughts, the teenager begins to blubber. "Please don't do this, man," he begs, sobbing. "I didn't do nothing! I swear, I didn't do nothing—"

"Shut up." I stare at him, letting the anticipation build. "Do you know why you're here?"

He shakes his head. "No! No, I swear," he babbles. "I don't know nothing. I was in this club, and there was this girl, and I don't know what happened 'cause I just woke up in this warehouse, and I didn't do nothing—"

"You didn't touch the girl in the yellow dress?" I cock my head to the side, twirling the knife between my fingers. I know exactly how cats feel when they play with mice; this kind of thing is fun.

The young man's eyes widen. "What? No! Fuck, no! I swear, I didn't have nothing to do with that! I told Sean it was a bad idea—"

"So you knew they were going to do it?"

Instantly realizing what he's admitted to, the boy starts babbling again, tears and snot running down his battered face. "No! I mean, they don't ever tell me nothing until they do it, so I didn't know! I swear, I didn't know until we were there, and they said to watch the door, and I told them it's not fair, and they said I should just do it, and then this other girl came, and I told her to go away—"

"Shut up." I press the sharp edge of the knife against his mouth. He falls silent instantly, his eyes white with fear. "All right," I say softly, "now listen to me carefully. You're going to tell me where your cousin Sean eats, sleeps, shits, fucks, and whatever else he does. I want a list of every place he might ever visit. Got it?"

He gives a tiny nod, and I move the knife away. Immediately, the boy starts spewing out names of restaurants, clubs, underground fighting gyms, hotels, and bars. I use my phone to record all that, and when he's done, I smile at him. "Good job."

His cracked lips quiver in a weak attempt at an answering smile. "So now you're going to let me go, right? 'Cause I swear I didn't have nothing to do with that."

"Let you go?" I look down at the knife in my hand, as if considering his words. Then I look up and smile again. "Why? Because you betrayed your cousin?"

"But ... but I told you everything!" His eyes are showing white again. "I don't know nothing else!"

"Yes, I know." I press the knife against his stomach. "And that means you're useless to me now."

"I'm not!" he begins yelling. "You can ransom me! I'm Jimmy Sullivan, Patrick Sullivan's nephew, and he'll pay to have me back! He will, I swear—"

"Oh, I'm sure he will." I let the knife's tip dig in, enjoying the sight of blood welling up around the blade. Tearing my eyes away from it, I meet the young man's petrified gaze. "It's too bad for you that his money is the last thing I need."

And as he lets out a terrified scream, I slice him open, watching the blood spill out in a dark, beautiful river of red.

* * *

After I wipe my hands on the towel someone thoughtfully left in the van, I open the door and jump out. Lucas is waiting for me, so I tell him to dispose of the body and head back into the house.

It's strange, but I don't feel much better. The kill should've relieved some of the pressure, eased the burning need for violence, but instead, it seems to have only added to it, the emptiness inside me growing and darkening with every moment.

I want Nora. I need her more than ever. But when I enter the house, the first thing I do is head into the shower. I'm covered in blood and gore, and I don't want her to see me like this.

Like the savage murderer her parents accused me of being.

When I emerge, the first thing I do is check the tracking app for Nora's location. To my intense disappointment, she's still in Rosa's room. I contemplate going there to retrieve her, but I decide to give her a few more minutes and catch up on some work in the meantime.

When I open my laptop, I see that my inbox is filled with the usual messages. Russians, Ukrainians, the Islamic State, supplier contract changes, a security leak at one of the Indonesian factories . . . I scan it all with disinterest until I come upon an email from Frank, my CIA contact.

Opening it, I read it swiftly—and my insides grow cold.

CHAPTER THIRTY-ONE

❖ NORA ❖

"Hey there." Balancing a tray with tea and sandwiches in my hands, I push open the door to Rosa's bedroom and approach her bed.

She's lying on her side, facing away from the door, a blanket wrapped tightly around her. Setting the tray down on the nightstand, I sit down on the edge of her bed and gently touch her shoulder. "Rosa? Are you okay?"

She rolls over to face me, and I almost flinch at the bruising on her face.

"Pretty bad, huh?" she asks, noticing my reaction. Her voice sounds a little scratchy, but she looks remarkably calm, her eyes dry in her swollen face.

"Well, I wouldn't say it's good," I say carefully. "How are you feeling?"

"Possibly better than you," she says quietly, looking at me. "I'm so sorry about the baby, Nora. I can't even imagine what you and Julian must be going through."

I nod, trying to ignore the stab of agony in my chest. "Thank you." I force a smile to my lips. "Now, are you hungry? I brought you something to eat."

Wincing, she sits up and glances dubiously at the tray. "You made this?"

"Of course. You know I'm capable of boiling water and putting cheese on bread, right? I used to do it all the time before Julian kidnapped me and made me live in luxury."

A ghost of a smile flits across Rosa's battered lips. "Ah, yes. Those dark times in the past when you had to fend for yourself."

"Exactly." I reach for a steaming cup of tea and carefully hand it to Rosa. "Here you go. Chamomile with honey. Should cure all ills, according to Ana."

Rosa takes a small sip and raises an eyebrow at me. "Impressive. Almost as good as Ana's."

"Hey now." I give her an exaggerated frown. "Almost? And here I thought I had this tea-making thing down."

Her smile is a shade brighter this time. "You're very close, I promise. Now let me try one of those sandwiches. I have to say, they look appetizing."

I give her a plate and watch as she eats her sandwich. "You're not joining me?" she asks halfway, and I shake my head.

"No, I grabbed a little something in the kitchen earlier," I explain.

"I shouldn't be hungry either," Rosa says after she polishes off most of her sandwich. "Lucas brought me an omelet earlier this morning."

"He did?" I blink at her in surprise. "I didn't know he can cook."

"I didn't know either." She takes the last few bites and hands the plate back to me. "That was really good, Nora, thank you."

"Of course." I stand up, ignoring the painful stiffness in my back. "Can I get anything else for you? Maybe a book to read?"

"No, that's okay." Wincing again, she pushes the blanket off, revealing a long T-shirt, and swings her feet to the floor. "I'm going to get up. I can't stay in bed all day."

I frown at her. "Of course you can. You should rest today, take it easy."

"Like you're resting?" She gives me a sardonic look and walks over to the dresser on the other side of the room. "I'm done lounging in bed. I want to talk to Lucas and find out what's being done about the fuckers who attacked us."

I look at her. "Rosa . . ." I hesitate, uncertain whether to proceed.

"You want to know what happened last night with those guys, right?" She pulls on a pair of jeans and stops to look at me, her eyes glittering. "You want to know what they did to me before you got there."

"Only if you want to tell me," I say quickly. "If you don't feel comfortable—"

She holds up her hand, silencing me mid-sentence. Then she takes a deep breath and says, "They followed me to the bathroom." There's only a hint of brittleness in her voice. "When I came out, they were there, both of them, and the older one, Sean, said there's a VIP room in the back that they want to show me. You know, like they sometimes have in the movies?"

I nod, feeling a growing lump in my throat.

"Well, idiot that I am, I believed them." She turns away, reaching into the dresser. I watch in silence as she pulls off her T-shirt and puts on a bra, followed by a black, long-sleeved shirt. There are scratches and bruises on her smooth skin, some in the shape of finger marks, and I have to hide my reaction as she turns back to face me and says, "I told them earlier that this was my first visit to this country, so I thought they wanted to show me a good time."

"Oh, Rosa . . ." I step toward her, my chest aching, but she holds up her hand.

"Don't." She swallows. "Just let me finish."

I stop a couple of feet from her, and she continues after a moment. "As soon as we got past the bathrooms, out of sight of the people standing in line, the younger one, Brian, jumped me and dragged me into that room. There was this teenage guy too, and he watched the whole thing before Sean told him to go stand out in the hallway and make sure no one came in. I think they were going to"—she stops to compose herself for a second—"going to give him a turn after they were both done."

As she speaks, the rage I felt in the club returns. It had gotten subsumed beneath the weight of grief, pushed aside by the agony of my own loss, but now I'm aware of it again. Sharp and burning hot, the anger fills me until I'm all but shaking with it, my hands clenching and unclenching by my sides.

"I think you know the rest of the story," Rosa continues, her voice growing more brittle by the second. "You came in just as I was trying to fight off Sean. If it hadn't been for you . . ." Her face crumples, and this time I can't hang back.

Closing the distance between us, I embrace her, holding her as she begins to shake. Underneath my anger, I feel helpless, utterly inadequate to the task at hand. What happened to Rosa is every woman's worst nightmare, and I have no idea how to console her. To an outsider, what Julian did to me on the island might seem the same, but even during that traumatic first time, he had given me some semblance of tenderness. I'd felt violated, but also cherished, as incongruous as that combination might be.

I've never felt the way Rosa must be feeling now.

"I'm sorry," I whisper, stroking her hair. "I'm so sorry. Those bastards will pay. We'll make them pay."

She sniffles and pulls away, her eyes shimmering with tears. "Yes." Her voice is choked as she steps back. "I want them to, Nora. I want it more than anything."

"Me too," I whisper, staring at her. I want Rosa's attackers dead. I want them eliminated in the most brutal way possible. It's wrong, it's sick, but I don't care. Images of the man Julian killed last night float through my mind, bringing with them a peculiar sense of satisfaction. I want the other one—Sean—to pay the same way.

I want to unleash Julian on him and watch my husband work his savage magic.

A knock on the door startles us both.

"Come in," Rosa calls out, using her sleeve to wipe the tears from her face.

To my surprise, Julian enters the room, his expression tense and oddly worried. He's changed clothes since this morning, and his hair looks wet, as though he just took a shower.

"What's wrong?" I ask immediately, my heart rate spiking. "Did something happen?"

"No," Julian says, crossing the room. "Not yet. But we may need to expedite your departure." He stops in front of me. "I just learned that an artist's sketch of the three of us is being circulated in the local FBI's office. The brother who got away must have a good memory for faces. The Sullivans are looking for us, and if they're as well connected as we think, we don't have much time."

Fear wraps like barbed wire around my chest. "Do you think they already know about my parents?"

"I have no idea, but it's not entirely out of the question. Call them now, and tell them to pack what they can. We'll pick them up in an hour, and I'll bring all of you to the airport."

"Wait a minute." I stare at Julian. "All of *us*? What about you?"

"I need to deal with the Sullivan threat. Lucas and I will remain behind along with most of the guards."

"What?" I find it hard to breathe all of a sudden. "What do you mean, you'll remain behind?"

"I need to clean up this mess," Julian says impatiently. "Now, are we going to waste time talking about this, or are you calling your parents?"

I swallow the bitter objections rising in my throat. "I'm going to call them now," I say tightly, reaching for my phone.

Julian is right; now is not the time to argue about this. However, if he thinks I'm going to meekly go along with this, he's deeply mistaken.

I will do whatever it takes not to lose him again.

CHAPTER THIRTY-TWO

❖ JULIAN ❖

The drive to Nora's parents' house passes in tense silence. I'm busy coordinating the security logistics with my team, and Nora is furiously texting with her parents, who seem to be bombarding her with questions about the sudden change of plans. Rosa watches us both quietly, the black-and-blue swelling on her face hiding her expression.

As soon as we arrive, Nora hurries into the house, and I follow her in, not wanting to leave her alone for even a half hour. Rosa remains in the car with Lucas, explaining that she doesn't want to be in the way.

When I walk in, I see that Rosa was right to stay outside.

Inside, the Lestons' place is a madhouse. Gabriela is rushing around, trying to stuff as many items as possible into a huge suitcase, and her husband is speaking loudly on the phone, explaining to someone that yes, he has to leave the country now, and no, he's sorry he couldn't give more notice.

"They're going to fire me," he mutters darkly as he hangs up, and I resist the urge to say that no job is worth his life.

"If they fire you, I'll help you find another position, Tony," I say instead, sitting down at the kitchen table. Nora's father shoots me an angry glare in response, but I ignore him, focusing on the dozens of emails that managed to pile up in my inbox in the last few hours.

Forty minutes later, Nora finally gets the Lestons to stop packing.

"We have to go, Mom," she insists as her mother remembers yet another thing she forgot to take. "We have bug spray at the compound, I promise. And whatever else you need, we'll order and have it delivered for you. We don't live in a complete wilderness, you know."

Gabriela seems mollified by that, so I help her close the huge suitcase and haul it out to the car. The thing weighs at least two-hundred-and-fifty pounds, and I grunt with effort as I lift it into the trunk of the limo.

In the meantime, Nora's father brings out a second, smaller suitcase.

"I'll take it," I say, reaching for it, but he jerks it away.

"I've got it," he says sharply, so I step away to let him handle it on his own. If he wants to continue stewing, that's his business.

Once everything is loaded, Nora's parents climb into the car, and Rosa goes to sit in the front next to Lucas. "To give the four of you more room," she explains, as though the back of the limo can't easily accommodate ten people.

"Do all these cars need to be here?" Nora's mother asks as I take a seat next to Nora. "I mean, is it really that unsafe?"

"Probably not, but I don't want to risk it," I say as we pull out of the driveway. In addition to the twenty-three guards split between seven SUVs—all of which are currently idling on this quiet block—I also have a stash of weapons under our seat. It's overkill for a peaceful trip to Chicago, but now that there's trouble, I'm worried that it's not enough. I should've brought more men, more weapons, but I didn't want Frank and company thinking I was here to do a deal.

"This is insane," Tony mutters, looking out the back window at the procession of cars following us. "I can't even imagine what our neighbors are thinking."

"They're thinking you're a VIP, Dad," Nora says with forced cheerfulness. "Haven't you ever wondered what it must be like for the President, always traveling with the Secret Service?"

"No, I can't say I have." Nora's father turns back to face us, his expression softening as he looks at his daughter. "How are you feeling, honey?" he asks her. "You should probably be resting instead of dealing with this craziness."

"I'm fine, Dad." Nora's face tightens. "And I'd rather not talk about it, if you don't mind."

"Of course, honey," her mother says, blinking rapidly—I presume to stop herself from crying. "Whatever you wish, my love."

Nora attempts to give her mother a smile, but fails miserably. Unable to resist, I reach out and drape my arm over her shoulders, pulling her against me. "Relax, baby," I murmur into her hair as she nestles against my side. "We'll be there soon, and you can sleep on the plane, okay?"

Nora lets out a sigh and mumbles into my shoulder, "Sounds good." She seems tired, so I stroke her hair, enjoying its silky softness. I could sit like this forever, feeling the warmth of her small body, smelling her sweet, delicate scent. For the first time since the miscarriage, some of the heaviness in my chest lifts, the dark, bitter grief easing slightly. The violence still pulses in my veins, but the awful emptiness is filled for the moment, the painful void no longer expanding within.

I don't know how long we sit like this, but when I glance across the limo aisle, I see Nora's parents watching us strangely. Gabriela, especially, seems fascinated. I frown at them and position Nora more comfortably at my side. I don't like that they're witnessing this. I don't want them to know how much I depend on my pet, how desperately I need her.

At my glare, they both look away, and I resume stroking Nora's hair as we get off the interstate onto a two-lane highway.

"How much longer until we get there?" Nora's father asks a couple of minutes later. "We're going to a private airport, right?"

"Right," I confirm. "We're not too far now, I believe. There's no traffic, so we'll be there in about twenty minutes. One of my men has gone ahead to prepare the plane, so as soon as we get there, we'll be able to take off."

"And we can depart like this? Without going through customs?" Nora's mother asks. She still seems to be unusually interested in the way I'm embracing Nora. "Nobody will prevent us from re-entering the country or anything?"

"No," I say. "I have a special arrangement with—" Before I can finish explaining, the car picks up speed. The acceleration is so sharp and sudden that I barely manage to remain upright and hold on to Nora, who gasps and clutches at my waist. Her parents aren't so lucky; they fall onto their sides, nearly flying off the long limo seat.

The panel separating us from the driver rolls down, revealing Lucas's grim face in the rearview mirror.

"We have a tail," he says tersely. "They're onto us, and they're coming with everything they've got."

CHAPTER THIRTY-THREE

❖ NORA ❖

My heart stops beating for a second; then adrenaline explodes in my veins.

Before I have a chance to react, Julian is already in motion. Unbuckling my seatbelt, he grabs my arm and drags me off the seat onto the limo floor.

"Stay there," he barks, and I watch in shock as he lifts the seat, revealing an enormous stash of weapons.

"What—" my mom gasps, but at that moment, the limo swerves, knocking me against the side of the stuffed leather seat. My parents cry out, clutching desperately at each other, and Julian grabs the edge of the raised seat to prevent himself from falling.

And then I hear it.

The *rat-tat-tat* of automatic gunfire.

Somebody is shooting at us.

"Gabriela!" My dad's face is stark white. "Hold on to me!"

The limo swerves again, causing my mom to let out a frightened scream. Somehow Julian remains upright, bending over the stash as the limo accelerates even more. From my position on the floor, all I can see through the windows are the tree tops flashing by. We must be flying down this highway at breakneck speed.

Another burst of gunfire, and the trees flash by faster, the greenery blurring in my vision. I can hear the drumming of my pulse; it almost drowns out the squeal of tires in the distance.

"Oh my God!" At my mom's panicked screech, I grab onto a seat and rise up on my knees to look out the back window.

The sight that greets me is like something out of a *Fast and Furious* movie.

Behind our guards' seven SUVs, there's a whole cavalcade of cars. About a dozen are SUVs and vans, but there are also three Hummers with giant guns mounted on their roofs. Men with assault rifles are hanging out of the cars' windows, exchanging fire with our guards—who are doing the same. As I watch in shock, I see one of the pursuers' cars gain on the last of our SUVs and smash into its side in an apparent effort to force it off the road. Both cars waver off course, sparks flying where their sides scrape together, and I hear another burst of gunfire, followed by the pursuers' car careening off the road and flipping over.

One down, fifteen-plus to go.

The math is crystal-clear in my mind. *Fifteen cars versus eight, counting our limo.* The odds are not in our favor. My heart beats wildly as the high-speed battle continues, the cars smashing together amidst a hail of bullets.

Boom! The deafening sound vibrates through me, rattling every bone in my body. Stunned, I watch the guards' SUV in the back fly up, exploding in mid-air. Its gas tank must've been hit, I think dazedly, and then I hear Julian shouting my name.

My ears ringing, I turn and see him thrusting something bulky at me. "Put this on!" he roars before throwing two of the same items at my parents.

Bulletproof vests, I realize in disbelief.

He just handed us bulletproof vests.

The thing is heavy, but I manage to get it on, even with the limo swerving all over the place. I can hear my parents frantically instructing one another, and I turn to see Julian already wearing his own vest.

He's also holding an AK-47—which he thrusts into my hands before turning to lift a big, unusual-looking weapon out of the stash. I stare at it, puzzled, but then I recognize what it is.

A handheld grenade launcher. Julian had shown it to me once on the estate.

Shaking off my shock, I climb up on the seat, cradling the assault rifle with unsteady hands. I have to do my part, no matter how terrifying it may be. But before I can roll down the window and start shooting, Julian pulls me down to the floor again.

"Stay down," he roars at me. "Don't fucking move!"

I nod, trying to control my rapid breathing. The adrenaline sizzling through me both speeds everything up and slows it down, my perception foggy and sharp at the same time. I can hear my mom sobbing and Rosa and Lucas yelling something at the front, and then I see Julian's face change as he turns toward the front window.

"Fuck!" The expletive bursts out of his throat, terrifying me with its vehemence.

Unable to stay still, I rise up on my knees again . . . and my lungs cease working.

On the road ahead of us, just a few hundred feet away, is a police blockade—and we're barreling toward it at race-car speed.

CHAPTER THIRTY-FOUR

❖ JULIAN ❖

The cold, rational part of my mind instantly registers two things: there's nowhere for us to turn, and the four police cars blocking our way are surrounded by men wearing SWAT gear.

They were expecting us—which means they're in Sullivan's pocket and here to kill us all.

The thought fills me with terrified rage. I'm not afraid for myself, but the knowledge that Nora may die today, that I may never hold her again—

No. Fuck, no. Ruthlessly, I push the paralyzing thought aside and quickly assess the situation.

In less than twenty seconds, we'll reach the police barricade. I know what Lucas intends: to ram into the two cars that have the widest gap between them. The gap is only two feet wide, but we're going 120 miles an hour and the car is heavily armored, which means momentum is on our side.

All we need to do is survive the collision.

Gripping the grenade launcher in my right hand, I yell at Nora's parents, "Brace yourselves!" and drop to the floor, surrounding Nora with my body.

A few seconds later, our limo slams into the police cars with bone-jarring force. I can hear Nora's parents screaming, feel the inertia of the impact dragging me forward, and I tense every muscle in my body in an effort to stop the slide.

It works, barely. My left shoulder slams into the side of the seat, but I keep Nora safe underneath me. I have no doubt I'm crushing her with my weight, but it's better than the alternative. I can hear the metallic ding of bullets hitting the side and windows of the car, and I know they're firing at us.

If we were in a regular car, we'd already be riddled with holes.

As soon as I feel the limo speeding up again, I jump to my feet, noting out of the corner of my eye that Nora's parents seem to have survived the impact. Tony is cradling his arm with a pained grimace, but Gabriela seems merely dazed.

I don't have time to look closer, though. If we're to have any chance of surviving this, we need to take care of Sullivan's men, and we need to do it now.

The grenade launcher is still in my hand, so I press a button on the side of the door to activate the hidden opening in the roof. Then I stand up in the middle of the aisle, my head and shoulders sticking out of the car. Lifting the weapon, I point it at the cars pursuing us—which now include one police cruiser on top of the fifteen Sullivan vehicles.

No, *thirteen* Sullivan vehicles, I correct myself after doing a quick count. My men managed to take out two more of them in the last couple of minutes.

It's time to even out the odds some more.

Bullets whizz by my head, but I ignore them as I aim carefully. I only have six shots in this launcher, so I have to make each one count.

Boom! The first shot goes off with a hard kick. The recoil hits my shoulder, but the grenade finds its target—the police cruiser that's right on our tail. The car flies up, exploding in the air, and lands on its side, burning. One of the Hummers slams into it, and I watch in grim satisfaction as both cars blow up, causing one of Sullivan's vans to careen off the road.

Eleven enemy vehicles left.

I aim again. This time my target is more ambitious: one of the remaining Hummers farther back. It has a single-shot grenade launcher mounted on its roof; that's what took out one of our SUVs earlier, and I know they'll use the weapon again as soon as they reload.

Boom! Another hard recoil—and to my disgust, I miss. At the last second, the Hummer swerves sharply, ramming into one of our SUVs with brutal force. I watch in helpless rage as my men's car flips over, rolling off the road.

We're now down to five guard SUVs and our limo.

Pushing aside all traces of emotions, I aim the next shot at a closer van. *Boom!* This time, I'm spot-on. The vehicle flips, exploding in the process, and the two Sullivan SUVs directly behind it smash into it at full speed.

Eight enemy vehicles left.

I point the launcher again, doing my best to compensate for the constant zig-zagging of the limo. I know that Lucas is weaving all over the road in an effort to make us a more difficult target, but that also makes *them* more difficult targets for me.

Boom! I take the shot, and another Sullivan SUV explodes, taking out the one behind it in the process.

Six enemy vehicles left, and I have two more grenades to launch.

Taking a deep breath, I aim again—and at that moment, both Hummers spit fire. Two of our SUVs fly into the air, rolling off the side of the road.

Three guard SUVs left.

Suppressing my fury, I hold the weapon steady and aim at the Hummer that's gaining on us. One, two . . . *boom!* The grenade hits its target, and the massive car careens off the road, smoke rising from its hood.

One Hummer and four enemy SUVs left.

I have one last grenade.

Taking a deep breath, I aim, but before I can squeeze the trigger, one of the enemy cars swerves and crashes into another. My men must've shot the driver, improving our chances some more. The Sullivan forces are now down to one Hummer and two SUVs.

Relieved, I take aim again . . . and then I hear it.

The unmistakable roar of helicopter blades in the distance.

Looking up, I see a police chopper coming from the west.

Fuck.

It's either more dirty cops, or the US authorities caught wind of this skirmish.

Either way, it doesn't bode well for us.

CHAPTER THIRTY-FIVE

❖ NORA ❖

As the new sound reaches my ears, my adrenaline levels spike. I didn't know it was possible to feel like this—numb and acutely alive at the same time. My heart is racing a million miles a minute, and my skin is tingling with prickles of icy fear. However, the panic that gripped me earlier is gone; it disappeared at some point between the second and third explosion.

Apparently one can get used to anything, even cars blowing up.

Gripping the weapon Julian gave me, I hold on to the seat with my free hand, unable to look away from the battle taking place outside the car window. The road behind us is like something out of a war zone, with crashed and burning cars littering the empty stretch of narrow highway.

It's as if we're in a video game, except the casualties are real.

Boom! One press of a controller button, and a car goes flying. *Boom!* Another car. *Boom! Boom!* I catch myself mentally directing each grenade, as though I can guide Julian's aim with my thoughts.

A game. Just a realistic shooting game with stunning sound effects. If I frame it like that, I can cope. I can pretend there aren't dozens of burning corpses behind us, both on our side and on theirs. I can tell myself the man I love isn't standing in the middle of the limo holding a grenade launcher, his head and upper body exposed to the hail of gunfire outside.

Yes, a game—in which there's now a helicopter. I can hear it, and when I climb up on the seat and lean closer to the window, I can see it too.

It's a police chopper, heading directly for us.

It should be a relief that the authorities are trying to intercede—except the blockade we just went through didn't seem like an attempt to restore law and order. I saw the police cruiser pursuing us right alongside Sullivan's forces; they weren't trying to arrest all the criminals involved in this deadly chase.

They were trying to take us out.

A new wave of terror washes over me, puncturing my false calm. This is *not* a game. There are people dying all around us, and if it weren't for the armor on this limo and Lucas's driving skills, we'd already be dead too. If it were just me, it wouldn't matter as much. But everyone I love is in this car. If something happens to them—

No, stop. I feel myself starting to hyperventilate, and I force the thought away. I can't afford to panic now. Glancing toward the front, I see my parents huddling together on the seat, gripping their seatbelts. They're so pale, they look almost green. I think they're both in shock now, since my mom is no longer screaming.

The limo takes a sharp right turn, nearly throwing me off the seat.

"I'm going for the hangar!" Lucas yells from the front, and I realize we just turned off the highway onto an even narrower road. The small airport looms directly ahead, beckoning with the promise of salvation. The roar of the helicopter is directly above us now, but if we can get to our plane and take off—

Boom! My vision goes dark, all sounds fading for a second. Gasping, I clutch at the edge of the seat, desperately trying to hang on as the limo swerves and speeds up even more. As my senses return, I realize that the guards' SUV directly behind us was hit. There's now a gaping, smoking hole in its roof. I watch in horrified shock as it careens into another one of our cars, colliding with it with shattering force. Tires squeal, and then both cars are rolling off the road in a tangle of crushed metal.

The police chopper shot at us, I realize with a jolt of panic. It shot at us and took out two of our cars, leaving only one guard vehicle to protect us.

Turning, I cast a frantic glance at the front window again. The hangar where our plane is parked is close, so close. Just a few hundred yards, and we'll be there. Surely we can survive that long—

Boom! My ears ringing, I twist to see the Hummer behind us go up in flames. Julian must've hit it, I realize with relief. There's just the helicopter and two SUVs pursuing us now, and we still have guards in that last SUV. Another couple of shots like that, and we'll be safe—

"Nora!" Powerful arms wrap around my waist, dragging me down to the floor. A furious Julian is kneeling over me, his face like thunder. "I fucking told you to stay down!"

In a split second, I register two things: he's uninjured, and his hands are empty.

The grenade launcher must be out of ammunition.

Boom! A blast rocks the limo, sending us both flying. I'm vaguely aware that Julian twists around me, protecting me with his body, but I still feel the brutal impact as we slam into the partition. All air leaves my lungs, and the interior of the car spins around me, my vision blurring as something sharp bites at my skin. My head is pounding from the inside, as though my brain is struggling to get out.

"Nora!" Julian's voice reaches through the ringing whine in my ears. Dazed, I try to focus in on him. As some of the blurriness clears, I realize we're on the floor again, with him lying on top of me. His face is covered with blood; it's trickling down, dripping on me. He's also saying something, but his words don't register in my mind.

All I see is the vicious, deadly red of his blood.

"You're hurt." The terrified croak bears little resemblance to my voice. "Julian, you're hurt—"

He grips my jaw, hard, stunning me into silence. "Listen to me," he grits out. "In exactly a minute, I'm going to need you to run. Do you understand me? Run straight for the fucking plane and don't stop, no matter what."

I stare at him, uncomprehending. *Drip. Drip. Drip.* The red drops keep coming down. I can feel the wetness on my face, taste the metallic warmth on my lips. His eyes are bright blue amidst all that red, blue and incredibly beautiful . . .

"Nora!" he roars, shaking me. "Do you understand me?"

Some of the ringing in my skull abates, and the meaning of his words finally reaches me.

Run. He wants me to run.

"What about—" *you*, I want to say, but he cuts me off.

"You'll take your parents, and you will *all* fucking run." His voice is sharp enough to cut through steel, his gaze burning into me. "You'll have the gun with you, but I don't want you playing hero. Do you understand, Nora?"

I manage a small nod. "Yes." Through the pounding in my temples, I realize the car is still going, still driving despite whatever it was that hit us. I can hear the helicopter hovering over us, but we're alive for now. "Yes, I understand."

"Good." He holds my gaze for a couple of moments longer, and then, as if unable to resist, he lowers his head and takes my mouth in a hard, searing kiss. I taste the salt and metal of his blood, and the unique flavor that is Julian, and I want him to keep kissing me, to make me forget the nightmare we're in. All too soon, though, his lips move over to my neck, and I feel the warmth of his breath as he whispers in my ear, "Please get yourself and your parents to the plane, baby. Thomas is already there, and he can pilot the plane if need be. Lucas will take care of Rosa. This is our only chance to get out of this alive, so when I tell you to run, you run. I'll be right behind you, okay?"

And before I can say anything, he jumps up and pulls me to my knees, handing me the AK-47 that I'd dropped. My head spins from the sudden movement, but I shake off the dizziness, gripping the weapon with all my strength. Everything feels off, my body strangely uncooperative, but I'm able to focus enough to see that the rear window is gone and there's smoke rising from the back of the car. To my relief, my parents are still strapped into their seats, bleeding and dazed-looking but alive.

The back window must've shattered, sending fragments of glass flying into the car—which explains the blood on them and Julian.

The limo begins slowing down, and Julian grips my jaw again, bringing my attention back to him. "In ten seconds," he says harshly, "I'm going to open this door and come out. In that moment, you escape through the other door. Understand, Nora? You jump out and run like hell."

I nod, and when he releases me, I turn to my parents. "Take off your seatbelts," I say hoarsely. "We're going to make a run for the plane as soon as the car stops."

My mom doesn't react, her face blank with shock, but my dad begins fumbling with the seatbelt buckles. Out of the corner of my eye, I see the hangar coming up, and I frantically begin helping my parents, determined to free them before the car stops.

I succeed in unbuckling my mom's seatbelt, but my dad's seems stuck, and we both desperately tug at it, our hands in each other's way as the limo barrels through a tall, open gate into a warehouse-like building.

"Hurry!" Julian shouts as the limo screeches to a halt. I'm nearly thrown again, but I manage to hang on to the seatbelt strap.

"Now, Nora!" Julian yells, throwing open his door. "Go now!"

The seatbelt buckle finally pops loose, and I grab my dad's hand as he grabs my mom's. Pushing open the opposite door, we scramble out of the car, falling onto our hands and knees. My heart pounding, I swivel my head, looking for our plane, and then I see it.

It's standing near the exit on the opposite side of the hangar, with a dozen other planes between us and it.

"This way!" I jump to my feet, tugging at my dad. "Come on, we have to go!"

We start running. Behind us, there is another screech of brakes, followed by a furious burst of gunfire. Twisting my head, I see Julian and Lucas shooting at an SUV that just barreled into the building behind us. Rosa is running too; she's right on our heels. My heart hammering, I slow down, everything inside me screaming to turn back, to help Lucas and Julian, but then I recall his words.

Our best chance of survival lies in getting everyone to that plane. Even with my help, my parents are barely functioning as is.

So I suppress the urge to rush back toward the limo and instead yell, "Hurry!" to Rosa, who's nearly caught up with us. Then the four of us are running again, my dad towing my mom along. He's deathly pale and his eyes look wild, but he's putting one foot in front of another, and that's all I need him to do at the moment. If we get through this, I'll worry about the impact on my parents' psyche and agonize about my role in all this.

For now, our only task is survival.

Still, even knowing this, I can't stop myself from casting frantic glances behind us as we run. Fear for Julian is a giant knot in my stomach. I can't imagine losing him again. I don't think I'd survive it.

The first time I glance back, I see that Julian and Lucas took shelter behind the limo and are exchanging fire with men hiding behind the SUV. There are already two corpses on the ground, and a bloody hole in the SUV's windshield.

Even in my panic, I feel a flash of pride. My husband and his right-hand man know what they're doing when it comes to taking lives.

The second glance I steal reveals an even better situation. Four enemy corpses and Lucas making his way around the limo to get at the remaining shooter while Julian provides cover fire.

By the third glance, the final shooter is eliminated, and the gunfire stops, the hangar oddly silent after all the racket. I see Lucas and Julian on their feet, apparently uninjured, and tears of joy start rolling down my cheeks.

We did it. We survived.

We're already by the plane, and I see Thomas, the driver from my hair appointment, standing by the open door. "Please get them inside," I tell him in a shaking voice, and he nods, shepherding my parents and Rosa up the stairs. "I'll be with you in a second," I tell my dad when he tries to get me to join them. "I just need a moment." Liberating myself from his grip, I turn back toward the limo.

"Julian!" Raising the AK-47 above my head, I wave at him with the weapon. "Over here! Come, let's go!"

He looks at me, and I see a huge smile light up his face.

Half-laughing, half-crying, I begin to run toward him, cognizant of nothing but my joy—and then the wall next to the limo explodes, sending him and Lucas flying.

CHAPTER THIRTY-SIX

❖ JULIAN ❖

Pain. Darkness.

For a second, I'm back in that windowless room, with Majid's knife slicing through my face. My stomach heaves, vomit rising in my throat. Then my mind clears, and I become cognizant of a dull ringing in my ears.

That didn't happen in Tajikistan.

I didn't feel this hot there, either.

Too hot. So hot I'm burning.

Fuck! A spurt of adrenaline chases away all traces of mental fog. Moving with lightning speed, I roll several times, putting out the flames eating at my vest. Nausea grips at my insides, my head throbbing with agony, but when I stop, the fire is gone.

Panting furiously, I lie still and try to regain my senses. What the fuck just happened?

The ringing in my head eases slightly, and I pry open my eyelids to see burning pieces of rubble all around me.

An explosion. It must've been an explosion.

As soon as the realization comes to me, I hear it.

A burst of gunfire, followed by answering shots.

My heart stops beating. *Nora!*

The jolt of panic is so intense, it supersedes everything. No longer cognizant of pain, I surge to my feet, stumbling as my knees buckle for a second before stiffening to support my weight.

641

Whipping my head from side to side, I look for the source of gunshots, and then I see it.

A small figure darting behind a large plane after letting loose another volley of shots. Behind her is a group of four armed men, all dressed in SWAT gear.

In a split second, I take in the rest of the scene. The hangar wall near the limo is gone, blown into pieces, and through the opening, I see the police chopper sitting on the grass, its blades now still and silent.

My men in that last SUV must've lost the fight, leaving us exposed to Sullivan's remaining forces.

Before that thought is fully formed in my mind, I'm already on the move. The limo is burning next to me, but the fire is in the front, not the back, so I still have a few seconds. Leaping toward the car, I wrench open one of the doors and climb inside. The weapons are still in the stash, so I grab two machine guns and jump out, knowing the car could blow up at any moment. As I do so, I notice Lucas struggling to get to his feet a dozen yards away. He's alive; I register that with a distant sense of relief.

I don't have time to dwell on it more. A hundred yards away, Nora is weaving around the planes, exchanging shots with her pursuers. My tiny pet against four armed men—the thought fills me with sickening terror and rage.

Gripping both weapons, one in each hand, I begin running. The second I have a clear line of sight at Sullivan's men, I open fire.

Rat-tat-tat! One man's head explodes. *Rat-tat-tat!* Another man goes down.

Realizing what's happening, the two surviving men turn around and begin firing at me. Ignoring the bullets whizzing around me, I continue running and shooting, doing my best to zig-zag around the planes. Even with the vest protecting my chest, I'm far from immune to gunfire.

Rat-tat-tat! Something slices across my left shoulder, leaving a burning trail in its wake. Cursing, I grip the guns tighter and return fire, causing one of the men to jump behind a small service truck. The second one continues shooting at me, and as I run, I see Nora step out from behind one of the planes and take aim, her eyes dark and enormous in her pale face.

Pop! The shooter's head explodes with a bang. Her bullet hit its target. Twisting, she turns and fires at the one hiding behind the truck.

Using the distraction she's providing, I change my course, snaking around the truck where the remaining man is taking shelter. As I come up behind him, I see him aiming at Nora—and with a bellow of rage, I squeeze the trigger, peppering him with bullets.

He slides down the side of the truck, a bloody mass of lifeless meat.

There are no more shots, the resulting silence almost startling.

Panting, I lower my guns and step out from behind the truck.

CHAPTER THIRTY-SEVEN

❖ NORA ❖

As Julian emerges from behind the truck, bloodied but alive, I drop the AK-47, my fingers no longer able to hold on to the heavy weapon. The emotion filling my chest goes beyond happiness, beyond relief.

It's elation. Stunning, savage elation that we killed our enemies and survived.

When the wall exploded and armed men ran into the hangar, I thought that Julian had been killed. Gripped by blinding fury, I opened fire on them, and when they began shooting at me, I ran mindlessly, operating on pure instinct.

I knew I wouldn't last more than a couple of minutes, and I didn't care. All I wanted was to live long enough to kill as many as I could.

But now Julian is here, in front of me, as alive and vital as ever.

I don't know if I run toward him, or if he runs toward me, but somehow I end up in his embrace, held so tightly that I can barely breathe. He's raining hot, burning kisses all over my face and neck, his hands roaming over my body in search of injuries, and all the horror of the past hour disappears, pushed away by wild joy.

We survived, we're together, and nothing will ever tear us apart again.

* * *

"These two were near the chopper," Lucas says when we come out of the hangar in search of him. Like Julian, he's bloodied and unsteady on his feet, but no less deadly for that—as evidenced by the state of the two men lying on the grass. They're both groaning and crying, one clutching his bleeding arm and the other attempting to contain blood spurting out of his leg.

"Is that who I think it is?" Julian asks hoarsely, nodding toward the older man, and Lucas smiles savagely.

"Yes. Patrick Sullivan himself, along with his favorite—and last remaining—son Sean."

I gaze at the younger man, now recognizing his contorted features. It's Rosa's assailant, the one who got away.

"I'm guessing they came in the chopper to observe the action and swoop in at the right time," Lucas continues, grimacing as he holds his ribs. "Except the right time never came. They must've learned who you were and called in all the cops who owed them favors."

"The men we killed were cops?" I ask, beginning to shake as my adrenaline-fueled high starts to fade. "The ones in the Hummers and the SUVs, too?"

"Judging by their gear, many of them were," Julian replies, wrapping his right arm around my waist. I'm grateful for his support, as my legs are beginning to feel like cooked noodles. "Some were probably dirty, but others just blindly following orders from their higher-ups. I have no doubt they were told we were highly dangerous criminals. Maybe even terrorists."

"Oh." My head starts hurting at the thought, and I suddenly become aware of all my aches and bruises. The pain hits me like a tidal wave, followed by an exhaustion so intense that I lean against Julian, my vision going gray.

"Fuck." With that muttered expletive, my world tilts, turning horizontal, and I realize that Julian picked me up, lifting me against his chest. "I'm going to take her to the plane," I hear him saying, and I use all of my remaining strength to shake my head.

"No, I'm fine. Please let me down," I request, pushing at his shoulders, and to my surprise, Julian complies, carefully setting me on my feet. He keeps one arm around my back, but lets me stand on my own.

"What is it, baby?" he asks, looking down at me.

I gesture toward the two bleeding men. "What are you going to do with them? Are you going to kill them?"

"Yes," Julian says. His blue eyes gleam coldly. "I will."

I take a slow breath and release it. The girl Julian brought to the island would've objected, offered him some reason to spare them, but I'm not that girl anymore. These men's suffering doesn't touch me. I've felt more sympathy for a beetle turned onto its back than for these people, and I'm glad Julian is about to take care of the threat they present.

"I think Rosa should be here for this," Lucas says. "She'll want to see justice served."

Julian glances at me, and I nod in agreement. It may be wrong, but in this moment, it seems right for her to be here, to see the one who hurt her come to this end.

"Bring her here," Julian orders, and Lucas heads back into the hangar, leaving Julian and me alone with the Sullivans.

We watch our captives in grim silence, neither one of us feeling like speaking. The older man is already unconscious, having passed out from heavy bleeding, but Rosa's attacker is quite vocal in his pleas for mercy. Sobbing and writhing on the ground, he promises us money, political favors, introduction to all the US cartels . . . whatever we want if only we would let him go. He swears he won't touch any woman again, says it was a mistake—he didn't know, didn't realize who Rosa was . . . When neither Julian nor I react, his bargaining attempts turn into threats, and I tune him out, knowing nothing he says will change either of our minds. The anger within me is ice-cold, leaving no room for pity.

For what he's done to Rosa and for the child we lost, Sean Sullivan deserves nothing less than death.

A minute later, Lucas comes back, leading a shaky-looking Rosa out of the hangar. The second she lays eyes on the two men, however, her face regains color and her gaze hardens. Approaching her attacker, she stares down at him for a couple of seconds before raising her eyes to us.

"May I?" she asks, holding out her hand, and Lucas smiles coldly, handing her his rifle. Her hands steady, she aims at her assailant.

"Do it," Julian says, and I watch yet another man die as his face is blown apart. Before the echo from Rosa's shot fades, Julian steps toward unconscious Patrick Sullivan and releases a round of bullets into his chest.

"We're done here," he says, turning away from the corpse, and the four of us walk back to the plane.

* * *

On the way home, Thomas pilots the plane while Lucas rests in the main cabin with Julian, myself, and Rosa. Upon seeing all of us alive, my mom breaks down in hysterical sobs, so Julian leads my parents into the plane's bedroom, telling them to take a shower and relax there. I want to go see how they are, but the combination of exhaustion and post-adrenaline slump finally catches up to me.

As soon as we're in the air, I pass out in my seat, my hand held tightly in Julian's grip.

I don't remember landing or getting to the house. The next time I open my eyes, we're already in our bedroom at home, and Dr. Goldberg is cleaning and bandaging my scrapes. I vaguely recall Julian washing the blood off me on the plane, but the rest of the trip is a blur in my mind.

"Where are my parents?" I ask as the doctor uses tweezers to get a small piece of glass out of my arm. "How are they feeling? And what about Rosa and Lucas?"

"They're all sleeping," Julian says, watching the procedure. His face is gray with exhaustion, his voice as weary as I've ever heard it. "Don't worry. They're fine."

"I examined them upon arrival," Dr. Goldberg says, bandaging the sullenly bleeding wound on my arm. "Your father bruised his elbow pretty badly, but he didn't break anything. Your mother was in shock, but other than a few scratches from the broken glass and a bit of whiplash, she's fine, as is Ms. Martinez. Lucas Kent has a couple of cracked ribs and a few burns, but he'll recover."

"And Julian?" I ask, glancing at my husband. He's already clean and bandaged, so I know the doctor must've seen to him while I was sleeping.

"A mild concussion, same as you, along with first-degree burns on his back, a few stitches in the arm where a bullet grazed him, and some bruising. And, of course, these little wounds from the flying glass." Taking another piece of glass out of my arm, the doctor pauses, looking at us both as if trying to decide how to proceed. Finally, he says quietly, "I heard about the miscarriage. I'm so sorry."

I nod, fighting to contain a sudden swell of tears. The pity in Dr. Goldberg's gaze hurts more than any shard of glass, reminding me of what we lost. The agonizing grief I'd buried during our fight for survival is back, sharper and stronger than ever.

We might've survived, but we didn't emerge unscathed.

"Thank you," Julian says thickly, getting up and walking over to stand by the window. His movements are stiff and jerky, his posture radiating tension. Apparently realizing his blunder, the doctor finishes treating me in silence and departs with a murmured "good night," leaving us alone with our pain.

As soon as Dr. Goldberg is gone, Julian returns to the bed. I've never seen him this tired. He's all but swaying as he walks.

"Did you sleep at all on the plane?" I ask, watching as Julian pulls off the T-shirt and sweatpants he must've changed into when we got home. My chest aches at the sight of his injuries. "Some bruising" is a serious understatement. He's black and blue all over, with much of his muscular back and torso wrapped in white gauze.

"No, I wanted to keep an eye on you," he replies wearily, climbing onto the bed next to me. Lying down facing me, he drapes one arm over my side and draws me closer. "I guessed you might be concussed from that tumble you took in the car," he murmurs, his face mere inches from mine.

"Oh, I see." I can't look away from the intense blue of his gaze. "But you also have a concussion, from the explosion."

He nods. "Yes, I figured as much. Another reason for me to stay awake earlier."

I stare at him, my ribcage tightening around my lungs. I feel like I'm drowning in his eyes, getting sucked deeper into those hypnotic blue pools. Unbidden, recollections of the explosion slither into my mind, bringing with them the full horror of these recent events. Julian flying from the blast, Rosa's rape, the miscarriage, my parents' terrified faces as we speed down the highway amidst a hail of bullets . . . The horrible scenes jumble together in my brain, filling me with suffocating grief and guilt.

Because I dragged us to that club, in a span of two short days I lost my baby and nearly lost everyone else who matters to me.

The tears that come feel like blood squeezed out of my soul. Each drop burns through my tear ducts, the sounds bursting out of my throat hoarse and ugly. My new world isn't just dark; it's black, utterly without hope.

Squeezing my eyes shut, I attempt to curl into a ball, to make myself as small as possible to keep the pain from exploding outward, but Julian doesn't let me. Wrapping his arms around me, he holds me as I break apart, his big body warming me as he strokes my back and whispers into my hair that we survived, that everything will be all right and we'll soon go back to normal . . . The low, deep sound of his voice surrounds me, filling my ears until I can't help but listen, the words providing comfort despite my awareness of their falseness.

I don't know how long I cry like this, but eventually the worst of the pain ebbs, and I become cognizant of Julian's touch, of his enormous strength. His embrace, once my prison, is now my salvation, keeping me from drowning in despair.

As my tears ease, I become aware that I'm holding him just as tightly as he's gripping me, and that he also seems to derive comfort from my touch. He's consoling me, but I'm consoling him in return—and somehow that fact lessens my agony, lifting some of the dark fog pressing down on me.

He's held me while I cried before, but never like this. Directly or indirectly, he's always been the cause of my tears. We haven't been united in our pain before, have never gone through joint agony. The closest we've come to experiencing loss together was Beth's gruesome death, but even then, we didn't have a chance to mourn together. After the warehouse explosion, I mourned Beth and Julian on my own, and by the time he came back for me, there was more anger than grief within me.

This time, it's different. My loss is his loss. More *his* loss, in fact, since he wanted this child from the very beginning. The tiny life that was growing within me—the one he guarded so fiercely—is gone, and I can't even imagine how Julian must feel.

How much he must hate me for what I've done.

The thought shatters me again, but this time, I manage to hold the agony in. I don't know what's going to happen tomorrow, but for now, he's comforting me, and I'm selfish enough to accept it, to rely on his strength to get me through this.

Letting out a shuddering sigh, I burrow closer to my husband, listening to the strong, steady beating of his heart.

Even if Julian hates me now, I need him.

I need him too much to ever let him go.

CHAPTER THIRTY-EIGHT

❖ JULIAN ❖

As Nora's breathing slows and evens out, her body relaxes against mine. An occasional shudder still ripples through her, but even that stops as she sinks deeper into sleep.

I should sleep too. I haven't closed my eyes since the night before Nora's birthday—which means I've been awake for over forty-eight hours.

Forty-eight hours that count among the worst of my life.

We survived. Everything will be all right. We'll soon go back to normal. My reassurances to Nora ring hollow in my ears. I want to believe my own words, but the loss is too fresh, the agony too sharp.

A child. A baby that was part me and part Nora. It should've been nothing, just a bundle of cells with potential, but even at ten weeks, the tiny creature had made my chest overflow with emotion, twisting me around its minuscule, barely formed finger.

I would've done anything for it, and it hadn't even been born.

It died before it had a chance to live.

Dark, bitter fury chokes me again, this time directed solely at myself. There are so many things I could've—should've—done to prevent this outcome. I know it's pointless to dwell on it, but my exhausted brain refuses to let it go. The useless what-ifs keep spinning round and round, until I feel like a hamster in a wheel, running in place and getting nowhere. What if I'd kept Nora on the estate? What if I'd gotten to the bathroom faster? What if, what if... My mind

651

spins faster, the void looming underneath me once more, and I know if I didn't have Nora with me, I'd tumble into madness, the emptiness swallowing me whole.

Tightening my grip on her small, warm body, I stare into the darkness, desperately wishing for something unattainable, for an absolution I don't deserve and will never find.

Nora sighs in her sleep and rubs her cheek on my chest, her soft lips pressing against my skin. On a different night, the unconscious gesture would've turned me on, awakening the lust that always torments me in her presence. Tonight, however, the tender touch only intensifies the pressure building in my chest.

My child is dead.

The stark finality of it hits me, smashing through the shields numbing me since childhood. There's nothing I can do, nothing anyone can do. I could annihilate all of Chicago, and it wouldn't change a thing.

My child is dead.

The pain rushes up uncontrollably, like a river cresting over a dam. I try to fight it, to hold it back, but it just makes it worse. The memories come at me in a tidal wave, the faces of everyone I've lost swimming through my mind. *The baby, Maria, Beth, my mother, my father as he had been during those rare moments when I loved him . . .* The surge of grief is overwhelming, crowding out everything but awareness of this new loss.

My child is dead.

The anguish sears through me, excruciating but somehow purifying too.

My child is dead.

Shaking, I hold on to Nora as I stop fighting and let the pain in.

PART IV: THE AFTERMATH

CHAPTER THIRTY-NINE

❖ NORA ❖

Two weeks after our arrival home, Julian deems it safe for my parents to return to Oak Lawn.

"I'll have extra security around them for a few months," he explains as we walk toward the training area. "They'll need to put up with some restrictions when it comes to malls and other crowded places, but they should be able to return to work and resume most of their usual activities."

I nod, not particularly surprised to hear that. Julian has been keeping me informed of his efforts in this area, and I know the Sullivans are no longer a threat. Utilizing the same ruthless tactics he employed with Al-Quadar, my husband accomplished what the authorities have been unsuccessfully trying to do for decades: he rid Chicago of its most prominent crime family.

"What about Frank?" I ask as we pass two guards wrestling on the grass. "I thought the CIA didn't want any of us coming back to the country."

"They relented yesterday. It took some convincing, but your parents should be able to return without anyone standing in their way."

"Ah." I can only imagine what kind of "convincing" Julian had to do in light of the devastation we left behind. Even the cover-up crew dispatched by the CIA hadn't been able to keep the story of our high-speed battle under wraps. The area around the private airport might not have been densely populated, but the explosions and gunfire hadn't gone unnoticed. For the past couple of weeks, the clandestine Chicago operation to "apprehend the deadly arms dealer" has been all anyone's talked about on the news.

As Julian speculated in the car, the Sullivans had indeed called in some serious favors to organize that attack. The police chief— formerly a Sullivan mole and currently bloody goo swimming in lye— took the information the Sullivans dug up about us and used the "arms dealer smuggling explosives into the city" pretext to hurriedly assemble a team of SWAT operatives. The Sullivan men joining them were explained away as "reinforcements from another area," and the entire rushed operation was kept secret from the other law enforcement agencies—which is how they were able to catch us off-guard.

"Don't worry," Julian says, misreading my tense expression. "Besides Frank and a few other high-level officials, nobody knows your parents were involved in what happened. The extra security is just a precaution, nothing more."

"I know that." I look up at him. "You wouldn't let them return if it weren't safe."

"No," Julian says softly, stopping at the entrance to the fighting gym. "I wouldn't." His forehead gleams with sweat from the humid heat, his sleeveless shirt clinging to his well-defined muscles. There are still a few half-healed scars from the shards of glass on his face and neck, but they do little to detract from his potent appeal.

Standing less than two feet away and watching me with his piercing blue gaze, my husband is the very picture of vibrant, healthy masculinity.

Swallowing, I look away, my skin crawling with heat at the memory of how I woke up this morning. We might not have had intercourse since the miscarriage, but that doesn't mean Julian has been abstaining from sex with me. *On my knees with his cock in my mouth, tied down with his tongue on my clit* . . . The images in my mind make me burn even as the ever-present guilt presses down on me.

Why does Julian keep being so nice to me? Ever since our return, I've been waiting for him to punish me, to do something to express the anger he must feel, but so far, he's done nothing. If anything, he's been unusually tender with me, even more caring in some ways than during my pregnancy. It's subtle, this shift in his behavior—a few extra kisses and touches during the day, full-body massages every evening, asking Ana to make more of my favorite foods... It's nothing he hasn't done before; it's just that the frequency of these little gestures has gone up since we came back from America.

Since we lost our child.

My eyes prickle with sudden tears, and I duck my head to hide them as I slip past Julian into the gym. I don't want him to see me crying again. He's had plenty of that in the past couple of weeks. That's probably why he's holding off on punishing me: he thinks I'm not strong enough to take it, afraid I'll turn back into the panic-attack-stricken wreck I was after Tajikistan.

Except I won't. I know that now. Something about this time is different.

Something within *me* is different.

Walking over to the mats, I bend over and stretch, using the time to compose myself. When I turn back to face Julian, my face shows nothing of the grief that ambushes me at random moments.

"I'm ready," I say, positioning myself on the mat. "Let's do this."

And for the next hour, as Julian trains me how to take down a two-hundred-pound man in seven seconds, I succeed in pushing all thoughts of loss and guilt out of my mind.

* * *

After the training session, I return to the house to shower and then go down to the pool to tell my parents the news. My muscles are tired, but I'm humming with endorphins from the hard workout.

"So we can return?" My dad sits up in his lounge chair, distrust warring with relief on his face. "What about all those cops? And those gangsters' connections?"

"I'm sure it's fine, Tony," my mom says before I can answer. "Julian wouldn't send us back if it weren't all taken care of."

Dressed in a yellow one-piece swimsuit, she looks tan and rested, as though she's spent the past couple of weeks on a resort—which, in a way, is not that far from the truth. Julian has gone out of his way to ensure my parents' comfort and make them feel like they're truly on vacation. Books, movies, delicious food, even fruity drinks by the pool—it's all been provided for them, causing my dad to admit reluctantly that my life at an arms dealer's compound is not as horrible as he'd imagined.

"That's right, he wouldn't," I confirm, sitting down on a lounge chair next to my mom's. "Julian says you're free to leave whenever you want. He can have the plane ready for you tomorrow—though, obviously, we'd love it if you stayed longer."

As expected, my mom shakes her head in refusal. "Thank you, honey, but I think we should head home. Your dad's been anxious about his job, and my bosses have been asking daily when I'll be able to return . . ." Her voice trailing off, she gives me an apologetic smile.

"Of course." I smile back at her, ignoring the slight squeezing in my chest. I know what's behind their desire to leave, and it's not their jobs or their friends. Despite all the comforts here, my parents feel confined, hemmed in by the watch towers and the drones circling over the jungle. I can see it in the way they eye the armed guards, in the fear that crosses their faces when they pass by the training area and hear gunshots. To them, living here is like being in a luxurious jail, complete with dangerous criminals all over the place.

One of those criminals being their own daughter.

"We should go inside and pack," my dad says, rising to his feet. "I think it's best if we fly out first thing tomorrow morning."

"All right." I try not to let his words sting me. It's silly to feel rejected because my parents want to return home. They don't belong here, and I know it as well as they do. Their bodies might've healed from the bruises and scratches they sustained during the car chase, but their minds are a different matter.

It will take more than a few hours of therapy with Dr. Wessex for my suburban parents to get over seeing cars blow up and people die.

"Do you want me to help you pack?" I ask as my dad drapes a towel around my mom's shoulders. "Julian's talking to his accountant, and I don't have anything to do before dinner."

"It's okay, honey," my mom says gently. "We'll manage. Why don't you take a swim before dinner? The water's nice and cool."

And leaving me standing by the pool, they hurry into the air-conditioned comfort of the house.

* * *

"They're leaving tomorrow morning?" Rosa looks surprised when I inform her of my parents' upcoming departure. "Oh, that's too bad. I didn't even have a chance to show your mom that lake you were telling them about."

"That's okay," I say, picking up a laundry basket to help her load the washer. "Hopefully, they'll come visit us again."

"Yes, hopefully," Rosa echoes, then frowns as she sees what I'm doing. "Nora, put that down. You shouldn't—" She abruptly stops.

"Shouldn't lift heavy things?" I finish, giving her an ironic smile. "You and Ana keep forgetting that I'm no longer an invalid. I can lift weights again, and fight and shoot and eat whatever I want."

"Of course." Rosa looks contrite. "I'm sorry"—she reaches for my basket—"but you still shouldn't do my job."

Sighing, I relinquish it to her, knowing she'll only get upset if I insist on helping. She's been particularly touchy about that since our return, determined not to have anyone treat her any differently than before.

"I was raped; I didn't have my arms amputated," she snapped at Ana when the housekeeper tried to assign her lighter cleaning tasks. "Nothing will happen to me if I vacuum and use a mop."

Of course that made Ana burst into tears, and Rosa and I had to spend the next twenty minutes trying to calm her down. The older woman has been very emotional since our return, openly grieving my miscarriage and Rosa's assault.

"She's taking it worse than my own mother," Rosa told me last week, and I nodded, not surprised. Though I'd only met Mrs. Martinez a couple of times, the plump, stern woman had struck me as an older version of Beth, with the same tough shell and cynical outlook on life. How Rosa managed to remain so cheerful with a mother like that is something that will always be a mystery to me. Even now, after everything she's been through, my friend's smile is only a bit more brittle, the sparkle in her eyes just a shade less bright. With her bruises nearly healed, one would never know that Rosa survived something so traumatic—especially given her fierce insistence on being treated as normal.

Sighing again, I watch as she loads the washer with brisk efficiency, separating out the darker clothes and placing them into a neat pile on the floor. When she's done, she turns to face me. "So did you hear?"

she says. "Lucas located the interpreter girl. I think he'll go after her after he flies your parents home."

"He told you that?"

She nods. "I ran into him this morning and asked how that's going. So yeah, he told me."

"Oh, I see." I don't see, not in the least, but I decide against prying. Rosa's been increasingly closemouthed about her strange non-relationship with Lucas, and I don't want to press the issue. I figure she'll tell me when she's ready—if there's anything to tell, that is.

She turns back to start the washer, and I debate whether I should share with her what I learned yesterday . . . what I still haven't shared with Julian. Finally, I decide to go for it, since she already knows part of the story.

"Do you remember the pretty young doctor who treated me at the hospital?" I ask, leaning against the dryer.

Rosa turns back toward me, looking puzzled at the change of topic. "Yes, I think so. Why?"

"Her last name is Cobakis. I remember reading it on her name tag and thinking that it seemed familiar, like I'd come across it before."

Now Rosa looks intrigued. "And did you? Come across it, that is?"

I nod. "Yes. I just couldn't remember where—and then yesterday, it came to me. There was a man by the name of George Cobakis on the list I gave to Peter."

Rosa's eyes widen. "The list of people responsible for what happened to his family?"

"Yes." I take a deep breath. "I wasn't sure, so I checked my email last night, and sure enough, there it was. George Cobakis from Homer Glen, Illinois. I noticed that name originally because of the location."

"Oh, wow." Rosa stares at me, mouth open. "You think that nice doctor is somehow connected to this George?"

"I know she is. I looked up George Cobakis last night, and she came up in search results. She's his wife. A local newspaper wrote about a fundraiser for veterans and their families, and they had their picture in there as a couple who's done a lot for that organization. He's apparently a journalist, a foreign correspondent. I can't imagine how his name ended up on that list."

"Shit." Rosa looks both horrified and fascinated. "So what are you going to do?"

"What can I do?" The question has been tormenting me ever since I learned of the connection. Before, the names on that list were just that: names. But now one of those names has a face attached to it. A photo of a smiling dark-haired man standing next to his smart, pretty wife.

A wife whom I'd met.

A woman who'll be a widow if Julian's former security consultant gets his revenge.

"Have you spoken to your husband about this?" Rosa asks. "Does he know?"

"No, not yet." Nor am I sure that I want Julian to know. A few weeks ago, I told Rosa about the list I sent to Peter, but I didn't tell her that I did it against Julian's wishes. That part—and what happened after we learned of my pregnancy—is too private to share. "I'm guessing Julian will say there's nothing to be done now that the list is in Peter's hands," I say, trying to imagine my husband's reaction.

"And he'll probably be right." Rosa gives me a steady look. "It's unfortunate that we met the woman and all, but if her husband was somehow involved in what happened to Peter's family, I don't see how we can interfere."

"Right." I take another deep breath, trying to let go of the anxiety I've been feeling since yesterday. "We can't. We shouldn't."

Even though I gave Peter that list.

Even though whatever's going to happen will be my fault once again.

"This is not your problem, Nora," Rosa says, intuiting my concern. "Peter would've learned about those names one way or another. He was too determined for it not to happen. You're not responsible for what he's going to do to those people—Peter is."

"Of course," I murmur, attempting a smile. "Of course, I know that."

And as Rosa resumes sorting through the laundry, I change the topic to our newest guard recruits.

CHAPTER FORTY

❖ JULIAN ❖

After wrapping up the conversation with my accountant, I get up and stretch, feeling the loosening of tension in my muscles. Immediately, my thoughts turn to Nora, and I pull up her location on my phone. I do that at least five times a day now, the habit as deeply ingrained as brushing my teeth in the morning.

She's in the house, which is exactly where I expected her to be. Satisfied, I put the phone away and close my laptop, determined to be done for the evening. Between all the paperwork for a new shell corporation and the interviews I've been conducting with potential guard replacements, I've been working upward of twelve hours a day. Once, that wouldn't have mattered—business was all I had to live for—but now work is an unwelcome distraction.

It prevents me from spending time with my beautiful, strangely distant wife.

I'm not sure when I first noticed it, the way Nora's eyes constantly slide away from mine. The way she withholds something of herself even during sex. At first, I ascribed her withdrawn manner to grief and the aftermath of trauma, but as the days wore on, I realized there's something more.

It's subtle, barely discernible, this distance between us, but it's there. She talks and acts as if things are normal, but I can tell they're not. Whatever secret she's keeping from me, it's weighing on her, causing her to erect barriers between us. I could sense them during our training today, and it solidified my determination to get to the bottom of the matter.

According to the doctors, she's finally fully healed from the miscarriage—and one way or another, tonight she's going to tell me everything.

* * *

At dinner, I watch Nora as she interacts with her parents, hungrily taking in every minute movement of her hands, every flicker of her long eyelashes. I would've thought it impossible, but my obsession with her has reached a new peak since our return. It's as if all the grief, rage, and pain inside me coalesced into one heart-ripping sensation, a feeling so intense it tears me from within.

A longing that's entirely focused on her.

As we finish the main course, I realize I've hardly said a word, spending most of the meal absorbed in the sight of her and the sound of her voice. It's probably just as well, given that it's Nora's parents' last evening here. Although her father is no longer openly hostile toward me, I know both Lestons still wish they could free their daughter from my clutches. I would never let them take her from me, of course, but I don't have a problem with the three of them spending some time on their own.

To that end, as soon as Ana brings out the dessert, I excuse myself by saying I'm full and go to the library, letting them finish the meal without me.

When I get there, I take a seat on a chaise by the window and spend a few minutes answering emails on my phone. Then the puzzle of Nora's uncharacteristic distance creeps into my mind again. The way she's been these past couple of weeks reminds me of when I first forced the trackers on her. It's as if she's upset with me—except this time, I have no idea why.

Glancing at the clock on the wall, I realize that it's already been a half hour since I left the table. Hopefully, Nora's already gone upstairs. When I check her location, however, I see she's still in the dining room.

Mildly annoyed, I contemplate getting a book to read while I wait, but then I get a better idea.

Pulling up a different app on my phone, I activate the hidden audio feed from the dining room, put on my Bluetooth headset, and lean back in the chaise to listen.

A second later, Gabriela's frustrated voice fills my ears.

"—people died," she argues. "How can that not bother you? There were police officers among those criminals, good men who were just following orders—"

"And they would've killed us by following those orders." Nora's tone is unusually sharp, causing me to sit up and listen more intently. "Is it better to die by the bullet of a good man than to defend yourself and live? I'm sorry that I'm not showing the remorse you expect, Mom, but I'm *not* sorry that all of us are alive and well. It's not Julian's fault that any of that happened. If anything—"

"He's the one who killed that gangster's son," Tony interrupts. "If he'd done the civilized thing, called nine-one-one instead of resorting to murder—"

"If he'd done the civilized thing, I would've been raped and Rosa would've suffered even more before the police got there." There is a hard, brittle note in Nora's voice. "You weren't there, Dad. You don't understand."

"Your dad understands perfectly well, honey." Gabriela's voice is calmer now, edged with weariness. "And yes, maybe your husband couldn't stand by and wait for the cops to arrive, but you know as well as I do that he could've abstained from killing that man."

Abstained from killing the man who hurt and nearly raped Nora? My blood boils with sudden fury. The fucking bastard's lucky I didn't castrate him and stuff his balls into his bowels. The only reason he died so easily was because Nora was there, and my worry for her was greater than my rage.

"Maybe he could've." Nora's tone matches her mother's. "But there's every reason to believe the Sullivans would've walked free, given their connections. Is that what you want, Mom, for men like that to continue doing this to other women?"

"No, of course not," Tony says. "But that doesn't give Julian the right to set himself up as judge, jury, and executioner. When he killed that man, he didn't know who he was, so you can't use that excuse. Your husband killed because he wanted to and for no other reason."

For a few tense seconds, there's silence in my headset. The fury inside me grows, the anger coiling and tightening as I wait to hear what Nora has to say. I don't give a fuck what Nora's parents think about me, but I very much care that they're trying to turn their daughter against me.

Finally, Nora speaks. "Yes, Dad, you're right, he did." Her voice is calm and steady. "He killed that man for hurting me without giving it a second thought. Do you want me to condemn him for that? Well, I can't. I won't. Because if I could've, I would've done the same thing."

Another prolonged silence. Then: "Honey, when you left the plane and there were all those gunshots, was that you?" Gabriela asks quietly. "Did you shoot anyone?" A short pause, then an even softer, "Did you kill anyone?"

"Yes." Nora's tone doesn't change. I can picture her sitting there, facing her parents without flinching. "Yes, Mom, I did."

A sharply indrawn breath, then another few beats of silence.

"I told you, Gabs." It's Tony who speaks now, his voice weighed down by sadness. "I told you she must've. Our daughter's changed—he's changed her."

There's a scraping noise, like that of a chair moving across the floor, and then a shaky, "Oh, honey." It's followed by a choked sob and Nora's voice murmuring, "Don't cry, Mom. Please, don't cry. I'm sorry I've disappointed you. I'm so sorry . . ."

I can't bear to listen anymore. Jumping off the chaise, I stride out of the library, determined to collect Nora and bring her upstairs. This guilt-tripping is the last thing she needs, and if I have to protect her from her own parents, so be it.

As I walk, I hear them speak again, and I slow down in the hallway, listening despite myself.

"You didn't disappoint us, honey," Nora's father says thickly. "It's not that, not at all. It's just that we see now that you're no longer the same girl . . . that even if you came back to us, it wouldn't be the same."

"No, Dad," Nora replies quietly. "It wouldn't be."

A couple more seconds pass, and then her mother speaks again. "We love you, honey," she says in a low, strained voice. "Please, don't ever doubt that we love you."

"I know, Mom. And I love you, both of you." Nora's voice cracks for the first time. "I'm sorry that things have worked out this way, but I belong here now."

"With *him*." Curiously, Gabriela doesn't sound bitter, just resigned. "Yes, we see that now. He loves you. I never would've thought I'd say that, but he does. The way the two of you are together, the way he looks at you . . ." She lets out a shaky laugh. "Oh, honey, we'd give an arm and a leg for it to be someone else for you. A good man, a kind man, someone who'd hold down a normal job and buy you a house near us—"

"Julian did buy me a house near you," Nora says, and her mother laughs again, sounding a little hysterical.

"That's true," she says when she calms down. "He did, didn't he?"

Now the two women laugh together, and I let out a relieved breath. Maybe Nora doesn't need my interference after all.

Another sound of a chair scraping across the floor, and then Tony says gruffly, "We're here for you, honey. No matter what, we're always here for you. If anything ever changes, if you ever want to leave him and come home—"

"I won't, Dad." The quiet confidence in Nora's voice warms me, chasing away the remnants of my anger. I'm so pleased that I nearly miss it when she adds softly, "Not unless he wants me to."

"Oh, he won't," Nora's father says, and he does sound bitter. "That much is obvious. If that man had his way, you'd never be more than ten feet away from him."

I only half-listen to his words, mulling over Nora's strange statement instead. *Not unless he wants me to.* She sounded almost as if she's afraid that's the case. Or is it that she *wants* it to be the case? An ugly suspicion snakes through me. Is that why she's been so distant in recent days—because she wants me to let her go? Because she no longer wants to be with me and hopes that I'll let her leave as a way to atone for what happened?

My chest tightens with sudden pain even as a new kind of anger kindles within me. Is that what my pet expects? Some sort of grand gesture where I give her freedom? Where I beg her for forgiveness and feign regret for having taken her in the first place?

Fuck that.

I tear the headset out of my ear, dark fury rolling through me as I turn and take the stairs two steps at a time.

If Nora thinks I'm that far gone, she couldn't be more mistaken.

She's mine, and she'll stay that way for the rest of our lives.

CHAPTER FORTY-ONE

❖ NORA ❖

Tired yet hyper after talking to my parents, I walk up the stairs toward our bedroom. Though a part of me still wishes I could've shielded my family from my new life, I'm relieved that they now know the truth.

That they know the woman I've become and still love me.

Reaching the bedroom, I open the door and step inside. No lights are on in the room, and as I close the door behind me, I wonder where Julian might be. While I'm glad I got the chance to clear the air with my parents, the fact that he left dinner without a good explanation worries me. Did something happen, or did he simply get tired of us?

Did he get tired of *me*?

Just as the devastating thought crosses my mind, I notice a dark shadow standing by the window.

My pulse jumps, my skin prickling with primitive terror as I fumble for the light switch.

"Leave it." Julian's voice comes out of the darkness, and my knees almost buckle with relief.

"Oh, thank God. For a second, I didn't realize it was—" I begin, and then his harsh tone registers. "You," I finish uncertainly.

"Who else would it be?" My husband turns and crosses the room, approaching me with the silent gait of a predator. "It's our bedroom. Or have you forgotten that?" He places his hands on both sides of the wall behind me, caging me in.

I draw in a startled breath, pressing my palms against the cold wall. Julian is clearly in a mood, and I have no idea what set him off. "No, of course not," I say slowly, staring at his shadowed features. There's so little light that all I can make out is the faint glitter of his eyes. "What do you—"

He steps closer, molding his lower body to mine, and I gasp as I feel his hard cock against my belly. He's naked and already aroused, his hot male scent surrounding me as he holds me trapped in place. Even through the separating layer of my dress, I can feel the lust pulsing within him—lust and something much, much darker.

My body awakens with a jolt, my pulse quickening on a surge of fear. This must be it: the punishment I've been expecting. With the doctors having deemed me healed earlier today, my reprieve is over.

"Julian?" His name comes out on a choked breath as he grips the nape of my neck, his long fingers nearly encircling my throat. His huge body is all muscle, hard and uncompromising around me. One squeeze of those steely fingers, and he'd crush my throat. The thought chills me, yet a hollow ache coils in my core, my nipples peaking with harsh arousal. The anger coming off him is palpable, and it calls to something savage inside me, fueling the dark fire simmering within.

If he's decided to finally punish me, I'm going to make damn sure I get what I deserve.

He leans into me, his breath warm on my face, and at that moment, I make my move. My right hand forms a fist at my side, and I swing upward with all my strength, striking the underside of his chin. At the same time, I twist to the right, breaking his grip on my neck, and duck under his extended arm, whirling around to hit him in the back.

Except he's no longer there.

In the half-second it took me to turn, Julian moved, as quick and deadly as any assassin. Instead of connecting with his back, the sharp edge of my palm slams into his elbow, and I cry out as the impact sends a shock of pain through my arm.

"Fuck!" His furious hiss is accompanied by a blurringly fast movement. Before I can react, he's got me encircled in his arms, my wrists crossed in front of my chest and his left leg wrapped around my knees to prevent me from kicking. With him holding me from behind, I can't bite him, and my attempts to head-butt his chin fall woefully short as he keeps his face out of my reach.

All that training, and he subdued me in three seconds flat.

Frustration mingles with adrenaline, adding to the fury brewing inside me. Fury at him for taunting me with tenderness these two weeks, and most of all, fury at myself.

My fault, my fault, it's all my fault. The words are a vicious drumbeat in my mind. Guilt, bitter and thick, rises in my throat, choking me as it mixes with the aching grief.

Rosa. Our baby. Dozens of men dead.

The sound that bursts out of my throat is something between a growl and a sob. Despite the futility of it, I begin to fight, bucking and twisting in Julian's iron hold. I don't have much leverage, but with one of his legs restraining mine, my frantic, jerky movements are enough to push him off-balance.

With a loud curse, he falls backward, still gripping me tightly. His back takes the brunt of the fall. I hardly feel the impact as he grunts and immediately rolls over, pinning me to the hard wooden floor. Disregarding his heavy weight on top of me, I continue fighting, struggling with all my strength. The cold wood presses into my face, but the discomfort barely registers.

My fault, my fault, all my fault.

Half-panting, half-sobbing, I try to kick back, to scratch him, to make him feel even a tiny fraction of the pain consuming me inside. My muscles scream with strain, but I don't stop—not when Julian wrenches my wrists back and ties them at the small of my back with his belt, and not even when he drags me up by my elbow and hauls me to the bed.

I fight as he tears off my dress and underwear, as he fists his hand in my hair and forces me up on my knees. I fight as though I'm fighting for my life, as though the man holding me is my worst enemy instead of my greatest love. I fight because he's strong enough to take the fury inside me.

Because he's strong enough to take it away from me.

As I writhe in his brutal hold, his knee forces apart my legs, and his cock presses against my entrance. In one savage thrust, he penetrates me from behind, and I cry out at the pain, at the unutterable relief of his possession. I'm wet, but not enough, not nearly enough, and each punishing thrust scrapes me raw, hurting me, healing me. My thoughts scatter, the chant inside my mind disappearing, and all that's left is the feel of his body inside mine, the pain and the agonizing pleasure of our need.

I'm rushing toward orgasm when Julian begins talking to me, growling that he'll always keep me, that I'll never belong to anyone but him. There is a dark threat implicit in his words, a promise that he'll stop at nothing. His ruthlessness should terrify me, yet as my body explodes in release, fear is the last thing on my mind.

All I'm cognizant of is sheer and utter bliss.

He flips me onto my back then, releasing my wrists, and I realize that at some point, I did stop fighting. The fury's gone, and in its place is deep exhaustion and relief.

Relief that Julian still wants me. That he'll punish me, but won't send me away.

So when he grips my ankles and props them on his shoulders, I don't resist. I don't fight when he leans forward, nearly folding me in half, and I don't struggle when he scoops the abundant moisture from my sex and smears it between my ass cheeks. It's only when I feel his thickness poised at that other opening that I utter a wordless sound of protest, my sphincter tightening as my hands move to push against his hard chest. It's a weak, mostly symbolic gesture—I can't possibly move Julian off me that way—but even that slight hint of resistance seems to enrage him.

"Oh, no, you don't," he growls, and in the faint light from the window, I see the dark glitter of his eyes. "You don't get to deny me this, to deny me anything. I own you... every inch of you." He presses forward, his massive cock forcing me open as he whispers harshly, "If you don't relax that ass, my pet, you'll regret it."

I shudder with perverse arousal, my nails digging into his chest as the tight ring of muscle gives in to the merciless pressure. The burning invasion is agonizing, my insides roiling as he pushes in deeper and deeper. It's been months since he's taken me like this, and my body's forgotten how to handle this, how to relax into the overly full sensation. Squeezing my eyelids shut, I attempt to breathe through it, to remain strong, but tears, stupid, betraying tears, come anyway, trickling out from the corners of my eyes.

It's not the pain that makes me cry, though, or my body's twisted response to it.

It's the knowledge that my punishment isn't over, that Julian still hasn't forgiven me.

That he may never forgive me.

"Do you hate me?" The question escapes before I can hold it back. I don't want to know, but at the same time, I can't bear to keep silent. Opening my eyes, I stare at the dark figure above me. "Julian, do you hate me?"

He stills, his cock lodged deep within me. "Hate you?" His big body tenses, his lust-roughened voice filling with disbelief. "What the fuck, Nora? Why would I hate you?"

"Because I miscarried." My voice quavers. "Because our child died because of me."

For a second, he doesn't respond, and then, with a low curse, he pulls out, making me gasp in pain.

"Fuck!" He releases me, moving back on the bed. The sudden absence of his heat and his heavy weight over me is startling, as is the light from the bedside lamp he turns on. It takes a moment before my eyes adjust to the brightness and I make out the expression on his face.

"You think I blame you for what happened?" he asks hoarsely, sitting back on his haunches. His eyes burn with intensity as he stares at me, his cock still fully erect. "You think it was somehow your fault?"

"Of course it was." I sit up, feeling the stinging soreness deep inside, where he was just buried. "I'm the one who wanted to go to Chicago, to go to that club. If not for me, none of this would've—"

"Stop." His harsh command vibrates through me even as his features contort with something resembling pain. "Just stop, baby, please."

I fall silent, staring at him in confusion. Wasn't that what this whole scene was about? My punishment for disappointing him? For endangering myself and our child?

Still holding my gaze, he takes a deep breath and moves toward me. "Nora, my pet . . ." He takes my face in his large palms. "How could you possibly think that I hate you?"

I swallow. "I'm hoping you don't, but I know you're angry—"

"You think I'm angry because you wanted to see your parents? To go out dancing and have fun?" His nostrils flare. "Fuck, Nora, if the miscarriage is anyone's fault, it's mine. I shouldn't have let you go to that bathroom on your own—"

"But you couldn't have known—"

"And neither could you." He takes a deep breath and lowers his hands to my lap, clasping my palms in his warm grasp. "It wasn't your fault," he says roughly. "None of it was your fault."

I dampen my dry lips. "So then why—"

"Why was I angry?" His beautiful mouth twists. "Because I thought you wanted to leave me. Because I misinterpreted something you said to your parents tonight."

"What?" My eyebrows pull together in a frown. "What did I— Oh." I recall my offhand comment, born of fear and insecurity. "No, Julian, that's not what I meant," I begin, but he squeezes my hands before I can explain further.

"I know," he says softly. "Believe me, baby, now I know."

We stare at each other in silence, the air thick with echoes of violent sex and dark emotions, with the aftermath of lust and pain and loss. It's strange, but in this moment, I understand him better than ever. I see the man behind the monster, the man who needs me so much he'll do anything to keep me with him.

The man I need so much I'll do anything to stay with him.

"Do you love me, Julian?" I don't know what gives me the courage to pose the question now, but I have to know, once and for all. "Do you love me?" I repeat, holding his gaze.

For a few moments, he doesn't move, doesn't say anything. His grip on my hands is tight enough to hurt. I can feel the struggle within him, the longing warring with the fear. I wait, holding my breath, knowing he may never open himself up like this, may never admit the truth even to himself. So when he speaks, I'm almost caught off-guard.

"Yes, Nora," he says hoarsely. "Yes, I love you. I love you so fucking much it hurts. I didn't know it, or maybe I just didn't want to know it, but it's always been there. I spent most of my life trying not to feel, trying not to let people get close to me, but I fell for you from the very beginning. It just took me two years to realize it."

"What made you realize it?" I whisper, my heart aching with relieved joy. *He loves me.* Up until this moment, I didn't know how desperately I needed the words, how much their lack weighed on me. "When did you know?"

"It was the night we came back home." His muscular throat moves as he swallows. "It was when I lay here next to you. I let myself truly feel it then—the pain of losing our baby, the pain of losing all those other people in my life—and I realized I'd been trying to protect myself from the agony of losing *you*. Trying to keep myself from loving you so it wouldn't destroy me. Except it was too late. I was already in love with you. I had been for a long time. Obsession, addiction, love—it's all the same thing. I can't live without you, Nora. Losing you *would* destroy me. I can survive anything but that."

"Oh, Julian . . ." I can't imagine what it took for this strong, ruthless man to admit this. "You won't lose me. I'm here. I'm not going anywhere."

"I know you're not." His eyes narrow, all traces of vulnerability fading from his features. "Just because I love you doesn't mean I'll ever let you go."

A shaky laugh escapes my throat. "Of course. I know that."

"Ever." He seems to feel the need to emphasize that.

"I know that too."

He stares at me then, his hands holding mine, and I feel the pull of his wordless command. He wants me to admit my feelings too, to bare my soul to him as he's just bared his to me. And so I give him what he demands.

"I love you, Julian," I say, letting him see the truth of that in my gaze. "I'll always love you—and I don't want you to ever let me go."

I don't know if he moves toward me then, or if I make the move first, but somehow his mouth is on mine, his lips and tongue devouring me as he holds me in his inescapable embrace. We come together in pain and pleasure, in violence and passion.

We come together in our kind of love.

* * *

The next morning, I stand next to the runway and watch as the plane carrying my parents home takes off. When it's nothing more than a small dot in the sky, I turn to Julian, who's standing beside me holding my hand.

"Tell me again," I say softly, looking up at him.

"I love you." His eyes gleam as he meets my gaze. "I love you, Nora, more than life itself."

I smile, my heart lighter than it's been in weeks. The shadow of grief is still with me, as is the lingering feeling of guilt, but the darkness no longer clouds everything. I can picture a day when the pain will fade, when all I'll feel is contentment and joy.

Our troubles aren't over—they can't be, with us being who we are—but the future no longer frightens me. Soon, I'll need to bring up the pretty doctor and Peter's plan for revenge, and at some point later, we'll have to discuss the possibility of another child and how to deal with the ever-present danger of our lives.

For now, though, we don't need to do anything but enjoy each other.

Enjoy being alive and in love.

EPILOGUE

❖ JULIAN ❖

Three Years Later

"Nora Esguerra!"

As the president of Stanford University calls out her name, I watch my wife walk across the stage, garbed in the same black cap and gown as the rest of the graduates. The robe billows around her petite frame, hiding the small, but already visible bump of her stomach—the child we both eagerly await this time.

Stopping in front of the university official, Nora shakes his hand to the sound of applause and then turns to smile for the camera, her delicate face glowing in the bright morning sun.

The flash goes off, startling me even though I knew it was coming.

Catching myself clutching the gun at my waist, I force my hand to uncurl and move away from the weapon. With a hundred of our best guards securing the field, my gun isn't necessary. Still, I feel better having it on me—and I know Nora is glad her semi-automatic is tucked inside her purse. Though the opening of her second art show in Paris went off without a hitch last year, we're both more than a little paranoid today, determined to do whatever it takes to ensure the safety of our unborn daughter.

Another flash goes off beside me. Glancing at the seats to my right, I see Nora's parents taking pictures with their new camera. They look as proud as I feel. Sensing my gaze on them, Nora's mother looks in my direction, and I give her a warm smile before turning my attention back to the stage.

The next graduate is already up, but I don't notice who it is. All I see is my pet, carefully making her way down the left side of the stage. The leather folder with the diploma is in her hands, and the tassel on her cap is hanging on the other side of her face, signifying her new diploma-recipient status.

She's beautiful, even more beautiful than at her high school graduation five years earlier.

As she makes her way through the rows of graduates and their families, our eyes meet, and I feel my heart expanding, filling with the mixture of dark possessiveness and tender love she always evokes in me.

My captive. My wife. My entire world.

I will love her to the end of time, and I will never, ever let her go.

FROM THE AUTHOR

Thank you for reading! If you would consider leaving a review, it would be greatly appreciated.

While *Hold Me* concludes Nora & Julian's story, there will be a spin-off about Lucas and the Russian interpreter. It will be called *Capture Me*. If you'd like to be notified when the book is out, please sign up for my new release email list at www.annazaires.com.

I love to hear from readers, so be sure to:
-Friend me on Facebook
-Like my Facebook page
-Follow me on Twitter
-Connect with me on Goodreads

And now please turn the page for a little taste of *Close Liaisons* (the start of Mia & Korum's story) and some of my other works.

EXCERPT FROM *CLOSE LIAISONS*

Author's Note: *Close Liaisons* is the first book in my erotic sci-fi romance trilogy, the Krinar Chronicles. While not as dark as *Twist Me*, it does have some elements that readers of dark erotica may enjoy.

* * *

A dark and edgy romance that will appeal to fans of erotic and turbulent relationships . . .

In the near future, the Krinar rule the Earth. An advanced race from another galaxy, they are still a mystery to us—and we are completely at their mercy.

Shy and innocent, Mia Stalis is a college student in New York City who has led a very normal life. Like most people, she's never had any interactions with the invaders—until one fateful day in the park changes everything. Having caught Korum's eye, she must now contend with a powerful, dangerously seductive Krinar who wants to possess her and will stop at nothing to make her his own.

How far would you go to regain your freedom? How much would you sacrifice to help your people? What choice will you make when you begin to fall for your enemy?

* * *

Breathe, Mia, breathe. Somewhere in the back of her mind, a small rational voice kept repeating those words. That same oddly objective part of her noted his symmetric face structure, with golden skin stretched tightly over high cheekbones and a firm jaw. Pictures and videos of Ks that she'd seen had hardly done them justice. Standing no more than thirty feet away, the creature was simply stunning.

As she continued staring at him, still frozen in place, he straightened and began walking toward her. Or rather stalking toward her, she thought stupidly, as his every movement reminded her of a jungle cat sinuously approaching a gazelle. All the while, his eyes never left hers. As he approached, she could make out individual yellow flecks in his light golden eyes and the thick long lashes surrounding them.

She watched in horrified disbelief as he sat down on her bench, less than two feet away from her, and smiled, showing white even teeth. No fangs, she noted with some functioning part of her brain. Not even a hint of them. That used to be another myth about them, like their supposed abhorrence of the sun.

"What's your name?" The creature practically purred the question at her. His voice was low and smooth, completely unaccented. His nostrils flared slightly, as though inhaling her scent.

"Um . . ." Mia swallowed nervously. "M-Mia."

"Mia," he repeated slowly, seemingly savoring her name. "Mia what?"

"Mia Stalis." Oh crap, why did he want to know her name? Why was he here, talking to her? In general, what was he doing in Central Park, so far away from any of the K Centers? *Breathe, Mia, breathe.*

"Relax, Mia Stalis." His smile got wider, exposing a dimple in his left cheek. A dimple? Ks had dimples? "Have you never encountered one of us before?"

"No, I haven't," Mia exhaled sharply, realizing that she was holding her breath. She was proud that her voice didn't sound as shaky as she felt. Should she ask? Did she want to know?

She gathered her courage. "What, um—" Another swallow. "What do you want from me?"

"For now, conversation." He looked like he was about to laugh at her, those gold eyes crinkling slightly at the corners.

Strangely, that pissed her off enough to take the edge off her fear. If there was anything Mia hated, it was being laughed at. With her short, skinny stature and a general lack of social skills that came from an awkward teenage phase involving every girl's nightmare of braces, frizzy hair, and glasses, Mia had more than enough experience being the butt of someone's joke.

She lifted her chin belligerently. "Okay, then, what is *your* name?"

"It's Korum."

"Just Korum?"

"We don't really have last names, not the way you do. My full name is much longer, but you wouldn't be able to pronounce it if I told you."

Okay, that was interesting. She now remembered reading something like that in *The New York Times*. So far, so good. Her legs had nearly stopped shaking, and her breathing was returning to normal. Maybe, just maybe, she would get out of this alive. This conversation business seemed safe enough, although the way he kept staring at her with those unblinking yellowish eyes was unnerving. She decided to keep him talking.

"What are you doing here, Korum?"

"I just told you, making conversation with you, Mia." His voice again held a hint of laughter.

Frustrated, Mia blew out her breath. "I meant, what are you doing here in Central Park? In New York City in general?"

He smiled again, cocking his head slightly to the side. "Maybe I'm hoping to meet a pretty curly-haired girl."

Okay, enough was enough. He was clearly toying with her. Now that she could think a little again, she realized that they were in the middle of Central Park, in full view of about a gazillion spectators. She surreptitiously glanced around to confirm that. Yep, sure enough, although people were obviously steering clear of her bench and its otherworldly occupant, there were a number of brave souls staring their way from further up the path. A couple were even cautiously filming them with their wristwatch cameras. If the K tried anything with her, it would be on YouTube in the blink of an eye, and he had to know it. Of course, he may or may not care about that.

Still, going on the assumption that since she'd never come across any videos of K assaults on college students in the middle of Central

Park, she was relatively safe, Mia cautiously reached for her laptop and lifted it to stuff it back into her backpack.

"Let me help you with that, Mia—"

And before she could blink, she felt him take her heavy laptop from her suddenly boneless fingers, gently brushing against her knuckles in the process. A sensation similar to a mild electric shock shot through Mia at his touch, leaving her nerve endings tingling in its wake.

Reaching for her backpack, he carefully put away the laptop in a smooth, sinuous motion. "There you go, all better now."

Oh God, he had touched her. Maybe her theory about the safety of public locations was bogus. She felt her breathing speeding up again, and her heart rate was probably well into the anaerobic zone at this point.

"I have to go now . . . Bye!"

How she managed to squeeze out those words without hyperventilating, she would never know. Grabbing the strap of the backpack he'd just put down, she jumped to her feet, noting somewhere in the back of her mind that her earlier paralysis seemed to be gone.

"Bye, Mia. I will see you later." His softly mocking voice carried in the clear spring air as she took off, nearly running in her haste to get away.

* * *

If you'd like to find out more, please visit my website at www.annazaires.com. All three books in the Krinar Chronicles trilogy are now available.

EXCERPT FROM *THE THOUGHT READERS* BY DIMA ZALES

Author's Note: If you want to try something different—and especially if you like urban fantasy and science fiction—you might want to check out *The Thought Readers*, the first book in the *Mind Dimensions* series that I'm collaborating on with Dima Zales, my husband. But be warned, there is not much romance or sex in this one. Instead of sex, there's mind reading. The book is now available at most retailers.

* * *

Everyone thinks I'm a genius.

Everyone is wrong.

Sure, I finished Harvard at eighteen and now make crazy money at a hedge fund. But that's not because I'm unusually smart or hard-working.

It's because I cheat.

You see, I have a unique ability. I can go outside time into my own personal version of reality—the place I call "the Quiet"—where I can explore my surroundings while the rest of the world stands still.

I thought I was the only one who could do this—until I met *her*.

My name is Darren, and this is how I learned that I'm a Reader.

* * *

Sometimes I think I'm crazy. I'm sitting at a casino table in Atlantic City, and everyone around me is motionless. I call this the *Quiet*, as though giving it a name makes it seem more real—as though giving it a name changes the fact that all the players around me are frozen like statues, and I'm walking among them, looking at the cards they've been dealt.

The problem with the theory of my being crazy is that when I 'unfreeze' the world, as I just have, the cards the players turn over are the same ones I just saw in the Quiet. If I were crazy, wouldn't these cards be different? Unless I'm so far gone that I'm imagining the cards on the table, too.

But then I also win. If that's a delusion—if the pile of chips on my side of the table is a delusion—then I might as well question everything. Maybe my name isn't even Darren.

No. I can't think that way. If I'm really that confused, I don't want to snap out of it—because if I do, I'll probably wake up in a mental hospital.

Besides, I love my life, crazy and all.

My shrink thinks the Quiet is an inventive way I describe the 'inner workings of my genius.' Now that sounds crazy to me. She also might want me, but that's beside the point. Suffice it to say, she's as far as it gets from my datable age range, which is currently right around twenty-four. Still young, still hot, but done with school and pretty much beyond the clubbing phase. I hate clubbing, almost as much as I hated studying. In any case, my shrink's explanation doesn't work, as it doesn't account for the way I know things even a genius wouldn't know—like the exact value and suit of the other players' cards.

I watch as the dealer begins a new round. Besides me, there are three players at the table: Grandma, the Cowboy, and the Professional, as I call them. I feel that now almost-imperceptible fear that accompanies the phasing. That's what I call the process: phasing into the Quiet. Worrying about my sanity has always facilitated phasing; fear seems helpful in this process.

I phase in, and everything gets quiet. Hence the name for this state.

It's eerie to me, even now. Outside the Quiet, this casino is very loud: drunk people talking, slot machines, ringing of wins, music—the only place louder is a club or a concert. And yet, right at this moment, I could probably hear a pin drop. It's like I've gone deaf to the chaos that surrounds me.

Having so many frozen people around adds to the strangeness of it all. Here is a waitress stopped mid-step, carrying a tray with drinks.

There is a woman about to pull a slot machine lever. At my own table, the dealer's hand is raised, the last card he dealt hanging unnaturally in midair. I walk up to him from the side of the table and reach for it. It's a king, meant for the Professional. Once I let the card go, it falls on the table rather than continuing to float as before—but I know full well that it will be back in the air, in the exact position it was when I grabbed it, when I phase out.

The Professional looks like someone who makes money playing poker, or at least the way I always imagined someone like that might look. Scruffy, shades on, a little sketchy-looking. He's been doing an excellent job with the poker face—basically not twitching a single muscle throughout the game. His face is so expressionless that I wonder if he might've gotten Botox to help maintain such a stony countenance. His hand is on the table, protectively covering the cards dealt to him.

I move his limp hand away. It feels normal. Well, in a manner of speaking. The hand is sweaty and hairy, so moving it aside is unpleasant and is admittedly an abnormal thing to do. The normal part is that the hand is warm, rather than cold. When I was a kid, I expected people to feel cold in the Quiet, like stone statues.

With the Professional's hand moved away, I pick up his cards. Combined with the king that was hanging in the air, he has a nice high pair. Good to know.

I walk over to Grandma. She's already holding her cards, and she has fanned them nicely for me. I'm able to avoid touching her wrinkled, spotted hands. This is a relief, as I've recently become conflicted about touching people—or, more specifically, women—in the Quiet. If I had to, I would rationalize touching Grandma's hand as harmless, or at least not creepy, but it's better to avoid it if possible.

In any case, she has a low pair. I feel bad for her. She's been losing a lot tonight. Her chips are dwindling. Her losses are due, at least partially, to the fact that she has a terrible poker face. Even before looking at her cards, I knew they wouldn't be good because I could tell she was disappointed as soon as her hand was dealt. I also caught a gleeful gleam in her eyes a few rounds ago when she had a winning three of a kind.

This whole game of poker is, to a large degree, an exercise in reading people—something I really want to get better at. At my job, I've been told I'm great at reading people. I'm not, though; I'm just good at using the Quiet to make it seem like I am. I do want to learn how to read people for real, though. It would be nice to know what everyone is thinking.

What I don't care that much about in this poker game is money. I do well enough financially to not have to depend on hitting it big gambling. I don't care if I win or lose, though quintupling my money back at the blackjack table was fun. This whole trip has been more about going gambling because I finally can, being twenty-one and all. I was never into fake IDs, so this is an actual milestone for me.

Leaving Grandma alone, I move on to the next player—the Cowboy. I can't resist taking off his straw hat and trying it on. I wonder if it's possible for me to get lice this way. Since I've never been able to bring back any inanimate objects from the Quiet, nor otherwise affect the real world in any lasting way, I figure I won't be able to get any living critters to come back with me, either.

Dropping the hat, I look at his cards. He has a pair of aces—a better hand than the Professional. Maybe the Cowboy is a professional, too. He has a good poker face, as far as I can tell. It'll be interesting to watch those two in this round.

Next, I walk up to the deck and look at the top cards, memorizing them. I'm not leaving anything to chance.

When my task in the Quiet is complete, I walk back to myself. Oh, yes, did I mention that I see myself sitting there, frozen like the rest of them? That's the weirdest part. It's like having an out-of-body experience.

Approaching my frozen self, I look at him. I usually avoid doing this, as it's too unsettling. No amount of looking in the mirror—or seeing videos of yourself on YouTube—can prepare you for viewing your own three-dimensional body up close. It's not something anyone is meant to experience. Well, aside from identical twins, I guess.

It's hard to believe that this person is me. He looks more like some random guy. Well, maybe a bit better than that. I do find this guy interesting. He looks cool. He looks smart. I think women would probably consider him good-looking, though I know that's not a modest thing to think.

It's not like I'm an expert at gauging how attractive a guy is, but some things are common sense. I can tell when a dude is ugly, and this frozen me is not. I also know that generally, being good-looking requires a symmetrical face, and the statue of me has that. A strong jaw doesn't hurt, either. Check. Having broad shoulders is a positive, and being tall really helps. All covered. I have blue eyes—that seems to be a plus. Girls have told me they like my eyes, though right now, on the frozen me, the eyes look creepy—glassy. They look like the eyes of a lifeless wax figure.

Realizing that I'm dwelling on this subject way too long, I shake my head. I can just picture my shrink analyzing this moment. Who would imagine admiring themselves like this as part of their mental illness? I can just picture her scribbling down *Narcissist*, underlining it for emphasis.

Enough. I need to leave the Quiet. Raising my hand, I touch my frozen self on the forehead, and I hear noise again as I phase out.

Everything is back to normal.

The card that I looked at a moment before—the king that I left on the table—is in the air again, and from there it follows the trajectory it was always meant to, landing near the Professional's hands. Grandma is still eyeing her fanned cards in disappointment, and the Cowboy has his hat on again, though I took it off him in the Quiet. Everything is exactly as it was.

On some level, my brain never ceases to be surprised at the discontinuity of the experience in the Quiet and outside it. As humans, we're hardwired to question reality when such things happen. When I was trying to outwit my shrink early on in my therapy, I once read an entire psychology textbook during our session. She, of course, didn't notice it, as I did it in the Quiet. The book talked about how babies as young as two months old are surprised if they see something out of the ordinary, like gravity appearing to work backwards. It's no wonder my brain has trouble adapting. Until I was ten, the world behaved normally, but everything has been weird since then, to put it mildly.

Glancing down, I realize I'm holding three of a kind. Next time, I'll look at my cards before phasing. If I have something this strong, I might take my chances and play fair.

The game unfolds predictably because I know everybody's cards. At the end, Grandma gets up. She's clearly lost enough money.

And that's when I see the girl for the first time.

She's hot. My friend Bert at work claims that I have a 'type,' but I reject that idea. I don't like to think of myself as shallow or predictable. But I might actually be a bit of both, because this girl fits

Bert's description of my type to a T. And my reaction is extreme interest, to say the least.

Large blue eyes. Well-defined cheekbones on a slender face, with a hint of something exotic. Long, shapely legs, like those of a dancer. Dark wavy hair in a ponytail—a hairstyle that I like. And without bangs—even better. I hate bangs—not sure why girls do that to themselves. Though lack of bangs is not, strictly speaking, in Bert's description of my type, it probably should be.

I continue staring at her. With her high heels and tight skirt, she's overdressed for this place. Or maybe I'm underdressed in my jeans and t-shirt. Either way, I don't care. I have to try to talk to her.

I debate phasing into the Quiet and approaching her, so I can do something creepy like stare at her up close, or maybe even snoop in her pockets. Anything to help me when I talk to her.

I decide against it, which is probably the first time that's ever happened.

I know that my reasoning for breaking my usual habit—if you can even call it that—is strange. I picture the following chain of events: she agrees to date me, we go out for a while, we get serious, and because of the deep connection we have, I come clean about the Quiet. She learns I did something creepy and has a fit, then dumps me. It's ridiculous to think this, of course, considering that we haven't even spoken yet. Talk about jumping the gun. She might have an IQ below seventy, or the personality of a piece of wood. There can be twenty different reasons why I wouldn't want to date her. And besides, it's not all up to me. She might tell me to go fuck myself as soon as I try to talk to her.

Still, working at a hedge fund has taught me to hedge. As crazy as that reasoning is, I stick with my decision not to phase because I know it's the gentlemanly thing to do. In keeping with this unusually chivalrous me, I also decide not to cheat at this round of poker.

As the cards are dealt again, I reflect on how good it feels to have done the honorable thing—even without anyone knowing. Maybe I should try to respect people's privacy more often. As soon as I think this, I mentally snort. *Yeah, right.* I have to be realistic. I wouldn't be where I am today if I'd followed that advice. In fact, if I made a habit of respecting people's privacy, I would lose my job within days—and with it, a lot of the comforts I've become accustomed to.

Copying the Professional's move, I cover my cards with my hand as soon as I receive them. I'm about to sneak a peek at what I was dealt when something unusual happens.

The world goes quiet, just like it does when I phase in . . . but I did nothing this time.

And at that moment, I see *her*—the girl sitting across the table from me, the girl I was just thinking about. She's standing next to me, pulling her hand away from mine. Or, strictly speaking, from my frozen self's hand—as I'm standing a little to the side looking at her.

She's also still sitting in front of me at the table, a frozen statue like all the others.

My mind goes into overdrive as my heartbeat jumps. I don't even consider the possibility of that second girl being a twin sister or something like that. I know it's her. She's doing what I did just a few minutes ago. She's walking in the Quiet. The world around us is frozen, but we are not.

A horrified look crosses her face as she realizes the same thing. Before I can react, she lunges across the table and touches her own forehead.

The world becomes normal again.

She stares at me from across the table, shocked, her eyes huge and her face pale. Her hands tremble as she rises to her feet. Without so much as a word, she turns and begins walking away, then breaks into a run a couple of seconds later.

Getting over my own shock, I get up and run after her. It's not exactly smooth. If she notices a guy she doesn't know running after her, dating will be the last thing on her mind. But I'm beyond that now. She's the only person I've met who can do what I do. She's proof that I'm not insane. She might have what I want most in the world.

She might have answers.

* * *

If you'd like to learn more about our fantasy and science fiction books, please visit Dima Zales's website at www.dimazales.com and sign up for his new release email list. You can also connect with him on Facebook, Google Plus, Twitter, and Goodreads.

ABOUT THE AUTHOR

Anna Zaires is a *New York Times, USA Today,* and international bestselling author of sci-fi romance and contemporary dark erotic romance. She fell in love with books at the age of five, when her grandmother taught her to read. Since then, she has always lived partially in a fantasy world where the only limits were those of her imagination. Currently residing in Florida, Anna is happily married to Dima Zales (a science fiction and fantasy author) and closely collaborates with him on all their works.

To learn more, please visit www.annazaires.com.